CHEAPER BY THE DOZEN

BY FRANK B. GILBRETH, JR.
AND
ERNESTINE GILBRETH CAREY

Illustrations by Donald McKay

BANTAM BOOKS
NEW YORK • TORONTO • LONDON • SYDNEY • AUCKLAND

This edition contains the complete text of the original hardcover edition.
NOT ONE WORD HAS BEEN OMITTED.

RL 5, IL age 11 and up

CHEAPER BY THE DOZEN
A Bantam Starfire Book / published by arrangement with Harper & Row, Publishers Inc.

PUBLISHING HISTORY

Crowell edition published January 1949
Book-of-the-Month Club edition published January 1949
Excerpts published in Ladies Home Journal *January 1949*
Reader's Digest *version published March 1949*
Bantam edition / December 1951
New Bantam edition / October 1959

Bantam Pathfinder edition / April 1963

Bantam edition / September 1975

The Starfire logo is a registered trademark of Bantam Books, a division of Bantam Doubleday Dell Publishing Group, Inc.

For information address: Harper & Row, Publishers Inc., 10 East 53rd Street, New York, N.Y. 10022.

ISBN 0-553-27250-0

Printed simultaneously in the United States and Canada

Bantam Books are published by Bantam Books, a division of Bantam Doubleday Dell Publishing Group, Inc. Its trademark, consisting of the words "Bantam Books" and the portrayal of a rooster, is Registered in U.S. Patent and Trademark Office and in other countries. Marca Registrada. Bantam Books, 1540 Broadway, New York, New York 10036.

PRINTED IN THE UNITED STATES OF AMERICA

OPM 70

ONE FOR THE ROAD

We were en route from Montclair to New Bedford, Massachusetts, and Frank, Jr., was left behind by mistake in a restaurant in New London. His absence wasn't discovered until near the end of the trip.

Dad wheeled the car around frantically and sped back to New London, breaking every traffic rule then on the books. We had stopped in the New London restaurant for lunch, and it had seemed a respectable enough place. It was night time when we returned, however, and the place was garish in colored lights. Dad left us in the car and entered. After the drive in the dark, his eyes were squinted in the bright lights, and he couldn't see very well.

A pretty young lady, looking for business, was drinking a highball in the second booth. Dad peered in, flustered.

"Hello, Pops," she said. "Don't be bashful. Are you looking for a naughty little girl?"

Dad was caught off guard. "Goodness, no," he stammered, with all of his ordinary poise shattered. "I'm looking for a naughty little boy."

CHEAPER BY THE DOZEN

"Instructive, funny and very readable."

—*Library Journal*

"Gay and lighthearted. . . . One of the most amusing books of the season."

—*The Chicago Sun*

Bantam Starfire Books by Frank B. Gilbreth, Jr. and Ernestine Gilbreth Carey

BELLES ON THEIR TOES
CHEAPER BY THE DOZEN

To DAD

who only reared twelve children

and

To MOTHER

who reared twelve only children

Foreword

Mother and Dad, Lillian Moller Gilbreth and Frank Bunker Gilbreth, were industrial engineers. They were among the first in the scientific management field and the very first in motion study. From 1910 to 1924, their firm of Gilbreth, Inc., was employed as "efficiency expert" by many of the major industrial plants in the United States, Britain, and Germany. Dad died in 1924. After that, Mother carried the load by herself and became perhaps the foremost woman industrial engineer. She is still active today after rearing twelve children. But that's another story. This book is about the Gilbreth family before Dad died.

Contents

CHAPTER 1

Whistles and Shaving Bristles

Dad was a tall man, with a large head, jowls, and a Herbert Hoover collar. He was no longer slim; he had passed the two-hundred-pound mark during his early thirties, and left it so far behind that there were times when he had to resort to railway baggage scales to ascertain his displacement. But he carried himself with the self-assurance of a successful gentleman who was proud of his wife, proud of his family, and proud of his business accomplishments.

Dad had enough gall to be divided into three parts, and the ability and poise to backstop the front he placed before the world. He'd walk into a factory like the Zeiss works in Germany or the Pierce Arrow plant in this country and announce that he could speed up production by one-fourth. He'd do it, too.

One reason he had so many children—there were twelve of us—was that he was convinced anything he and Mother teamed up on was sure to be a success.

Dad always practiced what he preached, and it was just about impossible to tell where his scientific management company ended and his family life began. His office was always full of children, and he often took two or three of us, and sometimes all twelve, on business trips. Frequently, we'd tag along at his side, pencils and notebooks in our hands, when Dad toured a factory which had hired him as an efficiency expert.

On the other hand, our house at Montclair, New Jersey, was a sort of school for scientific management and the elimination of wasted motions—or "motion study," as Dad and Mother named it.

Dad took moving pictures of us children washing dishes, so that he could figure out how we could reduce our motions and thus hurry through the task. Irregular jobs, such as painting the back porch or removing a stump from the front lawn, were awarded on a low-bid basis. Each child who wanted extra pocket money submitted a sealed bid saying what he would do the job for. The lowest bidder got the contract.

Dad installed process and work charts in the bathrooms. Every child old enough to write—and Dad expected his offspring to start writing at a tender age—was required to initial the charts in the morning after he had brushed his teeth, taken a bath, combed his hair, and made his bed. At night, each child had to weigh himself, plot the figure on a graph, and initial the process charts again after he had done his homework, washed his hands and face, and brushed his teeth. Mother wanted to have a place on the charts for saying prayers, but Dad said as far as he was concerned prayers were voluntary.

It was regimentation, all right. But bear in mind the trouble most parents have in getting just one child off to school, and multiply it by twelve. Some regimentation was necessary to prevent bedlam. Of course there were times when a child would initial the charts without actually having fulfilled the requirements. However, Dad had a gimlet eye and a terrible swift sword. The combined effect was that truth usually went marching on.

Yes, at home or on the job, Dad was always the efficiency expert. He buttoned his vest from the bottom up, instead of from the top down, because the bottom-to-top process took him only three seconds, while the top-to-bottom took seven. He even used two shaving brushes to lather his face, because he found that by so doing he could cut seventeen seconds off his shaving time. For a while he tried shaving with two razors, but he finally gave that up.

"I can save forty-four seconds," he grumbled, "but I wasted two minutes this morning putting this bandage on my throat."

It wasn't the slashed throat that really bothered him. It was the two minutes.

Some people used to say that Dad had so many children he couldn't keep track of them. Dad himself used to tell a story about one time when Mother went off to fill a lecture engagement and left him in charge at home. When Mother returned, she asked him if everything had run smoothly.

"Didn't have any trouble except with that one over there," he replied. "But a spanking brought him into line."

Mother could handle any crisis without losing her composure.

"That's not one of ours, dear," she said. "He belongs next door."

None of us remembers it, and maybe it never happened. Dad wasn't above stretching the truth, because there was nothing he liked better than a joke, particularly if it were on him and even more particularly if it were on Mother. This much is certain, though. There were two red-haired children who lived next door, and the Gilbreths all are blondes or red heads.

Although he was a strict taskmaster within his home, Dad tolerated no criticism of the family from outsiders. Once a neighbor complained that a Gilbreth had called the neighbor's boy a son of an unprintable word.

"What are the facts of the matter?" Dad asked blandly. And then walked away while the neighbor registered a double take.

But Dad hated unprintable words, and the fact that he had stood up for his son didn't prevent him from holding a full-dress court of inquiry once he got home, and administering the called-for punishment.

Dad was happiest in a crowd, especially a crowd of kids. Wherever he was, you'd see a string of them trailing him—and the ones with plenty of freckles were pretty sure to be Gilbreths.

He had a way with children and knew how to keep them on their toes. He had a respect for them, too, and didn't mind showing it.

He believed that most adults stopped thinking the day they left school—and some even before that. "A child, on the other hand, stays impressionable and eager to learn. Catch one young enough," Dad insisted, "and there's no limit to what you can teach."

Really, it was love of children more than anything else that made him want a pack of his own. Even with a dozen, he

wasn't fully satisfied. Sometimes he'd look us over and say to Mother:

"Never you mind, Lillie. You did the best you could."

We children used to suspect, though, that one reason he had wanted a large family was to assure himself of an appreciative audience, even within the confines of the home. With us around, he could always be sure of a full house, packed to the galleries.

Whenever Dad returned from a trip—even if he had been gone only a day—he whistled the family "assembly call" as he turned in at the sidewalk of our large, brown home in Montclair. The call was a tune he had composed. He whistled it, loud and shrill, by doubling his tongue behind his front teeth. It took considerable effort and Dad, who never exercised if he could help it, usually ended up puffing with exhaustion.

The call was important. It meant drop everything and come running—or risk dire consequences. At the first note, Gilbreth children came dashing from all corners of the house and yard. Neighborhood dogs, barking hellishly, converged for blocks around. Heads popped out of the windows of near-by houses.

Dad gave the whistle often. He gave it when he had an important family announcement that he wanted to be sure everyone would hear. He gave it when he was bored and wanted some excitement with his children. He gave it when he had invited a friend home and wanted both to introduce the friend to the whole family and to show the friend how quickly the family could assemble. On such occasions, Dad would click a stopwatch, which he always carried in his vest pocket.

Like most of Dad's ideas, the assembly call, while something more than a nuisance, made sense. This was demonstrated in particular one day when a bonfire of leaves in the driveway got out of control and spread to the side of the house. Dad whistled, and the house was evacuated in fourteen seconds—eight seconds off the all-time record. That occasion also was memorable because of the remarks of a frank neighbor, who watched the blaze from his yard. During the height of the excitement, the neighbor's wife came to the front door and called to her husband:

"What's going on?"

"The Gilbreths' house is on fire," he replied, "thank God!"

"Shall I call the fire department?" she shouted.

"What's the matter, are you crazy?" the husband answered incredulously.

Anyway, the fire was put out quickly and there was no need to ask the fire department for help.

Dad whistled assembly when he wanted to find out who had been using his razors or who had spilled ink on his desk. He whistled it when he had special jobs to assign or errands to be run. Mostly, though, he sounded the assembly call when he was about to distribute some wonderful surprises, with the biggest and best going to the one who reached him first.

So when we heard him whistle, we never knew whether to expect good news or bad, rags or riches. But we did know for sure we'd better get there in a hurry.

Sometimes, as we all came running to the front door, he'd start by being stern.

"Let me see your nails, all of you," he'd grunt, with his face screwed up in a terrible frown. "Are they clean? Have you been biting them? Do they need trimming?"

Then out would come leather manicure sets for the girls and pocket knives for the boys. How we loved him then, when his frown wrinkles reversed their field and became a wide grin.

Or he'd shake hands solemnly all around, and when you took your hand away there'd be a nut chocolate bar in it. Or he'd ask who had a pencil, and then hand out a dozen automatic ones.

"Let's see, what time is it?" he asked once. Out came wrist watches for all—even the six-week-old baby.

"Oh, Daddy, they're just right," we'd say.

And when we'd throw our arms around him and tell him how we'd missed him, he would choke up and wouldn't be able to answer. So he'd rumple our hair and slap our bottoms instead.

CHAPTER 2

Pierce Arrow

There were other surprises, too. Boxes of Page and Shaw candy, dolls and toys, cameras from Germany, wool socks from Scotland, a dozen Plymouth Rock hens, and two sheep that were supposed to keep the lawn trimmed but died, poor creatures, from the combined effects of saddle sores, too much petting, and tail pulling. The sheep were fun while they lasted, and it is doubtful if any pair of quadrupeds ever had been sheared so often by so many.

"If I ever bring anything else alive into this household," Dad said, "I hope the Society for the Prevention of Cruelty to Animals hales me into court and makes me pay my debt to society. I never felt so ashamed about anything in my life as I do about those sheep. So help me."

When Dad bought the house in Montclair, he described it to us as a tumbled-down shanty in a run-down neighborhood. We thought this was another one of his surprises, but he finally convinced us that the house was a hovel.

"It takes a lot of money to keep this family going," he said. "Food, clothes, allowances, doctors' bills, getting teeth straightened, and buying ice cream sodas. I'm sorry, but I just couldn't afford anything better. We'll have to fix it up the best we can, and make it do."

We were living at Providence, Rhode Island, at the time. As we drove from Providence to Montclair, Dad would point to every termite-trap we passed.

"It looks something like that one," he would say, "only it has a few more broken windows, and the yard is maybe a little smaller."

As we entered Montclair, he drove through the worst section of town, and finally pulled up at an abandoned structure that even Dracula wouldn't have felt at home in.

"Well, here it is," he said. "Home. All out."

"You're joking, aren't you, dear?" Mother said hopefully.

"What's the matter with it? Don't you like it?"

"If it's what you want, dear," said Mother, "I'm satisfied. I guess."

"It's a slum, that's what's the matter with it," said Ernestine.

"No one asked your opinion, young lady," replied Dad. "I was talking to your Mother, and I will thank you to keep out of the conversation."

"You're welcome," said Ernestine, who knew she was treading on thin ice but was too upset to care. "You're welcome, I'm sure. Only I wouldn't live in it with a ten-foot pole."

"Neither would I," said Martha. "Not with two ten-foot poles."

"Hush," said Mother. "Daddy knows best."

Lill started to sob.

"It won't look so bad with a coat of paint and a few boards put in where these holes are," Mother said cheerfully.

Dad, grinning now, was fumbling in his pocket for his notebook.

"By jingo, kids, wait a second," he crowed. "Wrong address. Well, what do you know. Pile back in. I thought this place looked a little more run down than when I last saw it."

And then he drove us to 68 Eagle Rock Way, which was an old but beautiful Taj Mahal of a house with fourteen rooms, a two-story barn out back, a greenhouse, chicken yard, grape arbors, rose bushes, and a couple of dozen fruit trees. At first we thought that Dad was teasing us again, and that this was the other end of a scale—a house much better than the one he had bought.

"This is really it," he said. "The reason I took you to that other place first, and the reason I didn't try to describe this place to you is—well, I didn't want you to be disappointed. Forgive me?"

We said we did.

Dad had bought the automobile a year before we moved. It was our first car, and cars still were a novelty. Of course, that had been a surprise, too. He had taken us all for a walk and had ended up at a garage where the car had been parked.

Although Dad made his living by redesigning complicated machinery, so as to reduce the number of human motions required to operate it, he never really understood the mechanical intricacies of our automobile. It was a gray Pierce Arrow, equipped with two bulb horns and an electric Klaxon, which Dad would try to blow all at the same time when he wanted to pass anyone. The engine hood was long and square, and you had to raise it to prime the petcocks on cold mornings.

Dad had seen the car in the factory and fallen in love with it. The affection was entirely one-sided and unrequited. He named it Foolish Carriage because, he said, it was foolish for any man with as many children as he to think he could afford a horseless carriage.

The contraption kicked him when he cranked, spat oil in his face when he looked into its bowels, squealed when he mashed the brakes, and rumbled ominously when he shifted gears. Sometimes Dad would spit, squeal, and rumble back. But he never won a single decision.

Frankly, Dad didn't drive our car well at all. But he did drive it fast. He terrified all of us, but particularly Mother. She sat next to him on the front seat—with two of the babies on her lap—and alternated between clutching Dad's arm and closing her eyes in supplication. Whenever we rounded a corner, she would try to make a shield out of her body to protect the babies from what she felt sure would be mutilation or death.

"Not so fast, Frank, not so fast," she would whisper through clenched teeth. But Dad never seemed to hear.

Foolish Carriage was a right-hand drive, so whoever sat to the left of Mother and the babies on the front seat had to be on the lookout to tell Dad when he could pass the car ahead.

"You can make it," the lookout would shout.

"Put out your hand," Dad would holler.

Eleven hands—everybody contributing one except Mother and the babies—would emerge from both sides of the car; from the front seat, rear seat, and folding swivel chairs amidships. We had seen Dad nick fenders, slaughter chickens, square away with traffic policemen, and knock down full-grown trees, and we weren't taking any chances.

The lookout on the front seat was Dad's own idea. The

other safety measures, which we soon inaugurated as a matter of self-preservation, were our own.

We would assign someone to keep a lookout for cars approaching on side streets to the left; someone to keep an identical lookout to the right; and someone to kneel on the rear seat and look through the isinglass window in the back.

"Car coming from the left, Dad," one lookout would sing out.

"Two coming from the right."

"Motorcycle approaching from astern."

"I see them, I see them," Dad would say irritably, although usually he didn't. "Don't you have any confidence at all in your father?"

He was especially fond of the electric horn, an ear-splitting gadget which bellowed "kadookah" in an awe-inspiring, metallic baritone. How Dad could manage to blow this and the two bulb horns, step on the gas, steer the car, shout "road hog, road hog," and smoke a cigar—all at the same time—is in itself a tribute to his abilities as a motion study expert.

A few days after he bought the car, he brought each of us children up to it, one at a time, raised the hood, and told us to look inside and see if we could find the birdie in the engine. While our backs were turned, he'd tiptoe back to the driver's seat—a jolly Santa Claus in mufti—and press down on the horn.

"Kadookah, Kadookah." The horn blaring right in your ear was frightening and you'd jump away in hurt amazement. Dad would laugh until the tears came to his eyes.

"Did you see the birdie? Ho, ho, ho," he'd scream. "I'll bet you jumped six and nine-tenths inches. Ho, ho, ho."

One day, while we were returning from a particularly trying picnic, the engine balked, coughed, spat, and stopped.

Dad was sweaty and sleepy. We children had gotten on his nerves. He ordered us out of the car, which was overheated and steaming. He wrestled with the back seat to get the tools. It was stuck and he kicked it. He took off his coat, rolled up his sleeves, and raised the left-hand side of the hood.

Dad seldom swore. An occasional "damn," perhaps, but he believed in setting a good example. Usually he stuck to such phrases as "by jingo" and "holy Moses." He said them both now, only there was something frightening in the way he rolled them out.

His head and shoulders disappeared into the inside of the hood. You could see his shirt, wet through, sticking to his back.

Nobody noticed Bill. He had crawled into the front seat. And then—"Kadookah. Kadookah."

Dad jumped so high he actually toppled into the engine, leaving his feet dangling in mid-air. His head butted the top of the hood and his right wrist came up against the red-hot exhaust pipe. You could hear the flesh sizzle. Finally he managed to extricate himself. He rubbed his head, and left grease across his forehead. He blew on the burned wrist. He was livid.

"Jesus Christ," he screamed, as if he had been saving this oath since his wedding day for just such an occasion. "Holy Jesus Christ. Who did that?"

"Mercy, Maud," said Mother, which was the closest she ever came to swearing, too.

Bill, who was six and always in trouble anyway, was the only one with nerve enough to laugh. But it was a nervous laugh at that.

"Did you see the birdie, Daddy?" he asked.

Dad grabbed him, and Bill stopped laughing.

"That was a good joke on you, Daddy," Bill said hopefully. But there wasn't much confidence in his voice.

"There is a time," Dad said through his teeth, "and there is a place for birdies. And there is a time and place for spankings."

"I'll bet you jumped six and nine-tenths inches, Daddy," said Bill, stalling for time, now.

Dad relaxed and let him go. "Yes, Billy, by jingo," he said. "That was a good joke on me, and I suspect I did jump six and nine-tenths inches."

Dad loved a joke on himself, all right. But he loved it best a few months after the joke was over, and not when it was happening. The story about Bill and the birdie became one of his favorites. No one ever laughed harder at the end of the story than Dad. Unless it was Bill. By jingo.

CHAPTER 3

Orphans in Uniform

When Dad decided he wanted to take the family for an outing in the Pierce Arrow, he'd whistle assembly, and then ask:

"How many want to go for a ride?"

The question was purely rhetorical, for when Dad rode, everybody rode. So we'd all say we thought a ride would be fine.

Actually, this would be pretty close to the truth. Although Dad's driving was fraught with peril, there was a strange fascination in its brushes with death and its dramatic, traffic-stopping scenes. It was the sort of thing that you wouldn't have initiated yourself, but wouldn't have wanted to miss. It was standing up in a roller coaster. It was going up on the stage when the magician called for volunteers. It was a back somersault off the high diving board.

A drive, too, meant a chance to be with Dad and Mother. If you were lucky, even to sit with them on the front seat. There were so many of us and so few of them that we never could see as much of them as we wanted. Every hour or so, we'd change places so as to give someone else a turn in the front seat with them.

Dad would tell us to get ready while he brought the car around to the front of the house. He made it sound easy—as if it never entered his head that Foolish Carriage might not *want* to come around front. Dad was a perpetual optimist, confident that brains someday would triumph over inanimate steel; bolstered in the belief that he entered the fray with clean hands and a pure heart.

While groans, fiendish gurglings and backfires were emitting from the barn, the house itself would be organized confusion, as the family carried out its preparations in accordance with prearranged plans. It was like a newspaper on election night; general staff headquarters on D-Day minus one.

Getting ready meant scrubbed hands and face, shined shoes, clean clothes, combed hair. It wasn't advisable to be late, if and when Dad finally came rolling up to the porte-cochere. And it wasn't advisable to be dirty, because he'd inspect us all.

Besides getting himself ready, each older child was responsible for one of the younger ones. Anne was in charge of Dan, Ern in charge of Jack, and Mart in charge of Bob. This applied not only to rides in the car but all the time. The older sister was supposed to help her particular charge get dressed in the morning, to see that he made his bed, to put clean clothes on when he needed them, to see that he was washed and on time for meals, and to see that his process charts were duly initialed.

Anne, as the oldest, also was responsible for the deportment and general appearance of the whole group. Mother, of course, watched out for the baby, Jane. The intermediate children, Frank, Bill, Lill and Fred, were considered old enough to look out for themselves, but not old enough to look after anyone else. Dad, for the purpose of convenience (his own), ranked himself with the intermediate category.

In the last analysis, the person responsible for making the system work was Mother. Mother never threatened, never shouted or became excited, never spanked a single one of her children—or anyone else's, either.

Mother was a psychologist. In her own way, she got even better results with the family than Dad. But she was not a disciplinarian. If it was always Dad, and never Mother, who suggested going for a ride, Mother had her reasons.

She'd go from room to room, settling fights, drying tears, buttoning jackets.

"Mother, he's got my shirt. *Make* him give it to me."

"Mother, can I sit up front with you? I *never* get to sit up front."

"It's mine; you gave it to me. You wore mine yesterday."

When we'd all gathered in front of the house, the girls in dusters, the boys in linen suits, Mother would call the roll. Anne, Ernestine, Martha, Frank and so forth.

We used to claim that the roll-call was a waste of time and motion. Nothing was considered more of a sin in our house than wasted time and motions. But Dad had two vivid memories about children who had been left behind by mistake.

One such occurrence happened in Hoboken, aboard the liner *Leviathan*. Dad had taken the boys aboard on a sightseeing trip just before she sailed. He hadn't remembered to count noses when he came down the gangplank, and didn't notice, until the gangplank was pulled in, that Dan was missing. The *Leviathan's* sailing was held up for twenty minutes until Dan was located, asleep in a chair on the promenade deck.

The other occurrence was slightly more lurid. We were en route from Montclair to New Bedford, Massachusetts, and Frank, Jr., was left behind by mistake in a restaurant in New London. His absence wasn't discovered until near the end of the trip.

Dad wheeled the car around frantically and sped back to New London, breaking every traffic rule then on the books. We had stopped in the New London restaurant for lunch, and it had seemed a respectable enough place. It was night time when we returned, however, and the place was garish in colored lights. Dad left us in the car, and entered. After the drive in the dark, his eyes were squinted in the bright lights, and he couldn't see very well. But he hurried back to the booths and peered into each one.

A pretty young lady, looking for business, was drinking a highball in the second booth. Dad peered in, flustered.

"Hello, Pops," she said. "Don't be bashful. Are you looking for a naughty little girl?"

Dad was caught off guard.

"Goodness, no," he stammered, with all of his ordinary poise shattered. "I'm looking for a naughty little boy."

"Whoops, dearie," she said. "Pardon *me*."

All of us had been instructed that when we were lost we were supposed to stay in the same spot until someone returned for us, and Frank, Jr., was found, eating ice cream with the proprietor's daughter, back in the kitchen.

Anyway, those two experiences explain why Dad always insisted that the roll be called.

As we'd line up in front of the house before getting into the car, Dad would look us all over carefully.

"Are you all reasonably sanitary?" he would ask.

Dad would get out and help Mother and the two babies into

the front seat. He'd pick out someone whose behavior had been especially good, and allow him to sit up front too, as the left-hand lookout. The rest of would pile in the back, exchanging kicks and pinches under the protection of the lap robe as we squirmed around trying to make more room.

Finally, off we'd start. Mother, holding the two babies, seemed to glow with vitality. Her red hair, arranged in a flat pompadour, would begin to blow out in wisps from her hat. As long as we were still in town, and Dad wasn't driving fast, she seemed to enjoy the ride. She'd sit there listening to him and carrying on a rapid conversation. But just the same her ears were straining toward the sounds in the back seats, to make sure that everything was going all right.

She had plenty to worry about, too, because the more cramped we became the more noise we'd make. Finally, even Dad couldn't stand the confusion.

"What's the matter back there?" he'd bellow to Anne. "I thought I told you to keep everybody quiet."

"That would require an act of God," Anne would reply bitterly.

"You are going to think God is acting if you don't keep order back there. I said quiet and I want quiet."

"I'm trying to make them behave, Daddy. But no one will listen to me."

"I don't want any excuses; I want order. You're the oldest. From now on, I don't want to hear a single sound from back there. Do you all want to walk home?"

By this time, most of us did, but no one dared say so.

Things would quiet down for a while. Even Anne would relax and forget her responsibilities as the oldest. But finally there'd be trouble again, and we'd feel pinches and kicks down underneath the robe.

"Cut it out, Ernestine, you sneak," Anne would hiss.

"You take up all the room," Ernestine would reply. "Why don't you move over. I wish you'd stayed home."

"You don't wish it half as much as I," Anne would say, with all her heart. It was on such occasions that Anne wished she were an only child.

We made quite a sight rolling along in the car, with the top down. As we passed through cities and villages, we caused a stir equaled only by a circus parade.

This was the part Dad liked best of all. He'd slow down to five miles an hour and he'd blow the horns at imaginary obstacles and cars two blocks away. The horns were Dad's calliope.

"I seen eleven of them, not counting the man and the woman," someone would shout from the sidewalk.

"You missed the second baby up front here, Mister," Dad would call over his shoulder.

Mother would make believe she hadn't heard anything, and look straight ahead.

Pedestrians would come scrambling from side streets and children would ask their parents to lift them onto their shoulders.

"How do you grow them carrot-tops, Brother?"

"These?" Dad would bellow. "These aren't so much, Friend. You ought to see the ones I left at home."

Whenever the crowds gathered at some some intersection where we were stopped by traffic, the inevitable question came sooner or later.

"How do you feed all those kids, Mister?"

Dad would ponder for a minute. Then, rearing back so those on the outskirts could hear, he'd say as if he had just thought it up:

"Well, they come cheaper by the dozen, you know."

This was designed to bring down the house, and usually it did. Dad had a good sense of theater, and he'd try to time this apparent ad lib so that it would coincide with the change in traffic. While the peasantry was chuckling, the Pierce Arrow would buck away in clouds of gray smoke, while the professor up front rendered a few bars of Honk Honk Kadookah.

Leave 'em in stitches, that was us.

Dad would use that same "cheaper by the dozen" line whenever we stopped at a toll gate, or went to a movie, or bought tickets for a train or boat.

"Do my Irishmen come cheaper by the dozen?" he'd ask the man at the toll bridge. Dad could take one look at a man and know his nationality.

"Irishmen is it? And I might have known it. Lord love you, and it takes the Irish to raise a crew of red-headed Irishmen like that. The Lord Jesus didn't mean for any family like that to pay toll on my road. Drive through on the house."

STOP
TOLL
10¢
ADDITIONAL
PASSENGERS
5¢

"If he knew you were a Scot he'd take a shillalah and wrap it around your tight-fisted head," Mother giggled as we drove on.

"He probably would," Dad agreed. "Bejabers."

And one day at the circus.

"Do my Dutchmen come cheaper by the dozen?"

"Dutchmen? Ach. And what a fine lot of healthy Dutchmen."

"Have you heard the story about the man with the big family who took his children to the circus?" asked Dad. " 'My kids want to see your elephants,' said the man. 'That's nothing,' replied the ticket-taker, 'my elephants want to see your kids.' "

"I heard it before," said the circus man. "Often. Just go in that gate over there where there ain't no turnstile."

Mother only drew the line once at Dad's scenes in Foolish Carriage. That was in Hartford, Connecticut, right in the center of town. We had just stopped at a traffic sign, and the usual crowd was beginning to collect. We heard the words plainly from a plump lady near the curb.

"Just look at those poor, adorable little children," she said. "Don't they look sweet in their uniforms?"

Dad was all set to go into a new act—the benevolent superintendent taking the little orphan tykes out for a drive.

"Why bless my soul and body," he began loudly, in a jovial voice. "Why bless my buttons. Why bless . . ."

But for once Mother exploded.

"That," she said, "is the last straw. Positively and emphatically the ultimate straw."

This was something new, and Dad was scared. "What's the matter, Lillie?" he asked quickly.

"Not the penultimate, nor yet the ante-penultimate," said Mother. "But the ultimate."

"What's the matter, Lillie? Speak to me, girl."

"The camel's back is broken," Mother said. "Someone has just mistaken us for an orphanage."

"Oh, that," said Dad. "Sure, I know it. Wasn't it a scream?"

"No," said Mother. "It wasn't."

"It's these dusters we have to wear," Anne almost wept. "It's these damned, damned dusters. They look just like uniforms."

"Honestly, Daddy," said Ernestine, "it's so embarrassing to go riding when you always make these awful scenes."

The crowd was bigger than ever now.

"I," said Martha, "feel like Lady Godiva."

Mother was upset, but not too upset to reprimand Anne for swearing. Dad started to shake with laughter, and the crowd started laughing, too.

"That's a good one," somebody shouted. "Lady Godiva. You tell him, Sis. Lady Godiva!"

The boys began showing off. Bill sat on the top of the back seat as if he were a returning hero being cheered by a welcoming populace. He waved his hat aloft and bowed graciously to either side, with a fixed, stagey smile on his face. Frank and Fred swept imaginary ticker tape off his head and shoulders. But the girls, crimson-faced, dived under the lap robe.

"Get down from there, Bill," said Mother.

Dad was still roaring. "I just don't understand you girls," he wheezed. "That's the funniest thing I ever heard in my life. An orphanage on wheels. And me the superintendent. Gilbreth's Retreat for the Red-Haired Offspring of Unwed but Repentant Reprobates."

"Not humorous," said Mother. "Let's get out of here."

As we passed through the outskirts of Hartford, Dad was subdued and repentant; perhaps a little frightened.

"I didn't mean any harm, Lillie," he said.

"Of course you didn't, dear. And there's no harm done."

But Ernestine wasn't one to let an advantage drop.

"Well, we're through with the dusters," she announced from the back seat. "We'll never wear them again. Never again. Quoth the raven, and I quoth, 'Nevermore,' and I unquoth."

Dad could take it from Mother, but not from his daughters.

"Who says you're through with the dusters?" he howled. "Those dusters cost a lot of money, which does not grow on grape arbors. And if you think for a minute that . . ."

"No, Frank," Mother interrupted. "This time the girls are right. No more dusters."

It was a rare thing for them to disagree, and we all sat there enjoying it.

"All right, Lillie," Dad grinned, and everything was all right now. "As I always say, you're the boss. And I unquoth, too."

CHAPTER 4

Visiting Mrs. Murphy

Roads weren't marked very well in those days, and Dad never believed in signs anyway.

"Probably some kid has changed those arrows around," he would say, possibly remembering his own youth. "Seems to me that if we turned that way, the way the arrow says, we'd be headed right back where we came from."

The same thing happened with the Automobile Blue Book, the tourist's bible in the early days of the automobile. Mother would read to him:

"Six-tenths of a mile past windmill, bear left at brick church and follow paved road."

"That must be the wrong windmill," Dad would say. "No telling when the fellow who wrote that book came over this road to check up on things. My bump of direction tells me to turn right. They must have torn down the windmill the book's talking about."

Then, after he'd turned right and gotten lost, he'd blame Mother for giving him the wrong directions. Several times, he called Anne up to the front seat to read the Blue Book for him.

"Your Mother hasn't a very good sense of direction," he'd say loudly, glaring over his pince-nez at Mother. "She tells me to turn left when the book says to turn right. Then she blames me when we get lost. Now you read it to me just like it says. Don't change a single word, understand? And don't be making up anything about windmills that aren't there, or non-existent brick churches, just to confuse me. Read it just like it says."

But he wouldn't follow Anne's directions, either, and so he'd get lost just the same.

When things looked hopeless, Dad would ask directions at

a store or filling station. He'd listen, and then usually drive off in exactly the opposite direction from the one his informant had indicated.

"Old fool," Dad would mutter. "He's lived five miles from Trenton all his life and he doesn't even know how to get there. He's trying to route me back to New York."

Mother was philosophical about it. Whenever she considered that Dad was hopelessly lost, she'd open a little portable ice box that she kept on the floor of the car under her feet, and hand Jane her bottle. This was Mother's signal that it was time to have lunch.

"All right, Lillie," Dad would say. "Guess we might as well stop and eat, while I get my bearings. You pick out a good place for a picnic."

While we were eating, Dad would keep looking around for something that might be interesting. He was a natural teacher, and believed in utilizing every minute. Eating, he said, was "unavoidable delay." So were dressing, face-washing, and hair-combing. "Unavoidable delay" was not to be wasted.

If Dad found an ant hill, he'd tell us about certain colonies of ants that kept slaves and herds of cows. Then we'd take turns lying on our stomachs, watching the ants go back and forth picking up crumbs from sandwiches.

"See, they all work and they don't waste anything," Dad would say, and you could tell that the ant was one of his favorite creatures. "Look at the teamwork, as four of them try to move that piece of meat. That's motion study for you."

Or he'd point out a stone wall and say it was a perfect example of engineering. He'd explain about how the glaciers passed over the earth many years ago, and left the stone when they melted.

If a factory was nearby, he'd explain how you used a plumb line to get the chimney straight and why the windows had been placed a certain way to let in the maximum light. If the factory whistle blew, he'd take out his stopwatch and time the difference between when the steam appeared and when we heard the sound.

"Now take out your notebooks and pencils and I'll show you how to figure the speed of sound," he'd say.

He insisted that we make a habit of using our eyes and ears every single minute.

"Look there," he'd say. "What do you see? Yes, I know, it's a tree. But look at it. Study it. What do you *see?*"

But it was Mother who spun the stories that made the things we studied really unforgettable. If Dad saw motion study and team-work in an ant hill, Mother saw a highly complex civilization governed, perhaps, by a fat old queen who had a thousand black slaves bring her breakfast in bed mornings. If Dad stopped to explain the construction of a bridge, she would find the workman in his blue jeans, eating his lunch high on the top of the span. It was she who made us feel the breathless height of the structure and the relative puniness of the humans who had built it. Or if Dad pointed out a tree that had been bent and gnarled, it was Mother who made us sense how the wind, eating against the tree in the endless passing of time, had made its own relentless mark.

We'd sit there memorizing every word, and Dad would look at Mother as if he was sure he had married the most wonderful person in the world.

Before we left our picnic site, Dad would insist that all of the sandwich wrappings and other trash be carefully gathered, stowed in the lunch box, and brought home for disposal.

"If there's anything I can't stand, it's a sloppy camper," he'd say. "We don't want to leave a single scrap of paper on this man's property. We're going to leave things just like we found them, only even more so. We don't want to overlook so much as an apple peel."

Apple peels were a particularly sore subject. Most of us liked our apples without skins, and Dad thought this was wasteful. When he ate an apple, he consumed skin, core and seeds, which he alleged were the most healthful and most delectable portions of the fruit. Instead of starting at the side and eating his way around the equator, Dad started at the North Pole, and ate down through the core to the South.

He didn't actually forbid us to peal our apples or waste the cores, but he kept referring to the matter so as to let us know that he had noticed what we were doing.

Sometimes, in order to make sure that we left no rubbish behind, he'd have us form a line, like a company front in the army, and march across the picnic ground. Each of us was expected to pick up any trash in the territory that he covered.

The result was that we often came home with the leavings of countless previous picnickers.

"I don't see how you children can possibly clutter up a place the way you do," Dad would grin as he stuffed old papers, bottles, and rusty tin cans into the picnic box.

"That's not our mess, Daddy. You know that just as well as we do. What would we be doing with empty whiskey bottles and a last year's copy of the Hartford *Courant?*"

"That's what I'd like to know," he'd say, while sniffing the bottles.

Neither Dad nor Mother thought filling station toilets were sanitary. They never elaborated about just what diseases the toilets contained, but they made it plain that the ailments were both contagious and dire. In comparison, leprosy would be no worse than a bad cold. Dad always opened the door of a public rest room with his coattail, and the preparations and precautions that ensued were "unavoidable delay" in its worst aspect.

Once he and Mother had discarded filling stations as a possibility, the only alternative was the woods. Perhaps it was the nervous strain of enduring Dad's driving; perhaps it was simply that fourteen persons have different personal habits. At any rate, we seemed to stop at every promising clump of trees.

"I've seen dogs that paid less attention to trees," Dad used to groan.

For family delicacy, Dad coined two synonyms for going to the bathroom in the woods. One was "visiting Mrs. Murphy." The other was "examining the rear tire." They meant the same thing.

After a picnic, he'd say:

"How many have to visit Mrs. Murphy?"

Usually nobody would. But after we had been under way ten or fifteen minutes, someone would announce that he had to go. So Dad would stop the car, and Mother would take the girls into the woods on one side of the road, while Dad took the boys into the woods on the other.

"I know every piece of flora and fauna from Bangor, Maine, to Washington, D.C.," Dad exclaimed bitterly.

On the way home, when it was dark, Bill used to crawl up

into a swivel seat right behind Dad. Every time Dad was intent on steering while rounding a curve, Bill would reach forward and clutch his arm. Bill was a perfect mimic, and he'd whisper in Mother's voice, "Not so fast, Frank. Not so fast." Dad would think it was Mother grabbing his arm and whispering to him, and he'd make believe he didn't hear her.

Sometimes Bill would go into the act when the car was creeping along at a dinified thirty, and Dad finally would turn to Mother disgustedly and say:

"For the love of Mike, Lillie! I was only doing twenty."

He automatically subtracted ten miles an hour from the speed whenever he discussed the matter with Mother.

"I didn't say anything, Frank," Mother would tell him.

Dad would turn around, then, and see all of us giggling into our handkerchiefs. He'd give Bill a playful cuff and rumple his hair. Secretly, Dad was proud of Bill's imitations. He used to say that when Bill imitated a bird he (Dad) didn't dare to look up.

"You'll be the death of me yet, boy," Dad would say to Bill.

As we'd roll along, we'd sing three-and-four part harmony, with Mother and Dad joining in as soprano and bass. "Bobolink Swinging on the Bow," "Love's Old Sweet Song," "Our Highland Goat," "I've Been Working on the Railroad."

"What do only children *do* with themselves?" we'd think.

Dad would lean back against the seat and cock his hat on the side of his head. Mother would snuggle up against him as if she were cold. The babies were asleep now. Sometimes Mother turned around between songs and said to us: "Right now is the happiest time in the world." And perhaps it was.

CHAPTER 5

Mister Chairman

Dad was born in Fairfield, Maine, where his father ran a general store, farmed, and raised harness-racing horses. John Hiram Gilbreth died in 1871, leaving his three-year-old son, two older daughters, and a stern and rockbound widow.

Dad's mother, Grandma Gilbreth, believed that her children were fated to make important marks in the world, and that her first responsibility was to educate them so they would be prepared for their rendezvous with destiny.

"After that," she told her Fairfield neighbors, with a knowing nod, "blood will tell."

Without any business ties to hold her in Maine, she moved to Andover, Massachusetts, so that the girls could attend Abbott Academy. Later, when her oldest daughter showed a talent for music, Grandma Gilbreth decided to move again. Every New Englander knew the location of the universe's seat of culture, and it was to Boston that she now journeyed with her flock.

Dad wanted, more than anything else, to be a construction engineer, and his mother planned to have him enter Massachusetts Institute of Technology. By the time he finished high school, though, he decided this would be too great a drain on the family finances, and would interfere with his sisters' studies. Without consulting his mother, he took a job as a bricklayer's helper.

Once the deed was done, Grandma Gilbreth decided to make the best of it. After all, Mr. Lincoln had started by splitting rails.

"But if you're going to be a bricklayer's helper," she said, "for mercy sakes be a good bricklayer's helper."

"I'll do my best to find a good bricklayer to help," Dad grinned.

If Grandma thought Dad was going to be a good helper, his new foreman thought he was the worst he had encountered in forty years, man and boy, of bricklaying.

During Dad's first week at work he made so many suggestions about how brick could be laid faster and better that the foreman threatened repeatedly to fire him.

"You're the one who came here to learn," the foreman hollered at him. "For Christ's sake don't try to learn us."

Subtle innuendoes like that never worried Dad. Besides, he already knew that motion study was his element, and he had discovered something that apparently had never attracted the attention of industry before. He tried to explain it to the foreman.

"Did you ever notice that no two men use exactly the same way of laying bricks?" he asked. "That's important, and do you know why?"

"I know that if you open your mouth about bricklaying again, I'll lay a brick in it."

"It's important because if one bricklayer is doing the job the right way, then all the others are doing the job the wrong way. Now if I had your job, I'd find who's laying brick the right way, and make all the others copy him."

"If you had my job," shouted the livid-faced foreman, "the first thing you'd do is fire the red-headed unprintable son of a ruptured deleted who tried to get *your* job. And that's what I think you're trying to do."

He picked up a brick and waved it menacingly.

"I may not be smart enough to know who my best bricklayer is, but I know who my worst hod-carrier is. I'm warning you, stop bothering me or this brick goes in your mouth—edgewise."

Within a year, Dad designed a scaffold that made him the fastest bricklayer on the job. The principle of the scaffold was that loose bricks and mortar always were at the level of the top of the wall being built. The other bricklayers had to lean over to get their materials. Dad didn't.

"You ain't smart," the foreman scoffed. "You're just too Goddamned lazy to squat."

But the foreman had identical scaffolds built for all the men on the job, and even suggested that Dad send the original to the Mechanics Institute, where it won a prize. Later, on the foreman's recommendation, Dad was made foreman of a crew of his own. He achieved such astonishing speed records that he was promoted to superintendent, and then went into the contracting business for himself, building bridges, canals, industrial towns, and factories. Sometimes, after the contract work was finished, he was asked to remain on the job to install his motion study methods within the factory itself.

By the time he was twenty-seven, he had offices in New York, Boston, and London. He had a yacht, smoked cigars, and had a reputation as a snappy dresser.

Mother came from a well-to-do family in Oakland, California. She had met Dad in Boston while she was en route to

Europe on one of those well-chaperoned tours for fashionable young ladies of the 'nineties.

Mother was a Phi Beta Kappa and a psychology graduate of the University of California. In those days women who were scholars were viewed with some suspicion. When Mother and Dad were married, the Oakland paper said:

"Although a graduate of the University of California, the bride is nonetheless an extremely attractive young woman."

Indeed she was.

So it was Mother the psychologist and Dad the motion study man and general contractor, who decided to look into the new field of the psychology of management, and the old field of psychologically managing a houseful of children. They believed that what would work in the home would work in the factory, and what would work in the factory would work in the home.

Dad put the theory to a test shortly after we moved to Montclair. The house was too big for Tom Grieves, the handyman, and Mrs. Cunningham, the cook, to keep in order. Dad decided we were going to have to help them, and he wanted us to offer the help of our own accord. He had found that the best way to get cooperation out of employees in a factory was to set up a joint employer-employee board, which would make work assignments on a basis of personal choice and aptitude. He and Mother set up a Family Council, patterned after an employer-employee board. The council met every Sunday afternoon, immediately after dinner.

At the first session, Dad got to his feet formally, poured a glass of ice water, and began a speech.

"You will notice," he said, "that I am installed here as your chairman. I assume there are no objections. The chair, hearing no objections, will . . ."

"Mr. Chairman," Anne interrupted. Being in high school, she knew something of parliamentary procedure, and thought it might be a good idea to have the chairman represent the common people.

"Out of order," said Dad. "Very much out of order when the chair has the floor."

"But you said you heard no objections, and I want to object."

"Out of order means sit down, and you're out of order,"

Dad shouted. He took a swallow of ice water, and resumed his speech. "The first job of the Council is to apportion necessary work in the house and yard. Does the chair hear any suggestions?"

There were no suggestions. Dad forced a smile and attempted to radiate good humor.

"Come, come, fellow members of the Council," he said. "This is a democracy. Everybody has an equal voice. How do you want to divide the work?"

No one wanted to divide the work or otherwise be associated with it in any way, shape, or form. No one said anything.

"In a democracy everybody speaks," said Dad, "so, by jingo, start speaking." The Good Humor Man was gone now. "Jack, I recognize you. What do you think about dividing the work? I warn you, you'd better think something."

"I think," Jack said slowly, "that Mrs. Cunningham and Tom should do the work. They get paid for it."

"Sit down," Dad hollered. "You are no longer recognized."

Jack sat down amid general approval, except that of Dad and Mother.

"Hush, Jackie," Mother whispered. "They may hear you and leave. It's so hard to get servants when there are so many children in the house."

"I wish they would leave," said Jack. "They're too bossy."

Dan was next recognized by the chair.

"I think Tom and Mrs. Cunningham have enough to do," he said, as Dad and Mother beamed and nodded agreement. "I think we should hire more people to work for us."

"Out of order," Dad shouted. "Sit down and be quiet!"

Dad saw things weren't going right. Mother was the psychologist. Let her work them out.

"Your chairman recognizes the assistant chairman," he said, nodding to Mother to let her know he had just conferred that title upon her person.

"We could hire additional help," Mother said, "and that might be the answer."

We grinned and nudged each other.

"But," she continued, "that would mean cutting the budget somewhere else. If we cut out all desserts and allowances, we could afford a maid. And if we cut out moving pictures, ice cream sodas, and new clothes for a whole year, we could afford a gardener, too."

"Do I hear a motion to that effect?" Dad beamed. "Does anybody want to stop allowances?"

No one did. After some prodding by Dad, the motion on allotting work finally was introduced and passed. The boys would cut the grass and rake the leaves. The girls would sweep, dust and do the supper dishes. Everyone except Dad would make his own bed and keep his room neat. When it came to apportioning work on an aptitude basis, the smaller girls were assigned to dust the legs and lower shelves of furniture; the older girls to dust table tops and upper shelves. The older boys would push the lawnmowers and carry leaves. The younger ones would do the raking and weeding.

The next Sunday, when Dad convened the second meeting of the Council, we sat self-consciously around the table, biding our time. The chairman knew something was in the air, and it tickled him. He had trouble keeping a straight face when he called for new business.

Martha, who had been carefully coached in private caucus, arose.

"It has come to the attention of the membership," she began, "that the assistant chairman intends to buy a new rug for the dining room. Since the entire membership will be required to look upon, and sit in chairs resting upon, the rug, I move that the Council be consulted before any rug is purchased."

"Second the motion," said Anne.

Dad didn't know what to make of this one. "Any discussion?" he asked, in a move designed to kill time while he planned his counter attack.

"Mr. Chairman," said Lillian. "We have to sweep it. We should be able to choose it."

"We want one with flowers on it," Martha put in. "When you have flowers, the crumbs don't show so easily, and you save motions by not having to sweep so often."

"We want to know what sort of a rug the assistant chairman intends to buy," said Ernestine.

"We want to make sure the budget can afford it," Fred announced.

"I recognize the assistant chairman," said Dad. "This whole Council business was your idea anyway, Lillie. What do we do now?"

"Well," Mother said doubtfully, "I had planned to get a plain violet-colored rug, and I had planned to spend a hundred dollars. But if the children think that's too much, and if they want flowers, I'm willing to let the majority rule."

"I move," said Frank, "that not more than ninety-five dollars be spent."

Dad shrugged his shoulders. If Mother didn't care, he certainly didn't.

"So many as favor the motion to spend only ninety-five dollars, signify by saying aye."

The motion carried unanimously.

"Any more new business?"

"I move," said Bill, "that we spend the five dollars we have saved to buy a collie puppy."

"Hey, wait a minute," said Dad. The rug had been somewhat of a joke, but the dog question was serious. We had wanted a dog for years. Dad thought that any pet which didn't lay eggs was an extravagance that a man with twelve children could ill afford. He felt that if he surrendered on the dog question, there was no telling what the Council might vote next. He had a sickening mental picture of a barn full of ponies, a roadster for Anne, motorcycles, a swimming pool, and, ultimately, the poor house or a debtors' prison, if they still had such things.

"Second the motion," said Lillian, yanking Dad out of his reverie.

"A dog," said Jack, "would be a pet. Everyone in the family could pat him, and I would be his master."

"A dog," said Dan, "would be a friend. He could eat scraps of food. He would save us waste and would save motions for the garbage man."

"A dog," said Fred, "would keep burglars away. He would sleep on the foot of my bed, and I would wash him whenever he was dirty."

"A dog," Dad mimicked, "would be an accursed nuisance. He would be our master. He would eat me out of house and home. He would spread fleas from the garret to the porte-cochere. He would be positive to sleep on the foot of *my* bed.

Nobody would wash his filthy, dirty, flea-bitten carcass."

He looked pleadingly at Mother.

"Lillie, Lillie, open your eyes," he implored. "Don't you see where this is leading us? Ponies, roadsters, trips to Hawaii, silk stockings, rouge, and bobbed hair."

"I think, dear," said Mother, "that we must rely on the good sense of the children. A five-dollar dog is not a trip to Hawaii."

We voted, and there was only one negative ballot—Dad's. Mother abstained. In after years, as the collie grew older, shed hair on the furniture, bit the mailman, and did in fact try to appropriate the foot of Dad's bed, the chairman was heard to remark on occasion to the assistant chairman:

"I give nightly praise to my Maker that I never cast a ballot to bring that lazy, disreputable, ill-tempered beast into what was once my home. I'm glad I had the courage to go on record as opposing that illegitimate, shameless flea-bag that now shares my bed and board. You abstainer, you!"

CHAPTER 6

Touch System

Like most of Dad's and Mother's ideas, the Family Council was basically sound and, although it verged sometimes on the hysterical, brought results. Family purchasing committees, duly elected, bought the food, clothes, furniture, and athletic equipment. A utilities committee levied one-cent fines on wasters of water and electricity. A projects committee saw that work was completed as scheduled. Allowances were decided by the Council, which also meted out rewards and punishment. Despite Dad's forebodings, there were no ponies or roadsters.

One purchasing committee found a large department store which gave us wholesale rates on everything from underwear to baseball gloves. Another bought canned goods directly from a manufacturer, in truckload lots.

It was the Council, too, which worked out the system of submitting bids for unusual jobs to be done.

When Lill was eight, she submitted a bid of forty-seven cents to paint a long, high fence in the back yard. Of course it was the lowest bid, and she got the job.

"She's too young to try to paint that fence all by herself," Mother told Dad. "Don't let her do it."

"Nonsense," said Dad. "She's got to learn the value of money and to keep agreements. Let her alone."

Lill, who was saving for a pair of roller skates and wanted the money, kept insisting she could do it.

"If you start it, you'll have to finish it," Dad said.

"I'll finish it, Daddy. I know I can."

"You've got yourself a contract, then."

It took Lill ten days to finish the job, working every day after school and all day week ends. Her hands blistered, and some nights she was so tired she couldn't sleep. It worried Dad so that some nights he didn't sleep very well either. But he made her live up to her contract.

"You've got to let her stop," Mother kept telling him. "She'll have a breakdown or something—or else you will."

"No," said Dad. "She's learning the value of money and she's learning that when you start something it's necessary to finish it if you want to collect. She's got to finish. It's in her contract."

"You sound like Shylock," Mother said.

But Dad stood firm.

When Lill finally completed the job, she came to Dad in tears.

"It's done," she said. "I hope you're satisfied. Now can I have my forty-seven cents?"

Dad counted out the change.

"Don't cry, honey," he said. "No matter what you think of your old Daddy, he did it for your own good. If you go look under your pillow you'll find that Daddy really loved you all the time."

The present was a pair of roller skates.

Fred headed the utilities committee and collected the fines.

Once, just before he went to bed, he found that someone had left a faucet dripping and that there was a bathtub full of hot water. Jack had been asleep for more than an hour, but Fred woke him up.

"Get in there and take a bath," he said.

"But I had a bath just before I went to bed."

"I know you did, and you left the faucet dripping," Fred told him. "Do you want to waste that perfectly good water?"

"Why don't you take a bath?" Jack asked.

"I take my baths in the morning. You know that. That's the schedule."

Jack had two baths that night.

One day Dad came home with two victrolas and two stacks of records. He whistled assembly as he hit the front steps, and we helped him unload.

"Kids," he said, "I have a wonderful surprise. Two victrolas and all these lovely records."

"But we have a victrola, Daddy."

"I know that, but the victrola we have is the downstairs victrola. Now we are going to have two upstairs victrolas. Won't that be fun?"

"Why?"

"Well from now on," said Dad, "we are going to try to do away with unavoidable delay. The victrolas will go in the bathrooms—one in the boys' bathroom and the other in the girls' bathroom. I'll bet we'll be the only family in town with a victrola in every bath. And when you are taking a bath, or brushing your teeth, or otherwise occupied, you will play the victrolas."

"Why?"

"Why, why, why," mimicked Dad. "Why this and why that. Does there have to be a why for everything?"

"There doesn't have to be, Daddy," Ernestine explained patiently. "But with you there usually is. When you start talking about unavoidable delay and victrolas, dance music is not the first thing that pops into our minds."

"No," Dad admitted. "It's not dance music. But you're going to find this is just as good in a way, and more educational."

"What kind of records are they?" Anne asked.

"Well," Dad said, "they are very entertaining. They are

French and German language lesson records. You don't have to listen to them consciously. Just play them. And they'll finally make an impression."

"Oh, no!"

Dad soon tired of diplomacy and psychology.

"Shut up and listen to me," he roared. "I have spent one hundred and sixty dollars for this equipment. Did I get it for myself? I most emphatically by jingo well did not. I happen already to be able to speak German and French with such fluency that I frequently am mistaken for a native of both of those countries."

This was at best a terribly gross exaggeration, for while Dad had studied languages for most of his adult life, he never had become very familiar with French, although he could stumble along fairly well in German. Usually he insisted that Mother accompany him as an interpreter on his business trips to Europe. Languages came naturally to Mother.

"No," Dad continued, "I did not buy this expenisve equipment for myself, although I must say I would like nothing better than to have my own private victrola and my own private language records. I bought it for you, as a present. And you are going to use it. If those two victrolas aren't going every morning from the minute you get up until you come down to breakfast, I'm going to know the reason why."

"One reason," said Bill, "might be that it is impossible to change records while you are in the bathtub."

"A person who applies motion study can be in and out of the tub in the time it takes one record to play."

That was perfectly true. Dad would sit in the tub and put the soap in his right hand. Then he'd place his right hand on his left shoulder and run it down the top of his left arm, back up the bottom of his left arm to his armpit, down his side, down the outside of his left leg, and then up the inside of his left leg. Then he'd change the soap to his left hand and do the same thing to his right side. After a couple of circular strokes on his midsection and his back, and some special attention to his feet and face, he'd duck under for a rinse and get out. He had all the boys in the bathroom several times to demonstrate just how he did it, and he sat in the middle of the living room rug one day, with all his clothes on, to teach the girls.

So there was no more unavoidable delay in the bathroom, and it wasn't long before we were all speaking at least a pidgin variety of French and German. For ten years, the victrolas ground out their lessons on the second floor of our Montclair house. As we became fairly fluent, we often would speak the languages at the dinner table. Dad was left out of the conversation when the talk was in French.

"Your German accents are not so bad," he said. "I can understand most of what you say when you talk German. But your French accents are so atrocious that no one but yourselves could possibly understand you. I believe you've developed some exotic language all your own, which has no more relation to French than it does to Pig Latin."

We giggled, and he turned furiously to Mother.

"Don't you think so, Lillie?"

"Well, dear," she said. "I don't think anyone would mistake them for natives of France, but I can usually make out what they're getting at."

"That," said Dad, with some dignity, "is because you learned your French in this country, where everybody talks with an accent, whereas my knowledge of the language came straight from the streets of Paris."

"Maybe so, dear," said Mother. "Maybe so."

That night, Dad moved the boys' bathroom victrola into his bedroom, and we heard him playing French records, far into the night.

At about the time that he brought home the victrolas, Dad became a consultant to the Remington typewriter company and, through motion study methods, helped Remington develop the world's fastest typist.

He told us about it one night at dinner—how he had put little flashing lights on the fingers of the typist and taken moving pictures and time exposures to see just what motions she employed and how those motions could be reduced.

"Anyone can learn to type fast," Dad concluded. "Why I've got a system that will teach touch typing in two weeks. Absolutely guaranteed."

You could see the Great Experiment hatching in his mind.

"In two weeks," he repeated. "Why I could even teach a child to type touch system in two weeks."

"Can you type touch system, Daddy?" Bill asked.

"In two weeks," said Dad. "I could teach a child. Anybody can do it if he will do just exactly what I tell him to do."

The next day he brought home a new, perfectly white typewriter, a gold knife, and an Ingersoll watch. He unwrapped them and put them on the dining room table.

"Can I try the typewriter, Daddy?" asked Mart.

"Why is the typewriter white?" Anne wanted to know. "All typewriters I've ever seen were black. It's beautiful, all right, but why is it white?"

"It's white so that it will photograph better," Dad explained. "Also, for some reason, anyone who sees a white typewriter wants to type on it. Don't ask me why. It's psychology."

All of us wanted to use it, but Dad wouldn't let anyone touch it but himself.

"This is an optional experiment," he said. "I believe I can teach the touch system in two weeks. Anyone who wants to learn will be able to practice on the white machine. The one who can type the fastest at the end of two weeks will receive the typewriter as a present. The knife and watch will be prizes awarded on a handicap basis, taking age into consideration."

Except for the two youngest, who still weren't talking, we all said we wanted to learn.

"Can I practice first, Daddy?" Lill asked.

"No one practices until I say 'practice.' Now first I will show you how the typewriter works." Dad got a sheet of paper. "The paper goes in here. You turn this—so-oo. And you push the carriage over to the end of the line—like this."

And Dad, using two fingers, hesitatingly pecked out the first thing that came to his mind—his name.

"Is that the touch system, Daddy?" Bill asked.

"No," said Dad. "I'll show you the touch system in a little while."

"Do you know the touch system, Daddy?"

"Let's say I know how to teach it, Billy boy."

"But do you know it yourself, Daddy?"

"I know how to teach it," Dad shouted. "In two weeks, I can teach it to a child. Do you hear me? I have just finished helping to develop the fastest typist in the world. Do you hear that? They tell me Caruso's voice teacher can't sing a by jingoed note. Does that answer your question?"

"I guess so," said Bill.

"Any other questions?"

There weren't. Dad then brought out some paper diagrams of a typewriter keyboard, and passed one to each of us.

"The first thing you have to do is to memorize that keyboard. QWERTYUIOP. Those are the letters in the top line. Memorize them. Get to know them forward and backwards. Get to know them so you can say them with your eyes closed. Like this."

Dad closed his right eye, but kept his left open just a slit so that he could still read the chart.

"QWERTYUIOP. See what I mean? Get to know them in your sleep. That's the first step."

We looked crestfallen.

"I know. You want to try out that white typewriter. Pretty, isn't it?"

He clicked a few keys.

"Runs as smoothly as a watch, doesn't it?"

We said it did.

"Well, tomorrow or the next day you'll be using it. First you have to memorize the keyboard. Then you've got to learn what fingers to use. Then you'll graduate to Moby Dick here. And one of you will win him."

Once we had memorized the keyboard, our fingers were colored with chalk. The little fingers were colored blue, the index fingers red and so forth. Corresponding colors were placed on the key zones of the diagrams. For instance, the Q, A and Z, all of which are hit with the little finger of the left hand, were colored blue to match the blue little finger.

"All you have to do now is practice until each finger has learned the right color habit," Dad said. "And once you've got that, we'll be ready to start."

In two days we were fairly adept at matching the colors on our fingers with the colors on the keyboard diagrams. Ernestine was the fastest, and got the first chance to sit down at the white typewriter. She hitched her chair up to it confidently, while we all gathered around.

"Hey, no fair, Daddy," she wailed. "You've put blank caps on all the keys. I can't see what I'm typing."

Blank caps are fairly common now, but Dad had thought

up the idea and had had them made specially by the Remington company.

"You don't have to see," Dad said. "Just imagine that those keys are colored, and type just like you were typing on the diagram."

Ern started slowly, and then picked up speed, as her fingers jumped instinctively from key to key. Dad stood in back of her, with a pencil in one hand and a diagram in the other. Every time she made a mistake, he brought the pencil down on the top of her head.

"Stop it Daddy. That hurts. I can't concentrate knowing that that pencil's about to descend on my head."

"It's meant to hurt. Your head has to teach your fingers not to make mistakes."

Ern typed along. About every fifth word, she'd make a mistake and the pencil would descend with a bong. But the bongs became less and less frequent and finally Dad put away the pencil.

"That's fine, Ernie," he said. "I believe I'll keep you."

By the end of the two weeks, all children over six years old and Mother knew the touch system reasonably well. Dad said he knew it, too. We were a long way from being fast—because nothing but practice gives speed—but we were reasonably accurate.

Dad entered Ernestine's name in a national speed contest, as a sort of child prodigy, but Mother talked him out of it and Ern never actually competed.

"It's not that I want to show her off," he told Mother. "It's just that I want to do the people a favor—to show them what can be done with proper instructional methods and motion study."

"I don't think it would be too good an idea, dear," Mother said. "Ernestine is high strung, and the children are conceited enough as it is."

Dad compromised by taking moving pictures of each of us, first with colored fingers practicing on the paper diagrams and then actually working on the typewriter. He said the pictures were "for my files," but about a month later they were released in a newsreel, which showed everything except the pencil descending on our heads. And some of us today recoil every time we touch the backspace key.

Since Dad thought eating was a form of unavoidable delay, he utilized the dinner hour as an instruction period. His primary rule was that no one could talk unless the subject was of general interest.

Dad was the one who decided what subjects were of general interest. Since he was convinced that everything he uttered was interesting, the rest of the family had trouble getting a word in edgewise.

"Honestly, we have the stupidest boy in our history class," Anne would begin.

"Is he cute?" Ernestine asked.

"Not of general interest," Dad roared.

"I'm interested," Mart said.

"But I," Dad announced, "am bored stiff. Now if Anne had seen a two-headed boy in history class, that would have been of general interest."

Usually at the start of a meal, while Mother served up the plates at one end of the table, Dad served up the day's topic of conversation at the other end.

"I met an engineer today who had just returned from India," he said. "What do you think he told me? He believes India has fewer industries for its size than has any other country in the world."

We knew, then, that for the duration of that particular meal even the dullest facts about India would be deemed of exceptional general interest; whereas neighboring Siam, Persia, China, and Mongolia would, for some reason, be considered of but slight general interest, and events which had transpired in Montclair, New Jersey, would be deemed of no interest whatsoever. Once India had been selected as the destination, Dad would head toward it as relentlessly as if Garcia were waiting there, and we had the message.

Sometimes, the topic of conversation was a motion study project, such as clearing off the dishes from the table. Motion study was always of great general interest.

"Is it better to stack the dishes on the table, so that you can carry out a big pile?" Dad asked. "Or is it better to take a few of them at a time into the butler's pantry, where you can rinse them while you stack? After dinner we'll divide the table into two parts, and try one method on one part and the other method on the other. I'll time you."

Also of exceptional general interest was a series of tricks whereby Dad could multiply large numbers in his head, without using pencil and paper. The explanation of how the tricks are worked is too complicated to explain in detail here, and two fairly elementary examples should suffice.

1. To multiply forty-six times forty-six, you figure how much greater forty-six is than twenty-five. The answer is twenty-one. Then you figure how much less forty-six is than fifty. The answer is four. You can square the four and get sixteen. You put the twenty-one and the sixteen together, and the answer is twenty-one sixteen, or 2,116.

2. To multiply forty-four times forty-four, you figure how much greater forty-four is than twenty-five. The answer is nineteen. Then you figure how much less forty-four is than fifty. The answer is six. You square the six and get thirty-six. You put the nineteen and the thirty-six together, and the answer is nineteen thirty-six, or 1,936.

"I want to teach all of you how to multiply two-digit numbers in your head," Dad announced at dinner.

"Not of general interest," said Anne.

"Now if you had learned to multiply a two-digit number by a two-headed calf," Ern suggested.

"Those who do not think it is of general interest may leave the table and go to their rooms," Dad said coldly, "and I understand there is apple pie for dessert."

Nobody left.

"Since everyone now appears to be interested," said Dad, "I will explain how it's done."

It was a complicated thing for children to understand, and it involved memorizing the squares of all numbers up to twenty-five. But Dad took it slowly, and within a couple of months the older children had learned all the tricks involved.

While Mother carved and served the plates—Dad sometimes carved wood for a hobby, but he never touched a carving knife at the table—Dad would shout out problems in mental arithmetic for us.

"Nineteen times seventeen."

"Three twenty-three."

"Right. Good boy, Bill."

"Fifty-two times fifty-two."

"Twenty-seven zero four."

"Right. Good girl, Martha."

Dan was five when this was going on, and Jack was three. One night at supper, Dad was firing questions at Dan on the squares of numbers up to twenty-five. This involved straight memory, and no mental arithmetic.

"Fifteen times fifteen," said Dad.

"Two twenty-five," said Dan.

"Sixteen times sixteen," said Dad.

Jack, sitting in his high chair next to Mother, gave the answer. "Two fifty-six."

At first Dad was irritated, because he thought one of the older children was butting in.

"I'm asking Dan," he said, "you older children stop showing off and . . ." Then he registered a double take.

"What did you say, Jackie boy?" Dad cooed.

"Two fifty-six."

Dad drew a nickel out of his pocket and grew very serious. "Have you been memorizing the squares as I asked the questions to the older children, Jackie?"

Jack didn't know whether that was good or bad, but he nodded.

"If you can tell me what seventeen times seventeen is, Jackie boy, this nickel is yours."

"Sure, Daddy," said Jack. "Two eighty-nine."

Dad passed him the nickel and turned beaming to Mother. "Lillie," he said, "we'd better keep that boy, too."

Martha, at eleven, became the fastest in the family at mental mathematics. Still feeling frustrated because he hadn't been able to take Ernestine to the speed typing contest, Dad insisted on taking Martha to an adding machine exhibition in New York.

"No, Lillie," he told Mother. "This one is not high strung. I was willing to compromise on moving pictures of the typing, but you can't take movies of this. She goes to New York with me."

Martha stood up on a platform at the adding machine show, and answered the problems quicker than the calculators could operate. Dad, of course, stood alongside her. After the final applause, he told the assemblage modestly:

"There's really nothing to it. I've got a boy named Jack at

home who's almost as good as she is. I would have brought him here with me, but Mrs. Gilbreth said he's still too young. Maybe next year, when he's four . . ."

By this time, all of us had begun to suspect that Dad had his points as a teacher, and that he knew what he was talking about. There was one time, though, when he failed.

"Tomorrow," he told us at dinner, "I'm going to make a cement bird bath. All those who want to watch me should come home right after school, and we'll make it in the late afternoon."

Dad had long since given up general contracting, to devote all of his time to scientific management and motion study, but we knew he had been an expert bricklayer and had written a book on reinforced concrete.

The next afternoon he built a mold, mixed his concrete confidently, and poured his bird bath.

"We'll let it set for awhile, and then take the mold off," he said.

Dad had to go out of town for a few weeks. When he returned, he changed into old clothes, whistled assembly, and led us out into the yard.

"I've had this bird bath on my mind all the time I was away," he said. "It should be good and hard now."

"Will the birds come and take a bath in it, Daddy?" Fred asked.

"I would say, Freddy, that birds will come for miles to take a bath in it. Indeed, on Saturday nights I would say the birds will be standing in line to use our lovely bathtub."

He leaned over the mold. "Stand back, everybody," he said. "We will now unveil the masterpiece. Get your towels ready, little birdies, it's almost bathing time."

We stood hushed and waiting. But as he lifted the bird bath out of the mold, there was an unbelievable grating sound, and a pile of dust and rubble lay at our feet. Dad stood deflated and silent. He took it so seriously that we felt sorry for him.

"Never mind, Daddy," Lill said. "We know you tried, anyway."

"Bill," Dad said sternly. "Did you?"

"Did I what, Daddy?"

"Did you touch my bird bath?"

"No, Daddy, honest."

Dad reached down and picked up some of the concrete. It crumbled into dust between his fingers.

"Too much sand," he muttered. And then to Bill. "No, it's my fault. Too much sand. I know you didn't touch it, and I'm sorry I implied that you did."

But you couldn't keep Dad down for long.

"Well," he said, "that didn't work out so very well. But I've built some of the finest and tallest buildings in the whole world. And some bridges and roads and canals that stretch for miles and miles."

"Is a bird bath harder to build than a tall building, Daddy?" asked Dan.

Dad, deflated all over again, kicked the rubble with his toe and started toward the house.

"Too much sand," he muttered.

CHAPTER 7

Skipping Through School

Mother saw her children as a dozen individuals, a dozen different personalities, who eventually would have to make their ways separately in the world. Dad saw them as an all-inclusive group, to be brought up under one master plan that would be best for everybody. What was good for Anne, he believed, would be good for Ernestine, for Bill, for Jack.

Skipping grades in school was part of Dad's master plan. There was no need, he said, for his children to be held back by a school system geared for children of simply average parents.

Dad made periodic surprise visits to our schools to find out if and when we were ready to skip. Because of his home-training program—spelling games, geography quizzes, and the arithmetic and languages—we sometimes were prepared to skip; but never so prepared as Dad thought we should be.

The standard reward for skipping was a new bicycle. None of us used to like to jump grades, because it meant making new friends and trailing behind the rest of the class until we could make up the work. But the bicycle incentive was great, and there was always the fear that a younger brother or sister would skip and land in your class. That would be the disgrace supreme. So whenever it looked as if anyone down the family line was about to skip, every older child would study frantically so that he could jump ahead, too.

Mother saw the drawbacks. She knew that, while we were advanced for our age in some subjects, we were only average or below in some intangibles such as leadership and sociability. She knew, too, that Dad, who was in his fifties, wanted to get as many of his dozen as possible through school and college before he died.

As for report cards, members of the family who brought home good grades were feted and rewarded.

"Chip off the old block," Dad would crow. "Youngest in his class, and he brings home all A's. I used to lead my class in the fifth grade, too, and I was always the one picked to draw the turkey on the blackboard come Thanksgiving. My only bad subject was spelling. Never learned to spell until I was a grown man. I used to tell the teachers that I'd be able to hire a bunch of stenographers to do my spelling for me."

Then he'd lean back and roar. You couldn't tell whether he was really bragging, or just teasing you.

Children who brought home poor grades were made to study during the afternoon, and were tutored by the older ones and Mother and Dad. But Dad seldom scolded for this offense. He was convinced that the low marks were merely an error of judgment on the teacher's part.

"That teacher must not know her business," he'd grumble for Mother's benefit. "Imagine failing one of my children. Why she doesn't even have the sense to tell a smart child from a moron."

When we moved to Montclair, the business of enrolling us in the public schools was first on the agenda. Dad loaded seven of us in the Pierce Arrow and started out.

"Follow me, Live Bait," he said. "I'm going to enjoy this. We are going to descend upon the halls of learning. Remember, this is one of the most important experiences of your life. Make the most of it and keep your eyes and ears open. Let me do the talking."

The first stop was Nishuane, the elementary school, an imposing and forbidding structure of dark red brick. At its front were two doors, one marked "Boys," the other "Girls."

"Frank, Bill, Lill and Fred—this is your school," said Dad. "Come on, in we go. No dying cow looks. Hold your shoulders straight and look alive."

We piled out, hating it.

"You older girls, too," said Dad. "We may as well make an impression."

"Oh, no, Daddy."

"What's the matter with you? Come on!"

"But this isn't our school."

"I know it, but we may as well show them what a real family looks like. Wonder if I have time to run home and get your Mother and the babies."

That was enough to cause the older girls to jump quickly out of the car.

As we approached the door marked "Boys," the girls turned and started for the other entrance.

"Here, where are you girls going?" Dad asked.

"This is the girls' door over this way."

"Nonsense," said Dad. "We don't have to pay any attention to those foolish rules. What are they trying to do here, anyway? Regiment the kids?"

"Hush, Daddy. They'll hear you."

"Suppose they do. They're going to hear from me soon enough, anyway."

We all went in through the door marked "Boys." Classes already were in session, and you could see the children watching us through the open doors as we walked down the corridor to the principal's office. One teacher came gasping to the doorway.

"Good morning, Miss," said Dad, bowing with a flourish. "Just a Gilbreth invasion—or a partial invasion, I should say, since I left most of them at home with their mother. Beautiful morning, isn't it?"

"It certainly is," she smiled.

The principal of Nishuane was an elderly lady, almost as

plump as Dad, and much shorter. She had the most refined voice in the Middle Atlantic States. Probably she was a very kind, gracious woman, but she was a principal, and we were scared of her. All but Dad.

"Good morning, Ma'am," he said, with another bow. "I'm Gilbreth."

"How do you do. I've heard of you."

"Only four of them enroll here," Dad said, nodding toward us. "I brought the other three along so that you could get a better idea of the crop we're raising. Red heads mostly. Some blondes. All speckled."

"Just so. I'll take care of everything, Mr. Gilbreth. And I'm glad you dropped in."

"Wait a minute," said Dad. "I'm not just dropping in. I want to meet their teachers and see what grades they're going in. I'm not in any hurry. I've arranged my schedule so that I can give you my entire morning."

"I'll be glad to introduce you to the teachers, Mr. Gilbreth. As to the classes they will enter, that depends on their ages."

"Hold on, hold on," Dad put in. "Depends on age, yes. Mental age. Come here, Bill. How old are you? Eight, isn't it?"

Bill nodded.

"What grade do eight-year-olds usually belong in?"

"The third," the principal replied.

"I want him in the fifth, please."

"The fourth," said the principal. But you could tell that she was beaten.

"Ma'am," said Dad. "Do you know the capital of Colombia? Do you know the population of Des Moines, according to the 1910 census? I know you do, being the principal. So does Bill, here. So does little Jackie, but I had to leave him home. It's time for his bottle."

"The fifth," said the principal.

After we were enrolled came the surprise visits that we used to dread, because Dad seemed to break all the school rules. He went in doors marked "Out," he went up stairs marked "Down," and he sometimes even wore his hat in the corridors. For any one of these offenses, a child might be kept after school for a week; for all three, he might be sent to reform school until his beard grew down to his knees. But the teachers always seemed to enjoy Dad's visits and the attention he gave them, and the principals—even the Nishuane principal—always were after him to speak at the school assemblies.

"If you had half the sense, or the manners, of your father or your mother," the teachers used to say, when they'd scold one of us.

Sometimes the class would be right in the middle of saluting the flag, when in would burst Dad, with a grin stretching from ear to ear. Even the kindergarten children knew of the inflexible rule against entering a room while the flag was being saluted. No pupil would have dared to do so, even to spread an alarm of fire, monsoon or the black plague. Yet, there was Dad. The floor seemed to rock while you waited for Miss Billsop to bare her fangs and spring. But, instead, Miss Billsop would grin right back at him. Then Dad would salute the flag, too, and you'd hear his deep voice booming over that of the class: "One nation, indivisible, with liberty and justice for all."

Everybody in school knew that the Lord's Prayer followed the salute to the flag, and after that "justice for all" you were supposed to sit down and bow your head on your desk, with your eyes closed, waiting for the teacher to lead off with "Our Father, Who art in Heaven." And there was Dad.

"Good morning, Miss Billsop," he'd say. Then—and this was the worst of all—"Hello, Frank, Junior. I see you hiding behind that book. Sort of a surprise visit, eh? Hello, shavers. Excuse me for interrupting you. I'm Frank, Junior's, father. I won't take up much of your teacher's time. Then she can get back to the lessons I know you love so well."

The class would laugh, and Dad would laugh with them. He really loved kids.

"How is he getting alone, Miss Billsop?" (Once he called her Milksop, by mistake, and sent her a dozen roses later that morning, as an apology.) "What's the story? Is he keeping up with his work? Does he need to study more at home? You're doing a fine job with him, and he's always quoting you around the house. Do you think he can skip the next grade? If he doesn't behave himself, just let me know."

Dad would listen to Miss Billsop for a few minutes, then drop you what might have been a wink, and burst out of the room again, to go to the classroom of another Gilbreth child.

Miss Billsop would still be smiling when she'd turn to the class.

"Now children, we will bow our heads, close our eyes, and repeat the Lord's Prayer."

You'd wait anxiously for recess, knowing that you were going to have to fight if anyone so much as hinted that your father was a fat man, or that he didn't know the school rules even as well as a kindergarten child. But, instead, a couple of the kids would come up shyly and tell you:

"Gee, your old man is the cat's, all right. He's not scared of anything."

"Yeah," you'd say.

Sometimes you'd try to tell Dad after such a visit that his popping in like that was embarrassing.

"Embarrassing?" he would ask a little hurt. "What's embarrassing about it?" Then he'd sort of pinch you on the shoulder and say, "Well, maybe it is a little embarrassing for me, too, Old Timer. But you've got to learn not to show it, and once you've learned that, it doesn't matter any more. The important thing is that dropping in like that gets results. The teachers lap it up."

They did, too.

Since Dad went to church only if one of us was being christened—in other words, about once a year—Mother had to carry the ball when it came to enrolling us in Sunday school. Dad said he believed in God, but that he couldn't stand clergymen.

"They give me the creeps," he said. "Show me a man with a loud mouth, a roving eye, a fat rear, and an empty head, and I'll show you a preacher."

Dad had crossed to Europe once on a liner carrying a delegation to a ministers' convention. It was on this trip that he had acquired most of his distaste for the reverends.

"They monopolized all the conversation at dinner," he complained—and it was obvious that this was the real sin he could never forgive. "They crawled out of every argument by citing the Lord God Jehovah as their authority. I was asked on an average of eight times a day, for eight miserable and consecutive days, to come to Jesus, whatever that is. And a stewardess told me that her behind had been pinched surreptitiously so many times between Hoboken and Liverpool that she had to eat off a mantelpiece."

Dad believed in Sunday school, though, because he thought everyone should have some knowledge of the Bible.

"The successful man knows something about everything," he said.

He used to drive Mother and us to Sunday school, and then sit outside in the car, reading *The New York Times* and ignoring the shocked glares of passing churchgoers.

"You at least might come in where it's warm," Mother told him. "You'll catch your death out here."

"No," Dad replied. "When I go to meet my Maker, I want to be able to tell Him that I did my praying on my own, halted by neither snow nor sleet nor icy stares, and without the aid of any black-frocked, collar-backwards cheerleader."

"You might at least park where they won't all see you."

"All the glares in Christendom won't force me to retreat," Dad said. "Besides, I'll bet I have half the town praying to save my soul."

Dad told Mother that the only church he'd even consider joining was the Catholic church.

"That's the only outfit that would give me some special credit for having such a large family," he said. "Besides, most priests whom I have known do not appear to be surreptitious pinchers."

"Like this," said Ernestine, pinching Anne where she sat down.

"You stop that," said Mother, shocked. And turning to Dad.

"You're really going to have to watch the stories you tell in front of the children. They don't miss a thing."

"The sooner they know what to expect from preachers, the better," said Dad. "Do you want to have them all eating off the mantelpiece?"

Although Mother always claimed that she liked church, she usually was ready to go home immediately after Sunday school.

"What's the matter, Lillie?" Dad would ask. "Stay around awhile. I'll take the children home and come back for you."

"No, I guess not this morning."

"You're not going to be able to get past St. Peter just on the strength of going to Sunday school, you know."

"Well, I'd be miserable up there anyway without you," Mother would smile. "Come on. Let's go home. I'll go to church next Sunday."

Mother did take an active part in the Sunday school work, though. She didn't teach a class, but she served on a number of committees. Once she called on a woman who had just moved to town, to ask her to serve on a fund-raising committee.

"I'd be glad to if I had the time," the woman said. "But I have three young sons and they keep me on the run. I'm sure if you have a boy of your own, you'll understand how much trouble three can be."

"Of course," said Mother. "That's quite all right. And I do understand."

"Have you any children, Mrs. Gilbreth?"

"Oh, yes."

"Any boys?"

"Yes, indeed."

"May I ask how many?"

"Certainly. I have six boys."

"Six boys!" gulped the woman. "Imagine a family of six!"

"Oh, there're more in the family than that. I have six girls, too."

"I surrender," whispered the newcomer. "When is the next meeting of the committtee? I'll be there, Mrs. Gilbreth. I'll be there."

One teacher in the Sunday school, a Mrs. Bruce, had the next-to-largest family in Montclair. She had eight children, most of whom were older than we. Her husband was very successful in business, and they lived in a large house, about two miles from us. Mother and Mrs. Bruce became great friends.

About a year later, a New York woman connected with some sort of national birth control organization came to Montclair to form a local chapter. Her name was Mrs. Alice Mebane, or something like that. She inquired among her acquaintances as to who in Montclair might be sympathetic to the birth control movement. As a joke, someone referred her to Mrs. Bruce.

"I'd be delighted to cooperate," Mother's friend told Mrs. Mebane, "but you see I have several children myself."

"Oh, I had no idea," said Mrs. Mebane. "How many?"

"Several," Mrs. Bruce replied vaguely. "So I don't think I would be the one to head up any birth control movement in Montclair."

"I must say, I'm forced to agree. We should know where we're going, and practice what we preach."

"But I do know just the person for you," Mrs. Bruce continued. "And she has a big house that would be simply ideal for holding meetings."

"Just what we want," purred Mrs. Mebane. "What is her name?"

"Mrs. Frank Gilbreth. She's civic minded, and she's a career woman."

"Exactly what we want. Civic minded, career woman, and—most important of all—a large house. One other thing—I suppose it's too much to hope for—but is she by any chance an organizer? You know, one who can take things over and militantly drive ahead?"

"The description," gloated Mrs. Bruce, "fits her like a glove."

"It's almost too good to be true," said Mrs. Mebane, wringing her hands in ecstasy. "May I use your name and tell Mrs. Gilbreth you sent me?"

"By all means," said Mother's friend. "Please do. I shall be disappointed, if you don't."

"And don't think that I disapprove of your having children," laughed Mrs. Mebane. "After all, many people do, you know."

"Careless of them," remarked Mrs. Bruce.

The afternoon that Mrs. Mebane arrived at our house, all of us children were, as usual, either upstairs in our rooms or playing in the back yard. Mrs. Mebane introduced herself to Mother.

"It's about birth control," she told Mother.

"What about it?" Mother asked, blushing.

"I was told you'd be interested."

"Me?"

"I've just talked to your friend, Mrs. Bruce, and she was certainly interested."

"Isn't it a little late for her to be interested?" Mother asked.

"I see what you mean, Mrs. Gilbreth. But better late than never, don't you think?"

"But she has eight children," said Mother.

Mrs. Mebane blanched, and clutched her head.

"My God," she said. "Not really."

Mother nodded.

"How perfectly frightful. She impressed me as quite normal. Not at all like an eight-child woman."

"She's kept her youth well," Mother conceded.

"Ah, there's work to be done, all right," Mrs. Mebane said. "Think of it, living right here within eighteen miles of our national birth control headquarters in New York City, and her having eight children. Yes, there's work to be done, Mrs. Gilbreth, and that's why I'm here."

"What sort of work?"

"We'd like you to be the moving spirit behind a Montclair birth control chapter."

Mother decided at this point that the situation was too ludicrous for Dad to miss, and that he'd never forgive her if she didn't deal him in.

"I'll have to ask my husband," she said. "Excuse me while I call him."

Mother stepped out and found Dad. She gave him a brief explanation and then led him into the parlor and introduced him.

"It's a pleasure to meet a woman in such a noble cause," said Dad.

"Thank you. And it's a pleasure to find a man who thinks of it as noble. In general, I find the husbands much less sympathetic with our aims than the wives. You'd be surprised at some of the terrible things men have said to me."

"I love surprises," Dad leered. "What do you say back to them?"

"If you had seen, as I have," said Mrs. Mebane, "relatively young women grown old before their time by the arrival of unwanted young ones. And population figures show . . . Why, Mr. Gilbreth, what are you doing?"

What Dad was doing was whistling assembly. On the first note, feet could be heard pounding on the floors above. Doors slammed, there was a landslide on the stairs, and we started skidding into the parlor.

"Nine seconds," said Dad pocketing his stopwatch. "Three short of the all-time record."

"God's teeth," said Mrs. Mebane. "What is it? Tell me quickly. It is a school? No. Or is it . . .? For Lord's sakes. It is!"

"It is what?" asked Dad.

"It's your family. Don't try to deny it. They're the spit and image of you, and your wife, too."

"I was about to introduce you," said Dad. "Mrs. Mebane, let me introduce you to the family—or most of it. Seems to me like there should be some more of them around here someplace."

"God help us all."

"How many head of children do we have now, Lillie, would you say off hand?"

"Last time I counted, seems to me there was an even dozen of them," said Mother. "I might have missed one or two of them, but not many."

"I'd say twelve would be a pretty fair guess," Dad said.

"Shame on you! And within eighteen miles of national headquarters."

"Let's have tea," said Mother.

But Mrs. Mebane was putting on her coat. "You poor dear, " she clucked to Mother. "You poor child." Then turning to Dad. "It seems to me that the people of this town have pulled my leg on two different occasions today."

"How revolting," said Dad. "And within eighteen miles of national headquarters, too."

CHAPTER 8

Kissing Kin

The day the United States entered the first World War, Dad sent President Wilson a telegram which read: "Arriving Washington 7:03 p.m. train. If you don't know how to use me, I'll tell you how."

Whether or not this heartening intelligence took some of the weight off Mr. Wilson's troubled shoulders, Dad never made entirely plain. But he was met at the train and taken over to the War Department. The next time we saw him, he was in uniform, assigned to motion study training in assembling and disassembling the Lewis machine gun and other automatic weapons. He had what probably was the most G.I. haircut in the entire armed forces, and when he walked into the parlor and shouted "Attention!" he wanted to hear our heels click.

Mother had been planning for several years to take all of us to California to visit her family. When Dad was ordered to Fort Sill, Oklahoma, the time seemed opportune.

Mother's family was genteel and well-to-do. She was the oldest of nine children, only three of whom were married. The other six, two brothers and four sisters, lived with their parents in a spacious house at 426 Twenty-Ninth Street, in Oakland. The house was fringed with palm trees, magnificent gardens, and concealed but nonetheless imposing outbuildings in which the family indulged its various hobbies. There were a billiard hall, radio shack, greenhouse, pigeon roost, and a place where prize-winning guinea pigs were raised.

The Mollers had three Packards, a French chauffeur named Henriette, a gardener, Chinese cook, first-story maid, and second-story maid. The Mollers managed, somehow, in spite of their worldly goods, to live fairly simply. They were quiet, introverted, and conservative. They seldom raised their voices and referred to each other as "Dear Elinor, Dear Mable, Dear Gertrude," and so on. Mother was "Dear Lillie."

Mother was the only one in her family who had moved from California. Mother had left home after her marriage, as introverted and conservative, and possibly even more shy and bookish, than any of the others. In ten years, she had seven children. She was lecturing around the country. She was a career woman and her name kept bobbing up in the newspapers. Frankly, the Mollers didn't know exactly what to make of Dear Lillie. But they knew they loved her.

Even before we visited California, we knew all about the household at Oakland and its inhabitants, because Mother used to like to tell us about her girlhood. We knew the arrangement of the house, even down to the full-length mirror on the hall door, which Mother's younger sisters used to open at just the right angle so that they could watch Dad's courting technique.

Hearing Mother tell about the courtship, the sparking on the sofa, we used to wonder what Mother's parents had thought when Dad first came to call.

He had met Mother in Boston, about a year before, when she was on that well-chaperoned tour to Europe, with several other Oakland girls. The chaperone, who was Dad's cousin, had introduced him to all the girls, but he had selected Miss Lillie as the one on whom to shower his attention.

He took Mother for a ride in his first automobile, some early ancestor of Foolish Carriage. As Dad and Mother, dressed in dusters and wearing goggles, went scorching through the streets of Boston, bystanders tossed insults and ridicule in their direction.

"Get a horse, get a horse."

Dad started to shout back an answer, but thought better of it. He was already in love with Mother, and was anxious to make a good impression. Mother's shyness and ladylike demeanor had a quieting effect on him, and he was displaying his most genteel behavior.

"Get a horse. Twenty-three skiddoo."

It was almost more than Dad could bear, but he didn't answer.

"Say, Noah, what are you doing with that Ark?"

That did it. Dad slowed the car and cocked his checkered cap belligerently over one eye.

"Collecting animals like the good Lord told me," he screamed back. "All I need now is a jackass. Hop in."

After that, Dad decided he might as well be himself, and his breezy personality and quick laugh made Mother forget her shyness and reserve. Soon she found herself laughing almost as loud and as long at his jokes as he.

As was its custom, the automobile inevitably broke down, and crowds of children gathered around. Mother stopped them from breathing down Dad's neck by taking them aside and telling them stories. When the car was fixed and they were on their way again, Dad asked her how she had managed to hold the children's attention.

"I told them some stories from *Alice in Wonderland,*"

Mother said. "You see, I have eight younger brothers and sisters, and I know what children like."

"Alice in Wonderland," Dad exclaimed. "You mean kids really like that? They must be raising different kinds of kids than when I was a boy. I never could get into it, myself."

"Of course they like it; they love it," Mother said. "You really should read it. I think everybody should. It's a classic."

"If you say so, Miss Lillie," said Dad, who had already made up his mind she was going to be Mrs. Gilbreth, "I'll read it."

Mother went on to Europe. After her return, Dad followed her out to the West Coast.

When he arrived at Oakland, he telephoned the Mollers' house.

"Hello," he said, "who do you think this is?"

"Really, I have no idea."

"Well guess, can't you?"

"No, I'm sorry, I have no idea."

"Aw, you know who it is," said Dad, who now had read the book that Mother said everyone should read. "It's the White Rabbit from Boston."

"The who?"

"The White Rabbit from Boston."

"Oh, I see. I think you must want to talk with one of my daughters."

"My God," said Dad, who didn't stop swearing until after he was married. "Who's this?"

"This is Mrs. Moller. To whom did you wish to speak?"

"May I please speak with Miss Lillie?" Dad asked meekly.

"Who should I say is calling?"

"You might say Mr. Rabbit, please," said Dad. "Mr. W. Rabbit, of Boston."

A few days later, Dad was invited to Mother's house for tea, where he met her mother and father and most of her brothers and sisters. A workman was building a new fireplace in the living room, and as Dad was escorted through that room he stopped to watch the man laying bricks.

"Now there's an interesting job," Dad in a conversational tone to the Mollers. "Laying brick. It looks easy to me. Dead easy. I don't see why these workmen claim that laying brick is skilled labor. I'll bet anyone could do it."

"Right this way, Mr. Gilbreth," said Mother's father. "We're having tea on the porch."

Dad wouldn't be hurried. "It seems to me," he continued in his flat New England twang, "that all you do is pick up a brick, put some mortar on it, and put it in the fireplace."

The bricklayer turned around to survey the plump but dapper dude from the East.

"Nothing personal meant," said Dad, with his most patronizing smile, "my good man."

"Sure, that's all right," said the workman, but he was furious. "Dead easy, eh? Like to try it, Mister?"

Dad, who had set his sights on just such an invitation, said he guessed not. Mother tugged at his sleeve and fidgeted.

"The porch is right this way," her father repeated.

"Here," the bricklayer said, handing Dad the trowel. "Try it."

Dad grinned and took the trowel. He grabbed a brick, flipped it into position in his hand, slapped on the mortar with a rotary motion of the trowel, placed the brick, scraped off the excess mortar, reached for a second brick, flipped it, and was about to slap on more mortar when the workman reached out and took back his trowel.

"That's enough, you old hod-carrier," he shouted, cuffing Dad affectionately on the back. "Dude from the East you might be. But it's many a thousand brick you've laid in your life, and don't try to tell me different."

Dad dusted off his hands gingerly with a spotless handkerchief.

"Dead easy," he said, "my good man."

Dad behaved himself pretty well during the tea, but on later visits he'd sometimes interrupt Mother's parents in the middle of sentences and go over and pick up Mother from her chair.

"Excuse me just a minute," he'd tell his future in-laws. "I think Miss Lillie would look more decorative up here."

He'd swing her up and place her on the top of a bookcase or china closet, and then go back and sit down. Mother was afraid to move for fear of upsetting her perch, and would remain up there primly, determined not to lose her dignity. Dad pretended he had forgotten all about her, as he resumed the conversation.

We knew, too, that the first time Dad had been invited to spend a weekend at the Mollers he had thrown himself with a wheeze and a sigh onto his bed, which had collapsed and enveloped him in a heavy, be-tasseled canopy.

"The things your daddy shouted before Papa and your Uncle Fred could untangle him from the tassels!" Mother tittered. "I can tell you, it was an education for us girls and, I suspect, for the boys too. Thank goodness he's stopped talking like that."

"And what did your family really think of him?" we asked her. "Really."

"I never could understand it," Mother said, glancing over at Dad, who was at his smuggest, "but they thought he was simply wonderful. Mama said it was like a breath of fresh air when he walked into a room. And Papa said the business of laying bricks wasn't just showing off, but was your father's way of telling them that he had started out by making a living with his hands."

"Is that what you were trying to tell them, Daddy?" we asked.

"Trying to tell them nothing," Dad shouted. "Anybody who knows anything about New England knows the Bunkers and the Gilbreths, or Galbraiths, descend through Governor Bradford right to the *Mayflower*. I wasn't trying to tell them anything."

"What did you lay the brick for then?" we insisted.

"When some people walk into a parlor," Dad said, "they like to sit down at the piano and impress people by playing Bach. When I walk into a parlor, I like to lay brick, that's all."

There were seven children in the family when we set out with Mother for California. Fred was the baby, and was train sick all the way from Niagara Falls to the Golden Gate. Lill, the next to youngest, had broken a bone in her foot three weeks before, and had to stay in her berth. Mother was expecting another baby in three months, and didn't always feel too well herself.

The chance to return with her children to her parents' home meant more to Mother than any of us realized, and she was anxious to show us off in the best possible light and to have her family approve of us.

"I know you're going to be good and quiet, and do what your grandparents and your aunts and uncles tell you," Mother kept saying. "You want to remember that they're very affectionate, but they're not accustomed to having children around any more. They're going to love you, but they're not used to noise and people running around."

Mother had spent a good bit of money buying us new outfits so that we would make a good impression in California, and she thought she ought to economize on train accommodations. We were jammed, two in a berth, into a drawing room and two sections. She brought along a Sterno cooking outfit and two suitcases of food, mostly cereals and graham crackers. We ate almost all our meals in the drawing room, journeying to the dining car only on those infrequent occasions when Mother yielded to our complaints that scurvy was threatening to set in.

She spent most of her time trying to make Lill comfortable and trying to find some kind of milk that would stay on Fred's stomach. She had little oppportunity to supervise the rest of us, and we wandered up and down the train sampling the contents of the various ice water tanks, peeking into berths and, in the case of Frank and Bill, turning somersaults and wrestling with each other in the aisles.

At each stop, Mother would leave Anne in charge of the broken foot and upset stomach department, while she rushed into the station to buy milk, food, and Sterno cans. The rest of us would get off the train to stretch our legs and see whether a new engine had been switched on. Once the train started up again, Mother would insist upon a roll call.

After four days on the train, with no baths except for the sponge variety, we were not very sanitary when we reached California. Mother wanted us to look our best when we got off the train, and she planned to give each of us a personal scrubbing and see that we had on clean clothes, an hour or so before we got to Oakland.

Her oldest brother, Uncle Fred, surprised her and us by boarding the train at Sacramento. He found us in the drawing room, in the middle of a meal. Suitcases were open on the floor, and there was a pile of diapers in a corner. The baby, still train sick, was crying in Mother's arms. Lill's foot was hurting, and she was crying on the couch. Bill was doing acrobatics on the bed. There were bowls of Cream of Wheat and graham crackers on a card table. The place smelled of Sterno and worse.

Uncle Fred used to joke about it when we were older—it reminded him of a zoo, he said. But at the time you never would have known he noticed anything unusual.

"Lillie, dear, it's good to see you," he said. "You look simply radiant. Not a day older."

"Oh, Fred, Fred." Mother put down the baby, wiped her eyes apologetically, and clung to her brother. "It's ridiculous to cry, isn't it? But it means so much having you here."

"Was it a hard trip, dear?"

Mother was already bustling around, straightening up the drawing room.

"I wouldn't want to do it every day," she admitted. "But it's almost over and you're here. You're my first taste of home."

Uncle Fred turned to us. "Welcome to California," he said. "Don't tell me now. I can name each of you. Let's see, the baby here making all the noise, he's my namesake, Fred. And here's little Lill, of course, with the broken foot, and Billy . . ."

"You're just like we imagined you," Martha told him, hanging onto his hand. "Are we like you imagined us?"

"Just exactly," he said gravely. "Right down to the last freckle."

"I hope you didn't imagine them like this," Mother said, but she was happy now. "Never mind. You'll never know them in a few minutes. You take the boys out into the car, and I'll start getting the girls cleaned up right now. Of course, none of them will be really clean until I can get them into a tub."

We were presentable and on our best behavior when we finally arrived in Oakland, where Mother's sisters and other brothers were waiting with the three limousines. It was a wonderful welcome, but we thought our aunts were the kissingest kin in the world.

"They must think we're sissies," whispered Bill, who was five and didn't like to be kissed by anyone except Mother, and only then in the privacy of his boudoir.

"Lillie, dear, it's good to see you, and the dear children," they kept repeating.

Each of us had a godparent among Mother's brothers and

sisters, and now the godparents began sorting us out.

"Here, little Ernestine, you come with me, dear," said Aunt Ernestine.

"Come, Martha, dear," said Aunt Gertrude. "You're mine."

"Give me your hand, Frank, dear," said Aunt Elinor.

"Dear this and dear that," Billy whispered scornfully.

"Where's dear Billy?" asked Aunt Mabel.

"Right here, dear," said Bill.

But Bill, like the rest of us, felt happy and warm inside because of the welcome.

The aunts led us over to the automobiles, where Henriette, in black puttees and with a stiff-brimmed cap tucked under his arm, was standing at rigid attention. Uncle Frank and Uncle Bill got behind the wheels of the other two machines.

The glassed-in cars seemed formal and luxurious as we drove from the station to Twenty-ninth Street, and Henriette managed to remain at attention even when sitting down. We wondered what Daddy would say about Henriette. Certainly rigid attention wasn't the most efficient way to drive an automobile. Anyone with half an eye could see the posture was fatiguing to the point of exhaustion. It was some class, though.

Frank and Bill started to crank down the windows so they could put out their hands when he turned the corners, but Anne and Ernestine shook their heads.

"And the first one who hollers 'road hog' is going to get a punch in the nose," Ernestine whispered.

Mother's father and mother—Papa and Grosie, we called them—were waiting for us on the steps of the house. We thought they were picture-book grandparents. Papa was tall, lean and courtly, with a gates-ajar collar, string tie, and soft, white moustache. Grosie was short and fragile, with a gray pompadour and smiling brown eyes. Grosie kissed us and called us "dears." Papa shook hands, and said that each day we stayed in his house he was going to take all of us down to a toy shop and let us pick out a toy apiece.

"Honestly," Anne bubbled, "it's like stepping into a fairy tale three-deep with godmothers and with wishes that come true."

"That's the way we want it to be for Lillie's dear children," Grosie said. "Now what's your very first wish. Tell me, and I'll see if I can make it come true."

That was easy. After four days of Mother's drawing room cookery, with only infrequent trips to the dining car, what we wanted most was something good to eat; a real home-cooked meal.

"I hate to say it after the way Mother's been slaving over a hot Sterno can," said Ernestine, "but we're starving."

"If my wish would come true," Mother hastened to change the subject, "you'd all be sitting in bathtubs right this minute, washing soot out of your hair."

Grosie said we were going to have a big dinner in about an hour and a half, and that she didn't want to spoil our appetites.

"How about just a little snack right now," she suggested, "and then baths and dinner? How about some graham crackers with milk? I know how much little children like graham crackers, and we have a great big supply of them."

The mention of graham crackers took away our appetities, and we said we guessed we'd skip the snack and get our baths.

"Such dear children," Grosie squeezed us. "They want their dear Mother's wish to come true!"

CHAPTER 9

Chinese Cooking

We were so impressed by the comforts and quiet organization of the Mollers' home that we were subdued and on our best behavior. But the biggest change was in Mother. Ensconced again in the bedroom in which she had grown up, she seemed to shed her responsibilities and become again "one of the Moller girls." Automatically, she found herself depending on her father to make the important decisions, and on her mother to advise her on social engagements and the proper clothes to wear. She seemed to have forgotten all about motion study, her career, and the household back East. Her principal worries seemed to be whether her parents had slept well, how they were feeling, whether they were sitting in drafts.

"Mama, dear," she'd say, "are you sure that shawl is warm enough? Let me run upstairs and get you another."

Since Mother seemed so concerned about Grosie and Papa, we held them in awe. We tiptoed in their presence and talked only in whispers.

The respect in which we held Grosie was heightened the day after our arrival, when she gave Mother a quiet reprimand which Mother accepted just as if she were a little girl again. Anybody who could have that effect on Mother, we thought, must be a very important person.

The reprimand came about after Grosie handed Mother a list of six close friends of the family, and suggested that Mother call to pay her respects that afternoon.

"Do you really think it's necessary, Mama, dear?" Mother asked.

"I think it would be nice, dear."

"What do you think I should wear?"

"I would think the dress you wore to dinner last night would be just right, dear."

Mother set out to make the calls, and returned about two hours later.

"There," she said, coming smiling into the living room. "Thank goodness that's out of the way. It didn't take me long, did it? Six calls in two hours! Wasn't I efficient?"

To be efficient, in the Gilbreth family, was a virtue on a par with veracity, honesty, generosity, philanthropy, and tooth-brushing. We agreed that Mother had, indeed, been exceptionally efficient. But Grosie looked disapproving.

"Don't you think I was efficient, Mama, dear?"

"Perhaps, Lillie, dear," Grosie said slowly, "perhaps you were a little—too—efficient."

Our grandparents became worried by our exemplary behavior. They told Mother they didn't think it was natural, and that it made them nervous the way we tiptoed and whispered.

"They don't act at all the way I pictured them," Papa said. "From your letters, I thought they whooped and hollered around. I don't believe they feel at home."

"They'll feel at home soon enough," Mother warned. "I'm

scared that when they decide to feel at home they may decide all at once. If they do, it's Katey bar the door."

We decided to feel at home on the day that Grosie gave a formal tea in Mother's honor. Our godmothers had bathed us with sweet-smelling soap and were dressing us in new outfits that Grosie had approved. For the girls, it was dotted Swiss and matching hair ribbons and sashes; for the boys, blue serge suits and Buster Brown collars, with red, generous bow ties.

The boys' trousers were shorts, rather than knickers, and buttoned down the sides, instead of down the front. That was bad enough, Frank and Bill thought. But the crowning indignity was a little flap, like the tongue of a shoe sewed on sideways, that served as a fly at the front of the trousers.

"We're all going to be so proud of you today, dears," the aunts told us. "I know you're going to make such a lovely impression on all the guests."

"Not in these pants," Bill said. "I look sissy and I'm not going to wear them."

"Why Billy, dear," said Aunt Mabel, his godmother. "You look lovely. You look just like Little Lord Fauntleroy."

"I don't want to look like him," Bill shouted. "I'm not going to wear these clothes."

"Of course you're going to wear them, Billy, dear. What do you think your father would say to hear you talk like that?"

"I think he'd say they were sissy, too," said Bill. "I think he'd laugh at the flap on the front of my pants."

"Be a good boy, now, dear. You don't want to worry your mother and Grosie and Papa."

"I do too," said Bill. "I'm sick of not worrying people. I say to heck with them."

The godmothers froze.

"Why Billy Gilbreth," said Aunt Mabel. "Where did you learn such an *ugly* word?"

We thought for just a moment that we saw a trace of a grin pass over Aunt Mabel's face, and that Aunt Gertrude nudged Aunt Ernestine, but we dismissed the notion as highly improbable and extremely out-of-character.

Bill finally was prevailed upon to dress in his new outfit. But he was sullen, and so were the rest of us when we received our instructions about the party.

"First the grownups will have a little chat and visit by

themselves, dears. Then we want you children to come in and meet the guests. Remember, some of these people are your mother's oldest friends, and she wants to be proud of you, so do be careful about your clothes. Now run along out into the garden, and we'll call you when it's time."

Left by ourselves, we walked out on the lawn, where we formed a starched, uncomfortable, and resentful group. We were tired of being on our best behavior, and we wished Daddy were there to stir up some excitement.

"At home," Martha whispered to the rest of us, "the children visit when the grownups visit. They don't have to go stand in the garden like darned lepers."

"Why, Martha, dear," Ern mimicked, in shocked tones, "Where did you learn such an *ugly* word?"

"At home," said Martha, "they think the children have enough sense to fix their own hair. And they don't have to wear hair ribbons tied so tight that they can't wiggle their eyebrows."

"Look at the flap in the front of the pants," said Bill, pointing.

A sprinkler was watering in the lawn nearby. Martha jerked off her hair ribbon, threw it on the ground, walked deliberately to the sprinkler and stood under it.

Anne and Ernestine were horrified. "Martha," they shouted. "Are you crazy? Come out of there."

Martha put her head back and laughed. She opened her mouth and caught water in it. She wiggled her now free eyebrows in ecstasy. The starch went out of her clothes, and her hair streamed over her face.

Frank and Bill joined Martha under the sprinkler. Then Ernestine came in, thus leaving Anne, the oldest, in what for her was a fairly familiar dilemma: whether to cast her lot with us or with the adults. She knew that being the oldest she'd be held responsible, whichever course she took.

"Come in and get wet," we shouted. "Don't be a traitor. The water's fine."

Anne sighed, untied her hair ribbon and came in.

"All right, dears," one of the aunts called from the house. "It's time to meet the guests now."

We filed, into the living room, where our dripping clothes made puddles on Grosie's Persian rug.

"I think they feel at home now," Mother said a little ruefully. "You children listen to me. Go upstairs and change your clothes. No nonsense, now. I want you down here, dry, in ten minutes. Do you understand?"

We understood. That was the kind of talk we understood.

Everybody liked it better now that we went shouting through the house, playing hide-and-go-seek, and sliding down the banisters. Only during the afternoons, when Grosie was taking a nap, Papa asked us to be quiet.

"Try to keep it down to a dull roar for just two hours, dears," he told us. "Your grandmother really needs her rest."

Our godmothers waited on us hand and foot, and we began to enjoy and even revel in the attention. They were willing to drop anything to amuse us, to play games with us, to help us plant a flower garden, to paste in our scrap books, to collect California seeds which we intended to plant in our yard when we returned home. They took us to the movies, on sightseeing tours to Chinatown in San Francisco, and away for weekends at their summer cottage at Inverness. It seemed natural now for them to call us "dears," and we began to return the salutation without sarcasm or affectation. When dear Aunt Gertrude had herself hospitalized because she was afraid she was coming down with whooping cough and didn't want to infect us, we mourned her departure almost as if she had been Mother herself.

Bill, meanwhile, had found a devoted friend and ally in the kitchen, where Chew Wong's word was law. Chew Wong was set in his ways and unamenable to suggestion. He was sinister looking and uncommunicative, and had a terrible temper. He understood English fairly well, except when someone tried to criticize him or tell him what to do. In such cases he launched into hissing Chinese, brandished skillets, and then turned his back and walked away. He was a wonderful cook. It was tacitly understood in the Moller family that the less one knew about his cooking methods and what he put into the food, the better for all concerned.

Of the Mollers, only Aunt Elinor, who planned the menus, ventured into the kitchen. We children were advised to keep out of it unless we wished to invoke Oriental wrath, die in agony from some exotic poison, touch off a tong war, or go through life with the responsibility of hara-kiri hanging over our heads.

Although aware of the possible consequences, Bill couldn't resist the smell of cakes and pies, and began to spend a good deal of his time in the kitchen. At first Aunt Elinor would hustle him out. But Chew Wong had taken a liking to him, and sulked when Bill was removed. Whenever Chew Wong sulked, his cooking suffered, and it finally was decided to allow Bill the run of the kitchen.

Chew Wong outdid himself then with the meals that he served up, and the kitchen rang with pidgin English and cackling laughter.

"Pleez now, Bleely, open mouth. Hi-hi-hi-hi-hi. Good boy, Bleely."

We questioned Bill about what he opened his mouth for. He told us that when Chew Wong iced a cake he put the frosting in a cornucopia made of newspaper, bit off the end and squeezed the frosting onto the cake. At intervals, Bill would open his mouth and the cornucopia would be inserted. When the rest of us dropped into the kitchen to get a turn at the business end of the cornucopia, Chew Wong drove us out with a skillet, while he and Bill screamed with laughter. Hi-hi-hi-hi-hi.

Sometimes, when Bill got into mischief in the kitchen, Chew Wong scolded him, picked him up, and threatened to put him in the oven. The cook opened the oven door and put Bill part way in it, where he could feel the heat on his face.

"Blad boy, Bleely. Putee in oven and cookee brown and eatee. Hi-hi-hi."

Bill knew it was a game, but it used to scare him, and he struggled and kicked.

One afternoon Chew Wong opened the oven door and was leaning in, on tiptoe, to see whether a cake was browning on all sides. Bill crept up behind him, placed a shoulder against his rear and hunched. Then he held him there.

"Blad boy, Wong," he said in a sing-song imitation of the cook. "Bleely putee in oven and cookee brown and eatee. Hi-hi-hi-hi."

Aunt Elinor was in the pantry and heard the conversation and Chew Wong's screams. By the time she rushed into the kitchen, the cook had extricated himself, had both hands under the cold water faucet, and was squealing with rage. Other Mollers and Gilbreths converged on the kitchen from various parts of the house.

Since she was responsible for the kitchen, Aunt Elinor decided it was up to her to take Bill to task.

"Billy Gilbreth," she said almost sternly. "You haven't behaved like a gentleman."

The visit came to an end, and we put on our traveling clothes and climbed again into the limousines. We were accustomed to them now, and we didn't hesitate to roll down the windows, put out our hands, and tell road hogs what we thought of them. The Mollers didn't seem to mind; they seemed to enjoy it. Even Henriette, still at rigid attention, grinned when hands popped out as he wheeled his car sedately around the corners.

We said goodbye on the station platform. It didn't seem sissy to Bill to be kissed now. He returned the kisses.

We got on the train and pressed our noses against the glass.

"One thing I can't get over," Anne said. "They really hate to see us go. Imagine! They're crying just as hard as we are."

The train pulled out of the station, and Mother did her best to cheer us up.

"I didn't bring a single Sterno can with me," she said. "Things will be much better going home than they were coming out. Lill's foot is all better, and I don't think Freddy's going to be sick any more. We can go into the diner and . . ."

"Whoop," Martha coughed. "Whoop. Whoop."

"You don't suppose that child's caught whooping cough, do you?" Mother asked. "Let me feel your forehead."

By the time we reached Salt Lake City, all seven of us had whooping cough. Our berths couldn't be made up, and no one in the same car with us got much sleep.

Dad had managed to obtain leave from Fort Sill, and surprised us by boarding the train at Chicago. He helped with a bucket and mop Mother had borrowed from the porter, and brought us soup heated over recently acquired Sterno cans.

"Thank you, Daddy, dear," we told him.

"Daddy, dear?" he said. "Daddy, dear? Well! I guess I ought to send you kids to California every summer."

"Not with me, you don't," Mother put in. "I can't tell you how much I enjoyed seeing the dear folks. But the next time you take the children out West, and I'll go to war."

CHAPTER 10

Motion Study Tonsils

Dad thought the best way to deal with sickness in the family was simply to ignore it.

"We don't have time for such nonsense," he said. "There are too many of us. A sick person drags down the performance of the entire group. You children come from sound pioneer stock. You've been given health, and it's your job to keep it. I don't want any excuses. I want you to stay well."

Except for measles and whooping cough, we obeyed orders. Doctors' visits were so infrequent we learned to identify them with Mother's having a baby.

Dad's mother, who lived with us for awhile, had her own secret for warding off disease. Grandma Gilbreth was born in Maine, where she said the seasons were Winter, July and August. She claimed to be an expert in combatting cold weather and in avoiding head colds.

Her secret prophylaxis was a white bag, filled and saturated with camphor, which she kept hidden in her bosom. Grandma's bosom offered ample hiding space not only for the camphor but for her eyeglasses, her handkerchief, and, if need be, for the bedspread she was crocheting.

Each year, as soon as the first frost appeared, she made twelve identical white, camphor-filled bags for each of us.

"Mind what Grandma says and wear these all the time," she told us. "Now if you bring home a cold it will be your own blessed fault, and I'll skin you alive."

Grandma always was threatening to skin someone alive, or

draw and quarter him, or scalp him like a red Indian, or spank him till his bottom blistered.

Grandma averred she was a great believer in "spare the rod and spoil the child." Her own personal rod was a branch from a lilac bush, which grew in the side lawn. She always kept a twig from this bush on the top of her dresser.

"I declare, you're going to catch it now," she would say. "Your mother won't spank you and your father is too busy to spank you, but your grandma is going to spank you till your bottom blisters."

Then she would swing the twig with a vigor which belied her years. Most of her swings were aimed so as merely to whistle harmlessly through the air. She'd land a few lights licks on our legs, though, and since we didn't want to hurt her feelings we'd scream and holler as if we were receiving the twenty-one lashes from a Spanish inquisitor. Sometimes she'd switch so vigorously at nothing that the twig would break.

"Ah, you see? You were so bad that I had to break my whip on you. Now go right out in the yard and cut me another one for next time. A big, thick one that will hurt even more than this one. Go along now. March!"

On the infrequent occasions when one of us did become sick enough to stay in bed, Grandma and Dad thought the best treatment was the absent treatment.

"A child abed mends best if left to himself," Grandma said, while Dad nodded approval. Mother said she agreed, too, but then she proceeded to wait on the sick child hand and foot.

"Here, darling, put my lovely bed jacket around your shoulders," Mother would tell the ailing one. "Here are some magazines, and scissors and paste. Now how's that? I'm going down to the kitchen and fix you a tray. Then I'll be up and read to you."

A cousin brought measles into the house, and all of us except Martha were stricken simultaneously. Two big adjoining bedrooms upstairs were converted into hospital wards—one for the boys and the other for the girls. We suffered together for two or three miserable, feverish, itchy days, while Mother applied cocoa butter and ice packs. Dr. Burton, who had delivered most of us, said there was nothing to worry about.

He was an outspoken man, and he and Dad understood each other.

"I'll admit, Gilbreth, that your children don't get sick very often," Dr. Burton said, "but when they do it messes up the public health statistics for the entire state of New Jersey."

"How come, Mr. Bones?" Dad asked.

"I have to turn in a report every week on the number of contagious diseases I handle. Ordinarily, I handle a couple of cases of measles a week. When I report that I had eleven cases in a single day, they're liable to quarantine the whole town of Montclair and close up every school in Essex County."

"Well, they're probably exceptionally light cases," Dad said. "Pioneer stock, you know."

"As far as I'm concerned, measles is measles, and they've got the measles."

"Probably even pioneers got the measles," Dad said.

"Probably so. Pioneers had tonsils, too, and so do your kids. Really ugly tonsils. They ought to come out."

"I never had mine out."

"Let me see them," Dr. Burton ordered.

"There's nothing the matter with them."

"For God's sake don't waste my time," said Dr. Burton. "Open your mouth and say 'Ah'."

Dad opened his mouth and said "Ah."

"I thought so," Dr. Burton nodded. "Yours ought to come out too. Should have had them taken out years ago. I don't expect you to admit it, but you have sore throats, don't you? You have one right this minute, haven't you?"

"Nonsense," said Dad. "Never sick a day in my life."

"Well, let yours stay in if you want. You're not hurting anybody but yourself. But you really should have the children's taken out."

"I'll talk it over with Lillie," Dad promised.

Once the fever from the measles had gone, we all felt fine, although we still had to stay in bed. We sang songs, told continued stories, played spelling games and riddles, and had pillow fights. Dad spent considerable time with us, joining in the songs and all the games except pillow fights, which were illegal. He still believed in letting sick children alone, but with all of us sick—or all but Martha, at any rate—he became so lonesome he couldn't stay away.

He came into the wards one night after supper, and took a chair over in a corner. We noticed that his face was covered with spots.

"Daddy," asked Anne, "what's the matter with you? You're all broken out in spots."

"You're imagining things," said Dad, smirking. "I'm all right."

"You've got the measles."

"I'm all right," said Dad. "I can take it."

"Daddy's got the measles, Daddy's got the measles." Dad sat there grinning, but our shouts were enough to bring Grandma on the run.

"What's the matter here?" she asked. And then to Dad. "Mercy sakes, Frank, you're covered with spots."

"It's just a joke," Dad told his mother, weakly.

"Get yourself to bed. A man your age ought to know better. Shame on you."

Grandma fumbled down her dress and put on her glasses. She peered into Dad's face.

"I declare, Frank Gilbreth," she told him, "sometimes I think you're more trouble than all of your children. Red ink! And you think it's a joke to scare a body half to death. Red ink!"

"A joke," Dad repeated.

"Very funny," Grandma muttered as she stalked out of the room. "I'm splitting my sides."

Dad sat there glumly.

"Is it red ink, Daddy?" we asked, and we agreed with him that it was, indeed, a very good joke. "Is it? You really had us fooled."

"You'll have to ask your grandma," Dad sulked. "She's a very smart lady. She knows it all."

Martha, who appeared immune to measles, nevertheless wasn't allowed to come into the wards. She couldn't go to school, since the house was quarantined, and the week or two of being an "only child" made her so miserable that she lost her appetite. Finally, she couldn't stand it any more, and sneaked into the sick rooms to visit us.

"You know you're not allowed in here," said Anne. "Do you want to get sick?"

Martha burst into tears. "Yes," she sobbed. "Oh, yes."

"Don't tell us you miss us? Why I should think it would be wonderful to have the whole downstairs to yourself, and to be able to have Mother and Dad all by yourself at dinner."

"Dad's no fun any more," said Mart. "He's nervous. He says the quiet at the table is driving him crazy."

"Tell him that's not of general interest," said Ern.

It was shortly after the measles epidemic that Dad started applying motion study to surgery to try to reduce the time required for certain operations.

"Surgeons really aren't much different from skilled mechanics," Dad said, "except that they're not so skilled. If I can get to study their motions, I can speed them up. The speed of an operation often means the difference between life and death."

At first, the surgeons he approached weren't very cooperative.

"I don't think it will work," one doctor told him. "We aren't dealing with machines. We're dealing with human beings. No two human beings are alike, so no set of motions could be used over and over again."

"I know it will work," Dad insisted. "Just let me take some moving pictures of operations and I'll show you."

Finally he got permission to set up his movie equipment in an operating room. After the film was developed he put it in the projector which he kept in the parlor and showed us what he had done.

In the background was a cross-section screen and a big clock with "GILBRETH" written across its face and a hand which made a full revolution every second. Each doctor and nurse was dressed in white, and had a number on his cap to identify him. The patient was on an operating table in the foreground. Off to the left, clad in a white sheet, was something that resembled a snow-covered Alp. When the Alp turned around, it had a stopwatch in its hand. And when it smiled at the camera you could tell through the disguise that it was Dad.

It seemed to us, watching the moving pictures, that the doctors did a rapid, business-like job of a complicated abdominal operation. But Dad, cranking the projector in back of us, kept hollering that it was "stupidity incorporated."

"Look at that boob—the doctor with No. 3 on his cap. Watch what he's going to do now. Walk all the way around the operating table. Now see him reach way over there for that instrument? And then he decides that he doesn't want that one after all. He wants this one. He should call the instrument's names, and that nurse—No. 6, she's his caddy—should hand it to him. That's what she's there for. And look at his left hand—dangling there at his side. Why doesn't he use it? He could work twice as fast."

The result of the moving picture was that the surgeons involved managed to reduce their ether time by fifteen per cent. Dad was far from satisfied. He explained that he needed to take moving pictures of five or six operations, all of the same type, so that he could sort out the good motions from the wasted motions. The trouble was that most patients refused to be photographed, and hospitals were afraid of law suits.

"Never mind, dear," Mother told him. "I'm sure the opportunity will come along eventually for you to get all the pictures that you want."

Dad said that he didn't like to wait; that when he started a project, he hated to put it aside and pick it up again piecemeal whenever he found a patient, hospital, and doctor who didn't object to photographs. Then an idea hit him, and he snapped his fingers.

"I know," he said. "I've got it. Dr. Burton has been after me to have the kids' tonsils out. He says they really have to come out. We'll rig up an operating room in the laboratory here, and take pictures of Burton."

"It seems sort of heartless to use the children as guinea pigs," Mother said doubtfully.

"It does for a fact. And I won't do it unless Burton says it's perfectly all right. If taking pictures is going to make him nervous or anything, we'll have the tonsils taken out without the motion study."

"Somehow or other I can't imagine Dr. Burton being nervous," Mother said.

"Me either. I'm going to call him. And you know what? I

feel a little guilty about this whole deal. So, as conscience balm, I'm going to let the old butcher take mine out, too."

"I feel a little guilty about the whole deal, too," said Mother. "Only thank goodness I had mine taken out when I was a girl."

Dr. Burton agreed to do the job in front of a movie camera.

"I'll save you for the last, Old Pioneer," he told Dad. "The best for the last. Since the first day I laid eyes on your great, big, beautiful tonsils, I knew I wouldn't be content until I got my hands on them."

"Stop drooling and put away your scalpel, you old flatterer you," said Dad. "I intend to be the last. I'll have mine out after the kids get better."

Dr. Burton said he would start with Anne and go right down the ladder, through Ernestine, Frank, Bill and Lillian.

Martha alone of the older children didn't need to have her tonsils out, the doctor said, and the children younger than Lillian could wait awhile.

The night before the mass operation, Martha was told she would sleep at the house of Dad's oldest sister, Aunt Anne.

"I don't want you underfoot," Dad informed her. "The children who are going to have their tonsils out won't be able to have any supper tonight or breakfast in the morning. I don't want you around to lord it over them."

Martha hadn't forgotten how we neglected her when she finally came down with the measles. She lorded it over us plenty before she finally departed.

"Aunt Anne always had apple pie for breakfast," she said, which we all knew to be perfectly true, except that sometimes it was blueberry instead of apple. "She keeps a jar of doughnuts in the pantry and she likes children to eat them." This, too, was unfortunately no more than the simple truth. "Tomorrow morning, when you are awaiting the knife, I will be thinking of you. I shall try, if I am not too full, to dedicate a doughnut to each of you."

She rubbed her stomach with a circular motion, and puffed out her cheeks horribly as if she were chewing on a whole doughnut. She opened an imaginary doughnut jar and helped herself to another, which she rammed into her mouth.

"My goodness, Aunt Anne," she said, pretending that that lady was in the room, "those doughnuts are even more delicious than usual." . . . "Well, why don't you have another, Martha?" . . . "Thanks, Aunt Anne, I believe I will." . . . "Why don't you take two or three, Martha?" . . . "I'm so full of apple pie I don't know whether I could eat two more, Aunt Anne. But since it makes you happy to have people eat your cooking, I will do my best."

"Hope you choke, Martha, dear," we told her.

The next morning, the five of us selected to give our tonsils for motion study assembled in the parlor. As Martha had predicted, our stomachs were empty. They growled and rumbled. We could hear beds being moved around upstairs, and we knew the wards were being set up again. In the laboratory, which adjoined the parlor, Dad, his movie cameraman, a nurse, and Dr. Burton were converting a desk into an operating table, and setting up the cross-section background and lights.

Dad came into the parlor, dressed like an Alp again. "All right, Anne, come on." He thumped her on the back and smiled at the rest of us. "There's nothing to it. It will be over in just a few minutes. And think of the fun we'll have looking at the movies and seeing how each of you looks when he's asleep."

As he and Anne went out, we could see that his hands were trembling. Sweat was beginning to pop through his white robe. Mother came in and sat with us. Dad had wanted her to watch the operations, but she said she couldn't. After awhile we heard Dad and a nurse walking heavily up the front stairs, and we knew Anne's operation was over and she was being carried to bed.

"I know I'm next, and I won't say I'm not scared," Ernestine confided. "But I'm so hungry all I can think of is Martha and that pie. The lucky dog."

"And doughnuts," said Bill. "The lucky dog."

"Can we have pie and doughnuts after our operations?" Lill asked Mother.

"If you want them," said Mother, who had had her tonsils out.

Dad came into the room. His robe was dripping sweat now. It looked as if a spring thaw had come to the Alps.

"Nothing to it," he said. "And I know we got some great movies. Anne slept just like a baby. All right, Ernestine, girl. You're next; let's go."

"I'm not hungry any more," she said. "Now I'm just scared."

A nurse put a napkin saturated with ether over Ern's nose. The last thing she remembered was Mr. Coggin, Dad's photographer, grinding away at the camera. "He should be cranking at two revolutions a second," she thought. "I'll count and see if he is. And one and two and three and four. That's the way Dad says to count seconds. You have to put the 'and' in between the numbers to count at the right speed. And one and two and three . . ." She fell asleep.

Dr. Burton peered into her mouth.

"My God, Gilbreth," he said. "I told you I didn't want Martha."

"You haven't got Martha," Dad said. "That's Ernestine."

"Are you sure?"

"Of course I'm sure, you jackass. Don't you think I know my own children?"

"You must be mistaken," Dr. Burton insisted. "Look at her carefully. There, now, isn't that Martha?"

"You mean to say you think I can't tell one child from another?"

"I don't mean to say anything, except if that isn't Martha we've made a horrible mistake."

"We?" Dad squealed. "We? I've made no mistake. And I hope I'm wrong in imagining the sort of a mistake you've made."

"You see, all I know them by is their tonsils," said Dr. Burton. "I thought these tonsils were Martha. They were the only pair that didn't have to come out."

"No," moaned Dad. "Oh, no!" Then growing indignant: "Do you mean to tell me you knocked my little girl unconscious for no reason at all?"

"It looks as if I did just that, Gilbreth. I'm sorry, but it's done. It was damned careless. But you do have an uncommon lot of them, and they all look just alike to me."

"All right, Burton," Dad said. "Sorry I lost my temper. What do we do?"

"I'm going to take them out anyway. They'd have to come out eventually at any rate, and the worst part of an operation is dreading it before hand. She's done her dreading, and there's no use to make her do it twice."

As Dr. Burton leaned over Ernestine, some reflex caused her to knee him in the mouth.

"Okay, Ernestine, if that's really your name," he muttered. "I guess I deserved that."

As it turned out, Ernestine's tonsils were recessed and bigger than the doctor had expected. It was a little messy to get at them, and Mr. Coggin, the movie cameraman, was sick in a waste basket.

"Don't stop cranking," Dad shouted at him, "or your tonsils will be next. I'll pull them out by the roots, myself. Crank, by jingo, crank."

Mr. Coggin cranked. When the operation was over, Dad and the nurse carried Ernestine upstairs.

When Dad came in the parlor to get Frank, he told Mother to send someone over to Aunt Anne's for Martha.

"Apple pie, doughnuts or not, she's going to have her tonsils out," he said. "I'm not going to go through another day like this one again in a hurry."

Frank, Bill, and Lillian had their tonsils out, in that order. Then Martha arrived, bawling, kicking, and full of pie and doughnuts.

"You said I didn't have to have my tonsils out, and I'm not going to have my tonsils out," she screamed at the doctor. Before he could get her on the desk which served as the operting table, she kicked him in the stomach.

"The next time I come to your house," he said to Dad as soon as he could get his breath, "I'm going to wear a chest protector and a catcher's mask." Then to the nurse: "Give some ether to Martha, if that's really her name."

"Yes, I'm Martha," she yelled through the towel. "You're making a mistake."

"I told you she was Martha," Dad said triumphantly.

"I know," Dr. Burton said. "Let's not go into that again. She's Martha, but I've named her tonsils Ernestine. Open your mouth, Martha, you sweet child, and let me get Ernestine's tonsils. Crank on Mr. Coggin. Your film may be the first photographic record of a man slowly going berserk."

All of us felt terribly sick that afternoon, but Martha was in agony.

"It's a shame," Grandma kept telling Martha, who was named for her and was her especial pet. "They shouldn't have let you eat all that stuff and then brought you back here for the butchering. I don't care whether it was the doctor's fault or your father's fault. I'd like to skin them both alive and then scalp them like red Indians."

While we were recuperating, Dad spent considerable time with us, but minimized our discomforts, and kept telling us we were just looking for sympathy.

"Don't tell me," he said. "I saw the operations, didn't I? Why there's only the little, tiniest cut at the back of your throat. I don't understand how you can do all that complaining. Don't you remember the story about the Spartan boy who kept his mouth shut while the fox was chewing on his vitals?"

It was partly because of our complaining, and the desire to show us how the Spartan boy would have had his tonsils out, that Dad decided to have only a local anesthetic for his operation. Mother, Grandma, and Dr. Burton all advised against it. But Dad wouldn't listen.

"Why does everyone want to make a mountain out of a molehill over such a minor operation?" he said. "I want to keep an eye on Burton and see that he doesn't mess up the job."

The first day that we children were well enough to get up, Dad and Mother set out in the car for Dr. Burton's office. Mother had urged Dad to call a taxi. She didn't know how to drive, and she said Dad probably wouldn't feel like doing the driving on the way home. But Dad laughed at her qualms.

"We'll be back in about an hour," Dad called to us as he tested his three horns to make sure he was prepared for any emergency. "Wait lunch for us. I'm starving."

"You've got to hand it to him," Anne admitted as the Pierce Arrow bucked up Wayside Place. "He's the bee's knees, all right. We were all scared to death before our operations. And look at him. He's looking forward to it."

Two hours later, a taxicab stopped in front of the house, and the driver jumped out and opened the door for his passengers. Then Mother emerged, pale and red-eyed. She and the driver helped a crumpled mass of moaning blue serge to alight. Dad's hat was rumpled and on sideways. His face was gray and sagging. He wasn't crying, but his eyes were watering. He couldn't speak and he couldn't smile.

"He's sure got a load on all right, Mrs. Gilbreth," said the driver enviously. "And still early afternoon, too. Didn't even know he touched the stuff, myself."

We waited for the lighting to strike, but it didn't. The seriousness of Dad's condition may be adjuged by the fact that he contented himself with a withering look.

"Keep a civil tongue in your head," said Mother, in one of the sharpest speeches of her career. "He's deathly ill."

Mother and Grandma helped Dad up to his room. We could hear him moaning, all the way downstairs.

Mother told us all about it that night, while Dad was snoring under the effects of sleeping pills. Mother had waited in Dr. Burton's ante-room while the tonsillectomy was being performed. Dad had felt wonderful while under the local anesthetic. When the operation was half over, he had come out into the ante-room, grinning and waving one tonsil in a pair of forceps.

"One down and one to go, Lillie," he had said. "Completely painless. Just like rolling off a log."

After what had seemed an interminable time, Dad had come out into the waiting room again, and reached for his hat and coat. He was still grinning, only not so wide as before.

"That's that," he said. "Almost painless. All right, boss, let's go. I'm still hungry."

Then, as Mother watched, his high spirits faded and he began to fall to pieces.

"I'm stabbed," he moaned. "I'm hemorrhaging. Burton, come here. Quick. What have you done to me?"

Dr. Burton came out of his office. It must be said to his credit that he was sincerely sympathetic. Dr. Burton had had his own tonsils out.

"You'll be all right, Old Pioneer," he said. "You just had to have it the hard way."

Dad obviously couldn't drive, so Mother had called the taxi. A man from the garage towed Foolish Carriage home later that night.

"I tried to drive it home," the garage man told Mother, "but I couldn't budge it. I got the engine running all right, but it just spit and bucked every time I put it in gear. Durndest thing I ever saw."

"I don't think anyone but Mr. Gilbreth understands it," Mother said.

Dad spent two weeks in bed, and it was the first time any of us remembered his being sick. He couldn't smoke, eat, or talk. But he could glare, and he glared at Bill for two full minutes when Bill asked him one afternoon if he had had his tonsils taken out like the Spartans used to have theirs removed.

Dad didn't get his voice back until the very day that he finally got out of bed. He was lying there, propped up on pillows, reading his office mail. There was a card from Mr. Coggin, the photographer.

"Hate to tell you, Mr. Gilbreth, but none of the moving pictures came out. I forgot to take off the inside lens cap. I'm terribly sorry. Coggin. P.S. I quit."

Dad threw off the covers and reached for his bathrobe. For the first time in two weeks, he spoke:

"I'll track him down to the ends of the earth," he croaked. "I'll take a blunt button hook and pull his tonsils out by the by jingoed roots, just like I promised him. He doesn't quit. He's fired."

CHAPTER 11

Nantucket

We spent our summers at Nantucket, Massachusetts, where Dad bought two lighthouses, which had been abandoned by the government, and a ramshackle cottage, which looked as if it had been abandoned by Coxey's Army. Dad had the lighthouses moved so that they flanked the cottage. He and Mother used one of them as an office and den. The other served as a bedroom for three of the children.

He named the cottage *The Shoe,* in honor of Mother, who, he said, reminded him of the old woman who lived in one.

The cottage and lighthouses were situated on a flat stretch

of land between the fashionable Cliff and the Bathing Beach. Besides our place, there was only one other house in the vicinity. This belonged to an artist couple named Whitney. But after our first summer at Nantucket, the Whitneys had their house jacked up, placed on rollers, and moved a mile away to a vacant lot near the tip of Brant Point. After that, we had the strip of land all to ourselves.

Customarily, en route from Montclair to Nantucket, we spent the night in a hotel in New London, Connecticut. Dad knew the hotel manager and all of the men at the desk, and they used to exchange loud and good-natured insults for the benefit of the crowds that followed us in from the street.

"Oh, Lord, look what's coming," the manager called when we entered the door. And then to an assistant. "Alert the fire department and the house detective. It's the Gilbreths. And take that cigar cutter off the counter and lock it in the safe."

"Do you still have that dangerous guillotine?" Dad grinned. "I know you'll be disappointed to hear that the finger grew in just as good as new. Show the man your finger, Ernestine."

Ernestine held up the little finger of her right hand. On a previous visit, she had pushed it inquisitively into the cigar cutter, and had lost about an eighth of an inch of it. She had bled considerably on a rug, while Dad tried to fashion a tourniquet and roared inquiries about whether there was a doctor in the house.

"Tell me," Dad remarked as he picked up a pen to register in the big book, "do my Irishmen come cheaper by the dozen?"

"Irishmen! If I were wearing a sheet, you'd call them Arabs. How many of them are there, anyway? Last year, when I went to make out your bill, you claimed there were only seven. I can count at least a dozen of them now."

"It's quite possible there may have been some additions since then," Dad conceded.

"Front, boy. Front, boy. Front, boy. Front, boy. You four boys show Mr. and Mrs. Gilbreth and their seven—or so—Irishmen to 503, 504, 505, 506, and 507. And mind you take good care of them, too."

When we first started going to Nantucket, which is off the tip of Cape Cod, automobiles weren't allowed on the island,

and we'd leave the Pierce Arrow in a garage at New Bedford, Massachusetts. Later, when the automobile ban was lifted, we'd take the car with us on the *Gay Head* or the *Sankaty*, the steamers which plied between the mainland and the island. Dad had a frightening time backing the automobile up the gangplank. Mother insisted that we get out of the car and stand clear. Then she'd beg Dad to put on a life preserver.

"I know you and it are going into the water one of these days," she warned.

"Doesn't anybody, even my wife, have confidence in my driving?" he would moan. Then on a more practical note. "Besides, I can swim."

The biggest problem, on the boat and in the car, was Martha's two canaries, which she had won for making the best recitation in Sunday school. All of us, except Dad, were fond of them. Dad called one of them Shut Up and the other You Heard Me. He said they smelled so much that they ruined his whole trip, and were the only creatures on earth with voices louder than his children. Tom Grieves, the handyman, who had to clean up the cage, named the birds Peter Soil and Maggie Mess. Mother wouldn't let us use those full names, she said they were "Eskimo." (Eskimo was Mother's description of anything that was off-color, revolting, or evil-minded.) We called the birds simply Peter and Maggie.

On one trip, Fred was holding the cage on the stern of the ship, while Dad backed the car aboard. Somehow, the wire door popped open and the birds escaped. They flew to a piling on the dock, and then to a roof of a warehouse. When Dad, with the car finally stowed away, appeared on deck, three of the younger children were sobbing. They made so much noise that the captain heard them and came off the bridge.

"What's the trouble now, Mr. Gilbreth?" he asked.

"Nothing," said Dad, who saw a chance to put thirty miles between himself and the canaries. "You can shove off at any time, captain."

"No one tells me when to shove off until I'm ready to shove off," the captain announced stubbornly. He leaned over Fred. "What's the matter, son?"

"Peter and Maggie," bawled Fred. "They've gone over the rail."

"My God," the captain blanched. "I've been afraid this

would happen ever since you Gilbreths started coming to Nantucket."

"Peter and Maggie aren't Gilbreths," Dad said irritatedly. "Why don't you just forget about the whole thing and shove off?"

The captain leaned over Fred again. "Peter and Maggie who? Speak up, boy!"

Fred stopped crying. "I'm not allowed to tell you their last names," he said. "Mother says they're Eskimo."

The captain was bewildered. "I wish someone would make sense," he complained. "You say Peter and Maggie, the Eskimos, have disappeared over the rail?"

Fred nodded. Dad pointed to the empty cage. "Two canaries," Dad shouted, "known as Peter and Maggie and by other aliases, have flown the coop. No matter. We wouldn't think of delaying you further."

"Where did they fly to, sonny?"

Fred pointed to the roof of the warehouse. The captain sighed.

"I can't stand to see children cry," he said. He walked back to the bridge and started giving orders.

Four crew members, armed with crab nets, climbed to the roof of the warehouse. While passengers shouted encouragement from the rail, the men chased the birds across the roof, back to the dock, onto the rigging of the ship, and back to the warehouse again. Finally Peter and Maggie disappeared altogether, and the captain had to give up.

"I'm sorry, Mr. Gilbreth," he said. "I guess we'll have to shove off without your canaries."

"You've been too kind already," Dad beamed.

Dad felt good for the rest of the trip, and even managed to convince Martha of the wisdom of throwing the empty, but still smelly, bird cage over the side of the ship.

The next day, after we settled in our cottage, a cardboard box arrived from the captain. It was addressed to Fred, and it had holes punched in the top.

"You don't have to tell *me* what's in it," Dad said glumly. "I've got a nose." He reached in his wallet and handed Martha a bill. "Take this and go down to the village and buy another cage. And after this, I hope you'll be more careful of your belongings."

Our cottage had one small lavatory, but no hot water, shower, or bathtub. Dad thought that living a primitive life in the summer was healthful. He also believed that cleanliness was next to godliness, and as a result all of us had to go swimming at least once a day. The rule was never waived, even when the temperature dropped to the fifties, and a cold, gray rain was falling. Dad would lead the way from the house to the beach, dog-trotting, holding a bar of soap in one hand, and beating his chest with the other.

"Look out, ocean, here comes a tidal wave. Brrr. Last one in is Kaiser Bill."

Then he'd take a running dive and disappear in a geyser of spray. He'd swim under water a ways, allow his feet to emerge, wiggle his toes, swim under water some more, and then come up head first, grinning and spitting a thin stream of water through his teeth.

"Come on," he'd call. "It's wonderful once you get in." And he'd start lathering himself with soap.

Mother was the only non-swimmer, except the babies. She hated cold water, she hated salt water, and she hated bathing suits. Bathing suits itched her, and although she wore the most conservative models, with long sleeves and black stockings, she never felt modest in them. Dad used to say Mother put on more clothes than she took off when she went swimming.

Mother's swims consisted of testing the water with the tip of a black bathing shoe, wading cautiously out to her knees, making some tentative dabs in the water with her hands, splashing a few drops on her shoulders, and, finally, in a moment of supreme courage, pinching her nose and squatting down until the water reached her chest. The nose-pinch was an unnecessary precaution, because her nose never came within a foot of the water.

Then, with teeth chattering, she'd hurry back to the house, where she'd take a cold water sponge bath, to get rid of the salt.

"My, the water was delightful this morning, wasn't it?" she'd say brightly at the lunch table.

"I've seen fish who found the air more delightful than you do the water," Dad would remark.

As in every other phase of teaching, Dad knew his business as a swimming instructor. Some of us learned to swim when we were as young as three years old, and all of us had learned by the time we were five. It was a sore point with Dad that Mother was the only pupil he ever had encountered with whom he had no success.

"This summer," he'd tell Mother at the start of every vacation, "I'm really going to teach you, if it's the last thing I do. It's dangerous not to know how to swim. What would you do if you were on a boat that sank? Leave me with a dozen children on my hands, I suppose! After all, you should have some consideration for me."

"I'll try again," Mother said patiently. But you could tell she knew it was hopeless.

Once they had gone down to the beach, Dad would take her hand and lead her. Mother would start out bravely enough, but would begin holding back about the time the water got to her knees. We'd form a ring around her and offer her what encouragement we could.

"That's the girl, Mother," we'd say. "It's not going to hurt you. Look at me. Look at me."

"Please don't splash," Mother would say. "You know how I hate to be splashed."

"For Lord's sakes, Lillie," said Dad. "Come out deeper."

"Isn't this deep enough?"

"You can't learn to swim if you're hard aground."

"No matter how deep we go, I always end up aground anyway."

"Don't be scared, now. Come on. This time it will be different. You'll see."

Dad towed her out until the water was just above her waist. "Now the first thing you have to do," he said, "is to learn the dead man's float. If a dead man can do it, so can you."

"I don't even like its name. It sounds ominous."

"Like this, Mother. Look at me."

"You kids clear out," said Dad. "But, Lillie, if the children can do it, you, a grown woman, should be able to. Come on now. You can't help but float, because the human body, when inflated with air, is lighter than water."

"You know I always sink."

"That was last year. Try it now. Be a sport. I won't let anything happen to you."

"I don't want to."

"You don't want to show the white feather in front of all the kids."

"I don't care if I show the whole albatross," Mother said. "But I don't suppose I'll have another minute's peace until I try it. So here goes. And remember, I'm counting on you not to let anything happen to me."

"You'll float. Don't worry."

Mother took a deep breath, stretched herself out on the surface, and sank like a stone. Dad waited a while, still convinced that under the laws of physics she must ultimately rise. When she didn't, he finally reached down in disgust and fished her up. Mother was gagging, choking up water, and furious.

"See what I mean?" she finally managed.

Dad was furious, too. "Are you sure you didn't do that on purpose?" he asked her.

"Mercy, Maud," Mother sputtered. "Mercy, mercy, Maud. Do you think I like it down there in Davey Jones' locker?"

"Davey Jones' locker," scoffed Dad. "Why you weren't even four feet under water. You weren't even in his attic."

"Well, it seemed like his locker to me. And I'm never going down there again. You ought to be convinced by now that Archimedes' principle simply doesn't apply, so far as I am concerned."

Coughing and blowing her nose, Mother started for the beach.

"I still don't understand it," Dad muttered. "She's right. It completely refutes Archimedes."

Dad had promised before we came to Nantucket that there would be no formal studying—no language records and no school books. He kept his promise, although we found he was always teaching us things informally, when our backs were turned.

For instance, there was the matter of the Morse code.

"I have a way to teach you the code without any studying," he announced one day at lunch.

We said we didn't want to learn the code, that we didn't want to learn anything until school started in the fall.

"There's no studying," said Dad, "and the ones who learn it first will get rewards. The ones who don't learn it are going to wish they had."

After lunch, he got a small paint brush and a can of black enamel, and locked himself in the lavatory, where he painted the alphabet in code on the wall.

For the next three days Dad was busy with his paint brush, writing code over the whitewash in every room in *The Shoe.* On the ceiling in the dormitory bedrooms, he wrote the alphabet together with key words, whose accents were a reminder of the code for the various letters. It went like this: A, dot-dash, a-BOUT; B, dash-dot-dot-dot, BOIS-ter-ous-ly; C, dash-dot-dash-dot, CARE-less CHILD-ren; D, dash-dot-dot, DAN-ger-ous, etc.

When you lay on your back, dozing, the words kept going through your head, and you'd find yourself saying, "DAN-ger-ous, dash-dot-dot, DAN-ger-ous."

He painted secret messages in code on the walls of the front porch and dining room.

"What do they say, Daddy?" we asked him.

"Many things," he replied mysteriously. "Many secret things and many things of great humor."

We went into the bedrooms and copied the code alphabet on pieces of paper. Then, referring to the paper, we started translating Dad's messages. He went right on painting, as if he were paying no attention to us, but he didn't miss a word.

"Lord, what awful puns," said Anne. "And this, I presume, is meant to fit into the category of 'things of great humor.' Listen to this one: 'Bee it ever so bumble there's no place like comb.' "

"And we're stung," Ern moaned. "We're not going to be satisfied until we translate them all. I see dash-dot-dash-dot, and I hear myself repeating CARE-less CHILD-ren. What's this one say?"

We figured it out: "When igorots is bliss, 'tis folly to be white." And another, by courtesy of Mr. Irvin S. Cobb, "Eat, drink and be merry for tomorrow you may diet." And still another, which Mother made Dad paint out, "Two maggots were fighting in dead Ernest."

"That one is Eskimo," said Mother. "I won't have it in my dining room, even in Morse code."

"All right, boss," Dad grinned sheepishly. "I'll paint over it. It's already served its purpose, anyway."

Every day or so after that, Dad would leave a piece of paper, containing a Morse code message, on the dining room table. Translated, it might read something like this: "The first one who figures out this secret message should look in the right hand pocket of my linen knickers, hanging on a hook in my room. Daddy." Or: "Hurry up before someone beats you to it, and look in the bottom, left drawer of the sewing machine."

In the knickers' pocket and in the drawer would be some sort of reward—a Hershey bar, a quarter, a receipt entitling the bearer to one cocolate ice cream soda at Coffin's Drug Store, payable by Dad on demand.

Some of the Morse code notes were false alarms. "Hello, Live Bait. This one is on the house. No reward. But there may be a reward next time. When you finish reading this, dash off like mad so the next fellow will think you are on some hot clue. Then he'll read it, too, and you won't be the only one who got fooled. Daddy."

As Dad had planned, we all knew the Morse code fairly well within a few weeks. Well enough, in fact, so that we could tap out messages to each other by bouncing the tip of a fork on a butter plate. When a dozen or so persons all attempt to broadcast in this manner, and all of us preferred sending to receiving, the accumulation is loud and nerve-shattering. A present-day equivalent might be reproduced if the sound-effects man on *Gangbusters* and Walter Winchell should go on the air simultaneously, before a battery of powerful amplifiers.

The wall-writing worked so well in teaching us the code that Dad decided to use the same system to teach us astronomy. His first step was to capture our interest, and he did this by fashioning a telescope from a camera tripod and a pair of binoculars. He'd tote the contraption out into the yard on clear nights, and look at the stars, while apparently ignoring us.

We'd gather around and nudge him, and pull at his clothes, demanding that he let us look through the telescope.

"Don't bother me," he'd say, with his nose stuck into the glasses. "Oh, my golly, I believe those two stars are going to collide! No. Awfully close, though. Now I've got to see what the Old Beetle's up to. What a star, what a star!"

"Daddy, give us a turn," we'd insist. "Don't be a pig."

Finally, with assumed reluctance, he agreed to let us look through the glasses. We could see the ring on Saturn, three moons on Jupiter, and the craters on our own moon. Dad's favorite star was Betelgeuse, the yellowish red "Old Beetle" in the Orion constellation. He took a personal interest in her, because some of his friends were collaborating in experiments to measure her diameter by Michelson's interferometer.

When he finally was convinced he had interested us in astronomy, Dad started a new series of wall paintings dealings with stars. On one wall he made a scale drawing of the major planets, ranging from little Mercury, represented by a circle about as big as a marble, to Jupiter, as big as a basketball. On another, he showed the planets in relation to their distances from the sun, with Mercury the closest and Neptune the farthest away—almost in the kitchen. Pluto still hadn't been discovered, which was just as well, because there really wasn't room for it.

Dr. Harlow Shapley of Harvard gave Dad a hundred or more photographs of stars, nebulae and solar eclipses. Dad hung these on the wall, near the floor. He explained that if they were up any higher, at the conventional level for pictures, the smaller children wouldn't be able to see them.

There was still some wall space left, and Dad had more than enough ideas to fill it. He tacked up a piece of cross-section graph paper, which was a thousand lines long and a thousand lines wide, and thus contained exactly a million little squares.

"You hear people talk a lot about a million," he said, "but not many people have ever seen exactly a million things at the same time. If a man has a million dollars, he has exactly as many dollars as there are little squares on that chart."

"Do you have a million dollars, Daddy?" Bill asked.

"No," said Dad a little ruefully. "I have a million children, instead. Somewhere along the line, a man has to choose between the two."

He painted diagrams in the dining room showing the difference between meters and feet, kilograms and pounds, liters and quarts. And he painted seventeen mysterious-looking symbols, representing each of the Therbligs, on a wall near the front door.

The Therbligs were discovered, or maybe a better word would be diagnosed, by Dad and Mother. Everybody has seventeen of them, they said, and the Therbligs can be used in such a way as to make life difficult or easy for their possessor.

A lazy man, Dad believed, always makes the best use of his Therbligs because he is too indolent to waste motions. Whenever Dad started to do a new motion study project at a factory, he'd always begin by announcing he wanted to photograph the motions of the laziest man on the job.

"The kind of fellow I want," he'd say, "is the fellow who is so lazy he won't even scratch himself. You must have one of those around some place. Every factory has them."

Dad named the Therbligs for himself—Gilbreth spelled backwards, with a slight variation. They were the basic theorems of his business and resulted indirectly in such things as foot levers to open garbage cans, special chairs for factory workers, redesign of typewriters, and some aspects of the assembly line technique.

Using Therbligs, Dad had shown Regal Shoe Company clerks how they could take a customer's shoe off in seven seconds, and put it back on again and lace it up in twenty-two seconds.

Actually, a Therblig is a unit of motion or thought. Suppose a man goes into the bathroom to shave. We'll assume that his face is all lathered and he is ready to pick up his razor. He knows where the razor is, but first he must locate it with his eye. That is "search," the first Therblig. His eye finds it and comes to rest—that's "find," the second Therblig. Third comes "select," the process of sliding the razor prior to the fourth Therblig, "grasp." Fifth is "transport loaded," bringing the razor up to the face, and sixth is "position," getting the razor set on the face. There are eleven other Therbligs—the last one is "think!"

When Dad made a motion study, he broke down each operation into a Therblig, and then tried to reduce the time taken to perform each Therblig. Perhaps certain parts to be assembled could be painted red and others green, so as to reduce the time required for "search" and "find."

Perhaps the parts could be moved closer to the object being assembled, so as to reduce the time required for "transport loaded."

Every Therblig had its own symbol, and once they were painted on the wall Dad had us apply them to our household chores—bedmaking, dishwashing, sweeping, and dusting.

Meanwhile, *The Shoe* and the lighthouses had become a stop on some of the Nantucket sightseeing tours. The stop didn't entail getting out of the carriages or, later, the buses. But we'd hear the drivers giving lurid and inaccurate accounts of the history of the place and the family which inhabited it. Some individuals occasionally would come up to the door and ask if they could peek in, and if the house was presentable we'd usually show them around.

Then, unexpectedly, the names of strangers started appearing in a guest book which we kept in the front room.

"Are these friends of yours?" Dad asked Mother.

"I never heard of them before. Maybe they're friends of the children."

When we said we didn't know them, Dad questioned Tom Grieves, who admitted readily enough that he had been showing tourists through the house and lighthouses, while we were at the beach. Tom's tour included the dormitories; Mother's and Dad's room, where the baby stayed; and even the lavatory, where he pointed out the code alphabet. Some of the visitors, seeing the guest book on the table, thought they were supposed to sign. Tom stood at the front door as the tourists filed out, and frequently collected tips.

Mother was irked. "I never heard of such a thing in all my born days. Imagine taking perfect strangers though our bedrooms, and the house a wreck, most likely."

"Well," said Dad, who was convinced the tourists had come to see his visual education methods, "there's no need for us to be selfish about the ideas we've developed. Maybe it's not a bad plan to let the public see what we're doing."

He leaned back reflectively in his chair, an old mahogany pew from some church. Dad had found the pew, disassembled, in the basement of our cottage. He had resurrected it reverently, rubbed it down, put it together, and varnished it. The pew was his seat of authority in *The Shoe,* and the only chair which fitted him comfortably and in which he could place complete confidence.

"I wonder how much money Tom took in," he said to Mother. "Maybe we could work out some sort of an arrangement so that Tom could split tips from future admissions . . ."

"The idea!" said Mother. "There'll be no future admissions. The very idea."

"Can't you take a joke? I was only joking. Where's your sense of humor?"

"I know." Mother nodded her head. "I'm not supposed to have any. But did you ever stop to think that there might be some women, somewhere, who might think their husbands were joking if they said they had bought two lighthouses and . . ."

Dad started to laugh, and as he rocked back and forth he shook the house so that loose whitewash flaked off the ceiling and landed on the top of his head. When Dad laughed, everybody laughed—you couldn't help it. And Mother, after a losing battle to remain severe, joined in.

"By jingo," he wheezed. "And I guess there are some women, somewhere, who wouldn't want the Morse code, and planets, and even Therbligs, painted all over the walls of their house, either. Come over here, boss, and let me take back everything I ever said about your sense of humor."

Mother walked over and brushed the whitewash out of what was left of his hair.

CHAPTER 12

The *Rena*

Dad acquired the *Rena* to reward us for learning to swim. She was a catboat, twenty feet long and almost as wide. She was docile, dignified, and ancient.

Before we were allowed aboard the *Rena,* Dad delivered a series of lectures about navigation, tides, the magnetic compass, seamanship, rope-splicing, right-of-way, and nautical terminology. Radar still had not been invented. It is doubtful if, outside the Naval Academy at Annapolis, any group of Americans ever received a more thorough indoctrination before setting foot on a catboat.

Next followed a series of dry runs, on the front porch of *The Shoe.* Dad, sitting in a chair and holding a walking stick as if it were a tiller, would bark out orders while maneuvering his imaginary craft around a tricky harbor.

We'd sit in line on the floor along side of him, pretending we were holding down the windward rail. Dad would rub imaginary spray out of his eyes, and scan the horizon for possible sperm whale, Flying Dutchmen, or floating ambergris.

"Great Point Light off the larboard bow," he'd bark. "Haul in the sheet and we'll try to clear her on this tack."

He'd ease the handle of the cane over toward the imaginary leeward rail, and two of us would haul in an imaginary rope.

"Steady as she goes," Dad would command. "Make her fast."

We'd make believe twist the rope around a cleet.

"Coming about," he'd shout. "Low bridge. Ready about, hard a'lee."

This time he'd push the cane handle all the way over toward the leeward side. We'd duck our heads and then scramble across the porch to man the opposite rail.

"Now we'll come up and pick up our mooring. You do that at the end of every sail. Good sailors always make the mooring on the first try. Landlubbers sometimes have to go around three or four times before they can catch it."

He'd stand up in the stern, the better to squint at the imaginary mooring.

"Now. Let go your sheet, Bill. Stand by the centerboard, Mart. Up on the bow with the boat hook, Anne and Ernestine, and mind you grab that mooring. Stand by the throat, Frank. Stand by the peak, Fred. . . ."

We'd scurry around the porch going through our duties,

until at last Dad was satisfied his new crew was ready for the high seas.

Dad was never happier than when aboard the *Rena*. From the moment he climbed into our dory to row out to *Rena's* mooring, his personality changed. On the *Rena*, we were no longer his flesh and blood, but a crew of landlubberly scum shanghaied from the taverns and fleshpots of many exotic ports. *Rena* was no scow-like catboat, but a sleek four-master, bound around the Horn with a bone in her teeth in search of rare spices and the priceless treasure of the Indies. He insisted that we address him as Captain, instead of Daddy, and every remark must needs be civil and end with a "sir."

"It's just like when he was in the Army," Ernestine whispered. "Remember those military haircuts for Frank and Bill, and all that business of snapping to attention and learning to salute, and the kitchen police?"

"Avast there, you swabs," Dad hollered. "No mutinous whispering on the poop deck!"

Anne, being the oldest, was proclaimed first mate of the *Rena*. Ernestine was second mate, Martha third, and Frank fourth. All the younger children were able-bodied seamen who, presumably, ate hardtack and bunked before the mast.

"Seems to be blowing up, mister," Dad said to Anne. "I'll have a reef in that mains'il."

"Aye, aye, sir."

"The *Rena's* just got one sail, Daddy," Lill said. "Is that the mains'il?"

"Quiet, you landlubber, or you'll get the merrie rope's end. Of course it's the mains'il."

The merrie rope's end was no idle threat. Able-bodied seamen or mates who failed to leap when Dad barked an order did in fact receive a flogging with a piece of rope. It hurt, too.

Dad's mood was contagious, and soon the mates were as dogmatic and as full of invective as he, when dealing with the sneaking pickpockets and rum-palsied derelicts who were their subordinates. And, somehow, Dad passed along to us the illusion that placid old *Rena* was a taunt ship.

"I'll have those halliards coiled," he told Anne.

"Aye, aye, sir. Come on you swabs. Look alive now, or shiver my timbers if I don't keel haul the lot of you."

Sometimes, without warning, Dad would start to bellow out tuneless chanties about the fifteen men on a dead man's chest and, especially, one that went, "He said heave her to, she replied make it three."

If there had been any irons aboard, they would have been occupied by the fumbling landlubber or scurvy swab who forgot his duties and made Dad miss the mooring. Dad felt that to have to make a second try for the mooring was the supreme humiliation, and that fellow yachtsmen and professional sea captains all along the waterfront were splitting their sides laughing at him. He'd drop the tiller, grow red in the face, and advance rope in hand on the offender. More than once, the scurvy swab made a panic-stricken dive over the side, preferring to swim ashore, where he would cope ultimately with Dad, instead of meeting the captain on the latter's own quarterdeck.

On one occasion, when Dad blamed missing a mooring on general inefficiency and picked up a merrie rope's end to inflict merrie mass punishment, the entire crew leaped simultaneously over the side in an unrehearsed abandon-ship maneuver. Only the captain remained at the helm, from which vantage point he hurled threatening reminders about the danger of sharks and the penalties of mutiny. On that occasion, he brought *Rena* up to the mooring by himself, without any trouble, thus proving something we had long suspected—that he didn't really need our help at all, but enjoyed teaching us and having a crew to order around.

Through the years, old *Rena* remained phlegmatic, paying no apparent attention to the bedlam which had intruded into her twilight years. She was too old a seadog to learn new tricks.

Only once, just for a second, did she display any sign of temperament. It was after a long sail. A fog had come up, and *Rena* was as clammy as a shower curtain. We had missed the mooring on the first go-round, and the captain was in an ugly mood. We made the mooring all right on the second try. The captain, as was his custom, was standing in the stern, merrie rope in hand, shouting orders about lowering the sail. Just before the sail came down, a squall hit *Rena,* and she retaliated by whipping her boom savagely across the hull. The captain saw it coming, but didn't have time to duck. The boom caught him on the side of the head with a terrific clout, a blow hard enough to lift him off his feet and tumble him, stomach first, into the water.

The captain didn't come up for almost a minute. The crew, while losing little love for their captain, become frightened for their Daddy. We were just about to dive in after him when a pair of feet emerged from the water and the toes wiggled. We knew everything was all right then. The feet disappeared, and a few moments later Dad came up head first. His nose was bleeding, but he was grinning and didn't forget to spit the fine stream of water through his front teeth.

"The bird they call the elephant," he whispered weakly, and he was Dad then. But not for long. As soon as his head cleared and his strength came back, he was the captain again.

"All right, you red lobsters, avast there," he bellowed. "Throw your captain a line and help haul me aboard. Or, shiver my timbers, I'll take a belaying pin to the swab who lowered the boom on me."

CHAPTER 13

Have You Seen the Latest Model?

It was an off year that didn't bring a new Gilbreth baby. Both Dad and Mother wanted a large family. And if it was Dad who set the actual target of an even dozen, Mother as readily agreed.

Dad mentioned the dozen figure for the first time on their wedding day. They had just boarded a train at Oakland,

California, after the ceremony, and Mother was trying to appear blasé, as if she had been married for years. She might have gotten away with it, too, if Dad had not stage whispered when she took off her hat prior to sitting down:

"Good Lord, woman, why didn't you tell me your hair was red?"

The heads of leering, winking passengers craned around. Mother slid into the seat and wiggled into a corner, where she tried to hide behind a magazine. Dad sat down next to her. He didn't say anything more until the train got underway and they could talk without being heard throughout the car.

"I shouldn't have done that," he whispered. "It's just —I'm so proud of you I want everyone to look at you, and to know you're my wife."

"That's all right, dear. I'm glad you're proud of me."

"We're going to have a wonderful life, Lillie. A wonderful life and a wonderful family. A great big family."

"We'll have children all over the house," Mother smiled. "From the basement to the attic."

"From the floorboards to the chandelier."

"When we go for our Sunday walk we'll look like Mr. and Mrs. Pied Piper."

"Mr. Piper, shake hands with Mrs. Piper. Mrs. Piper, meet Mr. Piper."

Mother put the magazine on the seat between her and Dad, and they held hands beneath it.

"How many would you say we should have, just an estimate?" Mother asked.

"Just as an estimate, many."

"Lots and lots."

"We'll sell out for an even dozen," said Dad. "No less. What do you say to that?"

"I say," said Mother, "a dozen would be just right. No less."

"That's the minimum."

"Boys or girls?"

"Well, boys would be fine," Dad whispered. "A dozen boys would be just right. But . . . well, girls would be all right too. Sure. I guess."

"I'd like to have half boys and half girls. Do you think it would be all right to have half girls?"

"If that's what you want," Dad said, "we'll plan it that way. Excuse me a minute while I make a note of it." He took out his memorandum book and solemnly wrote: "Don't forget to have six boys and six girls."

They had a dozen children, six boys and six girls, in seventeen years. Somewhat to Dad's disappointment, there were no twins or other multiple births. There was no doubt in his mind that the most efficient way to rear a large family would be to have one huge litter and get the whole business over with at one time.

It was a year or so after the wedding, when Mother was expecting her first baby, that Dad confided to her his secret conviction that all of their children would be girls.

"Would it make much difference to you?" Mother asked him.

"Would it make much difference?" Dad asked in amazement. "To have a dozen girls and not a single boy?" And then realizing that he might upset Mother, he added quickly: "No, of course not. Anything you decide to have will be just fine with me."

Dad's conviction that he would have no boys was based on a hunch that the Gilbreth Name, of which he was terribly proud, would cease to exist with him; that he was the last of the Gilbreths. Dad was the only surviving male of the entire branch of his family. There were two or three other Gilbreths in the country, but apparently they were no relation to Dad. The name Gilbreth, in the case of Dad's family, was a fairly recent corruption of Galbraith. A clerk of court, in a small town in Maine, had mispelled Galbraith on some legal document, and it had proved easier for Dad's grandfather to change his name to Gilbreth—which was how the clerk had spelled it—than to change the document.

So when Anne was born, in New York, Dad was not in the least bit disappointed, because he had known all along she would be a girl. It is doubtful if any father ever was more insane about an offspring. It was just as well that Anne was a girl. If she had been a boy, Dad might have toppled completely off the deep end, and run amok with a kris in his teeth.

Dad had long held theories about babies and, with the arrival of Anne, he was anxious to put them to a test. He believed that children, like little monkeys, were born with certain instincts of self-preservation, but that the instincts vanished because babies were kept cooped up in a crib. He was convinced that babies started learning things from the very minute they were born, and that it was wrong to keep them in a nursery. He always forbade baby talk in the presence of Anne or any of his subsequent offspring.

"The only reason a baby talks baby talk," he said, "is because that's all he's heard from grownups. Some children are almost full grown before they learn that the whole world doesn't speak baby talk."

He also thought that to feel secure and wanted in the family circle, a baby should be brought up at the side of its parents. He put Anne's bassinet on a desk in his and Mother's bedroom, and talked to her as if she were an adult, about concrete, and his new houseboat, and efficiency, and all the little sisters she was going to have.

The German nurse whom Dad had employed was scornful. "Why she can't understand a thing you say," the nurse told Dad.

"How do you know?" Dad demanded. "And I wish you'd speak German, like I told you to do, when you talk in front of the baby. I want her to learn both languages."

"What does a two-week-old baby know about German?" said the nurse, shaking her head.

"Never mind that," Dad replied. "I hired you because you speak German, and I want you to speak it." He picked up Anne and held her on his shoulder. "Hang on now, Baby. Imagine you are a little monkey in a tree in the jungle. Hang on to save your life."

"Mind now," said the nurse. "She can't hang on to anything. She's only two weeks old. You'll drop her. Mind, now."

"I'm minding," Dad said irritably. "Of course she can't hang on, the way you and her mother coddle her and repress all her natural instincts. Show the nurse how you can hang on, Anne, baby."

Anne couldn't. Instead, she spit up some milk on Dad's shoulder.

"Now is that any way to behave?" he asked her. "I'm surprised at you. But that's all right, honey. I know it's not your fault. It's the way you've been all swaddled up around here. It's enough to turn anybody's stomach."

"You'd better give her to me for awhile," Mother said. "That's enough exercise for one day."

A week later, Dad talked Mother into letting him see whether new babies were born with a natural instinct to swim.

"When you throw little monkeys into a river, they just automatically swim. That's the way monkey mothers teach their young. I'll try out Anne in the bathtub. I won't let anything happen to her."

"Are you crazy or something," the nurse shouted. "Mrs. Gilbreth, you're not going to let him drown that child."

"Keep quiet and maybe you'll learn something," Dad told her.

Anne liked the big bathtub just fine. But she made no effort to swim and Dad finally had to admit that the experiment was a failure.

"Now if it had been a boy," he said darkly to the nurse, when Mother was out of hearing.

The desk on which Anne's bassinet rested was within reach of the bed and was piled high with notes, *Iron Age* magazines, and the galley proofs of a book Dad had just written on reinforced concrete. Mother utilized the "unavoidable delay" of her confinement to read the proofs. At night, when the light was out, Dad would reach over into the bassinet and stroke the baby's hand. And once Mother woke up in the middle of the night and saw him leaning over the bassinet and whispering distinctly:

"Is ou a ittle bitty baby? Is ou Daddy's ittle bitty girl?"

"What was that, dear?" said Mother, smiling into the sheet.

Dad cleared his throat. "Nothing. I was just telling this noisy, ill-behaved, ugly little devil that she is more trouble than a barrel of monkeys."

"And just as much fun?"

"Every bit."

Dad and Mother moved to another New York apartment on Riverside Drive, where Mary and Ernestine were born. Then the family moved to Plainfield, New Jersey, where

Martha put in an appearance. With four girls, Dad was reconciled to his fate of being the Last of the Gilbreths. He was not bitter; merely resigned. He kept repeating that a dozen girls would suit him just fine, and he made hearty jokes about "my harem." When visitors came to call, Dad would introduce Anne, Mary and Ernestine. Then he'd get Martha out of her crib and bring her into the living room. "And this," he'd say, "is the latest model. Complete with all the improvements. And don't think that's all; we're expecting the 1911 model some time next month."

Although Mother's condition made the announcement unnecessary, he came out with it anyway. He never understood why this embarrassed Mother.

"I just don't see why you mind," he'd tell her later. "It's something to be proud of."

"Well, of course it is. Maybe I'm old-fashioned, but it seems to me a mistake to proclaim it from the housetops, or confide it to comparative strangers, until the baby arrives."

Still, Mother knew very well that Dad had to talk about his children, the children who had already arrived and those who were expected.

In spite of Mother's protests, Dad decided that the fifth child would be named for her. Mother didn't like the name Lillian, and had refused to pass the name along to any of the first four girls.

"No nonsense, now," Dad said. "We're running low on names, and this one is going to be named for you. Whether you like it or not, I want a little Lillian."

"But it could be a boy, you know."

"Boys!" Dad grunted. "Who wants boys?"

"Sooner or later there'll be a boy," Mother said. "Look what happened in my family." Mother's mother had six girls before she produced a boy.

"Sure," sighed Dad, "but your father wasn't the Last of the Gilbreths."

When Dr. Hedges came out of Mother's bedroom and announced that Mother and the fifth baby were doing nicely, Dad told him that "The Latest Model" was to be named Lillian.

"I think that's nice," Dr. Hedges said sympathetically.

"Real nice. Of course, the other boys in his class may tease him about having a girl's name, but . . ."

"Yes, that's true," said Dad. "I hadn't thought of . . ." He grabbed the doctor by the shoulders and shook him. "Other boys?" he shouted. "Did you say other boys? Boys?"

"I hate to disappoint you, Mr. Gilbreth," grinned Dr. Hedges. "Especially since you've been telling everyone how much you wanted a fifth girl for your harem. But this one . . ."

Dad pushed him out of the way and rushed into the bedroom, where his first son was sleeping in a by now battered bassinet, on a desk once again covered with galley proofs. Dad and Mother timed their books to coincide with Mother's annual intervals of unavoidable delay.

"Chip off the old block," Dad cooed into the bassinet. "Every inch a Gilbreth. Oh, Lillie, how did you ever manage to do it?"

"Do you think he's all right?" Mother whispered.

"He's one I think we'd better keep," said Dad. "Do you know something? I didn't come right out and say so before, because I didn't want to upset you, and I knew you were doing the best you could. But I really wanted a boy all the time. I was just trying to make you feel better when I said I wanted a fifth girl."

Mother managed to keep a straight face. "Mercy, Maud, you certainly had everybody fooled," she said. "I thought you'd be simply furious if little 'Lillian' turned out to be a boy. You seemed so set on naming this one for me. Are you sure you're not disappointed?"

"Gee whiz," was all Dad could manage.

"What should we name him?"

Dad wasn't listening. He was still leaning over the bassinet, cooing. There was little doubt in Mother's mind, anyway, about what the baby would be named, and Dad clinched the matter by the next remark which he addressed to the baby.

"I've got to leave you now for a few minutes, Mr. Frank Bunker Gilbreth, Junior," he said, rolling out the name and savoring its sound. "I've got to make a few telephone calls and send some wires. And I've got to get some toys suitable for a boy baby. All the toys we have around this house are girl baby toys. Behave yourself while I'm gone and take care of your mother. That's one of your jobs from now on." And over his shoulder to Mother, "I'll be back in a few minutes, Lillie."

"Farewell, Next to Last of the Gilbreths," Mother whispered. But Dad still wasn't listening. As he closed the door carefully, Mother heard him bellowing:

"Anne, Mary, Ernestine, Martha. Did you hear the news? It's a boy. Frank Bunker Gilbreth, Junior. How do you like the sound of that? Every inch a Gilbreth. Chip off the old block. Hello, central? Central? Long Distance, please. It's a boy."

Having fathered one son, Dad took it pretty much for granted that all the rest of his children would be boys.

"The first four were just practice," he'd say to Mother, while glaring with assumed ferocity at the girls. "Of course, I suppose we ought to keep them. They might come in handy some day to scrub the pots and pans and mend the socks of the men folk. But I don't see that we need any more of them."

The girls would rush at him and Dad would let them topple him over on the rug. Martha, using his vest pockets for fingerholds, would climb up on his stomach and the other three would tickle him so that Martha would be joggled up and down when he laughed.

Number Six was born in Providence, where the family had moved in 1912. As Dad had assumed, the new addition was a boy. He was named William for Mother's father and one of her brothers.

"Good work, Lillie," Dad told Mother. But this time there was no elaborate praise and his tone of voice indicated that Mother merely had done the sort of competent job that one might expect from a competent woman. "There's our first half-dozen."

And when his friends asked him whether the new baby was a boy or a girl, he replied matter of factly: "Oh, we had another boy."

Dad hadn't been there during the delivery. Both he and Mother agreed that it didn't help matters for him to be pacing up and down the hall, and Dad's business was placing more and more demands upon his time.

Mother had her first half-dozen babies at home, instead of in hospitals, because she liked to run the house and help Dad with his work, even during the confinements. She'd supervise the household right up until each baby started coming. There was a period of about twenty-four hours, then, when she wasn't much help to anybody. But she had prepared all the menus in advance, and the house ran smoothly by itself during the one day devoted to the delivery. For the next ten days to two weeks, while she remained in bed, we'd file in every morning so that she could tie the girls' hair ribbons and make sure the boys had washed properly. Then we'd come back again at night to hold the new baby and listen to Mother read *The Five Little Peppers*. Mother enjoyed the little Peppers every bit as much as we, and was particularly partial to a character named Phronsie, or something like that.

When Dad's mother came to live with us, Mother decided to have Number Seven in a Providence hospital, since Grandma could run the house for her. Six hours after Mother checked into the hospital, a nurse called our house and told Dad that Mrs. Gilbreth had had a nine-pound boy.

"Quick work," Dad told Grandma. "She really has found the one best way of having babies."

Grandma asked whether it was a boy or a girl, and Dad replied: "A boy, naturally, for goodness sakes. What did you expect?"

A few moments later, the hospital called again and said there had been some mistake. A Mrs. Gilbert, not Gilbreth, had had the baby boy.

"Well, what's *my* wife had?" Dad asked. "I'm not interested in any Mrs. Gilbert, obstetrically or any other way."

"Of course you're not," the nurse apologized. "Just a moment, and I'll see about Mrs. Gilbreth." And then a few minutes later. "Mrs. Gilbreth seems to have checked out of the hospital."

"Checked out? Why she's only been there six hours. Did she have a boy or a girl?"

"Our records don't show that she had either."

"It's got to be one or the other," Dad insisted. "What else is there?"

"I mean," the nurse explained, "she apparently checked out before the baby arrived."

Dad hung up the receiver. "Better start boiling water," he said to Grandma. "Lillie's on the way home."

"With that new baby?"

"No." Dad was downcast. "Somebody else claimed that baby. Lillie apparently put off having hers for the time being."

Mother arrived at the house about half an hour later. She was carrying a suitcase and had walked all the way. Grandma was furious.

"My goodness, Lillie, you have no business out in the street in your condition. And carrying that heavy suitcase. Give it to me. Now get upstairs to bed where you belong. A girl your age should know better. What did you leave the hospital for?"

"I got tired of waiting and I was lonesome. I decided I'd have this one at home, too. Besides, that nurse—she was a fiend. She hid my pencils and notebook and wouldn't even let me read. I never spent a more miserable day."

Lill was born the next day, in Dad's and Mother's room, where pencils and notebooks and proofs were within easy reach of Mother's bed.

"I had already told everybody it was going to be a boy," Dad said, a little resentfully. "But I know it's not your fault, and I think a girl's just fine. I was getting a little sick of boys, anyway. Well, this one will be named for you."

The older children, meanwhile, were becoming curious about where babies came from. The only conclusion we had reached was that Mother always was sick in bed when the babies arrived. About four months after Lill was born, when Mother went to bed early one night with a cold, we were sure a new brother or sister would be on hand in the morning. As soon as we got up, we descended on Dad's and Mother's room.

"Where's the baby? Where's the baby?" we shouted.

"What's all the commotion?" Dad wanted to know. "What's got into you? She's right over there in her crib." He pointed to four-month-old Lill.

"But we want to see the *latest* model," we said. "Come on, Daddy. You can't fool us. Is it a boy or a girl? What are we going to name this one? Come on, Daddy. Where have you hidden him?"

We began looking under the bed and in a half-open bureau drawer.

"What in the world are you talking about?" Mother said. "There isn't any new baby. Stop pulling all your father's clothes out of that drawer. For goodness sakes, whatever gave you the idea there was a new baby?"

"Well, you were sick, weren't you?" Anne asked.

"I had a cold, yes."

"And every time you're sick, there's always a baby."

"Why, babies don't come just because you're sick," Mother said. "I thought you knew that."

"Then when do they come?" Ern asked. "They always came before when you were sick. You tell us, Daddy."

We had seldom seen Dad look so uncomfortable. "I've got business in town, kids," he said. "In a hurry. Your Mother will tell you. I'm late now." He turned to Mother. "I'd be glad to explain it to them if I had the time," he said. "You go ahead and tell them, Lillie. It's time they knew. I'm sorry I'm rushed. You understand, don't you?"

"I certainly do," said Mother.

Dad hurried down the front stairs and out the front door. He didn't even stop by the dining room for a cup of coffee.

"I'm glad you children asked that question," Mother began. But she didn't look glad at all. "Come and sit here on the bed. It's time we had a talk. In the first place, about the stork—he doesn't really bring babies at all, like some children think."

"We knew that!"

"You did?" Mother seemed surprised. "Well, that's fine. Er—what else do you know?"

"That you have to be married to have babies, and it takes lots of hot water, and sometimes the doctor does things to you that make you holler."

"But not very loud?" Mother asked anxiously. "Never very loud or very often. Am I right?"

"No, never loud or very often."

"Good. Now first let's talk about flowers and bees and . . ."

When she was through, we knew a good deal about botany and something about apiology, but nothing about how babies came. Mother just couldn't bring herself to explain it.

"I don't know what's the matter with Mother," Anne said afterwards. "It's the first time she's ever kept from answering a question. And Daddy went rushing out of the room like he knew where something was buried."

Later we asked Tom Grieves about it. But the only reply we elicited from him was to: "Stop that nasty kind of talk, you evil-minded things you, or I'll tell your father on you."

Dad assumed Mother had told us. Mother assumed she had made her point in the flowers and bees. And we still wondered where babies came from.

Fred was born in Buttonwoods, Rhode Island, where we spent a summer. A hurricane knocked out communications and we couldn't get a doctor. A next-door neighbor who came over to help became so frightened at the whole thing that she kept shouting to Mother:

"Don't you dare have that baby until the doctor comes."

"I'm trying not to," Mother assured her calmly. "There's no use to get all excited. You mustn't get yourself all worked up. It's not good for you. Sit down here on the side of the bed and try to relax."

"Who's having this baby, anyway?" Dad asked the neighbor. "A big help you are!"

He departed for the kitchen to boil huge vats of water, most of which was never used.

Fred, Number Eight, arrived just as the doctor did.

Dan and Jack were born in Providence, and Bob and Jane in Nantucket. Dan and Jack came into the world in routine enough fashion, but Bob arrived all of a sudden. Tom Grieves had to pedal through Nantucket on a bicycle to find the doctor. Since Tom was in pajamas, having been routed from his bed, most of the island knew about Bob's birth. Once again, it was a case of the baby and the doctor arriving simultaneously.

By that time, all the family names for boys had been exhausted. The names of all the uncles, both grandfathers, and the four great grandfathers had been used. Great uncles were being resurrected from the family Bible and studied carefully.

"Now let's run over the names of the Bunker men again," Dad said, referring to Grandma Gilbreth's brothers. "Samuel?

Never could tolerate that name. Nathaniel? Too bookish. Frederick? We got one already. Humphrey? Ugh. Daniel? We got one. Nothing there."

"How about the middle names?" Mother suggested. "Maybe we'll get an idea from the Bunkers' middle names."

"All right. Moses? Too bullrushy. William? We got one. Abraham? They'd call him Abie. Irving? Over my dead body, which would be quite a climb."

"What was your father's name again?" Mother asked.

"John," said Dad. "We got one."

"No, I know that. I mean his middle name."

"You know what it was," said Dad. "We're not having any."

"Oh, that's right," Mother giggled. "Hiram, wasn't it?"

Dad started thumbing impatiently through the Bible. "Jacob? No. Saul? Job, Noah, David? Too sissy. Peter? Paul? John? We got one."

"Robert," Mother said. "That's it. We'll call him Robert."

"Why Robert? Who's named Robert?" Dad looked over the top of his glasses at Mother, and she reddened.

"No one in particular. It's just a beautiful name, that's all. This one will be Robert."

Dad started to tease. "I knew you had a strange collection of beaux during your college days, but which one was Robert? I don't believe I remember your mentioning him. Was he the one whose picture you had with the blazer and mandolin? Or was he the one your sisters told me about who stuttered?"

"Stop it, Frank," said Mother. "You know that's ridiculous."

We took our cue from Dad. "Oh, Mother, Rob-bert is such a beautiful name. Why didn't you name me Rob-bert? May I carry your books home from college, Lillie, dear? Why Rob-bert, you do say the *nicest* things. And so clever, too."

Dad, who knew that Mother's favorite poet was Browning and suspected where the Robert came from, nevertheless bunched the fingers of his right hand, kissed their tips, and threw his hand into the air.

"Ah, Robert," he intoned, "if I could but taste the nectar of thy lips."

"When you're all quite through," Mother said coldly, "I

suggest we have a vote on the name I have proposed. And when it comes to discussing old flames, it might be borne in mind that that is a game two can play. I recall . . ."

"We wouldn't think of blighting any school girl romance, would we, kids?" Dad put in hastily. "What do you say we make it 'Robert' unanimously?"

We voted and it was unanimous.

Bob, Number Eleven, made the count six boys and five girls. There was considerable partisanship among the family as to the desired sex of the next baby. The boys wanted to remain in the majority; the girls wanted to tie the count at six-all. Dad, of course, wanted another boy. Mother wanted to please Dad, but at the same time thought it would be nice to have a girl for her last child.

Number Twelve was due in June, 1922, and that meant we would be in Nantucket. Mother had vowed she wasn't going to have another baby in our summer house, because the facilities were so primitive. For a time, she debated whether to remain behind at Montclair and have the baby at home there, or whether to go to Nantucket with us and have the baby in a hospital. Finally, with some foreboding because of her previous experience in Providence, she chose the latter alternative. Jane, Number Twelve, was born in the Nantucket Cottage Hospital.

Mother's ten days in the hospital were pure misery for Dad. He fidgeted and sulked, and said he couldn't get any work done without her. Dad's business trips to Europe sometimes kept him away from home for months, but then he was on the go and in a different environment. Now, at home with the family where he was accustomed to have Mother at his side, he felt frustrated, and seized every opportunity to go down to the hospital and visit.

His excuse to us, when we complained we were being neglected, was that he had to get acquainted with his new daughter.

"I won't be gone long," he'd say. "Anne, you're in charge while I'm away." He'd jump into the car and we wouldn't see him again for hours.

He had never taken such care with his dress. His hair was smoothed to perfection, his canvas shoes a chaste white, and he looked sporty in his linen knickers, his belted coat with a boutonniere of Queen Anne's Lace, and his ribbed, knee-length hose.

"Gee, Daddy, you look like a groom," we told him.

"Bride or stable?"

"A bridegroom."

"You don't have to tell me I'm a handsome dude," he grinned. "I've got a mirror, you know. Well, I've got to make a good impression on that new daughter of mine. What did we name her? Jane."

At the hospital, he'd sit next to Mother's bed and discuss the work he'd planned for the autumn.

"Now I want you to stay here until you feel good and strong. Get a good rest; it's the first rest you've had since the children started coming." And then in the same breath. "I'll certainly be glad when you're back home. I can't seem to get any work accomplished when you're not there."

Mother thought the hospital was marvellous. "I would have to wait until my dozenth baby was born to find out how much better it is to have them in a hospital. The nurses here wait on me hand and foot. You don't know what a comfort it is to have your baby in the hospital."

"No," said Dad, "I don't. And I hope to Heaven I never find out!"

What Mother liked best about the hospital, although she didn't tell Dad, was the knowledge that if she made any noise during the delivery, it didn't matter.

When Dad finally drove Mother and Jane home, he lined all of us up by ages on the front porch. Jane, in her bassinet, was at the foot of the line.

"Not a bad-looking crowd if I do say so myself," he boasted, strutting down the line like an officer inspecting his men. "Well, Lillie, there you have them, and it's all over. Have you stopped to think that by this time next year we won't need a bassinet any more? And by this time two years from now, there won't be a diaper in the house, or baby bottles, or play pens, or nipples—when I think of the equipment we've amassed during the years! Have you thought what it's going to be like not to have a baby in our room? For the first time in seventeen years, you'll be able to go to bed without setting the alarm clock for a two o'clock feeding."

"I've been thinking about that," said Mother. "It's certainly going to be a luxury, isn't it?"

Dad put his arm around her waist, and tears came to her eyes.

Later that summer, when company came to call, Dad would whistle assembly and then introduce us.

"This one is Anne," he'd say, and she'd step forward and shake hands. "And Ernestine, Martha. . . ."

"Gracious, Mr. Gilbreth. And all of them are yours?"

"Hold on, now. Wait a minute." He'd disappear into the bedroom and come out holding Jane. "You haven't seen the latest model."

But some of the enthusiasm had gone out of his tone, because he knew the latest model really was the last model, and that he would never again be able to add the clincher, which so embarrassed Mother, about how another baby was underway.

CHAPTER 14

Flash Powder and Funerals

Next to motion study and astronomy, photography was the science nearest to Dad's heart. He had converted most of the two-story barn in Montclair into a photographic laboratory. It was here that Mr. Coggin, Dad's English photographer, held forth behind a series of triple-locked doors. Children made Mr. Coggin nervous, particularly when they opened the door of his darkroom when he was in the middle of developing a week's supply of film. Even in front of Dad and Mother, he referred to us as blighters and beggars. Behind their backs, he called us 'orse thieves, bloody barsteds, and worse.

At one time, shortly after Dad had had an addition built on our cottage at Nantucket, he told Mr. Coggin:

"I want you to go up there and get some pictures of the ell on the house."

"Haw," said Mr. Coggin. "I've taken many a picture of the 'ell *in* your 'ouse. But this will be the first time I've taken one of the 'ell *on* your 'ouse."

When Mr. Coggin departed after the unfortunate debacle concerning our tonsils, a series of other professional cameramen came and went. Dad always thought, and with some justification, that none of the professionals were as good a photographer as he. Consequently, when it came to taking pictures of the family, Dad liked to do the job himself.

He liked to do the job as often as possible, rain or shine, day or night, summer or winter, and especially on Sundays. Most photographers prefer sunlight for their pictures. But Dad liked it best when there was no sun and he had an excuse to take his pictures indoors. He seemed to have a special affinity for flashlight powder, and the bigger the flash the more he enjoyed it.

He'd pour great, gray mountains of the powder into the pan at the top of his T-shaped flash gun, and hold this as far over his head as possible with his left hand, while he burrowed beneath a black cloth at the stern of the camera. In his right hand, he'd hold the shutter release and a toy of some kind, which he'd shake and rattle to get our attention.

Probably few men have walked away from larger flashlight explosions than those Dad set off as a matter of routine. The ceilings of some of the rooms in Montclair bore charred, black circles, in mute testimony to his intrepidity as an exploder. Some of the professional photographers, seeing him load a flash gun, would blanch, mutter, and hasten from the room.

"I know what I'm doing," Dad would shout after them irritably. "Go ahead, then, if you don't want to learn anything. But when I'm through, just compare the finished product with the kind of work you do."

The older children had been through it so often that, while somewhat shellshocked, they were no longer terrified. It would be stretching a point to say they had developed any real confidence in Dad's indoor photography. But at least they had adopted a fatalistic attitude that death, if it came, would be swift and painless. The younger children, unfortunately, had no such comforting philosophy to fall back on. Even the Latest Model was aware that all hell was liable to break loose at any time after Dad submerged under the black cloth. They'd behave pretty well right up to the time Dad was going to take the picture. Then they'd start bellowing.

"Lillie, stop those children from crying," Dad would shout from under the black cloth. "Dan, open your eyes and take your fingers out of your ears! The idea! Scared of a little flash! And stop that fidgeting, all of you."

He'd come up in disgust from under the cloth. It was hot under there, and the bending over had made the blood run to his head.

"Now stop crying, all of you," he'd say furiously. "Do you hear me? Next time I go under there I want to see all of you smiling."

He'd submerge again. "I said stop that crying. Now smile, or I'll come out and give you something to cry about. Smile so I can see the whites of your teeth. That's more like it."

He'd slip a plate holder into the back of the camera.

"Ready? Ready? Smile now. Hold it. Hold it. Hooold it."

He'd wave the toy furiously and then there'd be an awful, blinding, roaring flash that shook the room and deposited a fine ash all over us and the floor. Dad would come up, sweaty but grinning. He'd look to see whether the ceiling was still there, and then put down the flash gun and go over and open the windows to let out a cloud of choking smoke that made your eyes water.

"I think that was a good picture," he'd say. "And this new flash gun certainly works fine. Don't go away now. I want to take one more as soon as the smoke clears. I'm not sure I had quite enough light that time."

For photographs taken in the sunlight, Dad had a delayed-action release that allowed him to click the camera and then run and get into the picture himself before the shutter was released. While outdoor pictures did away with the hazard of being blown through the ceiling, they did not eliminate the hazards connected with Dad's temper.

The most heavily relied upon prop for outdoor pictures was the family Pierce Arrow, parked with top down in the driveway.

Once we were seated to Dad's satisfaction, he would focus, tell us to smile, click the delayed-action release, and race for the driver's seat. He'd arrive there panting, and the car would lurch as he jumped in. When conditions were ideal, there would be just enough time for Dad to settle himself and smile pleasantly, before the camera clicked off the exposure.

Conditions were seldom ideal, for the delayed action release was unreliable. Sometimes it went off too soon, thus featuring Dad's blurred but ample stern as he climbed into the car. Sometimes it didn't go off for a matter of minutes, during which we sat tensely, with frozen-faced smiles, while we tried to keep the younger children from squirming. Dad, with the camera side of his mouth twisted into a smile, would issue threats from the other side about what he was going to do to all of us if we so much as twitched a muscle or batted an eyelash.

Occasionally, when the gambling instinct got the better of him, he'd try to turn around and administer one swift disciplinary stroke, and then turn back again in time to smile before the camera went off. Once, when he lost the gamble, an outstanding action picture resulted, which showed Dad landing a well-aimed and well-deserved clout on the side of Frank's head.

Any number of pictures showed various members of the family, who had received discipline within a matter of seconds before the shutter clicked, looking anything but pleasant in the swivel seats of the car. The swivel seat occupants received most of the discipline, because they were the easiest for Dad to reach, and no one liked to sit there when it was picture taking time.

Sometimes newspaper photographers and men from Underwood and Underwood would come to the house to take publicity pictures. Dad would whistle assembly, take out his stopwatch, and demonstrate how quickly we could gather. Then he would show the visitors how we could type, send the Morse code, multiply numbers, and speak some French, Ger-

man, and Italian. Sometimes he'd holler *"fire"* and we'd drop to the floor and roll up in rugs.

Everything seemed to go much smoother when Dad was on our side of the camera, for now he too was ordered where to stand, when to lick his lips, and, occasionally, to stop fidgeting. The rest of us had no trouble looking pleasant after the photographer lectured Dad. In fact we looked so pleasant we almost popped.

"Mr. Gilbreth, will you please stand still? And take your hands out of your pockets. Move a little closer to Mrs. Gilbreth, No, not that close. Look. I want you right here." The photographer would take him by the arm and place him. "Now try to look pleasant, please."

"By jingo, I am looking pleasant," Dad finally would say impatiently.

"I can't understand one thing," a man from Underwood and Underwood told Dad one time after the picture-taking was over. "I've been out here several times now. Everything always seems to be going fine until I put my head under the black cloth to focus. Then, just as if it's a signal, the four youngest ones start to cry and I can never get them to stop until I put the cloth out of sight."

"Is that a fact?" was all the information Dad volunteered.

Dad had a knack for setting up publicity pictures that tied in with his motion-study projects. While he was working for the Remington people, there were the news reels of us typing touch system on Moby Dick, the white typewriter with the blind keys. Later, when he got a job with an automatic pencil company, he decided to photograph us burying a pile of wooden pencils.

We were in Nantucket at the time. Tom Grieves built a realistic-looking black coffin out of a packing case. For weeks we bought and collected wooden pencils, until we had enough to fill the coffin.

We carried the casket to a sand dune between *The Shoe* and the ocean, where Dad and Tom dug a shallow grave. It was a desolate, windswept spot. The neighbors on the Cliff, doubtless concluding that one of us had fallen down and had had to be destroyed, watched our actions through binoculars.

Dad set up a still camera on a tripod, connected the delayed-action attachment, and took a series of pictures showing us lowering the coffin into the grave and covering it with sand.

"We'll have to dig up the coffin now and do the same thing all over again so we can get the movies," Dad said. "We're going to hit them coming and going with this one."

We dug, being careful not to scratch up the coffin, and then sifted the sand from the pencils. Tom cranked the movie camera while we went through the second funeral. Fortunately, it was before the days of sound movies, because Dad kept hollering instructions.

"Turn that crank twice a second, Tom. And one and two and three and four. Get out from in front of the camera, Ernestine. Marguerite Clark and Mary Pickford have things pretty well lined up out there, you know. Now then, everybody pick up the shovels and heave in the sand. Look serious. This is a sad burial. The good are often interred with their bones. So may it be with pencils. And one and two and . . ."

When we were through with the second funeral, Dad told us we'd have to dig up the coffin again.

"You're not going to take any more pictures, are you?" we begged. "We've taken the stills and the movies."

"Of course not," said Dad. "But you don't think we're going to waste all those perfectly good wooden pencils, do you? Dig them up and take them back into the house. They should last us for years."

In justification to Dad, it should be said that automatic pencils always were used once the supply of wooden ones was exhausted. Dad simply couldn't stand seeing the wooden ones wasted.

The next summer, when Dad was hired as a consultant by a washing machine company, we went through the same procedure with the washboard and hand-wringer at Nantucket. This time, though, Tom was prepared.

"Wait a minute, Mr. Gilbreth," he said. "Before you bury my wringer I want to oil it good, so I can get the sand off it when we dig it up again."

"That might not be a bad idea," Dad admitted. "After all," he added defensively, "I bought you a washing machine for Montclair. I can't have washing machines scattered all along the Atlantic seaboard, you know."

"I didn't say nothing," said Tom. "I just said I wanted to oil my wringer good, that's all. I didn't say nothing about a washing machine for Nantucket." He started to mutter. "Efficiency. All I hear around this house is efficiency. I'd like to make one of them lectures about efficiency. The one best way to ruin a wringer is to bury the God-damned thing in the sand, and then dig it up again. That's motion study for you!"

"What's that?" asked Dad. "Speak up if you have anything to say, and if you haven't keep quiet."

Tom continued muttering. "Motion study is burying a God-damned wringer in the sand and getting the parts all gummed up so that it breaks your back to turn it. That's motion study, as long as it's someone else's motions you're studying, and not your own. Lincoln freed the slaves. All but one. All but one."

The pictures and writeups sometimes put us on the defensive in school and among our friends.

"How come you write with a wooden pencil in school, when I saw in the newsreel how your father and all you kids buried a whole casket of them in a grave?"

Sometimes, and this was worst of all, the teachers would read excerpts from writeups about the process charts in the bathroom, the language records, and the decisions of the Family Council. We'd blush and squirm, and wish Dad had a nice job selling shoes somewhere, and that he had only one or two children, neither of whom was us.

The most dangerous reporters, from our standpoint, were the women who came to interview Mother for human interest stories. Mother usually got Dad to sit in on such interviews, because she liked to be able to prove to him and us that she didn't say any of the things they attributed to her, or at least not many of them.

Dad derived considerable pleasure from reading these interviews aloud at the supper table, with exaggerated gestures and facial expressions that were supposed to be Mother's.

"There sat Mrs. Gilbreth, surrounded by her brood, reading aloud a fairy tale," Dad would read. "The oldest, almost debutante Anne, wants to be a professional violinist. Ernestine intends to be a painter, Martha and Frank to follow in their father's footsteps."

" 'Tell me about your honorary degrees,' I asked this remarkable mother of twelve. A flush of crimson crept modestly to her cheeks, and she made a depreciating moue."

Here Dad would stop long enough to give his version of a depreciating moue, and hide his face coyly behind an upraised elbow. He resumed reading:

" 'I am far more proud of my dozen husky, red-blooded American children than I am of my two dozen honorary degrees and my membership in the Czechoslovak Academy of Science,' Mrs. Gilbreth told me."

"Mercy, Maud," Mother exploded. "I never said anything like that. You were there during that interview, Frank. Where did that woman get all that? If my mother should see that article, I don't know what she'd think of me. That woman never asked me about honorary degrees. And two dozen? No one ever had two dozen, unless it was poor Mr. Wilson. And I never said a thing about Czechoslovakia. And I hate and detest people who make depreciating moues. I never made one in my life, or at any rate not since I've been old enough to know better."

Meanwhile, both Anne and Ern were near tears.

"I can't go back to school tomorrow," Anne said. "How can I face the class after that business about the violin?"

"How about me?" moaned Ern. "At least you own a violin and can make noises come out of it. 'Ernestine wants to be a painter.' How *could* you tell her that, Mother? And my teacher is sure to read it out loud. She always does."

"I didn't tell her that or anything else in the article," Mother insisted. "Where do you suppose she dreamed up those things, Frank?"

Dad grinned and went on reading.

"Mr. Gilbreth, the time study expert, entered the room on tiptoe so as not to disturb his wife's train of thought. Plump but dynamic, Mr. Gilbreth . . ."

The grin faded and Dad tossed the newspaper from him in disgust. "What unspeakable claptrap," he grunted. "Of all the words in the English language, the one I like least is 'plump.' The whole article is just a figment of the imagination."

One newsreel photographer, who visited us in Nantucket, deliberately set out to make us look ridiculous. It wasn't a difficult job. If he was acting under instructions from his employers, he should have been paid a bonus.

In good faith, Dad moved the dining room table, the chairs and his pew out onto the beach grass at the side of our cottage, where the newsreel man said the light would be best. There, amid the sandflies, we ate dinner while the cameraman took pictures.

The newsreel, as shown in the movie houses, opened with a caption which said, "The family of Frank B. Gilbreth, time-saver, eats dinner." The rest of it was projected at about ten times the normal speed. It gave the impression that we raced to the table, passed plates madly in all directions, wolfed our food, and ran away from the table, all in about forty-five seconds. In the background was the reason the photographer wanted us outside—the family laundry with, of course, the diapers predominating.

We saw the newsreel at the Dreamland Theater in Nantucket, and it got much louder laughs than the comedy, which featured a fat actor named Lloyd Hamilton. Everyone in the Dreamland turned around and gaped at us, and we were humiliated and furious. We didn't even want to go to Coffin's Drug Store for a soda, when Dad extended a half-hearted invitation after the show.

"I hope it never comes to the Wellmont in Montclair," we kept repeating. "How can we ever go back to school?"

"Well," Dad said, "it was a mean trick, all right, and I'd like to get my hands on that photographer. But it could have been worse. Do you know what I kept thinking all the way through it? I kept thinking that when it was over they probably were going to show it again, backwards, so that it would look as if we were regurgitating our food back on our plates. I'll swear, if they had done that I was going to wreck the place."

"And I would have helped you," said Mother. "Honestly!"

"Come on, it's water over the dam," Dad shrugged. "Let's forget it. Let's go up to Coffin's after all and get those sodas. I'm ready for a double chocolate soda. What do you say?"

Under such relentless arm-twisting, we finally gave in and allowed ourselves to be taken to Coffin's.

CHAPTER 15

Gilbreths and Company

Dad's theories ranged from Esperanto, which he made us study because he thought it was the answer to half the world's problems, to immaculate conception, which he said wasn't supported by available biological evidence. His theories on social poise, although requiring some minor revision as the family grew larger, were constant to the extent that they hinged on unaffectation.

A poised, unaffected person was never ridiculous, at least in his own mind, Dad told us. And a man who didn't feel ridiculous could never lose his dignity. Dad seldom felt ridiculous, and never admitted losing his dignity.

The part of the theory requiring some revision was that guests would feel at home if they were treated like one of our family. As Mother pointed out, and Dad finally admitted, the only guest who could possibly feel like a member of our family was a guest who, himself, came from a family of a dozen, headed by a motion study man.

When guests weren't present, Dad worked at improving our table manners. Whenever a child within his reach took too large a mouthful of food, Dad's knuckles would descend sharply on the top of the offender's head, with a thud that made Mother wince.

"Not on the head, Frank," she protested in shocked tones. "For mercy sakes, not on the head!"

Dad paid no attention except when the blow had been unusually hard. In such cases he rubbed his knuckles ruefully and replied:

"Maybe you're right. There must be softer places."

If the offender was at Mother's end of the table, out of

Dad's reach, he'd signal her to administer the skull punishment. Mother, who never disciplined any of us or even threatened discipline, ignored the signals. Dad then would catch the eye of a child sitting near the offender and, by signals, would deputize him to carry out the punishment.

"With my compliments," Dad would say when the child with the full mouth turned furiously on the one who had knuckled him. "If I've told you once, I've told you a hundred times to cut your food up into little pieces. How am I going to drive that into your skull?"

"Not on the head," Mother repeated. "Mercy, Maud, not on the head!"

Anyone with an elbow on the table might suddenly feel his wrist seized, raised and jerked downward so that his elbow hit the table hard enough to make the dishes dance.

"Not on the elbow, Frank. That's the most sensitive part of the body. Any place but on the elbow."

Mother disapproved of all forms of corporal punishment. She felt, though, that she could achieve better results in the long run by objecting to the part of the anatomy selected for punishment, rather than the punishment itself. Even when Dad administered vitally needed punishment on the conventional area, the area where it is supposed to do the most good, Mother tried to intervene.

"Not on the end of the spine," she'd say in a voice indicating her belief that Dad was running the risk of crippling us for life. "For goodness sakes, not on the end of the spine!"

"Where, then?" Dad shouted furiously in the middle of one spanking. "Not on the top of the head, not on the side of the ear, not on the back of the neck, not on the elbow, not across the legs, and not on the seat of the pants. Where did your father spank you? Across the soles of the by jingoed feet like the heathen Chinese?"

"Well, not on the end of the spine," Mother said. "You can be sure of that."

Skull-rapping and elbow-thumping became a practice in which everybody in the family, except Mother, participated until Dad deemed our table manners satisfactory. Even the youngest child could mete out the punishment without fear of reprisal. All during meals, we watched each other, and particularly Dad, for an opportunity. Sometimes the one who spotted a perched elbow would sneak out of his chair and walk all the way around the table, so that he could catch the offender.

Dad was quite careful about his elbows, but every so often would forget. It was considered a feather in one's cap to thump any elbow. But the ultimate achievement was to thump Dad's. This was considered not just a feather in the cap, but the entire head-dress of a full Indian chief.

When Dad was caught and his elbow thumped, he made a great to-do over it. He grimaced as if in excruciating pain, sucked in air through his teeth, rubbed the elbow, and claimed he couldn't use his arm for the remainder of the meal.

Occasionally, he would rest an elbow purposely on the edge of the table, and make believe he didn't notice some child who had slipped out of a chair and was tiptoeing toward him. Just as the child was about to reach out and grab the elbow, Dad would slide it into his lap.

"I've got eyes in the back of my head," Dad would announce.

The would-be thumper, walking disappointedly back to his chair, wondered if it wasn't just possible that Dad really did.

Both Dad and Mother tried to impress us that it was our responsibility to make guests feel at home. There were guests for meals almost as often as not, particularly business friends of Dad's, since his office was in the house. There was no formality and no special preparations except a clean napkin and an extra place at the table.

"If a guest is sitting next to you, it's your job to keep him happy, to see that things are passed to him," Dad kept telling us.

George Isles, a Canadian author, seemed to Lillian to be an unhappy guest. Mr. Isles was old, and told sad but fascinating stories.

"Once upon a time there was an ancient, poor man whose joints hurt when he moved them, whose doctor wouldn't let him smoke cigars, and who had no little children to love him," Mr. Isles said. He continued with what seemed to us to be a tale of overwhelming loneliness, and then concluded:

"And do you know who that old man was?"

We had an idea who it was, but we shook our heads and said we didn't. Mr. Isles looked sadder than ever. He slowly raised his forearm and tapped his chest with his forefinger.

"Me," he said.

Lillian, who was six, was sitting next to Mr. Isles. It was her responsibility to see that he was happy, and she felt somehow that she had failed on the job. She threw her arms around his neck and kissed his dry, old man's cheek.

"You do too have little children who love you," she said, on the brink of tears. "You do too!"

Whenever Mr. Isles came to call after that, he always brought one box of candy for Mother and us, and a separate box for Lillian. Ernestine used to remark, in a tone tinged with envy, that Lill was probably New Jersey's youngest gold digger, and that few adult gold diggers ever had received more, in return for less.

Dad was an easy-going host, informal and gracious, and we tried to pattern ourselves after him.

"Any more vegetables, boss?" he'd ask Mother. "No? Well, how about mashed potatoes? Lots of them. And plenty of lamb. Fine. Well, Sir, I can't offer you any vegetables, but how about . . . ?"

"Oh, come on, have some more beef," Frank urged a visiting German engineer. "After all, you've only had three helpings."

"There's no need to gobble your grapefruit like a pig," Fred told a woman professor from Columbia University, who had arrived late and was trying to catch up with the rest of us. "If we finish ahead of you, we'll wait until you're through."

"I'm sorry, but I'm afraid I can't pass your dessert until you finish your lima beans," Dan told a guest on another occasion. "Daddy won't allow it, and you're my responsibility. Daddy says a Belgian family could live a week on what's thrown away in this house every day."

"Daddy, do you think that what Mr. Fremonville is saying is of general interest?" Lill interrupted a long discourse to ask.

Dad and Mother, and most of the guests, laughed away remarks like these without too much embarrassment. Dad would apologize and explain the family rule involved, and the reason for it. After the guests had gone, Mother would get us together and tell us that while family rules were important, it was even more important to see that guests weren't made uncomfortable.

Sometimes after a meal, Dad's stomach would rumble and, when there weren't any guests, we'd tease him about it. The next time it rumbled, he'd look shocked and single out one of us.

"Billy," he said. "Please! I'm not in the mood for an organ recital."

"That was your stomach, not mine, Daddy. You can't fool me."

"You children have the noisiest stomachs I've ever heard. Don't you think so, Lillie?"

Mother looked disapprovingly over her mending.

"I think," she said, "there are Eskimos in the house."

One night, Mr. Russell Allen, a young engineer, was a guest for supper. Jack, in a high chair across the table from him, accidentally swallowed some air and let out a belch that resounded through the dining room and, as we found out later, was heard even in the kitchen by Mrs. Cunningham. It was such a thorough burp, and had emerged from such a small subject, that all conversation was momentarily suspended in amazement. Jack, more surprised than anybody, looked shocked. He reached out his arm and pointed a chubby and accusing forefinger at the guest.

"Mr. Allen," he said in offended dignity. "Please! I'm not in the mood for an organ recital."

"Why, Jackie!" said Mother, almost in tears. "Why, Jackie. How could you?"

"Out," roared Dad. "Skiddoo. Tell Mrs. Cunningham to give you the rest of your supper in the kitchen. And I'll see you about this later."

"Well, you say it," Jack sobbed as he disappeared toward the kitchen. "You say it when your stomach rumbles."

Dad was blushing. The poise which he told us he valued so highly had disappeared. He shifted uneasily in his seat and fumbled with his napkin. Nobody could think of a way to break the uneasy silence.

Dad cleared his throat with efficient thoroughness. But the silence persisted, and it hung heavily over the table.

"Lackaday," Dad finally said. The situation was getting desperate, and he tried again. "Lack a couple of days," Dad said with a weak, artificial laugh. We felt sorry for him and for Mother and Mr. Allen, who were just as crimson as Dad. The silence persisted.

Dad suddenly flung his napkin on the table and walked out into the kitchen. He returned holding Jack by the hand. Jack was still crying.

"All right, Jackie," Dad said. "Come back and sit down. You're right, you learned it from me. First you apologize to Mr. Allen. Then we'll tell him the whole story. And then none of us will ever say it again. As your Mother told us, it all comes from having Eskimos in the house."

Dad's sister, Aunt Anne, was an ample Victorian who wore full, sweeping skirts and high ground-gripper shoes. She was older than Dad, and they were much alike and devoted to each other. She was kindly but stern, big bosomed, and every inch a lady. Like Dad, she had reddish brown hair and a reddish brown temper. She, her husband, and their grown children, whom we worshipped, lived a few blocks from us in Providence. Aunt Anne was an accomplished pianist and gave music lessons at her house at 26 Cabot Street. Dad thought it would be nice if all of us learned to play something. Dad admitted he was as green as any valley when it came to music, but he had a good ear and he liked symphonies.

Aunt Anne must have sensed almost immediately that we had no talent. She knew, though, that any such admission would have a depressing effect on Dad, who took it for granted that his children had talent for everything. Consequently, Aunt Anne stuck courageously to a losing cause for six years, in an unusual display of devotion and fortitude above and beyond the regular call of family duty.

When she finally became convinced of the hopelessness of teaching us the piano, she shifted us to other instruments. Although we had no better success, the other instruments at least were quieter than the piano and, more important, only one person could play them at a time.

Our Anne was shifted to the violin, Ernestine to the mandolin, and Martha and Frank to the 'cello. It was awful at home when we practiced, and Dad would walk smirking through the house with wads of cotton sticking prominently from his ears.

"Never mind," he said, when we told him we didn't seem to be making any progress. "You stick with it. You'll thank me when you're my age."

Unselfishly jeopardizing her professional reputation as a teacher, Aunt Anne always allowed each of us to play in the annual recitals at her music school. Usually we broke down in the middle, and always had a demoralizing effect on the more talented children, and on their parents in the audience.

To salvage what she could of her standing as a teacher, Aunt Anne used to tell the audience before we went on stage that we had only recently shifted from the piano to stringed instruments. The implication, although not expressed in so many words, was that we had already mastered the piano and were now branching out along other musical avenues.

Just before we started to play, she affixed mutes to our strings and whispered:

"Remember, your number should be played softly, softly as a little brook tinkling through a still forest."

The way we played, it didn't tinkle. As Dad whispered to Mother at one recital: "If I heard that coming from the back fence at night, I'd either report it to the police or heave shoes at it."

Aunt Anne was good to us and we loved her and her family, but like Dad she insisted on having her own way. While we reluctantly accepted Dad's bossing as one of the privileges of his rank as head of the family, we had no intention of accepting it from anybody else, including his oldest sister.

After we moved to Montclair, Aunt Anne came to stay with us for several days while Mother and Dad were away on a lecture tour. She made it plain from the start that she was not a guest, but the temporary commander-in-chief. She even used the front stairs, leading from the front hall to the second floor, instead of the back stairs, which led from the kitchen to a hallway near the girls' bathroom. None of us was allowed to use the front stairs, because Dad wanted to keep the varnish on them looking nice.

"Daddy will be furious if he comes home and finds you've been using his front stairs," we told Aunt Anne.

"Nonsense," she cut us off. "The back stairs are narrow and steep, and I for one don't propose to use them. As long as I'm here, I'll use any stairs I have a mind to. Now rest your features and mind your business."

She sat at Dad's place at the foot of the table, and we resented this, too. Ordinarily, Frank, as the oldest boy, sat in Dad's place, and Anne, as the oldest girl, sat at Mother's. We also disapproved of Aunt Anne's blunt criticism of how we kept our bedrooms, and some of the changes she made in the family routine.

"What do you do, keep pigeons in here?" she'd say when she walked into the bedroom shared by Frank and Bill. "I'm coming back in fifteen minutes, and I want to find this room in apple-pie order."

And: "I don't care what time your regular bedtime is. As long as I'm in charge, we'll do things my way. Off with you now."

Like Grandma and Dad, Aunt Anne thought that all Irishmen were shiftless and that Tom Grieves was the most shiftless of all Irishmen. She told him so at least once a day, and Tom was scared to death of her.

Experience has established the fact that a person cannot move from a small, peaceful home into a family of a dozen without having something finally snap. We saw this happen time after time with Dad's stenographers and with the cooks who followed Mrs. Cunningham. In order to reside with a family of a dozen it is necessary either (1) to be brought up from birth in such a family, as we were; or (2) to become accustomed to it as it grew, as Dad, Mother, and Tom Grieves did.

It was at the dinner table that something finally snapped in Aunt Anne.

We had spent the entire meal purposely making things miserable for her. Bill had hidden under the table, and we had removed his place and chair so she wouldn't realize he was missing. While we ate, Billy thumped Aunt Anne's legs with the side of his hand.

"Who's kicking me?" she complained. "Saints alive!"

We said no one.

"Well, you don't have a dog, do you?"

We didn't, and we told her so. Our collie had died some time before this.

"Well somebody's certainly kicking me. Hard."

She insisted that the child sitting on each side of her slide his chair toward the head of the table, so that no legs could possibly reach her. Bill thumped again.

"Somebody *is* kicking me," Aunt Anne said, "and I intend to get to the bottom of it. Literally."

Bill thumped again. Aunt Anne picked up the table cloth and looked under the table, but Bill had anticipated her and retreated to the other end. The table was so long you couldn't see that far underneath without getting down on your hands and knees, and Aunt Anne was much too dignified to stoop to any such level. When she put the table cloth down again, Bill crawled forward and licked her hand.

"You do too have a dog," Aunt Anne said accusingly, while she dried her hand on a napkin. "Speak up now! Who brought that miserable cur into the house?"

Bill thumped her again and retreated. She picked up the table cloth and looked. She put it down again, and he licked her hand. She looked again, and then dangled her hand temptingly between her knees. Bill couldn't resist this trap, and this time Aunt Anne was ready for him. When he started to lick, she snapped her knees together like a vise, trapped his head in the folds of her skirt, and reached down and grabbed him by the hair.

"Come out of there, you scamp you," she shouted. "I've got you. You can't get away this time. Come out, I say."

She didn't give Bill a chance to come out under his own power. She yanked, and he came out by the hair of his head, screaming and kicking.

In those days, Bill was not a snappy dresser. He liked old clothes, preferably held together with safety pins, and held up by old neckties. When he wore a necktie around his neck, which was as seldom as possible, he sometimes evened up the ends by trimming the longer with a pair of scissors. His knickers usually were partially unbuttoned in the front—what the Navy calls the commodore's privilege. They were completely unfastened at the legs and hung down to his ankles. During the course of a day, his stockings rode gradually down his legs and, by dinner, had partially disappeared into his sneakers. When Mother was at home, she made him wear such appurtenances as a coat and a belt. In her absence, he had grown slack.

When Aunt Anne jerked him out, a piece of string connecting a buttonhole in his shirt with a buttonhole in the front of his trousers suddenly broke. Bill grabbed for his pants, but it was too late.

"Go to your room, you scamp you," Aunt Anne said, shaking him. "Just wait until your father comes home. He'll know how to take care of you."

Bill picked up his knickers and did as he was told. He had a new respect for Aunt Anne, and the whole top of his head was smarting from the hair-pulling.

Aunt Anne sat down with deceptive calm, and gave us a disarming smile.

"I want you children to listen carefully to me," she almost whispered. "There's not a living soul here, including the baby, who is cooperative. I've never seen a more spoiled crowd of children."

As she went on, her voice grew louder. Much louder. Tom Grieves opened the pantry door a crack and peeked in.

"For those of you who like to believe that an only child is a selfish child, let me say you are one hundred per cent wrong. From what I have seen, this is the most completely selfish household in the entire world."

She was roaring now, wide open, and it was the first time we had ever seen her that way. Except that her voice was an octave higher, it might have been Dad, sitting there in his own chair.

"From this minute on, pipe down every last one of you, or I'll lambaste the hides off you. I'll fix you so you can't sit down for a month. Do you understand? Does everybody understand? In case you don't realize it, *I've had enough!*"

With that, determined to show us she wasn't going to let us spoil her meal, she put a piece of pie in her mouth. But she was so upset that she choked, and slowly turned a deep pur-

ple. She clutched at her throat. We were afraid she was dying, and were ashamed of ourselves.

Tom, watching at the door, saw his duty. Putting aside his fear of her, he ran into the dining room and slapped her on the back. Then he grabbed her arms and held them high over her head.

"You'll be all right in a minute, Aunt Anne," he said.

His system worked. She gurgled and finally caught her breath. Then, remembering her dignity, she jerked her arms out of his hands and drew herself up to her full height.

"Keep your hands to yourself, Grieves," she said in a tone that indicated her belief that his next step would be to loosen her corset. "Don't ever let me hear you make the fatal mistake of calling me 'Aunt Anne' again. And after this, mind your own"—she looked slowly around the table and then decided to say it anyway—"*damned* business."

There was no doubt after that about who was boss, and Aunt Anne had no further trouble with us. When Dad and Mother returned home, all of us expected to be disciplined. But we had misjudged Aunt Anne.

"You look like you've lost weight," Dad said to her. "The children didn't give you any trouble, did they?"

"Not a bit," said Aunt Anne. "They behaved beautifully, once we got to understand each other. We got along just fine, didn't we, children?"

She reached out fondly and rumpled Billy's hair, which didn't need rumpling.

"Ouch," Billy whispered to her, grinning in relief. "It still hurts. Have a heart."

We had better success with another guest whom we set out deliberately to discourage. She was a woman psychologist who came to Montclair every fortnight from New York to give us intelligence tests. It was her own idea, not Dad's or Mother's, but they welcomed her. She was planning to publish a paper about the effects of Dad's teaching methods on our intelligence quotients.

She was thin and sallow, with angular features and a black moustache, not quite droopy enough to hide a horsey set of upper teeth. We hated her and suspected that the feeling was mutual.

At first her questions were legitimate enough: Arithmetic, spelling, languages, geography, and the sort of purposeful confusion—about ringing numbers and underlining words—in which some psychologists place particular store.

After we had completed the initial series of tests, she took us one by one into the parlor for personal interviews. Even Mother and Dad weren't allowed to be present.

The interviews were embarrassing and insulting.

"Does it hurt when your mother spanks you?" she asked each of us, peering searchingly into our eyes and breathing into our faces. "You mean your mother never spanks you?" She seemed disappointed. "Well, how about your father? Oh, he does?" That appeared to be heartening news. "Does your mother pay more attention to the other children than she does to you? How many baths do you take a week? Are you sure? Do you think it would be nice to have still another baby brother? You do? Goodness!"

We decided that if Dad and Mother knew the kinds of questions we were being asked, they wouldn't like them any better than we did. Anne and Ernestine had made up their minds to explain the situation to them, when destiny delivered the psychologist into our hands, lock, stock and moustache.

Mother had been devising a series of job aptitude tests, and the desk by her bed was piled with pamphlets and magazines on psychology. Ernestine was running idly through them one night, while Mother was reading aloud to us from *The Five Little Peppers and How they Grew,* when she came across a batch of intelligence tests. One of them was the test which the New York woman was in the process of giving us—not the embarrassing personal questions, but the business of circling numbers, spelling, and filling in blanks. The correct answers were in the back.

"Snake's hips," Ernestine crowed. "Got it!"

Mother looked up absently from her book. "Don't mix up my work, Ernie," she said. "What are you after?"

"Just want to borrow something," Ern told her.

"Well, don't forget to put it back when you're through with

it, will you? Where was I? Oh, I remember. Joel had just said that if necessary he could help support the family by selling papers and shining shoes down at the depot."

She resumed her reading.

The psychologist had already given us the first third of the test. Now Anne and Ernestine tutored us on the second third, until we could run right down a page and fill in the answers without even reading the questions. The last third was an oral word-association test, and they coached us on that, too.

"We're going to be the smartest people she ever gave a test to," Ern told us. "And the queerest, too. Make her think we're smart, but uncivilized because we haven't had enough individual attention. That's what she wants to think, anyway."

"Act nervous and queer," Anne said. "While she's talking to you, fidget and scratch yourself. Be as nasty as you can. That won't require much effort from most of you; there's no need our tutoring you on that."

The next time the psychologist came out from New York, she sat us at intervals around the walls of the parlor, with books on our laps to write on. She passed each of us a copy of the second third of the test.

"When I say commence, work as quickly as you can," she told us. "You have half an hour, and I want you to get as far along in the tests as you can. If any of you should happen to finish before the time is up, bring your papers to me." She looked at her watch. "Ready? Now turn your test papers over and start. Remember, I'm watching you, so don't try to look at your neighbor's paper."

We ran down the pages, filling in the blanks. The older children turned in their papers within ten minutes. Lillian, the youngest being examined, finally turned hers in within twenty.

The psychologist looked at Lillian's paper, and her mouth dropped open.

"How old are you, dearie?" she asked.

"Six," said Lill. "I'll be seven in June."

"There's something radically wrong here," the visitor said. "I haven't had a chance to grade all of your paper, but do you know you have a higher I.Q. than Nicholas Murray Butler?"

"I read a lot," Lill said.

The psychologist glanced at the other tests and shook her head.

"I don't know what to think," she sighed. "You've certainly shown remarkable improvement in the last two weeks. Maybe we'd better get on to the last third of the test. I'm going to go around the room and say a word to each of you. I want you to answer instantly the first word that comes into your mind. Now won't that be a nice little game?"

Anne twitched. Ernestine scratched. Martha bit her nails.

"We'll go by ages," the visitor continued. "Anne first."

She pointed to Anne. "Knife," said the psychologist.

"Stab, wound, bleed, slit-throat, murder, disembowel, scream, shriek," replied Anne, without taking a breath and so fast that the words flowed together.

"Jesus," said the psychologist. "Let me get that down. You're just supposed to answer one word, but let me get it all down anyway." She panted in excitement as she scribbled in her pad.

"All right, Ernestine. Your turn. Just one word. 'Black.'"

"Jack," said Ernestine.

The visitor looked at Martha. "Foot."

"Kick," said Martha.

"Hair."

"Louse," said Frank.

"Flower."

"Stink," said Bill.

The psychologist was becoming more and more excited. She looked at Lill.

"Droppings," said Lill, upsetting the apple cart.

"But I haven't even asked you your word yet," the visitor exclaimed. "So that's it. Let me see what your word was going to be. I thought so. Your word was 'bird.' And they told you to say 'droppings,' didn't they?"

Lill nodded sheepishly.

"And they told you just how to fill out the rest of the test, didn't they? I suppose the answers were given to you by your Mother, so you would impress me with how smart you are."

We started to snicker and then to roar. But the psychologist didn't think it was funny.

"You're all nasty little cheats," she said. "Don't think for a minute you pulled the wool over my eyes. I saw through you from the start."

She picked up her wraps and started for the front door. Dad had heard us laughing, and came out of his office to see what was going on. If there was any excitement, he wanted to be on it.

"Well," he beamed, "it sounds as if it's been a jolly test. Running along so soon? Tell me, frankly, what do you think of my family?"

She looked at us and there was an evil glint in her eye.

"I'm glad you asked me that," she whinnied. "Unquestionably, they are smart. Too damned smart for their breeches. Does that answer your question? As to whether they were aided and abetted in an attempted fraud, I cannot say. But my professional advice is to bear down on them. A good thrashing right now, from the oldest to the youngest, might be just the thing."

She slammed the front door, and Dad looked glumly at us.

"All right," he sighed. "What have you been up to? That woman's going to write a paper on the family. What did you do to her?"

Anne twitched. Ernestine scratched. Martha bit her nails. Dad was getting angry.

"Hold still and speak up. No nonsense!"

"Do you want another baby brother?" Anne asked.

"Does it hurt when your Mother spanks you?" said Ernestine.

"When did you have your last bath?" Martha inquired. "Are you sure? Hmmm?"

Dad raised his hands in surrender and shook his head. He looked old and tired now.

"Sometimes I don't know if it's worth it," he said. "Why didn't you come and tell your Mother and me about it, if she was asking questions like that. Oh, well . . . On the other hand . . . Why the bearded old goat!"

Dad started to smile.

"If she writes a paper about any of that I'll sue her for

everything she owns, including her birth certificate. If she has one."

He opened the door into his office.

"Come in and give me all the frightful details."

"After you, Dr. Butler," Ernestine told Lill.

A few minutes later, Mother came into the office, where we were perched on the edges of her and Dad's desks. The stenographers had abandoned their typewriters and were crowded around us.

"What's the commotion, Frank?" she asked Dad. "I could hear you bellowing all the way up in the attic."

"Oh, Lord," Dad wheezed. "Start at the beginning, kids. I want your mother to hear this, too. The bearded old goat—not you, Lillie."

CHAPTER 16

Over the Hill

On Friday nights, Dad and Mother often went to a lecture or a movie by themselves, holding hands as they went out to the barn to get Foolish Carriage.

But on Saturday nights, Mother stayed home with the babies, while Dad took the rest of us to the movies. We had early supper so that we could get to the theater by seven o'clock, in time for the first show.

"We're just going to stay through one show tonight," Dad told us on the way down. "None of this business about seeing the show through a second time. None of this eleven o'clock stuff. No use to beg me."

When the movie began, Dad became as absorbed as we, and noisier. He forgot all about us, and paid no attention when we nudged him and asked for nickels to put in the candy vendors on the back of the seats. He laughed so hard at the comedies that sometimes he embarrassed us and we tried to tell him that people were looking at him. When the feature was sad, he kept trumpeting his nose and wiping his eyes.

When the lights went on at the end of the first show, we always begged him to change his mind, and let us stay and see it again. He put on an act of stubborn resistance, but always yielded in the end.

"Well, you were less insolent than usual this week," he said. "But I hate to have you stay up until all hours of the night."

"Tomorrow's Sunday. We can sleep late."

"And your mother will give me Hail Columbia when I bring you home late."

"If you think it's all right, Mother will think it's all right."

"Well, all right. We'll make an exception this time. Since your hearts are so set on it, I guess I can sit through it again."

Once, after a whispered message by Ernestine had passed along the line, we picked up our coats at the end of the first show and started to file out of the aisle.

"What are you up to?" Dad called after us in a hurt tone, and loud enough so that people stood up to see what was causing the disturbance. "Where do you think you're going? Do you want to walk home? Come back here and sit down."

We said he had told us on the way to the theater that we could just sit through one show that night.

"Well, don't you want to see it again? After all, you've been good as gold this week. If your hearts are set on it, I guess I could sit through it again. I don't mind, particularly."

We said we were a little sleepy, that we didn't want to be all tired out tomorrow and that we didn't want Mother to be worried because we had stayed out late.

"Aw, come on," Dad begged. "Don't be spoil sports. I'll take care of your mother. Let's see it again. The evening's young. Tomorrow's Sunday. You can sleep late."

We filed smirking back to our seats.

"You little fiends," Dad whispered as we sat down. "You spend hours figuring out ways to gang up on me, don't you? I've got a good mind to leave you all home next week and come to the show by myself."

The picture that made the biggest impression on Dad was a

twelve-reel epic entitled *Over the Hill to the Poor House,* or something like that. It was about a wispy widow lady who worked her poor old fingers to the bone for her children, only to end her days in the alms house after they turned against her.

For an hour and a half, while Dad manned the pumps with his handkerchief, the woman struggled to keep her family together. She washed huge vats of clothes. She ironed an endless procession of underwear. Time after time, ingle-handed and on her hands and knees, she emptied all the cuspidors and scrubbed down the lobby of Grand Central Station.

Her children were ashamed of her and complained because they didn't have store-bought clothes. When the children were grown up, they fought over having her come to live with them. Finally, when she was too old to help even with the housework, they turned her out into the street. There was a snowstorm going on, too.

The fade-out scene, the one that had Dad actually wringing out his handkerchief, showed the old woman, shivering in a worn and inadequate hug-me-tight, limping slowly up the hill to the poor house.

Dad was still red-eyed and blowing his nose while we were drinking our sodas after the movie, and all of us felt depressed.

"I want all of you to promise me one thing," he choked. "No matter what happens to me, I want you to take care of your mother."

After we promised, Dad felt better. But the movie remained on his mind for months.

"I can see myself twenty years from now," he'd grumble when we asked him for advances on our allowances. "I can see myself, old, penniless, unwanted, trudging up that hill. I wonder what kind of food they have at the poor house and whether they let you sleep late in the mornings?"

Even more than the movies, Dad liked the shows that we staged once or twice a year in the parlor, for his and Mother's benefit. The skits, written originally by Anne and Ernestine, never varied much, so we could give them without rehearsal.

The skits that Dad liked best were the imitations of him and Mother.

Frank, with a couple of sofa pillows under his belt and a straw hat on the back of his head, played the part of Dad leading us through a factory for which he was a consultant. Ernestine, with stuffed bosom and flowered hat, played Mother. Anne took the part of a superintendent at the factory and the younger children played themselves.

"Is everybody here?" Frank asked Ernestine. She took out a notebook and called the roll. "Is everybody dry? Do you all have your notebooks? All right, then. Follow me."

We paraded around the room a couple of times in lockstep, like a chain gang, with Frank first, Ernestine next, and the children following by ages. Then we pretended to walk up a flight of stairs, to indicate that we had entered the factory. Anne, the superintendent, came forward and shook hands with Dad.

"Christmas," she said. "Look what followed you in. Are those your children, or is it a picnic?"

"They're my children," Ernestine said indignantly. "And it was no picnic."

"How do you like my little Mongolians?" Frank leered. "Mongolians come cheaper by the dozen, you know. Do you think I should keep them all?"

"I think you should keep them all home," Anne said. "Tell them to stop climbing over my machinery."

"They won't get hurt," Frank assured her. "They're all trained engineers. I trained them myself."

Anne shrieked. "Look at that little Mongolian squatting over my buzz saw." She covered her eyes. "I can't watch him. Don't let him squat any lower. Tell him to stop squatting."

"The little rascal thinks it's a bicycle," Frank said. "Leave him alone. Children have to learn by doing."

Someone off stage gave a dying scream.

"I lose more children in factories," Ernestine complained. "Now the rest of you keep away from that buzz saw, you hear me?"

"Someone make a note of that so we can tell how many places to set for supper," Frank said. He turned to Fred. "Freddy boy, I want you to take your fingers out of your mouth, and then explain to the superintendent what's inefficient about this drill press here."

"That thing a drill press?" Fred said with an exaggerated lisp. "Haw."

"Precisely," said Frank. "Explain it to him, in simple language."

"The position of the hand lever is such that there is waste motion both after transport loaded and transport empty," Fred lisped. "The work plane of the operator is at a fatiguing level and . . ."

Sometimes we made believe we were on an auditorium platform at an engineering meeting, at which Dad was to speak. Anne played the chairman who was introducing him.

"Our next speaker," she said, "is Frank Bunker Gilbreth. Wait a minute now. Please keep your seats. Don't be frightened. He's promised, this time, to limit himself to two hours, and not to mention the 'One Best Way to Do Work' more than twice in the same sentence."

Frank, with pillows in front again, walked to the edge of the platform, adjusted a pince-nez which hung from a black ribbon around his neck, smirked, reached under his coat, and pulled out a manuscript seven inches thick.

"For the purpose of convenience," he began pompously, "I have divided my talk tonight into thirty main headings and one hundred and seventeen sub-headings. I will commence with the first main heading. . . ."

At this point, the other children, who were seated as if they were the engineers in Dad's audience, nudged each other, arose, and tiptoed out of the room. Frank droned on, speaking to an empty hall.

When Frank finally sat down, the audience returned, and the chairman introduced Mother, played again by Ernestine.

"Our next guest is Dr. Lillian Moller Gilbreth. She's not going to make a speech, but she will be glad to answer any questions."

Ernestine swept forward in a wide-brimmed hat and floor-length skirt. She was carrying a suitcase-sized pocketbook, from which protruded a pair of knitting needles, some mending, crochet hook, baby's bottle, and copy of the *Scientific American.*

She smiled for a full minute, nodding to friends in the audience. "Hello, Grace, I like your new hat. Why, Jennie, you've bobbed your hair. Hello, Charlotte, so glad you could be here."

Dressed in a collection of Mother's best hats, Martha, Frank, Bill and Lill started jumping up with questions.

"Tell us, Mrs. Gilbreth, did you really want such a large family, and if so why?"

"Any other questions?" asked Ernestine.

"Who really wears the pants in your household, Mrs. Gilbreth? You or your husband?"

"Any other questions?" asked Ernestine.

"One thing more, Mrs. Gilbreth. Do Bolivians really come cheaper by the dozen?"

After the skits, Dad sometimes would put on a one-man minstrel show for us, in which he played the parts of both the Messrs. Jones and Bones. We knew the routine by heart, but we always enjoyed it, and so did Dad.

With his lower lip protruding and his hands hanging down to his knees, he shuffled up and down the parlor floor.

"Does you know how you gets de water in de watermelon?"

"I don't know, how does you get the water in the watermelon?"

"Why you plants dem in de spring." Dad slapped his knee, folded his arms in front of his face, and rolled his head to the left and right in spasms of mirth. "Yak. Yak."

"And does you know Isabelle?"

"Isabelle?"

"Yeah, Isabelle necessary on a bicycle."

"And does you know the difference between a pretty girl and an apple? Well, one you squeeze to git cider, and the odder you git 'sider to squeeze. Yak. Yak."

When the show was over, Dad looked at his watch.

"It's way past your bedtime," he complained. "Doesn't anybody pay any attention to the rules I make? You older children should have been in bed an hour ago, and you little fellows three hours ago."

He took Mother by the arm.

"My throat is as hoarse as a frog's from all that reciting," he said. "The only thing that will soothe it is a nice, sweet, cool, chocolate ice cream soda. With whipped cream. Ummm." He rubbed his stomach. "Go to bed, children. Come on, Boss. I'll go get the car and you and I will go down to the drug store. I couldn't sleep a wink with this hoarse throat."

"Take us, Daddy?" we shouted. "You wouldn't go without us? Our throats are hoarse as frogs' too. We wouldn't sleep a wink either."

"See?" Dad asked. "When it comes to sodas, you're right on the job, up and ready to go. But when it comes to going to bed, you're slow as molasses!"

He turned to Mother. "What do you say, Boss?"

Mother protruded her lower lip, sagged her shoulders and let her hands hang down to her knees.

"Did you say mo' 'lasses, Mr. Bones?" she squeaked in a querulous falsetto. "Mo' 'lasses? Why, Honey, I ain't had no 'lasses. Git yo' coats on, chillen. Yak. Yak."

"Thirteen sodas at fifteen cents apiece," Dad muttered. "I can see the handwriting on the wall. Over the Hill to the Poor House."

CHAPTER 17

Four Wheels, No Brakes

By the time Anne was a senior in high school, Dad was convinced that the current generation of girls was riding, with rouged lips and rolled stockings, straight for a jazzy and probably illicit rendezvous with the greasy-haired devil.

Flaming youth had just caught fire. It was the day of the flapper and the sheik, of petting and necking, of flat chests and dimpled knees. It was yellow slickers with writing on the back, college pennants, and plus fours. Girls were beginning to bob their hair and boys to lubricate theirs. The college boy was a national hero, and collegiate was the most complimentary adjective in the American vocabulary. The ukulele was a social asset second only to the traps and saxophone. It was "Me and the Boy Friend," "Clap Hands Here Comes Charlie" and "Jadda, Jadda, Jing, Jing, Jing." The accepted mode of transportation was the stripped-down Model T Ford, preferably inscribed with such witticisms as "Chicken, Here's Your Roost," "Four Wheels, No Brakes" and "The Mayflower—Many a Little Puritan Has Come Across In It."

It was the era of unfastened galoshes and the shifters club. It was the start of the Jazz Age.

If people the world over wanted to go crazy, that was their affair, however lamentable. But Dad had no intention of letting his daughters go with them. At least, not without a fight.

"What's the matter with girls today?" Dad kept asking. "Don't they know what those greasy-haired boys are after? Don't they know what's going to happen to them if they go around showing their legs through silk stockings, and with bare knees, and with skirts so short that the slightest wind doesn't leave anything to the imagination?"

"Well, that's the way everybody dresses today," Anne insisted. "Everybody but Ernestine and me; we're school freaks. Boys don't notice things like that when everybody dresses that way."

"Don't try to tell me about boys," Dad said in disgust. "I know all about what boys notice and what they're after. I can see right through all this collegiate stuff. This petting and necking and jazzing are just other words for something that's been going on for a long, long time, only nice people didn't used to discuss it or indulge in it. I hate to tell you what would have happened in my day if girls had come to school dressed like some girls dress today."

"What?" Anne asked eagerly.

"Never you mind. All I know is that even self-respecting streetwalkers wouldn't have dressed . . ."

"Frank!" Mother interrupted him. "I don't like that Eskimo word."

The girls turned to Mother for support, but she agreed with Dad.

"After all, men don't want to marry girls who wear makeup and high heels," Mother said. "That's the kind they run around with before they're married. But when it comes to picking out a wife, they want someone they can respect."

"They certainly respect me," Anne moaned. "I'm the most respected girl in the whole high school. The boys respect me so much they hardly look at me. I wish they'd respect me a little less and go out with me a little more. How can you expect me to be popular?"

"Popular!" Dad roared. "Popular. That's all I hear. That's the magic word, isn't it? That's what's the matter with this generation. Nobody thinks about being smart, or clever, or sweet or even attractive. No, sir. They want to be skinny and flat-chested and popular. They'd sell their soul and body to be popular, and if you ask me a lot of them do."

"We're the only girls in the whole high school who aren't allowed to wear silk stockings," Ernestine complained. "It just isn't fair. If we could just wear silk stockings it wouldn't be so bad about the long skirts, the sensible shoes, and the cootie garages."

"No, by jingo." Dad pounded the table. "I'll put you both in a convent first. I will, by jingo. Silk stockings indeed! I don't want to hear another word out of either of you, or into the convent you go. Do you understand?"

The convent had become one of Dad's most frequently used threats. He had even gone so far as to write away for literature on convents, and he kept several catalogues on the tea table in the dining room, where he could thumb through them and wave them during his arguments with the older girls.

"There seems to be a nice convent near Albany," he'd tell Mother after making sure that Anne and Ernestine were listening. "The catalogue says the wall around it is twelve feet high, and the sisters see to it that the girls are in bed by nine o'clock. I think that's better than the one at Boston. The wall of the Boston one is only ten feet high."

The so-called cootie garages, which Anne and Ernestine now detested, had been the style several years before, and still were worn by girls who hadn't bobbed their hair. The long hair was pulled forward and tied into two droppy pugs which protruded three or four inches from each ear. If a girl didn't have enough hair to do the trick, she used rags, rats, or switches to fill up the insides of the ear muffs.

Anne decided that she could never get Dad's permission to dress like the other girls in her class, and that it was up to her to take matters into her own hands. She felt a certain amount of responsibility to Ernestine and the younger girls, since she knew they would never be emancipated until she paved the way. She had a haunting mental picture of Jane, fifteen years hence, still wearing pugs over her ears, long winter drawers, and heavy ribbed stockings.

"Convent, here I come," she told Ern. "I mean the Albany convent with the twelve-foot wall."

She disappeared into the girls' bathroom with a pair of scissors. When she emerged, her hair was bobbed and shingled up the back. It wasn't a very good-looking job, but it was good and short. She tiptoed, unnoticed, into Ernestine's room.

"How do I look?" she asked. "Do you think I did a good job?"

"Good Lord," Ernestine screamed. "Get out of here. It might be catching."

"I'll catch it when Dad gets ahold of me, I know that. But how does it look?"

"I didn't know any human head of hair could look like that," Ernestine said. "I like bobbed hair, but yours looks like you backed into a lawn-mower. My advice is to start all over again, and this time let the barber do it."

"You're not much help," Anne complained. "After all, I did it as much for you as for me."

"Well, don't do anything like that for me again. I'm not worth it. It's too big a sacrifice to expect you to go around like that until the end of your days, which I suspect are numbered."

"You're going to back me up, aren't you, when Dad sees it? After all, you want to bob your hair, don't you?"

"I'll back you up," said Ern, "to the hilt. But I don't want to bob my hair. I want a barber to bob it for me. What I'm wondering is who's going to back up Dad. Somebody had better be there to catch him."

"I have a feeling," Anne said, "that I'm in for a fairly disagreeable evening. Oh, well, somebody had to do it, and I'm the oldest."

They sat in Ernestine's room until supper time, and then went downstairs together. Mother was serving the plates, and dropped peas all over the tablecloth.

"Anne," she whispered. "Your beautiful hair. Oh, oh, oh. Just look at yourself."

"I have looked at myself," Anne said. "Please don't make me look at myself again. I don't want to spoil my appetite."

Mother burst into tears. "You've already spoiled mine," she sobbed.

Dad hadn't paid any attention when Anne and Ernestine entered the dining room.

"What's the trouble now?" he asked. "Can't we have a little peace and quiet around here for just one meal? All I ask is . . ." He saw Anne and choked.

"Go back upstairs and take that thing off," he roared. "And don't you ever dare to come down here looking like that again. The idea! Scaring everybody half to death and making your Mother cry. You ought to be ashamed of yourself."

"It's done, Daddy," Anne said. "I'm afraid we're all going to have to make the best of it. The moving finger bobs, and having bobbed, moves on."

"I think it looks snakey," Ern hastened to do her duty to her older sister. "And listen, Daddy, it's ever so much more efficient. It takes me ten minutes to fix these pugs in the morning, and Anne can fix her hair now in fifteen seconds."

"What hair?" Dad shouted. "She doesn't have any hair to fix."

"How could you do this to me?" Mother sobbed.

"How could she do it to an Airedale, let alone to herself or you and me?" said Dad. "The Scarlet Letter. How Hester won her 'A.' Well, I won't have it, do you understand? I want your hair grown back in and I want it grown back in fast. Do you hear me?"

Anne had tried to keep up a bold front, but the combined attack was too much and she burst into tears.

"Nobody in this family understands me," she sobbed. "I wish I were dead."

She ran from the table. We heard her bedroom door slam, and muffled, heartbroken sobs.

Dad reached over and picked up his convent catalogues, but he couldn't put any enthusiasm into them, and he finally tossed them down again. Neither he nor Mother could eat anything, and there was an uneasy, guilty silence, punctuated by Anne's sobs.

"Listen to that poor, heartbroken child," Mother finally said. "Imagine her thinking that no one in the world understands her. Frank, I think you were too hard on her."

Dad put his head in his hands. "Maybe I was," he said. "Maybe I was. Personally, I don't have anything much against bobbed hair. Like Ernestine says, it's more efficient. But when I saw how upset it made you, I lost my temper, I guess."

"I don't have anything against bobbed hair either," Mother said. "It certainly would eliminate a lot of brushing and combing. But I knew you didn't like it, and . . ."

Anne appeared at dessert time, red-eyed and disheveled. Without a word she sat down and picked up her knife and fork. Minutes later, she smiled enchantingly.

"That was good," she said, passing her plate. "If you don't mind, Mother, I'll have another helping of everything. I'm positively starved tonight."

"I don't mind, dear," said Mother.

"I like to see girls eat," said Dad.

That weekend, Mother took the girls down to Dad's barber shop in the Claridge Building in Montclair.

"I want you to trim this one's hair, please," she said, pointing to Anne, "and to bob the hair of the others."

"Any special sort of bob, Mrs. Gilbreth?" the barber asked.

"No. No, I guess just a regular bob," Mother said slowly. "The shorter the better."

"And how about you, Mrs. Gilbreth?"

"What about me?"

"How about your hair?"

"No, sir," the girls shouted indignantly. "You don't touch a hair on her head. The idea!"

Mother pretended to consider the suggestion. "I don't know, girls," she smiled. "It might look very chic. And it certainly would be more efficient. What do you think?"

"I think," said Ernestine, "it would be disgraceful. After all, a mother's a mother, not a silly flapper."

"I guess not today, thank you," Mother told the barber. "Five bobbed-haired bandits in the family should be enough."

Having capitulated on the hair question, Dad put up an even sterner resistance against any future changes in dress. But Anne and Ernestine broke him down a little at a time. Anne got a job in the high-school cafeteria, saved her money, and bought silk stockings, two short dresses and four flimsy pieces of underwear known as teddies. These she unwrapped with some ceremony in the living room.

"I don't want to be a sneak," she said, "so I'm going to show these to everybody right now. If you won't let me wear them at home, I'll change into them on the way to school. I'm never going to wear long underwear again."

"Oh no you don't," Dad shouted. "Take those things back to the store. It embarrasses me to look at them, and I won't have them in my house."

He picked up a teddy and held the top of it against his shoulders. It hung down to his belt.

"You mean that's all the underwear women wear nowadays?" he asked incredulously. "When I think of . . . well, never mind that. No wonder you read about all those crimes and love nests, like that New Brunswick preacher and the choir singer. Well, you take the whole business right back to the store."

"No," Anne insisted. "I bought these clothes with my own money and I'm going to wear them. I'm not going to be the only one in the class with long underwear and a flap in the back. It's disgusting."

"It's not so disgusting as having no back of the underwear to sew a flap on," said Dad. "I just can't believe that everybody in your class wears these teddybear, or bare-teddy things. There must be some sane parents besides your mother and me." He shook his head. But he was weakening.

"I don't see why you object to teddies," Anne said. "They don't show, you know."

"Of course they don't show, that's just the trouble. It's what does show that I'm talking about."

"There's only one other girl in high school besides Anne and me who doesn't wear teddies," Ernestine put in. "If you don't believe us, come to school and see for yourself."

"That won't be necessary," Dad blushed. "I'm willing to take your word for it."

"I should say not," said Mother.

"Aside from the possibility of being arrested for indecent exposure every time they crossed their legs or stood in a breeze," Dad muttered, "I'd think they'd die of pneumonia."

"Well, I'm glad there's one other sensible girl in school besides you two," Mother said, clutching at a straw. "She sounds like a nice girl. Do I know her?"

"I don't believe so," Ernestine whispered. "She doesn't even wear a teddy. And if you don't believe me . . ."

"I know," Dad blushed again. "And it still won't be necessary."

He picked up one of the stockings and slipped his hand into it.

"You might as well go bare-legged as to wear these. You can see right through them. It's like the last of the seven veils. And those arrows at the bottom—why do they point in that direction?"

"Those aren't arrows, Daddy," Anne said. "They're clocks. And it seems to me that you're going out of your way to find fault with them."

"Well, why couldn't the hands of the clock have stopped at quarter after three or twenty-five of five, instead of six o'clock?"

"Be sensible, Daddy," Anne begged him. "You don't want us to grow up to be wallflowers, do you?"

"I'd a lot rather raise wallflowers than clinging vines or worse. The next thing I know you'll be wanting to paint."

"Everybody uses make-up nowadays," Ern said. "They don't call it painting any more."

"I don't care what they call it," Dad roared. "I'll have no painted women in this house. Get that straight. The bare-teddies and six o'clock stockings are all right, I guess, but no painting, do you understand?"

"Yes, Daddy."

"And no high heels or pointed toes. I'm not going to have a lot of doctor's bills because of foot troubles."

Anne and Ernestine decided that half a loaf was better than none, and that they had better wait until Dad got used to the silk stockings and short skirts before they pressed the make-up and shoe question.

But it turned out that Dad had given all the ground he intended to, and the girls found Mother a weak reed on which to lean.

"Neither my sisters nor I have ever used face powder," Mother told Anne and Ernestine, when they asked her to intervene in their behalf. "Frankly girls, I consider it nonessential."

"Don't tell me you'd rather see a nose full of freckles!"

"At least that looks natural. And when it comes to the matter of high heels, I don't see how your father can be expected to travel around the world talking about eliminating fatigue, while you girls are fatiguing yourself with high-heel shoes."

Dad kept a sharp lookout for surreptitious painting, and was especially suspicious whenever one of the girls looked particularly pretty.

"What's got into you tonight?" he'd ask, sniffing the air for traces of powder or perfume.

Ernestine, after playing outside most of the afternoon, came to supper one evening with flushed cheeks.

"Come over here, young lady," Dad yelled. "I warned you about painting. Let me take a look at you. I declare, you girls pay no more attention to me than if I were a cigar store Indian. A man's got to wear grease in his hair and gray flannel trousers to get any attention in this house nowadays."

"I haven't got on make-up, Daddy."

"You haven't eh? Don't think you can fool me. And don't think I'm fooling you when I tell you you've just about painted your way into that convent."

"The one with the twelve-foot wall, or the one with the ten-foot wall?" Ern asked.

"Don't be impudent." He pulled out a handkerchief and held a corner of it out to Ern. "Spit on that."

He took the wet part of the handkerchief, rubbed her cheeks and examined it.

"Well, Ernestine," he said after a minute. "I see that it isn't rouge, and I apologize. But it might have been, and I won't have it, do you hear?"

Dad prided himself on being able to smell perfume as soon as he walked into a room, and on being able to pick the offender out of a crowd.

"Ernestine, are you the one we have to thank for that smell?" he asked. "Good Lord. It smells like a French . . . like a French garbage can."

"What smell, Daddy?"

"By jingo, don't tell me you're indulging in perfume now!"

"Why not, Daddy? Perfume isn't painting or make-up. And it smells so good!"

"Why not? Because it stinks up good fresh air, that's why not. Now go up and wash that stuff off before I come up and wash it off for you. Don't you know what men think when they smell perfume on a woman?"

"All I know is what one man thinks," Ernestine complained. "And he thinks I should wash it off."

"Thinks, nothing," said Dad. "He knows. And he's telling you. Now get moving."

Clothes remained a subject of considerable friction, but the matter that threatened to affect Dad's stability was jazz. Radios were innocuous, being still in the catwhisker and headphone stage, and featuring such stimulating programs as the Arlington Time Signals. But five- and six-piece dance bands were turning out huge piles of graphophone records, and we tried to buy them all.

We already had an ample supply of graphophones, because of the ones Dad had acquired for the language records. And we still weren't allowed to neglect our language lessons. But once we had played the required quota of French, German, and Italian records, we switched to "Stumbling," "Limehouse Blues," "Last Night on the Back Porch," "Charlie, My Boy," "I'm Forever Blowing Bubbles," and "You've Got to See Mama Every Night or You Can't See Mama at All." Not only did we listen to them, we sang with them, imitated them, and rolled back the rugs and danced to them.

Dad didn't particularly object to jazz music. He thought some of it was downright catchy. But he felt that we devoted far too much time to it, that the words were something more than suggestive, and that the kind of dancing that went with it might lead to serious consequences. As he walked from room to room in the house, jazz assailed him from phonograph after phonograph, and he sometimes threw up his hands in disgust.

"Da-da, de-da-da-da," he bellowed sarcastically. "If you spent half as much time improving your minds as you do memorizing those stupid songs, you could recite *The Koran* forwards and backwards. Wind up the victrola and let's have some more jazz. Da-da, de-da-da-da. Let's have that record about 'I love my sweetie a hundred times a night.' "

"You made that song up," we told him. "That's not a record, Daddy."

"Maybe it's not a record," he said. "But take it from me, it's well above average. Da-da, de-da-da-da."

When Anne came home from school one afternoon and announced that she had been invited to her first dance, she seemed so happy that both Dad and Mother were happy for her.

"I told you that if I started dressing like the other girls everything would be all right and that I would be popular with the boys," Anne crowed. "Joe Scales has asked me to go with him to the prom next Friday night."

"That's lovely, dear," Mother said.

"That's just fine," Dad smiled. "Is he a nice boy?"

"Nice? Gee, I'll say. He's a cheerleader and he has a car."

"Two mighty fine recommendations," Dad said. "If only he had a raccoon coat I suppose he'd be listed in the year book as the one most likely to succeed."

The sarcasm was lost on Anne. "He's going to get his raccoon coat next year when he goes to Yale," she hastened to assure Dad. "His father's promised it to him if he passes his work."

"That takes a load off my mind," said Dad. "It used to be that a father promised his son a gold watch if he didn't smoke until he was twenty-one. Now the kids get a raccoon coat as a matter of routine if they manage to stumble through high school."

He shook his head and sighed. "Honestly, I don't know

what the world's coming to," he said. "I really don't. Friday night, you say?" He pulled a notebook out of his pocket and consulted it. "It's all right. I can make it."

"You can make what?" Anne asked him suspiciously.

"I can make the dance," said Dad. "You didn't think for a minute I was going to let you go out by yourself, at night, with that—that cheerleader, did you?"

"Oh, Daddy," Anne moaned. "You wouldn't spoil everything by doing something like that, would you? What's he going to think of me?"

"He'll think you're a sensible, well-brought-up child, with sensible parents," Mother put in. "I'm sure that if I called up his mother right now, she'd be glad to hear that your father was going along as a chaperone."

"Don't you trust your own flesh and blood?"

"Of course we trust you," Dad said. "I know you've been brought up right. I trust all my daughters. It's that cheerleader I don't trust. Now you might as well make up your mind to it. Either I go, or you don't."

"Do you think it would help if I called up his mother and explained the situation to her?" Mother asked.

Anne had become philosophic about breaking Dad down a little at a time, and she had suspected all along that there was going to be a third person on her first date.

"No, thanks, Mother," she said. "I'd better announce the news myself, in my own way. I guess I'll have to tell him about some people still being in the dark concerning the expression that two's company and three's a crowd. I don't know what he's going to say, though."

"He'll probably be tickled to death to have someone along to pay for the sodas," Dad told her.

"Shall I tell him we'll go in his car, or ours?" Anne asked.

"His car? I haven't seen it, but I can imagine it. No doors, no fenders, no top, and a lot of writing about in case of fire throw this in. I wouldn't be seen dead in it, even if the dance was a masquerade and I was going as a cheerleader. No sir. We'll go in Foolish Carriage."

"Sometimes," Anne said slowly, "it's hard to be the oldest. When I think of Ernestine, Martha, Lillian, Jane—they won't have to go through any of this. I wonder if they'll just take things for granted, or whether they'll appreciate what I've suffered for them."

On the night of Anne's first date, we stationed ourselves at strategic windows so we could watch Joe Scales arrive. It wasn't every day that a cheerleader came to call.

As Dad had predicted, Anne's friend drove up to the house in an ancient Model T, with writing on it. We could hear the car several blocks before it actually hove into sight, because it was equipped with an exhaust whistle that was allowed to function as a matter of routine. When the car proceeded at a moderate speed, which was hardly ever, the whistle sounded no worse than an hellish roar. But when young Mister Scales stepped on the gas, the roar became high pitched, deafening, and insane.

As the Model T bumped down Eagle Rock Way, heads popped out of the windows of neighboring houses, dogs raced into the woods with their tails between their legs, and babies started to scream.

The exhaust whistle, coupled with the natural engine noises, precluded the necessity of Mister Scales' giving any further notice about the car's arrival at its destination. But etiquette of the day was rigid, and he followed it to the letter. First he turned off the engine, which automatically and mercifully silenced the whistle. Then, while lounging in the driver's seat, he tooted and re-tooted the horn until Anne finally came to the front door.

"Come on in, Joe," Anne called.

"Okay, baby. Is your pop ready?"

Dad was peeking at the arrival from behind a curtain in his office. "If he 'pops' me, I'll pop him." Dad whispered to Mother. "My God, Lillie. I mean, Great Caesar's ghost. Come here and look at him. It's Joe College in the flesh. And he just about comes up to Anne's shoulder."

Anne's sheik was wearing a black-and-orange-striped blazer, gray Oxford bags, a bow tie on an elastic band, and a brown triangular porkpie hat, pinched into a bowsprit at the front.

"You and I are going to the dance," Joe shouted to Anne, "And so's your Old Man. Get it? So's your Old Man."

"Of course she gets it, wise guy," Dad grumbled for Mother's benefit. "What do you think she is, a moron? And let me hear you refer to me tonight as the 'Old Man' and you'll get it, too. I promise you."

"Hush," Mother warned him, coming over to peek out the curtain. "He'll hear you. Actually, he's kind of cute, in a sort of vest-pocket way."

"Cute?" said Dad. "He looks like what might happen if a pigmy married a barber pole. And look at that car. What's that written on the side? 'Jump in sardine, here's your tin.' "

"Well don't worry about the car," Mother told him. "You'll be riding in yours, not that contraption."

"Thank the Lord for small favors. You stall him and Anne off until I can get the side curtains put up. I'm not going to drive through town with that blazer showing. Someone might think he was one of our kids."

Dad disappeared in the direction of the barn, and Mother went into the living room to meet the caller. As she entered, Joe was demonstrating to Frank and Bill how the bow tie worked.

"It's a William Tell tie," he said, holding the bow away from his neck and allowing it to pop back into position. "You pull the bow and it hits the apple."

Both Frank and Bill were impressed.

"You're the first cheerleader we ever saw up close," Frank said. "Gee."

Joe was sitting down when he was introduced to Mother. Remembering his manners, he tipped his hat, unveiling for just a moment a patent-leather hairdo, parted in the middle.

"Will you lead some cheers for us?" Bill begged. "We know them all. Anne and Ernestine taught them to us."

Joe leaped to his feet. "Sure thing," he said. He cupped his hands over his mouth and shouted in an adolescent baritone that cracked and made Mother shudder:

"Let's have a hoo, rah, ray and a tiger for Montclair High. A hoo, rah, ray and a tiger. I want to hear you holler now. Readddy?"

He turned sideways to us, dropped on one knee and made his fists go in a circle, like a squirrel on a treadmill.

"Hoo," he screamed, at the top of his voice. "Rah. Ray . . ."

It was at this point that Dad entered the room. He stood

viewing the proceedings with disgust, lips pursed and hands on hips. At the end of the cheer, he sidled over toward Mother.

"The car won't start," he whispered, "and I can't say that I blame it. What shall I do?"

"You could go in his car."

"With that insane calliope and those signs?" Dad hissed. "Do I look like a sardine looking for a tin to leap into?"

"Not exactly," Mother conceded. "Why don't you call a cab, then?"

"Look at him," Dad whispered. "He doesn't come up to her shoulder. He wouldn't dare get funny with her—she'd knock him cold."

Dad walked over to where Joe and Anne were sitting.

"I hope you youngsters won't mind," he said, "but I won't be able to go to the dance with you."

"No, we don't mind at all, Daddy," said Anne. "Do we Joe?"

"A hoo, rah, ray and a tiger for me, is that it?" Dad asked.

Joe made no attempt to hide his elation. "That's it," he said. "Come on, baby. Let's shake that thing. We're running late."

"Now I want you to be home at midnight," Dad said to Anne. "I'm going to be right here waiting for you, and if you're not here by one minute after midnight I'm coming looking for you. Do you understand?"

"All right, Daddy," Anne grinned. "Good old Foolish Carriage saved the day, didn't it?"

"That," said Dad, "and the way certain other matters"—he looked pointedly down at Scales—"shaped up."

"Come on, Cinderella," said Scales, "before the good fairy turns things into field mice and pumpkins."

He and Anne departed, and he didn't forget to tip his hat.

"Do you guess he meant me?" Dad asked Mother. "Why the little . . . I ought to break his neck."

"Of course not. He was speaking in generalities, I'm sure."

The hellish whistle could be heard gradually disappearing in the distance.

CHAPTER 18

Motorcycle Mac

Once the ice was broken, Anne started having dates fairly often, and Ernestine and Martha followed suit. Dad acted as chaperone whenever the pressure of business permitted. Although he had decided that Joe Scales was small enough to be above suspicion, he had no confidence in the football heroes and other sheiks who soon were pitching their tents and woo upon the premises. When Dad couldn't act as chaperone himself, he sent Frank or Bill along as his proxy.

"It's bad enough to have you tagging along on a date," Ernestine told Dad. "But to have a kid brother squirming and giggling on the back seat is simply unbearable. I don't know why the boys in school bother with us."

"Well, I know, even if you don't," Dad said. "And that's exactly why Frank and Bill are there. And let me tell you, if those sheiks would stop bothering you and find some other desert to haunt, it would suit me just right."

Frank and Bill didn't like the chaperone job any more than the girls liked having them for chaperones.

"For Lord's sake, Daddy," Frank complained, "I feel just like a third wheel sitting in the back seat all by myself."

"That's just what you're supposed to be—the third wheel. I don't expect you to be able to thrash those fullbacks if they start trying to take liberties with your sisters. But at least you'll be able to run for help."

The girls complained to Mother, but as usual she sided with Dad.

"If you ask me," Anne told her, "it's a dead give away to be as suspicious as Daddy. It denotes a misspent youth."

"Well nobody asked you," Mother said, "so perhaps you'd better forego any further speculation. It's not a case of suspicion. Just because other parents won't face up to their responsibilities is no reason for your father or me to forget ours."

At the dances, Dad would sit by himself against a wall, as far away from the orchestra as possible, and work on papers he had brought along in a brief case. At first no one paid much attention to him, figuring perhaps that if he was ignored he might go away. But after a few months he was accepted as a permanent fixture, and the girls and boys went out of their way to speak to him and bring him refreshments. People, even sheiks, couldn't be around Daddy without liking him. And Daddy couldn't be in the midst of people without being charming.

"Do you see what's happening?" Anne whispered to Ernestine one night, pointing to the crowd around Dad's chair. "By golly, he's become the belle of the high school ball. What do you think of that?"

"I think it's a pain in the neck," Ernestine said. "But it's kind of cute, isn't it?"

"Not only cute, it's our salvation. You wait and see."

"What do you mean?"

"When Daddy gets to know the boys, and sees that they're pretty good kids, he'll decide this chaperone business is a waste of time. He really hates being here, away from Mother. And if he can find a way to quit gracefully, he'll quit."

Dad resigned as chaperone the next day, at Sunday dinner.

"I'm all through wet nursing you," he told the girls. "If you want to go to the dogs—or at any rate to the tea hounds—you're going to have to go by yourselves from now on. I can't take any more of it."

"They're really not bad kids, are they Daddy?" Anne grinned.

"Bad kids? How do I know whether they're bad kids? Naturally they behave when I'm around. But that's not the point. The point is they're making a character out of me. They're setting me up as the meddlesome but harmless old duffer, a kind of big-hearted, well-meaning, asinine, mental eunuch. The boys slap me on the back and the girls pinch me on my cheek and ask me to dance with them. If there's anything I hate, it's a Daddy-Long-Legs kind of father like that."

He turned to Mother.

"I know it's not your fault, Boss, but things would have been a whole lot easier if we had had all boys, like I suggested, instead of starting out with the girls."

From that day on, about the only contact Dad had with the sheiks was over the telephone.

"Some simpleton with pimples in his voice wants to speak to Ernestine," he grumbled to Mother when he answered the phone. "I'll swear, I'm going to have that instrument taken out of here. These tea hounds are running me crazy. I wish they'd sniff around someone else's daughters for awhile, and give us some peace."

Libby Holton, one of the girls in Anne's class, was from Mississippi and had only recently moved with her family to Montclair. She was pretty, mature for her age, and even the straight silhouette styles couldn't hide her figure. She was a heavy painter and wore the highest heels and the shortest skirts in the school. She looked like everything Dad said his daughters shouldn't look like.

Libby was charming and popular. She and Anne became good friends, and Anne finally had her over for lunch. Libby's place was next to Dad's, and she was loaded with perfume—you could smell it the minute she walked into the house. Knowing how Dad disliked make-up and perfume, we were afraid he was going to make Anne's friend change her place at the table or, worse still, order her to go upstairs and wash herself.

We might have saved ourselves the worry, because it soon became apparent that while Dad didn't like perfume on his own daughters, he didn't object to it on other people's daughters.

"My, that smells good," he told Libby after he had been introduced. "I'm glad you're going to sit right here next to me, where I can keep an eye and a nose on you."

"Why, I declare," said Libby. "Anne Gilbreth, you hussy you, why didn't you tell me you had such a gallant Daddy? And so handsome, too."

"Oh, boy," groaned Bill.

Libby turned to Bill and dropped him a slow, fluttering wink. "Ain't I the limit?" she laughed.

"Oh, boy," said Bill. But this time it was more of a yodel than a groan.

Both Anne and Libby worked hard on Dad all during lunch. He saw through them, but he enjoyed it. He imitated Libby's southern accent, called her Honey Chile and You-All, and outdid himself telling stories and jokes.

"I heard from some of the other girls in school about how cute you were," said Libby. "They said the nicest things about you. And they said you used to come to all the dances, too."

"That's right. And if I had known about the Mississippi invasion I would have started going to the dances all over again."

After dessert, we sat around the table wondering what came next. We knew, and so did Dad, that it was a build up for something. Just as Dad finally pushed back his chair, Anne cleared her throat.

"You know, Daddy, there's something I've been wanting to ask you for a long time."

"And now, having been flattered, fattened, and fussed over, the sucker is led forward for the shake-down," Dad grinned. "Well, speak up girls. What is it?"

"Why don't you take this afternoon off and teach Libby and me how to drive the car? We're almost old enough to get licenses, and it would be a big convenience for the whole family if someone besides you knew how to drive."

"Is that all? You didn't need all the sweet-talk for that. I thought you were going to ask me to let you spend the week-end at Coney Island or something." He looked at his watch. "I'm going to have to put some more Neatsfoot oil on the clutch. I'll have the car out front in exactly twelve minutes."

Libby and Anne both threw their arms around his neck.

"I never thought he'd do it," Anne said.

"I told you he'd say yes," Libby grinned. "Mr. Gilbreth, you're a sweet old duck." She planted a kiss on his cheek, leaving two red, lipsticked smears.

The girls rushed out of the dining room to get ready, and Dad rolled his eyes.

"Well, Lillie," he said to Mother, "I guess my spring

chicken days are over. When you start getting pecks on the cheek from your daughters' friends, you're on the decline."

"The first thing I know you'll be greasing your hair and wearing one of those yellow slickers," Mother admonished him with mock severity. "Better wash the lipstick off your face before you go out, sheik."

Dad grinned vacantly, and walked so that his pants cuffs swished like Oxford bags.

"I'm going out and take the fenders off Foolish Carriage," he said. "Four Wheels, No Brakes. The Tin You Love to Touch."

Frank, Bill and Lillian, still in junior high school, resented the infiltration of the high school romeos. What they objected to principally was that the three oldest girls were being turned away from family activities. Anne, Ernestine, and Martha had less and less time for family games, for plays, and skits. It was the inevitable prelude to growing up. It was just a few bars, if you please, professor, of that sentimental little ditty entitled "Those Wedding Bells Are Breaking up That Old Gang of Mine." Marriage was still in the distant future, but the stage was being set.

Anne already had had her first proposal. Joe Scales had asked her to marry him. They were sitting in a hammock on the side porch when he popped the question. The porch was separated by French doors from the parlor and by windows from the office. Frank, Bill and Lillian, lying flat on the parlor floor and peeking through the doors, bore witness to the proposal and to Anne's none-too-original rejection.

"I like to think of you as a brother," she told Scales.

"A fine thing!" Frank whispered to Bill. "Imagine thinking of that wet smack in terms of us."

"You caught me," Scales told Anne. "I went for you, hook, line and sinker. What are you going to do with me?"

Anne was touched by this show of slavish devotion. "What am I going to do with you?" she echoed dramatically.

"Throw him back," Dad roared from the other side of the office window. "He's too small to keep."

Frank, Bill and Lill fought gamely against the invasion, but in vain. More effective, although unpremeditated, were the obstacles erected by the four little boys, Fred, Dan, Jack, and Bob, who kept running in and out of the rooms where the older girls were entertaining their callers.

"I'm living through what can only be described as a hell on earth," Anne moaned to Mother. "It's impossible to entertain at home with that troop of four berserk little boys. Something drastic has got to be done about them."

"What's the matter with them?"

"They're in and out of the porch all evening. Up in my lap, up in my friend's lap, under the hammock, over the hammock, in and out, up and down, over and under, until I'm about to go daft."

"Well, what do you suggest, dear?"

"Tie them down."

At the end of one particular evening, Anne became almost hysterical.

"I'm fed up to the eyeballs with that button brigade," she sobbed. "They're driving me screaming, screeching mad. How can you expect any boy to get into a romantic mood when you have to button and unbutton all evening?"

"They're not supposed to get into romantic moods," Dad said. "That's just what we don't want around here."

Anne paid no attention to him. "It's 'Andy, unbutton me, I have to get undressed.' It's 'Andy button me up, I'm cold.' It's 'Andy, it's three o'clock in the button factory.' I tell you, Mother, it's just too much of a handicap to endure. You're going to have to do something about it, unless you want all your daughters to be old maids."

"You're right," Mother conceded. "I'll do my best to keep them upstairs the next time you have company. I wonder what four sets of leg irons would cost?"

The opposition of Frank, Bill and Lill was less subtle.

"You want to speak to Martha?" Frank would say in an incredulous voice when one of her sheiks would telephone. "You're absolutely sure? You haven't got her mixed up with somebody else? You mean Martha Gilbreth, the one with all the freckles? Oh, mercy! Don't hang up, please. Are you still there? Thank goodness! Please don't hang up."

Then, holding the telephone so that the boy on the other

end could still hear him, Frank would shout desperately:

"Martha, come quick. Imagine! It's a boy calling for you. Isn't that wonderful? Hurry up. He might hang up."

"Give me that phone, you little snake-in-the-grass," Martha would scream in a white rage. "When I get through I'll tear your eyes out, you unspeakable little brat, you." And then, in a honeyed voice, into the mouthpiece. "Helloooo. Who? Well, good looking, where have you been all my life? You have? Well, I've been waiting too. Uh, huh."

One of Ernestine's admirers was shy and subdued, and never could bring himself to tell her what he thought of her. After he had been calling on her for almost a year, he finally mustered his courage and had a beautiful picture taken of himself. Then he inscribed across the bottom of the picture, in purple ink, a very special message.

The message said, "All My Fondest Thoughts Are of You, Dearest Ernestine."

He couldn't bring himself to give the picture to her personally, so he wrapped it up, insured it for one hundred dollars, and sent it through the mail.

Ern kept it hidden in a bureau drawer, but no hiding place in our house was any too safe, and the junior-high-school contingent finally discovered it, memorized it, put it to music, and learned a three-part harmony for it.

The next time the bashful boy came to call, Frank, Bill and Lill, hidden in a closet under the front steps, started to sing:

"All my fondest thoughts,
"(My fondest thoughts)
"Are of you,
"(Yes, nobody else but you)
"My Dearest Ernestine,
"(I don't mean Anne; I don't mean Mart)
"But Dearest Ernestine."

The shrinking sheik turned a bright crimson and actually cringed against the hatrack, while Ernestine picked up one of Dad's walking sticks and started after the younger set, bent on premeditated, cold-blooded mayhem.

As a matter of routine, Frank and Bill would answer the front door when a sheik came to call and subject him to a preliminary going over, designed to make him feel ill at ease for the balance of the evening.

"Look at the suit," Frank would say, opening the coat and examining the inside label. "I thought so. Larkey's Boys Store. Calling all lads to Larkey's College-cut clothes, with two pairs of trousers, for only seventeen fifty. This fellow's a real sport, all right."

"Pipe the snakey socks," Bill would say, lifting up the sheik's pant leg. "Green socks and a blue tie. And yellow shoes."

"You kids cut it out or I'll knock you into the middle of next week," the sheik would protest hopelessly. "Have a heart, will you? Beat it now, and tell your sister I'm here."

Frank brought out a folding ruler that he had slipped into his pocket a few minutes before, and measured the cuffs of the visitor's pants.

"Twenty-three inches," Frank told Bill. "That's collegiate, all right, but it's two inches less collegiate than the cuffs of Anne's sheik. Let's see that tie . . ."

"Let's see his underwear," Bill suggested.

"Hey, stop that," the sheik protested. "Get your hands off of me. Go tell your sister that I'm here, now, or there's going to be trouble."

One of Ernestine's sheiks drove a motorcycle madly around town, and used to buzz our place three or four times a night in hopes of catching sight of her. Mother and Dad didn't allow the boys to come calling on school nights, but there was always a chance Ernestine might be out in the yard or standing by a window.

One night he parked his motorcycle a couple of blocks away, crept up to the house, and climbed a cherry tree near Ernestine's bedroom window. Fortunately for the motorcyclist, Dad was out of town on business.

Ernestine was doing her homework, and had a spooky feeling she was being watched through the open window. It suddenly occurred to her that she hadn't heard the motorcycle go chugging by the house for several hours, and she immediately grew suspicious.

She walked into a dark room, peeked out from behind a

shade, and saw the sheik high up in the cherry tree silhouetted against the moon. She was furious.

"The sneaking peeping tom," she told Anne. "Good golly, I was just about to get undressed. There's no telling what he might have seen, if I hadn't had that creepy feeling I was being watched."

"The sight probably would have toppled him right out of the tree," Anne said a little sarcastically. "Do you think he knows you saw him?"

"I don't know, but I don't think so."

"Come on, we'll peek out that dark window again," Anne said. "If he's still there, I've got an idea."

He was still there, and Anne quickly rounded up Martha, Frank. Bill, and Lillian.

"There's a peeping tom in the cherry tree," Anne explained. "One of Ernestine's. He needs to be taught a lesson. If he gets away with it and tells the other boys around school, our cherry trees are going to look like the bleachers at the Polo Grounds."

"It would certainly play hob with the crop," Frank said.

"Now not a word to Mother," Anne continued, "because she'll play her part better if she doesn't know what's going on. Ernestine, go back into your room and tease him along. Don't pull down your shades. Comb your hair, take off your shoes and socks. Even fiddle around with the buttons on your dress, if you want to. Anything to keep him interested. The rest of you, come with me."

We went down into the cellar, where Anne took some wire and fastened a rag to the end of a stick. The rest of us loaded our arms with old newspapers, excelsior and packing boxes. Then outside Anne poured kerosene over the rag, lighted it, and led a torch parade from the cellar toward the cherry tree.

Ern's sheik was so interested in what seemed about to transpire in her bedroom that he didn't notice us at first. But as the parade drew closer, he looked down. We formed a ring around the base of the tree, and one by one deposited our combustibles at the trunk. As the pile of refuse grew, Anne swung her torch closer and closer to it.

"Christmas," the peeping tom shouted in terror. "Are you

trying to burn me to the stake? Don't set fire to that. You'll roast me alive."

"Precisely," said Anne. "Precisely what you deserve, too. If you know any prayers, start babbling them."

"It was just a prank," he pleaded. "Just a boyish prank, that's all. Watch out for that torch. Let me come down. I'll go quietly."

"Let you come down, nothing," said Martha. "You evil-minded thing you. Let you come down and spread the story all over town about how you climbed our cherry tree and put one over on the Gilbreth family? I should say not."

Anne swung the torch nearer the pile of refuse.

"Look out," the peeping tom shrieked. "You wouldn't roast me alive in cold blood, would you? By God, I believe you would!"

"Of course we would," Frank said. "Dead men tell no tales."

Ernestine stuck her head out of the window.

"Have you got him trapped?" she called. "Good. I've been fiddling with the buttons on my dress so long I'm about to wear all the skin off the tips of my fingers. Is he who I think he is?"

"None other," said Anne. "Motorcycle Mac himself, in the soon-to-be-seared flesh. Treed like a tree toad in a tree."

"Don't cremate him until I get down there," Ernestine begged. "I want to see the fun."

Motorcycle Mac was alternately whimpering and cursing when Ernestine joined the ring around the cherry tree.

"I always thought he was a nasty boy anyway," Ernestine said. "Sheiks are hard to find, and goodness knows I don't have too many of them. But he's one I'll be glad to sacrifice."

"I don't blame you," said Martha. "He's a particularly disagreeable one, all right. He's even a cry baby. I hope when it comes my time to cash in my chips I'll be able to go out with a trace of a smile on my beautiful lips, like Wally Reid."

"Yes," said Anne. "I have the feeling that if anyone has to be cremated, it couldn't happen to a more objectionable sheik."

We had counted on the commotion to attract Mother's

attention, and now she opened her window and put her head out.

"What in the world's going on out there?" she called. "What are you doing with that torch? Which one of you is swinging it? That doesn't look safe to me, children."

"I have it," Anne said. "It's all right, Mother. We've trapped a skunk up in the cherry tree, and we're trying to make him come down."

Mother sniffed the air suspiciously.

"I thought I smelled something," she said. "Now listen, children, I don't think you ought to burn up that cherry tree for any old skunk. Your father is devoted to that tree, and he's devoted to cherry pie. Just come on in the house, and let's see if the skunk won't come down and go away by itself."

"Oh, we weren't really going to burn the tree," Ernestine giggled. "We just wanted to scare hell out of the skunk."

"Ernestine, I forbid that kind of Eskimo language," Mother said, in a shocked tone. "Now I think you'd better come into the house, all of you. It's bedtime, and even a skunk is entitled to some peace and quiet. You've scared him enough for one night. I'll bet his eyes are about to pop out of his head with what he's seen tonight."

Mother disappeared inside the window.

"I'll bet," Ernestine said for the benefit of Motorcycle Mac, "that his eyes were about to pop out of his head with what he *thought* he was going to see. Now slink down out of that cherry tree, you rat you."

"If Dad were here," Bill said, "he'd probably blind him, like they did back in Lady Godiva's day."

"That's just what Dad would do," Anne agreed. "I wish we had thought of that ourselves."

"Should I go get a hatpin?" Frank asked hopefully.

"Too late now," Anne said. "It's past your bedtime. But maybe he'll come back again some other night."

CHAPTER 19

The Party Who Called You . . .

None of us children knew it, but Dad had had a bad heart for years, and now Dr. Burton told him he was going to die.

We noticed that Dad had grown thinner. For the first time in twenty-five years he weighed less than two hundred pounds. He joked about how strange it was to be able to see his feet again. His hands had begun to tremble a little and his face was gray. Sometimes, when he was playing baseball with the older boys or rolling on the floor with Bob and Jane, he'd stop suddenly and say he guessed he had had enough for today. There was a trace of a stagger as he walked away.

He was fifty-five years old, and we supposed his symptoms were those of approaching old age. Certainly it never occurred to any of us that Dad had any intention of dying until he was good and ready to die.

He had known about the bad heart even before Bob and Jane were born. He and Mother had discussed it, and the possibility that she would be left a widow with all the children.

"But I don't think those doctors know what they're talking about," Dad said.

Mother knew the answer Dad wanted.

"I don't see how twelve children would be much more trouble than ten," she told him, "and personally I like to finish what I start. I don't know about you."

The bad heart was one of the principal reasons for Dad's home instruction programs. It was also why he had organized the house on an efficiency basis, so that it would operate smoothly without supervision; so that the older children would be responsible for the younger ones. He knew a load was going to be thrown on Mother, and he wanted to lessen it as much as he could.

"Maybe tomorrow, maybe in six months," Dr. Burton told Dad now. "A year at the outside if you stop work and stay in bed."

"Don't think you can scare me," Dad said. "You doctors have been telling me for three years not to subscribe to any new magazines. Well, I don't believe a word of it. For one thing, I'm in my prime. And for another, I'm too busy."

"Still the Old Pioneer," Dr. Burton grinned.

"Don't think you can scare me," Dad repeated. "I'll be in the amen corner when they're laying you away. I'll see you in church, even if you don't see me."

Dad went home and wrote a letter to a friend, Miss Myrtell Canavan, the Boston brain specialist.

"Dear Mortuary Myrt: If and when I die, I'd like my brain to go to Harvard, where they are doing those brain experiments you told me about. I'd like you to handle the details. My hat size is seven and three-eighths, in case you want to get a jar ready. Don't think this letter means I'm getting ready to go any time soon, because I'm not. I'll leave a copy of this where Lillie will see it when the time comes, and she'll get in touch with you. The next time I see you, I don't want you casting any appraising glances at my cranium."

With the letter mailed, Dad shrugged thoughts of death out of his mind. The World Power Conference and the International Management Conference were going to meet in eight months in England and Czechoslovakia, respectively. Dad accepted invitations to speak at both.

The post-war industrial expansion had resulted in more and more emphasis being placed on motion study. For the first time, both Dad and Mother had more clients than they could handle. Dad went from factory to factory, installing his time-saving systems, reducing worker fatigue, so as to speed up production.

He died on June 14, 1924, three days before he was to sail for Europe for the two conferences.

Dad had walked from our house down to the Lackawanna

Station, a distance of about a mile, where he intended to catch a commuters' train for New York. He had a few minutes before the train left, and he telephoned home to Mother from a pay booth in the station.

"Say, Boss," he said, "on the way down here I had an idea about saving motions on packing those soapflakes for Lever Brothers. See what you think. . . ."

Mother heard a thud and the line went silent. She jiggled the receiver hook.

"I'm sorry," it was the voice of the operator. "The party who called you has hung up."

Jane, the baby, was two years old. Anne, the oldest, was taking her examinations at Smith, where she was a sophomore.

It was Saturday morning. The younger children were playing in the yard. Most of the older ones, members of the purchasing committees, were in town doing the marketing. Six or seven neighbors set out in automobiles to round up those who were missing. The neighbors wouldn't say what the trouble was.

"Your mother wants you home, dear," they told each of us. "There's been an accident. Just slide into the car and I'll drive you home."

When we arrived at the front of the house, we knew the accident was death. Fifteen or twenty cars were parked in the driveway and on the front lawn. Mother? It couldn't be Mother, because they had said Mother wanted us home. Daddy? Accidents didn't happen to Daddy. Somebody fell off his bicycle and was run over? Maybe. All the girls were terrible bicycle riders. Bill was a good rider but took too many chances.

We jumped out of the car and ran toward the house. Jackie was sitting on a terrace near the sidewalk. His face was smudged where he had rubbed his hands.

"Our Daddy's dead," he sobbed.

Dad was a part of all of us, and a part of all of us died then.

They dressed him in his Army uniform, and we went in and looked in the coffin. With his eyes closed and his face gone slack, he seemed stern and almost forbidding. There was no repose there and no trace left of the laugh wrinkles at the corners of his eyes.

We thought that when they came after him, Daddy must have given them a real fight. We bet they had their hands full with Daddy.

Mother found the carbon of the letter to Dad's friend, and the brain went to Harvard. After the cremation, Mother chartered a boat and went out into the Atlantic. Somewhere out there, standing alone in the bow, she scattered his ashes. That was the way Dad wanted it.

There was a change in Mother after Dad died. A change in looks and a change in manner. Before her marriage, all Mother's decisions had been made by her parents. After the marriage, the decisions were made by Dad. It was Dad who suggested having a dozen children, and that both of them become efficiency experts. If his interests had been in basket weaving or phrenology, she would have followed him just as readily.

While Dad lived, Mother was afraid of fast driving, of airplanes, of walking alone at night. When there was lightning, she went in a dark closet and held her ears. When things went wrong at dinner, she sometimes burst into tears and had to leave the table. She made public speeches, but she dreaded them.

Now, suddenly, she wasn't afraid any more, because there was nothing to be afraid of. Now nothing could upset her because the thing that mattered most had been upset. None of us ever saw her weep again.

It was two days after Dad's death, and the house still smelled of flowers. Mother called a meeting of the Family Council. It seemed natural now for her to sit at Dad's place in the chairman's chair, with a pitcher of ice water at her right.

Mother told us that there wasn't much money—most of it had gone back into the business. She said she had talked by telephone with her mother, and that her mother wanted all of us to move out to California.

Anne interrupted to say she planned to leave college anyway and get a job. Ernestine, who had graduated from high school the night before Dad died, said she didn't care anything about college either.

"Please wait until I'm finished," Mother said, and there

was a new note of authority in her voice. "There is another alternative, but it hinges on your being able to take care of yourselves. And it would involve some sacrifices from all of us. So I want you to make the decision.

"I can go ahead with your father's work. We can keep the office open here. We can keep the house, but we would have to let the cook go."

"Tom, too?" we asked. "We couldn't let Tom go, could we? He wouldn't go anyway."

"No, not Tom. But we would have to sell the car and live very simply. Still we could be together. And Anne would go back to college. You know your father wants all of you to go to college.

"Do you want to try it? Can you run the house and take care of things until I get back?"

"Get back from where, Mother?" we asked.

"If you want to try it here," she told us, and she actually rapped the table, "I'm going on that boat tomorrow; the one your father planned to take. He had the tickets. I'm going to give those speeches for him in London and Prague, by jingo. I think that's the way your father wants it. But the decision is up to you."

Ernestine and Martha went upstairs to help Mother pack. Anne disappeared into the kitchen to plan supper. Frank and Bill started down town to see the used car dealers about selling the automobile.

"Better tell them to bring a tow car," Lill called after the boys. "Foolish Carriage never starts for anybody but Daddy."

Someone once asked Dad: "But what do you want to save time *for?* What are you going to do with it?"

"For work, if you love that best," said Dad. "For education, for beauty, for art, for pleasure." He looked over the top of his pince-nez. "For mumblety-peg, if that's where your heart lies."

Seabirds of the World

A Photographic Guide

JEFF BLOOM

Seabirds of the World

A Photographic Guide

Peter Harrison

Princeton University Press

Princeton, New Jersey

JEFF BLOOM

Reprinted 1989, 1996, 2003

Published by Princeton University Press, 41 William Street, Princeton, New Jersey 08540

In the United Kingdom, published by Christopher Helm Publishers Ltd., a subsidiary of
A & C Black Publishers Ltd., 37 Soho Square, London, W1D 3QZ

ISBN 0-691-01551-1

This book has been composed in Century 8 pt

Printed in Hong Kong

10 9 8 7 6 5 4

Front cover: Northern Gannets *Sula bassana* (Mike Wilkes/Aquila)
Back cover: Red-faced Cormorants *Phalacrocorax urile* (David Beadle/Aquila)

CONTENTS

For Carol, Peta and Lea Anne

PREFACE

It should be stated from the outset that this pocket-sized guide cannot possibly hope to condense all the information contained in the 220,000-word-long text of *Seabirds: An Identification Guide* without discarding some information. This is not meant to be a standard work. It has been designed to be a pocket-sized book with the finest and largest collection of seabird photographs ever published.

My first book, *Seabirds: An Identification Guide*, was published in 1983. Since then there have been significant advances, not only in our understanding of seabird biology but also in that of the breeding and pelagic distribution of seabirds. A few months ago, for instance, while working aboard the *MS Society Explorer* as the ornithological lecturer, I, along with Dr Jo Jehl, discovered White-throated Storm-petrels breeding on Sala y Gomez, a range extension of some 1,800 miles (2,900 km). Even more remarkable were the exploits of Watling and Lewanavanua, who after several years of searching managed to find a Fiji Petrel on Gua Island in the Fiji group. This petrel, formerly called Macgillivray's, was known only from one specimen collected at the same island in 1855. Despite its having been seen only twice in 99 years, two photographs, thanks to Dick Watling, are published in this volume. Of equal importance was the discovery of a new albatross on Amsterdam Island in the Indian Ocean by Jean Paul Roux and colleagues. Only eight pairs attempt to breed annually, making it one of the rarest of all birds.

These discoveries are a few examples of the progress being made in our understanding of seabirds, their biology and distribution. In this volume, I have followed the latest taxonomic revisions of such bodies as the American Ornithologists' Union (AOU). Some species therefore have been either lumped or split. The Least Tern, for instance, formerly regarded as the American race of the European Little Tern *Sterna albifrons*, is now elevated to a distinct species *Sterna antillarum*, while Townsend's and Newell's Shearwaters are now lumped following Jehl (1982). In some cases, i.e. the Manx/Balearic/Levantine Shearwater group, I have tried to anticipate future changes and have split the Manx Shearwater as a separate species, treating Balearic/Levantine as dark and light representatives of a new species, the name for which has yet to be decided upon. From the foregoing, it will be seen that seabird taxonomy is vexed and continually changing.

This book has been designed as a pocket-sized companion volume to my first book, *Seabirds: An Identification Guide*. It differs in the exciting concept of using photographs to illustrate the 320 or so seabird species/forms. In total, 741 have been used, which is easily the largest and most complete collection of seabird photographs ever to be published. There has been a great deal of debate as to whether it is better to use photographs or artists' illustrations in bird guides. Both representations have their advantages and disadvantages. In this volume, although it is primarily a photographic guide, we employ black and white drawings in the tubenose identification keys (pp.286–309) — to enjoy the advantages and to offset the disadvantages of each. The black and white identification keys are also included to compensate for some of the minor errors in jizz and shape which indubitably occur in a few of the colour plates in *Seabirds: An Identification Guide*.

This volume, then, and my earlier work *Seabirds: An Identification Guide* are designed as companion volumes, one for the shelf and one for the pocket, to help researchers and amateur birders the world over to identify seabirds in their natural environment, the open ocean. Most importantly, it is hoped that this, my second book, will further help to promote and stimulate the growing interest in seabirds.

ACKNOWLEDGEMENTS

This book could not have been produced without the help of the several hundred photographers who submitted their work for possible inclusion in this guide. To all of those who submitted photographs, whether included in this guide or not, I record my sincere and grateful thanks. Particular mention should be made of photographers Bob Pitman, Ed Mackrill, Richard Webster and Jim Enticott, whose combined photographs account for nearly a third of the 741 photographs contained in this volume. My thanks, too, to David Cottridge, who carefully and masterfully duplicated and enlarged the photographs from the original transparencies.

Especial thanks go to the backroom staff at Christopher Helm Publishers, whose encouragement and help over the years has made the publication of this book possible. In particular, I wish to record my thanks to Christopher Helm and Jo Hemmings. Thanks are also in order to David Christie, long-time friend and copy editor, who has made many suggestions and comments for improvements to the text. David Flumm friend and birding companion for many years, has also been of great assistance, helping with proofreading, selection of photographs and research. Victor Tucker, expert birder and lifelong friend, once again has been most generous and helpful with his time and advice, devoting many hours to checking the manuscript: for all his advice and comments I record my earnest thanks.

As in my previous book, my greatest thanks are reserved for my wife Carol, without whose help this guide could not have been completed. Despite all the times that I have crept from my bed in the early hours of the morning to work on the manuscript, or those long winter months when I am working in the Antarctic or chasing seabirds over the world's oceans, her encouragement and devotion have never wavered. She has typed and re-typed draft upon draft of this manuscript, supervised the collection, duplication and return of many thousands of transparencies, and still found time for her other roles as mother and housewife. Few if any birders have been blessed with such a devoted, cheerful and supportive partner.

Photographic Credits

K. Atkin 41, 47, 519, 522, 529.
R.S. Bailey 255.
S. Bainbridge 181.
R. Barrett 731, 732.
G. Baudoin 204.
K. Beylevelt 475, 479, 543, 651, 725, 749, 751.
D. Boersma 33, 609.
M.A. Brazil 314, 359, 461, 474, 605, 695.
B. Breife 441.
N. Brothers 72.
G.V. Byrd 755, 756.
M.J. Carter 63, 64, 71, 78, 115, 122, 165, 219, 303, 331, 333, 583, 647, 684, 686.
G.P. Catley 39.
R.J. Chandler 516, 545.
D.T. Cheeseman, Jr. 323, 324.
S. Chester/J. Oetzel 34, 80, 157, 158, 227, 228, 289, 325, 326, 443, 450, 584.
N.R. Christensen 31, 32, 43, 349, 649.
R.B. Clapp 250, 253, 453, 511.
D. Clugston 291, 351, 360.
R.J. Connor 371, 372, 661.
C. Corben 116, 220.
D.M. Cottridge 45, 52, 439, 483, 485, 521, 530, 546, 645, 655.
T. Crabtree 56, 429, 541, 627, 754.
D.W. Crumb 427, 499, 501.
L. Cumming 50.
D. Cunningham 44, 51, 348, 405, 484, 491, 537, 639, 728, 764.
R.S. Daniel 59.
R.H. Day 460, 462, 539, 542.
K. de Korte 35, 83, 84, 278, 286, 377, 378, 401, 407, 696, 721.
A. de Kniff 560, 621, 622, 644, 648.
Denstone College Expeditions Trust 243.
J W. de Roever 6, 556, 557.
P. Doherty 524, 526, 553, 633, 660
C. Duncan 722.
N. Dymond 486, 620, 709, 719, 720.
D.W. Eades 119, 580, 634, 656.
M. Egawa 735.
J Enticott 12, 15, 68, 70, 75, 76, 89, 90, 98, 99, 107, 108, 124, 125, 127, 184, 186, 197, 198, 201, 202,

V. Fazio 514, 658.
A. Ferguson 691.
B. Fields 506, 520.
D.J. Fisher 295, 357, 358, 558.
D. Garrick 141, 142, 247, 317, 318.
G. Grant 179, 394, 478, 715.
M. Graybill 464, 734.
E. Greaves 200.
W.E. Harper 88, 196, 199, 510, 525, 632, 744, 745, 752.
M.P. Harris 9, 14, 35, 103, 128, 332, 341, 385, 438, 470.
P. Harrison 1, 2, 5, 7, 8, 10, 25, 58, 61, 65, 67, 69, 74, 77, 79, 94, 95, 96, 102, 104, 110, 111, 113, 114, 133, 139, 148, 153, 154, 155, 156, 163, 164, 195, 245, 246, 270, 271, 272, 290, 304, 305, 306, 330, 334, 336, 337, 339, 340, 350, 356, 364, 365, 368, 369, 389, 390, 391, 392, 395, 398, 399, 400, 413, 414, 415, 421, 422, 423, 435, 440, 442, 447, 448, 454, 465, 466, 480, 481, 496, 497, 568, 569, 571, 572, 574, 575, 577, 578, 588, 595, 598, 607, 617, 618, 636, 669, 670, 671, 672, 680, 699, 700, 702, 703, 707, 708, 723. *Coloured illustrations*: 117, 118, 132, 136, 168, 169, 170, 217, 218, 256, 274, 276, 319, 320, 327, 328, 665, 677, 678, 710, 713, 714, 740.
H. Hasegawa 85, 86, 216, 361, 362, 739.
J. Heino 452, 458, 518.
D.R. Herter 692.
S.J. Hingston 472, 473.
H. Huneker 352, 540, 753.
The late D.B. Hunt 236.
M. Imber 143, 144.
T. Ishikawa 603.
J.R. Jehl, Jr. 129, 131, 224, 275.
P. Johnson 717, 718.
L. Jonsson 648.
T. Keller 49, 55, 288, 446, 630, 657, 716.
A.R. Kitson 562.
A.J. Knystautas/H.Z. Sakalauskas 555.
P. Lansley 221.
L.E. Löfgren 48, 60, 129, 134, 173, 194, 273, 277, 379, 523, 565, 566, 596, 652.
T. Loseby 293, 404, 455, 544, 659.
A. McBride 161, 192, 428.
A. McGeehan 408, 409, 482, 493, 494, 508, 515, 534, 551.
E.J. Mackrill 105, 120, 193, 203, 287, 307, 308, 343, 344, 345, 347, 381, 419, 420, 433, 434, 503, 504, 505, 513, 547, 548, 549, 550, 552, 554, 567, 573, 591, 592, 593, 597, 600, 601, 602, 611, 612, 613, 614, 667, 674, 675, 676, 724.
S.C. Madge 625, 626, 662.
P. Malan 100, 101, 431, 663.
C. Mann 387.
F.W. Mantlik 282, 300, 403, 488, 507, 527, 531, 532.
K. Mauer 458.
P. Meeth 130, 135, 140, 150, 251, 252, 471.
P.L. Meininger 624.
A. Moon 561.
K. Mullarney 299, 375, 402, 451, 564.
K. Nakanure 175, 215, 736.
M. Naughton 146, 254.
R. Naveen 233, 240.
J.B. Nelson 315, 316, 386, 388.
P.J. Nikander, 457.
T. Palliser 425.
J.F. Parnell 370, 629, 641, 650.
D. Paulson 374, 459.
K. Pellow 234, 235.
W.R. Peterson 487.
U. Pfrien 666.
R.L. Pitman 62, 81, 82, 87, 92, 106, 109, 121, 126, 138, 147, 149, 159, 160, 166, 177, 178, 183, 187, 188, 189, 190, 207, 208, 211, 212, 223, 231, 232, 237, 238, 239, 241, 242, 249, 257, 258, 259, 260, 261, 265, 266, 268, 280, 283, 284, 285, 310, 311, 312, 313, 346, 393, 396, 397, 432, 463, 495, 500, 528, 599, 643, 668, 687, 698, 705, 706, 737, 743, 759, 760.
R. Pop 37, 38, 42.
M.K. Poulson 738.
P. Pyle 309, 635, 693, 694, 701.
M.J. Rauzon 17, 145, 176, 329, 338, 697.
D. Robertson 209, 262, 445, 498, 509, 586, 747.
B. Robertson 579, 581, 582.
D.G. Roseneau 533, 726, 741, 742.
J.P. Roux 11, 13, 16, 66, 91, 342, 416, 570, 576, 664, 679, 681.
K. Schafer 3, 467, 761.
O.L. Schmidt 477, 536, 757.
J.C. Sinclair 123, 185, 191, 292, 325, 559, 563, 619, 685.
C. Smith 29, 30, 363, 366, 367.
A. Smythe 222.
B.A. Sorrie 54, 57, 213, 424, 476, 538, 673, 733, 763.
L. Spear 748.
B. Spencer 180, 489.
P. Steyn 269.
K.B. Strann 535, 729, 730.
M.P. Sutherland 437.
J.D. Swenson 53, 279, 353, 355, 704, 727, 758.
I.C. Tait 354, 653.
Y. Tanaka 229, 230, 281.
R.P. Tipper 376, 604, 606, 688.
F. Todd 296, 297, 298, 410, 411, 417, 418, 590, 596, 608, 750, 762.
M. Tove 444.
P. Trull 646.
N. Tucker 373, 615, 616, 711, 712.
A.B. van den Berg 167, 174, 502, 623.
F. van Olphen 492, 610.
N. van Swelm 380, 436.
R.R. Veit 4, 73, 93, 97, 112, 137, 441, 490, 517.
C.R. Veitch 321, 322, 683, 689.
K. Voous 637, 638.
J. Warham 18, 19, 20, 21, 22, 23, 24, 26, 27, 28, 162, 248.
R. Watling 151, 152, 171, 172.
R.E. Webster 40, 46, 210, 214, 225, 226, 263, 264, 267, 406, 426, 449, 468, 469, 512, 518, 585, 587, 589, 628, 631, 642, 654, 690, 746.
D. Wingate 182.

INTRODUCTION

How to Use This Guide

SECTION 1 ACKNOWLEDGEMENTS
Mention is made of all those who have helped in the preparation of text, proofreading and the gathering of photographs, and a list is provided of the photographers and photographic credits.

SECTION 2 INTRODUCTION
This short introduction gives details of how to use this guide followed by a diagram with recognised names of parts of a typical seabird. The six seabird orders and their respective families are then discussed, with particular emphasis on what identification points to look for in each of the groups.

SECTION 3 PHOTOGRAPHIC PLATES
There are 741 colour photographs in this guide, easily the largest collection of seabird photographs ever to be published in a single volume. Most species are illustrated with two photographs, but in the more problematical groups — gulls, skuas/jaegers and frigatebirds — there are four photographs per species. Where possible, similar species which occur in the same geographical area have been grouped together for ease of reference. The month the photograph was taken, if known, is also included.

The photographs have been chosen to aid identification. Birds in flight, even though slightly blurred or at long range, have been chosen in preference to crisp portrait shots of sitting/standing birds as this is how most of them are seen over their environment, the ocean. Some reviewers would no doubt have preferred portraits, but this is a book intended for the field-glass fraternity and I make no apologies. In some species, e.g. Barau's Petrel, the photograph, although poor by some standards, is the best ever taken and, as seabirders, we are fortunate that such a rare, and little-known, petrel has at last been captured on film. In cases like Barau's Petrel one photograph has been included, and, to balance the treatment, an illustration has been included by the author. Where a species has been illustrated by two paintings instead of photographs this was because no photographs were available. I urge all bird photographers to try to capture these last remaining seabirds on film for possible inclusion in future editions of this book. Also, if you think that you have a better photograph than the one appearing in this book please let me know about it.

SECTION 4 DESCRIPTIVE TEXT AND DISTRIBUTION MAPS
Each species description begins with the English and the scientific name, followed by length (denoted L) and wingspan (denoted W). Thus L40cm/16in W92cm/36in reads length 40 centimetres/16 inches, wingspan 92 centimetres/32 inches. This is followed by a photographic reference number (denoted **P** plus page number), and, where appropriate, an identification-key number (**K** plus page number). The descriptive text is divided into four main sections:
IDENTIFICATION: The bird's general appearance and most important identification characters are noted. Where one species looks similar to another within the same geographical area, a brief, 'Differs from . . .' paragraph provides a list of characters to help avoid possible misidentifications. Where a species exhibits sexual dimorphism, males and females are described separately, as are seasonal differences under the headings of **Adult Winter**, **Adult Summer**. Juvenile/immature plumages are also

described, but it must be emphasised that this is only a pocket guide and is designed as a pocket-sized companion volume to *Seabirds: An Identification Guide.* A fuller, more expansive treatment of immature gulls, skuas/jaegers, frigatebirds etc will be found in that work and is outside the scope of this book. Nevertheless, the treatment given to these problematical groups is generally more comprehensive and detailed than in many guides. The identification characters to look for within each seabird family are given between pages 14 and 19.

HABITS: A brief account of habits is given: whether a colonial or solitary breeder; or an inveterate ship follower; or perhaps a note on whether a particular species is gregarious at sea. In many cases, e.g. storm-petrels, flight is an important identification character, and, where necessary, differences in flight between respective species are given. A general discussion on the habits of each of the seabird families can be found between pages 14 and 19.

DISTRIBUTION: This section should be read in conjunction with the maps at left of the main text. It gives a general account of the oceans/areas in which a particular species is found; where and at what time of year it breeds (unless breeding is protracted throughout year, depending on location); and brief notes on movements/ migration. Once again, serious students are urged to consult *Seabirds: An Identification Guide* for detailed accounts of breeding islands, egg-dates, fledging and departure dates, migration etc. It should also be noted that the maps should be regarded only as a basic summary of our incomplete knowledge. There is a great deal yet to be learnt about the pelagic distribution of many seabirds, and in the case of some we do not even know where they breed.

SIMILAR SPECIES: Lists those species with which the bird is most likely to be confused within its geographical area.

SECTION 5 IDENTIFICATION KEYS

For the first time in any publication, the Procellariiformes, comprising 92 species in 23 genera, have been arranged into 24 pages of identification keys. Wherever possible, species which look alike or which share the same geographical area have been grouped together for ease of reference. For speedy identification, arrows have been employed to draw the user's attention to the key field characters of each species. These points are further emphasised in the text.

SECTION 6 BIBLIOGRAPHY

A short bibliography is provided.

SECTION 7 INDEX

Fully cross-referenced index to scientific and all commonly used English names. The index in this guide includes check-off boxes beside the common name entry for each species; you can use this as your seabird checklist.

MAP KEY

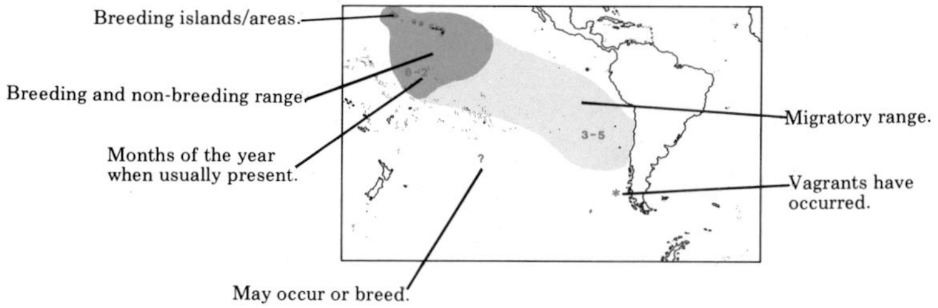

Topography of a Seabird

1 Upper mandible
2 Lower mandible
3 Iris
4 Legs/feet
5 Forehead
6 Crown
7 Nape
8 Hindneck
9 Ear-coverts/cheek
10 Chin
11 Gular stripe
12 Throat
13 Foreneck
14 Mantle
15 Back
16 Rump
17 Uppertail-coverts
18 Breast
19 Belly
20 Flank/side
21 Thigh
22 Ventral area
23 Undertail-coverts
24 Primaries
25 Secondaries
26 Primary-coverts
27 Alula
28 Greater coverts
29 Median coverts
30 Lesser coverts
31 Marginal coverts
32 Carpal joint
33 Underwing-coverts
34 Axillaries
35 Scapulars
36 Tail

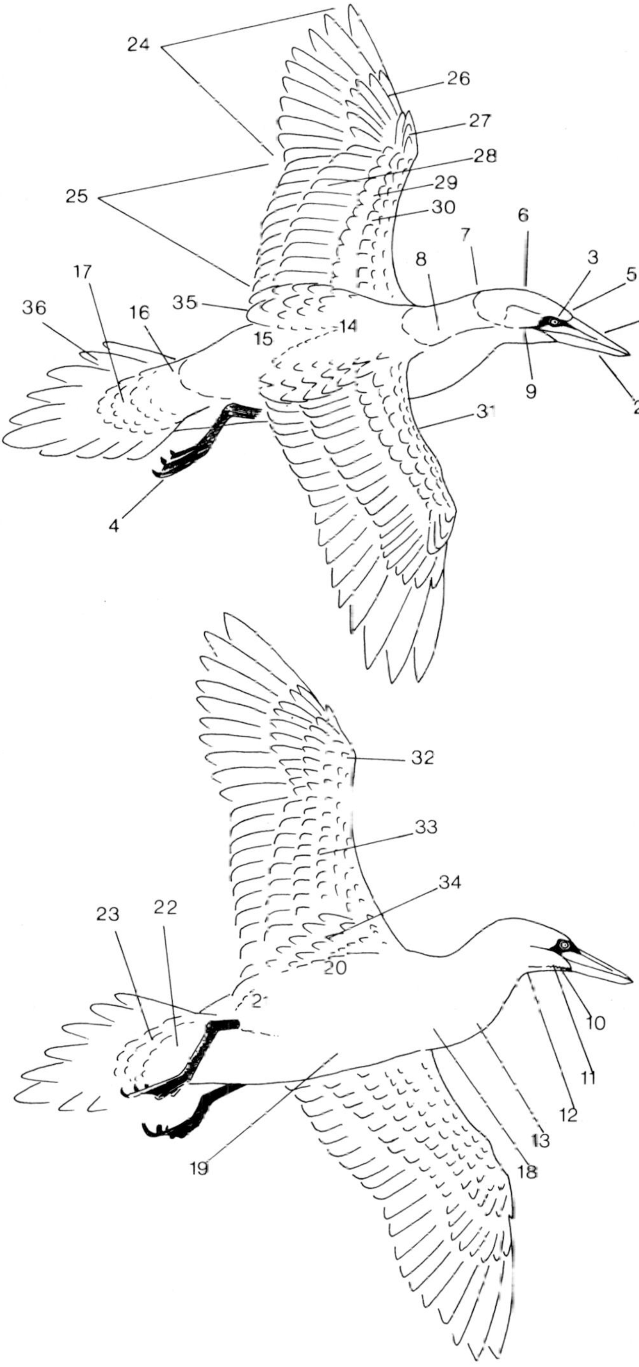

Seabird Orders

In zoological classification all birds are placed in the class Aves. This class is then divided into orders, which are further subdivided to form one or more families; these are then once again subdivided to yield species and subspecies. It should be noted that seabird taxonomy is vexed and not fully agreed upon; the number of species in a given family will therefore vary among different taxonomic authorities. In this guide I have followed the recent second edition of Peters's *Checklist of the Birds of the World* (Mayr & Cottrell 1979), although I have not followed the new sequence of orders and families. The nomenclature for Charadriiformes is based on Howard & Moore's *A Complete Checklist of the Birds of the World* (1980). In a number of cases I have 'split' or 'lumped' species, following more recent revisions by such authorities as the AOU.

Order SPHENISCIFORMES

Family SPHENISCIDAE Penguins

Six genera comprising 16-18 species, all flightless, stocky, aquatic birds. Their rigid flippers are modified wings which enable them to 'fly' through water with the ease with which most terrestrial species fly through the air. On land, however, they move awkwardly, with waddling gait or clumsy hop.

Most of the species occur in the bountiful Southern Oceans bordering Antarctica and its remote sub-Antarctic islands, although one, the Galapagos Penguin, occurs on the Equator, but in an area influenced by a cold-water current. They vary in size from the Emperor Penguin, standing over 1 metre high, to the diminutive Little Penguin, 40 centimetres high; sexes are outwardly similar, males averaging slightly larger.

Identification at colonies, where most penguins are tame and confiding, is straightforward, but not so at sea owing to their low profile and cryptic coloration; they also dive at the approach of ships. In all cases it is important accurately to record colours/patterns of head and bill and fleshy margins at base of bill.

Order GAVIIFORMES

Family GAVIIDAE Divers/loons

Single genus containing 4–5 species (status of *G. (a.) pacifica* currently under review). These are large, mainly fish-eating, foot-propelled swimming/diving birds which breed at freshwater locations in northern Holarctic area but disperse south to more marine locations during non-breeding season. In all species juvenile plumage is held through the first winter and first summer, during which time they resemble adults in non-breeding plumage but have more white on upperparts, giving them a scaly look.

Identification of birds in breeding plumage is straightforward, but more difficult in juvenile/non-breeding plumage. Key identification points to note are bill size, shape and colour; head shape and colour, whether lighter or darker than upperparts; amount of darkness on sides of neck, and whether a regular or irregular division.

All except Red-throated Diver require a long run to become airborne from both land and water but, once aloft, flight is swift and powerful with neck extended forward and down, imparting characteristic humpbacked jizz with feet projecting beyond tail. With experience, divers can be identified in flight by difference in height and speed of wing strokes plus overall jizz and colour.

Order PODICIPEDIFORMES

Family PODICIPEDIDAE Grebes

Six genera comprising about 50 distinct forms but usually reduced to some 20 species, one or more of which occur on all major landmasses except Antarctica. Unlike the treatment of this order in *Seabirds: An Identification Guide* (Harrison 1983), only the six Northern Hemisphere species (which are generally more marine in habits during non-breeding season) have been included in this pocket guide. They are small to medium-sized swimming/diving birds, rarely seen in flight, with lobed feet which act as a rudder both in flight and when swimming (all grebes lack a functional tail). Sexes are normally alike but may differ in size; most species have elaborate courtship displays.

All six species treated in this guide have a breeding and non-breeding plumage; juveniles resemble non-breeding adults, but usually have stripes on sides of face and neck. Identification of breeding birds straightforward, but more difficult in winter/juvenile plumages, when colour, length and proportions of bill, head and neck should be accurately recorded. It should be noted, however, that the jizz of a floating bird, particularly apparent length of neck, can vary depending on whether the bird is alert, alarmed or sleeping.

Order PROCELLARIIFORMES

Albatrosses, petrels and shearwaters, storm-petrels, diving-petrels

Family DIOMEDEIDAE Albatrosses

Two genera comprising 14 species, which includes the recently described Amsterdam Albatross *Diomedea amsterdamensis* (Roux *et al.* 1983). Some authorities, however, consider the three *cauta* subspecies as good species, which would make a total of 16 species. Albatrosses, the largest of all seabirds, are huge, long-winged birds which visit land only to breed, sometimes in large colonies, chiefly on remote oceanic islands. They are long-lived and normally pair for life. Sexes outwardly alike except in Wandering Albatross *Diomedea exulans*, females of which resemble immature males. Three species are to be found in the North Pacific, one in the tropical Pacific and ten in the Southern Hemisphere. Generally albatrosses are easily recognised by combination of great size (but see also giant petrels p.191) and peerless, soaring flight, their long, thin, stiffly held wings carrying them effortlessly over the ocean. In calm conditions, however, they have a ponderous flapping flight, preferring instead to roost on the water until more favourable conditions prevail. They feed chiefly on fish, squid and refuse from ships' galleys; most are thus inveterate ship followers, making them one of the more easily viewed and most familiar of Southern Hemisphere seabird groups.

Identifying albatrosses at sea can be problematical, particularly if inexperienced. In many species bill coloration is diagnostic, but difficult to record with medium- or long-range observations. Under these conditions concentrate chiefly on accurately recording overall colour patterns, particularly those of underwing in the smaller albatrosses, and if conditions permit use bill and head coloration to confirm identification.

Family PROCELLARIIDAE Fulmars, prions, petrels and shearwaters

The most diverse group within the order Procellariiformes; twelve genera comprising about 55 species ranging in size from the huge giant petrels to diminutive prions. Unlike albatrosses, which have single nostrils placed on each side of their hook-tipped bills, all Procellariidae have their nostrils united in a single tube and placed on the top of the bill (hence vernacular term tubenosed). They are highly pelagic, ranging over the ocean with bursts of rapid wingbeats followed by stiff-winged glides; they return to land only to breed. Like albatrosses they lay only one egg.

Sexes outwardly similar with (thankfully) little or no difference between breeding, non-breeding and immature plumages. The various forms can be divided into four natural groups:

Fulmars: Includes the two species of giant petrel, which can be difficult to identify at sea, but others within the group, the Pintado, Antarctic and Snow Petrels and two species of fulmar, are straightforward.

Prions: *Pachyptila* and monotypic *Halobaena* are small, blue-grey petrels, restricted to Southern Oceans, with distinctive 'M' mark across upperparts and black-tipped tails. They are difficult, almost impossible to identify at sea without comparative experience. Concentrate on bill proportions/colour, head pattern and extent of black on tail. The Blue Petrel is easily identified by its diagnostic white-tipped tail.

Gadfly-petrels: *Pterodroma* and *Bulweria* species present one of the most challenging of all seabird groups to identify; identification criteria for many are still evolving. They are widely distributed, but generally confined to tropical and subtropical seas, particularly in Pacific Ocean; some species, e.g. Kerguelen Petrel, range south to 50°S. Identification is fraught with problems, not least of which is the polymorphic tendencies of some species which then resemble similar sibling species. Difficulty of identification further enhanced in that most do not readily follow ships nor are attracted to galley waste; views are thus fleeting and at long range.

It is important accurately to record head markings, upperwing patterns and exact distribution of underwing margins. Some species have characteristic flight actions which aid identification .

Large petrels and shearwaters: *Procellaria, Calonectris* and *Puffinus* differ from the *Pterodroma* group in having long, slender (not short and stubby) bills, and straighter, stiffly held wings not angled and flexed at the wrist. In all sightings, bill and feet colour, plus underwing patterns, are important field characters. Some species have characteristic flight actions which aid identification.

Family OCEANITIDAE Storm-petrels

Smallest of Procellariiformes; seven genera comprising about 20 species arranged into two main groups, one in each of the hemispheres. The southern genera (*Oceanites, Garrodia, Pelagodroma, Fregetta* and *Nesofregetta*) are characterised by long legs and short rounded wings. The northern genera (*Hydrobates* and *Oceanodroma*) have short legs and, usually, longer and more pointed wings.

Owing to their small size and generally similar coloration, identification of storm-petrels is difficult, even for the experienced birder. In this respect, flight and feeding action are as important to note down as the degree and extent of white on rump and lateral undertail-coverts, wing markings and both wing and tail shape. It should be noted, however, that strong wind can often alter the normal flight of any seabird.

For all serious students the excellent four-part series on storm-petrel identification by Naveen (1981) is recommended for further reading.

Family PELECANOIDIDAE Diving-petrels

Four species, restricted to Southern Oceans. Diving-petrels are small, dumpy, short-winged seabirds, black above, white below. Flight is extremely fast and low over waves on whirring wings, occasionally flying through crests without so much as a pause. When entering water they simply crash or fall into waves and disappear; they emerge in the same manner, exploding in a flurry of whirring wings and making off in low, contour-hugging flight.

Identification of diving-petrels at sea is usually impossible owing to similarities in plumage, small size, and fast skimming flight which precludes observation of the critical features. Even in the hand some birds defy specific identification.

Order PELECANIFORMES

Pelicans, boobies, cormorants, frigatebirds, tropicbirds, anhingas

Family PHAETHONTIDAE Tropicbirds

Three species in single genus, the smallest members of the Pelecaniformes. They are distributed throughout tropical and subtropical latitudes of all three major oceans, where they are mainly pelagic outside breeding season and mostly solitary. They have a graceful, pigeon-like flight, fluttering wing strokes alternated with soaring glides producing characteristic 'butterfly progression'. Feed by plunge-diving, after which they often sit on water with their long tails (adults) cocked.

Tropicbirds are mostly white, and adults are identified by combination of bill and tail-streamer colour. Sexes are alike. There is no seasonal difference in plumage, but juveniles/immatures are strongly barred on upperparts, lack tail streamers and are difficult to distinguish from each other at sea.

Family PELECANIDAE Pelicans

Seven or eight species in single genus, distinctive owing to size. Plumage is mostly white and black (5 species); greyish (1 species); or brown (2 species). They are distributed throughout most tropical and temperate regions of both hemispheres and are social, often breeding, fishing and flying together. They have long bills with large distensible pouch which is used as a scoop net when fishing and not, as is popularly believed, to carry food in. They are found in both marine and freshwater locations.

Sexes alike; slight seasonal variations in plumage. Juveniles/immatures similar but marked with brown, grey or white and have different bare-part colours from adults. Where sympatric black-and-white-plumaged forms occur, identification should be based on extent of black on wings and bare-parts coloration.

Family SULIDAE Boobies, gannets

Nine species in single genus comprising 6 boobies and 3 species of gannet. Boobies are generally smaller than gannets and are found in tropical and subtropical oceans. Gannets are distributed in more temperate oceans, but range into or towards tropical regions during non-breeding season. All have long, narrow wings, tapered tail and tapered bill. All are gregarious, both at colonies and also during non-breeding season, when boobies return to land to roost whereas gannets rest on the open ocean. At sea, boobies and gannets are conspicuous owing to their large size, high flight over ocean, and spectacular plunge-diving habits, falling like spears to secure fish and squid. Flight is usually direct, with alternating periods of flapping broken by glides producing steady undulating progression, groups of birds often flying in lines.

Sexes usually alike; no marked seasonal variation, although juveniles and some immatures have markedly different plumage from adults. Identification of adults should be based on head, body, primary and tail coloration. Leg and bill colours are also useful to note, but only the Blue-footed and Red-footed Boobies have diagnostic bare-part colours. Juveniles/immatures are more difficult to identify, but present no real problems when head and underwing patterns are accurately recorded.

Family PHALACROCORACIDAE Cormorants/shags

The most successful and diverse family of the Pelecaniformes order. One genus (although *Nannopterum* sometimes retained for flightless Galapagos Cormorant) with 32 different forms, usually treated as 27 or 28 species. They are small to large-sized birds inhabiting both marine and freshwater localities along temperate and tropical coasts and inland waterways; some species are found in Arctic and Antarctic regions. All are underwater pursuit swimmers characterised by hooked bills, long necks, elongated bodies and longish tails. Some species are gregarious throughout the year, foraging and roosting together. Sexes normally alike, males averaging larger; seasonal variation, often marked, particularly in extent and colour of facial skin and prenuptial head plumes. Juveniles/immatures differ from adults.

Size and jizz, together with details of the colours of any facial skin (which is often diagnostic), crests, or white on head and neck should be accurately recorded.

Family FREGATIDAE Frigatebirds

Five species in single pantropical genus; they neither walk nor swim and are thus one of the most aerial of all seabirds. All are large and spectacular birds with long wings and deeply forked tails which soar high over ocean, from where they plummet to chase and harry boobies and terns or snatch at offal and fish. All are colonial breeders, usually in small groups, and are unusual in biennial breeding and long juvenile dependency period.

All five species are sexually dimorphic, which, coupled with the seemingly arbitrary variety of juvenile and immature plumages which can last up to six years, renders them one of the most difficult of all seabird groups to identify. There are no fewer than 60 recognisably different plumage patterns for the five species. Identification at sea is thus notoriously difficult. In all observations it is crucial accurately to record distribution of white on underparts and underwing (if present). Pay particular attention to how far the white extends towards vent and whether it encroaches onto the underwing as narrow 'spurs'. Breastbands, and their comparative width and shape are also important identification characters, together with head colour.

Unfortunately space prevents inclusion of the black and white frigatebird identification keys from *Seabirds: An Identification Guide* (Harrison 1983), but readers are urged to consult that work for further information regarding this difficult group.

Order CHARADRIIFORMES

Shorebirds, skuas, gulls, terns, skimmers, auks

Family PHALAROPODIDAE Phalaropes

Three species in single genus which breed in Northern Hemisphere and winter to the south. Two species, the Red and Red-necked, spend the non-breeding season at sea, where gregarious, floating like corks, occasionally spinning while picking at minute organisms on surface. The third species, Wilson's, winters on shores and lakes of South America. All three have lobed toes and are unusual in that the sexual roles are reversed, the females being larger and more colourful than the males, who incubate the eggs and care for the chicks. In winter, plumage of both sexes similar.

Breeding birds distinctive; in winter/juvenile plumage, colour of upperparts, wingbars and length and proportions of bill and head are important identification criteria.

Family STERCORARIIDAE Skuas/jaegers

Six or seven species in two genera; medium to large, brown or brown and white piratical seabirds which breed in higher latitudes of both hemispheres, migrating towards or to opposite hemisphere in their respective winters. Sexes similar but females in both genera average larger.

The larger *Catharacta* are robust, gull-like birds, with mostly brown plumage except for conspicuous white area at base of primaries. The smaller *Stercorarius* are more dashing and falcon-like and during the breeding season have elongated tail streamers, the shape of which is diagnostic. In all *Catharacta* observations it is important to note colour tones of plumage (cold or warm), presence of hackles or collar on head, paler tips (or lack of) to upperparts, contrast between underbody and underwings, elongation of tail feathers (some species, e.g. Chilean and South Polar, have noticeable rounded tail projections).

Stercorarius are just as taxing in winter/juvenile/immature plumages. Particular attention should be paid to degree of contrast on upperwing (see Long-tailed Skua), number and extent of white primary shafts, details of barring on uppertail- and undertail-coverts and, at close range, exact shape of tail projections. In the final analysis, however, it is often jizz, the combination of size, shape and form, that will provide the vital clues to enable identification. Unlike *Catharacta* species (except South Polar), the three *Stercorarius* species are dimorphic and differ further from all *Catharacta* in having a distinct non-breeding plumage. This complicates identification and, owing to some overlap in plumage features, specific identification is not always possible even when birds are seen well.

Family LARIDAE Gulls, terns, noddies

About 87 species in ten or twelve genera, although even the number of genera is not fully agreed upon by systematists.

The 45 species of gull are usually larger than terns, are found predominantly in the Northern Hemisphere and, in adult plumage, are mostly white and grey with black and white on the wingtips. All can be identified by wing and head pattern, bill and leg coloration. Males average larger than females but are otherwise similar; many have different winter/summer plumages. Maturity is reached in 2–4 years with several immature plumage stages, but head, wingtip and bare-parts coloration enables ready identification during these immature plumages.

Serious students are urged to consult Peter Grant's excellent work *Gulls: A Guide to Identification* (1982).

There are some 42 species of tern; they differ from gulls in generally smaller size, forked tail, longer, more slender and pointed wings giving more graceful proportions, and plunge-diving habits. Many, e.g. Arctic Tern (p.265), undertake long migrations. Like the gulls, they inhabit chiefly coastal or inshore waters, with some species on inland waterways, marshes etc. Males average larger than females, and most species have a different non-breeding plumage, usually relating to the extent of black on head. Juveniles/immatures are variably marked with brown and grey and have duller bare parts, but like the adults can be identified by bare-part colours, wing pattern and head colour.

Family RYNCHOPIDAE Skimmers

Three species in a single genus; one each in Americas, Africa and Asia. All three are mainly dark above and white below; characterised by long bill with knife-like mandibles compressed to thin blades, the lower mandible longer than the upper, a unique feature. When feeding, they fly low above the surface with tip of lower mandible ploughing shallowly through the water; when lower mandible strikes prey, bill snaps shut. Active mainly at dusk and dawn; sociable at all times.

Skimmers frequent coastal regions and larger inland rivers and lakes. As ranges of species do not overlap, locality of sighting usually sufficient for identification.

Family ALCIDAE Auks

Twenty-two species in eleven genera, confined to Northern Hemisphere. Most are black and white and usually have colourful bare parts and/or nuptial head plumes. Sexes are outwardly alike, males averaging slightly larger; most show some seasonal variation in plumage.

All are skilful divers and swimmers, using their wings to 'fly' underwater; they are the ecological counterpart of the Southern Oceans penguins. Most breed in huge colonies at sites ranging from mountain slopes to holes, burrows and ledges on sea cliffs.

Depending on conditions, but particularly when in flight at long range, identification can be problematical. Record accurately distribution of black and white, colours of bare parts, nuptial crests/ornaments etc, which are often diagnostic.

PHOTOGRAPHIC PLATES

(1) **King Penguin** (Adult; Apr)
Aptenodytes patagonicus Text p.176

(2) **King Penguin** (Imm.; Feb)
Aptenodytes patagonicus Text p.176

(3) **Emperor Penguin** (Adult; Mar)
Aptenodytes forsteri Text p.176

(4) **Emperor Penguin** (Adult; Feb)
Aptenodytes forsteri Text p.176

(5) **Gentoo Penguin** (Adult, chick; Jan)
Pygoscelis papua Text p.176

(6) **Gentoo Penguin** (Adult; juv.)
Pygoscelis papua Text p.176

(7) **Chinstrap Penguin** (Adult; Jan)
Pygoscelis antarctica Text p.177

(8) **Chinstrap Penguin** (Adult, chick; Feb)
Pygoscelis antarctica Text p.177

(9) **Adélie Penguin** (Adult; Feb)
Pygoscelis adeliae Text p.177

(10) **Adélie Penguin** (Adult, chick; Feb)
Pygoscelis adeliae Text. p.177

(11) **Macaroni Penguin** (Adult)
Eudyptes chrysolophus Text p.177

(12) **Macaroni Penguin** (Imm.)
Eudyptes chrysolophus Text p.177

(13) **Royal Penguin** (Adult; May)
Eudyptes (chrysolophus) schlegeli
Text p.178

(14) **Royal Penguin** (Adult, chick; Feb)
Eudyptes (chrysolophus) schlegeli
Text p.178

(15) **Rockhopper Penguin** (Adult)
Eudyptes c. chrysocome
Text p.178

(16) **Rockhopper Penguin** (Adult)
Eudyptes c. moseleyi
Text p.178

(17) **Fiordland Crested Penguin** (Adult; Mar)
Eudyptes pachyrhynchus Text p.178

(18) **Fiordland Crested Penguin** (Adult; Sep)
Eudyptes pachyrhynchus Text p.178

(19) **Snares Island Penguin** (Adult; Dec)
Eudyptes robustus Text p.179

(20) **Snares Island Penguin** (Imm; Nov)
Eudyptes robustus Text p.179

(21) **Erect-crested Penguin** (Adult; Feb)
Eudyptes sclateri Text p.179

(22) **Erect-crested Penguin** (Adult; Feb)
Eudyptes sclateri Text p.179

(23) **Yellow-eyed Penguin** (Adult)
Megadyptes antipodes Text p.179

(24) **Yellow-eyed Penguin** (Adult)
Megadyptes antipodes Text p.179

(25) **Little Penguin** (Adult)
Eudyptula minor Text p.180

(26) **Little Penguin** (Adult)
Eudyptula minor Text p.180

(27) **White-flippered Penguin** (Adult, chick; Nov)
Eudyptula (minor) albosignata Text p.180

(28) **White-flippered Penguin** (Adult; Nov)
Eudyptula (minor) albosignata Text p.180

(29) **Jackass Penguin** (Imm., adult; Oct)
Spheniscus demersus Text p.180

(30) **Jackass Penguin** (Adult; Nov)
Spheniscus demersus Text p.180

(31) **Humboldt Penguin** (Adult; Aug)
Spheniscus humboldti Text p.181

(32) **Humboldt Penguin** (Adult; Aug)
Spheniscus humboldti Text p.181

(33) **Magellanic Penguin** (Adult, imm; Oct)
Spheniscus magellanicus Text p.181

(34) **Magellanic Penguin** (Adult; Feb)
Spheniscus magellanicus Text p.181

(35) **Galapagos Penguin** (Imm., adult)
Spheniscus mendiculus Text p.181

(36) **Galapagos Penguin** (Adult)
Spheniscus mendiculus Text p.181

(37) **Great Northern Diver** (Adult; Jan)
Gavia immer Text p.182

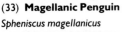

(38) **Great Northern Diver** (1st Winter; Jan)
Gavia immer Text p.182

(39) **White-billed Diver** (Adult; Feb)
Gavia adamsii Text p.182

(40) **White-billed Diver** (1st Winter; Dec)
Gavia adamsii Text p.182

(41) **Black-throated Diver** (Adult Winter)
Gavia arctica Text p.183

(42) **Black-throated Diver** (1st Winter)
Gavia arctica Text p.183

(43) **Pacific Diver** (Adult; June)
Gavia (arctica) pacifica Text p.182

(44) **Pacific Diver** (1st Summer, adult; May)
Gavia (arctica) pacifica Text p.182

(45) **Red-throated Diver** (Adult Summer)
Gavia stellata Text p.183

(46) **Red-throated Diver** (1st Winter; Jan)
Gavia stellata Text p.183

(47) **Great Crested Grebe** (Adult Summer)
Podiceps cristatus Text p.183

(48) **Great Crested Grebe** (Adult; June)
Podiceps cristatus Text p.183

(49) **Red-necked Grebe** (Adult Summer)
Podiceps grisegena Text p.185

(50) **Red-necked Grebe** (1st Winter)
Podiceps grisegena Text p.185

(51) **Horned Grebe** (Adult; May)
Podiceps auritus Text p.185

(52) **Horned Grebe** (Adult Winter)
Podiceps auritus Text p.185

(53) **Black-necked Grebe** (Adult; May)
Podiceps nigricollis Text p.185

(54) **Black-necked Grebe** (Adult; Mar)
Podiceps nigricollis Text p.185

(55) **Western Grebe** (Adult dark phase)
Aechmophorus occidentalis Text p.184

(56) **Western Grebe** (Adult light phase)
Aechmophorus o. clarkii Text p.184

(57) **Pied-billed Grebe** (Adult; Feb)
Podilymbus podiceps Text p.184

(58) **Pied-billed Grebe** (Adult; Feb)
Podilymbus podiceps Text p.184

(59) **Little Grebe** (Adult; May)
Tachybaptus ruficollis Text p.184

(60) **Little Grebe** (Adult Winter)
Tachybaptus ruficollis Text p.184

(61) **Wandering Albatross** (Adult)
Diomedea exulans Text p.186

(62) **Wandering Albatross** (Juv.; May)
Diomedea exulans Text p.186

(63) **Royal Albatross** (Adult)
Diomedea e. epomophora Text p.186

(64) **Royal Albatross** (Juv.; Aug)
Diomedea e. epomophora Text p.186

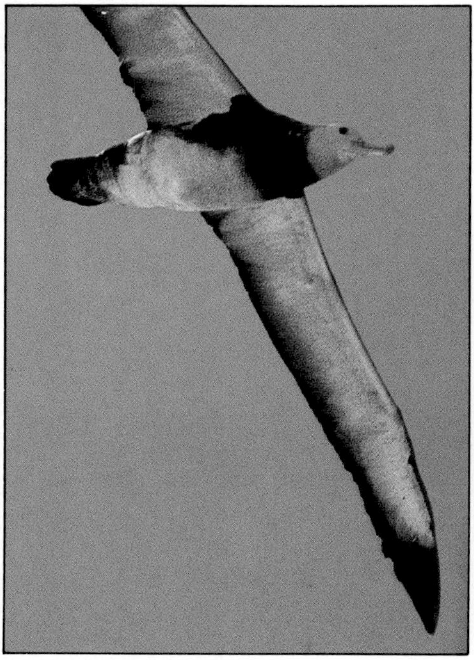

(65) **Amsterdam Albatross**
Diomedea amsterdamensis Text p.186

(66) **Amsterdam Albatross**
Diomedea amsterdamensis Text p.186

(67) **White-capped Albatross** (Adult)
Diomedea c. cauta Text p.187

(68) **White-capped Albatross** (Imm.)
Diomedea c. cauta Text p.187

(69) **Salvin's Albatross** (Adult)
Diomedea (cauta) salvini Text p.187

(70) **Salvin's Albatross** (Imm.)
Diomedea (cauta) salvini Text p.187

(71) **Chatham Island Albatross** (Adult; June)
Diomedea (cauta) eremita Text p.187

(72) **Chatham Island Albatross** (Adult; Jan)
Diomedea (cauta) eremita Text p.187

(73) **Black-browed Albatross** (Adult; Mar)
Diomedea melanophris Text p.188

(74) **Black-browed Albatross** (Juv.)
Diomedea melanophris Text p.188

(75) **Grey-headed Albatross** (Adult)
Diomedea chrysostoma Text p.188

(76) **Grey-headed Albatross** (Imm.)
Diomedea chrysostoma Text p.188

(77) **Yellow-nosed Albatross** (Adult)
Diomedea c. chlororhynchos Text p.188

(78) **Yellow-nosed Albatross** (imm., Sep)
Diomedea chlororhynchos bassi Text p.188

(79) **Buller's Albatross** (Adult)
Diomedea bulleri Text p.189

(80) **Buller's Albatross** (Adult; Feb)
Diomedea bulleri Text p.189

(81) **Laysan Albatross** (Apr)
Diomedea immutabilis Text p.189

(82) **Laysan Albatross**
Diomedea immutabilis Text p.189

(83) **Waved Albatross** (Adult)
Diomedea irrorata Text p.190

(84) **Waved Albatross** (Adult)
Diomedea irrorata Text p.190

(85) **Short-tailed Albatross** (Adult; Mar)
Diomedea albatrus Text p.189

(86) **Short-tailed Albatross** (Imm.)
Diomedea albatrus Text p.189

(87) **Black-footed Albatross** (Adult; May)
Diomedea nigripes Text p.190

(88) **Black-footed Albatross** (Imm.; Feb)
Diomedea nigripes Text p.190

(89) **Sooty Albatross** (Adult)
Phoebetria fusca Text p.190

(90) **Sooty Albatross** (Adult)
Phoebetria fusca Text p.190

(91) **Light-mantled Sooty Albatross** (Adult)
Phoebetria palpebrata Text p.191

(92) **Light-mantled Sooty Albatross** (Imm., adult)
Phoebetria palpebrata Text p.191

(93) **Northern Giant Petrel** (Adult; Mar)
Macronectes halli Text p.191

(94) **Northern Giant Petrel** (Adult; Feb)
Macronectes halli Text p.191

(95) **Southern Giant Petrel** (Adult)
Macronectes giganteus Text p.191

(96) **Southern Giant Petrel** (Adult; Feb)
Macronectes giganteus Text p.191

(97) **Antarctic Petrel**
Thalassoica antarctica Text p.192

(98) **Antarctic Petrel**
Thalassoica antarctica Text p.192

(99) **Pintado Petrel**
Daption capense Text p.192

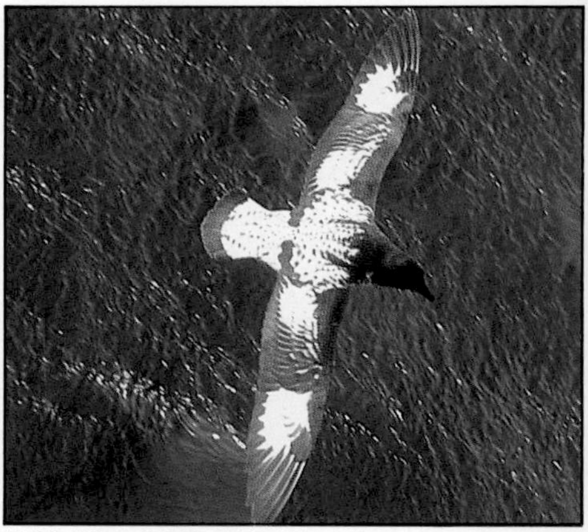

(100) **Pintado Petrel**
Daption capense Text p.192

(101) **Snow Petrel**
Pagodroma nivea Text p.193

(102) **Snow Petrel**
Pagodroma nivea Text p.193

(103) **Antarctic Fulmar**

Fulmarus glacialoides Text p.192

(104) **Antarctic Fulmar**

Fulmarus glacialoides Text p.192

(105) **Northern Fulmar** (July)

Fulmarus glacialis Text p.193

(106) **Northern Fulmar**

Fulmarus g. rodgersii Text p.193

(107) **Blue Petrel**

Halobaena caerulea Text p.193

(108) **Blue Petrel**

Halobaena caerulea Text p.193

PRIONS

(109) **Broad-billed Prion**
Pachyptila vittata Text p.194

(110) **Broad-billed Prion**
Pachyptila vittata Text p.194

(111) **Antarctic Prion**
Pachyptila (vittata) desolata Text p.194

(112) **Antarctic Prion**
Pachyptila (vittata) desolata Text p.194

(113) **Salvin's Prion**
Pachyptila (vittata) salvini Text p.194

(114) **Salvin's Prion**
Pachyptila (vittata) salvini Text p.194

(115) **Fairy Prion**
Pachyptila turtur Text p.195

(116) **Fairy Prion**
Pachyptila turtur Text p.195

(117) **Fulmar Prion**
Pachyptila (turtur) crassirostris Text p.195

(118) **Fulmar Prion**
Pachyptila (turtur) crassirostris Text p.195

(119) **Thin-billed Prion**
Pachyptila belcheri Text p.195

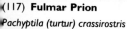

(120) **Thin-billed Prion** (July)
Pachyptila belcheri Text p.195

(121) **Great-winged Petrel** (May)
Pterodroma macroptera Text p.196

(122) **Great-winged Petrel** (Jan)
Pterodroma macroptera Text p.196

(123) **Kerguelen Petrel**
Pterodroma brevirostris Text p.196

(124) **Kerguelen Petrel**
Pterodroma brevirostris Text p.196

(125) **Soft-plumaged Petrel**
Pterodroma mollis Text p.196

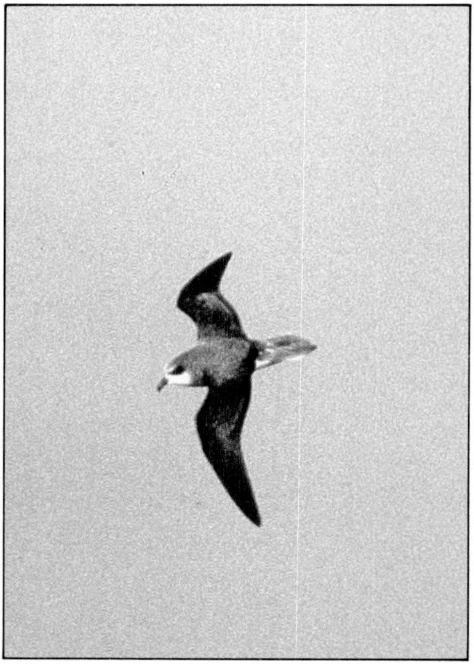

(126) **Soft-plumaged Petrel**
Pterodroma mollis Text p.196

(127) **Atlantic Petrel**
Pterodroma incerta Text p.197

(128) **Atlantic Petrel**
Pterodroma incerta Text p.197

(129) **Cook's Petrel**
Pterodroma cooki Text p.198

(130) **Cook's Petrel** (Dec)
Pterodroma cooki Text p.198

(131) **Masatierra Petrel**
Pterodroma (cooki) defilippiana Text p.198

(132) **Masatierra Petrel**
Pterodroma (cooki) defilippiana Text p.198

(133) **Stejneger's Petrel** (Feb)
Pterodroma longirostris Text p.198

(134) **Stejneger's Petrel**
Pterodroma longirostris Text p.198

(135) **Pycroft's Petrel** (Dec)
Pterodroma (longirostris) pycrofti Text p.199

(136) **Pycroft's Petrel**
Pterodroma (longirostris) pycrofti Text p.199

(137) **Mottled Petrel**
Pterodroma inexpectata Text p.201

(138) **Mottled Petrel**
Pterodroma inexpectata Text p.201

(139) **Black-winged Petrel**
Pterodroma nigripennis Text p.200

(140) **Black-winged Petrel** (Dec)
Pterodroma nigripennis Text p.200

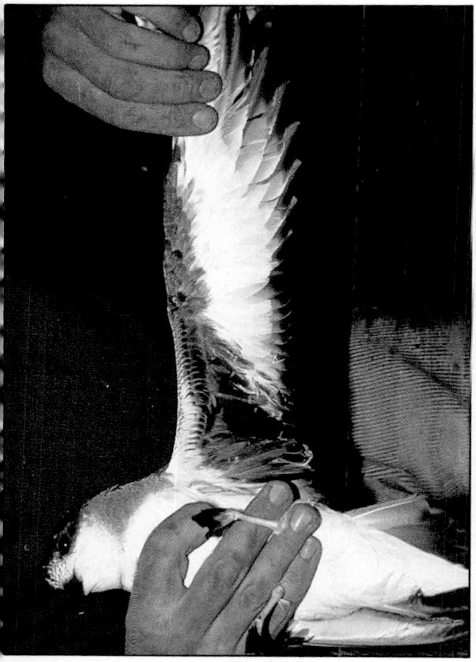

(141) **Chatham Island Petrel**
Pterodroma axillaris Text p.200

(142) **Chatham Island Petrel**
Pterodroma axillaris Text p.200

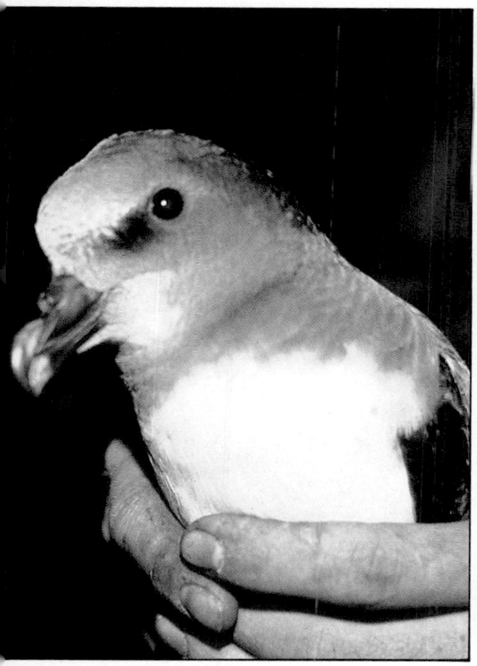

(143) **Magenta Petrel**
Pterodroma magentae Text p.201

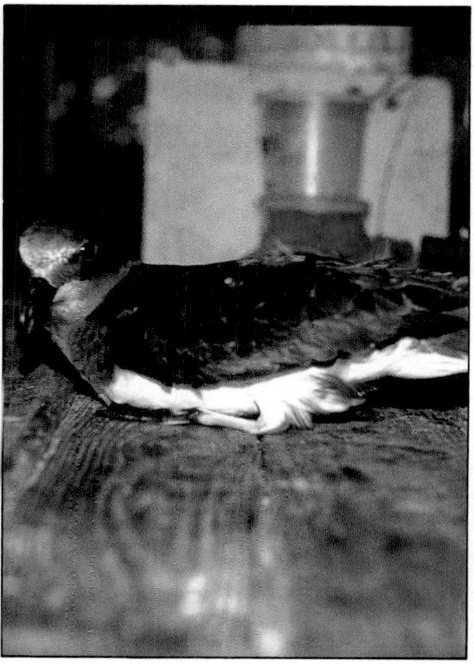

(144) **Magenta Petrel**
Pterodroma magentae Text p.201

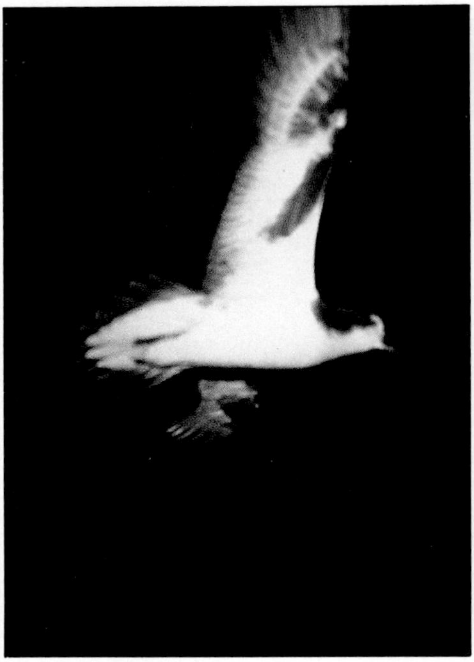

(145) **Bonin Petrel**
Pterodroma hypoleuca Text p.200

(146) **Bonin Petrel** (June)
Pterodroma hypoleuca Text p.200

(147) **Hawaiian Petrel**
Pterodroma phaeopygia Text p.204

(148) **Hawaiian Petrel**
Pterodroma phaeopygia Text p.204

(149) **Gould's Petrel**
Pterodroma leucoptera Text p.199

(150) **Gould's Petrel** (Dec)
Pterodroma leucoptera Text p.199

(151) **Collared Petrel**
Pterodroma (leucoptera) brevipes Text p.199

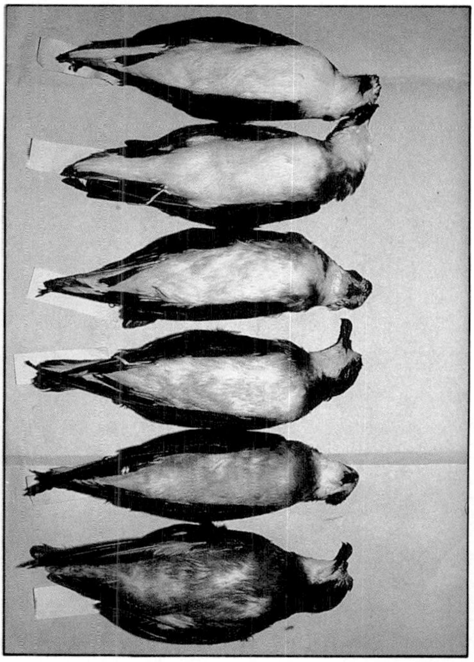

(152) **Collared Petrel** (Pale, intermediate and dark)
Pterodroma (leucoptera) brevipes Text p.199

(153) **Herald Petrel** (Intermediate morph)
Pterodroma arminjoniana Text p.202

(154) **Herald Petrel** (Intermediate morph)
Pterodroma arminjoniana Text p.202

(155) **Kermadec Petrel** (Pale morph)
Pterodroma neglecta Text p.202

(156) **Kermadec Petrel** (Dark morph)
Pterodroma neglecta Text p.202

(157) **Phoenix Petrel**
Pterodroma alba Text p.202

(158) **Phoenix Petrel**
Pterodroma alba Text p.202

(159) **Tahiti Petrel**
Pterodroma rostrata Text p.203

(160) **Tahiti Petrel**
Pterodroma rostrata Text p.203

(161) **Providence Petrel**
Pterodroma solandri Text p.203

(162) **Providence Petrel**
Pterodroma solandri Text p.203

(163) **Murphy's Petrel** (Mar)
Pterodroma ultima Text p.203

(164) **Murphy's Petrel** (Mar)
Pterodroma ultima Text p.203

(165) **White-headed Petrel**
Pterodroma lessonii Text p.197

(166) **White-headed Petrel** (Mar)
Pterodroma lessonii Text p.197

(167) **Barau's Petrel** (June)
Pterodroma baraui Text p.197

(168) **Barau's Petrel**
Pterodroma baraui Text p.197

(169) **Mascarene Petrel**
Pterodroma aterrima Text p.205

(170) **Mascarene Petrel**
Pterodroma aterrima Text p.205

(171) **Fiji Petrel**
Pseudobulweria macgillivrayi Text p.206

(172) **Fiji Petrel**
Pseudobulweria macgillivrayi Text p.206

(173) **Jouanin's Petrel** (Aug)
Bulweria fallax Text p.205

(174) **Jouanin's Petrel** (July)
Bulweria fallax Text p.205

(175) **Bulwer's Petrel**
Bulweria bulwerii Text p.205

(176) **Bulwer's Petrel** (Adult; June)
Bulweria bulwerii Text p.205

(177) **Juan Fernandez Petrel** (Apr)
Pterodroma externa Text p.201

(178) **Juan Fernandez Petrel** (June)
Pterodroma externa Text p.201

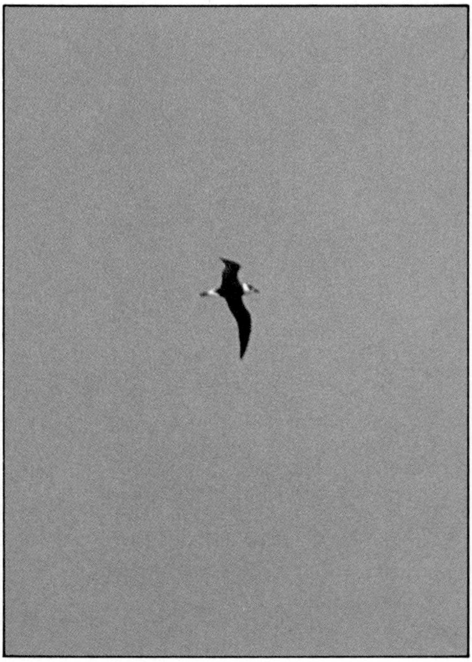

(179) **Black-capped Petrel**
Pterodroma hasitata Text p.204

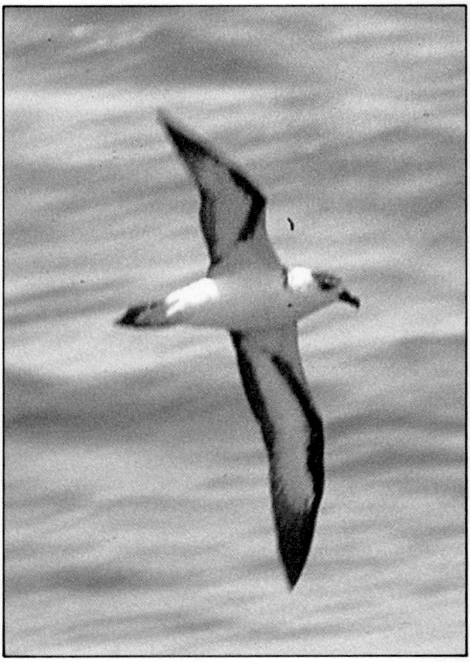

(180) **Black-capped Petrel** (May)
Pterodroma hasitata Text p.204

(181) **Bermuda Petrel** (July)
Pterodroma cahow Text p.204

(182) **Bermuda Petrel**
Pterodroma cahow Text p.204

(183) **Grey Petrel**
Procellaria cinerea Text p.207

(184) **Grey Petrel** (May)
Procellaria cinerea Text p.207

(185) **White-chinned Petrel**
Procellaria aequinoctialis Text p.206

(186) **White-chinned Petrel** (Sep)
Procellaria aequinoctialis Text p.206

(187) **Westland Petrel** (Apr)
Procellaria westlandica Text p.206

(188) **Westland Petrel** (Apr)
Procellaria westlandica Text p.206

(189) **Parkinson's Petrel** (July)
Procellaria parkinsoni Text p.207

(190) **Parkinson's Petrel** (July)
Procellaria parkinsoni Text p.207

(191) **Flesh-footed Shearwater**
Puffinus carneipes Text p.207

(192) **Flesh-footed Shearwater** (Jan)
Puffinus carneipes Text p.207

(193) **Cory's Shearwater** (May)
Calonectris diomedea Text p.208

(194) **Cory's Shearwater** (Mar)
Calonectris diomedea Text p.208

(195) **Great Shearwater**
Puffinus gravis Text p.208

(196) **Great Shearwater** (Aug)
Puffinus gravis Text p.208

(197) **Sooty Shearwater** (Sep)
Puffinus griseus Text p.208

(198) **Sooty Shearwater** (Sep)
Puffinus griseus Text p.208

(199) **Short-tailed Shearwater**
Puffinus tenuirostris Text p.211

(200) **Short-tailed Shearwater**
Puffinus tenuirostris Text p.211

(201) **Manx Shearwater** (Nov)
Puffinus puffinus Text p.209

(202) **Manx Shearwater**
Puffinus puffinus Text p.209

(203) **Balearic/Levantine Shearwater** (June)
Puffinus mauretanicus/yelkouan Text p.209

(204) **Balearic/Levantine Shearwater** (Sep)
Puffinus mauretanicus/yelkouan Text p.209

(205) **Little Shearwater**
Puffinus assimilis Text p.209

(206) **Little Shearwater**
Puffinus assimilis Text p.209

(207) **Audubon's Shearwater** (Aug)
Puffinus lherminieri Text p.212

(208) **Audubon's Shearwater** (Aug)
Puffinus lherminieri Text p.212

(209) **Pink-footed Shearwater** (Sep)
Puffinus creatopus Text p.210

(210) **Pink-footed Shearwater** (Aug)
Puffinus creatopus Text p.210

(211) **Wedge-tailed Shearwater** (Pale morph; July)
Puffinus pacificus Text p.210

(212) **Wedge-tailed Shearwater** (Dark morph; Apr)
Puffinus pacificus Text p.210

(213) **Buller's Shearwater** (Nov)
Puffinus bulleri Text p.210

(214) **Buller's Shearwater** (Sep)
Puffinus bulleri Text p.210

(215) **Streaked Shearwater**
Calonectris leucomelas Text p.211

(216) **Streaked Shearwater** (Mar)
Calonectris leucomelas Text p.211

(217) **Heinroth's Shearwater** (Pale)
Puffinus (lherminieri) heinrothi Text p.212

(218) **Heinroth's Shearwater** (Dark)
Puffinus (lherminieri) heinrothi Text p.212

(219) **Fluttering Shearwater** (Jan)
Puffinus gavia Text p.213

(220) **Fluttering Shearwater**
Puffinus gavia Text p.213

(221) **Hutton's Shearwater** (Mar)
Puffinus huttoni Text p.212

(222) **Hutton's Shearwater** (Nov)
Puffinus huttoni Text p.212

(223) **Townsend's Shearwater** (July)
Puffinus auricularis Text p.213

(224) **Townsend's Shearwater**
Puffinus auricularis Text p.213

(225) **Black-vented Shearwater** (Jan)
Puffinus opisthomelas Text p.213

(226) **Black-vented Shearwater** (Mar)
Puffinus opisthomelas Text p.213

(227) **Christmas Shearwater**
Puffinus nativitatis Text p.211

(228) **Christmas Shearwater**
Puffinus nativitatis Text p.211

(229) **Matsudaira's Storm-petrel**
Oceanodroma matsudairae Text p.219

(230) **Matsudaira's Storm-petrel**
Oceanodroma matsudairae Text p.219

(231) **Hornby's Storm-petrel** (Nov)
Oceanodroma hornbyi Text p.219

(232) **Hornby's Storm-petrel** (Nov)
Oceanodroma hornbyi Text p.219

STORM-PETRELS

(233) **Wilson's Storm-petrel** (Jan)
Oceanites oceanicus Text p.215

(234) **Wilson's Storm-petrel** (May)
Oceanites oceanicus Text p.215

(235) **British Storm-petrel** (Aug)
Hydrobates pelagicus Text p.214

(236) **British Storm-petrel**
Hydrobates pelagicus Text p.214

(237) **Leach's Storm-petrel** (Mar)
Oceanodroma leucorhoa Text p.214

(238) **Leach's Storm-petrel** (Aug)
Oceanodroma leucorhoa Text p.214

(239) **Madeiran Storm-petrel** (Jan)
Oceanodroma castro Text p.214

(240) **Madeiran Storm-petrel** (June)
Oceanodroma castro Text p.214

(241) **White-faced Storm-petrel** (Nov)
Pelagodroma marina Text p.215

(242) **White-faced Storm-petrel** (Aug)
Pelagodroma marina Text p.215

(243) **White-bellied Storm-petrel**
Fregetta grallaria Text p.218

(244) **White-bellied Storm-petrel**
Fregetta grallaria Text p.218

(245) **Black-bellied Storm-petrel**
Fregetta tropica Text p.218

(246) **Black-bellied Storm-petrel**
Fregetta tropica Text p.218

(247) **Grey-backed Storm-petrel** (Jan)
Garrodia nereis Text p.218

(248) **Grey-backed Storm-petrel** (Feb)
Garrodia nereis Text p.218

(249) **White-throated Storm-petrel** (Feb)
Nesofregetta fuliginosa Text p.219

(250) **White-throated Storm-petrel** (Oct)
Nesofregetta fuliginosa Text p.219

(251) **Markham's Storm-petrel** (Sep)
Oceanodroma markhami Text p.217

(252) **Markham's Storm-petrel** (Sep)
Oceanodroma markhami Text p.217

(253) **Tristram's Storm-petrel**
Oceanodroma tristrami Text p.220

(254) **Tristram's Storm-petrel** (May)
Oceanodroma tristrami Text p.220

(255) **Swinhoe's Storm-petrel** (Sep)
Oceanodroma monorhis Text p.220

(256) **Swinhoe's Storm-petrel**
Oceanodroma monorhis Text p.220

STORM-PETRELS

(257) **Elliot's Storm-petrel** (Aug)
Oceanites gracilis Text p.215

(258) **Elliot's Storm-petrel** (Aug)
Oceanites gracilis Text p.215

(259) **Wedge-rumped Storm-petrel** (Dec)
Oceanodroma tethys Text p.216

(260) **Wedge-rumped Storm-petrel** (Oct)
Oceanodroma tethys Text p.216

(261) **Fork-tailed Storm-petrel**
Oceanodroma furcata Text p.216

(262) **Fork-tailed Storm-petrel** (Aug)
Oceanodroma furcata Text p.216

(263) **Ashy Storm-petrel** (Aug)
Oceanodroma homochroa Text p.217

(264) **Ashy Storm-petrel** (Aug)
Oceanodroma homochroa Text p.217

(265) **Black Storm-petrel** (July)
Oceanodroma melania Text p.217

(266) **Black Storm-petrel** (July)
Oceanodroma melania Text p.217

(267) **Least Storm-petrel** (Oct)
Oceanodroma microsoma Text p.216

(268) **Least Storm-petrel** (Nov)
Oceanodroma microsoma Text p.216

DIVING-PETRELS

(269) **Common Diving-petrel**
Pelecanoides urinatrix Text p.221

(270) **Common Diving-petrel**
Pelecanoides urinatrix Text p.221

(271) **Georgian Diving-petrel** (Sep)
Pelecanoides georgicus Text p.221

(272) **Georgian Diving-petrel**
Pelecanoides georgicus Text p.221

(273) **Peruvian Diving-petrel** (July)
Pelecanoides garnoti Text p.220

(274) **Peruvian Diving-petrel**
Pelecanoides garnoti Text p.220

(275) **Magellan Diving-petrel** (July)
Pelecanoides magellani Text p.221

(276) **Magellan Diving-petrel**
Pelecanoides magellani Text p.221

(277) **Red-billed Tropicbird** (Adult)
Phaethon aethereus Text p.222

(278) **Red-billed Tropicbird** (Adult)
Phaethon aethereus Text p.222

(279) **Red-tailed Tropicbird** (Adult; Aug)
Phaethon rubricauda Text p.222

(280) **Red-tailed Tropicbird** (Imm.; Aug)
Phaethon rubricauda Text p.222

(281) **White-tailed Tropicbird** (Adult)
Phaethon lepturus Text p.222

(282) **White-tailed Tropicbird** (Adult)
Phaethon lepturus Text p.222

(283) **Brown Pelican** (Adult; Nov)
Pelecanus occidentalis Text p.223

(284) **Brown Pelican** (Imm.; Mar)
Pelecanus occidentalis Text p.223

(285) **Peruvian Pelican** (Adult; Nov)
Pelecanus (occidentalis) thagus Text p.223

(286) **Peruvian Pelican** (Imm., adult winter)
Pelecanus (occidentalis) thagus Text p.223

(287) **American White Pelican** (Adult; Aug)
Pelecanus erythrorhynchos Text p.223

(288) **American White Pelican** (Adult; Apr)
Pelecanus erythrorhynchos Text p.223

(289) **Australian Pelican** (Adult; Dec)
Pelecanus conspicillatus Text p.225

(290) **Australian Pelican** (Imm.)
Pelecanus conspicillatus Text p.225

(291) **Eastern White Pelican** (Adult; Feb)
Pelecanus onocrotalus Text p.224

(292) **Eastern White Pelican** (Adult; July)
Pelecanus onocrotalus Text p.224

PELICANS

(293) **Dalmatian Pelican**
Pelecanus crispus Text p.224

(294) **Dalmatian Pelican** (Adult, non-breeding)
Pelecanus crispus Text p.224

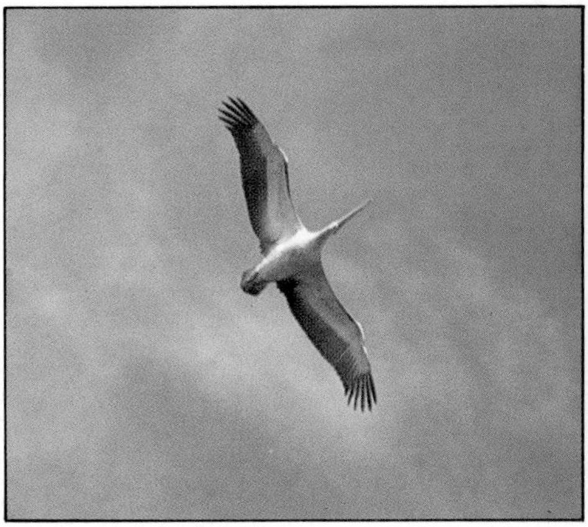

(295) **Pink-backed Pelican** (Dec)
Pelecanus rufescens Text p.224

(296) **Pink-backed Pelican**
Pelecanus rufescens Text p.224

(297) **Spot-billed Pelican** (Adult)
Pelecanus philippensis Text p.225

(298) **Spot-billed Pelican**
Pelecanus philippensis Text p.225

(299) **Northern Gannet** (Adult; May)
Sula bassana Text p.225

(300) **Northern Gannet** (Juv.)
Sula bassana Text p.225

(301) **Cape Gannet** (Adult; Sep)
Sula capensis Text p.226

(302) **Cape Gannet** (Adult; Sep)
Sula capensis Text p.226

(303) **Australasian Gannet** (Adult; Aug)
Sula serrator Text p.226

(304) **Australasian Gannet** (Adult)
Sula serrator Text p.226

(305) **Blue-footed Booby** (Adult)
Sula nebouxii Text p.228

(306) **Blue-footed Booby** (Adult)
Sula nebouxii Text p.228

(307) **Peruvian Booby** (Adult; June)
Sula variegata Text p.228

(308) **Peruvian Booby** (Adult; July)
Sula variegata Text p.228

(309) **Masked Booby** (Adult; Mar)
Sula dactylatra Text p.227

(310) **Masked Booby** (Imm.; June)
Sula dactylatra Text p.227

311) **Red-footed Booby** (Imm.; Mar)
ula sula Text p.227

(312) **Red-footed Booby** (Adult white morph; Mar)
Sula sula Text p.227

313) **Brown Booby** (Adult ♂, eastern form; June)
ula leucogaster Text p.227

(314) **Brown Booby** (Juv.)
Sula leucogaster Text p.227

315) **Abbott's Booby** (Adult)
ula abbotti Text p.226

(316) **Abbott's Booby** (Adult)
Sula abbotti Text p.226

CORMORANTS

(317) **New Zealand King Cormorant** (Adult; May)
Phalacrocorax carunculatus Text p.228

(318) **New Zealand King Cormorant** (Adult; May
Phalacrocorax carunculatus Text p.22

(319) **Stewart Island Cormorant** (Adult pale morph)
Phalacrocorax carunculatus chalconotus Text p.229

(320) **Stewart Island Cormorant** (Adult, intermediat
Phalacrocorax carunculatus chalconotus Text p.2

(321) **Chatham Island Cormorant** (Chick, adult)
Phalacrocorax carunculatus onslowi Text p.229

(322) **Chatham Island Cormorant** (Adult
Phalacrocorax carunculatus onslowi Text p.22

(323) **Campbell Island Cormorant** (Adult)
Phalacrocorax campbelli Text p.229

(324) **Campbell Island Cormorant** (Adult)
Phalacrocorax campbelli Text p.229

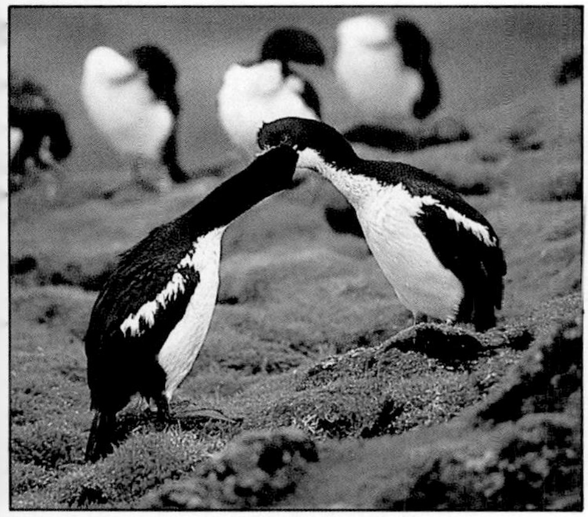

(325) **Auckland Island Cormorant** (Adult)
Phalacrocorax campbelli colensoi Text p.230

(326) **Auckland Island Cormorant** (Adult, imm.)
Phalacrocorax campbelli colensoi Text p.230

(327) **Bounty Island Cormorant** (Adult)
Phalacrocorax campbelli ranfurlyi Text p.230

(328) **Bounty Island Cormorant** (Adult)
Phalacrocorax campbelli ranfurlyi Text p.230

(329) **Pied Cormorant** (Adult)
Phalacrocorax varius Text p.232

(330) **Pied Cormorant** (Chick, adult)
Phalacrocorax varius Text p.232

(331) **Black-faced Cormorant** (Adult; Aug)
Phalacrocorax fuscescens Text p.231

(332) **Black-faced Cormorant** (Adult)
Phalacrocorax fuscescens Text p.231

(333) **Little Black Cormorant** (Adult; Jan)
Phalacrocorax sulcirostris Text p.231

(334) **Little Black Cormorant** (Adult)
Phalacrocorax sulcirostris Text p.231

(335) **Little Pied Cormorant** (Adult pale morph; Mar)
Phalacrocorax melanoleucos Text p.231

(336) **Little Pied Cormorant** (Juv. dark morph)
Phalacrocorax melanoleucos Text p.231

(337) **Spotted Shag** (Adult)
Phalacrocorax punctatus Text p.232

(338) **Spotted Shag** (Juv.)
Phalacrocorax punctatus Text p.232

(339) **Rock Shag** (Adult, chick; Jan)
Phalacrocorax magellanicus Text p.232

(340) **Rock Shag** (Imm.)
Phalacrocorax magellanicus Text p.232

(341) **Imperial Shag** (Adult; Jan)
Phalacrocorax atriceps Text p.230

(342) **Imperial Shag** (Adult, imm.; May)
Phalacrocorax atriceps Text p.230

(343) **Guanay Cormorant** (Adult; May)
Phalacrocorax bougainvillii Text p.233

(344) **Guanay Cormorant** (Imm.; May)
Phalacrocorax bougainvillii Text p.233

(345) **Red-legged Shag** (Adult; May)
Phalacrocorax gaimardi Text p.233

(346) **Red-legged Shag** (Adult; Nov)
Phalacrocorax gaimardi Text p.233

347) **Olivaceous Cormorant** (Adult; May)
'halacrocorax olivaceus Text p.233

(348) **Olivaceous Cormorant** (Adult; Feb)
Phalacrocorax olivaceus Text p.233

(349) **Double-crested Cormorant** (Adult; Apr)
Phalacrocorax auritus Text p.234

(350) **Double-crested Cormorant** (Imm.)
Phalacrocorax auritus Text p.234

(351) **Red-faced Cormorant** (Adult)
Phalacrocorax urile Text p.235

(352) **Red-faced Cormorant** (Adult)
Phalacrocorax urile Text p.235

(353) **Pelagic Cormorant** (Adult; May)
Phalacrocorax pelagicus Text p.234

(354) **Pelagic Cormorant** (Adult; May)
Phalacrocorax pelagicus Text p.234

(355) **Brandt's Cormorant** (Adult)
Phalacrocorax penicillatus Text p.234

(356) **Brandt's Cormorant** (Adult)
Phalacrocorax penicillatus Text p.234

(357) **Shag** (Adult)
Phalacrocorax aristotelis Text p.235

(358) **Shag** (Imm.)
Phalacrocorax aristotelis Text p.235

(359) **Great Cormorant** (Adult; June)
Phalacrocorax carbo Text p.235

(360) **Great Cormorant** (Adult; July)
Phalacrocorax carbo Text p.235

(361) **Japanese Cormorant** (Adult, imm.; Feb)
Phalacrocorax capillatus Text p.238

(362) **Japanese Cormorant** (Adult; Feb)
Phalacrocorax capillatus Text p.238

(363) **Bank Cormorant** (Adult)
Phalacrocorax neglectus Text p.236

(364) **Bank Cormorant** (Imm.)
Phalacrocorax neglectus Text p.236

CORMORANTS

(365) **Cape Cormorant** (Adult)
Phalacrocorax capensis Text p.236

(366) **Cape Cormorant** (Adult)
Phalacrocorax capensis Text p.236

(367) **Crowned Cormorant** (Adult, chick)
Phalacrocorax coronatus Text p.237

(368) **Crowned Cormorant** (Adult)
Phalacrocorax coronatus Text p.237

(369) **Long-tailed Cormorant** (Imm.)
Phalacrocorax africanus Text p.236

(370) **Long-tailed Cormorant** (Adult)
Phalacrocorax africanus Text p.236

(371) **Socotra Cormorant** (Adult)
Phalacrocorax nigrogularis Text p.237

(372) **Socotra Cormorant** (Juv.; June)
Phalacrocorax nigrogularis Text p.237

(373) **Pygmy Cormorant** (Adult; Sep)
Phalacrocorax pygmeus Text p.237

(374) **Pygmy Cormorant** (Adult; Nov)
Phalacrocorax pygmeus Text p.237

(375) **Javanese Cormorant** (Adult; Jan)
Phalacrocorax niger Text p.238

(376) **Javanese Cormorant** (Adult; July)
Phalacrocorax niger Text p.238

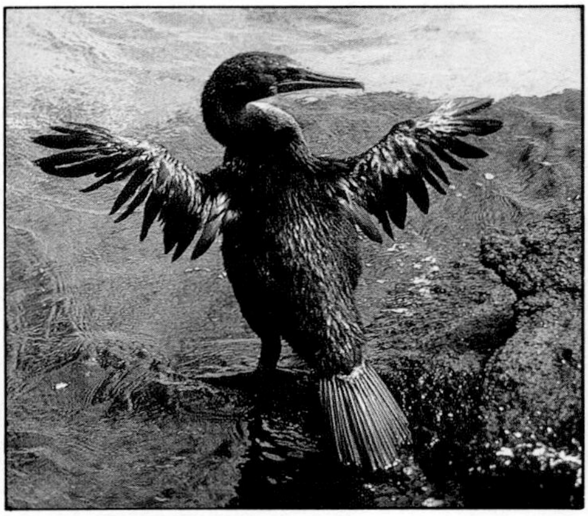

(377) **Galapagos Cormorant** (Adult)
Nannopterum (= Phalacrocorax) harrisi Text p.239

(378) **Galapagos Cormorant** (Adult)
Nannopterum (= Phalacrocorax) harrisi Text p.239

(379) **Indian Cormorant** (Adult)
Phalacrocorax fuscicollis Text p.238

(380) **Indian Cormorant** (Adult)
Phalacrocorax fuscicollis Text p.238

(381) **Ascension Frigatebird** (Juv.)
Fregata aquila Text p.239

(382) **Ascension Frigatebird** (Juv.)
Fregata aquila Text p.239

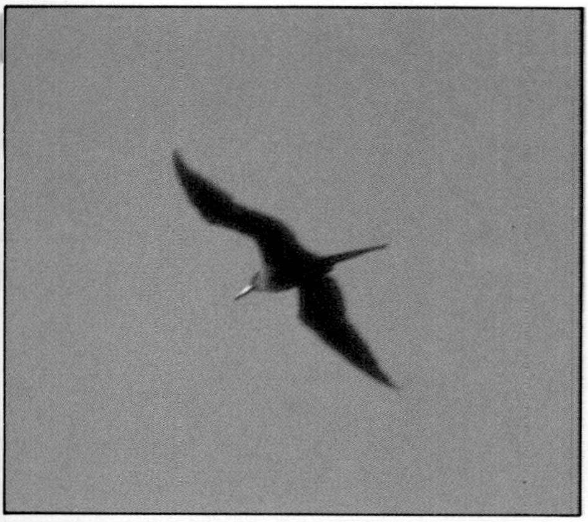

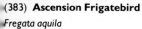

(383) **Ascension Frigatebird** (Adult ♀)
Fregata aquila Text p.239

(384) **Ascension Frigatebird** (Adult ♀)
Fregata aquila Text p.239

(385) **Christmas Frigatebird** (Adult ♀; Jan)
Fregata andrewsi Text p.240

(386) **Christmas Frigatebird** (Adult ♂)
Fregata andrewsi Text p.240

(387) **Christmas Frigatebird** (Juv.)
Fregata andrewsi Text p.240

(388) **Christmas Frigatebird** (Juv., adult ♀)
Fregata andrewsi Text p.240

(389) **Lesser Frigatebird** (Adult ♀)
Fregata ariel Text p.239

(390) **Lesser Frigatebird** (Adult ♂)
Fregata ariel Text p.239

(391) **Lesser Frigatebird** (Imm. ♂, 3rd stage)
Fregata ariel Text p.239

(392) **Lesser Frigatebird** (Juv., 2nd stage)
Fregata ariel Text p.239

(393) **Great Frigatebird** (Adult ♀; Jan)
Fregata minor Text p.240

(394) **Great Frigatebird** (Sub-adult ♂; Jan)
Fregata minor Text p.240

(395) **Great Frigatebird** (Imm. ♀)
Fregata minor Text p.240

(396) **Great Frigatebird** (Juv.; Apr)
Fregata minor Text p.240

(397) **Magnificent Frigatebird** (Adult ♀; July)
Fregata magnificens Text p.240

(398) **Magnificent Frigatebird** (Sub-adult ♀)
Fregata magnificens Text p.240

(399) **Magnificent Frigatebird** (Sub-adult ♂)
Fregata magnificens Text p.240

(400) **Magnificent Frigatebird** (Juv.)
Fregata magnificens Text p.240

(401) **Red Phalarope** (Adult ♀)
Phalaropus fulicarius Text p.241

(402) **Red Phalarope** (Adult; Oct)
Phalaropus fulicarius Text p.241

(403) **Red-necked Phalarope** (Adult ♂, Adult ♀)
Phalaropus lobatus Text p.241

(404) **Red-necked Phalarope** (Juv.)
Phalaropus lobatus Text p.241

(405) **Wilson's Phalarope** (Adult ♂♂, Adult ♀♀; Apr)
Phalaropus tricolor Text p.241

(406) **Wilson's Phalarope** (Adult Winter; Aug)
Phalaropus tricolor Text p.241

(407) **Great Skua** (Adult)
Catharacta skua Text p.242

(408) **Great Skua** (Adult)
Catharacta skua Text p.242

(409) **Great Skua** (Adult)
Catharacta skua Text p.242

(410) **Great Skua** (Adult)
Catharacta skua Text p.242

(411) **South Polar Skua** (Adult intermediate morph)
Catharacta maccormicki Text p.243

(412) **South Polar Skua** (Adult light morph)
Catharacta maccormicki Text p.243

(413) **South Polar Skua** (Adult atypical)
Catharacta maccormicki Text p.243

(414) **South Polar Skua** (Adult dark)
Catharacta maccormicki Text p.243

(415) **Antarctic Skua** (Adult)
Catharacta (skua) antarctica Text p.242

(416) **Antarctic Skua** (Adult)
Catharacta (skua)/antarctica hamiltoni Text p.242

(417) **Antarctic Skua** (Adult)
Catharacta (skua) antarctica Text p.242

(418) **Antarctic Skua** (Adult)
Catharacta (skua) antarctica Text p.242

(419) **Chilean Skua** (Adult; Sep)
Catharacta chilensis Text p.242

(420) **Chilean Skua** (Adult; Sep)
Catharacta chilensis Text p.242

(421) **Chilean Skua** (Adult)
Catharacta chilensis Text p.242

(422) **Chilean Skua** (Juv.)
Catharacta chilensis Text p.242

(423) **Arctic Skua** (Adult Summer, dark morph)
Stercorarious parasiticus Text p.243

(424) **Arctic Skua** (Pale morph; Oct)
Stercorarius parasiticus Text p.243

(425) **Arctic Skua** (Adult Winter; Feb)
Stercorarius parasiticus Text p.243

(426) **Arctic Skua** (Juv.; Nov)
Stercorarius parasiticus Text p.243

(427) **Long-tailed Skua** (Adult Summer; Aug)
Stercorarius longicaudus Text p.244

(428) **Long-tailed Skua** (Adult Winter; Jan)
Stercorarius longicaudus Text p.244

(429) **Long-tailed Skua** (Juv. light)
Stercorarius longicaudus Text p.244

(430) **Long-tailed Skua** (Juv. dark; Oct)
Stercorarius longicaudus Text p.244

(431) **Pomarine Skua** (Adult transitional; summer)
Stercorarius pomarinus Text p.243

(432) **Pomarine Skua** (Adult light morph, winter; Jan)
Stercorarius pomarinus Text p.243

(433) **Pomarine Skua** (2nd-winter light morph; Jan)
Stercorarius pomarinus Text p.243

(434) **Pomarine Skua** (Juv. light morph; Feb/Mar)
Stercorarius pomarinus Text p.243

435) **Swallow-tailed Gull** (Adult Summer)
arus furcatus Text p.260

(436) **Swallow-tailed Gull** (Adult transitional)
Larus furcatus Text p.260

437) **Swallow-tailed Gull** (Adult Summer/Winter)
arus furcatus Text p.260

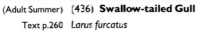

(438) **Swallow-tailed Gull** (Juv.)
Larus furcatus Text p.260

GULLS

(439) **Herring Gull** (Adult Summer)
Larus argentatus Text p.245

(440) **Herring Gull** (Adult Winter; Jan
Larus argentatus Text p.24

(441) **Herring Gull** (Juv.)
Larus argentatus Text p.245

(442) **Herring Gull** (1st Winter; Jan)
Larus argentatus Text p.245

(443) **Thayer's Gull** (Adult Summer; June)
Larus thayeri Text p.245

(444) **Thayer's Gull** (Adult; Feb)
Larus thayeri Text p.245

(445) **Thayer's Gull** (1st Winter; Mar)
Larus thayeri Text p.245

(446) **Thayer's Gull** (1st Winter; Mar)
Larus thayeri Text p.245

(447) **California Gull** (Adult Winter; Jan)
Larus californicus Text p.245

(448) **California Gull** (1st Winter; Jan)
Larus californicus Text p.245

(449) **California Gull** (1st Winter; Oct)
Larus californicus Text p.245

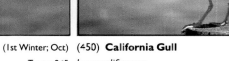

(450) **California Gull** (1st Winter; Jan)
Larus californicus Text p.245

(451) **Great Black-backed Gull** (Adult Summer; May)
Larus marinus Text p.252

(452) **Great Black-backed Gull** (Adult)
Larus marinus Text p.252

(453) **Great Black-backed Gull** (1st Winter; Jan)
Larus marinus Text p.252

(454) **Great Black-backed Gull** (1st Winter; Jan)
Larus marinus Text p.252

(455) **Lesser Black-backed Gull** (Adult Summer)
Larus fuscus Text p.252

(456) **Lesser Black-backed Gull** (1st Winter)
Larus fuscus Text p.252

(457) **Lesser Black-backed Gull** (Juv.)
Larus fuscus Text p.252

(458) **Lesser Black-backed Gull** (1st Winter)
Larus fuscus Text p.252

(459) **Slaty-backed Gull** (Adult transitional)
Larus schistisagus Text p.252

(460) **Slaty-backed Gull** (Adult Summer; May)
Larus schistisagus Text p.252

(461) **Slaty-backed Gull** (Imm.; Feb)
Larus schistisagus Text p.252

(462) **Slaty-backed Gull** (2nd Summer; May)
Larus schistisagus Text p.252

(463) **Western Gull** (Adult Summer; May)
Larus occidentalis Text p.244

(464) **Western Gull** (3rd Summer)
Larus occidentalis Text p.244

(465) **Western gull** (1st, 2nd Winter)
Larus occidentalis Text p.244

(466) **Western Gull** (1st Winter)
Larus occidentalis Text p.244

(467) **Yellow-footed Gull** (Adult Summer)
Larus livens Text p.244

(468) **Yellow-footed Gull** (Adult Summer, juv.; July)
Larus livens Text p.244

(469) **Yellow-footed Gull** (Juv; Aug)
Larus livens Text p.244

(470) **Yellow-footed Gull** (1st Summer)
Larus livens Text p.244

(471) **Black-tailed Gull** (Adult Winter; Jan)
Larus crassirostris Text p.258

(472) **Black-tailed Gull** (Adult Summer)
Larus crassirostris Text p.258

(473) **Black-tailed Gull** (Adult Summer)
Larus crassirostris Text p.258

(474) **Black-tailed Gull** (Adult Winter)
Larus crassirostris Text p.258

(475) **Glaucous-winged Gull** (Adult Summer)
Larus glaucescens Text p.250

(476) **Glaucous-winged Gull** (2nd Winter; Mar)
Larus glaucescens Text p.250

(477) **Glaucous-winged Gull** (1st Winter)
Larus glaucescens Text p.250

(478) **Glaucous-winged Gull** (1st Winter; Feb)
Larus glaucescens Text p.250

(479) **Glaucous Gull** (Adult Summer)
Larus hyperboreus Text p.250

(480) **Glaucous Gull** (2nd Winter)
Larus hyperboreus Text p.250

(481) **Glaucous Gull** (2nd Winter)
Larus hyperboreus Text p.250

(482) **Glaucous Gull** (1st Winter)
Larus hyperboreus Text p.250

(483) **Iceland Gull** (Adult Summer)
Larus glaucoides Text p.250

(484) **Iceland Gull** (2nd Winter; Mar)
Larus glaucoides Text p.250

(485) **Iceland Gull** (1st Winter)
Larus glaucoides Text p.250

(486) **Iceland Gull** (1st Winter; Mar)
Larus glaucoides Text p.250

(487) **Kumlien's Gull** (Adult Summer; Mar)
Larus (glaucoides) kumlieni Text p.251

(488) **Kumlien's Gull** (Adult)
Larus (glaucoides) kumlieni Text p.251

(489) **Kumlien's Gull** (Adult Winter; Jan)
Larus (glaucoides) kumlieni Text p.251

(490) **Kumlien's Gull** (1st Winter/Summer; Mar)
Larus (glaucoides) kumlieni Text p.251

(491) **Ivory Gull** (Adult Summer)
Pagophila eburnea Text p.251

(492) **Ivory Gull** (Adult Winter)
Pagophila eburnea Text p.251

(493) **Ivory Gull** (1st Winter)
Pagophila eburnea Text p.251

(494) **Ivory Gull** (1st Winter)
Pagophila eburnea Text p.251

(495) **Heermann's Gull** (Adult Summer; Feb)
Larus heermanni Text p.251

(496) **Heermann's Gull** (Adult Summer, 2nd Winter)
Larus heermanni Text p.251

(497) **Heermann's Gull** (1st Winter)
Larus heermanni Text p.251

(498) **Heermann's Gull** (Juv.)
Larus heermanni Text p.251

(499) **Laughing Gull** (Adult Summer; Feb)
Larus atricilla Text p.247

(500) **Laughing Gull** (2nd Winter; Mar)
Larus atricilla Text p.247

(501) **Laughing Gull** (1st Winter; Feb)
Larus atricilla Text p.247

(502) **Laughing Gull** (1st Winter; Jan)
Larus atricilla Text p.247

(503) **Franklin's Gull** (Adult Summer; May)
Larus pipixcan Text p.247

(504) **Franklin's Gull** (2nd Winter; Dec)
Larus pipixcan Text p.247

505) **Franklin's Gull** (1st Summer; May)
Larus pipixcan Text p.247

(506) **Franklin's Gull** (1st Winter; Jan)
Larus pipixcan Text p.247

(507) **Bonaparte's Gull** (Adult Summer)
Larus philadelphia Text p.247

(508) **Bonaparte's Gull** (Adult transitional summer)
Larus philadelphia Text p.247

(509) **Bonaparte's Gull** (Adult Winter; Nov)
Larus philadelphia Text p.247

(510) **Bonaparte's Gull** (1st Winter; Jan)
Larus philadelphia Text p.247

(511) **Ring-billed Gull** (Adult Winter; Jan)
Larus delawarensis Text p.246

(512) **Ring-billed Gull** (1st Winter; Nov
Larus delawarensis Text p.24

(513) **Ring-billed Gull** (1st Winter; Oct)
Larus delawarensis Text p.246

(514) **Ring-billed Gull** (1st Winter transitional; Mar
Larus delawarensis Text p.24

(515) **Common Gull** (Adult Winter)
Larus canus Text p.246

(516) **Common Gull** (Adult Winter; Jan
Larus canus Text p.24

(517) **Common Gull** (1st Winter; Jan)
Larus canus Text p.246

(518) **Common Gull** (1st Winter; Dec)
Larus canus Text p.246

(519) **Black-headed Gull** (Adult Summer)
Larus ridibundus Text p.246

(520) **Black-headed Gull** (1st Winter)
Larus ridibundus Text p.246

(521) **Black-headed Gull** (1st Winter)
Larus ridibundus Text p.246

(522) **Black-headed Gull** (Juv.)
Larus ridibundus Text p.246

(523) **Little Gull** (Adult Summer; May)
Larus minutus Text p.248

(524) **Little Gull** (1st Summer; July)
Larus minutus Text p.248

(525) **Little Gull** (1st Winter; Jan)
Larus minutus Text p.248

(526) **Little Gull** (Juv.; Aug)
Larus minutus Text p.248

(527) **Sabine's Gull** (Adult Summer)
Larus sabini Text p.248

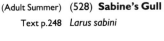

(528) **Sabine's Gull** (Adult Winter; Nov)
Larus sabini Text p.248

(529) **Sabine's Gull** (1st Summer)
Larus sabini
Text p.248

(530) **Sabine's Gull** (Juv.)
Larus sabini
Text p.248

(531) **Ross's Gull** (Adult Summer; June)
Rhodostethia rosea
Text p.248

(532) **Ross's Gull** (Adult Summer)
Rhodostethia rosea
Text p.248

(533) **Ross's Gull** (Adult Winter)
Rhodostethia rosea
Text p.248

(534) **Ross's Gull** (Adult Winter)
Rhodostethia rosea
Text p.248

(535) **Black-legged Kittiwake** (Adult Summer)
Larus tridactyla Text p.253

(536) **Black-legged Kittiwake** (Adult Summer)
Larus tridactyla Text p.253

(537) **Black-legged Kittiwake** (1st Winter; Apr)
Larus tridactyla Text p.253

(538) **Black-legged Kittiwake** (1st Winter; Mar)
Larus tridactyla Text p.253

(539) **Red-legged Kittiwake** (Adult Summer; July)
Larus brevirostris Text p.253

(540) **Red-legged Kittiwake** (Adult Summer)
Larus brevirostris Text p.253

(541) **Red-legged Kittiwake** (Adult)
Larus brevirostris Text p.253

(542) **Red-legged Kittiwake** (Adult Summer)
Larus brevirostris Text p.253

(543) **Mediterranean Gull** (Adult Summer)
Larus melanocephalus Text p.249

(544) **Mediterranean Gull** (2nd Winter)
Larus melanocephalus Text p.249

(545) **Mediterranean Gull** (1st Winter; Oct)
Larus melanocephalus Text p.249

(546) **Mediterranean Gull** (Juv.)
Larus melanocephalus Text p.249

(547) **Audouin's Gull** (Adult Summer; June)
Larus audouinii Text p.249

(548) **Audouin's Gull** (Adult Summer; July)
Larus audouinii Text p.249

(549) **Audouin's Gull** (2nd Summer; July)
Larus audouinii Text p.249

(550) **Audouin's Gull** (Juv. transitional; July)
Larus audouinii Text p.249

(551) **Slender-billed Gull** (Adult Summer)
Larus genei Text p.249

(552) **Slender-billed Gull** (Juv., adult summer; July)
Larus genei Text p.249

(553) **Slender-billed Gull** (1st Winter; Sep)
Larus genei Text p.249

(554) **Slender-billed Gull** (Juv.; July)
Larus genei Text p.249

(555) **Relict Gull** (Adult Summer, chick; June)
Larus relictus Text p.255

(556) **Relict Gull** (Adult Summer)
Larus relictus Text p.255

(557) **Relict Gull** (Adult Summer, 1st Summer)
Larus relictus Text p.255

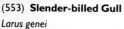

(558) **Relict Gull** (Adult Summer; June)
Larus relictus Text p.255

(559) **Great Black-headed Gull** (Adult Summer)
Larus ichthyaetus Text p.254

(560) **Great Black-headed Gull** (3rd Winter)
Larus ichthyaetus Text p.254

(561) **Great Black-headed Gull** (1st Winter; Jan)
Larus ichthyaetus Text p.254

(562) **Great Black-headed Gull** (Juv.; Aug)
Larus ichthyaetus Text p.254

(563) **Indian Black-headed Gull** (Adult Winter; Dec)
Larus brunnicephalus Text p.254

(564) **Indian Black-headed Gull** (Adult Winter; Jan)
Larus brunnicephalus Text p.254

(565) **Indian Black-headed Gull** (Adult Winter; Feb)
Larus brunnicephalus Text p.254

(566) **Indian Black-headed Gull** (1st Winter; Feb)
Larus brunnicephalus Text p.254

GULLS

(567) **Kelp Gull** (Adult Winter; June)
Larus dominicanus Text p.253

(568) **Kelp Gull** (Adult Summer; Dec)
Larus dominicanus Text p.253

(569) **Kelp Gull** (Adult Summer, 2nd Winter; Jan)
Larus dominicanus Text p.253

(570) **Kelp Gull** (1st Winter; Oct)
Larus dominicanus Text p.253

(571) **Grey-headed Gull** (Adult Summer; Sep)
Larus cirrocephalus Text p.255

(572) **Grey-headed Gull** (Adult Summer; Sep)
Larus cirrocephalus Text p.255

573) **Grey-headed Gull** (Adult Winter; Dec)
Larus cirrocephalus Text p.255

(574) **Grey-headed Gull** (Juv. transitional; Dec)
Larus cirrocephalus Text p.255

575) **Hartlaub's Gull** (Adult; Sep)
Larus hartlaubii Text p.255

(576) **Hartlaub's Gull** (Adult; Dec)
Larus hartlaubii Text p.255

577) **Hartlaub's Gull** (1st Winter; Sep)
Larus hartlaubii Text p.255

(578) **Hartlaub's Gull** (1st Winter; Sep)
Larus hartlaubii Text p.255

(579) **Pacific Gull** (Adult Summer; Jan)
Larus pacificus Text p.257

(580) **Pacific Gull** (3rd Winter; July
Larus pacificus Text p.257

(581) **Pacific Gull** (1st Winter; Sep)
Larus pacificus Text p.257

(582) **Pacific Gull** (1st Winter; Mar)
Larus pacificus Text p.257

(583) **Silver Gull** (Adult; May)
Larus novaehollandiae Text p.256

(584) **Silver Gull** (Adult; Feb)
Larus novaehollandiae Text p.256

(585) **Silver Gull** (1st Winter; May)
.arus novaehollandiae Text p.256

(586) **Silver Gull** (Juv.; Sep)
Larus novaehollandiae Text p.256

587) **Black-billed Gull** (Adult; May)
.arus bulleri Text p.257

(588) **Black-billed Gull** (Adult; Oct)
Larus bulleri Text p.257

(589) **Black-billed Gull** (2nd Winter; May)
.arus bulleri Text p.257

(590) **Black-billed Gull** (Adult)
Larus bulleri Text p.257

(591) **Andean Gull** (Adult Summer; June)
Larus serranus Text p.256

(592) **Andean Gull** (Adult Summer; Nov)
Larus serranus Text p.256

(593) **Andean Gull** (Adult Summer; Nov)
Larus serranus Text p.256

(594) **Andean Gull** (Adult Winter; July)
Larus serranus Text p.256

(595) **Brown-hooded Gull** (Adult Winter)
Larus maculipennis Text p.256

(596) **Brown-hooded Gull** (Adult Summer)
Larus maculipennis Text p.256

(597) **Brown-hooded Gull** (Adult Summer)
Larus maculipennis Text p.256

(598) **Brown-hooded Gull** (1st Winter; Feb)
Larus maculipennis Text p.256

(599) **Band-tailed Gull** (Adult Summer; Nov)
Larus belcheri Text p.257

(600) **Band-tailed Gull** (Adult Winter; June)
Larus belcheri Text p.257

(601) **Band-tailed Gull** (1st Winter; Sep)
Larus belcheri Text p.257

(602) **Band-tailed Gull** (Juv.; Apr)
Larus belcheri Text p.257

603) **Chinese Black-headed Gull** (Adult Winter; Dec)
arus saundersi Text p.254

(604) **Chinese Black-headed Gull** (Adult Winter; Apr)
Larus saundersi Text p.254

605) **Chinese Black-headed Gull** (Adult Winter; Dec)
arus saundersi Text p.254

(606) **Chinese Black-headed Gull** (1st Winter; Apr)
Larus saundersi Text p.254

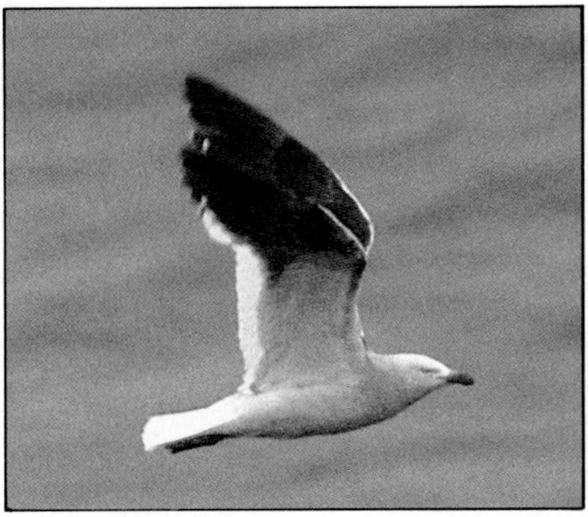

(607) **Dolphin Gull** (Adult Summer)
Larus scoresbii Text p.259

(608) **Dolphin Gull** (1st Winter
Larus scoresbii Text p.25

(609) **Dolphin Gull** (Adult Summer)
Larus scoresbii Text p.259

(610) **Dolphin Gull** (Adult Summer
Larus scoresbii Text p.25

(611) **Grey Gull** (Adult Summer; Dec)
Larus modestus Text p.259

(612) **Grey Gull** (Adult Winter, 1st Winter; Sep
Larus modestus Text p.25

(613) **Grey Gull** (1st Summer; Apr)
Larus modestus Text p.259

(614) **Grey Gull** (1st Summer; Apr)
Larus modestus Text p.259

(615) **Lava Gull** (Adult Summer)
Larus fuliginosus Text p.259

(616) **Lava Gull** (Adult Summer)
Larus fuliginosus Text p.259

(617) **Lava Gull** (Adult Summer)
Larus fuliginosus Text p.259

(618) **Lava Gull** (2nd Winter)
Larus fuliginosus Text p.259

(619) **Sooty Gull** (Adult Summer; Dec)
Larus hemprichii Text p.258

(620) **Sooty Gull** (3rd Winter; Feb)
Larus hemprichii Text p.258

(621) **Sooty Gull** (2nd Winter)
Larus hemprichii Text p.258

(622) **Sooty Gull** (1st Summer)
Larus hemprichii Text p.258

(623) **White-eyed Gull** (Adult Summer; June)
Larus leucophthalmus Text p.258

(624) **White-eyed Gull** (Adult Summer; Apr)
Larus leucophthalmus Text p.258

(625) **White-eyed Gull** (Adult Summer, 1st Summer)
Larus leucophthalmus Text p.258

(626) **White-eyed Gull** (Adult Summer, juv.)
Larus leucophthalmus Text p.258

(627) **Caspian Tern** (Juv., adult summer)
Sterna caspia Text p.262

(628) **Caspian Tern** (Adult Summer)
Sterna caspia Text p.262

(629) **Royal Tern** (Adult Summer transitional)
Sterna maxima Text p.262

(630) **Royal Tern** (1st Winter)
Sterna maxima Text p.262

(631) **Elegant Tern** (Adult Summer; Apr)
Sterna elegans Text p.263

(632) **Elegant Tern** (Adult Winter; Sep)
Sterna elegans Text p.263

(633) **Lesser Crested Tern** (Adult, 1st Winter; Nov)
Sterna bengalensis Text p.263

(634) **Lesser Crested Tern** (Juv.)
Sterna bengalensis Text p.263

(635) **Crested Tern** (Adult Summer; June)
Sterna bergii Text p.262

(636) **Crested Tern** (Adult transitional, juv.)
Sterna bergii Text p.262

(637) **Cayenne Tern** (Adult Summer; June)
Sterna (sandvicensis) eurygnatha Text p.264

(638) **Cayenne Tern** (Adult Summer; June)
Sterna (sandvicensis) eurygnatha Text p.264

(639) **Sandwich Tern** (Adult Winter; Sep)
Sterna sandvicensis Text p.264

(640) **Sandwich Tern** (Adult Summer; Apr)
Sterna sandvicensis Text p.264

(641) **Gull-billed Tern** (Adult Summer)
Sterna nilotica Text p.260

(642) **Gull-billed Tern** (Adult Summer)
Sterna nilotica Text p.260

TERNS

(643) **Common Tern** (Adult Summer; May)
Sterna hirundo Text p.264

(644) **Common Tern** (Juv.)
Sterna hirundo Text p.264

(645) **Arctic Tern** (Adult Summer)
Sterna paradisaea Text p.265

(646) **Arctic Tern** (Juv.)
Sterna paradisaea Text p.265

(647) **Roseate Tern** (Adult Summer; Nov)
Sterna dougallii Text p.265

(648) **Roseate Tern** (Juv.)
Sterna dougallii Text p.265

(649) **Forster's Tern** (Adult Summer)
Sterna forsteri Text p.263

(650) **Forster's Tern** (1st Winter)
Sterna forsteri Text p.263

(651) **Little Tern** (Adult Summer)
Sterna albifrons Text p.265

(652) **Little Tern** (Adult Summer; June)
Sterna albifrons Text p.265

(653) **Least Tern** (Adult Summer)
Sterna antillarum Text p.266

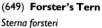

(654) **Least Tern** (Juv.)
Sterna antillarum Text p.266

(655) **Whiskered Tern** (Adult Summer)
Chlidonias hybridus Text p.261

(656) **Whiskered Tern** (Juv.; Jan)
Chlidonias hybridus Text p.261

(657) **Black Tern** (Adult Summer)
Chlidonias niger Text p.261

(658) **Black Tern** (Juv.)
Chlidonias niger Text p.261

(659) **White-winged Black Tern** (Juv. transitional)
Chlidonias leucopterus Text p.261

(660) **White-winged Black Tern** (Sep)
Chlidonias leucopterus Text p.261

(661) **White-cheeked Tern** (Adult Summer; June)
Sterna repressa Text p.268

(662) **White-cheeked Tern** (Adult Winter)
Sterna repressa Text p.268

(663) **Damara Tern** (Adult Summer)
Sterna balaenarum Text p.268

(664) **Damara Tern** (Juv.)
Sterna balaenarum Text p.268

(665) **Saunders' Little Tern** (Adult Summer)
Sterna saundersi Text p.268

(666) **Saunders' Little Tern** (Adult Summer)
Sterna saundersi Text p.268

(667) **Inca Tern** (Adult Summer; June)
Larosterna inca Text p.270

(668) **Inca Tern** (Juv.)
Larosterna inca Text p.270

(669) **Large-billed Tern** (Adult Summer; Oct)
Phaetusa simplex Text p.271

(670) **Large-billed Tern** (Adult Summer; Oct)
Phaetusa simplex Text p.271

(671) **Amazon Tern** (Adult Summer; Oct)
Sterna superciliaris Text p.271

(672) **Amazon Tern** (Adult Summer; Oct)
Sterna superciliaris Text p.271

(673) **Peruvian Tern** (Adult Summer)
Sterna lorata Text p.270

(674) **Peruvian Tern** (Adult Summer transitional)
Sterna lorata Text p.270

(675) **South American Tern** (Adult Summer; Aug)
Sterna hirundinacea Text p.270

(676) **South American Tern** (Adult, 1st Winter; Feb)
Sterna hirundinacea Text p.270

(677) **Trudeau's Tern** (Adult Summer)
Sterna trudeaui Text p.260

(678) **Trudeau's Tern** (Adult Winter)
Sterna trudeaui Text p.260

(679) **Antarctic Tern** (Adult Summer)
Sterna vittata Text p.267

(680) **Antarctic Tern** (Adult Winter)
Sterna vittata Text p.267

(681) **Kerguelen Tern** (Adult Summer)
Sterna virgata Text p.267

(682) **Kerguelen Tern** (Adult Summer)
Sterna virgata Text p.267

(683) **White-fronted Tern** (Adult Summer)
Sterna striata Text p.266

(684) **White-fronted Tern** (1st Summer; May)
Sterna striata Text p.266

(685) **Fairy Tern** (Adult Summer; Dec)
Sterna nereis Text p.266

(686) **Fairy Tern** (Juv. transitional; June)
Sterna nereis Text p.266

(687) **Black-naped Tern** (Adult)
Sterna sumatrana Text p.269

(688) **Black-naped Tern** (Adult, 1st Winter; July)
Sterna sumatrana Text p.269

(689) **Black-fronted Tern** (Adult Summer; Dec)
Sterna albostriata Text p.267

(690) **Black-fronted Tern** (Adult Winter; May)
Sterna albostriata Text p.267

(691) **Aleutian Tern** (Adult Summer)
Sterna aleutica Text p.272

(692) **Aleutian Tern** (Adult Summer; June)
Sterna aleutica Text p.272

(693) **Grey-backed Tern** (Adult Summer)
Sterna lunata Text p.272

(694) **Grey-backed Tern** (Adult Summer)
Sterna lunata Text p.272

(695) **Bridled Tern** (Adult)
Sterna anaethetus Text p.272

(696) **Bridled Tern** (Juv.)
Sterna anaethetus Text p.272

697) **Sooty Tern** (Adult Summer)
terna fuscata Text p.273

(698) **Sooty Tern** (1st Winter; Feb)
Sterna fuscata Text p.273

699) **White Tern** (Adult)
ygis alba Text p.273

(700) **White Tern** (Juv.; Aug)
Gygis alba Text p.273

701) **Grey Noddy** (Adult; May)
rocelsterna cerulea Text p.273

(702) **Grey Noddy** (Adult; Mar)
Procelsterna cerulea Text p.273

NODDIES

(703) **Brown Noddy** (Adult, juv.)
Anous stolidus Text p.274

(704) **Brown Noddy** (Adult
Anous stolidus Text p.27

(705) **Black Noddy** (Adult; May)
Anous minutus Text p.274

(706) **Black Noddy** (Juv.
Anous minutus Text p.27

(707) **Lesser Noddy** (Adult, typical)
Anous tenuirostris Text p.274

(708) **Lesser Noddy** (Adult, atypica
Anous tenuirostris Text p.27

709) **Black-bellied Tern** (Adult Summer)
terna melanogastra Text p.269

(710) **Black-bellied Tern** (Adult Summer)
Sterna melanogastra Text p.269

(711) **Indian River Tern** (Adult Summer)
Sterna aurantia Text p.269

(712) **Indian River Tern** (Adult Summer)
Sterna aurantia Text p.269

(713) **Chinese Crested Tern** (Adult Summer)
Sterna bernsteini Text p.271

(714) **Chinese Crested Tern** (Adult Winter)
Sterna bernsteini Text p.271

SKIMMERS

(715) **Black Skimmer** (Adult Summer; May)
Rynchops niger Text p.275

(716) **Black Skimmer** (Juv.; Sep)
Rynchops niger Text p.275

(717) **African Skimmer** (Adult Summer)
Rynchops flavirostris Text p.275

(718) **African Skimmer** (Adult)
Rynchops flavirostris Text p.275

(719) **Indian Skimmer** (Adult Summer)
Rynchops albicollis Text p.275

(720) **Indian Skimmer** (Adult Summer; Mar)
Rynchops albicollis Text p.275

(721) **Little Auk** (Adult Summer)
Alle alle Text p.277

(722) **Little Auk** (Dec)
Alle alle Text p.277

(723) **Atlantic Puffin** (Adult Summer)
Fratercula arctica Text p.278

(724) **Atlantic Puffin** (Adult Summer; July)
Fratercula arctica Text p.278

(725) **Brünnich's Guillemot** (Adult Summer)
Uria lomvia Text p.276

(726) **Brünnich's Guillemot** (Adult Summer; July)
Uria lomvia Text p.276

(727) **Guillemot** (Adult Summer; Apr)
Uria aalge Text p.276

(728) **Guillemot** (Adult Winter; Oct)
Uria aalge Text p.276

(729) **Razorbill** (Adult Summer)
Alca torda Text p.276

(730) **Razorbill** (Adult Summer)
Alca torda Text p.276

(731) **Black Guillemot** (Adult Summer)
Cepphus grylle Text p.277

(732) **Black Guillemot** (Adult Summer, 1st Summer)
Cepphus grylle Text p.277

(733) **Pigeon Guillemot** (Adult Summer)
Cepphus columba Text p.277

(734) **Pigeon Guillemot** (Adult Winter)
Cepphus columba Text p.277

(735) **Spectacled Guillemot** (Adult Summer)
Cepphus carbo Text p.278

(736) **Spectacled Guillemot** (Adult Winter)
Cepphus carbo Text p.278

(737) **Ancient Murrelet** (Adult Summer)
Synthliboramphus antiquum Text p.281

(738) **Ancient Murrelet** (Adult Winter)
Synthliboramphus antiquum Text p.281

(739) **Crested Murrelet** (Adult Summer; Mar)
Synthliboramphus wumizusume Text p.278

(740) **Crested Murrelet** (Adult Summer)
Synthliboramphus wumizusume Text p.278

(741) **Kittlitz's Murrelet** (Adult; July)
Brachyramphus brevirostris Text p.282

(742) **Kittlitz's Murrelet** (Adult; July)
Brachyramphus brevirostris Text p.282

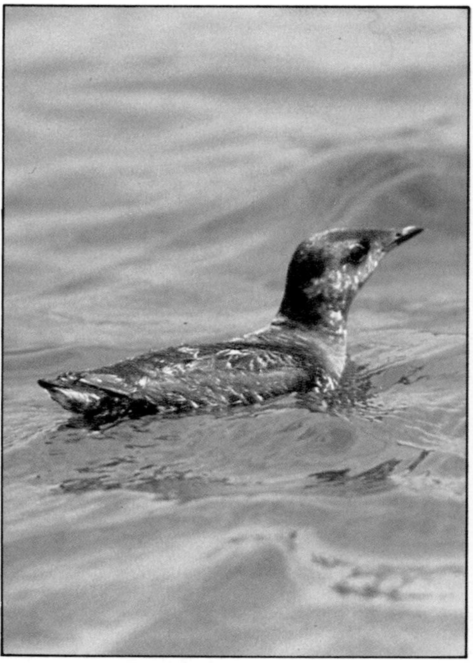

(743) **Marbled Murrelet** (Adult Summer; June)
Brachyramphus marmoratus Text p.282

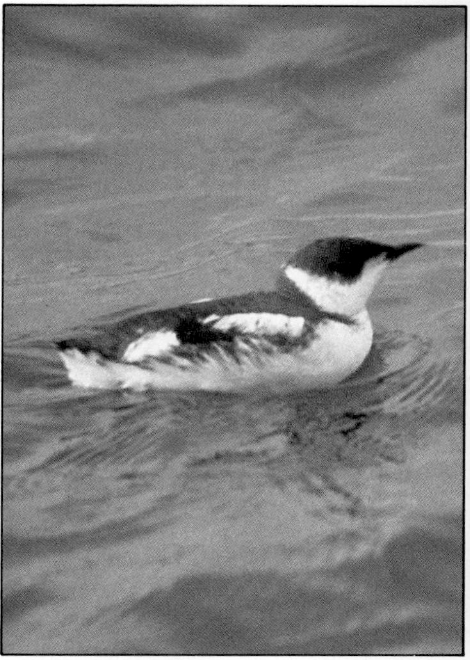

(744) **Marbled Murrelet** (Adult Winter; Feb)
Brachyramphus marmoratus Text p.282

(745) **Xantus' Murrelet** (Oct)
Synthliboramphus hypoleucus Text p.282

(746) **Xantus' Murrelet**
Synthliboramphus hypoleucus Text p.282

(747) **Craveri's Murrelet** (Oct)
Synthliboramphus craveri Text p.283

(748) **Craveri's Murrelet** (Adult, chick)
Synthliboramphus craveri Text p.283

(749) **Parakeet Auklet** (Adult Summer)
Cyclorrhynchus psittacula Text p.279

(750) **Parakeet Auklet** (Adult)
Cyclorrhynchus psittacula Text p.279

(751) **Crested Auklet** (Adult Summer)
Aethia cristatella Text p.279

(752) **Crested Auklet** (Adult Summer; June)
Aethia cristatella Text p.279

(753) **Least Auklet** (Adult Summer)
Aethia pusilla Text p.279

(754) **Least Auklet** (Adult Summer)
Aethia pusilla Text p.279

(755) **Whiskered Auklet** (Adult; May)
Aethia pygmaea Text p.280

(756) **Whiskered Auklet** (Adult; Aug)
Aethia pygmaea Text p.280

(757) **Cassin's Auklet** (Adult)
Ptychoramphus aleuticus Text p.280

(758) **Cassin's Auklet** (Juv.)
Ptychoramphus aleuticus Text p.280

(759) **Rhinoceros Auklet** (Adult Summer; June)
Cerorhinca monocerata Text p.280

(760) **Rhinoceros Auklet** (Adult Summer; June)
Cerorhinca monocerata Text p.280

761) **Horned Puffin** (Adult Summer)
ratercula corniculata Text p.281

(762) **Horned Puffin** (Adult Summer)
Fratercula corniculata Text p.281

763) **Tufted Puffin** (Adult Summer)
ratercula cirrhata Text p.281

(764) **Tufted Puffin** (Adult Summer)
Fratercula cirrhata Text p.281

SYSTEMATIC SECTION

King Penguin *Aptenodytes patagonicus* L94cm/37in **P** p. 22

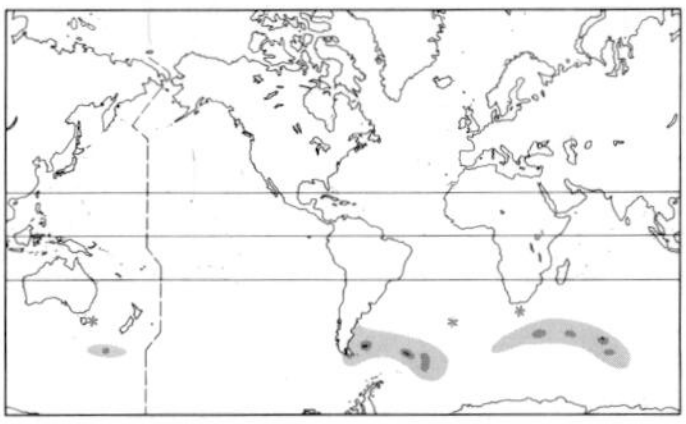

IDENTIFICATION: **Adult:** Smaller than Emperor Penguin, with different head pattern and bill colour. **Immature:** As adult, but head and dorsal area browner with pale yellow to white auricular patches and a pink stripe along base of lower mandible. At sea, immature Emperor and King Penguins can be difficult to separate, but King Penguins have pale yellow or whitish spoon-shaped auricular patches on sides of head whereas immature Emperor has dark head with white patch lower down on sides of neck. **Chick:** Dark brown.

HABITS: Gregarious, breeds twice every three years (unique), in large colonies on sub-Antarctic islands. Pelagic outside breeding season.

DISTRIBUTION: More northerly than Emperor Penguin but pelagic ranges may overlap off eastern South America. Pelagic range usually between 40°S and 55°S. Vagrants north to Gough Is, South Africa and Australia. Breeds Falkland, South Georgia, Marion, Prince Edward, Crozet, Kerguelen, Heard and Macquarie Is. May breed Staten Is.

SIMILAR SPECIES: Compare Emperor Penguin (below).

Emperor Penguin *Aptenodytes forsteri* L112cm/44in **P** p. 22

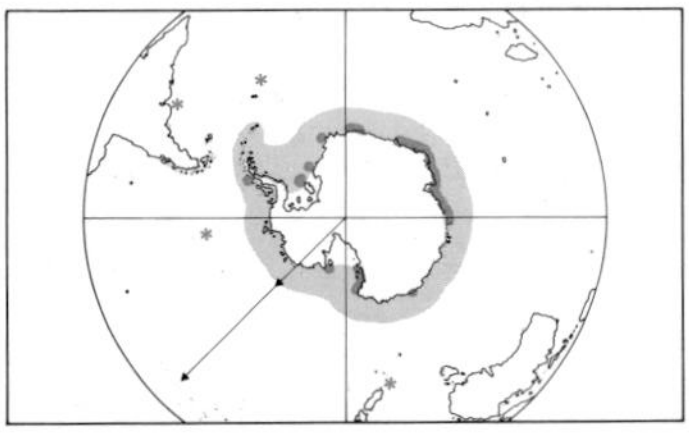

IDENTIFICATION: **Adult:** Differs from King Penguin in larger size, darker head, with pale lemon-yellow (not orange) patches on sides of neck, and proportionately shorter bill with pink or lilac stripe along base of lower mandible. **Immature:** Similar to adult but paler; patches on sides of neck whiter, stripe along lower mandible dull pinkish-orange. See King Penguin for separation of immatures at sea. **Chick:** Silvery-grey with black head and white face mask.

HABITS: Largest penguin, highly gregarious. Unique, the only penguin breeding on ice-shelf during Antarctic winter.

DISTRIBUTION: More southerly than King Penguin, usually confined to pack ice and adjacent seas but has been recorded off Patagonia at 40° 30′S (Rumboll & Jehl 1977). Breeds Mar–Dec at about 30 localities, including Dion Is, Antarctic Peninsula.

SIMILAR SPECIES: Compare King Penguin (above).

Gentoo Penguin *Pygoscelis papua* L81cm/42in **P** p. 23

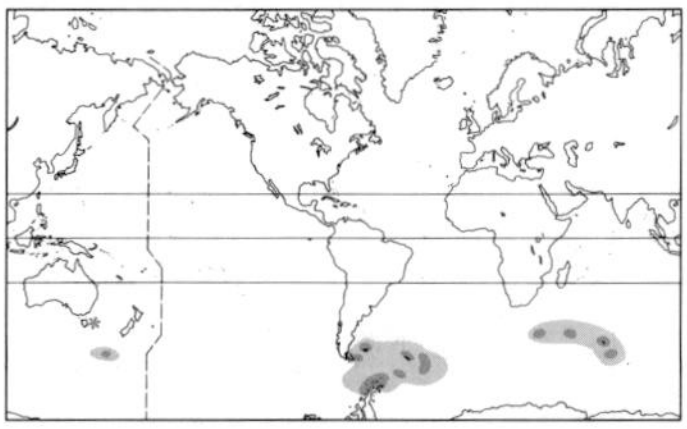

IDENTIFICATION: Third largest penguin. **Adult/Immature:** At any age the distinctive white patches over eyes separate this red-billed, medium-sized species from all other penguins. **Chick:** Brownish-grey above, white below.

HABITS: Breeds in small colonies, occasionally with other species.

DISTRIBUTION: Circumpolar in sub-Antarctic zone, from about 65°S on Antarctic Peninsula ranging north to 43°S off Argentina. Breeds Aug to Mar on islands adjacent to Antarctic Peninsula, Staten, Falkland, South Georgia, South Sandwich, South Orkney, South Shetland, Marion, Prince Edward, Crozet, Kerguelen, Heard and Macquarie Is.

SIMILAR SPECIES: Compare King, Yellow-eyed and Macaroni (p. 176, p. 179, p. 177).

Chinstrap Penguin *Pygoscelis antarctica* L68cm/27in

P p. 23

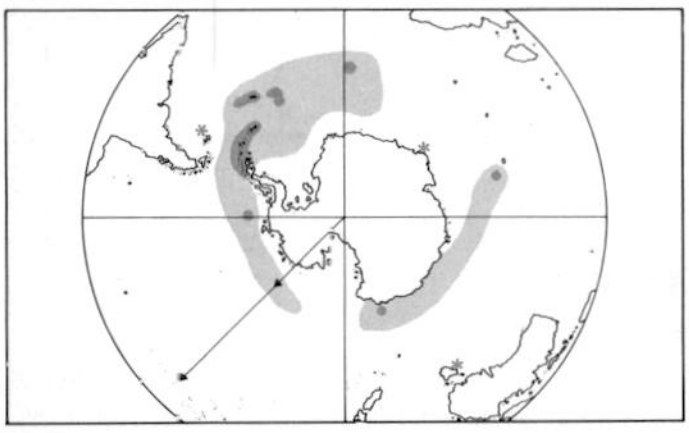

IDENTIFICATION: **Adult:** Medium-sized black and white penguin with diagnostic black line across white chin and sides of face. Unlike Adélie Penguin, demarcation between black and white occurs above eye. **Immature:** As adult but chin and throat speckled with dark grey. See notes on this page under Adélie Penguin for separation of immatures at sea. **Chick:** Greyish-brown above, paler below.
HABITS: Gregarious. Large colonies are usually in higher situations than those chosen by Adélie or Gentoo Penguins. Bold and aggressive.
DISTRIBUTION: Probably circumpolar in seas adjacent to Antarctic continent north to about 55°S. Vagrant north to Gough and Tasmania. Breeds Nov–Mar on islands adjacent to Antarctic Peninsula south to Anvers Is; and at South Orkney, South Shetland, South Georgia and South Sandwich Is. Smaller colonies occur Bouvet, Peter First, Heard and Balleny Is.
SIMILAR SPECIES: Compare Adélie Penguin (below).

Adélie Penguin *Pygoscelis adeliae* L71cm/28in

P p. 24

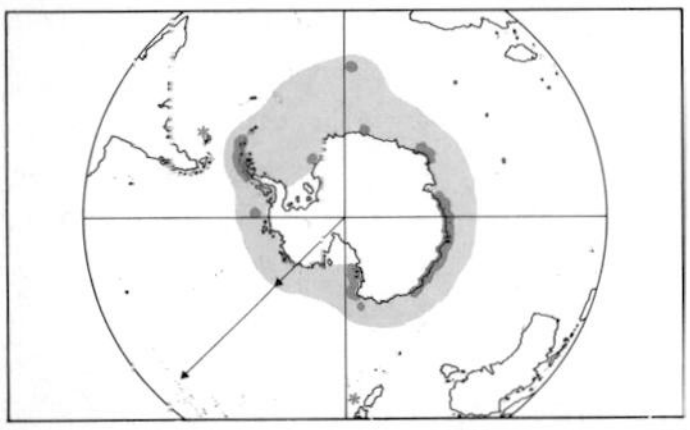

IDENTIFICATION: **Adult:** Medium-sized penguin with comical button-eyed appearance. Unlike both Gentoo and Chinstrap Penguins, head, including chin and throat, wholly black. **Immature:** As adult but chin and throat white; eye-ring dark at fledging but whitish at about one year of age. Immatures with white chins and throats resemble Chinstrap Penguins but demarcation between black and white occurs well below eye with more black on sides of neck; bill always much shorter, more stocky than that of Chinstrap. **Chick:** Wholly brownish-grey.
HABITS: Gregarious, breeds in large colonies. Bold and inquisitive.
DISTRIBUTION: Circumpolar in seas adjacent to Antarctic continent, north to about 60°S. Vagrant north to Falklands, Kerguelen and Macquarie Is. Breeds Oct–Feb along coasts and islands of Antarctic continent, South Shetlands, South Orkney, South Sandwich and Bouvet Is.
SIMILAR SPECIES: Compare Gentoo and Chinstrap Penguins (p. 176, p. 177).

Macaroni Penguin *Eudyptes chrysolophus* L70cm/28in

P p. 24

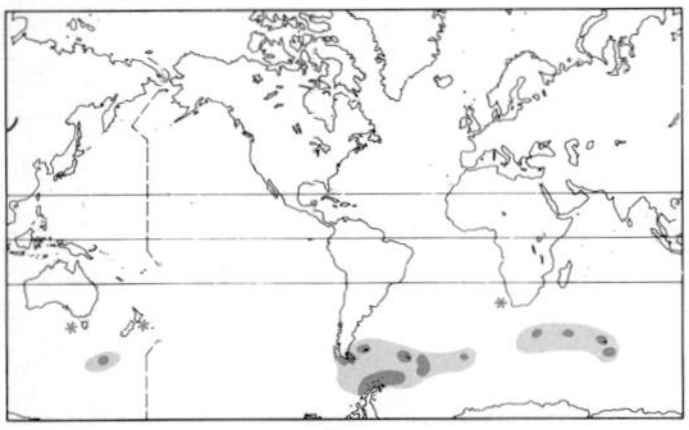

IDENTIFICATION: **Adult:** Larger than Rockhopper, differing from that and other crested penguins (except Royal) in that golden-yellow head plumes are joined across forehead. **Immature:** As adult, but orange head plumes reduced, more yellow in colour with greyer chin and throat. **Chick:** Brownish-grey above, white below.
HABITS: Gregarious, noisy and aggressive. Usually breeds in large colonies, but small numbers may occur in Rockhopper rookeries. Unlike Rockhopper, has waddling gait, rarely, if ever, hops.
DISTRIBUTION: Southern Oceans, but pelagic range poorly known, probably from 65°S north to about 45°S. Vagrants have reached South Africa. Breeds Sep–Mar Antarctic Peninsula, islands off Cape Horn, Falklands, South Georgia, South Sandwich, South Orkney, South Shetland, Bouvet, Prince Edward, Crozet, Marion, Kerguelen and Heard Is.
SIMILAR SPECIES: Compare Rockhopper and Royal Penguins (p. 178).

Royal Penguin *Eudyptes (chrysolophus) schlegeli* L76cm/30in **P** p. 25

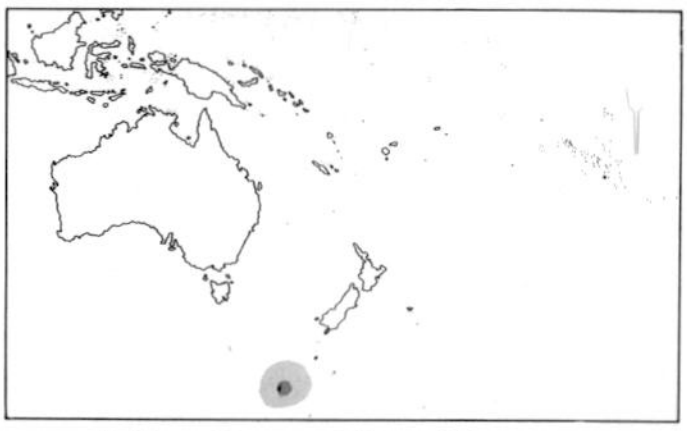

IDENTIFICATION: **Adult:** May be only a colour phase or race of Macaroni Penguin, from which it differs in larger size, more robust bill and in white or grey sides to face, chin and throat. **Immature:** As adult but head plumes shorter. **Chick:** Dark brownish-grey above, white below.
HABITS: As Macaroni Penguin.
DISTRIBUTION: Thought to be confined to Macquarie Is south of New Zealand, but birds with field characters resembling those of Royal have occurred at Marion Is, Indian Ocean. Intermediates between the two forms/species have also occurred at Macquarie and Marion Is.
SIMILAR SPECIES: Compare typical Macaroni and Rockhopper Penguins (p. 177, p. 178).

Rockhopper Penguin *Eudyptes chrysocome* L55cm/22in **P** p. 25

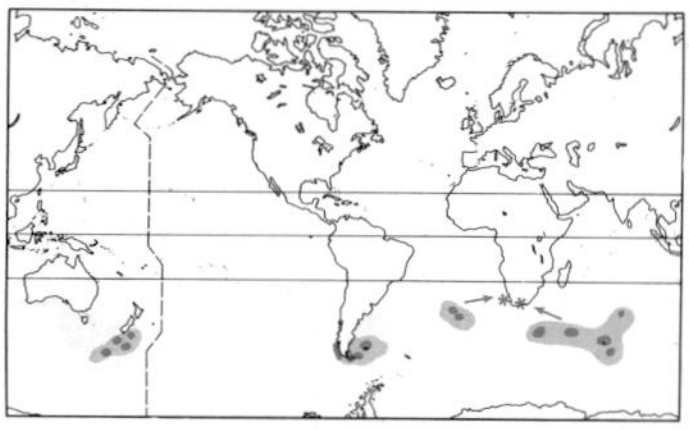

IDENTIFICATION: **Adult:** Smallest crested penguin, differing from all others in diagnostic black occipital crest and fact that the drooping golden crests neither reach the bill nor join across the forehead. Northern *E.c. moseleyi* has longer crest and darker underflipper pattern. Those at Heard, Campbell and Macquarie Is have pink area at gape inviting confusion with larger, more robust Macaroni Penguin, which, however, has more prominent fleshy gape and orange head plumes joining on forehead over bill. **Immature:** As adult but crest shorter. **Chick:** Brownish-grey above, white below.
HABITS: Gregarious, noisy and quarrelsome, usually breeds in huge colonies on steep cliffs. Progresses on land in series of stiff feet-together hops.
DISTRIBUTION: Circumpolar in sub-Antarctic zone, pelagic range probably from about 57°S north to about 35°S. Vagrants north to South Africa and Australia. Breeds Sep–Apr on islands off Cape Horn, Falklands, Tristan da Cunha, Gough, St Paul, Amsterdam, Prince Edward, Marion, Crozet, Kerguelen, Heard, Macquarie, Campbell, Auckland and Antipodes Is.
SIMILAR SPECIES: Compare Macaroni, Snares Island and Erect-crested Penguins (p. 177, p. 179).

Fiordland Crested Penguin *Eudyptes pachyrhynchus* L62cm/24in **P** p. 26

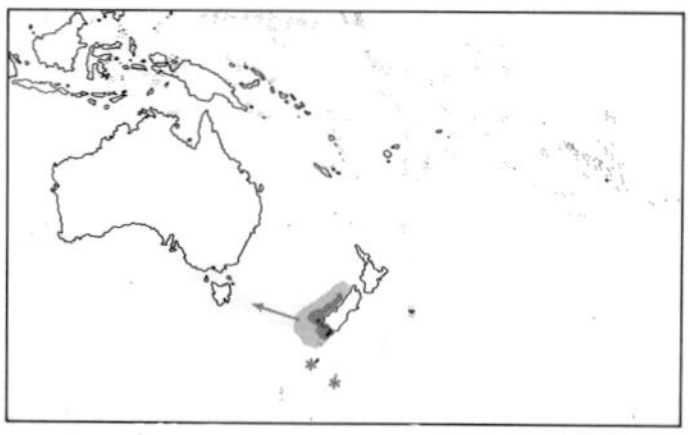

IDENTIFICATION: **Adult:** Medium-sized black and white penguin, differing from all other New Zealand penguins in absence of fleshy margins at base of bill. Sides of face usually show between two and five diagnostic white parallel stripes across dark cheeks. Unlike Snares Is and Erect-crested Penguins, the yellow crest lies flat on head (but this difference of doubtful value when crests are wet). **Immature:** As adult but crest shorter; first-year birds, recently fledged, have white chin and throat. At these ages very difficult to separate from similarly aged Snares Island Penguin at sea, but juveniles and immatures of latter species have a fleshy margin at base of bill. **Chick:** Sooty-brown above, white below.
HABITS: Loosely colonial, breeds in temperate rainforests.
DISTRIBUTION: Southern New Zealand, with post-breeding dispersal west to Tasmania and Australia and south to Snares Is. Breeds Jul–Nov South Is, from southern Westland south to Solander and Stewart Is.
SIMILAR SPECIES: Compare Erect-crested, Snares Island and Rockhopper (p. 179, p. 178).

Snares Island Penguin *Eudyptes robustus* L63cm/25in P p. 26

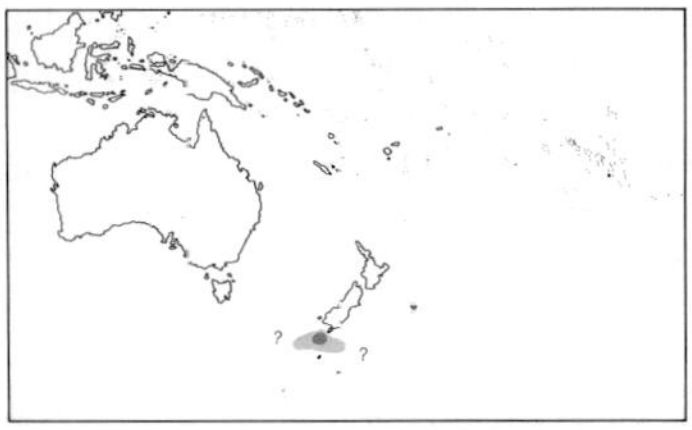

IDENTIFICATION: **Adult:** Medium-sized black and white crested penguin. Differs from similar but smaller-billed Fiordland Crested Penguin in prominent fleshy margin at base of bill, uniformly dark cheeks, and narrower, more upright crest with bushy end. Erect-crested Penguin has more upward-sweeping, brush-like crest and broader dark margins to underside of flipper. **Immature:** As adult but crest shorter. Recently fledged birds have white chin and throat mottled with black. See notes under Fiordland Crested Penguin for separation of non-adults (p. 178). **Chick:** Smoky-brown above, white below.

HABITS: Gregarious, breeds in large colonies, usually among trees or under dense bushes; occasionally roosts on branches of low trees.

DISTRIBUTION: Breeds only at Snares Is, south of New Zealand, Aug–Jan, dispersing to adjacent seas, but pelagic range unknown. Has occurred Australia (Warham pers. comm.).

SIMILAR SPECIES: Compare Fiordland Crested, Erect-crested and Rockhopper Penguins (p. 178, p. 179, p. 178).

Erect-crested Penguin *Eudyptes sclateri* L63cm/25in P p. 27

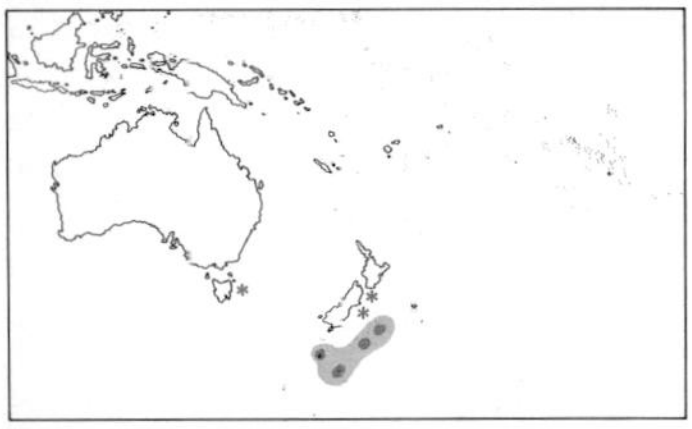

IDENTIFICATION: **Adult:** Medium-sized black and white penguin, differing from all other penguins in conspicuous upward-sweeping brush-like crest and broader dark margins to underside of flipper. **Immature:** As adult; crest less pronounced, but brush-like appearance and pattern of underflipper still enable separation from congeners. Recently fledged birds have white chin and throat. **Chick:** Sooty-black above, white below.

HABITS: Gregarious, breeds in large colonies on rocky coasts (unlike Snares and Fiordland Crested Penguins, which breed in forests).

DISTRIBUTION: Confined to sub-Antarctic islands south of New Zealand, with post-breeding dispersal north to Cook Strait, west to Tasmania and southern Australia (Serventy *et al.* 1971), and south to Macquarie Island. Breeds Sep–? in huge colonies at Bounty and Antipodes Is, New Zealand. Smaller numbers also breed at Campbell and Auckland Is.

SIMILAR SPECIES: Compare Rockhopper, Fiordland Crested and Snares Island Penguins (p. 178, p. 179).

Yellow-eyed Penguin *Megadyptes antipodes* L66cm/26in P p. 27

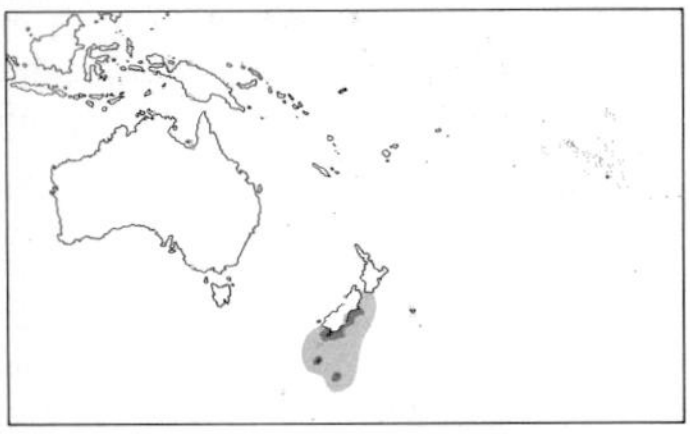

IDENTIFICATION: **Adult:** Medium-sized penguin with diagnostic pale yellow band stretching from behind eye to encircle hindcrown. No other penguin has this character, but see adult Gentoo Penguin (p. 176). **Immature:** As adult, but pale yellow band broken across nape; chin and throat mostly white. **Chick:** Wholly cocoa-brown, recalling that of King Penguin.

HABITS: Nests singly or in loose colonies in temperate forests or on grassy coastal cliffs, where it is timid and shy. At sea, usually seen singly or in small groups.

DISTRIBUTION: Sedentary, confined to southeast corner of South Island, New Zealand, but occasionally wanders to Cook Strait during non-breeding season. Breeds Aug–Mar from Oamaru, south to Stewart Island, also at Auckland and Campbell Is.

SIMILAR SPECIES: None, but compare Royal and Gentoo Penguins (p. 178, p. 176).

Little Penguin *Eudyptula minor* L40cm/16in **P** p. 28

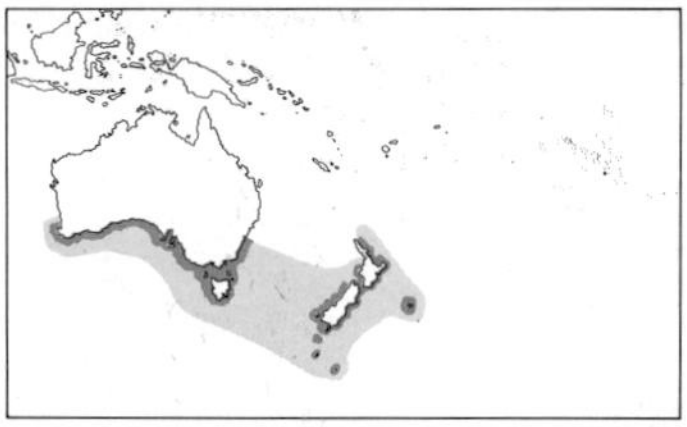

IDENTIFICATION: **Adult:** World's smallest penguin, which, with pale blue upperparts and uncrested head, should prevent confusion with all but White-flippered Penguin (see below). **Immature:** As adult but bill smaller, upperparts often bluer. **Chick:** Light greyish-chocolate above, whitish below.
HABITS: Gregarious, nests in burrows, hollows under bushes or rocks; usually returns to land at dusk.
DISTRIBUTION: Largely sedentary, confined to adjacent seas of southern Australia, Tasmania and New Zealand. Breeds Jun–Oct, occurring in Australia from Fremantle east to Port Stephens and coasts and offshore islands of New Zealand.
SIMILAR SPECIES: Compare with White-flippered Penguin (below).

White-flippered Penguin *Eudyptula (minor) albosignata* L41cm/16in **P** p. 28

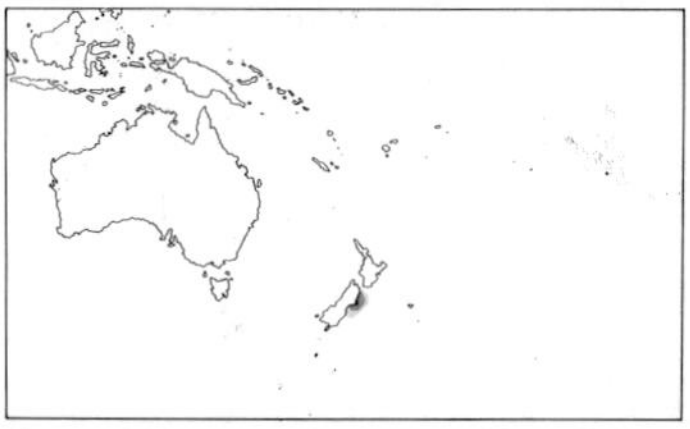

IDENTIFICATION: Usually regarded as a subspecies of Little Penguin. **Adult:** Differs from nominate form in slightly larger size, paler blue-grey upperparts, and broad white margins to both leading and trailing edges of upper flipper which, in males, may link across centre of flipper. **Immature:** As adult but bill smaller. **Chick:** Light greyish-chocolate above, whitish below.
HABITS: As for Little Penguin.
DISTRIBUTION: Restricted to Banks Peninsula, near Canterbury on east coast of South Is, New Zealand.
SIMILAR SPECIES: None, but compare with nominate form, Little Penguin (above).

Jackass Penguin *Spheniscus demersus* L70cm/28in **P** p. 29

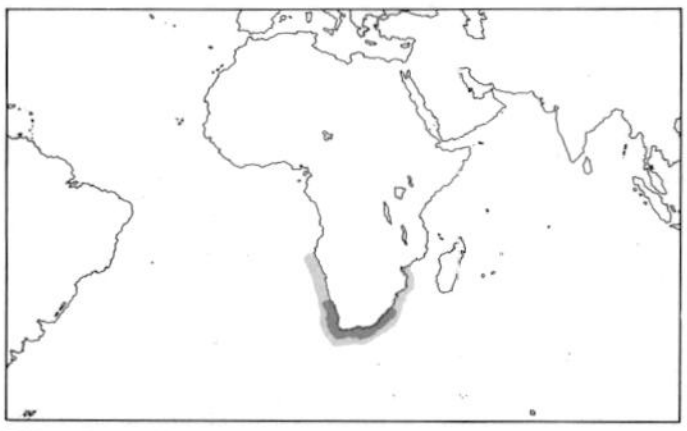

IDENTIFICATION: **Adult:** Distinctive. The only penguin occurring regularly off coasts of southern Africa. The diagnostic black and white head pattern distinguishes it from vagrant Rockhopper and Macaroni Penguins, which have yellow crests. Some individuals show a partial or second black breastband across white upper breast suggesting Magellanic Penguin (beware). **Immature:** Head mostly grey, thus lacks distinctive head pattern of adult. Breastband incomplete. **Chick:** Head and upperparts brown, underparts whitish.
HABITS: Gregarious, breeds in huge colonies in burrows. At sea, often seen in small groups, usually within 50km of shoreline.
DISTRIBUTION: Endemic to southern Africa; non-breeders often wander north to Angola and Mozambique. Breeds throughout year, chiefly May–Aug, on offshore islands of Namibia and South Africa, east to eastern Cape Province.
SIMILAR SPECIES: None in area, but compare Rockhopper and Macaroni Penguins (p. 178, p. 177).

Humboldt Penguin *Spheniscus humboldti* L65cm/26in P p. 29

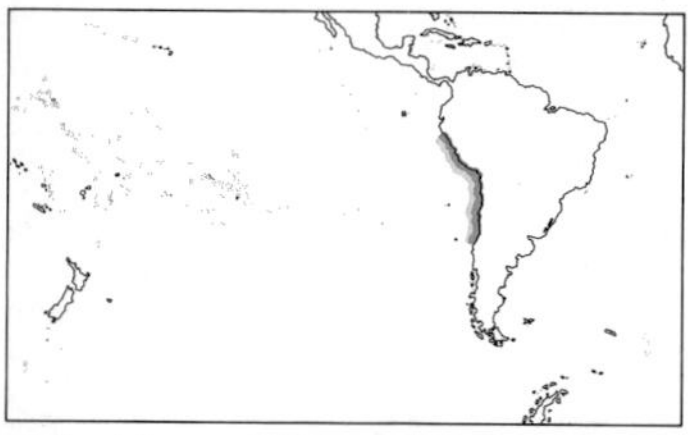

IDENTIFICATION: The only black and white penguin to occur regularly along coasts of Peru; in Chile, range overlaps with similar Magellanic Penguin off northern Chile. **Adult:** Differs from Magellanic in larger bill, more pink at base of bill, narrower white bands on the sides of head and only one black band across upper breast. **Immature:** Lacks adult's distinctive head pattern, head appearing mostly grey; no breastband. Differs from corresponding Magellanic Penguin in more pink at base of bill, and darker head colour extending to include upper breast. **Chick:** Head and upperparts dark grey, white below.

HABITS: Gregarious at colonies, where it nests in burrows; but less gregarious at sea, where it occurs singly or in small groups ranging up to 50km from landfall.

DISTRIBUTION: Confined to coasts of Peru and Chile; occasionally wanders north to Guayaquil and south to 37°S in Chile. Breeds throughout year from about 5°S in Peru southward to about 33°S near Valparaiso, Chile.

SIMILAR SPECIES: Compare Magellanic Penguin (below).

Magellanic Penguin *Spheniscus magellanicus* L70cm/28in P p. 30

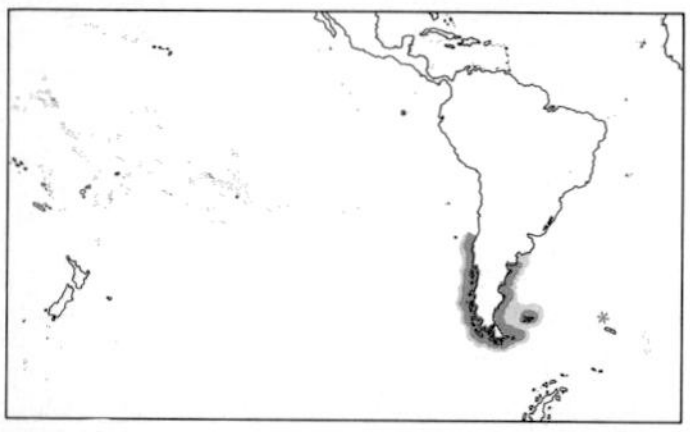

IDENTIFICATION: **Adult:** Distinctive white stripe on side of face should prevent confusion with all but Humboldt Penguin (see notes above). **Immature:** Lacks adult's distinctive head pattern; sides of face, chin and throat mostly whitish or pale grey giving slight capped effect, with indistinct grey band across white upper breast. Immature Humboldt has darker head with obvious pink at base of bill. **Chick:** Upperparts brown, underparts whitish.

HABITS: The most numerous *Spheniscus* penguin, gregarious and noisy at colonies but rather timid; nests in burrows. Perhaps more pelagic than Humboldt Penguin during breeding season, when usually encountered in small groups of up to 50 birds.

DISTRIBUTION: Atlantic and Pacific coasts of South America. During non-breeding season range extends north to 23°S off Brazil and to about 30°S off Chile. Vagrants have reached New Zealand and South Georgia (Watson 1975). Breeds Sep–Apr Falklands and along coasts of Chile from 37°S southwards to Cape Horn and then north to about 40°S in Patagonia.

SIMILAR SPECIES: Compare Humboldt Penguin (above).

Galapagos Penguin *Spheniscus mendiculus* L53cm/21in P p. 30

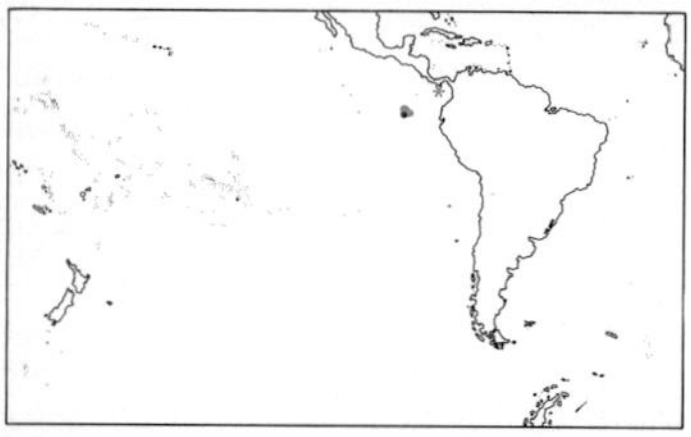

IDENTIFICATION: **Adult:** Virtually unmistakable, the only penguin of the region. Compared with Humboldt Penguin, much smaller with less distinct facial markings and breastband; lower mandible mostly pink. **Immature:** Lacks adult's distinctive head pattern and breastband. **Chick:** Undescribed.

HABITS: Gregarious but colonies often small, numbering up to about 40 pairs, and scattered.

DISTRIBUTION: Endemic to the Galapagos Islands, where it breeds on Fernandina and Isabela. Small parties also occur at James, Santa Cruz and Floreana.

SIMILAR SPECIES: None within normal range.

Great Northern Diver *Gavia immer* L76cm/30in W137/54in

P p. 30

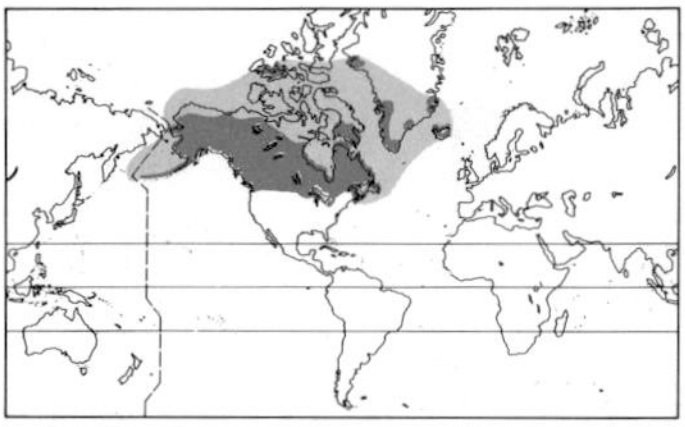

IDENTIFICATION: Summer adults distinctive, but separation from White-billed and Black-throated Divers in winter problematical. When swimming, appears larger than most Black-throated with heavier bill, thicker neck and flatter crown; flight more goose-like, with slower measured beats. **Adult Summer:** Combination of black bill, blackish head and neck with white necklace diagnostic. **Adult Winter:** Bill usually grey or whitish, inviting confusion with White-billed Diver, but culmen always dark; head usually darker. Compared with winter Black-throated Diver, area around eye usually paler, crown and hindneck darker than upperparts, more irregular dark/light division down side of neck and (in most birds) absence of white flank patch. **First Winter:** As adult winter, but upperparts scaled with white.

HABITS: Breeds singly at freshwater locations, but in winter moves to mainly coastal habitat where often seen in small groups.

DISTRIBUTION: Northern Hemisphere; breeds from Aleutian Is eastwards across North America to Greenland and Iceland. In winter may move as far south as about 30°N.

SIMILAR SPECIES: Compare Black-throated, Pacific and White-billed Divers (p. 183, p. 182), also swimming Great Cormorant (p. 235).

White-billed Diver *Gavia adamsii* L83cm/33in W147cm/58in

P p. 31

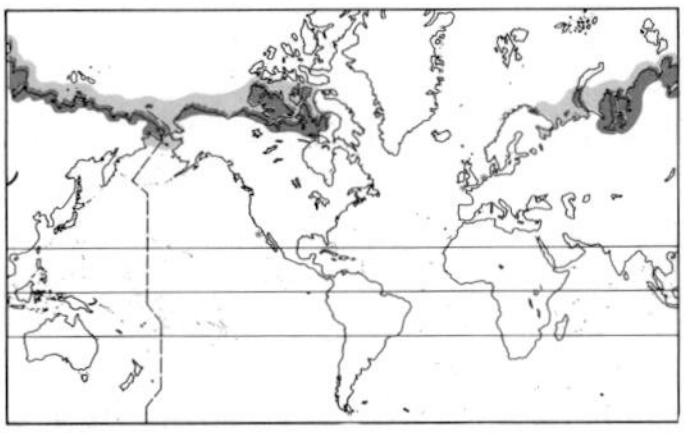

IDENTIFICATION: Largest diver. Characteristic upward tilt of bill and head recalls much smaller Red-throated Diver. Bill usually longer and larger than Great Northern, with almost straight culmen and sharp upwards angle from gonys to tip. White primary shafts diagnostic. **Adult Summer:** Combination of white or yellowish bill, black head and white necklace diagnostic. **Adult Winter:** Differs from Great Northern in longer, diagnostic upturned ivory bill and much paler crown and hindneck. Unlike Great Northern, head and neck usually appear paler than upperparts. **First Winter:** As adult winter, but paleness of head and hindneck further emphasised by conspicuously pale auricular patch and dark mark behind eye. Upperparts more distinctly scaled than in Great Northern Diver.

HABITS: Breeds singly at freshwater locations, moving to coasts in winter.

DISTRIBUTION: Northern Hemisphere; breeds high Arctic from Alaska east to northwest Canada and in Eurasia from Murmansk east to Siberia. In winter moves south to about 50°N.

SIMILAR SPECIES: Great Northern, Black-throated and Pacific Divers (p. 182, p. 183, p. 182).

Pacific Diver *Gavia (arctica) pacifica* L66cm/26in W118cm/46in

P p. 31

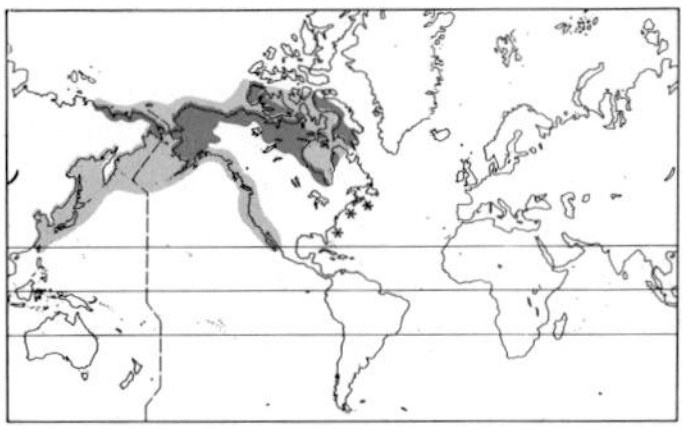

IDENTIFICATION: **Adult:** On present knowledge cannot be separated in winter or immature plumages from the slightly smaller Black-throated Diver, although appears to lack that species' white flank patch in winter/immature plumages; bill averages smaller. **Adult Summer:** Differs from Black-throated in purple (not greenish) gloss to throat patch and in more extensive whitish area on nape.

HABITS: As for Black-throated Diver.

DISTRIBUTION: Northern Hemisphere; breeds eastern Siberia, Alaska and Canada, moving during winter to coasts of Japan and western North America south to California.

SIMILAR SPECIES: Red-throated, Black-throated and Great Northern Divers (p. 183, p. 182).

Black-throated Diver *Gavia arctica* L68cm/27in W120cm/47in **P** p. 31

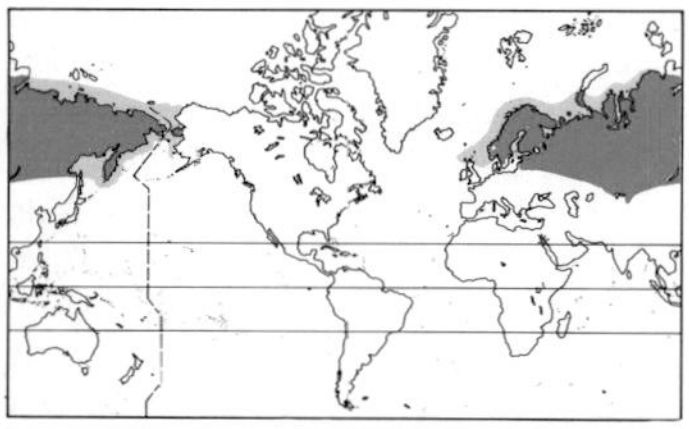

IDENTIFICATION: Size intermediate between Red-throated and Great Northern Divers. When swimming, differs from Red-throated in thicker neck and in straighter more dagger-like bill carried horizontally. Great Northern averages noticeably larger. **Adult Summer:** Combination of grey head, blackish-green throat patch and spangled upperparts separates from all but Pacific Diver (p. 182). **Adult Winter:** Unlike Great Northern, crown and nape paler than back with cap extending to eye; sides of neck have equal brown and white division; has white patch on flank. **First Winter:** As adult winter, but upperparts scaled white.
HABITS: Breeds singly at freshwater locations, moving to coast in winter where often forms loose flocks.
DISTRIBUTION: Breeds Apr–Aug in Northern Hemisphere, from Scotland, where rare, east to Siberia. In winter moves south to about 30°N.
SIMILAR SPECIES: Compare Pacific, Red-throated and Great Northern Divers (p. 182, p. 183, p. 182), also swimming Shag (p. 235).

Red-throated Diver *Gavia stellata* L61cm/24in W110cm/43in **P** p. 32

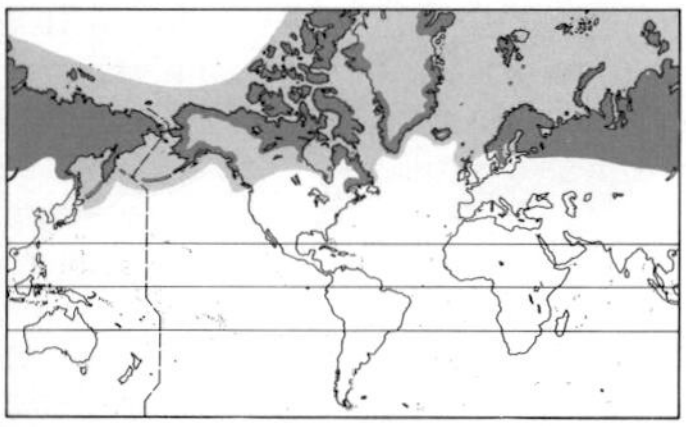

IDENTIFICATION: Smallest diver. At all ages, when swimming, small head coupled with slender neck and bill carried in characteristic upward tilt enables separation from Black-throated Diver. In flight, wingbeats higher, faster than Black-throated. **Adult Summer:** Combination of grey head, striped hindneck and red throat patch diagnostic; brown upperparts lack white blocking of congeners. **Adult Winter:** Upperparts spotted white, which with more extensive white on sides of face and neck enhance overall paler appearance than that of larger, darker Black-throated Diver. **First Winter:** As adult winter, but bill greyer, forehead darker, sides of neck speckled with brown.
HABITS: Most northerly diver, breeding singly at freshwater locations; in winter moves to coast, where often forms small flocks.
DISTRIBUTION: Circumpolar, breeds May–Sep, moving south in winter to about 30°N.
SIMILAR SPECIES: Compare Black-throated Diver and swimming Shag (p. 183, p. 235).

Great Crested Grebe *Podiceps cristatus* L49cm/19in W87cm/34in **P** p. 32

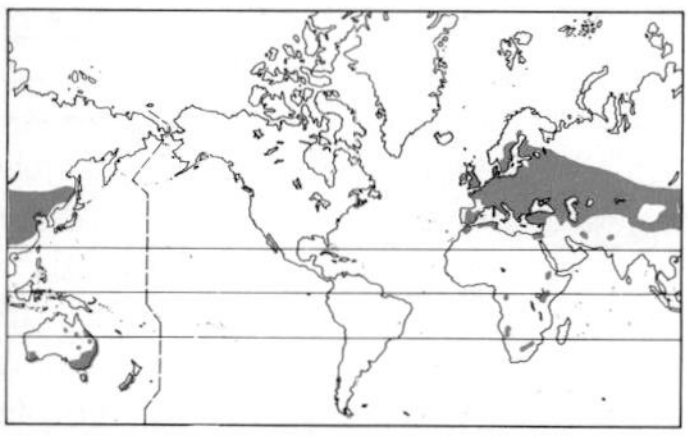

IDENTIFICATION: Unmistakable in summer, when crest and chestnut frills often erected during head-waggling and other displays. In winter, when swimming, usually appears much longer- and thinner-necked than Red-necked Grebe, with longer sloping crown and pinkish bill; body longer, usually flatter, not so hunched or rounded. **Adult Summer:** Combination of white sides of face, black crown extending to double crest, and chestnut frills diagnostic. **Adult Winter:** Resembles adult summer, but crest much reduced, crown greyer, no frills on sides of face. Unlike Red-necked Grebe, dark cap always separated from eye by white supercilium. **Juvenile:** As adult winter, but sides of face striped.
HABITS: Breeds freshwater locations, occasionally loosely colonial. Northern populations disperse to coasts during winter.
DISTRIBUTION: Throughout much of Europe and Asia; also Africa and Australia.
SIMILAR SPECIES: Compare Red-necked Grebe (p. 185).

Western Grebe *Aechmophorus occidentalis* L65cm/26in W90cm/35in P p. 33

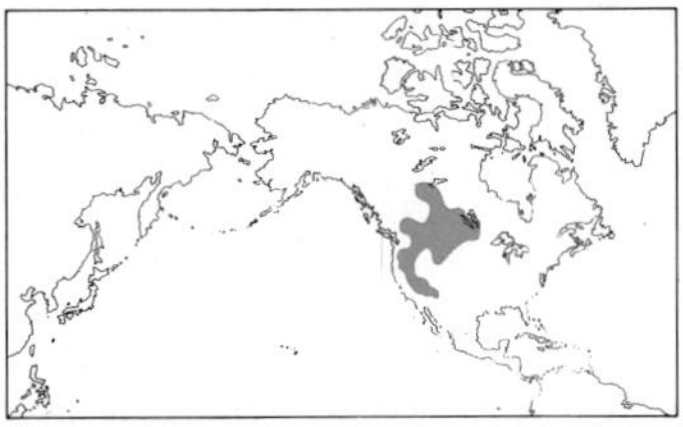

IDENTIFICATION: Largest North American grebe, with swan-like neck and long, slightly upturned bill. Two forms (sometimes treated as separate species), differing in extent of black on sides of face and mottling on flanks. Dark forms have greenish-yellow bills, pale forms yellowish-orange bills. **Adult Summer:** Large size, black crown and hindneck contrasting with white foreneck diagnostic. **Adult Winter:** Division between black and white sides of face less distinct. **Juvenile:** As adult winter, but crown and hindneck greyer.
HABITS: Highly colonial, breeds freshwater locations, dispersing to coasts and lakes in winter. Often forms large flocks.
DISTRIBUTION: Confined to western North America. Breeds Apr–Sep.
SIMILAR SPECIES: Compare Red-necked Grebe (p. 185).

Pied-billed Grebe *Podilymbus podiceps* L34cm/13in W59cm/23in P p. 34

IDENTIFICATION: Larger than Little Grebe, appears stocky when swimming, with short neck, large head and banded chicken-like bill. **Adult Summer:** Banded bill combined with black chin and throat diagnostic. **Adult Winter:** As adult summer, but band on bill faint or absent, chin and throat whitish. **Juvenile:** As adult winter, but sides of head and neck striped.
HABITS: Skulking and shy, breeds singly at freshwater locations. Winters on fresh or salt water, where more easily seen but not usually gregarious.
DISTRIBUTION: Breeds Mar–Aug throughout much of North and South America, dispersing to coasts and estuaries in winter.
SIMILAR SPECIES: Compare Little Grebe (below).

Little Grebe *Tachybaptus ruficollis* L27cm/11in W42cm/17in P p. 34

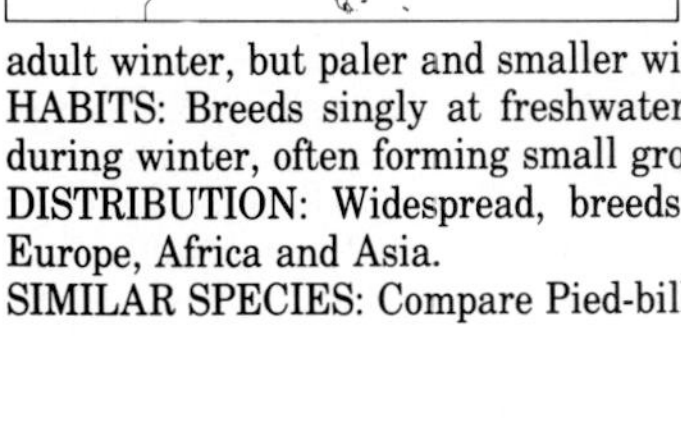

IDENTIFICATION: Smallest Old World grebe; swims buoyantly, rear end often with dumpy powder-puff appearance. Separated from winter Horned and Black-necked Grebes by structure, lack of any black and white contrasts, noticeable even at distance. **Adult Summer:** Yellowish gape patch combined with chestnut sides of face and foreneck diagnostic. **Adult Winter:** Crown, hindneck and upperparts dark olive-brown, sides of face and underparts sandy, ventral area white. **Juvenile:** As adult winter, but paler and smaller with striped head.
HABITS: Breeds singly at freshwater locations; northern birds disperse to lakes and coasts during winter, often forming small groups.
DISTRIBUTION: Widespread, breeds Feb–Oct depending on location, freshwater ponds of Europe, Africa and Asia.
SIMILAR SPECIES: Compare Pied-billed, Horned and Black-necked Grebes (p. 184, p. 185).

Red-necked Grebe *Podiceps grisegena* L45cm/18in W80cm/31in

P p. 32

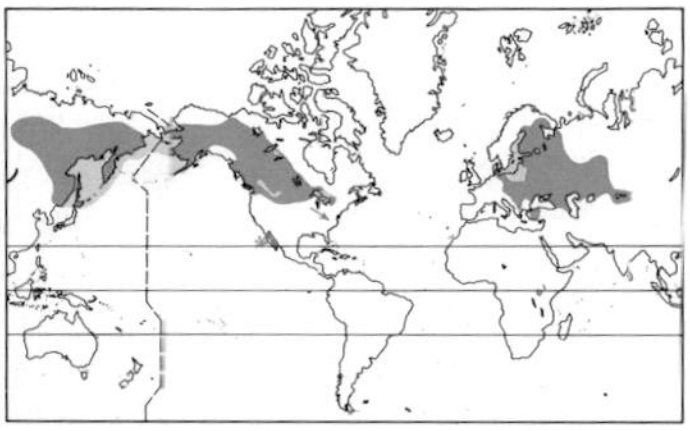

IDENTIFICATION: At all ages look for diagnostic yellow base to both mandibles. Smaller, more compact and rounded than Great Crested Grebe, bill shorter, less dagger-like, with proportionately larger more bulbous head; neck thicker and shorter. **Adult Summer:** Combination of black cap, pale grey cheeks and chestnut foreneck diagnostic. **Adult Winter:** As adult summer, but cap less distinct, sides of face mottled grey; most show whitish foreneck except for pale grey collar across upper neck. Unlike winter Great Crested, dark cap always extends to surround eye. More bulky than winter Horned Grebe, with darker cheeks and longer thicker bill, yellow at base. **Juvenile:** Resembles adult, sides of face striped.

HABITS: Breeds freshwater locations, moving to coastal habitat during winter where flocks often formed. When diving often jumps clear of water.

DISTRIBUTION: Breeds May–Aug western North America, parts of Europe and southeast Asia.

SIMILAR SPECIES: Compare Great Crested, Western and Horned Grebes (p. 183, p. 184, p. 185).

Horned Grebe *Podiceps auritus* L33cm/13in W60cm/24in

P p. 33

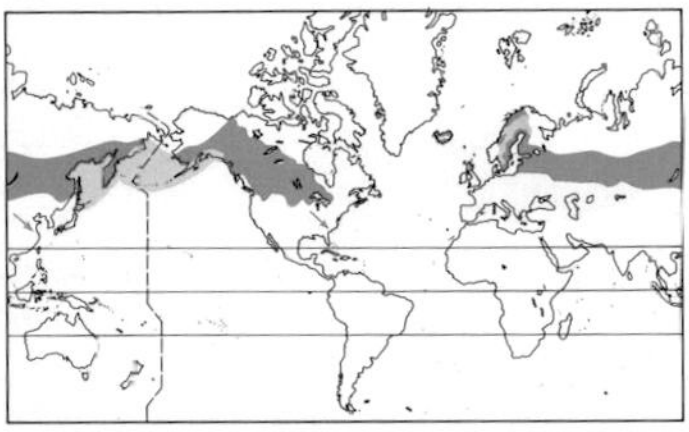

IDENTIFICATION: Breeding adults distinctive. Harder to separate in winter from Black-necked Grebe but, at all ages when swimming, less petite, head larger, crown flatter with thicker neck; stubby bill lacks upward tilt. Red-necked Grebe is larger with diagnostic bill. **Adult Summer:** Combination of black head, 'golden horns' and chestnut foreneck diagnostic. **Adult Winter:** Differs from Black-necked in diagnostic pale-tipped bill, grey spot on lores, black cap extending only to eye with much whiter sides of face and foreneck (beware birds in transitional plumage). **Juvenile:** As adult winter, but more diffuse division between dark cap and white cheeks.

HABITS: Breeds freshwater locations, moving south in winter to both coasts and lakes where often forms small flocks.

DISTRIBUTION: Breeds Apr–Aug throughout much of Northern Hemisphere, dispersing south to about 30°N in winter.

SIMILAR SPECIES: Compare Black-necked and Red-necked Grebes (this page).

Black-necked Grebe *Podiceps nigricollis* L30cm/12in W57cm/22in

P p. 33

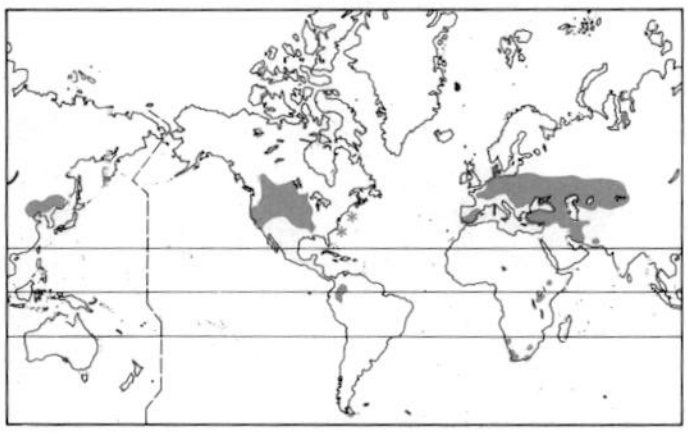

IDENTIFICATION: Breeding adults distinctive. In winter, compared with Horned Grebe, head smaller with steeply rising forecrown, more peaked crown, and longer, thinner bill with distinctive upward tilt; neck thinner, usually sits higher in water. **Adult Summer:** Combination of yellow ear tufts and black foreneck diagnostic. **Adult Winter:** Separated from winter Horned Grebe by all-dark bill, dark cap extending well below eye, white chin extending up as narrow crescent behind eye, and duskier foreneck. **Juvenile:** As adult winter, but sides of face and base of foreneck duskier.

HABITS: More gregarious than Horned, breeds colonially at freshwater locations, moving in winter to both coasts and lakes where often forms flocks.

DISTRIBUTION: Breeds Apr–Aug in western North America, Eurasia east to Mongolia; isolated populations South America, Africa and China. Northern birds disperse south to 30°N in winter.

SIMILAR SPECIES: Compare Red-necked and Horned Grebes (above).

Wandering Albatross *Diomedea exulans*

L115cm/45in W330cm/130in **P** p. 35 **K** p. 287

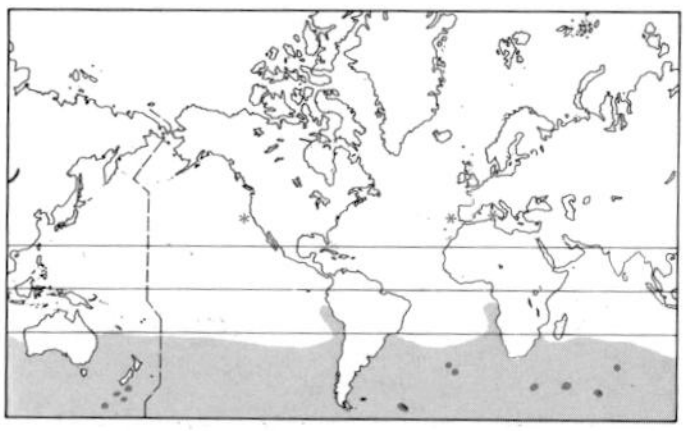

IDENTIFICATION: Plumage variable, beginning as mostly dark brown juvenile and becoming progressively whiter. Separation from Royal Albatross always difficult, but in Wandering the dark upperwing whitens from a central wedge outwards to the leading edge of wing whereas in nominate Royal wing whitens from leading edge backwards. Any large white-backed albatross with brown on head, breast and back or black sides to tail will be Wandering. Many birds retain this intermediate plumage, but others attain mostly white appearance at which stage difficult to tell from Royal. See identification keys p. 286, p. 287 for differences in plumage.

HABITS: Wandering, Royal and Amsterdam Albatrosses are the largest of all seabirds, with magnificent soaring flight on long stiffly held wings. Wandering is habitual ship follower. Breeds in loose colonies on grassy headlands and plateaux of oceanic islands.

DISTRIBUTION: Circumpolar in Southern Hemisphere north to Tropic of Capricorn, but occasionally to 10°S in cold-water zones. Biennial 13-month cycle Nov–Dec; breeds South Georgia, Inaccessible, Gough, Amsterdam, Marion, Prince Edward, Heard (?), Crozet, Kerguelen, Macquarie, Auckland, Campbell and Antipodes Is.

SIMILAR SPECIES: Compare Royal and Amsterdam Albatrosses (below).

Royal Albatross *Diomedea epomophora*

L114cm/45in W330cm/130in **P** p. 35 **K** p. 286

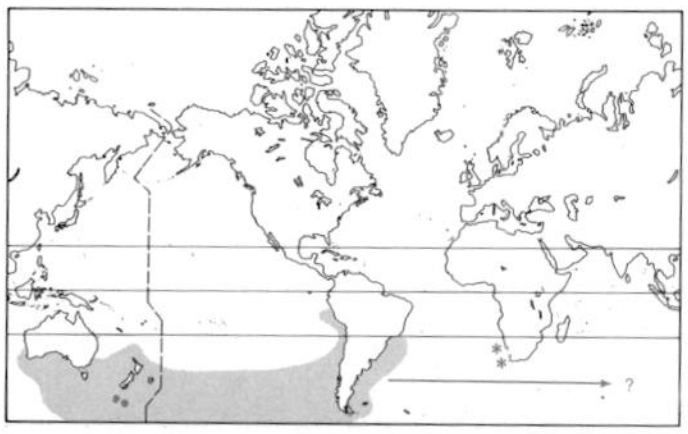

IDENTIFICATION: Two races with variable plumages, but, unlike Wandering, body and tail mostly white at all ages. In nominate race, juveniles fledge with blackish upperwing and small dark tips to tail; in subsequent plumage tail becomes white and upperwing whitens from leading edge backwards (cf. Wandering). Race *sanfordi* fledges with brown speckling on crown and across lower back and, at all ages, has a diagnostic black leading edge on underwing near carpal.

HABITS: Much as Wandering Albatross, sweeping majestically over ocean.

DISTRIBUTION: Circumpolar in Southern Hemisphere north to Tropic of Capricorn, but occasionally to 10°S off western South America. Has 13-month biennial cycle Nov–Dec at Chatham, Auckland and Campbell Is, New Zealand, and at Taiaroa Head, South Island, New Zealand.

SIMILAR SPECIES: Compare Wandering and Amsterdam Albatrosses (this page).

Amsterdam Albatross *Diomedea amsterdamensis* L? W? **P** p. 36 **K** p. 286

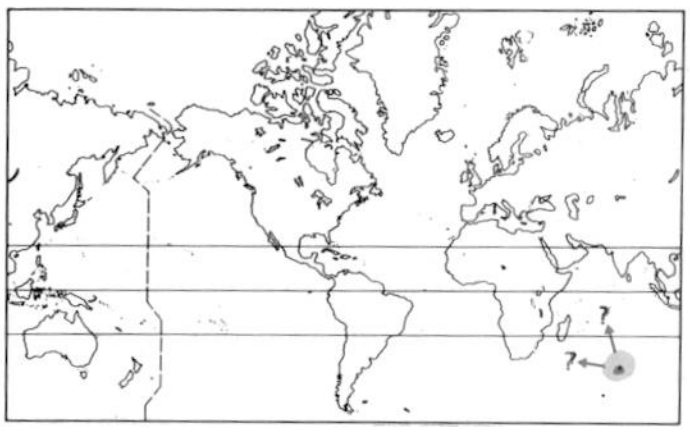

IDENTIFICATION: Following account based on Roux *et al.* (1983). Recently discovered species, perhaps averaging slightly smaller overall than Wandering Albatross. At all ages, plumages resemble the dark immature stage of Wandering. Can be distinguished by dark tip and cutting edges to bill; a dark line along leading edge of underwing at point where wing joins body, and (in darker-plumaged birds) a distinct dark patch extending from sides of body to leg.

HABITS: Probably as Wandering, but breeding cycle begins about 2 months later.

DISTRIBUTION: Nothing known of dispersal or movements; up to 8 pairs attempt breeding Amsterdam Is, Indian Ocean.

SIMILAR SPECIES: Compare Wandering and Royal Albatrosses (above).

White-capped Albatross *Diomedea cauta cauta*
L99cm/39in W256cm/101in **P** p. 36 **K** p. 288

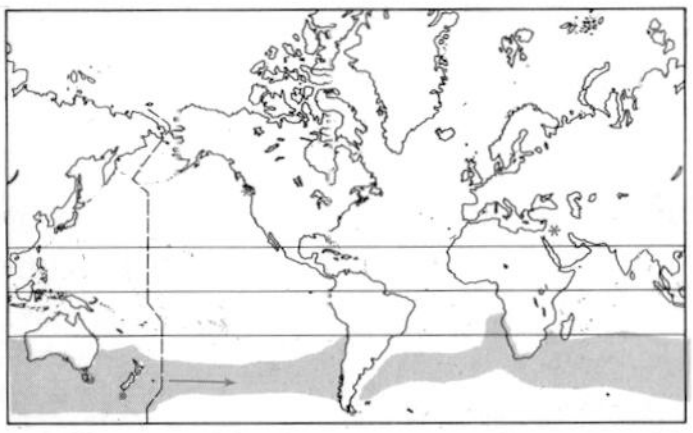

IDENTIFICATION: The three subspecies of *cauta* albatrosses are sometimes treated as separate species. They are the largest black-backed albatrosses, approaching Wandering Albatross in size. All three species/subspecies differ from all other albatrosses in narrow black margins to white underwing and diagnostic thumb mark at base of leading edge (see p. 288). **Adult:** Differs from *D.(c.) salvini* in greyer bill with yellow tip to both mandibles; mostly white head; smaller but blacker tip to underwing. **Immature:** At fledging, head grey; underwing markings as adult. In worn plumage, head mostly white with partial collar recalling Black-browed or Grey-headed Albatrosses, but easily separated by bill and underwing colours.
HABITS: Breeds colonially on oceanic islands; follows ships. Flight recalls that of Wandering.
DISTRIBUTION: Southern Oceans north to about 25°S, occurring on both coasts of South America and South Africa. Breeds Aug–Apr, Tasmania and Bass Strait region, also Auckland Is.
SIMILAR SPECIES: None; see Black-browed, Yellow-nosed and Grey-headed Albatrosses (p. 188). See below for subspecific separation from Salvin's and Chatham Is.

Salvin's Albatross *Diomedea (cauta) salvini*
L95cm/37in W250cm/98in **P** p. 37 **K** p. 288

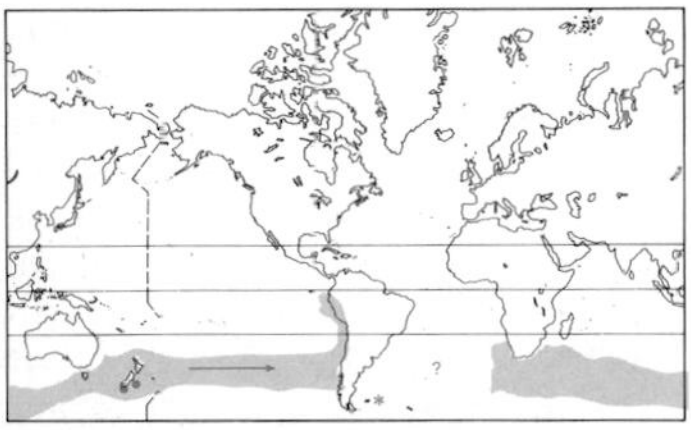

IDENTIFICATION: **Adult:** Similar to White-capped Albatross, differs in pronounced greyish-brown head contrasting with white forehead and larger, though greyer tip to underwing. From above thus resembles Buller's Albatross, but in latter species bill black and yellow and underwing pattern different. **Immature:** As for White-capped Albatross, differing only in amount of black on tip of underwing (see p. 288).
HABITS: In flight appears larger-headed than White-capped but otherwise similar.
DISTRIBUTION: Recently recorded in South Atlantic and central Indian Ocean, but not yet from Cape Horn; extends north to about 25°S in Atlantic, Indian and Pacific Oceans. Breeds Aug–Apr, Snares and Bounty Is, New Zealand.
SIMILAR SPECIES: Compare Buller's and Grey-headed Albatrosses (p. 189, p. 188).

Chatham Island Albatross *Diomedea (cauta) eremita*
L90cm/35in W220cm/87in **P** p. 37 **K** p. 288

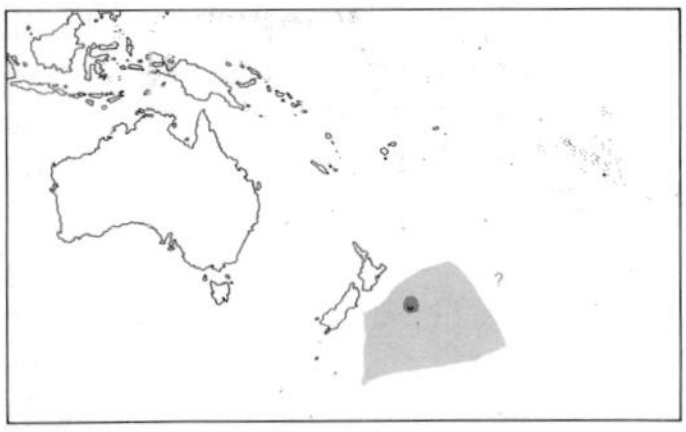

IDENTIFICATION: **Adult:** Resembles Salvin's; differs in slightly smaller size, much darker head, and bright yellow bill with dark mark on tip of lower mandible. **Immature:** Resembles adult, but bill dark olive-brown with black tip to both mandibles; grey wash sometimes extends over upper breast.
HABITS: Probably more sedentary than other *cauta* albatrosses but otherwise similar.
DISTRIBUTION: Apparently disperses only to seas adjacent to Pyramid Rock, Chatham Is, its only breeding site.
SIMILAR SPECIES: Compare Buller's and Grey-headed Albatrosses (p. 189, p. 188).

Black-browed Albatross *Diomedea melanophris*
L88cm/35in W224cm/88in P p. 38 K p. 289

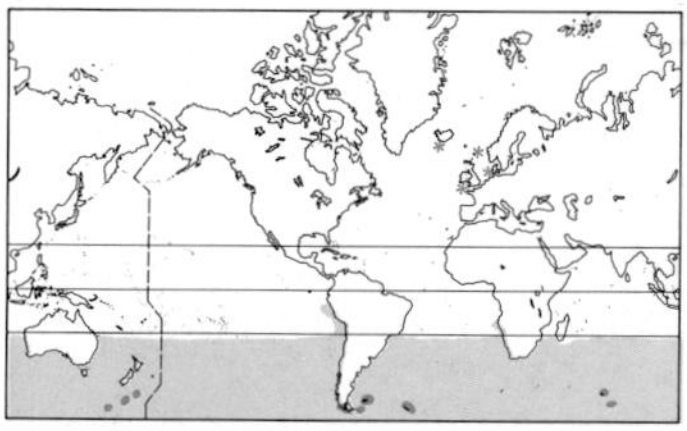

IDENTIFICATION: All albatrosses can be identified if bill, head and underwing pattern are accurately recorded. Separation of non-adult Black-browed from Grey-headed is more difficult as some overlap of plumage features occurs but, unlike Black-browed, juvenile/immature Grey-headed has mostly black bill. **Adult:** White head combined with yellow bill diagnostic; underwing white, black margins form wedge midway along leading edge. **Immature:** White head combined with blackish tip to dull yellow bill diagnostic. **Juvenile:** Bill dusky-horn with blackish tip. Head white, grey wash extends from nape across breast. Underwing dusky, but becoming paler with ghost image of adult's pattern.
HABITS: Habitual ship follower. Breeds colonially on grassy cliffs of oceanic islands; the most widespread and frequently encountered albatross.
DISTRIBUTION: Southern Oceans, breeds Aug–May Cape Horn, Staten, Falklands, South Georgia, Kerguelen, Heard, Antipodes, Macquarie and Campbell Is.
SIMILAR SPECIES: Compare Grey-headed, Buller's and Yellow-nosed (p. 188, p. 189, p. 188).

Grey-headed Albatross *Diomedea chrysostoma*
L81cm/32in W220cm/87in P p. 38 K p. 289

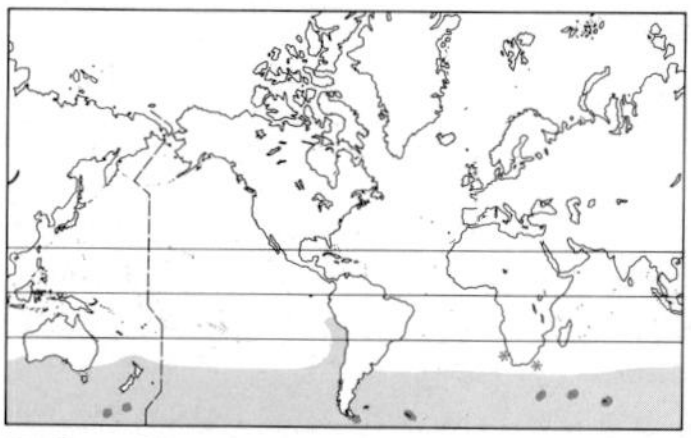

IDENTIFICATION: **Adult:** Combination of grey head plus black bill with bright yellow ridges to upper and lower mandibles diagnostic throughout much of range. In Australasia and South Pacific region beware Buller's Albatross, which has white forehead, darker head and narrower black underwing margins. **Juvenile/Immature:** Head darker than adult, underwing mostly dusky-grey. With wear/maturity, head often white with pronounced grey collar, underwings become whiter. Differs from immature Black-browed in blackish bill, darker collar.
HABITS: As Black-browed but prefers colder waters, less inclined to follow ships.
DISTRIBUTION: Circumpolar in Southern Oceans. Breeds Aug–May Cape Horn, South Georgia, Marion, Prince Edward, Crozets, Macquarie, Kerguelen and Campbell Is.
SIMILAR SPECIES: Compare Buller's, Yellow-nosed and Black-browed (p. 189, p. 188).

Yellow-nosed Albatross *Diomedea chlororhynchos*
L76cm/30in W203cm/80in P p. 39 K p. 289

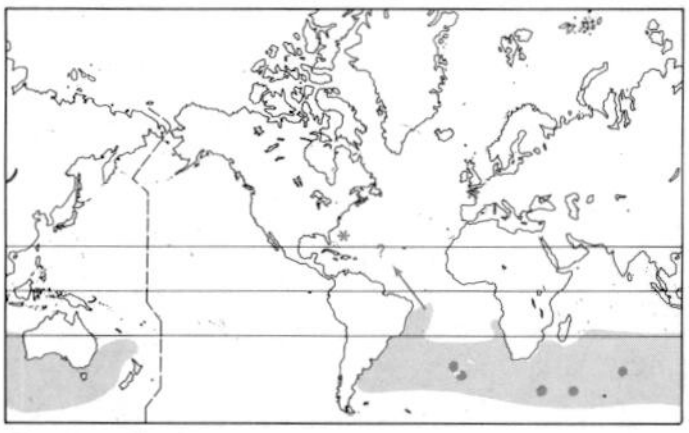

IDENTIFICATION: Smallest, most slender of the southern albatrosses. At all ages, dark underwing margins are narrower than Grey-headed, Black-browed or Buller's Albatrosses. **Adult:** Two races, one with grey head, the other with white head. White-headed forms easily identified, but beware confusing grey-headed form with Buller's or Grey-headed Albatrosses. Both forms differ in narrower black border to underwings, yellow confined to top edge of upper mandible. **Juvenile/Immature:** As adult, but head in both races white, some show partial grey collar; bill wholly black.
HABITS: Occasionally follows ships; breeds colonially on cliffs of oceanic islands.
DISTRIBUTION: Southern Indian and Atlantic Oceans, straying north to eastern USA. Breeds Aug–May Tristan da Cunha, Gough, St Paul, Amsterdam, Prince Edward and Crozets.
SIMILAR SPECIES: Compare Buller's, Grey-headed, Black-browed and Salvin's Albatrosses (p. 189, p. 188, p. 187).

Buller's Albatross *Diomedea bulleri* L78cm/31in W210cm/83in **P** p. 39 **K** p. 289

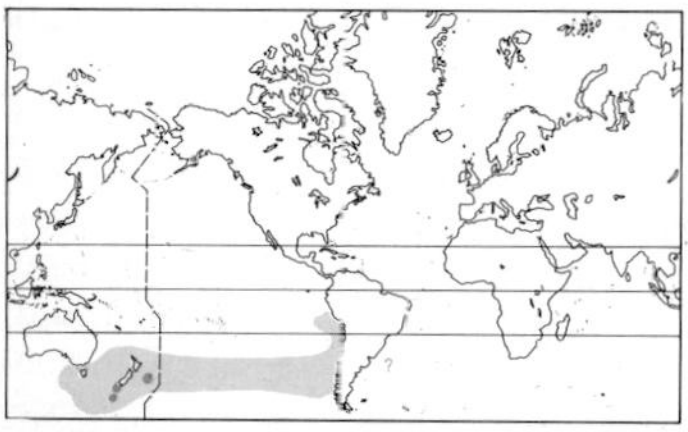

IDENTIFICATION: Superficially resembles adult Grey-headed Albatross; differs in whiter forehead and a narrow dark margin on leading edge of underwing recalling Yellow-nosed Albatross. At long range confusion always possible with Salvin's Albatross (p. 187), but latter species is much larger, longer-winged and has paler bill and diagnostic underwing pattern. **Juvenile:** As adult, but darker, more brownish head and dark-tipped brownish bill.
HABITS: Colonial breeder on oceanic islands; follows ships.
DISTRIBUTION: Australasian seas, dispersing east to Humboldt Current region west to Tasmania; rarely north of 30°S, but movements little known. Breeds Dec–Aug at Solander, Snares, Chatham Is, Three Kings, New Zealand.
SIMILAR SPECIES: Compare Grey-headed, Salvin's and Yellow-nosed (p. 188, p. 187, p. 188).

Laysan Albatross *Diomedea immutabilis* L80cm/31in W203cm/82in **P** p. 40 **K** p. 291

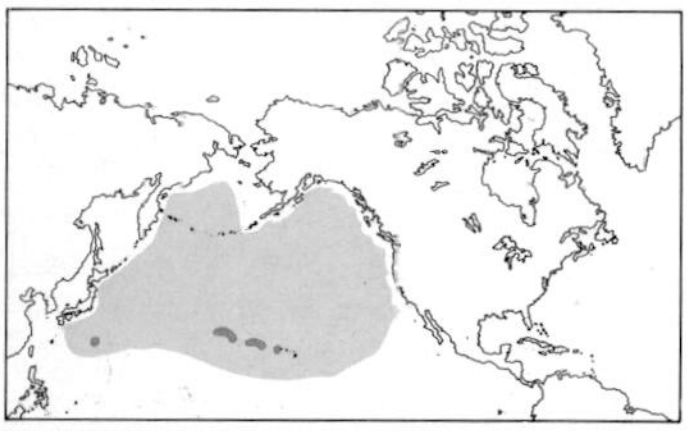

IDENTIFICATION: Superficially resembles Southern Oceans Black-browed Albatross, but underwing has narrower black margins and irregular blackish streaks across coverts. Thus easily separable from all-dark Black-footed Albatross and near-extinct Short-tailed Albatross, the only other North Pacific albatrosses. In flight feet project beyond tail.
HABITS: Breeds colonially on oceanic islands; follows ships, feeds on galley refuse, squid and fish.
DISTRIBUTION: North Pacific, pelagic range between about 30°N and 55°N from Japan north to Bering Sea and east to Washington and California where regular but rare. Most breed on Leeward Hawaiian Chain Oct–May; recently discovered breeding Bonin Is south of Japan (Kurata in Hasegawa 1978).
SIMILAR SPECIES: None within normal range, but see Black-browed Albatross (p. 188).

Short-tailed Albatross *Diomedea albatrus*
L89cm/35in W211cm/83in **P** p. 41 **K** p. 291

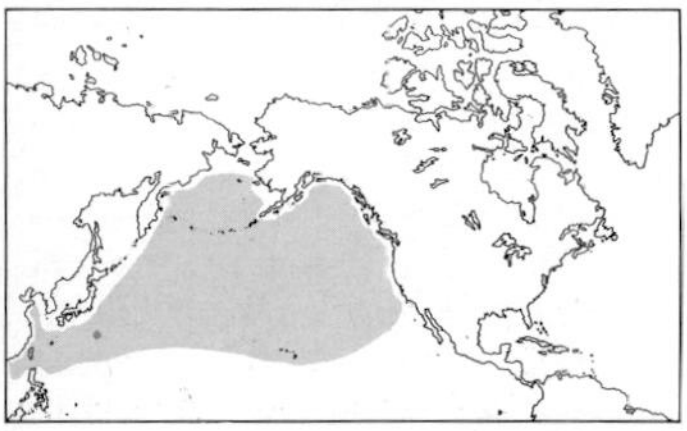

IDENTIFICATION: Plumage variable, beginning with all-brown fledgling, becoming progressively white towards maturity. At any age, huge pinkish bill and pale feet are good identification characters. **Adult:** Largest and only white-bodied albatross of the North Pacific. **Juvenile/Immature:** At fledging plumage all-brown, differing from Black-footed Albatross only in larger size, pink bill and feet. Subsequently face and underbody become white, producing plumage not unlike Laysan x Black-footed hybrid, but differs in bare-parts colour, lack of distinct breastband, and dark flanks and undertail-coverts. As maturity advances, head attains distinctive capped appearance with dark cervical collar, while underparts (except undertail-coverts) become progressively whiter and two diagnostic white patches appear on proximal portion of upperwing. Underwing- and undertail-coverts eventually become white.
HABITS: Endangered, population only about 250, breeds colonially; occasionally follows ships.
DISTRIBUTION: North Pacific, where formerly abundant but now breeds only Tori Shima, perhaps also Minami Kojima, south of Japan, Oct–May. Disperses north to Bering Sea and east to California, where extremely rare.
SIMILAR SPECIES: Compare Black-footed and Laysan Albatrosses (p. 190, p. 189).

Black-footed Albatross *Diomedea nigripes*
L81cm/32in W226cm/89in **P** p. 41 **K** p. 291

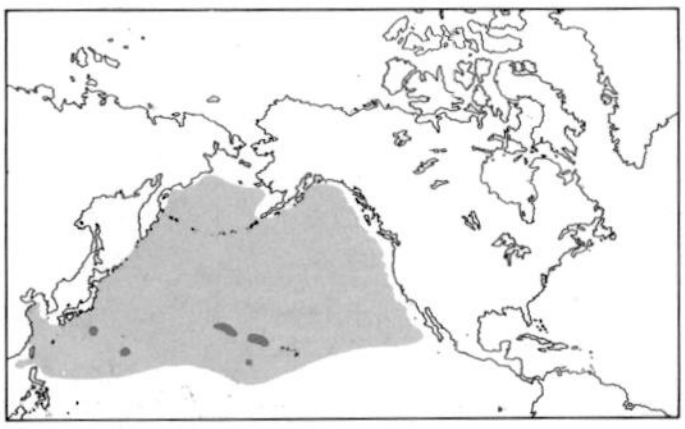

IDENTIFICATION: **Adult:** Mostly dusky-brown, except for narrow whitish area around base of bill, over base of tail and undertail-coverts. Typical forms are thus easily separable from Short-tailed and Laysan Albatrosses by mostly dark brown plumage. **Atypical:** Aged, aberrant birds or Black-footed x Laysan hybrids with paler bills and underparts can suggest immature Short-tailed, but are distinctly smaller with dark legs, head lacks capped effect and/or collar and the upperwings, while paler than typical Black-footed, lack the diagnostic white patches found in Short-tailed. **Juvenile:** As adult, but lacks white over tail and on undertail-coverts, area around bill darker.
HABITS: Breeds colonially on oceanic islands; often follows ships, feeding on garbage.
DISTRIBUTION: North Pacific. Most breed Oct–Jul at Leeward Chain of Hawaiian Is; smaller numbers Marshall, Johnston, and Tori Shima Is. Disperses over much of North Pacific between about 30°N and 55°N from Taiwan north to Bering Sea, and east to Baja California, where regular, particularly during summer.
SIMILAR SPECIES: Compare juvenile/immature Short-tailed Albatross (p. 189).

Waved Albatross *Diomedea irrorata* L89cm/35in W235cm/93in **P** p. 40 **K** p. 292

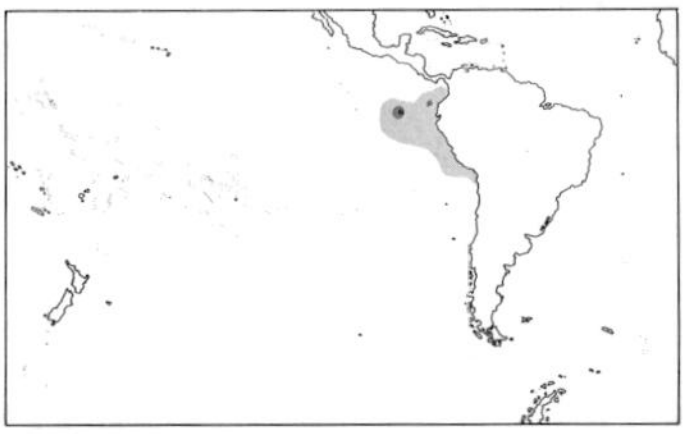

IDENTIFICATION: Virtually unmistakable, the only albatross of the Galapagos region. Large size coupled with distinctive whitish head, brown body and underwing pattern should prevent confusion with any other seabird of the region.
HABITS: The world's only exclusively tropical albatross. Breeds colonially; does not usually follow ships.
DISTRIBUTION: Confined to Galapagos and seas off Ecuador and Peru, mainly between 4°N and 12°S but occasionally south to Mollendo, Peru. Breeds Mar–Jan, Hood Is, Galapagos, and at Las Platas Is off Ecuador.
SIMILAR SPECIES: None within range, but see Southern Giant Petrel (p. 191).

Sooty Albatross *Phoebetria fusca* L86cm/34in W203cm/80in **P** p. 42 **K** p. 290

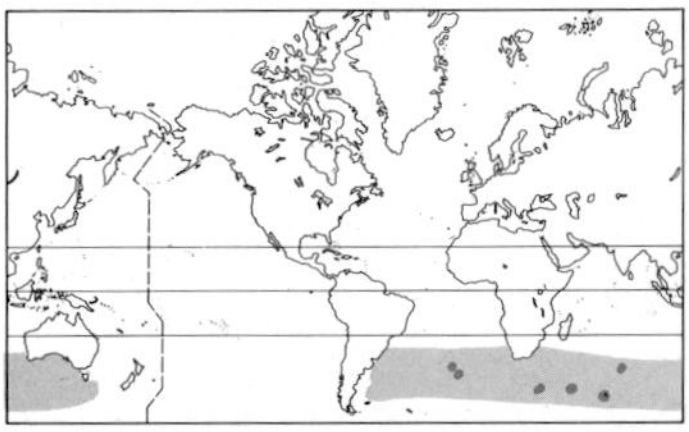

IDENTIFICATION: Both species of sooty albatross have narrow wings and elongated wedge-shaped tail, giving pointed appearance at both ends. Their slender overall jizz enables instant separation from the pale-billed, dark-plumaged, heavy-bodied giant petrels (p. 191). **Adult:** Sooty-brown overall. Differs from Light-mantled Sooty in uniformly dark upperparts and, at close range, cream or yellow stripe on side of black bill. **Immature** (and **Worn Adults**): Have a pale buff or whitish collar suggesting Light-mantled but, unlike that species, pale area does not extend to lower back.
HABITS: Breeds colonially on grassy cliffs of oceanic islands; follows ships.
DISTRIBUTION: Southern Atlantic and Indian Oceans from about 60°S north to about 30°S; has been recorded in eastern Pacific (Watson 1975). Breeds Sep–May at Tristan da Cunha, Gough, Amsterdam, St Paul, Marion, Prince Edward, Crozet and Kerguelen Is.
SIMILAR SPECIES: Compare Light-mantled Sooty Albatross, Northern and Southern Giant Petrels (p. 191).

Light-mantled Sooty Albatross *Phoebetria palpebrata*

L84cm/33in W215cm/85in

P p. 42 **K** p. 290

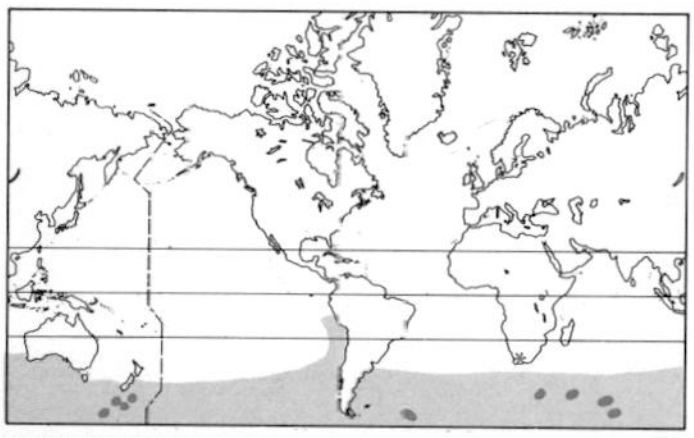

IDENTIFICATION: **Adult:** Differs from Sooty Albatross in ashy-grey hindneck, mantle and lower back contrasting with dark head, wings and tail. At close range, blue stripe on sides of black bill diagnostic. **Juvenile/ Immature:** Averages paler than corresponding Sooty Albatross, with mottled grey mantle extending to lower back.

HABITS: Breeds colonially on grassy cliffs of oceanic islands; follows ships.

DISTRIBUTION: Circumpolar in Southern Oceans from pack ice north to about 33°S, but to 20°S off Peru. Breeds Oct–May South Georgia, Marion, Prince Edward, Crozet, Kerguelen, Heard, Macquarie, Auckland, Campbell and Antipodes Is.

SIMILAR SPECIES: Compare Sooty Albatross, Northern and Southern Giant Petrels (p. 190, p. 191).

Northern Giant Petrel *Macronectes halli*

L87cm/34in W190cm/75in

P p. 43 **K** p. 290

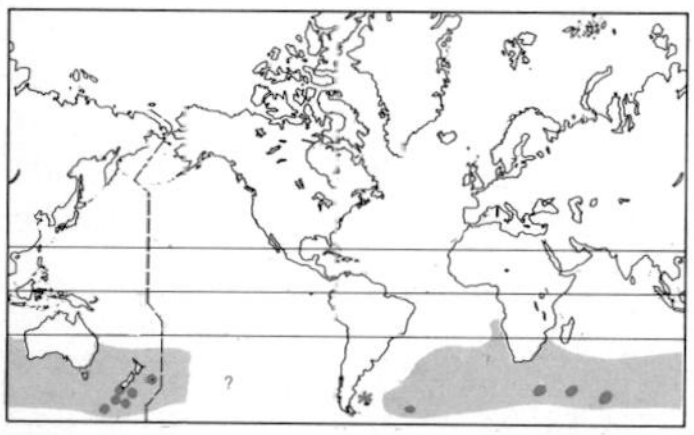

IDENTIFICATION: **Adult/Immature:** The two species of giant petrel (which occasionally hybridise) are similar in size to the smaller albatrosses, but with darker underwings, massive pale bill and a heavy, humpbacked appearance. Plumage in both species is variable, beginning wholly sooty-brown and becoming progressively paler with maturity. Adult Northern Giant Petrel appears more capped than Southern Giant Petrel and with paler underparts but, owing to variations within populations, the two species can be certainly identified (at any age) only by bill colour: Northern has a horn-coloured bill with reddish tip to both mandibles, giving a distinct darker-tipped appearance at sea, whereas the bill of Southern Giant Petrel has a pale green tip to both mandibles, appearing uniformly coloured at sea.

HABITS: A pugnacious, ungainly and uncouth scavenger, both on land and at sea. Breeds singly on oceanic islands; habitually follows ships.

DISTRIBUTION: Circumpolar in Southern Hemisphere from about 55°S north to 25°S, occasionally to 15°S in cold-water zones. Breeds Jul–Feb Prince Edward, Marion, Crozet, Kerguelen, Macquarie, Chatham, Stewart, Auckland, Antipodes and Campbell Is.

SIMILAR SPECIES: Compare Southern Giant Petrel and Sooty Albatross (p. 191, p. 190).

Southern Giant Petrel *Macronectes giganteus*

L87cm/34in W195cm/77in

P p. 43 **K** p. 290

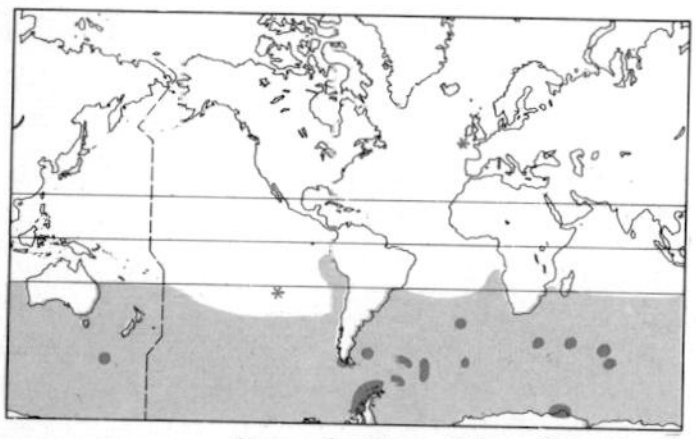

IDENTIFICATION: **Adult/Immature:** See discussion above under Northern Giant Petrel. At all ages can be certainly separated from Northern Giant Petrel only by horn-coloured bill with pale greenish (not red) tip to both mandibles.

HABITS: As for Northern Giant Petrel, but perhaps more migratory; breeds in small loose colonies.

DISTRIBUTION: Circumpolar in Southern Hemisphere from pack ice north to about 25°S, but to 10°S in cold-water zones. Breeds Sep–Mar South Georgia, South Sandwich, South Orkney, South Shetland, Antarctic Peninsula and scattered sites on continent; also Falklands, Gough, Bouvet, Prince Edward, Marion, Crozet, Kerguelen, Heard and Macquarie Is.

SIMILAR SPECIES: Compare Northern Giant Petrel and Sooty Albatross (p. 191, p. 190).

Antarctic Petrel *Thalassoica antarctica* L43cm/17in W102cm/40in **P** p. 44 **K** p. 293

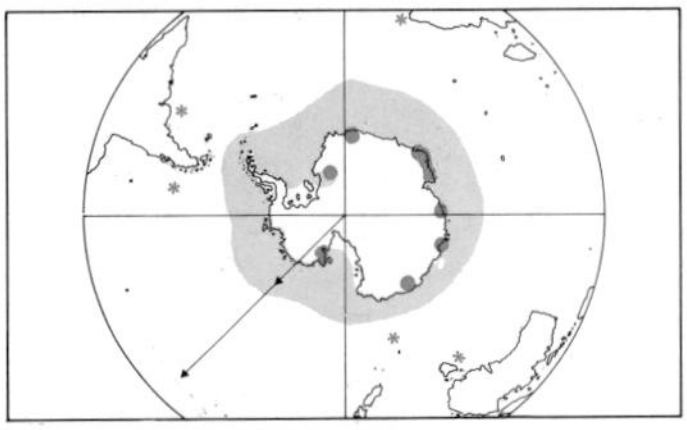

IDENTIFICATION: Conspicuous brown and white fulmarine petrel, can be confused only with Pintado Petrel. It differs in larger size and less chequered upperparts, with a distinctive, broad, white subterminal trailing edge to the upperwing which contrasts with dark brown forewing; white tail has narrower brown tip. In worn plumage, brown areas paler with whitish or buff hindcollar.
HABITS: Breeds in huge colonies on snow-free cliffs. Gregarious at sea, large flocks roosting on pack ice, often with other species.
DISTRIBUTION: Circumpolar in Southern Oceans, but usually confined to pack ice and adjacent seas north to about 63°N. Vagrant north to South America, South Africa and Australia. Breeds Oct–Mar on a few islands close to Antarctic continent and along Antarctic coast.
SIMILAR SPECIES: Compare Pintado Petrel (below).

Pintado Petrel *Daption capense* L39cm/15in W86cm/34in **P** p. 44 **K** p. 293

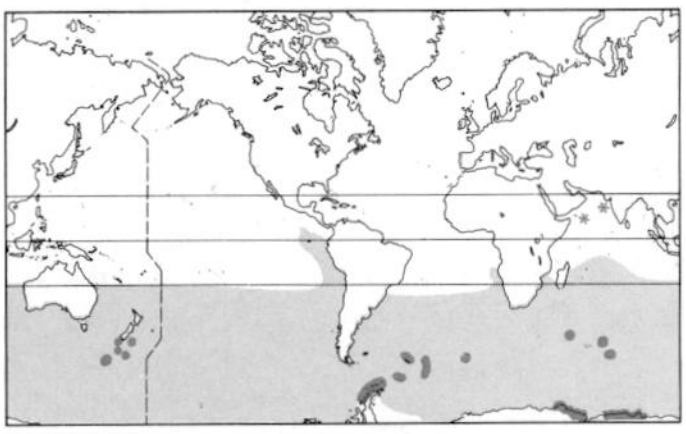

IDENTIFICATION: Virtually unmistakable with boldly chequered upperparts and white wing patches. Antarctic Petrel is larger and browner, with conspicuous white subterminal trailing edge to upperwings.
HABITS: Gregarious; one of the most familiar of all petrels owing to inveterate ship-following habits, alighting at galley waste where noisy and quarrelsome. Breeds colonially.
DISTRIBUTION: Circumpolar in Southern Oceans from pack ice to about 25°N, but north to Equator and Galapagos Is off western South America. Breeds Aug–Mar South Georgia, South Sandwich, South Orkney, South Shetland, Bouvet, Crozet, Kerguelen, Heard, Macquarie, Balleny, Peter First Is and at several sites on Antarctic Peninsula and continent; also at Snares, Antipodes, Bounty and Campbell Is.
SIMILAR SPECIES: Compare Antarctic Petrel (above).

Antarctic Fulmar *Fulmarus glacialoides* L48cm/19in W117cm/46in **P** p. 45 **K** p. 293

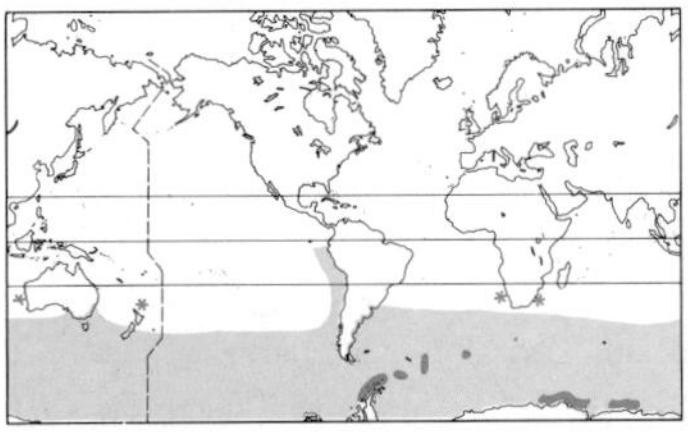

IDENTIFICATION: Easily separated from the predominantly brown petrels of the Southern Oceans by its pale grey, gull-like plumage and conspicuous white patch across inner primaries. At close range, the bright pinkish bill shows blackish tip.
HABITS: Breeds colonially on steep cliffs. Gregarious at sea, often with Pintado and Snow Petrels, but rarely follows ships; attends trawling operations. Flight typical of fulmarine petrels, with stiff-winged flaps and accomplished gliding, planing over waves on stiffly held wings.
DISTRIBUTION: Circumpolar in Southern Oceans from pack ice north to about 40°S, but 10°S off Peru; occasionally to South Africa, Australia and New Zealand during 'wreck' years. Breeds Oct–Apr South Sandwich, South Orkney, South Shetland, Bouvet and Peter Is; also at several locations on Antarctic Peninsula and continent.
SIMILAR SPECIES: None within range, but see Snow Petrel (p. 193).

Northern Fulmar *Fulmarus glacialis* L48cm/19in W107cm/42in **P** p. 45 **K** p. 293

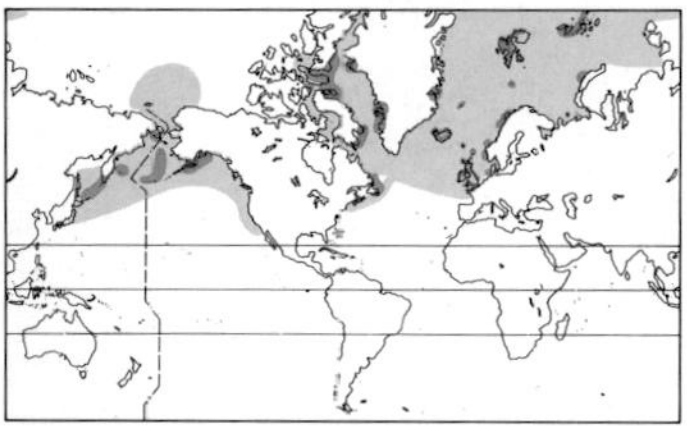

IDENTIFICATION: Plumage variable: pale morph predominates in Atlantic, dark morph in Pacific; intermediates also occur. **Pale Morph:** Upperwings pearl-grey, thus, with white head, neck and underparts, resembles gull spp. but, at close range, differs in stout, tubenosed bill, dark eye patch, whitish patch at base of primaries, and bull-necked, heavy-bodied jizz with stiff flap-and-glide flight recalling that of larger shearwaters. **Dark Morph:** Range from blue/grey upperparts with white underbodies to wholly dark plumbeous-brown, and, at distance, can suggest Flesh-footed, Pink-footed, or even Cory's Shearwaters.

HABITS: Breeds colonially along coasts, usually in shallow holes on cliff faces, but also holes or old burrows among dunes and grassy slopes. A noisy scavenger at trawling operations. Follows ships.

DISTRIBUTION: North Pacific, Atlantic and adjacent Arctic seas, ranging south to about 34°N. Breeds May–Sep in North Pacific from Kuriles to Alaska and north to Bering Sea; in North Atlantic from Arctic Canada south to Newfoundland and from Arctic regions of Atlantic south to Britain and France.

SIMILAR SPECIES: Compare with larger shearwater spp. or gull spp. (p. 208, p. 210; pp.245–250).

Snow Petrel *Pagodroma nivea* L32cm/13in W78cm/31in **P** p. 44 **K** p. 293

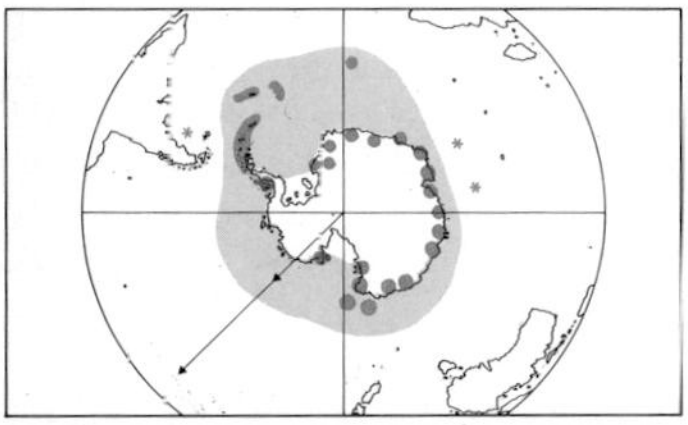

IDENTIFICATION: Unmistakable; the world's only wholly white petrel.

HABITS: Breeds colonially on sea and inland cliffs. Gregarious at sea, large groups roosting on ice floes, often with Pintado and Antarctic Petrels. Appears long-winged in flight with shallow bat-like wingbeats and infrequent glides, fluttering and jinking between ice floes and icebergs. Rarely settles on the sea.

DISTRIBUTION: Circumpolar in Southern Oceans, but range usually confined to pack ice and adjacent seas north to about 63°N. Breeds South Shetland, South Georgia, South Sandwich, South Orkney, Bouvet, Balleny and Scott Is; also at several localities on Antarctic Peninsula and continent.

SIMILAR SPECIES: None, but beware albino petrel spp.

Blue Petrel *Halobaena caerulea* L29cm/11in W62cm/24in **P** p. 45 **K** p. 299

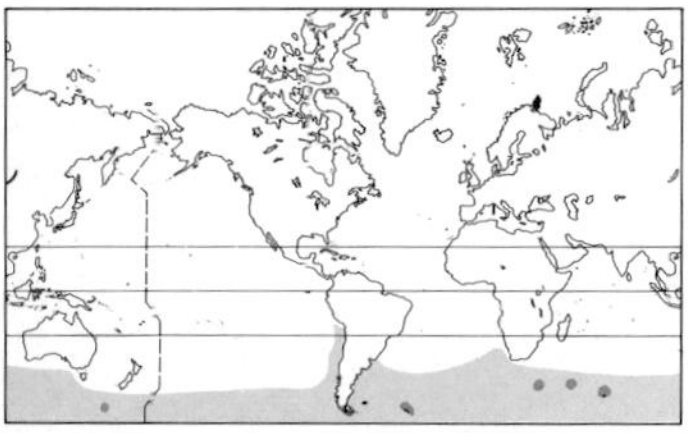

IDENTIFICATION: Superficially resembles smaller prion spp., but easily told by combination of conspicuous black cap which extends to sides of breast and by diagnostic white tip to tail (the only petrel with this character). At close range shows obvious 'M' mark across blue-grey upperparts. Unlike most prions, bill is black.

HABITS: Colonial breeder on sub-Antarctic islands. Gregarious at sea, sometimes up to 100 in groups, or with dense groups of prions. Does not usually follow ships. Flight faster and less erratic than that of prions, with higher arcs over waves.

DISTRIBUTION: Circumpolar in Southern Oceans north to about 30°S during austral winter, but to about 20°S off Peru (Meeth & Meeth 1977). Breeds Sep–Mar at Diego Ramirez, Cape Horn, South Georgia, Prince Edward, Marion, Crozet, Macquarie and Kerguelen Is.

SIMILAR SPECIES: Compare any prion sp. (p. 194, p. 195).

Broad-billed Prion *Pachyptila vittata* L28cm/11in W61cm/24in **P** p. 46 **K** p. 299

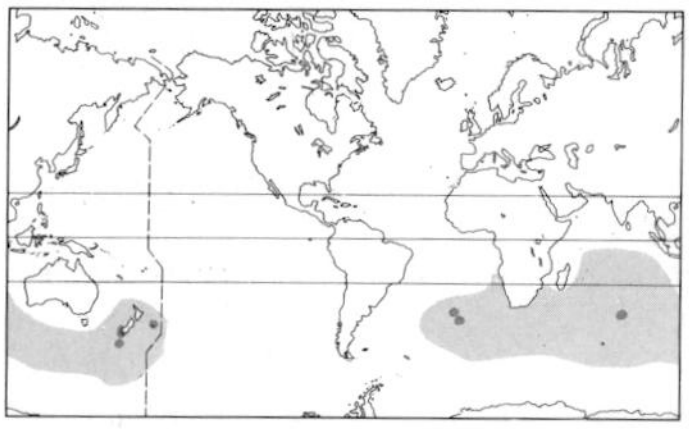

IDENTIFICATION: There are six forms/species of prion which can be treated as three species (Cox 1980) or as six species (Harper 1980). All are small blue-grey petrels with distinct 'M' mark across upperparts; at sea, even under optimum conditions, they are extremely difficult to separate. Broad-billed is the largest, with diagnostic black bill. In addition to colour and proportions of bill, it can be separated from both Fairy and Fulmar Prions by darker-headed appearance (caused by distinctly darker cap and blackish streak through eye), and less black in tail. Although Antarctic and Salvin's Prions have blue (not black) bills, separation from Broad-billed at sea is difficult, often impossible. For differences see notes below.
HABITS: Breeds colonially on sub-Antarctic islands. At sea highly gregarious, usually encountered in huge flocks; occasionally follows ships. All prions have characteristic, erratic weaving flight low over waves.
DISTRIBUTION: Southern Oceans, with post-breeding dispersal north towards tropics to about 10°S. Breeds Jul–Mar Marion, Prince Edward, Crozet, Tristan da Cunha, Gough, St Paul, Amsterdam, Snares, Chatham and Stewart Is; also coasts of South Island, New Zealand.
SIMILAR SPECIES: Compare with other prions and Blue Petrel (p. 194, p. 195, p. 193).

Antarctic Prion *Pachyptila (vittata) desolata* L27cm/11in W61cm/24in **P** p. 46 **K** p. 299

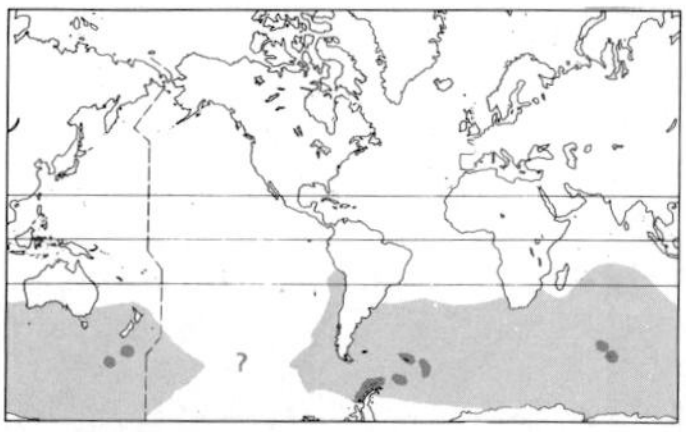

IDENTIFICATION: Very similar in all respects to Broad-billed Prion. It differs in its smaller bill, which is blue (not black), and more extensive mottling on sides of breast, extending as partial but distinctive collar. When viewed from the side or elevated position, foreshortening often imparts distinctive white-chinned appearance. Separated from Fulmar, Thin-billed and Fairy Prions by distinctly darker head and sides of breast.
HABITS: As Broad-billed Prion.
DISTRIBUTION: Southern Oceans, with post-breeding dispersal north towards tropics to about 10°S. Breeds Oct–Apr South Shetlands, South Orkney, South Sandwich, South Georgia, Kerguelen, Heard, Macquarie, Auckland, Scott Is and at Cape Denison, Antarctica.
SIMILAR SPECIES: Compare with other prions and Blue Petrel (p. 194, p. 195, p. 193).

Salvin's Prion *Pachyptila (vittata) salvini* L28cm/11in W57cm/22in **P** p. 46 **K** p. 299

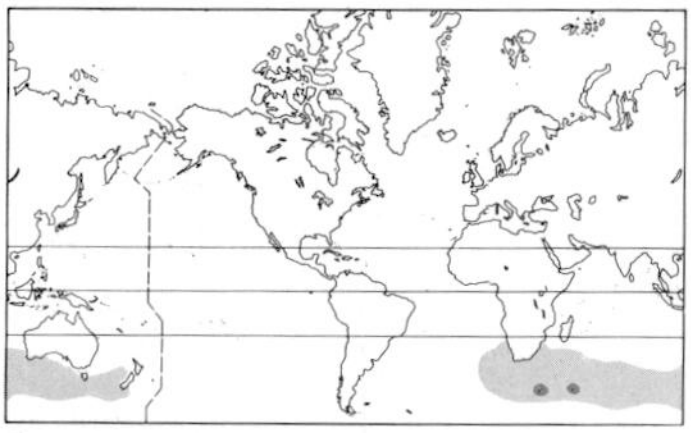

IDENTIFICATION: Virtually identical to both Broad-billed and Antarctic Prions, and perhaps impossible to distinguish from either at sea when differences are not always visible owing to distances/conditions. It differs from Antarctic Prion in cleaner, neater appearance, with less grey on sides of breast which ends in a neater division with white breast (can suggest Thin-billed Prion). Broad-billed Prion has a much larger black (not blue) bill and, at sea, looks distinctly larger-headed than Salvin's.
HABITS: As Broad-billed Prion.
DISTRIBUTION: Indian Ocean, dispersing to coasts of South Africa and Australia during winter. Breeds Jul–Mar Marion, Prince Edward and Crozet Is.
SIMILAR SPECIES: Compare with other prions and Blue Petrel (p. 194, p. 195, p. 193).

Fairy Prion *Pachyptila turtur* L25cm/10in W58cm/23in **P** p. 47 **K** p. 299

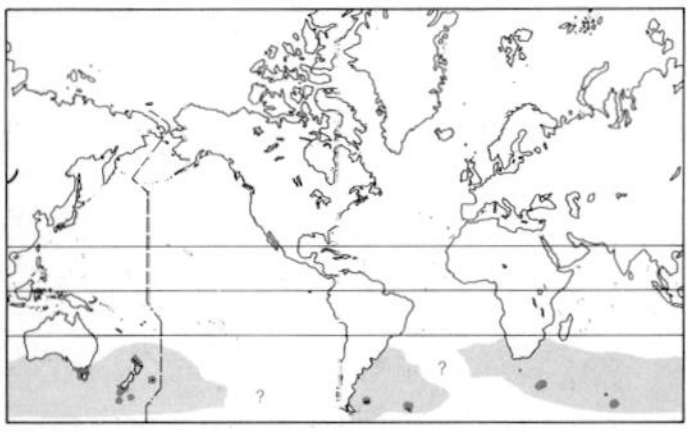

IDENTIFICATION: Smallest prion. Unlike Broad-billed and Antarctic Prions, head appears pale, lacking noticeable black streak through eye or noticeable darkening on crown, nape and sides of breast; uppertail has broader black tip. Very similar to Fulmar Prion at sea, but has a slightly darker head and thinner bill; flight less erratic.
HABITS: As Broad-billed Prion.
DISTRIBUTION: Southern Oceans. Breeds Aug–Feb Falklands, South Georgia, Marion and Prince Edward Is; also islands in Bass Strait and off Tasmania and New Zealand, including Chatham, Heard and Auckland Is.
SIMILAR SPECIES: Compare other prions and Blue Petrel (p. 194, p. 195, p. 193).

Fulmar Prion *Pachyptila (turtur) crassirostris*
L26cm/10in W58cm/23in **P** p. 47 **K** p. 299

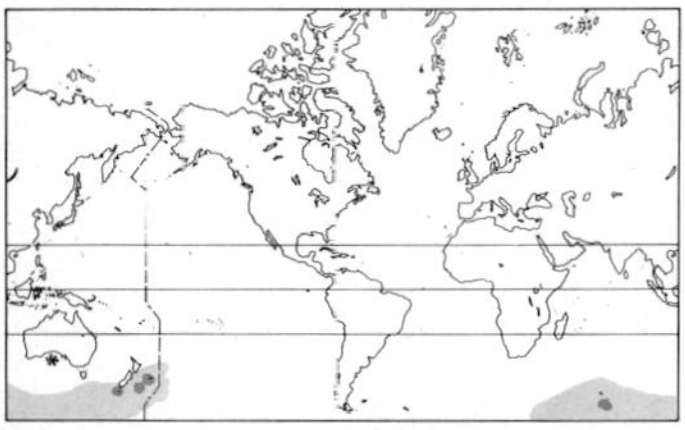

IDENTIFICATION: Very similar to Fairy Prion, of which it may be only a subspecies. It differs in stouter bill, slightly paler head with less distinct supercilium and more apparent 'M' mark across upperparts. Flight as Fairy Prion but more erratic, during which it habitually executes a remarkable 'loop-the-loop' manoeuvre high into air before rejoining original course.
HABITS: Much as Fairy Prion.
DISTRIBUTION: Breeds Aug–Feb near New Zealand at Bounty Is and at Pyramid Rock, Chatham Is. Thought to disperse only to adjacent seas, but movements largely unknown owing to difficulty of identification.
SIMILAR SPECIES: Compare other prions and Blue Petrel (p. 194, p. 195, p. 193).

Thin-billed Prion *Pachyptila belcheri* L26cm/10in W56cm/22in **P** p. 47 **K** p. 299

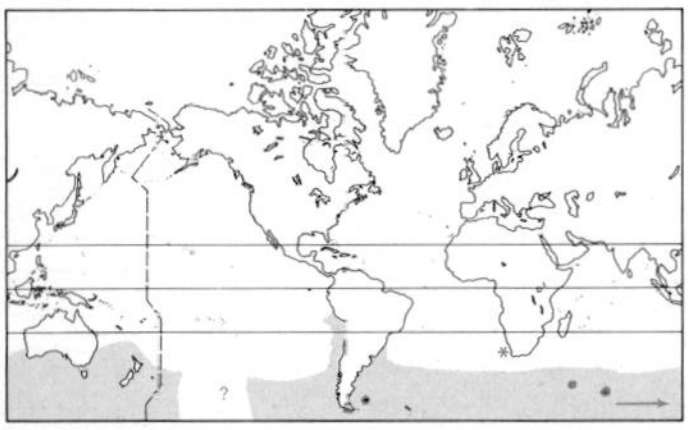

IDENTIFICATION: At sea, very similar to Fairy Prion in size and shape but head proportionately smaller, usually less rounded, with much more noticeable blackish streak through eye and long white supercilium giving face a distinct pattern. Upperparts usually paler and greyer than any other prion, with a paler, much less distinct 'M' mark across wings and back; uppertail shows less black than any other prion, with distinctly paler outer tail feathers. At close range, thin bill diagnostic.
HABITS: As Fairy Prion.
DISTRIBUTION: Southern Oceans, but distribution little known owing to difficulty in separating from other prions; disperses north to 15°S off Peru. Breeds Aug–Mar Falklands, Crozet and Kerguelen, perhaps Prince Edward.
SIMILAR SPECIES: Compare with other prions and Blue Petrel (p. 194, p. 195, p. 193).

Great-winged Petrel *Pterodroma macroptera*
L41cm/16in W97cm/38in **P** p. 48 **K** p. 300

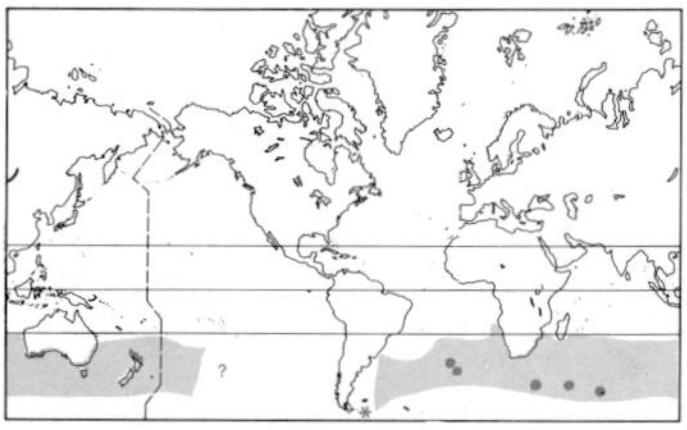

IDENTIFICATION: A wholly blackish-brown petrel with stubby black bill and dark feet; some show pale area around base of bill. Differs from Sooty and Short-tailed Shearwaters in stout bill, gadfly jizz and dark underwings. Flight impetuous, hurrying over ocean in high sweeping arcs. White-chinned Petrel is much larger, more thickset, with more languid, less dashing flight and pale bill.
HABITS: A winter breeder, singly or semi-colonially; occasionally follows ships.
DISTRIBUTION: Southern Oceans between 50°S and 30°S. Breeds Feb–Dec at Tristan da Cunha, Gough, Crozet, Marion, Prince Edward, Kerguelen, Amsterdam (?) and coasts of southwest Australia and North Island, New Zealand.
SIMILAR SPECIES: Compare Sooty and Short-tailed Shearwaters, White-chinned and Kerguelen Petrels (p. 208, p. 211, p. 206, p. 196).

Kerguelen Petrel *Pterodroma brevirostris* L36cm/14in W81cm/32in **P** p. 48 **K** p. 300

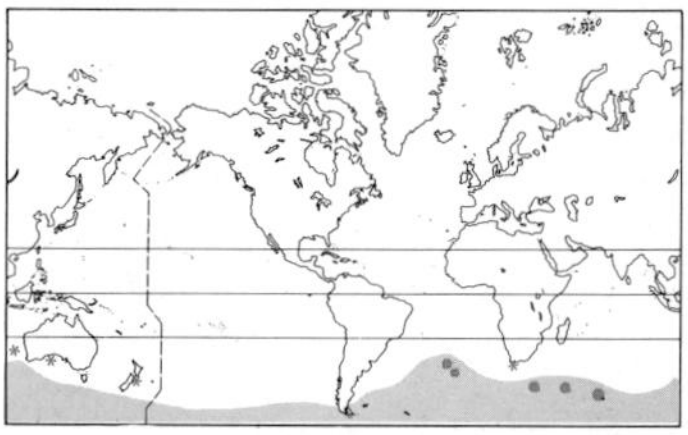

IDENTIFICATION: Similar to Great-winged Petrel, but smaller, more thickset with proportionately larger head, and has mostly dark, slate-grey (not brown) plumage. In sunlight plumage often appears silvery, particularly underside of primaries and leading edge of underwing, and, owing to shadow from steeply rising forehead, face often appears darker, giving hooded effect.
HABITS: Colonial breeder on sub-Antarctic islands; does not normally follow ships. Flight extremely fast and swooping, towering higher above waves than other gadfly-petrels where it often hangs motionless, suspended over ocean.
DISTRIBUTION: Circumpolar in Southern Oceans, ranging from pack ice north to about 30°S. Breeds Aug–Mar Tristan da Cunha group, Gough, Marion, Prince Edward, Crozet and Kerguelen Is.
SIMILAR SPECIES: Great-winged and dark morph of Soft-plumaged Petrels (this page).

Soft-plumaged Petrel *Pterodroma mollis*
L34cm/13in W89cm/35in **P** p. 49 **K** p. 305

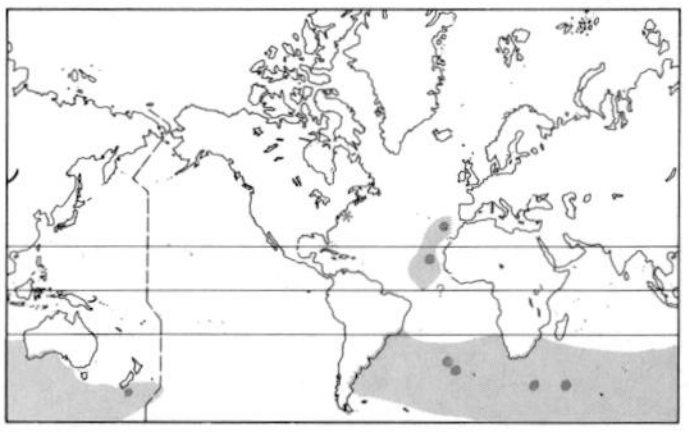

IDENTIFICATION: **Typical:** Medium-sized grey and white gadfly-petrel recalling Atlantic Petrel, but smaller, more dashing, with white throat and forehead; dark smudges on sides of breast sometimes form complete breastband. Brownish-grey upperparts usually show faint 'M' mark across wings and back. Underwing dark at long range, but with paler highlights across base of primaries and secondary coverts when closer. **Atypical:** Rare dark phase resembles Kerguelen, but has broader, more rounded wings and is mottled on belly; flight not so dashing or high.
HABITS: Colonial breeder on oceanic islands; occasionally follows ships.
DISTRIBUTION: Fragmented distribution in Atlantic and Indian Oceans. The two North Atlantic populations (sometimes considered as separate species) have staggered breeding throughout most of year at Cape Verde, Madeira and Desertas Is. In Southern Hemisphere breeds Sep–May at Gough, Tristan da Cunha, Prince Edward, Marion, Crozet and Antipodes, with post-breeding dispersal north to about 25°S.
SIMILAR SPECIES: Compare Atlantic, Grey and Kerguelen Petrels (p. 197, p. 207, p. 196).

Atlantic Petrel *Pterodroma incerta* L43cm/17in W104cm/41in **P** p. 49 **K** p. 304

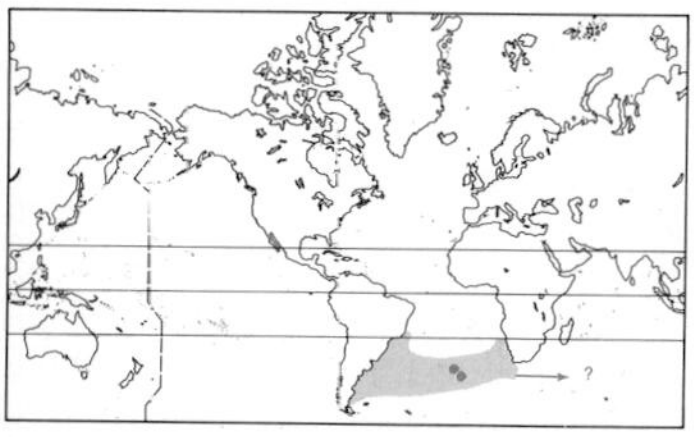

IDENTIFICATION: Medium-sized, rather robust, dark brown gadfly-petrel with conspicuous white lower breast and belly. Upperparts and underwing uniformly dark, lacking 'M' mark or obvious pale areas. In worn plumage head and breast paler, often with dark mask around eye. Differs from larger Grey Petrel in brown, not grey, plumage and in dark throat and upper breast. Magenta Petrel has pale throat and undertail-coverts. Soft-plumaged Petrel is smaller, has a white throat and dark breastband, and 'M' mark across greyer upperparts.
HABITS: Breeds colonially on oceanic islands; follows ships. Flight high and swooping, moving over ocean in high sweeping arcs.
DISTRIBUTION: Southern Atlantic from about 50°S to 20°S, but perhaps north to mouth of Amazon off Brazil at 5°S. Breeds Feb–? Tristan da Cunha group and Gough.
SIMILAR SPECIES: Compare Magenta, Soft-plumaged and Grey Petrels (p. 201, p. 196, p. 207).

White-headed Petrel *Pterodroma lessonii*
L43cm/17in W109cm/43in **P** p. 59 **K** p. 303

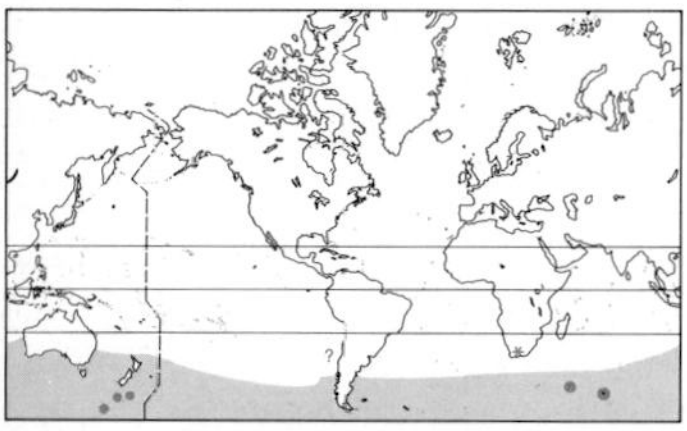

IDENTIFICATION: Large, rather robust gadfly-petrel, easily identified by combination of diagnostic white head and underbody contrasting with dark grey underwing. Greyish-brown upperparts usually show indistinct 'M' mark across wings and back. At close range, has distinctive black eye patch, partial grey collar and grey centre to white tail. Differs from larger Grey Petrel in white head and undertail.
HABITS: Colonial breeder on oceanic islands. Flight fast and swooping with wings held bowed and angled forward, moving over ocean in high sweeping arcs; does not normally follow ships. Usually solitary at sea.
DISTRIBUTION: Circumpolar in Southern Oceans from pack ice north to about 30°S. Breeds Aug–May Kerguelen, Crozet, Auckland, Antipodes and Macquarie; may breed Marion, Prince Edward and Campbell Is.
SIMILAR SPECIES: None, but compare Grey Petrel (p. 207).

Barau's Petrel *Pterodroma baraui* L38cm/15in W? **P** p. 59 **K** p. 303

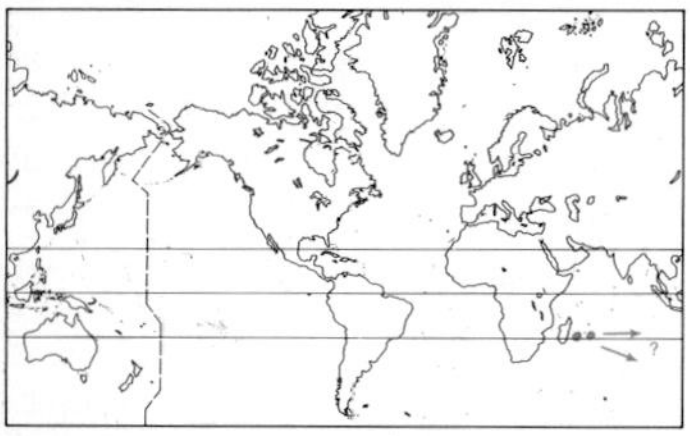

IDENTIFICATION: Medium-sized grey and white gadfly-petrel unlike any other of tropical Indian Ocean; easily identified by combination of white forehead, dark cap, white underparts and white underwings, latter with narrow black line running diagonally across coverts. Upperparts grey, with distinct dark 'M' mark across wings, and dark rump.
HABITS: This recently described petrel (Jouanin 1963) breeds on only one or two oceanic islands. Typical gadfly flight, fast and swooping; does not normally follow ships.
DISTRIBUTION: Indian Ocean, but pelagic range unknown; may disperse in subtropical convergence zone south of about 20°S. Breeds Nov–Apr on Rodriguez and probably Reunion, Indian Ocean.
SIMILAR SPECIES: None within range, but compare Herald, Mascarene and Soft-plumaged Petrels (p. 202, p. 205, p. 196).

Cook's Petrel *Pterodroma cooki* L26cm/10in W66cm/26in

P p. 50 **K** p. 301

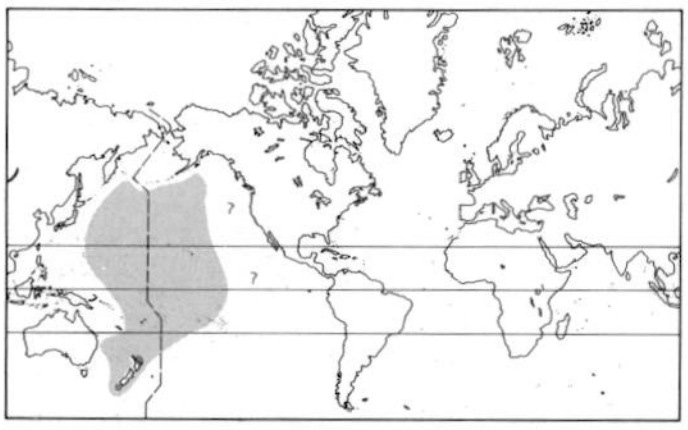

IDENTIFICATION: Small gadfly-petrel with pale grey upperparts and white underparts; difficult to separate, at any range, from Pycroft's and Stejneger's Petrels and, on present knowledge, perhaps impossible to separate from Masatierra Petrel. Differs from Pycroft's and Stejneger's in paler head, greyer upperparts with more obvious 'M' mark, and whiter outer tail feathers; from Gould's, Collared, Bonin, Black-winged and Chatham Island Petrels in much paler head, and lack of pronounced dark margin and diagonal stripe on underwing.
HABITS: Breeds oceanic islands; not normally attracted to ships. Flight typical of smaller gadfly-petrels, fast and swooping, weaving an erratic bat-like course.
DISTRIBUTION: Pacific transequatorial migrant. Breeds Oct–Apr Codfish, Little and Great Barrier Is, New Zealand, dispersing through central Pacific Apr–Sep to reach Aleutians and Baja California, where rare but probably regular.
SIMILAR SPECIES: Compare Masatierra, Pycroft's and Stejneger's (p. 198, p. 199, p. 198).

Masatierra Petrel *Pterodroma (cooki) defilippiana* L26cm/10in W66cm/26in

P p. 50 **K** p. 301

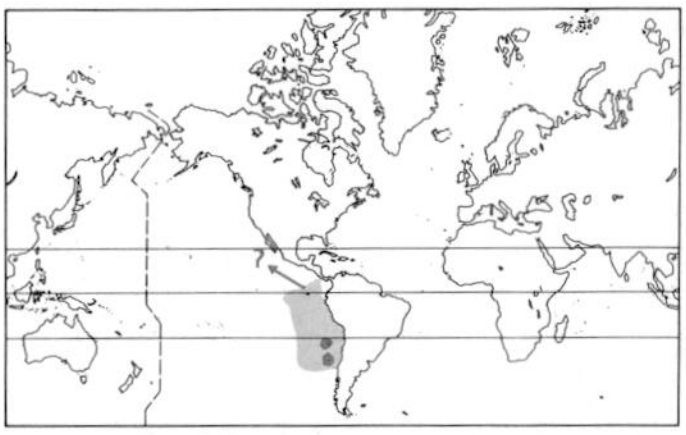

IDENTIFICATION: Closely resembles Cook's Petrel, of which it may be only a subspecies. Differs in larger bill and, usually, less white on inner webs of outer 2–4 tail feathers, but there is overlap in this character although no *defilippiana* shows wholly white outer web to outermost feathers as in some *cooki*. Thus a bird at sea showing indistinct white outer tail feathers could be either, but a bird with conspicuous white sides to tail would be *cooki* (Roberson pers. comm.). On average the eye patch of Cook's is smaller than that of Masatierra and contrasts less with head (Morlan pers. comm.).
HABITS: As for Cook's Petrel, but probably less migratory, though pelagic range unknown.
DISTRIBUTION: Tropical and subtropical Pacific, breeds Jun–Jan off Chile at San Ambrosio and San Felix and at Santa Clara and Robinson Crusoe Is. Disperses north towards Peruvian coast during Feb, but movements unknown owing to similarity to Cook's Petrel.
SIMILAR SPECIES: Compare Cook's, Pycroft's and Stejneger's Petrels (p. 198, p. 199, p. 198).

Stejneger's Petrel *Pterodroma longirostris* L26cm/10in W66cm/26in

P p. 51 **K** p. 301

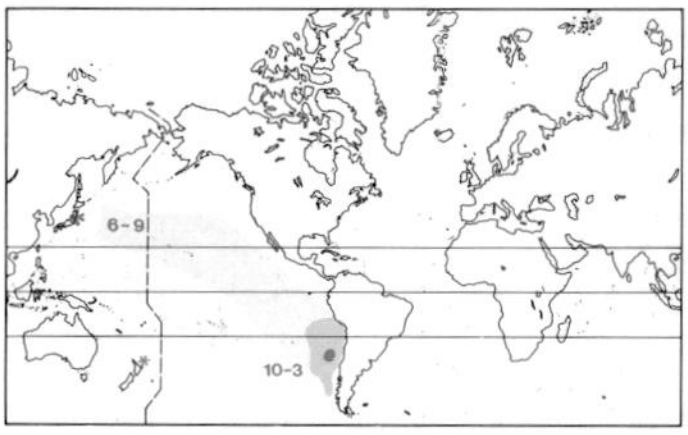

IDENTIFICATION: Small gadfly-petrel with pale greyish-brown upperparts and white underparts. In flight the upperparts, particularly when worn, are darker than in Cook's, and distinctly browner with a less distinct 'M' mark. White underwing shows a slightly wider, inconspicuous, black broken leading edge than Cook's and tail lacks white outer feathers. The best field character is, perhaps, the darker crown and nape which, in fresh plumage, appears blackish and contrasts strongly with paler grey mantle and upperparts. In flight, from below, the dark cap extends to sides of neck and forms a more definite division than in either Cook's or Pycroft's.
HABITS: Much as Cook's Petrel. Does not follow ships; flight probably less erratic.
DISTRIBUTION: Transequatorial Pacific migrant with post-breeding dispersal Apr–Sep north past California towards Japan, but movements largely unknown owing to difficulty of identification. Breeds Oct–Mar on Mas Afuera, Juan Fernandez, off Chile.
SIMILAR SPECIES: Compare Pycroft's, Cook's and Gould's Petrels (p. 199, p. 198, p. 199).

Pycroft's Petrel *Pterodroma (longirostris) pycrofti*
L26cm/10in W66cm/26in **P** p. 51 **K** p. 301

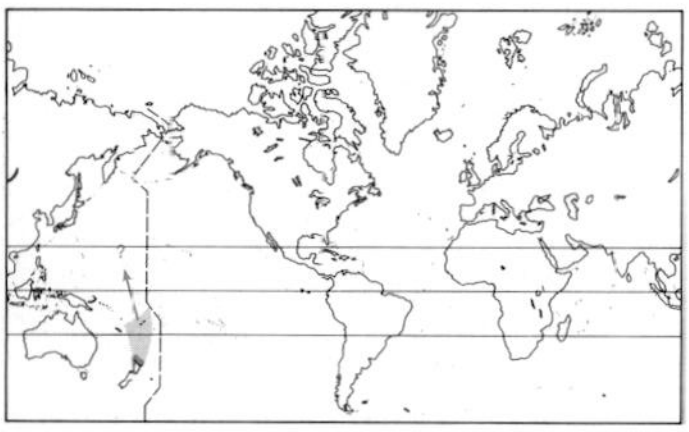

IDENTIFICATION: Closely resembles Cook's Petrel, differing only in darker grey crown and nape, giving darker cap, more noticeable dark mark through and below eye, less white on outer tail feathers. In flight the upperwings are browner than in Cook's, with less distinct 'M' mark, and contrast more with grey mantle, back and rump. Stejneger's Petrel differs in darker cap, contrasting with pale grey mantle.
HABITS: Colonial breeder on oceanic islands; does not normally follow ships.
DISTRIBUTION: Unconfirmed transequatorial migrant Apr–Sep in Pacific from New Zealand breeding grounds. Breeds Oct–Mar Hen, Chicken, Poor Knights, Mercury, Stanley and Stephenson Is off New Zealand.
SIMILAR SPECIES: Compare Cook's, Masatierra and Stejneger's Petrels (p. 198).

Gould's Petrel *Pterodroma leucoptera* L30cm/12in W71cm/28in **P** p. 55 **K** p. 302

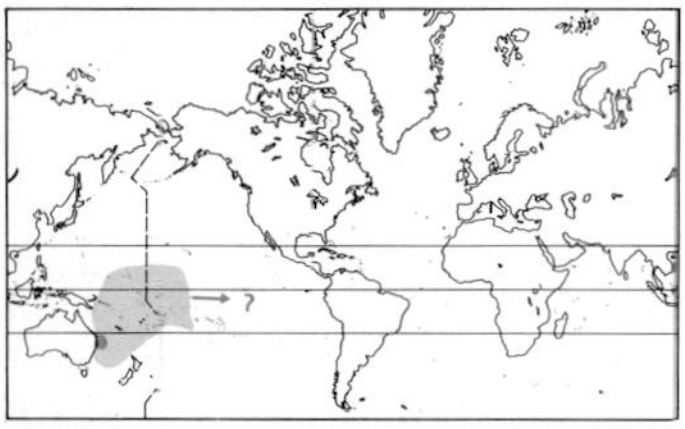

IDENTIFICATION: Medium-sized gadfly-petrel, easily told from all but Collared Petrel (which may be only a race) by combination of sooty-brown cap and hindneck contrasting with grey upperparts; the white underwing has conspicuous dark margins and diagonal bar across coverts. (Cook's, Pycroft's and Stejneger's have paler heads and mostly white underwings.) In flight, upperparts show broad 'M' across wings and back.
HABITS: Breeds oceanic islands; does not normally follow ships. Flight usually slower than Cook's Petrel, recalling small shearwater with shallower flight peaks, but often adopts erratic bat-like weaving, sprinting high over ocean.
DISTRIBUTION: Tropical and subtropical Pacific Ocean. Breeds Oct–Apr Cabbage Tree Is, Australia, dispersing east towards Galapagos Is May–Sep.
SIMILAR SPECIES: Compare Collared, Bonin and Black-winged Petrels (p. 199, p. 200).

Collared Petrel *Pterodroma (leucoptera) brevipes*
L30cm/12in W71cm/28in **P** p. 55 **K** p. 302

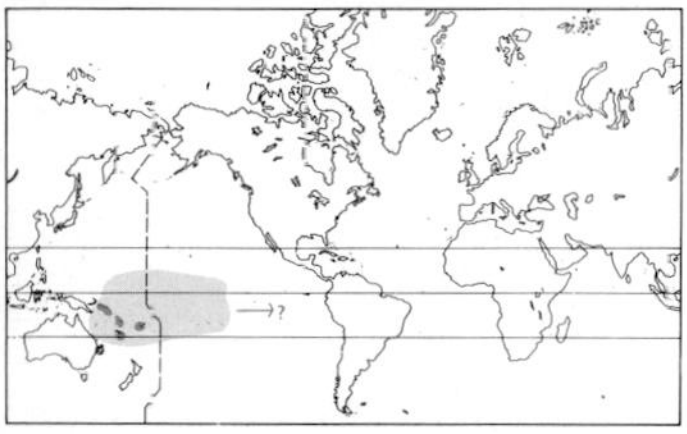

IDENTIFICATION: Medium-sized gadfly-petrel with polymorphic plumages; palest examples are virtually identical to Gould's Petrel (of which Collared may be only a race), whereas darkest examples have whole of underparts except chin, which is white, an even grey with blackish band across upper breast. These melanistic varieties differ further in that the white underwing is usually sullied with grey and the dark leading edge wider. Intermediates between these two extremes are commonplace. The upperparts of all varieties are grey, with obvious, broad open 'M' mark across wings and back.
HABITS: Breeds in loose colonies on oceanic islands; does not normally follow ships. May be less migratory than Gould's Petrel.
DISTRIBUTION: Tropical and subtropical Pacific Ocean. Probably breeds throughout year, as fledglings found Aug and Feb. Breeds Fijian Is of Gau, Kadavu, and Rarotonga, Cook Is; perhaps also Vanuatu, Vitelebu, Western Samoa, American Samoa, Tonga and the Solomons (see Watling 1986). Although thought to be more sedentary than Gould's Petrel, there are tentative sight records from central Pacific (Meeth pers. comm.).
SIMILAR SPECIES: Compare Gould's and Mottled Petrels (p. 199, p. 201).

Bonin Petrel *Pterodroma hypoleuca* L30cm/12in W67cm/26in P p. 54 K p. 302

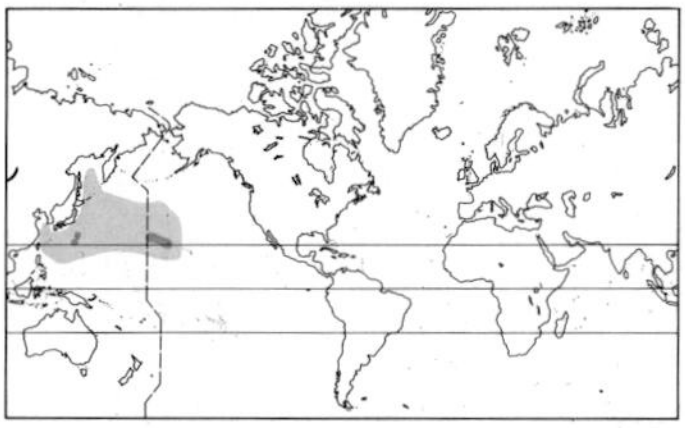

IDENTIFICATION: Medium-sized gadfly-petrel with greyish upperparts and white underparts. Easily identified by combination of blackish crown and nape and white underwing with diagnostic pattern of two blackish patches, the outermost across primary coverts, the second a thinner bar across median and secondary coverts. No other gadfly shows these markings. In flight, grey upperparts show obvious 'M' mark across wings and back.
HABITS: Colonial breeder on oceanic islands; does not normally follow ships. Flight fast and swooping.
DISTRIBUTION: Western north Pacific, breeds Aug–Jun Volcano, Bonin, and Leeward Hawaiian Is, dispersing north Jun–Jul towards central Pacific to about 30°N (Gould pers. comm.) and to Japan and Sakhalin.
SIMILAR SPECIES: Compare Black-winged, Chatham Island and Hawaiian Petrels (p. 200, p. 204).

Chatham Island Petrel *Pterodroma axillaris* L30cm/12in W67cm/26in P p. 53 K p. 302

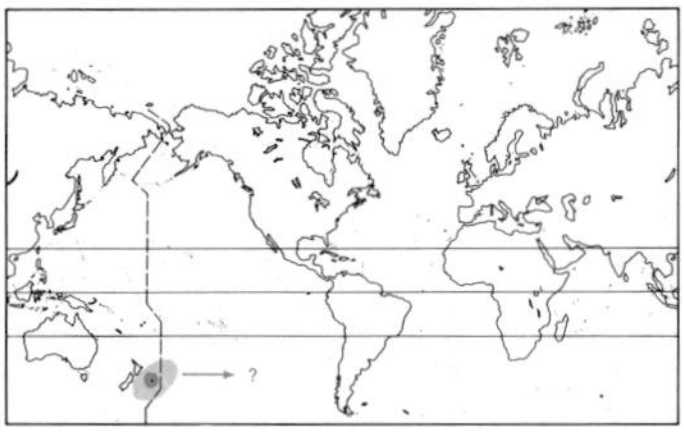

IDENTIFICATION: Medium-sized gadfly-petrel, grey above, white below, bearing superficial resemblance to Black-winged Petrel but differing from that and all other petrels by diagonal black bar extending across white underwing from carpal to axillaries. No other gadfly shows these characters. In flight, mantle and back frosty-grey with 'M' mark across brownish wings and back; partial grey collar on sides of breast. Mottled Petrel is larger, with grey or black belly patch.
HABITS: Colonial breeder on oceanic islands; does not normally follow ships. Flight fast and swooping.
DISTRIBUTION: Southwest Pacific, but pelagic range unknown. Breeds only at Chatham Is, New Zealand; egg dates Dec–Jan, fledging date unrecorded.
SIMILAR SPECIES: Compare Black-winged and Mottled Petrels (p. 200, p. 201).

Black-winged Petrel *Pterodroma nigripennis* L30cm/12in W67cm/26in P p. 52 K p. 302

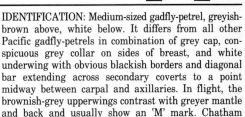

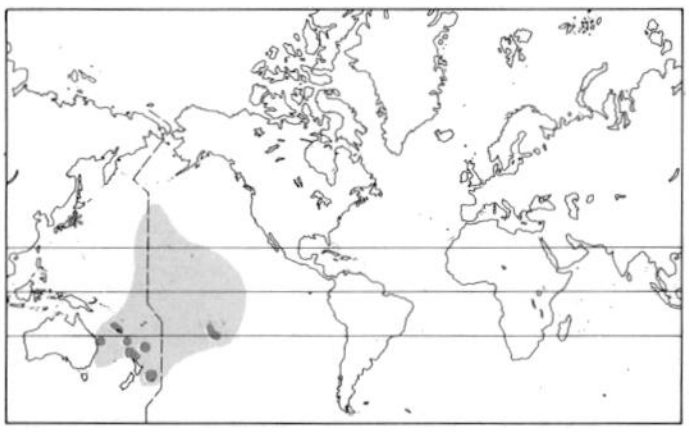

IDENTIFICATION: Medium-sized gadfly-petrel, greyish-brown above, white below. It differs from all other Pacific gadfly-petrels in combination of grey cap, conspicuous grey collar on sides of breast, and white underwing with obvious blackish borders and diagonal bar extending across secondary coverts to a point midway between carpal and axillaries. In flight, the brownish-grey upperwings contrast with greyer mantle and back and usually show an 'M' mark. Chatham Island Petrel differs in black axillaries; Bonin and Gould's Petrels have darker heads and different underwing patterns.
HABITS: Colonial breeder on oceanic islands; does not usually follow ships. Flight as Cook's Petrel, but often flies higher, hanging motionless over ocean.
DISTRIBUTION: Southwest Pacific. Breeds Oct–May New Caledonia, Lord Howe, Norfolk, Three Kings, Kermadec, Chatham and Austral Is. Post-breeding dispersal to central Pacific begins May, reaching north of Hawaii to about 30°N (Gould pers. comm.).
SIMILAR SPECIES: Compare Chatham Island, Bonin and Gould's Petrels (p. 200, p. 199).

Mottled Petrel *Pterodroma inexpectata* L34cm/13in W74cm/29in **P** p. 52 **K** p. 301

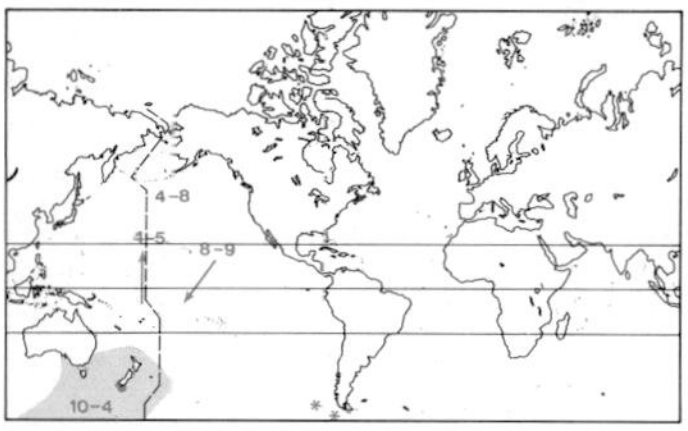

IDENTIFICATION: Large, thickset grey and white gadfly-petrel, easily identified by combination of diagnostic dark grey belly patch and white underwing with obvious broad black border on leading edge extending diagonally across underwing-coverts to a point midway between carpal and axillaries. At close range, head shows blackish eye patch with frosty-grey cap; upperparts have 'M' mark across wings and back. Melanistic Collared Petrels have dark undertail-coverts and greyer underwings.
HABITS: Breeds oceanic islands; does not usually follow ships. Flight wild and impetuous.
DISTRIBUTION: Pacific Ocean. Breeds only at islands in Foveaux Strait, off Stewart Is and at Chatham Is, New Zealand, Oct–Apr, ranging south to pack ice. Post-breeding dispersal begins Mar through central Pacific to southern Alaska, where regular in summer, but casual elsewhere.
SIMILAR SPECIES: None, but compare Great Shearwater, melanistic Collared (p. 208, p. 199).

Magenta Petrel *Pterodroma magentae* L? W? **P** p. 53 **K** p. 303

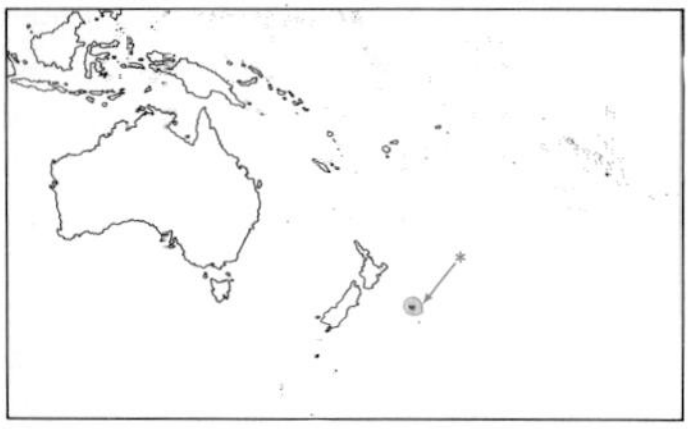

IDENTIFICATION: Medium-sized greyish-brown gadfly-petrel; the dark underwings contrast with white belly and undertail-coverts. Head and upper breast grey, giving hooded effect, but at close range shows variable degree of white mottling over base of bill, chin and throat, recalling smaller, more tropical Phoenix Petrel, of which Magenta Petrel may be only a southerly form (Fullagar and van Tets pers. comm.). In flight, upperparts appear mostly brownish-grey, wings browner and darker forming 'M' mark. Smaller Soft-plumaged Petrel differs in distinct eye patch, white underparts broken by diffuse breastband, and more obvious 'M' mark across upperparts.
HABITS: Unknown; thought to be extinct until rediscovery by David Crockett in 1978.
DISTRIBUTION: Thought to breed Chatham Is, New Zealand, southwest Pacific. Movements unknown: may move towards Pitcairn group, near where type specimen collected 1867.
SIMILAR SPECIES: Compare Soft-plumaged, Tahiti, Phoenix and Atlantic Petrels (p. 196, p. 203, p. 202, p. 197).

Juan Fernandez Petrel *Pterodroma externa*
L43cm/17in W97cm/38in **P** p. 62 **K** p. 305

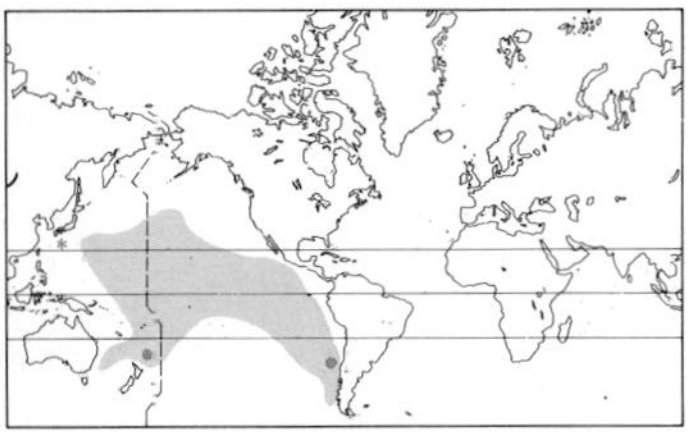

IDENTIFICATION: Large, long-winged gadfly-petrel with dark cap, grey upperparts and white underparts. In flight, upperparts grey with obvious 'M' mark and variable amount of white on rump. Kermadec population has conspicuous white cervical collar. Underwing appears wholly white at distance but, at close range, shows black tip to primaries and faint narrow bar spreading diagonally across coverts. Hawaiian Petrel has darker, more extensive cap, and obvious dark margins and diagonal bar on underwings.
HABITS: Colonial breeder on oceanic islands; does not usually follow ships. Compared with smaller gadfly-petrels, e.g. Cook's, flight is less vigorous and darting, not so fast or swooping.
DISTRIBUTION: Tropical and subtropical Pacific; breeds Oct–May Raoul, Kermadec Is, New Zealand, and at Mas Afuera, Juan Fernandez Is, Chile. Post-breeding dispersal begins May, reaching northern Pacific, but poorly documented; regular south to Gulf of Penas, Chile.
SIMILAR SPECIES: Compare Hawaiian Petrel and Buller's Shearwater (p. 204, p. 210).

Herald Petrel *Pterodroma arminjoniana* L37cm/15in W95cm/37in **P** p. 56 **K** p. 304

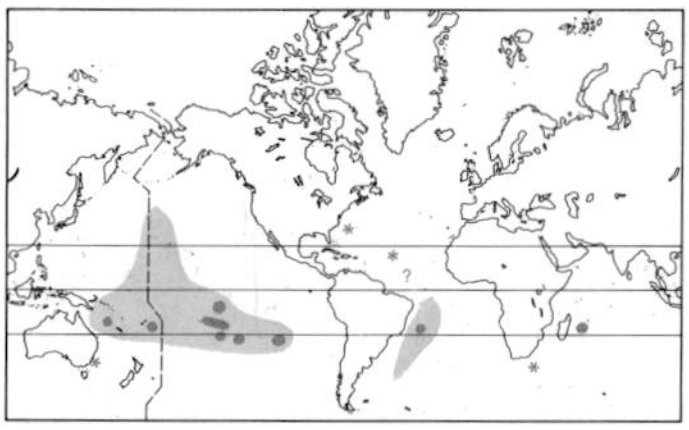

IDENTIFICATION: Large, long-winged, polymorphic gadfly-petrel which closely resembles corresponding phases of Kermadec Petrel. Underbody varies from wholly white to wholly brown; intermediates are white below with dark breastbands. All morphs have dark underwings with a white skua-like patch at base of primaries, which in some extends inwards across coverts. Upperwing of all morphs lacks Kermadec's white primary shafts.
HABITS: Colonial breeder on oceanic islands; occasionally follows ships.
DISTRIBUTION: Fragmented distribution in Pacific, Atlantic and Indian Oceans. Returns to colonies Oct, eggs Mar onwards, fledging ?. In Atlantic breeds Trinidade and Martin Vaz. In Indian Ocean at Round Is, Mauritius, perhaps Reunion. In Pacific at Chesterfield, Tonga, Marquesas, Tuamotu, Gambier, Pitcairn and Easter Is; may breed Raine Is, Australia.
SIMILAR SPECIES: Compare Kermadec, Murphy's and Providence Petrels (p. 202, p. 203).

Kermadec Petrel *Pterodroma neglecta* L38cm/15in W92cm/36in **P** p. 56 **K** p. 304

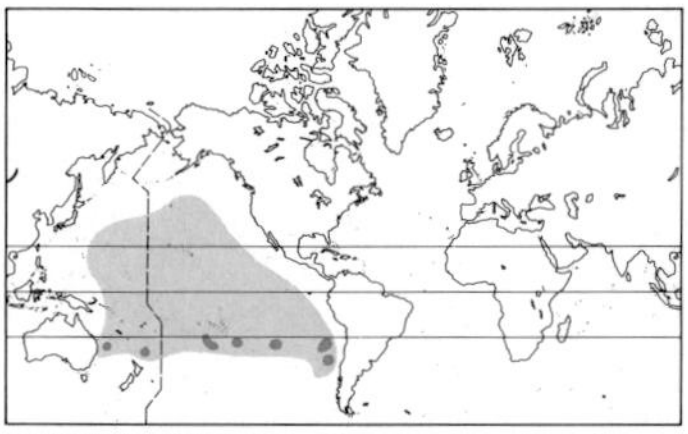

IDENTIFICATION: Large, long-winged, polymorphic gadfly-petrel, the phases of which closely resemble those of Herald Petrel. Differs in obvious white bases and shafts of primaries on upperwing which are easily seen, showing as skua-like flash. In flight, appears larger, stockier than Herald Petrel, with squarer tail, larger head.
HABITS: Breeds colonially on oceanic islands; does not normally follow ships.
DISTRIBUTION: Tropical and subtropical Pacific; egg-dates protracted, Oct–Feb. Breeds Lord Howe, Kermadec, Austral, Pitcairn, Easter, Juan Fernandez, San Ambrosio and San Felix, perhaps Tuamotu. Ranges north to about 40°N in central Pacific (Gould pers. comm.) and to 15°N off western USA.
SIMILAR SPECIES: Compare Herald, Providence and Murphy's Petrels (p. 202, p. 203), intermediate morphs with Tahiti and Phoenix Petrels (p. 203, p. 202).

Phoenix Petrel *Pterodroma alba* L35cm/14in W83cm/33in **P** p. 57 **K** p. 304

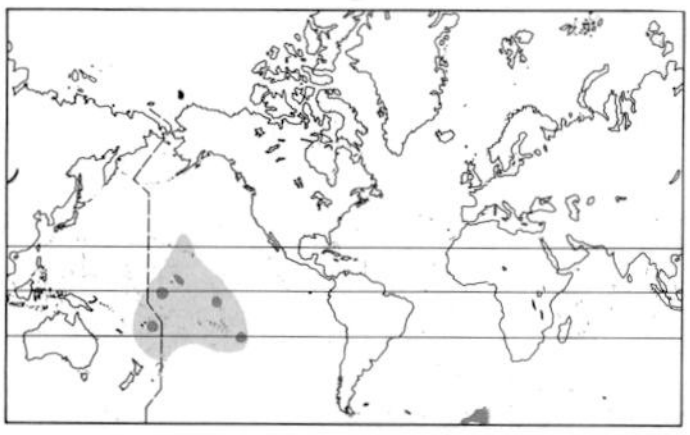

IDENTIFICATION: Large, white-bellied gadfly-petrel with uniform sooty-brown upperparts; difficult at any range to separate from Tahiti Petrel. It differs in whitish throat patch (often difficult to detect) and in narrow white leading edge to sooty-brown underwing, a character not found in Tahiti Petrel. Upperparts usually appear distinctly darker than those of Tahiti Petrel and, though slightly smaller overall, it has proportionately larger head and wider body, giving more thickset jizz. Differs from intermediate Kermadec and Herald Petrels in darker underwing.
HABITS: Breeds on oceanic islands; does not normally follow ships.
DISTRIBUTION: Tropical and subtropical Pacific; egg-dates protracted, Jan–Jul. Breeds Phoenix, Marquesas, Tonga, Line and Pitcairn Is, perhaps also Raoul. Pelagic range extends to seas north of Hawaiian Chain.
SIMILAR SPECIES: Compare Tahiti, Kermadec and Herald Petrels (p. 203, p. 202).

Tahiti Petrel *Pterodroma rostrata* L39cm/15in W84cm/33in **P** p. 57 **K** p. 304

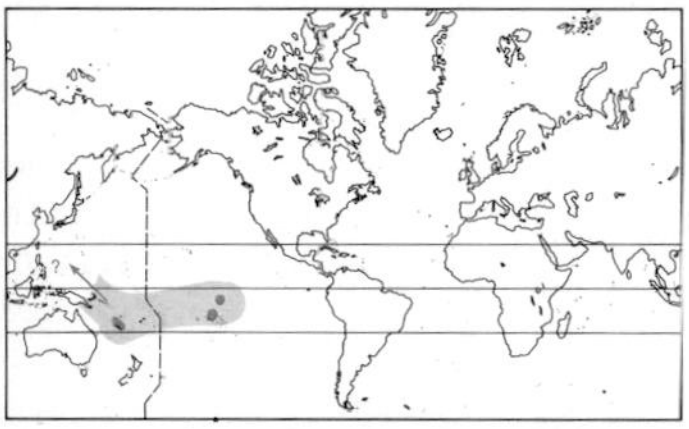

IDENTIFICATION: Medium-sized white-bellied gadfly-petrel with uniform sooty-brown upperparts; difficult at any range to separate from Phoenix Petrel. It differs in lack of white on throat and paler brown upperparts. The underwing lacks narrow white leading edge of Phoenix Petrel, and has a slightly paler base to primaries which extends back through secondaries along hindwing, giving two-toned appearance. In flight, appears smaller-headed and longer-necked than Phoenix, giving more attenuated jizz. Intermediate Kermadec and Herald Petrels have different underwing patterns.
HABITS: Breeds on oceanic islands; does not normally follow ships.
DISTRIBUTION: Tropical and subtropical central and western Pacific, perhaps dispersing northwest towards Taiwan. Egg-dates Oct, breeds New Caledonia, Marquesas and Society Is.
SIMILAR SPECIES: Compare Phoenix Petrel (p. 202), also intermediate Herald and Kermadec Petrels (p. 202).

Providence Petrel *Pterodroma solandri* L40cm/16in W94cm/37in **P** p. 58 **K** p. 300

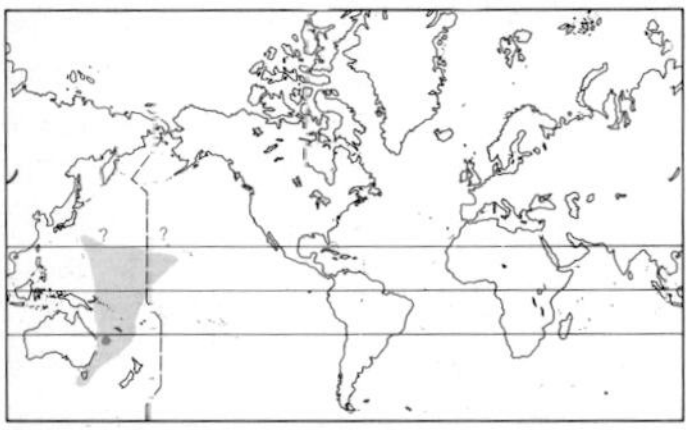

IDENTIFICATION: Large, thickset gadfly-petrel, appearing mostly dark greyish-brown except for conspicuous skua-like patch on underside of primaries. At close range, from below, head appears darker than rest of underbody, giving hooded appearance. Whitish flecking around bill imparts grey-faced appearance. Murphy's Petrel is similar, but greyer overall with indistinct 'M' mark across upper surfaces and paler secondaries on underwing. Dark forms of Herald and Kermadec Petrels lack grey-faced appearance of Providence, which differs further in distinct wedge-shaped tail (see photos p. 58).
HABITS: Breeds oceanic islands; does not normally follow ships.
DISTRIBUTION: Transequatorial migrant in Pacific; breeds May–Nov at Lord Howe Is, southwest Pacific, ranging southwest to seas off Australia. Post-breeding dispersal north towards Japan.
SIMILAR SPECIES: Compare Murphy's Petrel (below), dark morphs of Kermadec and Herald Petrels (p. 202).

Murphy's Petrel *Pterodroma ultima* L40cm/16in W97cm/38in **P** p. 58 **K** p. 300

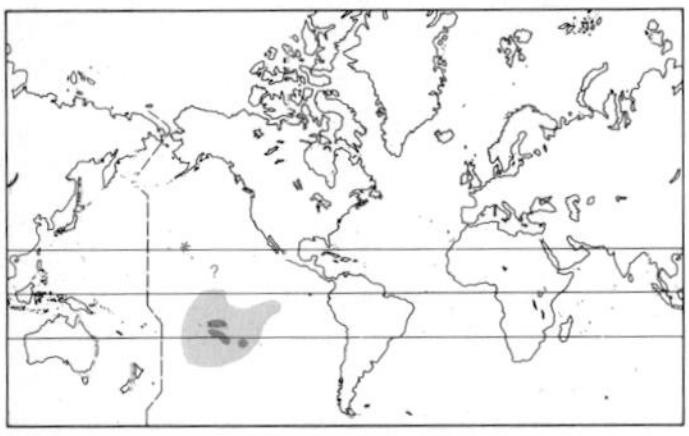

IDENTIFICATION: Large, thickset gadfly-petrel, appearing (*contra* Harrison 1986) mostly greyish-brown, rather featureless, except for indistinct 'M' mark across upperparts and pale base to underside of primaries which extends inwards along length of wing. At close range, variable mottling around bill gives indistinct grey- or white-faced appearance. Dark morph Kermadec and Herald Petrels are distinctly browner and lack grey-faced aspect. Providence has more obvious white crescent on underwing and lacks 'M' across upperparts.
HABITS: Breeds oceanic islands; does not normally follow ships.
DISTRIBUTION: Central tropical Pacific, but pelagic range poorly documented; has occurred Hawaiian Leeward Is, and California, suggesting northwards post-breeding dispersal. Present at colonies Mar–Apr, but breeding dates unknown; breeds Rapa and Oeno Is, Austral, Tuamotu and Pitcairn groups.
SIMILAR SPECIES: Compare Providence Petrel (above) and dark morphs of Kermadec and Herald Petrels (p. 202).

Hawaiian Petrel *Pterodroma phaeopygia* L43cm/17in W91cm/36in P p. 54 K p. 305

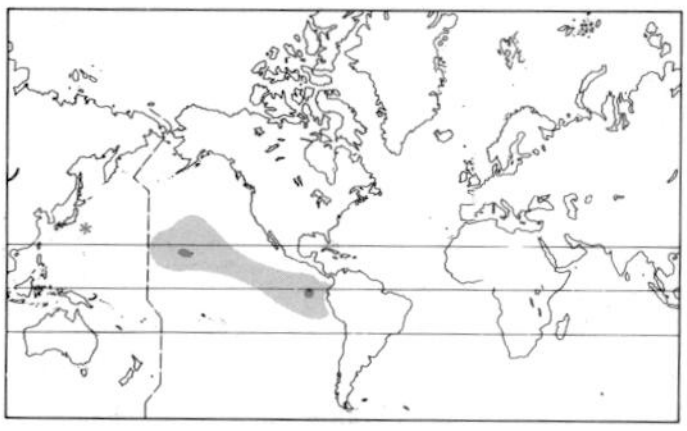

IDENTIFICATION: Large, long-winged gadfly-petrel, brownish-grey above with obvious dark cap extending to sides of face and variable white patches over tail. Underparts mostly white, except for distinct black border to underwing and diagonal bar across coverts; white axillaries show small but diagnostic blackish mark. Juan Fernandez Petrel is similar, but lacks the noticeable cap and underwing markings.
HABITS: Colonial breeder on oceanic islands; does not normally follow ships. Flight powerful, bounding over ocean in long, spectacular swoops.
DISTRIBUTION: Tropical Pacific, but pelagic range poorly known; breeds Apr–Dec Galapagos Is and Hawaiian Chain.
SIMILAR SPECIES: Compare Juan Fernandez Petrel (p. 201).

Black-capped Petrel *Pterodroma hasitata* L40cm/16in W95cm/37in P p. 62 K p. 305

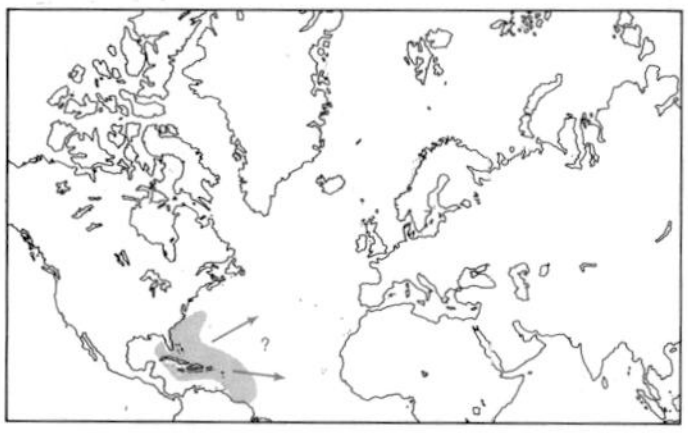

IDENTIFICATION: **Typical:** Large, long-winged gadfly-petrel, upperparts mostly blackish-brown contrasting with conspicuous white cervical collar and broad 'U' shaped band over rump; forehead white, with small blackish cap extending downwards to eye. Underparts mostly white, except for obvious blackish border to underwing and diagonal bar on leading edge. **Atypical:** As typical, except for reduced amount of white on nape and rump; darkest examples may thus be indistinguishable from Bermuda Petrel. Great Shearwater has similar plumage pattern, but has longer bill, less white on nape and rump, different underwing and flight characters.
HABITS: Colonial breeder in mountains and cliffs of oceanic islands; does not normally follow ships. Flight high and swooping, moving over ocean in high sweeping arcs; springs clear of water when flushed.
DISTRIBUTION: Caribbean Sea, dispersing north to eastern USA and south towards Brazil; may move east towards centre of Atlantic. Breeds Nov–May highlands of Hispaniola.
SIMILAR SPECIES: Compare Bermuda Petrel and Great Shearwater (p. 204, p. 208).

Bermuda Petrel *Pterodroma cahow* L38cm/15in W89cm/35in P p. 63 K p. 305

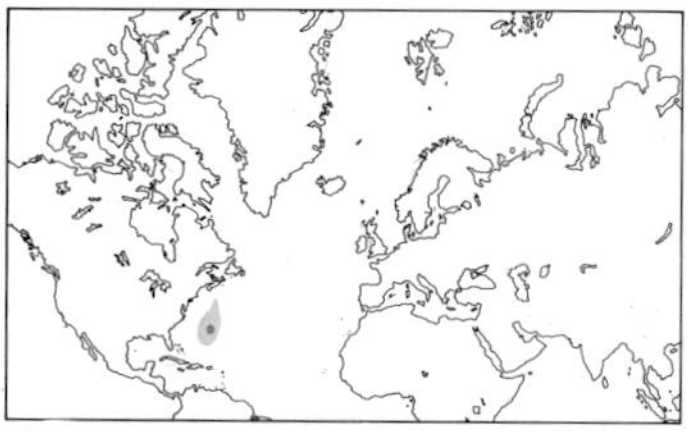

IDENTIFICATION: Large, long-winged gadfly-petrel, wholly blackish-brown above, thus differing from typical Black-capped Petrel in absence of white over rump or on hindneck. Underparts mostly white, except for dark sides of breast, on some extending to form complete breastband. Underwing as Black-capped Petrel.
HABITS: Colonial breeder on oceanic islands; does not normally follow ships. Flight as Black-capped Petrel (above), thus distinctly different from Great Shearwater.
DISTRIBUTION: Breeds only at Bermuda, Oct–May; pelagic dispersal unknown.
SIMILAR SPECIES: Compare Black-capped Petrel and Great Shearwater (p. 204, p. 208).

Mascarene Petrel *Pterodroma aterrima* L36cm/14in W? **P** p. 60 **K** p. 303

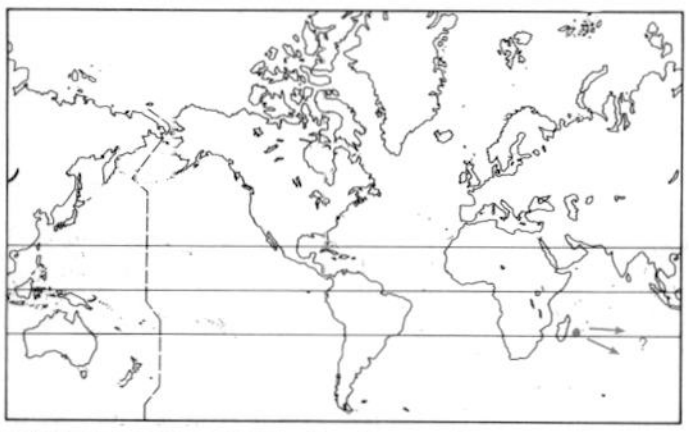

IDENTIFICATION: Status and identification of this petrel virtually unknown. Appears wholly blackish-brown, underwing may be greyish-black (Bourne & Dixon 1972). It differs from all-dark Wedge-tailed and Flesh-footed Shearwaters in large stubby bill, gadfly jizz and high swooping flight. Dark-morph Herald Petrel, which occurs in same area, has conspicuous white patch at base of primaries.
HABITS: Virtually unknown. Breeds oceanic islands.
DISTRIBUTION: Indian Ocean, but range and distribution unknown. Possible sight records off Reunion Is, where it may breed. Perhaps also on Mascarene Is. See Jouanin (1969).
SIMILAR SPECIES: Compare Wedge-tailed and Flesh-footed Shearwaters, also dark-morph Herald Petrel (p. 210, p. 207, p. 202).

Bulwer's Petrel *Bulweria bulwerii* L26cm/10in W67cm/26in **P** p. 61 **K** p. 306

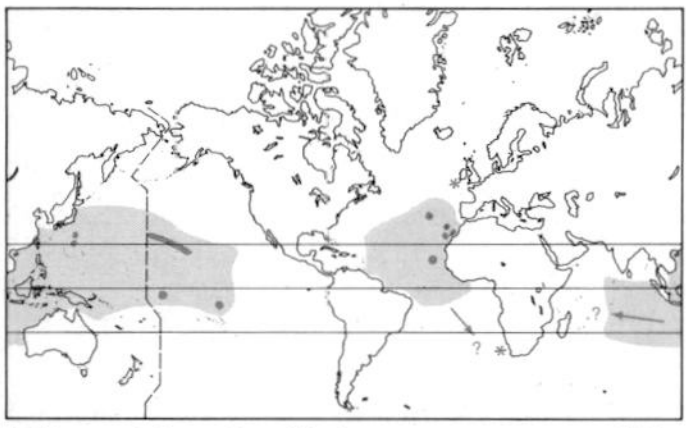

IDENTIFICATION: Between storm-petrels and smaller *Pterodroma* petrels in size, with diagnostic long, wedge-shaped tail which is usually held closed and appears long and pointed. Plumage blackish-brown, except for paler diagonal bar across median coverts of upperwing (normally invisible over 250m range). All-dark storm-petrels are smaller, with distinctly different tails. Jouanin's Petrel is much larger, with different flight.
HABITS: Breeds oceanic islands; does not normally follow ships. In flight, appears small-headed with long wings and long pointed tail, moving over ocean with buoyant twisting flight, wings held forward, weaving and twisting close to waves, rarely higher than 2m before dipping into trough. Over calm seas flight often direct and purposeful, a few wingbeats followed by a short glide with wings parallel to sea surface.
DISTRIBUTION: Tropical and subtropical waters of Pacific, Atlantic and Indian Oceans. Breeds Apr–Oct in Atlantic off Azores, Desertas, islands off Madeira, Salvage, Canary and Cape Verde Is. In Pacific breeds islands off Taiwan and China, and at Bonin, Marquesas, Johnston, Volcano, Hawaiian and Phoenix Is.
SIMILAR SPECIES: Compare Jouanin's Petrel (below).

Jouanin's Petrel *Bulweria fallax* L31cm/12in W79cm/31in **P** p. 61 **K** p. 306

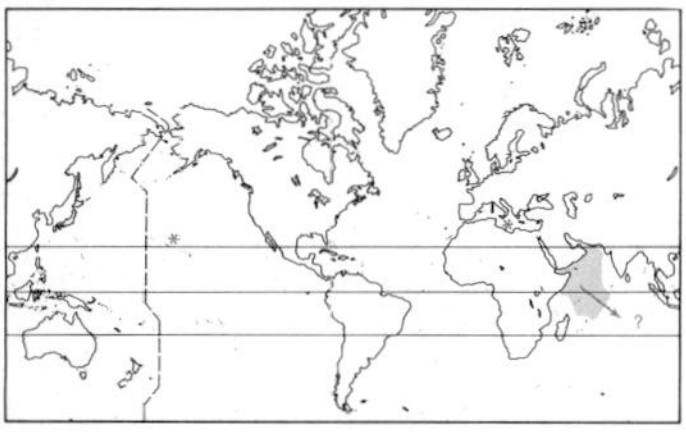

IDENTIFICATION: Wholly blackish-brown. Recalls Bulwer's Petrel, but distinctly larger with bigger bill, proportionately larger head and broader wings; tail broader, not so pointed or long, with curious midway 'step' formed by shorter outer feathers. At close range, area around bill paler; in worn plumage upperwing-coverts paler, forming pale upperwing diagonal as in Bulwer's Petrel. Mascarene Petrel is larger than Jouanin's, with thickset jizz and square tail. Wedge-tailed Shearwater is larger, with flap-and-glide flight, loose-winged jizz and long slender bill.
HABITS: Biology unknown; does not normally follow ships. Unlike Bulwer's Petrel, flight strong and swift, moving over ocean in broad sweeps 15–20m above waves, recalling gadfly-petrel.
DISTRIBUTION: Arabian Sea, Gulf of Aden and adjacent northwest Indian Ocean, east to 58°E and south to Equator. Breeding area unknown, perhaps islands off Arabia.
SIMILAR SPECIES: Compare Bulwer's and Mascarene Petrels, also Wedge-tailed Shearwater (p. 205, p. 210).

Fiji Petrel *Pseudobulweria macgillivrayi* L30cm/12in W? **P** p. 60 **K** p. 300

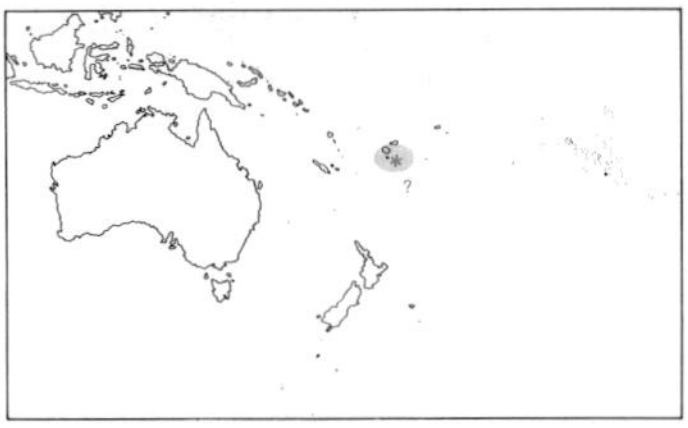

IDENTIFICATION: Formerly known as Macgillivray's Petrel. This 'lost' species was rediscovered on Gua in 1983. Recalls Bulwer's Pètrel, but plumage is wholly dark brown, without paler upperwing bars, and has a slightly darker head, giving hooded effect. It is larger, more bulky, than Bulwer's Petrel, with short, stout bill, shorter tail, more rounded wings and proportionately larger head, giving thickset jizz.
HABITS: Unknown.
DISTRIBUTION: Seas off Fiji, southwest Pacific, but pelagic distribution unknown. Known only from two specimens collected on Gua, Fiji Is, the first in 1855, the second in 1983.
SIMILAR SPECIES: None within area, but compare Bulwer's and Jouanin's Petrels (p. 205).

White-chinned Petrel *Procellaria aequinoctialis*
L55cm/22in W140cm/55in **P** p. 64 **K** p. 294

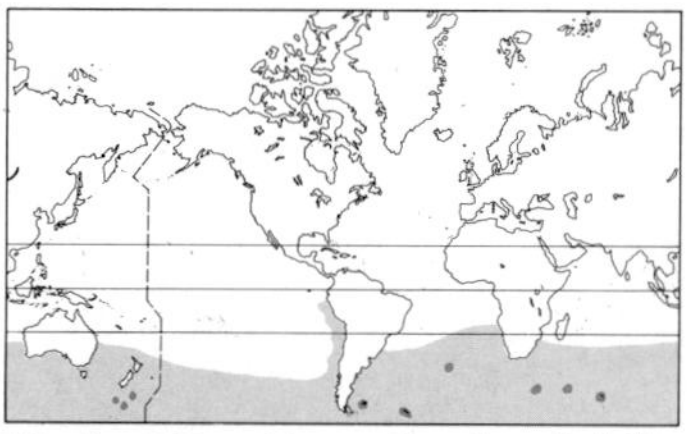

IDENTIFICATION: A large, uniformly dark, brownish-black petrel with white chin of variable extent, and large unmarked greenish-ivory bill. The South Atlantic form *conspicillata* usually has more white on chin, often extending to encircle cheeks, giving distinct spectacled appearance. Size intermediate between all-dark shearwaters and dark juveniles of the much larger giant petrels. Differs from all-dark shearwaters in larger size, bull-necked jizz, bill and leg colour. Separated from Westland Petrel by uniformly pale bill.
HABITS: One of the commonest, most widespread petrels of Southern Oceans, breeding on sub-Antarctic islands; habitually follows ships. Flight measured and purposeful, with slow wingbeats interspersed with sustained glides.
DISTRIBUTION: Circumpolar in the Southern Oceans, ranging from pack ice north to about 30°S but to 6°S in Humboldt Current. Usually breeds Oct–Apr Falklands, South Georgia, Inaccessible, Prince Edward, Marion, Crozet, Kerguelen, Auckland, Campbell and Antipodes; perhaps Gough and Macquarie Is.
SIMILAR SPECIES: Compare Westland and Parkinson's Petrels, also Flesh-footed Shearwater (p. 206, p. 207).

Westland Petrel *Procellaria westlandica* L51cm/20in W137cm/54in **P** p. 64 **K** p. 294

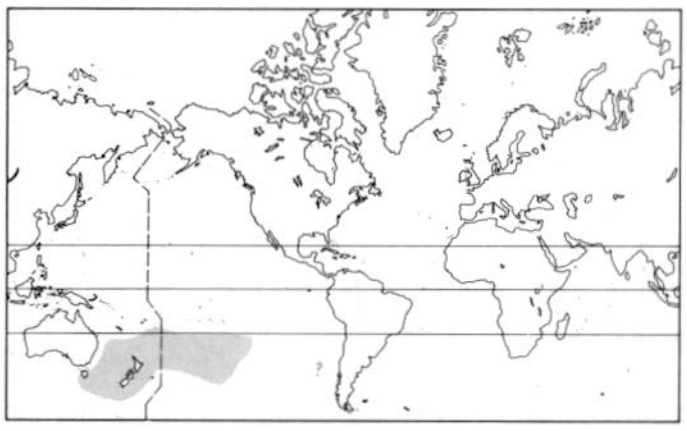

IDENTIFICATION: A large, uniformly dark blackish-brown petrel which can be reliably separated from the more widespread White-chinned Petrel only by the black tip to its ivory-coloured bill and by its dark chin (some White-chinned Petrels also have dark chins). Parkinson's Petrel differs only in smaller size. Flesh-footed Shearwater is smaller, with more slender bill and body and pink (not black) feet.
HABITS: Breeds colonially on forested hillsides. Flight as for White-chinned Petrel, but does not normally follow ships.
DISTRIBUTION: New Zealand seas; recent sightings, however, indicate post-breeding dispersal to at least 150°W in central Pacific (Pitman and Bartle pers. comm.). Breeds Mar–Dec forested hills near Barrytown, South Island, New Zealand.
SIMILAR SPECIES: Compare White-chinned, Parkinson's and Great-winged Petrels, also Flesh-footed Shearwater (p. 206, p. 207, p. 196, p. 207).

Parkinson's Petrel *Procellaria parkinsoni*
L46cm/18in W115cm/45in **P** p. 65 **K** p. 294

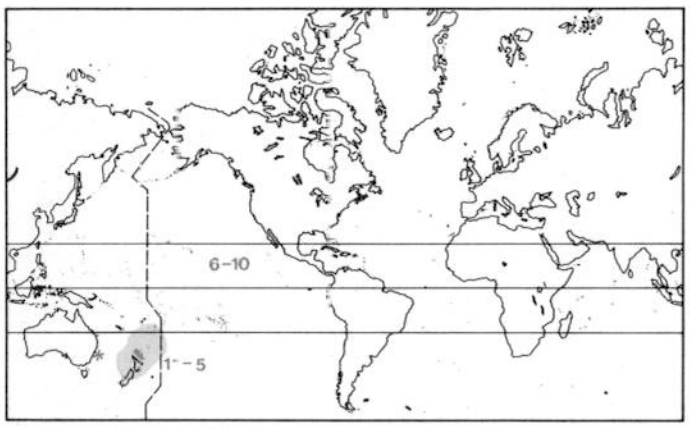

IDENTIFICATION: A medium-sized, uniformly dark, brownish-black petrel, differing from Westland Petrel only in its smaller size; separation at sea therefore problematical. Differs from Flesh-footed Shearwater in its stout bill, more thickset body, more rounded wings and blackish (not pink) feet. Great-winged Petrel is smaller, with different bill shape and colour.
HABITS: Colonial breeder on offshore islands; unlike Westland Petrel, breeds in austral summer. Does not normally follow ships. Flight less laboured than larger Westland or White-chinned Petrels, but difficult to separate from either at sea.
DISTRIBUTION: Subtropical Pacific. Breeds Nov–Jun at Little and Great Barrier Is, New Zealand; disperses east towards Galapagos and Mexico.
SIMILAR SPECIES: Compare White-chinned, Westland and Great-winged Petrels, also Flesh-footed Shearwater (p. 206, p. 196, p. 207).

Grey Petrel *Procellaria cinerea* L48cm/19in W120cm/47in **P** p. 63 **K** p. 294

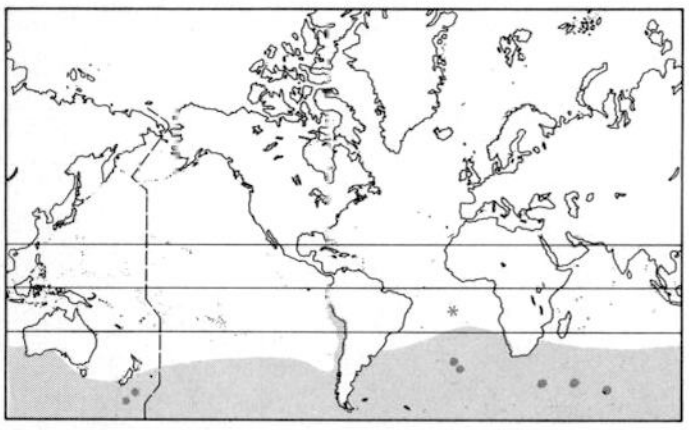

IDENTIFICATION: Large grey and white petrel with yellowish bill recalling Cory's Shearwater, but easily separated by white underbody contrasting with dark underwing and tail. Upperparts wholly grey, merging on sides of face into white chin and throat without obvious demarcation. Differs from smaller White-headed Petrel in darker head, upperparts and tail. Atlantic Petrel is smaller, with dark bill, throat and upper breast.
HABITS: Colonial breeder on sub-Antarctic islands; follows ships. Flight usually high and wheeling, with awkward, stiff, duck-like wingbeats followed by sustained gliding. Dives into sea from heights up to 10m.
DISTRIBUTION: Circumpolar, usually between 60°S and 25°S, but further north off western South America and South Africa. Breeds Feb–Sep Tristan da Cunha, Gough, Marion, Prince Edward, Crozet, Kerguelen, Campbell and Antipodes Is.
SIMILAR SPECIES: Compare White-headed and Atlantic Petrels, Cory's Shearwater (p. 197, p. 208).

Flesh-footed Shearwater *Puffinus carneipes*
L43cm/17in W103cm/41in **P** p. 65 **K** p. 297

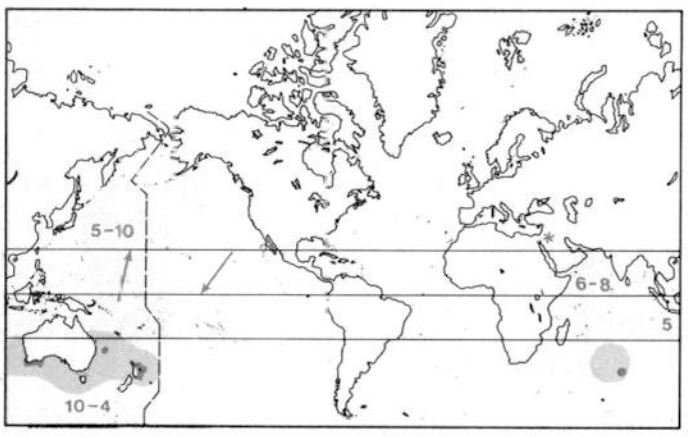

IDENTIFICATION: Large, wholly blackish-brown shearwater with diagnostic yellowish-pink or flesh-coloured bill and legs. At close range tip of bill dark. Very similar to dark-morph Wedge-tailed Shearwater, but has larger head, more thickset body, shorter more rounded tail. Differs from Sooty and Short-tailed Shearwaters in larger size, pale bill and feet, dark underwing; from Westland, Parkinson's and White-chinned Petrels in smaller size, more slender appearance, bill and leg colour.
HABITS: Breeds colonially on oceanic islands; does not usually follow ships. Flight slow and unhurried, with long glides on stiff wings broken by slow effortless flaps.
DISTRIBUTION: Transequatorial migrant in Pacific and Indian Oceans. Breeds Sep–May western Australia and St Paul Is, dispersing north to Arabian Sea, occasionally to seas off South Africa. New Zealand and Lord Howe breeders move north into Pacific past Japan to western USA, where rare but regular.
SIMILAR SPECIES: Compare dark-morph Wedge-tailed Shearwater, Westland, White-chinned and Parkinson's Petrels (p. 210, p. 206, p. 207).

Cory's Shearwater *Calonectris diomedea*
L46cm/18in W113cm/44in **P** p. 66 **K** p. 295

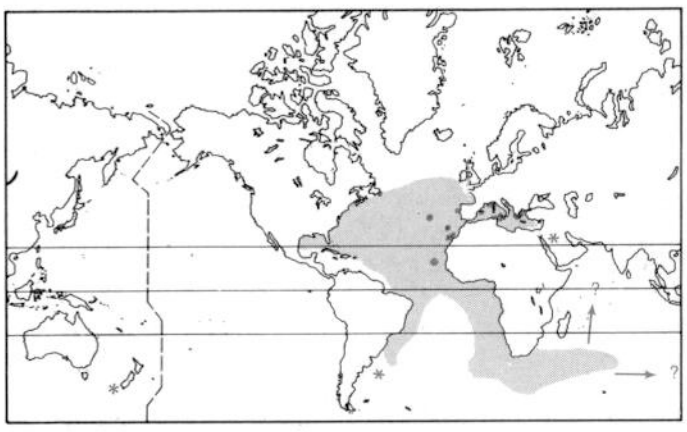

IDENTIFICATION: A large, heavy-bodied shearwater with ash-brown upperparts merging into white underparts without obvious demarcation. At close range, yellow bill shows dark tip with variable amount of white over tail. Differs from Great Shearwater in more uniform upperparts, lack of pronounced dark cap or white collar, less white over tail and, usually, whiter underwing-coverts contrasting with darker primary tips on underwing.
HABITS: Colonial breeder on marine islands. At sea, often forms large flocks; follows ships. Flight more languid than Great Shearwater, with broader wings held looser, more flexed, with characteristic bow from carpal to wingtip, skimming closer to water in long, low glides.
DISTRIBUTION: Widespread in North Atlantic during summer months, with post-breeding dispersal to coasts of Brazil, Uruguay and South Africa; vagrant Red Sea. Breeds Feb–Sep at islands in Mediterranean Sea, Azores, Madeira, Canary, Berlenga and Cape Verde Is.
SIMILAR SPECIES: Compare Great Shearwater and Grey Petrel (p. 208, p. 207).

Great Shearwater *Puffinus gravis* L47cm/19in W109cm/43in **P** p. 66 **K** p. 295

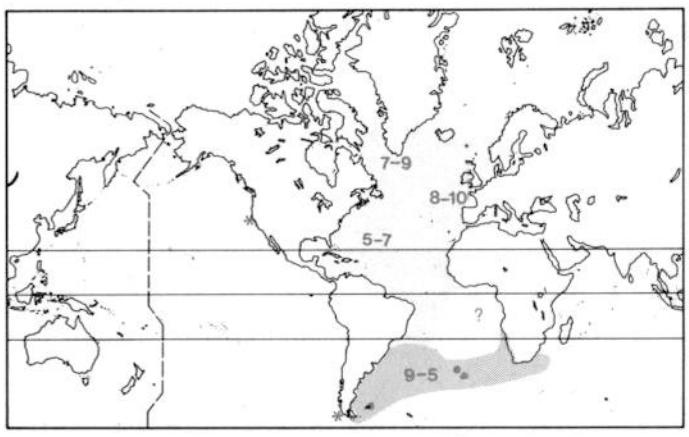

IDENTIFICATION: Large, long-winged brown and white shearwater. Differs from Cory's and Pink-footed in clear-cut, dark brown cap, white hindneck and prominent white band over uppertail-coverts (Cory's usually shows less white over uppertail-coverts). From below, white underwing shows narrow black border and variable diagonal bar across coverts and axillaries.
HABITS: Breeds colonially on oceanic islands; gregarious at sea, often follows ships. Flight stiffer-winged and more dynamic than Cory's Shearwater, higher arcs than those of the smaller shearwaters, with more powerful, slower wingbeats and longer, more forceful glides.
DISTRIBUTION: Transequatorial migrant in Atlantic, with post-breeding dispersal to coasts of America and Europe north to 66°N. Breeds Sep–Apr Tristan da Cunha group, Gough, Falklands.
SIMILAR SPECIES: Compare Cory's, Pink-footed and Buller's Shearwaters, also Black-capped Petrel (p. 208, p. 210, p. 204).

Sooty Shearwater *Puffinus griseus* L44cm/17in W105cm/41in **P** p. 67 **K** p. 297

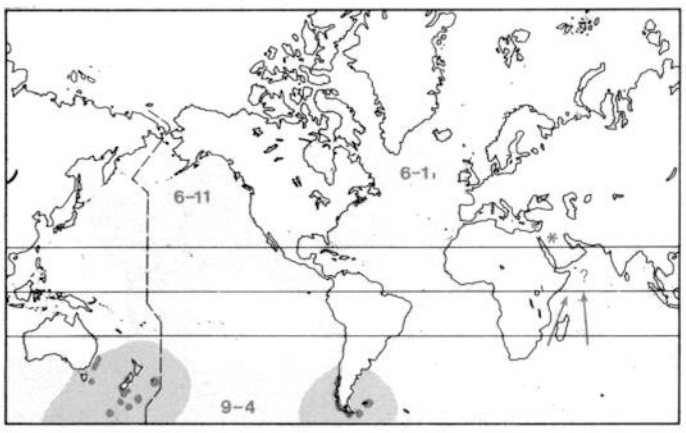

IDENTIFICATION: A large, dark brown, slender-bodied shearwater with long, narrow, swept-back wings. Plumage mostly sooty-brown, except for conspicuous but variable amount of white on underwing-coverts which appears as a white flash during flap-and-glide flight. Differs from Short-tailed Shearwater in longer bill and whiter underwing-coverts; from Flesh-footed and Wedge-tailed Shearwaters in white underwing-coverts, dark feet and faster, more direct flight. Some Balearic Shearwaters resemble Sooty, but have shorter, more rounded wings and mottled belly.
HABITS: Colonial breeder on sub-Antarctic islands. Does not normally follow ships; gregarious at sea. Flight strong and direct, with fast, mechanical wingbeats.
DISTRIBUTION: Transequatorial migrant in Pacific and Atlantic Oceans. Breeds Sep–May southern Chile, Australia and Tasmania, Snares, Auckland, Campbell, Chatham, Antipodes, Macquarie and Stewart Is, New Zealand. Also Tristan da Cunha (MacKenzie pers. comm.).
SIMILAR SPECIES: Short-tailed, Balearic and Flesh-footed Shearwaters, Great-winged Petrel (p. 211, p. 209, p. 207, p. 196).

Manx Shearwater *Puffinus puffinus* L34cm/13in W82cm/32in **P** p. 68 **K** p. 295

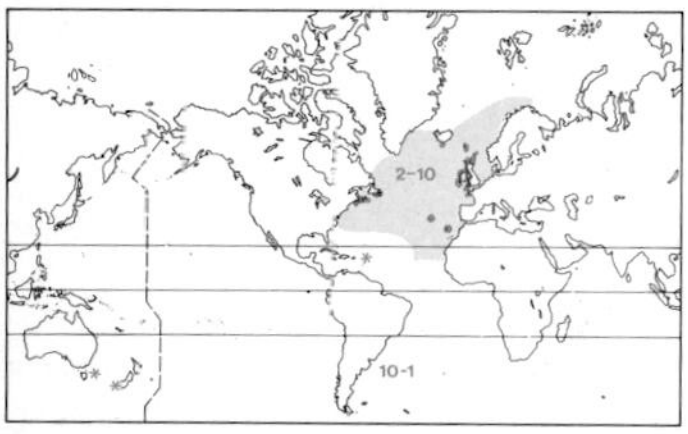

IDENTIFICATION: Medium-sized shearwater, black above, white below. At close range, black cap extends below eye, underwing shows blackish borders and tip with variable mottling on axillaries and flanks. Differs from smaller, shorter-billed Little Shearwater in broader underwing margins, sides of face are usually darker, distinctly different jizz and flight. See also Balearic and Levantine Shearwaters (below).

HABITS: Colonial breeder on islands and headlands; gregarious at sea, occasionally follows ships. In flight appears longer-necked and flatter-crowned than Little Shearwater, with bursts of rapid stiff-winged strokes alternating with shearing glides low over waves. In strong winds capable of sustained gliding with fewer wingbeats.

DISTRIBUTION: Transequatorial Atlantic migrant, dispersing from natal islands south to Chile and east to South Africa. Breeds Feb–Aug Cape Cod, USA, Iceland, Faeroes and Britain, with smaller colonies northwest France, Azores and Madeira.

SIMILAR SPECIES: Compare Little and Balearic/Levantine Shearwaters (below).

Balearic/Levantine Shearwaters *Puffinus mauretanicus/yelkouan* L37cm/15in W87cm/34in **P** p. 68 **K** p. 295

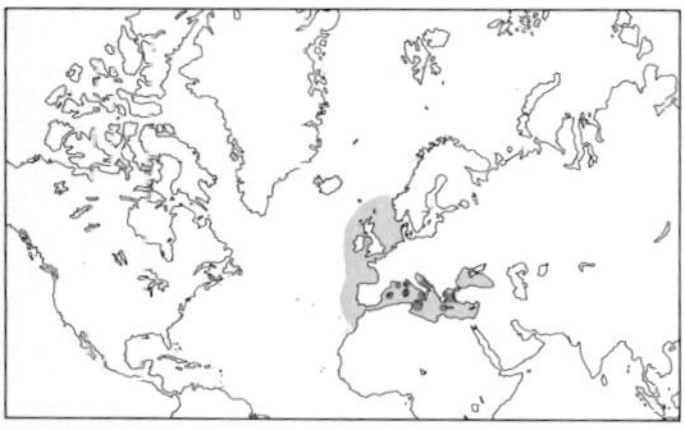

IDENTIFICATION: Taxonomy vexed; *mauretanicus* and *yelkouan* appear to indicate clinal variations, birds becoming darker, perhaps larger, from east to west. Plumage thus variable, ranging from those with characters of Sooty Shearwater to those resembling paler Manx types. Dark forms differ from Sooty in smaller size, shorter more rounded wings, slower, less direct flight; palest forms from Manx in browner upperparts, diffuse division between upperparts and underparts, darker flanks, undertail-coverts and axillaries.

HABITS: As for Manx, although *mauretanicus* has slower wingbeats giving smoother flight.

DISTRIBUTION: Breeds islands of Mediterranean Sea Mar–Aug. Darker *mauretanicus* appear to disperse into Atlantic, reaching north to Britain and Norway, whereas paler *yelkouan* appear to move only to western Mediterranean.

SIMILAR SPECIES: Compare Sooty and Manx Shearwaters (p. 208, p. 209).

Little Shearwater *Puffinus assimilis* L27cm/11in W62cm/24in **P** p. 69 **K** p. 298

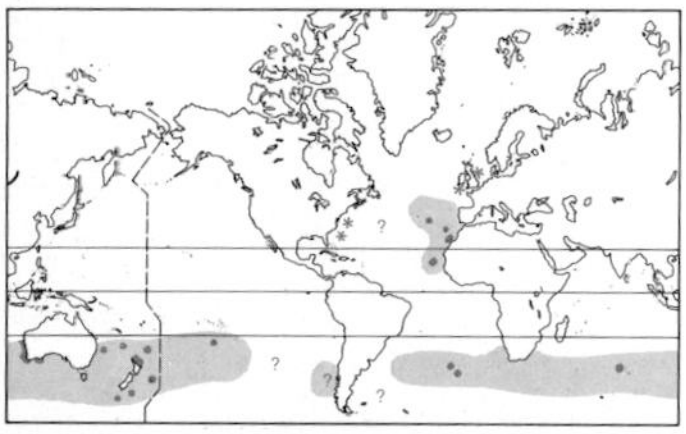

IDENTIFICATION: Very small black and white shearwater. Differs from Manx in size, small bill, demarcation between black and white in most forms above eye giving whiter-faced appearance, and narrower margins and smaller dark tip to underwings. From Audubon's in black upperparts, whiter face, underwing and undertail-coverts.

HABITS: Colonial breeder on marine islands; does not usually follow ships. Flight differs from Manx in lower, wave-hugging progression, with rapid, whirring wingbeats followed by brief glides on shorter, more rounded wings, held parallel to water's surface, giving auk-like jizz.

DISTRIBUTION: Widespread: breeds Azores, Desertas, Salvage, Canary and Cape Verde, Tristan da Cunha, Gough, St Paul, islands off western Australia and northern New Zealand, Kermadecs, Lord Howe, Norfolk and Rapa Is; dates dependent on location.

SIMILAR SPECIES: Compare Manx and Audubon's Shearwaters (p. 209, p. 212).

Pink-footed Shearwater *Puffinus creatopus*
L48cm/19in W109cm/43in **P** p. 70 **K** p. 296

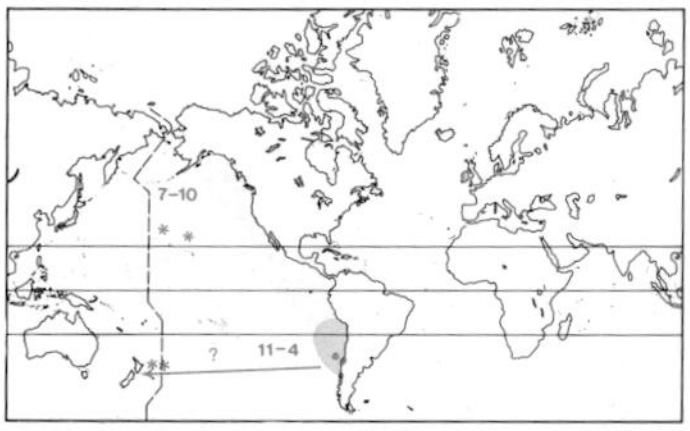

IDENTIFICATION: Large shearwater, dark greyish-brown above, mainly white below, with pale bill and feet. Differs from pale-morph Wedge-tailed Shearwater in more mottled sides to face and neck giving darker-headed impression; underwing margins average broader, more diffuse, with browner axillaries forming dark triangle across coverts at base of wing; appears more lumbering in flight, with larger head, bull-necked jizz and thickset body with broader wings and shorter tail. At close range, bill pink with dark tip.
HABITS: Colonial breeder on oceanic islands; solitary or gregarious at sea, often with other migratory species. Flight languid and unhurried.
DISTRIBUTION: Southeast Pacific, breeds Nov–Apr Mocha and Juan Fernandez Is off Chile, with post-breeding dispersal north towards Alaska. Recently photographed near New Zealand (Tunnicliffe 1982).
SIMILAR SPECIES: Compare Wedge-tailed and Cory's Shearwaters (p. 210, p. 208).

Wedge-tailed Shearwater *Puffinus pacificus*
L43cm/17in W101cm/40in **P** p. 70 **K** p. 296

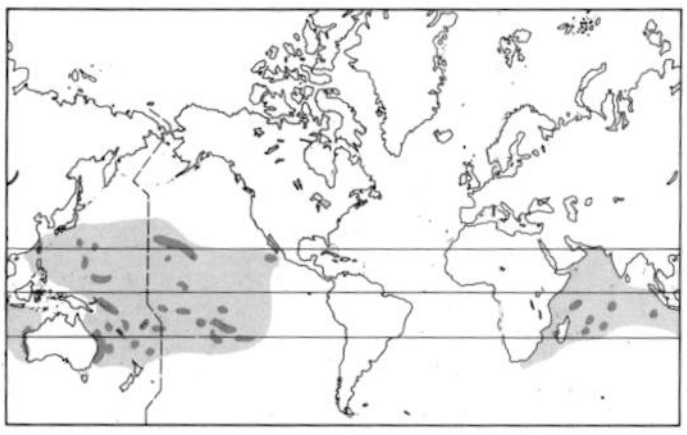

IDENTIFICATION: Large, slender-bodied dimorphic shearwater. Commoner dark morph differs from Flesh-footed Shearwater in darker bill and structure. Rarer pale morph differs from Pink-footed Shearwater in paler head and whiter underwing, with smaller head, more slender body and longer tail, which, although wedge-shaped during manoeuvres, normally appears long and pointed in level flight.
HABITS: Colonial breeder on oceanic islands. Often gregarious at sea, does not follow ships. Flight usually slow and unhurried, drifting over ocean.
DISTRIBUTION: Breeds throughout much of tropical and subtropical Pacific and Indian Oceans, ranging east to Mexico and west to South Africa; dates dependent on location.
SIMILAR SPECIES: Compare Flesh-footed and Pink-footed Shearwaters (p. 207, p. 210).

Buller's Shearwater *Puffinus bulleri* L46cm/18in W97cm/38in **P** p. 71 **K** p. 296

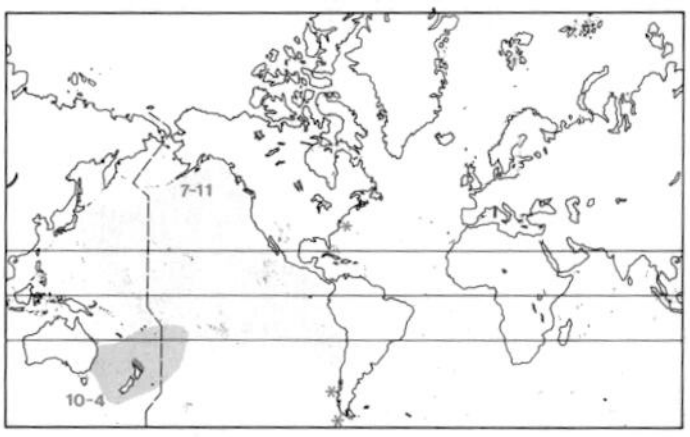

IDENTIFICATION: Large, slender-bodied shearwater with strikingly patterned upperwings, dark cap and white underparts. No other shearwater has these characters.
HABITS: Breeds colonially on oceanic islands; gregarious at sea, does not follow ships. Jizz and flight recalls that of Wedge-tailed Shearwater, with graceful, measured wingbeats followed by long effortless glides, banking and circling lazily over ocean.
DISTRIBUTION: Transequatorial Pacific migrant. Breeds Aug–Apr Poor Knights Is, New Zealand, with post-breeding dispersal to coasts of North and South America from Alaska south to Valparaiso, Chile, occasionally south to Cape Horn.
SIMILAR SPECIES: None, but see Juan Fernandez Petrel (p. 201).

Streaked Shearwater *Calonectris leucomelas*

L48cm/19in W122cm/48in **P** p. 71 **K** p. 296

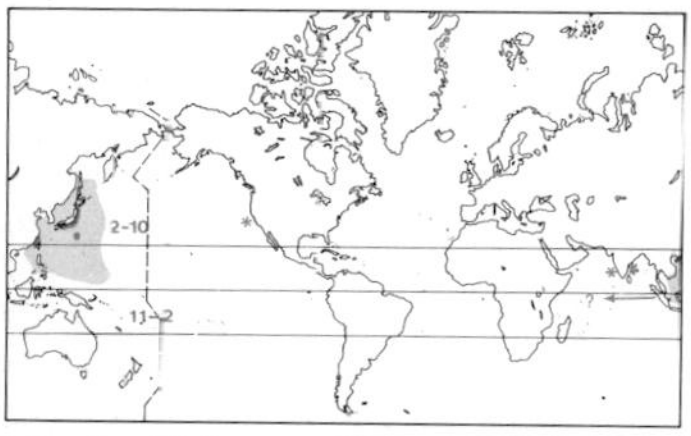

IDENTIFICATION: Large brown and white shearwater, easily identified by combination of whitish face, dark nape and broad, dark margins to white underwings. At close range, black streaks on white face diagnostic.

HABITS: Colonial breeder; gregarious at sea, often forms large flocks. Flight recalls Cory's Shearwater, languid but purposeful, with loose, rather angled wings.

DISTRIBUTION: Northwest Pacific. Breeds Feb–Oct on islands off Japan, China and Korea, with post-breeding dispersal to seas off New Guinea; has occurred off eastern Australia, with stragglers west to Sri Lanka and east to California.

SIMILAR SPECIES: None, but see Buller's and Pink-footed Shearwaters (p. 210).

Short-tailed Shearwater *Puffinus tenuirostris*

L42cm/17in W98cm/39in **P** p. 67 **K** p. 297

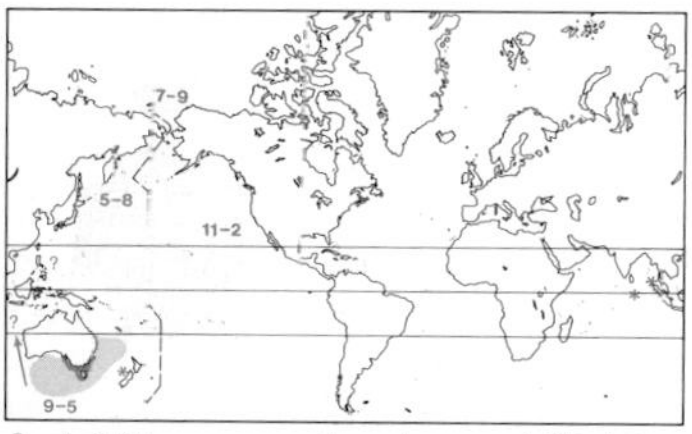

IDENTIFICATION: Medium-sized, uniform sooty-brown shearwater which lacks obvious plumage features. Differs from Sooty Shearwater in shorter bill, more steeply rising forehead and, usually, greyer, less silvery underwing-coverts. In winter quarters appears more uniformly coloured than Sooty, with darker cap and whitish chin. At long range, darker head may impart hooded appearance. Differs from Flesh-footed and Wedge-tailed Shearwaters in smaller size, short dark bill, grey underwing and flight.

HABITS: Colonial breeder on marine islands; occasionally follows ships, gregarious at sea. Flight fast and mechanical, bursts of short rapid wingbeats alternating with stiff-winged glides.

DISTRIBUTION: Transequatorial Pacific migrant. Breeds Sep–May southeast Australia and Tasmania, with figure-of-eight dispersal north to Bering Sea and California. May also occur off Thailand.

SIMILAR SPECIES: Compare Sooty, Wedge-tailed and Flesh-footed Shearwaters (p. 208, p. 210, p. 207).

Christmas Shearwater *Puffinus nativitatis*

L36cm/14in W76cm/30in **P** p. 74 **K** p. 297

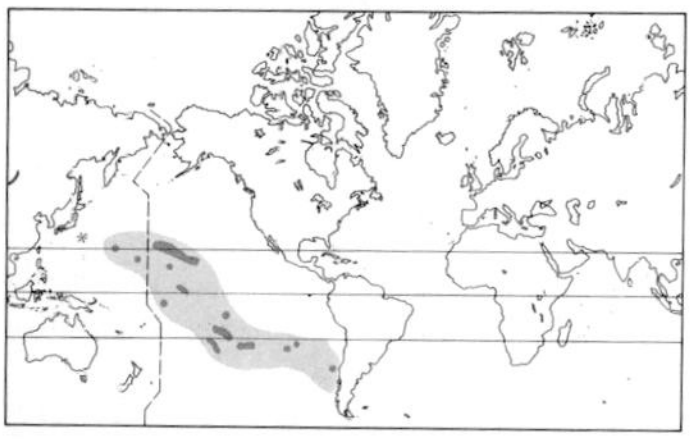

IDENTIFICATION: Small, uniformly sooty-brown shearwater. Differs from Sooty and Short-tailed Shearwaters in smaller size and darker underwings. Wedge-tailed and Flesh-footed Shearwaters are much larger, with pale feet.

HABITS: Colonial breeder; does not normally follow ships. Flight light and buoyant, bursts of fast, stiff wingbeats alternating with long glides close to surface.

DISTRIBUTION: Tropical Pacific. Breeding season protracted; breeds Hawaiian Is, Marcus, Christmas, Phoenix, Marquesas, Tuamotu, Austral, Pitcairn and Easter Is. Pelagic dispersal unknown, perhaps only to seas adjacent to breeding islands.

SIMILAR SPECIES: Compare Sooty and Short-tailed Shearwaters (p. 208, p. 211).

Audubon's Shearwater *Puffinus lherminieri*
L30cm/12in W69cm/27in **P** p. 69 **K** p. 298

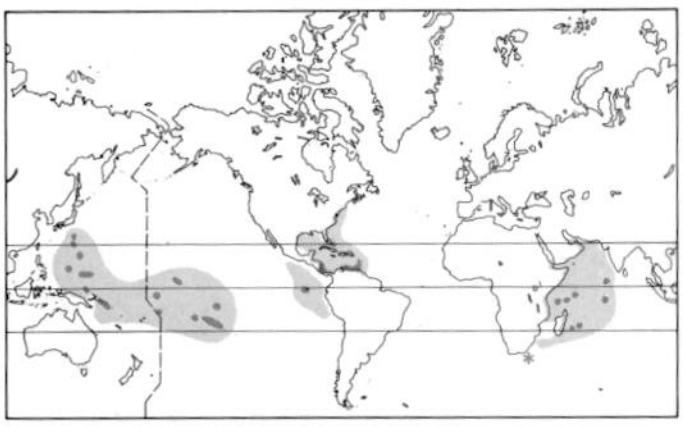

IDENTIFICATION: Small brown and white shearwater. Differs from Manx Shearwater in smaller size and from both Manx and Little in browner upperparts, dark undertail-coverts and distinctly broader underwing margins. At very close range, can be seen to have a longer bill than Little Shearwater. From Levantine Shearwater by smaller size, broader underwing margins and dark undertail-coverts. The race *persicus* differs from nominate in slightly larger size, longer bill, darker underwing and variable brown streaking to flanks and axillaries.
HABITS: Colonial breeder on marine islands. Gregarious at sea; does not usually follow ships. Appears shorter-winged and longer-tailed than Manx, progressing in a series of rapid flutters followed by a short glide low over waves.
DISTRIBUTION: Widespread in tropical oceans; time of breeding varies according to location. Pelagic range poorly documented, perhaps mostly sedentary except for limited feeding movements.
SIMILAR SPECIES: Compare Manx, Little and Levantine Shearwaters (p. 209).

Heinroth's Shearwater *Puffinus (lherminieri) heinrothi*
L27cm/11in W? **P** p. 72 **K** p. 298

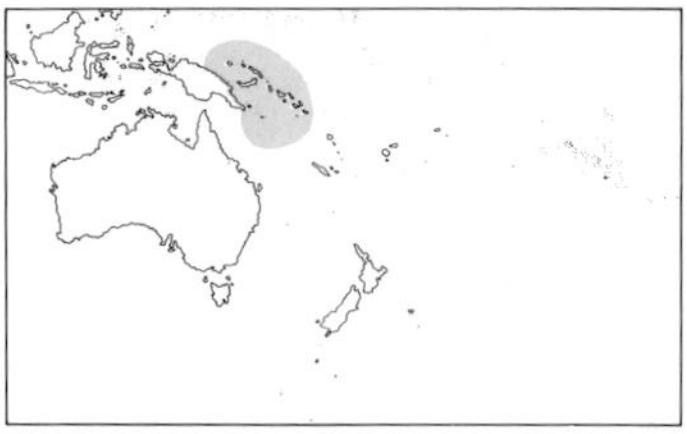

IDENTIFICATION: Small, variably plumaged shearwater which is treated as a melanistic form of Audubon's Shearwater by some authors. Darkest examples are wholly sooty-brown except for underwing-coverts, giving impression of miniature Sooty Shearwater. Paler examples have variable whitish belly patch. Differs from transient Sooty and Short-tailed Shearwaters in smaller size, whiter underwing, whitish belly patch (if present) and pink (not black) feet.
HABITS: Unknown; flight probably as for Audubon's Shearwater.
DISTRIBUTION: Known only from seas near Rabaul, New Britain. Breeding islands as yet undiscovered, but has been collected at night, on Bougainville, Solomon Is (Dr Mayr pers. comm.).
SIMILAR SPECIES: Compare Sooty and Short-tailed Shearwaters (p. 208, p. 211).

Hutton's Shearwater *Puffinus huttoni* L38cm/15in W90cm/35in **P** p. 73 **K** p. 298

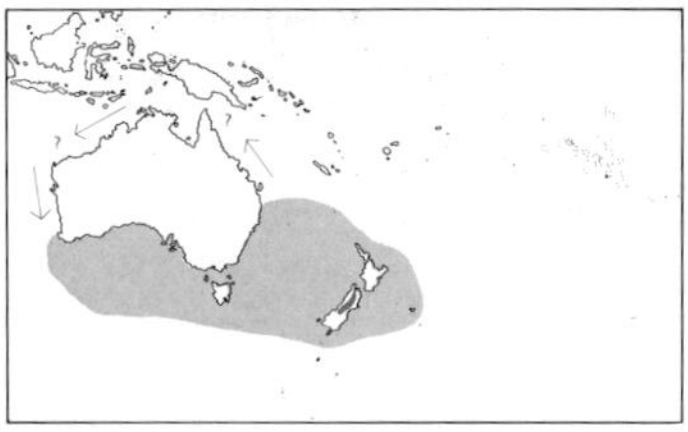

IDENTIFICATION: Medium-sized shearwater, brown above, white below except for dusky sides of neck and upper breast, which often causes head to look wholly dark at long distance. Differs from Fluttering Shearwater in consistently darker brown upperparts which merge into dull white underparts without obvious demarcation; duskier underwing-coverts and axillaries form a more solid dark triangle between carpal and body. Little Shearwater is smaller, with auk-like jizz and pure white underparts.
HABITS: Colonial breeder on high seaward-facing mountains; does not usually follow ships. Flight low and direct, often hugging waves, rising over crests with rapid wingbeats before scuttling into troughs. In strong winds flight higher and stronger, flapping less, gliding longer.
DISTRIBUTION: Australasian seas. Breeds Aug–Apr South Island, New Zealand, with post-breeding dispersal ranging from adjacent seas west to northwest Australia and north to New South Wales, Australia; may occur Torres Strait, suggesting circular route around Australia.
SIMILAR SPECIES: Compare Fluttering and Little Shearwaters (p. 213, p. 209).

Fluttering Shearwater *Puffinus gavia* L33cm/13in W76cm/30in P p. 72 K p. 298

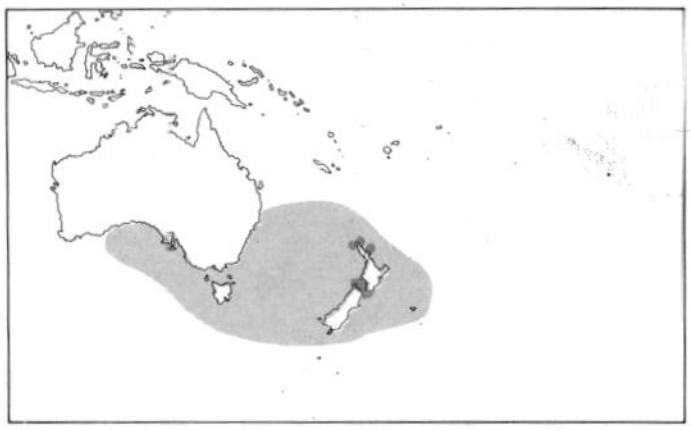

IDENTIFICATION: Small to medium-sized brown and white shearwater. Differs from Hutton's Shearwater in browner upperparts, which, when worn, become rusty in tone, and in whiter, cleaner underparts, which, at distance, appear to have definite demarcation on sides of neck and face below eye. Underwing-coverts whiter than in Hutton's, axillaries not so dark. From Little Shearwater by larger size, darker head, browner upperparts, broader dark margins on underwing.

HABITS: Colonial breeder on marine islands; does not normally follow ships. Flight as for Hutton's Shearwater.

DISTRIBUTION: Australasian seas. Breeds Aug–Mar offshore islands of New Zealand from Three Kings south to Cook Strait; post-breeding dispersal ranges from adjacent seas west to Tasmania and Queensland.

SIMILAR SPECIES: Compare Little and Hutton's Shearwaters (p. 209, p. 212).

Townsend's Shearwater *Puffinus auricularis*

L33cm/13in W76cm/30in P p. 73 K p. 298

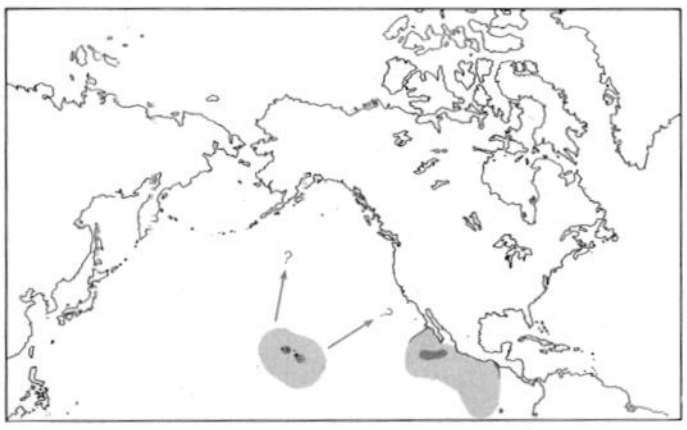

IDENTIFICATION: Small to medium-sized shearwater, blackish above, mostly white below except for blackish undertail-coverts and broad trailing edge to wing. Differs from Black-vented Shearwater in blacker upperparts, a conspicuous white flank patch extending upwards on to sides of rump, cleaner demarcation between black and white on head, and whiter axillaries. The race *newelli* (Jehl 1982) differs from nominate in slightly larger size, with longer tail and white or mixed black and white undertail-coverts. From Audubon's by larger size, blacker upperparts, white thigh patch, and underwing pattern.

HABITS: Colonial breeder on marine islands; occasionally follows ships.

DISTRIBUTION: Central and eastern Pacific; breeds Apr–Oct Kauai, Hawaii, and Revilla Gigedo, off western Mexico. Perhaps mostly sedentary, but recorded south to 8°N near Galapagos (Bourne & Dixon 1975).

SIMILAR SPECIES: Compare Black-vented and Audubon's Shearwaters (p. 213, p. 212).

Black-vented Shearwater *Puffinus opisthomelas*

L34cm/13in W82cm/32in P p. 74 K p. 298

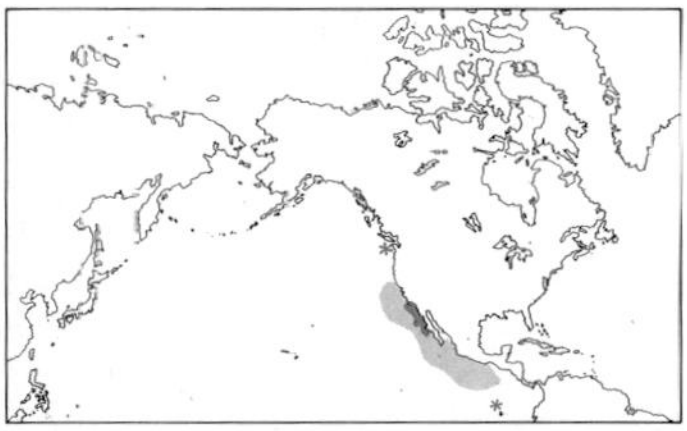

IDENTIFICATION: Medium-sized brown and white shearwater. Differs from Townsend's in slightly larger size, brown (not black) upperparts which fuse into white underparts without obvious demarcation, the neck often wholly dusky and extending across upper breast. Unlike Townsend's, there is no extension of white flanks onto sides of rump and axillaries are marked with brown. From Pink-footed Shearwater by small size, dark bill and different flight.

HABITS: Colonial breeder on marine islands; occasionally follows ships. Flight low and fast, recalling Little Shearwater but with less gliding, more fluttering.

DISTRIBUTION: Pacific coast of Mexico. Breeds Jan–Jul, islands of Baja California. Post-breeding dispersal north to Mendicino County, California, and south to Galapagos.

SIMILAR SPECIES: Compare Audubon's and Townsend's Shearwaters (p. 212, p 213).

British Storm-petrel *Hydrobates pelagicus* L15cm/6in W37cm/15in P p. 76 K p. 307

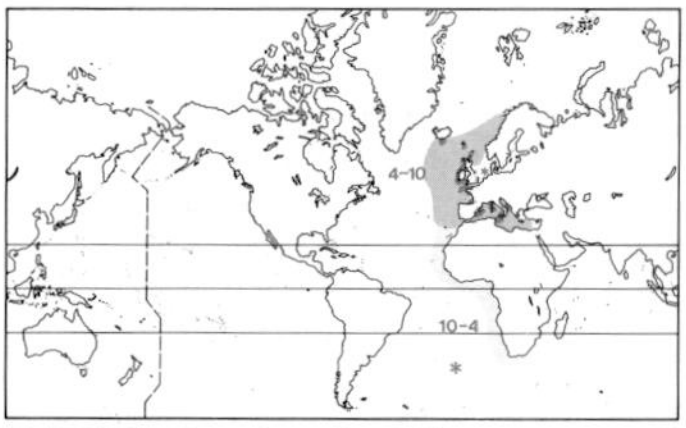

IDENTIFICATION: Smallest and darkest North Atlantic storm-petrel, with square white rump and diagnostic white stripe on underwing. Unlike congeners, upper-wing usually appears uniformly dark but, at very close range, paler edging to coverts may show as narrow pale line. Feet do not project beyond square tail. Differs from Wilson's, Leach's and Madeiran in smaller size, darker upperwings, shape and extent of rump patch and diagnostic white stripe across underwing-coverts.
HABITS: Breeds colonially; occasionally follows ships, usually gregarious at sea. Flight weak and fluttering, recalling that of a bat, with almost continuous wing action broken by short glides. Wing strokes distinctly faster, shallower than those of Leach's; foot-patters with wings raised.
DISTRIBUTION: Eastern North Atlantic and Mediterranean. Breeds Apr–Sep Iceland, Faeroes, Lofoten Is, Britain, France and islands in Mediterranean Sea, migrating south to South Atlantic.
SIMILAR SPECIES: Compare Wilson's, Leach's and Madeiran Storm-petrels (p. 215. p. 214).

Leach's Storm-petrel *Oceanodroma leucorhoa*
L20cm/8in W46cm/18in P p. 76 K p. 307

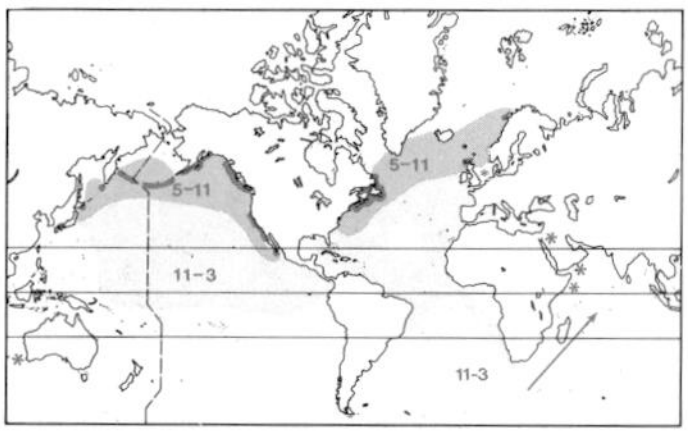

IDENTIFICATION: Medium-sized, white-rumped storm-petrel with long angular wings and forked tail. Plumage mostly dark brown, except for obvious pale bar across upperwing-coverts and smudgy white rump which, at very close range, usually shows diagnostic dark central division with much less side extension than in Wilson's, British or Madeiran Storm-petrels. (Some Pacific forms have darker rumps, see p. 307). Differs from Madeiran in longer, more angular wings, prominent wingbar, more erratic bounding flight; from Wilson's and British in wing shape, rump pattern, forked tail, and flight.
HABITS: Breeds colonially; does not normally follow ships. Flight buoyant and bounding with sudden changes of direction, weaving an irregular course between deep tern-like wingbeats and short shearing glides. Occasionally foot-patters.
DISTRIBUTION: North Pacific and Atlantic Oceans. Breeds May–Sep in Pacific from Japan northeast to Aleutian Is and Alaska and then south to Mexico. In Atlantic off eastern USA, Westmann, Faeroes, Lofoten and islands off Scotland.
SIMILAR SPECIES: Compare Madeiran, Wilson's and British Storm-petrels (p. 214, p. 215, p. 214).

Madeiran Storm-petrel *Oceanodroma castro*
L20cm/8in W43cm/17in P p. 77 K p. 307

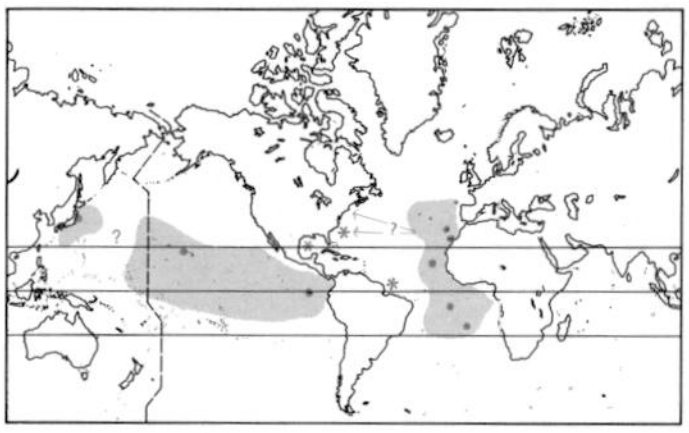

IDENTIFICATION: Medium-sized, white-rumped storm-petrel with angular wings and slightly forked tail. Plumage mostly blackish-brown, except for paler upper-wing bar and curving white rump patch which extends to lateral undertail-coverts. Wing shape intermediate between Leach's and Wilson's. Differs from Leach's in shorter wings, less noticeable upperwing bar, whiter more extensive rump patch, shallower tail fork, and less erratic flight. From Wilson's in larger size, wing shape, less noticeable wingbar, smaller white rump with less side extension, short legs, forked tail, and flight. From British in dark underwing, forked tail, and flight.
HABITS: Does not follow ships. Flight buoyant, often working steady zigzag progression between quick, deep wingbeats and low shearing glides. Patters with wings held horizontally; sits on water.
DISTRIBUTION: Breeds oceanic islands of tropical and subtropical Pacific and Atlantic Oceans.
SIMILAR SPECIES: Compare Leach's, Wilson's and British Storm-petrels (p. 214, p. 215, p. 214).

White-faced Storm-petrel *Pelagodroma marina*
L20cm/8in W42cm/17in **P** p. 77 **K** p. 308

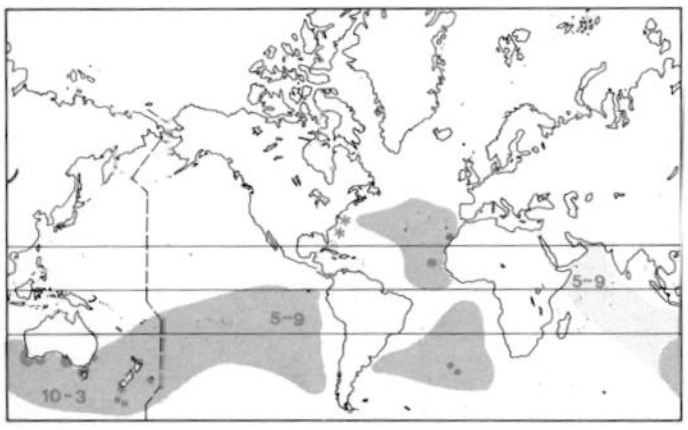

IDENTIFICATION: Large, grey-brown storm-petrel with patterned face, broad dark arcs on upperwing, grey rump and upperparts. At close range, white supercilium and dark eye patch diagnostic; feet project beyond forked tail in flight. Differs from White-throated Storm-petrel in smaller size, grey rump and lack of breastband; from Hornby's in paler, less patterned upperparts, grey rump and lack of breastband.
HABITS: Breeds colonially. Often gregarious at sea; does not normally follow ships. Non-feeding flight erratic, weaving and banking; feeding flight strong and direct, dancing along with short glides between splashdowns, body swinging wildly from side to side; occasionally 'walks' into strong headwinds, wings raised over back.
DISTRIBUTION: Widespread in all three oceans. Breeds Salvage, Cape Verde, Tristan da Cunha, Gough, Auckland, Chatham and Stewart Is, Australia and New Zealand.
SIMILAR SPECIES: Compare Hornby's and White-throated Storm-petrels (p. 219), also phalaropes (p. 241).

Wilson's Storm-petrel *Oceanites oceanicus* L17cm/7in W40cm/16in **P** p. 76 **K** p. 307

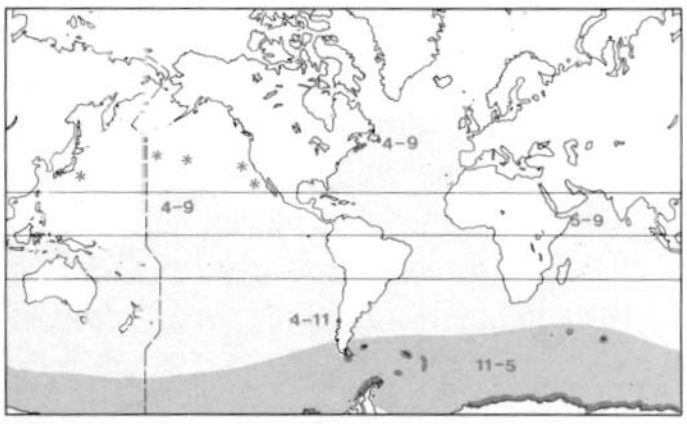

IDENTIFICATION: A small, dark brown storm-petrel with pale upperwing bar, and bold 'U' shaped band across rump which extends broadly onto lateral undertail-coverts and which is seemingly always in view whatever the angle of observation. Differs from Leach's and Madeiran in smaller size, shape and extent of white rump, shorter rounded wings which lack bend at carpal, square tail and projecting feet (webs of which yellow, but rarely seen). From British by larger size, obvious pale crescent on upperwing, darker underwing, shape and extent of white rump, projecting feet.
HABITS: Colonial breeder; usually gregarious at sea, habitually follows ships. While feeding 'walks on water' more than any other storm-petrel, skipping and hopping over surface, wings held vertically, legs trailing. Direct flight purposeful, lacking Leach's erratic bounding quality.
DISTRIBUTION: Breeds Nov–May on many sub-Antarctic islands and Antarctic coastline, with transequatorial migration to higher latitudes of Atlantic and Indian Oceans, less commonly Pacific, May–Oct.
SIMILAR SPECIES: Compare British, Leach's, Madeiran and Elliot's Storm-petrels (p. 214, p. 215).

Elliot's Storm-petrel *Oceanites gracilis* L15cm/6in W? **P** p. 80 **K** p. 309

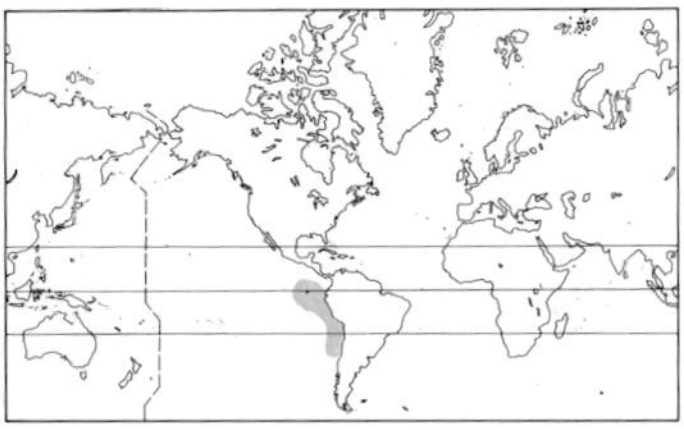

IDENTIFICATION: Small, mostly dark storm-petrel, similar to Wilson's but smaller, with pale suffusion on underwing and white patch of variable size on belly (sometimes difficult to see). Feet project slightly more beyond tail than in Wilson's (Sutherland pers. comm.).
HABITS: Only one nest has ever been found of this little-studied species. Gregarious at sea, follows ships. Flight as Wilson's but of a lighter quality, with rapid, fairly shallow wingbeats while hopping and splashing across surface.
DISTRIBUTION: Eastern Pacific. Breeding grounds unknown, but almost certainly breeds Galapagos and coasts/islands of Humboldt Current. Pelagic range extends from Galapagos and Ecuador south to Valparaiso, Chile.
SIMILAR SPECIES: Compare Wilson's Storm-petrel (above).

Least Storm-petrel *Oceanodroma microsoma*
L14cm/6in W32cm/13in **P** p. 81 **K** p. 309

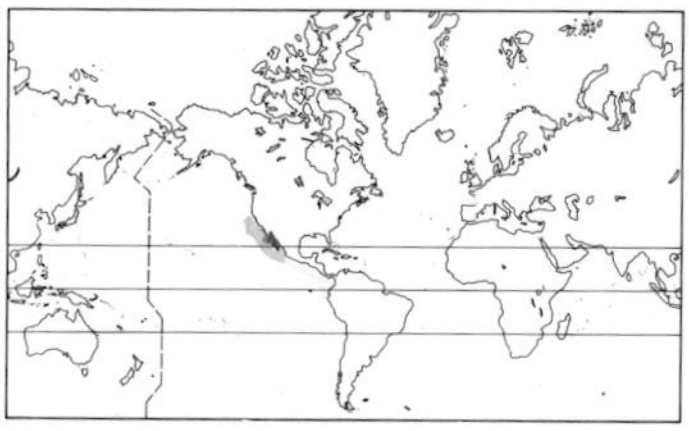

IDENTIFICATION: Smallest Pacific storm-petrel. Plumage wholly dark except for pale upperwing bar; unlike its dark-rumped congeners, has a diagnostic, short, rounded or wedge-shaped tail. Differs from Black and dark-rumped Leach's in smaller size and wedge-shaped (not forked) tail. From Ashy in darker underwing and wedge-shaped tail.
HABITS: Breeds on marine islands; gregarious at sea. Flight usually swift and direct with rather deep wingbeats similar to Black Storm-petrel but more rapid (Stallcup 1976). When feeding, wings held over back; does not usually foot-patter.
DISTRIBUTION: American Pacific coast. Egg-dates Jul, breeding on islands off western Baja California and on northern islands in Gulf of California. Disperses south to Colombia and Ecuador.
SIMILAR SPECIES: Compare Black, Ashy and dark-rumped forms of Leach's Storm-petrels (p. 217, p. 214).

Wedge-rumped Storm-petrel *Oceanodroma tethys* L19cm/7in W? **P** p. 80 **K** p. 307

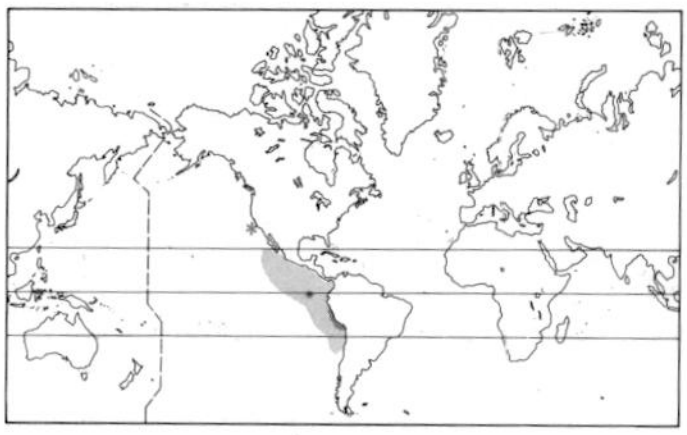

IDENTIFICATION: Combination of small size and diagnostic rump pattern enables separation from all other Pacific storm-petrels. Plumage mostly blackish, except for pale upperwing bar and huge, triangular-shaped white rump which begins on lower back, in line with trailing edge of wings, and extends almost to notch of tail. White rump thus largest and most conspicuous of all storm-petrels.
HABITS: Colonial breeder visiting colonies in daylight; occasionally follows ships, gregarious at sea. Flight fast, direct and forceful, often quite high above waves, with deep wingbeats with much twisting and banking. When feeding, has a skipping bounding flight dipping down to water, with legs occasionally trailing on surface or fully immersed.
DISTRIBUTION: Eastern Pacific. Breeds May–Aug Galapagos and Peruvian guano islands, dispersing north to coasts of Colombia and Mexico, occasionally to California.
SIMILAR SPECIES: None, but compare Elliot's and Wilson's Storm-petrels (p. 215).

Fork-tailed Storm-petrel *Oceanodroma furcata*
L22cm/9in W46cm/18in **P** p. 80 **K** p. 308

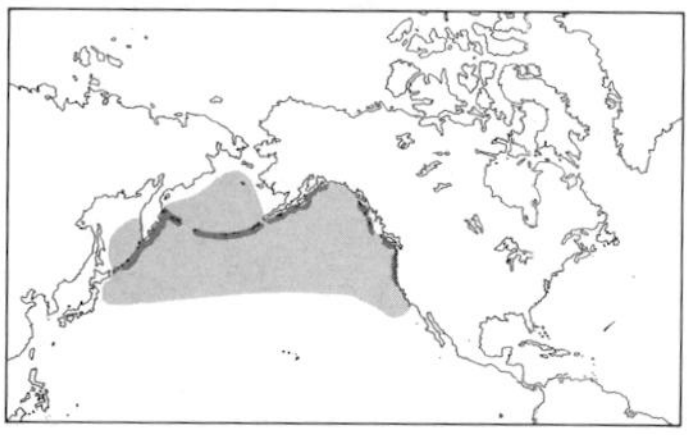

IDENTIFICATION: Distinctive medium-sized, grey-backed storm-petrel with blackish underwing-coverts. Combination of pale grey plumage and dark mask through eye diagnostic within range. Could be confused, only at a distance, with swimming phalaropes in winter plumage.
HABITS: Breeds colonially on marine islands; gregarious at sea, occasionally follows ships. Wave-hugging flight recalls Leach's, but not so buoyant or erratic, with shallower wingbeats and rather stiff-winged glides.
DISTRIBUTION: Northern Pacific and Bering Sea from 55°N south to about 35°N. Breeds May–Aug from Kurile and Commander Is south through Aleutians to Oregon and northern California; perhaps also Kamchatka Peninsula.
SIMILAR SPECIES: None, but see winter phalaropes (p. 241).

Black Storm-petrel *Oceanodroma melania*
L23cm/9in W48cm/19in **P** p. 81 **K** p. 306

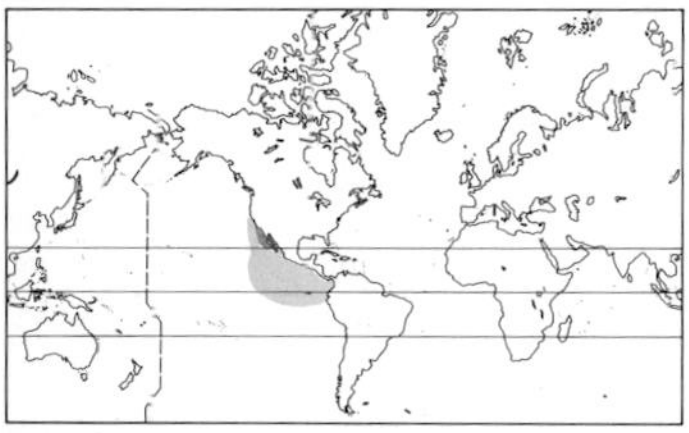

IDENTIFICATION: Large, long-winged storm-petrel with deeply forked tail. Plumage mostly sooty-brown, except for obvious pale bar across upperwing-coverts. Differs from Markham's in blacker plumage and less obvious pale bar across upperwing-coverts which does not extend to leading edge of wing. From Ashy in larger size and dark underwing; from Least in larger size and forked not wedge-shaped tail.
HABITS: Colonial breeder on marine islands; occasionally follows ships, gregarious at sea. Flight buoyant and deliberate, with steady wingbeats raised high and then deep to 60° above and below the horizontal; rhythm sometimes interrupted by shallower beats and occasional glides.
DISTRIBUTION: Northeast Pacific. Breeds Apr–Oct on islands off southern California, Baja California and in Gulf of California, dispersing north to Point Reyes and then south to seas off Ecuador and Peru.
SIMILAR SPECIES: Compare Markham's and Ashy Storm-petrels (below).

Ashy Storm-petrel *Oceanodroma homochroa* L20cm/8in W? **P** p. 81 **K** p. 308

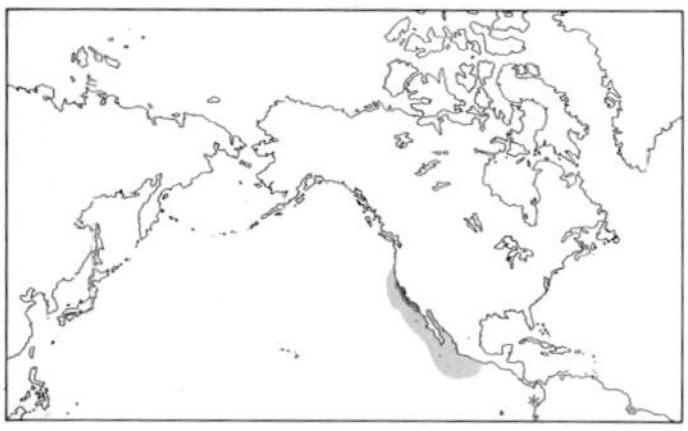

IDENTIFICATION: Medium-sized storm-petrel with long wings and forked tail. Plumage mostly sooty-brown, with pale bar on upperwing-coverts and diagnostic pale suffusion on underwing-coverts. Differs from Black Storm-petrel in smaller size, proportionately shorter, more rounded wings and pale suffusion on underwing. From Least in larger size, paler underwings and forked tail.
HABITS: Breeds colonially on marine islands; gregarious at sea. Flight more fluttering than that of Black Storm-petrel, with wingbeat rhythm between that of Black and Least Storm-petrels but shallower (except when accelerating to gain height).
DISTRIBUTION: Northeast Pacific. Breeds Jan–Aug offshore islands of California and Mexico. Pelagic dispersal not well known, probably only to adjacent waters with limited southwards dispersal.
SIMILAR SPECIES: Compare Black, Least and dark-rumped forms of Leach's Storm-petrels (p. 217, p. 216, p. 214).

Markham's Storm-petrel *Oceanodroma markhami* L23cm/9in W? **P** p. 79 **K** p. 306

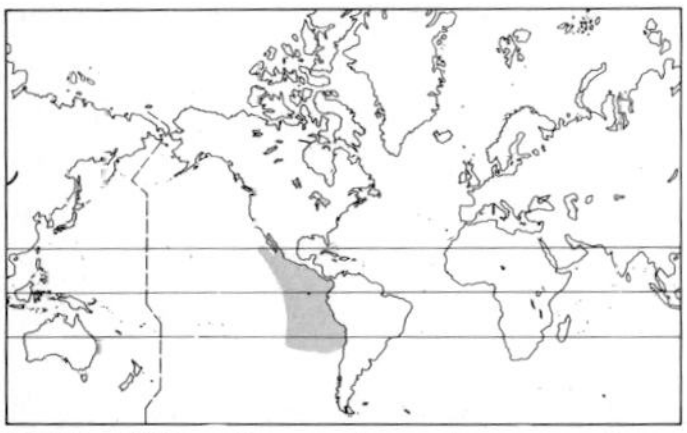

IDENTIFICATION: Large, long-winged storm-petrel with deeply forked tail. Plumage mostly dark brown, except for obvious pale bar across upperwing-coverts. Differs from Black Storm-petrel in browner plumage, longer pale bar on upperwing which reaches almost to carpal, deeper-forked tail.
HABITS: Breeding strategy unknown; does not normally follow ships.
DISTRIBUTION: Seas off Peru, ranging north to about 15°N off Mexico and south to northern Chile, but movements obscured by confusion with Black Storm-petrel, which moves south from California during autumn. Breeding area unknown, thought to be in Peruvian deserts.
SIMILAR SPECIES: Compare Black Storm-petrel (above)

Black-bellied Storm-petrel *Fregetta tropica*

L20cm/8in W46cm/18in **P** p. 78 **K** p. 308

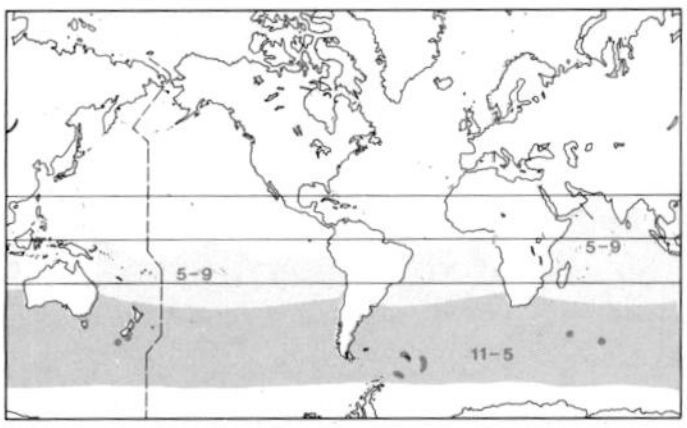

IDENTIFICATION: Large, blackish storm-petrel with pale upperwing bar, white rump and belly. At close range, shows diagnostic black line down centre of white belly, and broad dark margins to white underwing. The feet project slightly beyond tail in flight. Differs from White-bellied Storm-petrel in darker upperparts, more noticeable wingbar, black stripe through centre of belly and dark undertail-coverts. From Wilson's Storm-petrel in larger size, white belly and underwing.
HABITS: Loosely colonial. Often accompanies ships, but alongside or over bow wave rather than stern. Has distinctive, wave-hugging flight with legs dangling and body swinging from side to side, bouncing breast first into water and then springing clear; occasionally 'walks' on water.
DISTRIBUTION: Circumpolar in Southern Oceans, with post-breeding dispersal towards Equator. Breeds Dec–Apr South Georgia, South Orkney, South Shetland, Crozet, Kerguelen, Auckland, Bounty and Antipodes Is; perhaps Bouvet and Prince Edward.
SIMILAR SPECIES: Compare White-bellied and Wilson's Storm-petrels (p. 218. p. 215).

White-bellied Storm-petrel *Fregetta grallaria*

L20cm/8in W46cm/18in **P** p. 77 **K** p. 308

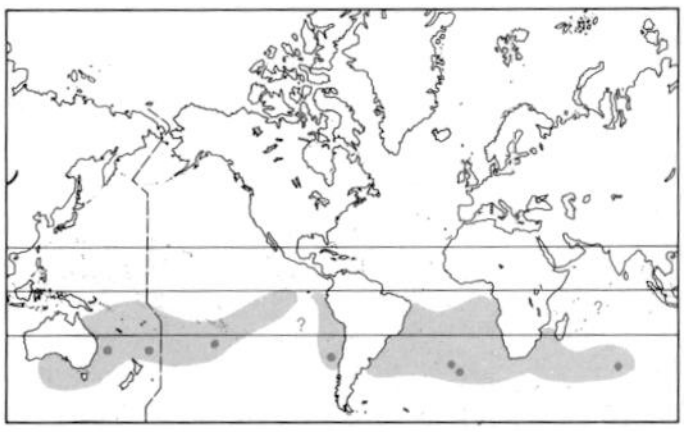

IDENTIFICATION: Large, blackish-brown storm-petrel with white rump and belly. At close range, upperparts have paler feather edges giving scaled appearance. It differs from Black-bellied Storm-petrel in paler brown upperparts, less noticeable upperwing bar, and an unmarked white belly. From Wilson's Storm-petrel in larger size, white belly and underwing.
HABITS: As for Black-bellied Storm-petrel (above).
DISTRIBUTION: Southern Oceans from about 35°S north to tropics. Breeds Tristan da Cunha, Gough, St Paul, Lord Howe, Kermadec, Rapa, Austral and Juan Fernandez Is; breeding dates vary depending on location.
SIMILAR SPECIES: Compare Black-bellied and Wilson's Storm-petrels (p. 218, p. 215).

Grey-backed Storm-petrel *Garrodia nereis*

L17cm/7in W39cm/15in **P** p. 78 **K** p. 309

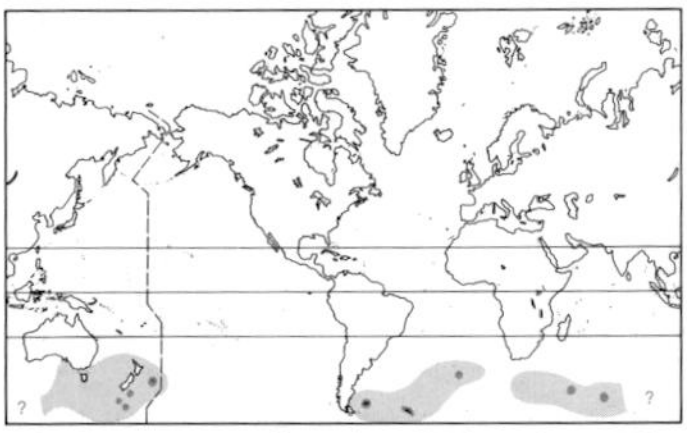

IDENTIFICATION: Small storm-petrel, readily identified by combination of blackish-grey upperparts, pale grey rump and white underparts. At close range, white underwing shows broad dark margins and feet project slightly beyond square tail. Differs from Black- and White-bellied Storm-petrels in smaller size, greyer upperparts with grey (not white) rump. White-faced Storm-petrel is larger and browner, with patterned face.
HABITS: Loosely colonial; occasionally follows ships. Flight can recall either Wilson's or Black-bellied Storm-petrels, particularly when hopping across surface, splashing down and springing clear.
DISTRIBUTION: Southern Oceans north to about 35°S. Breeds Oct–May Falklands, South Georgia, Gough, Crozet, Kerguelen, Chatham, Auckland and Antipodes; perhaps Macquarie and Prince Edward.
SIMILAR SPECIES: None, but compare White-bellied, Black-bellied and White-faced Storm-petrels (p. 218, p. 215).

White-throated Storm-petrel *Nesofregetta fuliginosa*
L25cm/10in W? **P** p. 78 **K** p. 308

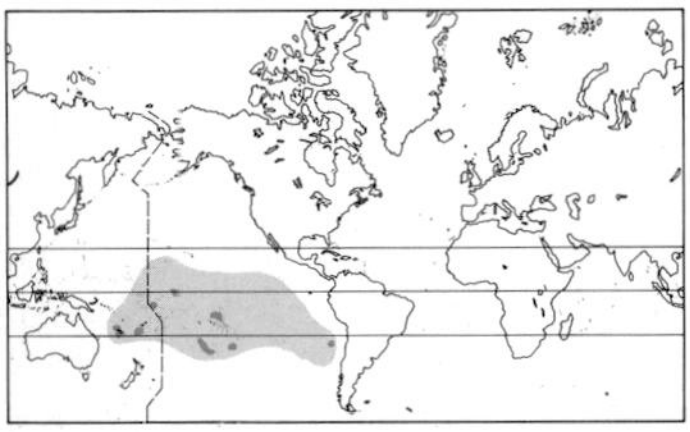

IDENTIFICATION: Largest storm-petrel; polymorphic, ranging from typical pale morph to those with wholly dark underparts. All three morphs have brown upperparts with short, pale bar across wing-coverts and narrow white band across rump. Pale forms are most typical, with white throat divided from white underparts by dark breastband; intermediates similar, but with varying amounts of dark streaking on underparts giving continuous gradation between light and dark forms. Darkest examples have wholly dark underparts.
HABITS: Breeds oceanic islands. In flight uses long legs to spring clear of water, sailing on broad, rounded wings for up to 30 seconds before splashing down and kicking off again. Feet project beyond long, forked tail during flight.
DISTRIBUTION: Tropical Pacific Ocean. Breeds New Hebrides, Fiji, Phoenix, Line, Austral, Marquesas, Gambier and Sala y Gomez; perhaps Samoa.
SIMILAR SPECIES: Compare White-faced Storm-petrel (p. 215).

Hornby's Storm-petrel *Oceanodroma hornbyi* L22cm/9in W? **P** p. 75 **K** p. 309

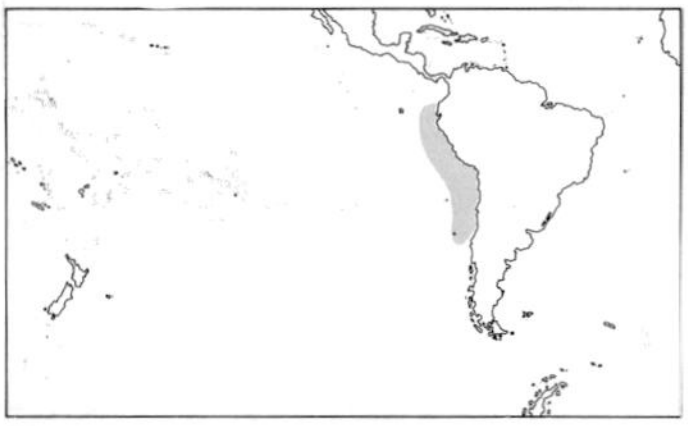

IDENTIFICATION: A large, distinctive, grey-backed storm-petrel; virtually unmistakable. No other storm-petrel has a combination of dark cap, broad upperwing bars, and dark grey breastband across white underparts. At close range, rump grey, tail deeply forked.
HABITS: Breeding strategy unknown; often gregarious at sea. Flight erratic and unpredictable; slow, rather deep wingbeats followed by sailing glides, skipping and bouncing breast first across waves.
DISTRIBUTION: Southeast Pacific from about 35°S off Chile, north to Equator. Breeding grounds unknown, thought to be in coastal deserts of Peru and northern Chile.
SIMILAR SPECIES: None, but beware winter phalarope spp. (p. 241).

Matsudaira's Storm-petrel *Oceanodroma matsudairae*
L24cm/9in W56cm/22in **P** p. 75 **K** p. 309

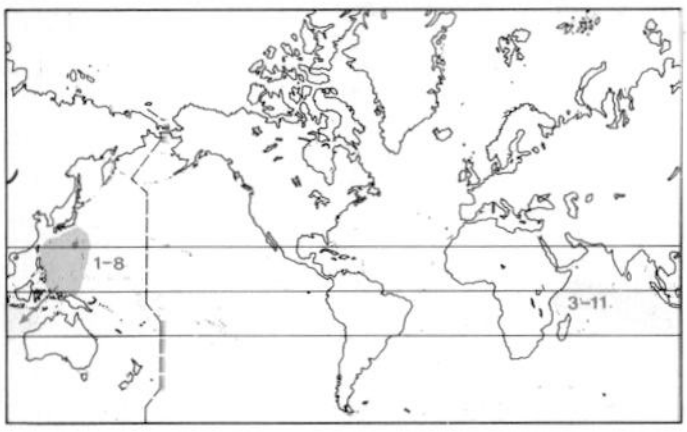

IDENTIFICATION: Large, long-winged storm-petrel with deeply forked tail. Plumage mostly sooty-brown, with pale bar across upperwing-coverts and diagnostic white bases to outermost 6 primaries forming a noticeable pale forewing patch. Differs from Swinhoe's in broader-based wings and white forewing patch. From Tristram's in smaller size, less pronounced pale bar on upperwing, and white forewing patch.
HABITS: Colonial breeder on oceanic islands; follows ships. Flight slower than that of Swinhoe's; flaps then glides for short distance, but at no great speed; rather lethargic. Occasionally, however, sprints off twisting over waves. When feeding, raises wings over back in shallow 'V'.
DISTRIBUTION: Subtropical western Pacific, migrating westwards to Indian Ocean to reach coasts of Kenya and Somalia. Breeds Jan–Jun Volcano Is, south of Japan.
SIMILAR SPECIES: Compare Tristram's and Swinhoe's Storm-petrels (p. 220).

Tristram's Storm-petrel *Oceanodroma tristrami*
L24cm/9in W56cm/22in **P** p. 79 **K** p. 306

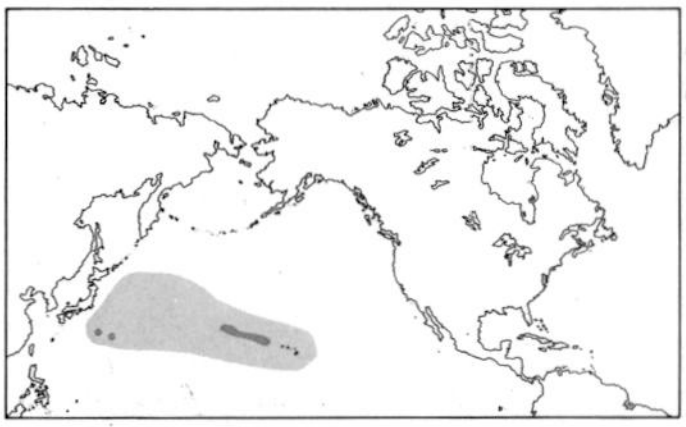

IDENTIFICATION: Large, long-winged storm-petrel with deeply forked tail. Plumage mostly sooty-brown with obvious pale bar across upperwing-coverts; when fresh, plumage has distinct grey or bluish cast, particularly mantle and back, which contrast with darker head giving hooded effect. Some occasionally show white on sides of rump or a pale greyish bar or paleness on rump. Differs from Swinhoe's Storm-petrel in distinctly larger size, more obvious upperwing bar, greyer plumage and more deeply forked tail. From Black and Markham's in greyer plumage, more obvious wingbar.
HABITS: Breeds on marine islands. Flight fairly strong, steep-banked arcs and glides interspersed with fluttering wingbeats (King 1967).
DISTRIBUTION: Western North Pacific; thought to disperse only to seas adjacent to natal islands. Breeding dates unknown; breeds Volcano, southern Izu and Leeward Hawaiian Is.
SIMILAR SPECIES: Compare Swinhoe's, Black, Markham's and dark-rumped Leach's Storm-petrels (p. 220, p. 217, p. 214).

Swinhoe's Storm-petrel *Oceanodroma monorhis*
L20cm/8in W45cm/18in **P** p. 79 **K** p. 306

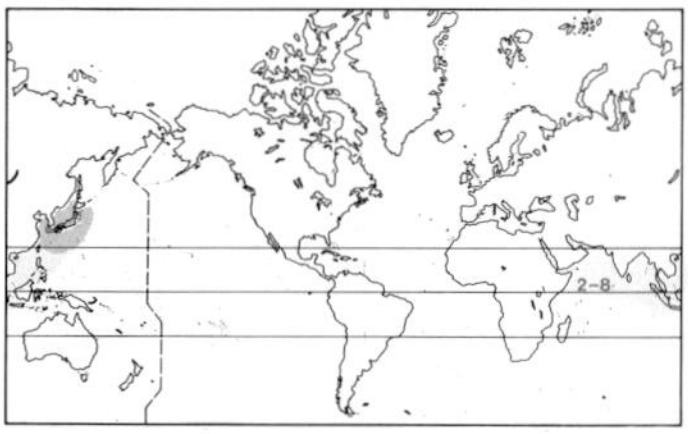

IDENTIFICATION: Medium-sized storm-petrel with long angular wings and forked tail. Plumage mostly blackish-brown, with paler bar across upperwing-coverts. Differs from Tristram's Storm-petrel in smaller size, less noticeable upperwing bar, browner plumage and shallower notch to tail. Matsudaira's is larger, with diagnostic white forewing patch.
HABITS: Breeds marine islands; does not normally follow ships. Flight recalls that of Leach's Storm-petrel, perhaps faster, more swooping.
DISTRIBUTION: Northwest Pacific, migrating west through South China Sea to northern Indian Ocean and Red Sea. Breeds islands of Japan, Korea and China; egg-dates May, fledging dates unrecorded.
SIMILAR SPECIES: Compare Tristram's and Matsudaira's Storm-petrels (p. 220, p. 219).

Peruvian Diving-petrel *Pelecanoides garnoti* L22cm/9in W? **P** p. 82 **K** p. 292

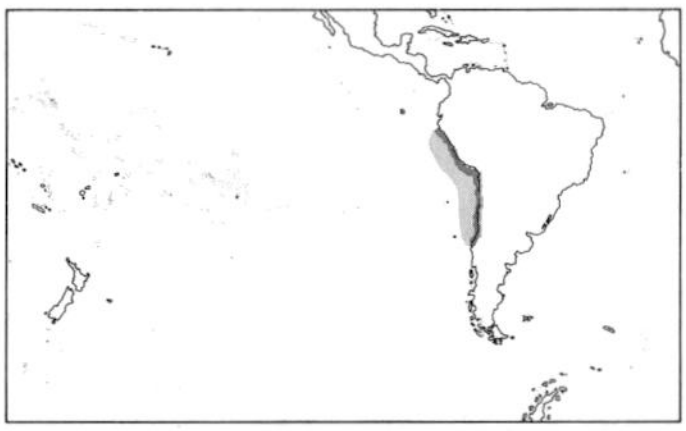

IDENTIFICATION: Range normally diagnostic, although in far south overlaps with Magellan Diving-petrel off central Chile. It differs from that species in lack of white half collar on side of neck and darker foreneck and sides of breast. (For identification in the hand see p. 292.)
HABITS: As for Georgian Diving-petrel p. 221.
DISTRIBUTION: The most northerly of all diving-petrels. Breeds throughout the year on islands off Peru and northern Chile from about 6°S to 37°S, dispersing to 42°S during Humboldt Current fluctuations.
SIMILAR SPECIES: Compare Magellan Diving-petrel (p. 221).

Common Diving-petrel *Pelecanoides urinatrix*
L23cm/9in W35cm/14in **P** p. 82 **K** p. 292

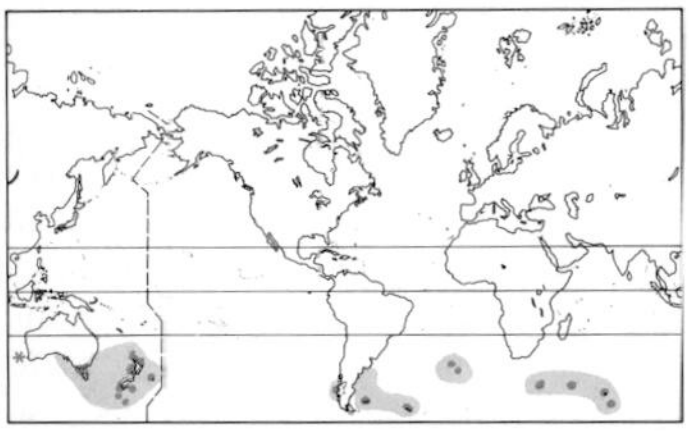

IDENTIFICATION: At sea, all four species of diving-petrel appear very small, with black and white plumage, short rounded wings and chunky auk-like jizz. Identification at sea is usually impossible, although Common Diving-petrel differs from Georgian (usually) in more pronounced mottling on throat and foreneck, greyer underwing-coverts, darker inner webs to primaries, and less obvious pale tips to scapulars. In the hand, can be identified by bill shape and measurements (see p. 292) and lack of a black line down the back of the leg, although it does usually show a small black spot on the back of the knee joint (Payne & Prince 1978).
HABITS: Breeds colonially. Often forms small flocks at sea; does not usually follow ships. Flight low and swift, wings in constant motion, buzzing and whirring over or through wave crests; typically enters or leaves water in full flight, exploding or disappearing in a flurry of wings.
DISTRIBUTION: Seas adjacent to sub-Antarctic breeding islands, occasionally met with in mid ocean. Most widespread of the diving-petrels. Breeds in summer, dates dependent on location, at Falklands, Tristan da Cunha, Gough, South Georgia, Marion, Prince Edward, Crozet, Heard, Kerguelen, Auckland, Antipodes, Chatham, Snares, islands of Bass Strait, coasts of Victoria, Tasmania and New Zealand; perhaps also Macquarie and Campbell Is, and Chile.
SIMILAR SPECIES: Compare other diving-petrels (p. 220, p. 221).

Georgian Diving-petrel *Pelecanoides georgicus*
L20cm/8in W32cm/13in **P** p. 82 **K** p. 292

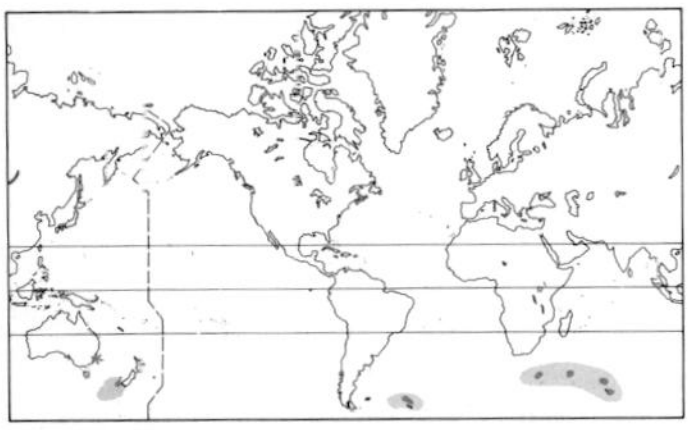

IDENTIFICATION: Virtually impossible to separate at sea from Common Diving-petrel, although on average it shows more obvious pale tips to scapulars, white (not grey) underwing-coverts, and paler inner webs to primaries; breastband averages paler. In the hand, differs from Common Diving-petrel in that the blue legs have a black line running along the back down to the blackish webs of feet. See p. 292 for differences in bill measurements.
HABITS: Breeds colonially, but, unlike Common Diving-petrel, which prefers to burrow beneath tussock grass on steep coastal slopes, Georgian Diving-petrel prefers stony soil with little or no vegetation (Payne & Prince 1978). Flight as for Common Diving-petrel.
DISTRIBUTION: Seas adjacent to sub-Antarctic breeding islands. Breeds Nov–Mar at South Georgia, Marion, Prince Edward, Crozet, Kerguelen, Heard and Codfish (near Stewart Is); perhaps Auckland and Macquarie Is.
SIMILAR SPECIES: Compare with other diving-petrels (p. 220, p. 221).

Magellan Diving-petrel *Pelecanoides magellani* L19cm/7in W? **P** p. 83 **K** p. 292

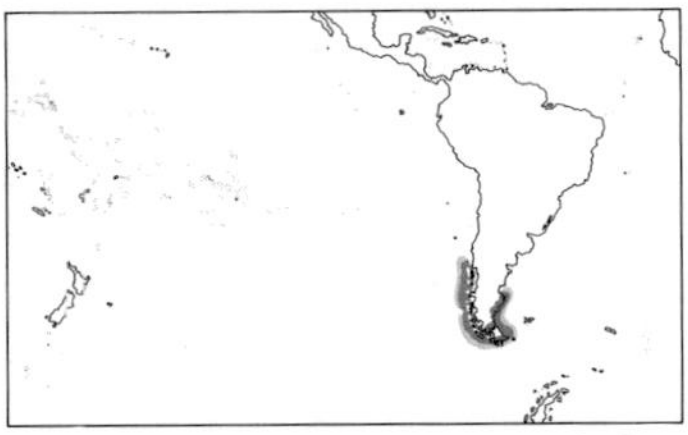

IDENTIFICATION: The only diving-petrel with distinctive plumage. It can be separated, at close range, from all other diving-petrels by its white foreneck and diagnostic, crescent-shaped half collar on sides of neck.
HABITS: As for Common Diving-petrel.
DISTRIBUTION: Coasts and fiords of southern Chile, Patagonia and Tierra del Fuego, from Staten Is and Cape Horn north to Chiloe Is; egg-dates Dec. Movements little known: occurs in Fuegian waters throughout year, with limited northwards dispersal during austral winter.
SIMILAR SPECIES: Compare Peruvian and Common Diving-petrels (p. 220, p. 221).

Red-billed Tropicbird *Phaethon aethereus* L98cm/39in W105cm/41in **P** p. 83

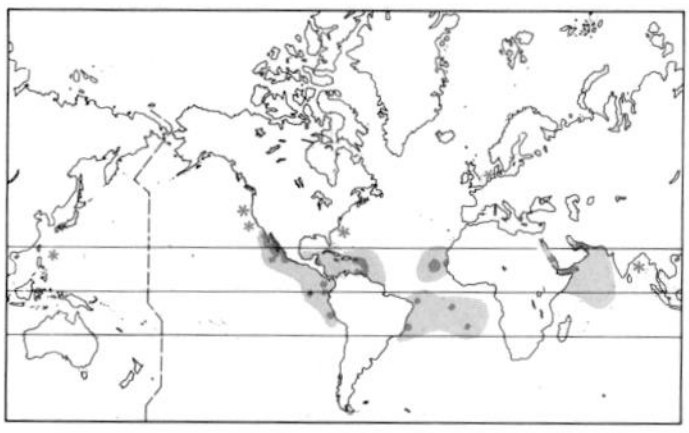

IDENTIFICATION: **Adult:** Combination of red bill, barred upperparts and long white tail streamers diagnostic. **Juvenile/Immature:** Differs from juvenile White- and Red-tailed Tropicbirds in finer, denser barring of upperparts and diagnostic broad eye-stripe extending across hindneck as a continuous nuchal collar. Bill yellow or orange.

HABITS: Loosely colonial. Solitary at sea; occasionally follows ships. In flight appears equal in size to Red-tailed Tropicbird but lighter in build, thus distinctly larger and broader-winged than White-tailed Tropicbird, with slower more purposeful wingbeats. Flies high over ocean with graceful pigeon-like flight. Feeds by first hovering and then plunging on half-closed wings in manner of a gannet (see also p. 17).

DISTRIBUTION: Tropical and subtropical zones of eastern Pacific, Atlantic and northwest Indian Oceans; breeding dates dependent upon location. Pelagic outside breeding season.

SIMILAR SPECIES: Compare White- and Red-tailed Tropicbirds (below).

White-tailed Tropicbird *Phaethon lepturus* L78cm/31in W92cm/36in **P** p. 84

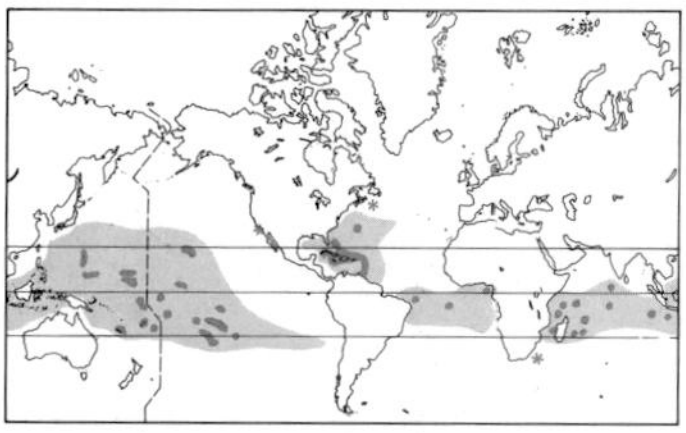

IDENTIFICATION: **Adult:** Combination of yellowish or orange bill, two black patches on each upperwing and long white tail streamers diagnostic. Christmas Island race in Indian Ocean has apricot wash to plumage. **Juvenile/Immature:** Differs from corresponding Red-tailed in blackish outermost primaries forming distinct black patch on outer wing; barring on upperparts slightly coarser, less dense, with smaller black tip to mostly yellow bill. From corresponding Red-billed in coarser barring and lack of black nuchal collar.

HABITS: As for Red-billed Tropicbird, but perhaps attracted more to ships. See also p. 17.

DISTRIBUTION: Tropical and subtropical Pacific, Atlantic and Indian Oceans; breeding dates dependent upon location. Mostly pelagic outside breeding season.

SIMILAR SPECIES: Compare Red-tailed and Red-billed Tropicbirds (this page).

Red-tailed Tropicbird *Phaethon rubricauda* L78cm/31in W107cm/42in **P** p. 83

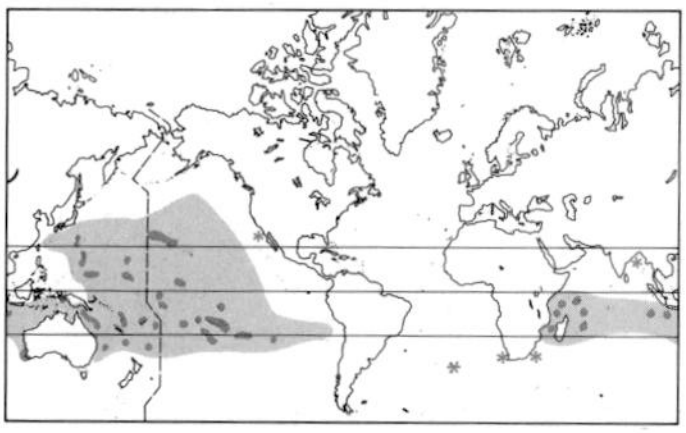

IDENTIFICATION: **Adult:** Whitest adult tropicbird, often with rosy tint on body or wings; combination of red bill and red tail streamers diagnostic. **Juvenile/Immature:** Differs from corresponding Red-billed in blackish bill with yellow base, much less black on outer primaries, coarser barring on upperparts, and lack of black nuchal collar. From White-tailed in blackish bill with yellow base, finer, denser barring on upperparts, less black on outer primaries.

HABITS: As for Red-billed Tropicbird. In flight appears broader-winged and shorter-tailed than other tropicbirds, with heavier body and less graceful, more laboured flight (see also p. 17).

DISTRIBUTION: Tropical and subtropical Pacific and Indian Oceans; breeding dates depend on location. Mostly pelagic outside breeding season.

SIMILAR SPECIES: Compare Red-billed and White-tailed Tropicbirds (above).

Brown Pelican *Pelecanus occidentalis* L114cm/45in W203cm/80in **P** p. 84

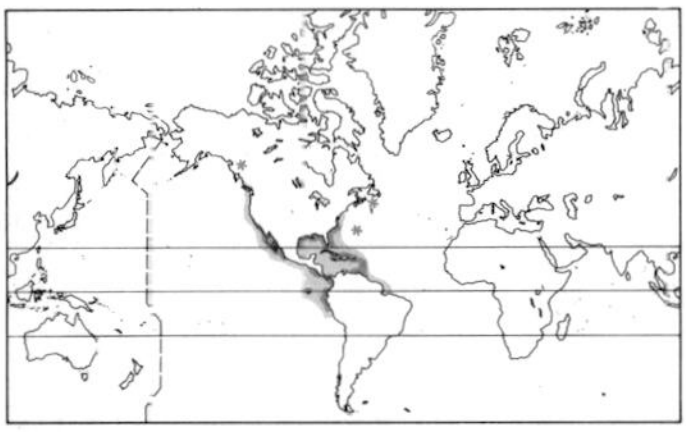

IDENTIFICATION: **Adult Summer:** Unmistakable throughout much of range; plumage mostly grey, with blackish belly, primaries and secondaries, yellowish head with chestnut nape and hindneck. **Adult Winter:** Similar, but bare parts duller; nape and hindneck mostly white, occasionally washed with yellow. Differs from Peruvian Pelican in much smaller size, duller bare parts, smaller crest, upperwing lacking pale forewing patch. **Juvenile/Immature:** Mostly brown above, merging into white breast and underparts; acquires adult plumage by third year.
HABITS: Breeds colonially; gregarious throughout year. This and Peruvian Pelican are the only true marine pelicans; they feed by diving from the wing, executing spectacular plunge-dives.
DISTRIBUTION: Both coasts of North and South America, from Washington south to Peru, including Galapagos Is, and in Atlantic from North Carolina south through West Indies to tropical Brazil; breeding dates vary according to location, most Mar–Aug.
SIMILAR SPECIES: Compare Peruvian Pelican (below).

Peruvian Pelican *Pelecanus (occidentalis) thagus* L152cm/60in W228cm/90in **P** p. 84

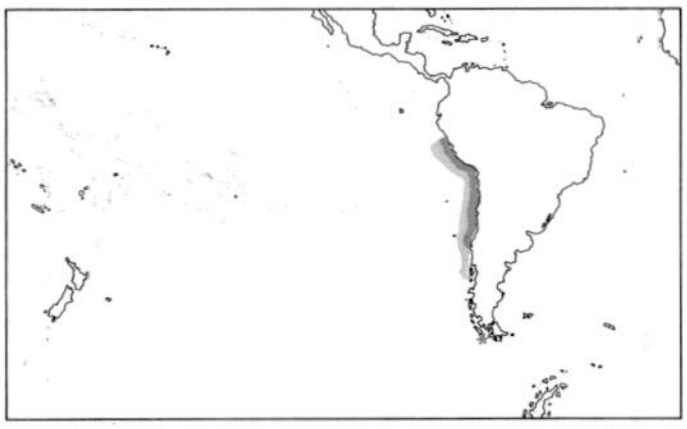

IDENTIFICATION: Huge; plumage recalls much smaller Brown Pelican, which some authors consider conspecific. **Adult Summer:** Differs from more widespread Brown Pelican in brighter bare parts and more pronounced yellow crest, with darker brown, almost black nape and hindneck. The secondaries and inner wing are darker and enclose a conspicuous pale rectangle on leading edge of upperwing during flight this diagnostic character is easily seen. **Adult Winter:** Similar, but bare parts duller, with white head and scattered white tips to scapulars, back and upperwing-coverts. Plumage thus more variable and contrasting than in winter Brown Pelican. **Juvenile/Immature:** Differs from Brown Pelican in larger size, darker brown upperparts.
HABITS: As for Brown Pelican.
DISTRIBUTION: Endemic to Humboldt Current region off coasts of Peru and Chile. Breeds from central Peru south to 33½°S in Chile; occasionally strays south to Tierra del Fuego.
SIMILAR SPECIES: Compare Brown Pelican (above).

American White Pelican *Pelecanus erythrorhynchos*
L152cm/60in W271cm/107in **P** p. 85

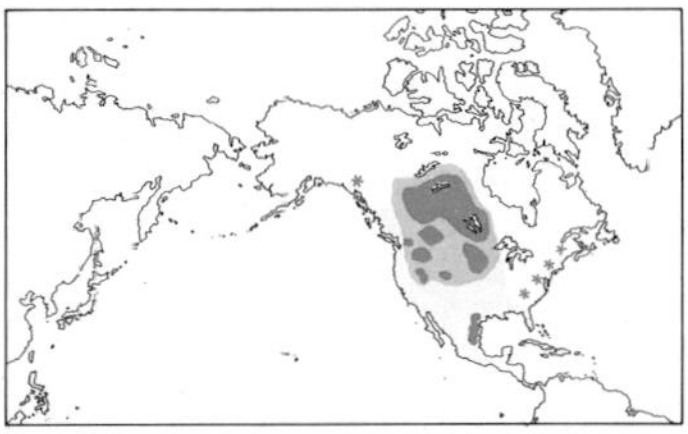

IDENTIFICATION: Unmistakable the only white North American pelican. **Adult Summer:** Plumage mostly white, except for black primaries and outer secondaries and pale yellow crest on nape; bill bright orange, with fibrous plate on upper mandible. **Adult Winter:** Similar, but crown and nape greyish; bill plate shed. **Juvenile/Immature:** Much as winter adult, except for more extensive brownish nape, secondaries and upperwing-coverts. Unlike Wood Stork, Whooping Crane or Snow Goose, white pelicans fly with their heads drawn back against the body.
HABITS: Breeds colonially at freshwater locations, dispersing during winter to estuaries and bays, where gregarious. Unlike Brown Pelican, feeds by dipping bill while swimming.
DISTRIBUTION: North America; breeds Apr–Sep mainly Prairie Provinces and in scattered colonies in east Washington south to coastal Texas. Disperses south to Texas, Mexico, coasts of central America, West Indies and Guatemala Sep–Mar.
SIMILAR SPECIES: None.

Eastern White Pelican *Pelecanus onocrotalus*
L157cm/62in W315cm/124in **P** p. 85

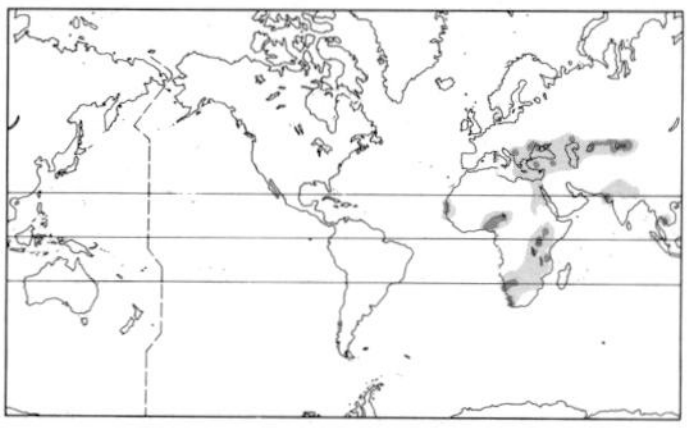

IDENTIFICATION: Large, mostly white pelican with black primaries and secondaries. **Adult:** Differs from larger Dalmatian Pelican in pink and blue bill with yellowish pouch, and black primaries and secondaries giving diagnostic underwing pattern. **Juvenile/ Immature:** Ashy-brown above, white below with conspicuous brown margins to white underwing. Differs from juvenile Dalmatian in darker upperparts and conspicuous underwing pattern.
HABITS: Not on oceans. Breeds colonially on freshwater lakes; gregarious throughout year. Second largest pelican. Flight consists of heavy flaps followed by a long glide; frequently soars on outstretched wings.
DISTRIBUTION: Eurasia and Africa. Breeds southeast Europe eastwards from Black, Caspian and Aral Seas to Lake Balkash; perhaps Indus Delta. Also in Africa from Mauritania and Ethiopia south to South Africa.
SIMILAR SPECIES: Compare Dalmatian and Pink-backed Pelicans (below).

Dalmatian Pelican *Pelecanus crispus* L170cm/67in W327cm/129in **P** p. 86

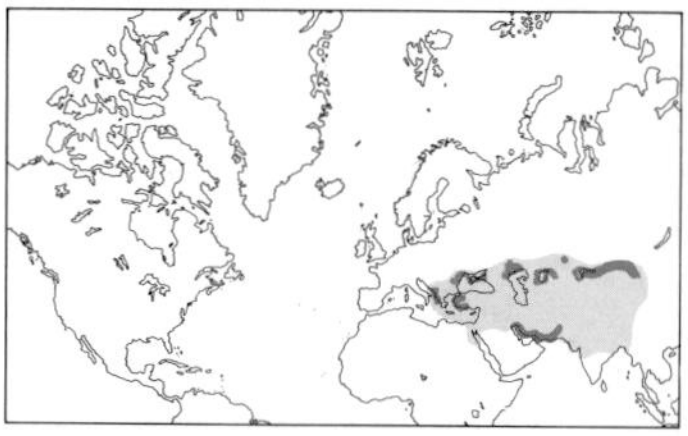

IDENTIFICATION: Largest Eurasian pelican; plumage mostly white, with dark grey primaries and outer secondaries. **Adult:** Differs from White Pelican in grey bill with reddish tip and bright orange pouch, greyer cast to underparts and lack of contrasting black and white pattern on underwing. **Juvenile/Immature:** Recalls Pink-backed Pelican, but is much larger with grey legs; underwing lacks darker secondaries.
HABITS: Not on ocean. Breeds colonially on freshwater lakes; gregarious throughout year. Flight as for Eastern White Pelican.
DISTRIBUTION: Eurasia; breeds southeast Europe east through Black and Caspian Seas, China and Mongolia and southern Iran. Dates vary according to location.
SIMILAR SPECIES: Compare Eastern White, Pink-backed and Spot-billed Pelicans (p. 224, p. 225).

Pink-backed Pelican *Pelecanus rufescens* L128cm/50in W277cm/109in **P** p. 86

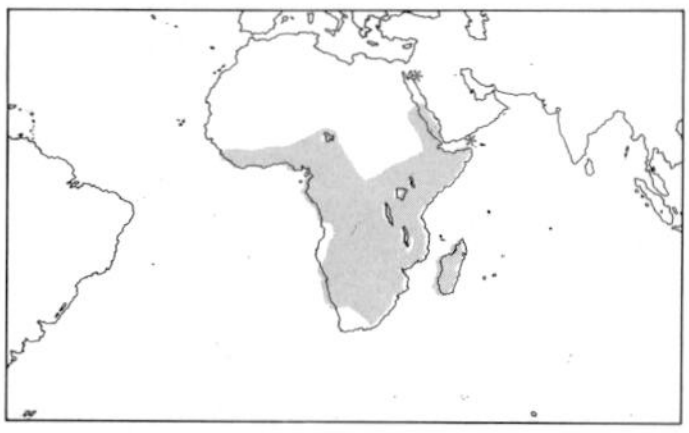

IDENTIFICATION: Small, rather dowdy pelican. **Adult:** Differs from Eastern White in much smaller size, greyer, dowdier plumage, pinkish bill with dark spot in front of eye, and less contrast on underwing. **Juvenile/Immature:** Recalls Dalmatian, but has pink bill, pale legs and darker secondaries.
HABITS: Not on ocean. Breeds colonially; gregarious throughout year. Unlike Eastern White, often roosts in trees.
DISTRIBUTION: Breeds throughout Africa south of Sahara, including Madagascar north to about 25°N in Red Sea; dates dependent upon location.
SIMILAR SPECIES: Compare Eastern White and Dalmatian Pelicans (above).

Spot-billed Pelican *Pelecanus philippensis* L139cm/55in W250cm/98in **P** p. 86

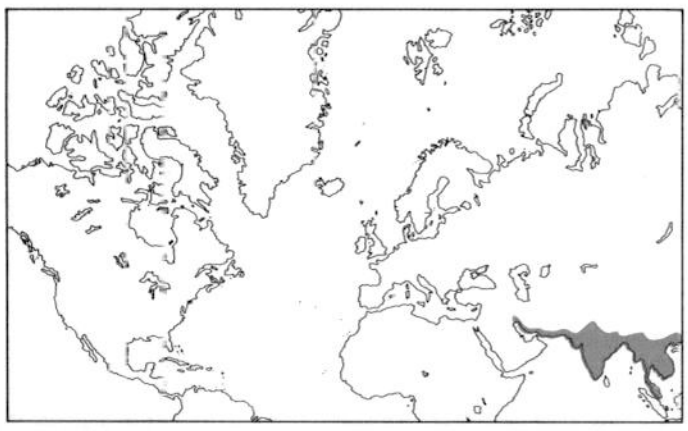

IDENTIFICATION: **Adult:** Mainly white, with brownish crest and hindneck and pink suffusion to back, rump, flanks and undertail-coverts. Differs from Dalmatian in smaller size, pinkish bill and grey pouch. **Juvenile/Immature:** Recalls Dalmatian, but smaller with paler legs (usually) and browner nape and hindneck.
HABITS: Not on oceans. Breeds colonially at freshwater locations. Gregarious throughout year.
DISTRIBUTION: Asiatic; breeds India, Sri Lanka, Burma, Malay Peninsula, southern China and the Philippines. Disperses widely over Indian subcontinent, with stragglers east to Japan.
SIMILAR SPECIES: Compare Pink-backed and Dalmatian Pelicans (p. 224).

Australian Pelican *Pelecanus conspicillatus* L167cm/66in W252cm/99in **P** p. 85

IDENTIFICATION: **Adult:** Unmistakable; the only Australian pelican. Plumage white, except for black upperwings which show conspicuous white patch extending from leading edge across coverts; from below, underwing white, primaries and secondaries black. Tail white, with broad, black tip. **Juvenile/Immature:** Similar to adult, but brown where adults are black.
HABITS: Breeds colonially mainly at freshwater locations, but also marine localities; gregarious throughout year. Flight and habits as for Eastern White Pelican.
DISTRIBUTION: Australasia. Breeds throughout Australia subject to local conditions; disperses widely (probably drought-related) to New Zealand, Lesser Sunda Is, Java and even north of Equator to Palau Is.
SIMILAR SPECIES: None.

Northern Gannet *Sula bassana* L93cm/37in W172cm/68in **P** p. 87

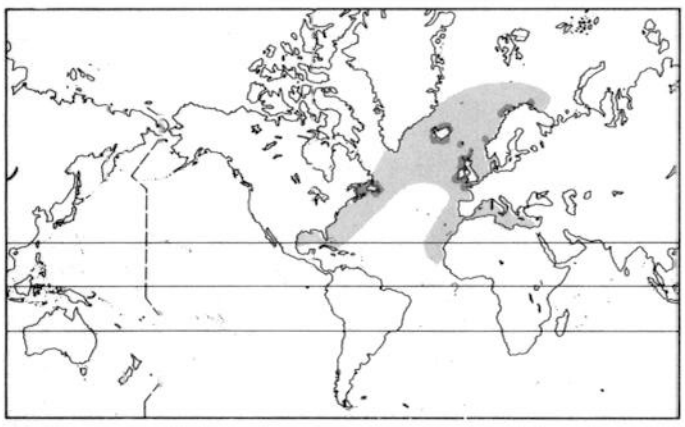

IDENTIFICATION: **Adult:** Large, mostly white seabird with straw-coloured head and black wingtips. Differs from adult Australasian and Cape Gannets and Masked Booby in all-white secondaries and tail. **Juvenile/Immature:** Fledges with mainly drab brownish plumage spotted with white, but paler on breast and belly with whitish 'V' over tail. Becomes progressively whiter over 4-year period, beginning with head, rump and underparts, then wings and tail.
HABITS: Largest indigenous seabird of North Atlantic; long neck and wedge-shaped tail impart distinctive jizz. Flight steady and purposeful, a series of shallow flaps between long glides. Groups often fly in long lines. In high winds wings angled, with more undulating, shearing flight: beware of confusing immatures with Cory's Shearwaters. Breeds colonially on headlands and marine islands; gregarious throughout year.
DISTRIBUTION: North Atlantic, dispersing from Iceland south towards Gulf of Mexico and seas off northwest Africa. Breeds Apr–Sep off eastern USA in Gulf of St Lawrence, Newfoundland and Labrador; also Iceland, the Faeroes, Norway, British Isles, the Channel Isles and Brittany, France.
SIMILAR SPECIES: Compare Cape and Australasian Gannets, also Masked Booby (p. 226, p. 227).

Cape Gannet *Sula capensis* L85cm/33in W? P p. 87

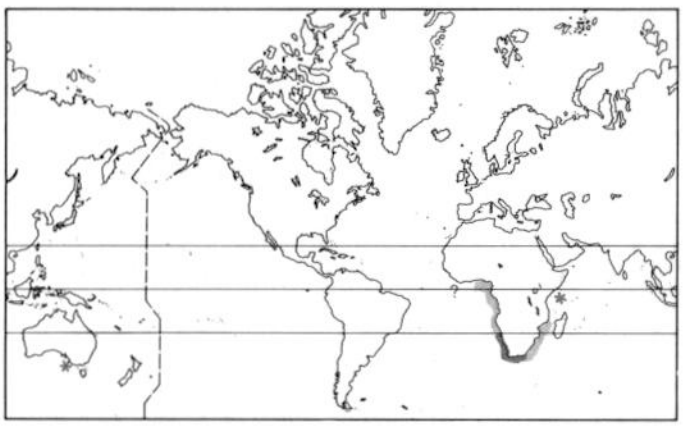

IDENTIFICATION: **Adult:** Recalls Northern Gannet; differs in smaller size, with wholly black secondaries and tail. From Australasian Gannet in wholly black tail. **Juvenile/Immature:** Undergoes similar progressive whitening of plumage over 3–4 years as Northern Gannet, but the secondaries and tail remain uniformly dark throughout all transitional plumages.
HABITS: Much as for Northern Gannet. See also p. 17.
DISTRIBUTION: Seas off southern Africa, with post-breeding dispersal north towards Gulf of Guinea and Mozambique. Breeds offshore islands of Namibia and Cape Province, South Africa; egg-dates Sep–Oct.
SIMILAR SPECIES: Compare Northern and Australasian Gannets, Masked Booby (p. 225, p. 226, p. 227).

Australasian Gannet *Sula serrator* L84cm/33in W170cm/67in P p. 87

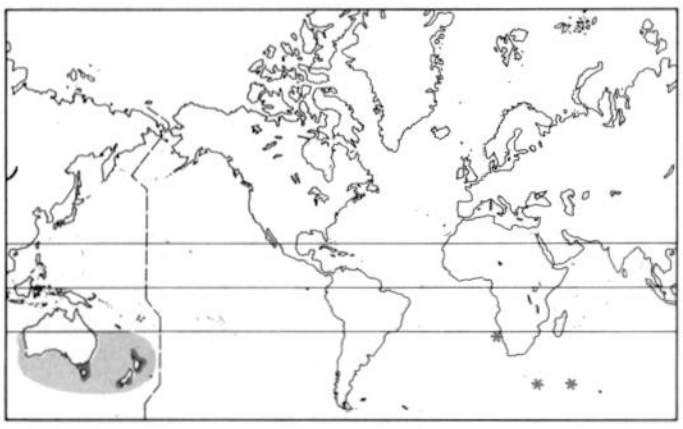

IDENTIFICATION: **Adult:** Resembles Cape Gannet in having dark secondaries, but only the 4 central tail feathers are black, outermost white. **Juvenile/ Immature:** As corresponding Cape Gannet; underparts average paler, but probably indistinguishable at sea.
HABITS: As for Cape Gannet. See also p. 17.
DISTRIBUTION: Australasian seas, with post-breeding dispersal north to Sharks Bay in the west and to Tropic of Capricorn in the east. Breeds Oct–May in Australia on islands off Tasmania and Victoria, also in New Zealand from Three Kings Is south to Little Solander, Foveaux Strait.
SIMILAR SPECIES: Compare Cape Gannet and Masked Booby (p. 226, p. 227).

Abbott's Booby *Sula abbotti* L71cm/28in W? P p. 89

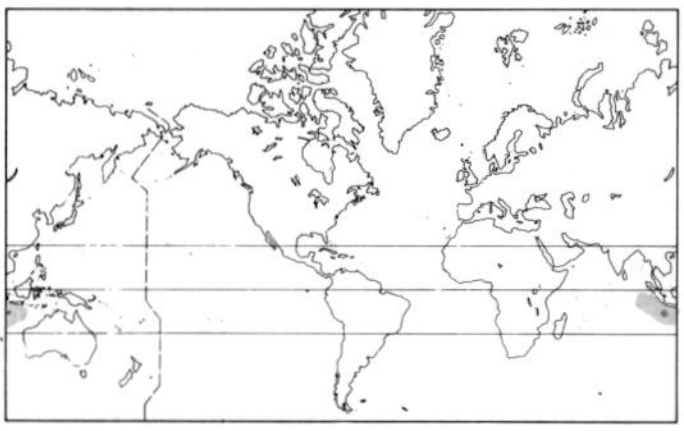

IDENTIFICATION: **Adult:** Distinctive Indian Ocean booby. Plumage white, except for blackish upperwing, thigh patch and tail; from below, in flight, white underwing shows distinct black tip. **Juvenile/Worn Adult:** Brown where fresh adults are black, and have grey bill.
HABITS: Tree-nesting sulid with biennial breeding season. Flight more leisurely than that of other boobies, with slow flaps and languid glides. The large head, long neck and narrow, rakish wings impart distinctive jizz.
DISTRIBUTION: Endemic to Christmas Is, Indian Ocean, where 2,000–3,000 pairs breed in tall trees on central plateau. Egg-dates Apr–Jul. Pelagic dispersal poorly understood, but certainly occurs off coasts of Java where there are rich upwellings.
SIMILAR SPECIES: None.

Masked Booby *Sula dactylatra* L86cm/34in W152cm/60in

P p. 88

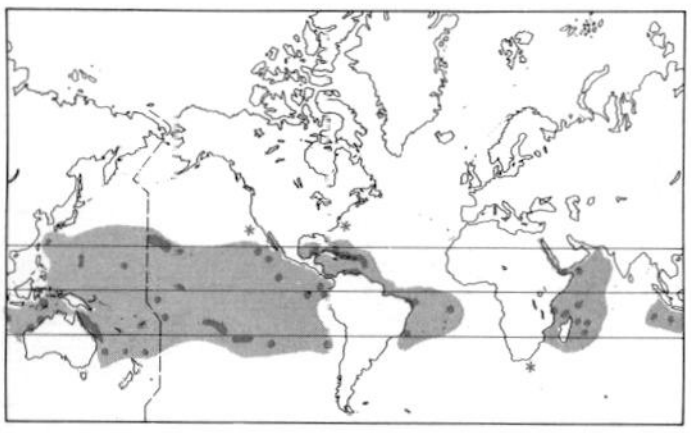

IDENTIFICATION: **Adult:** Superficially resembles gannet spp., but has all-white head, black face mask, and broader, more extensive trailing edge to wings. Unlike Northern Gannet, tail black. **Juvenile:** Head and upperparts brown with narrow white cervical collar, and striped underwing recalling juveniles of both Brown and Blue-footed Boobies. Differs from Brown in paler, more mottled brown upperparts, white cervical collar, white foreneck and upper breast, different underwing pattern. From juvenile Blue-footed in white cervical collar, dark uppertail-coverts and different underwing pattern. **Immature:** Attains adult plumage over 2 years; back whitens first, then scapulars, mantle and upperwing-coverts.
HABITS: Largest and heaviest booby; prefers deep water for fishing, executing near-vertical plunge-dives. Colonial breeder on marine islands; loosely gregarious at sea, does not usually follow ships.
DISTRIBUTION: Pantropical; breeding dates vary according to location.
SIMILAR SPECIES: Compare adult with gannet spp. (p. 225, p. 226); compare juvenile/immature with Brown and Blue-footed Boobies (p. 227, p. 228).

Brown Booby *Sula leucogaster* L69cm/27in W141cm/56in

P p. 89

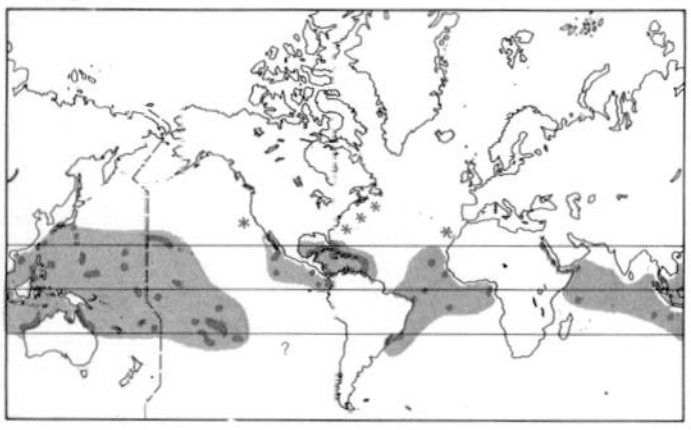

IDENTIFICATION: **Adult:** Head, neck and upperparts uniformly dark brown, terminating across upper breast in clear-cut division at junction with white underparts. No other booby has this pattern. In eastern Pacific, males have pale grey to white head and grey, not yellow bill. **Juvenile:** Much as adult, but underparts whitish-brown. Differs from juvenile/immature Northern Gannet in smaller size, uniformly dark head, neck and upper breast, whiter stripe on underwing. Attains adult plumage over 2–3 years.
HABITS: Smaller than Northern Gannet, with lighter jizz, quicker wing action and proportionately longer tail. Usually feeds inshore, securing prey by raking plunge-dives; freely perches on buoys. Colonial breeder on marine islands. Gregarious.
DISTRIBUTION: Pantropical; possibly commonest and most widespread booby. Breeding dates vary with location.
SIMILAR SPECIES: Compare with juvenile of Northern Gannet, and of Blue-footed and Masked Boobies (p. 225, p. 228, p. 227).

Red-footed Booby *Sula sula* L71cm/28in W152cm/60in

P p. 89

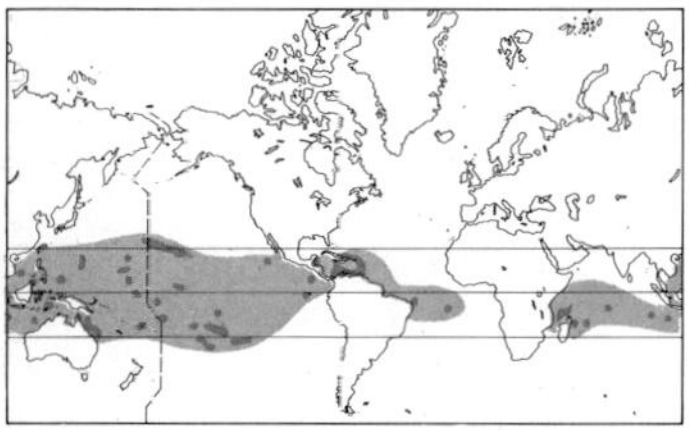

IDENTIFICATION: Small polymorphic booby, but all morphs have diagnostic red feet and pink base to bill. **Adult White Morph:** Differs from Masked Booby in diagnostic black carpal patch on white underwing and wholly white tail (at Galapagos, however, tail black: beware). **Intermediate Morph:** Head, neck and underparts dull white or pale buff, with brown upperwings and white rump, tail and undertail-coverts. **Dark Morph:** Wholly ash-brown, head and neck sometimes with golden wash. **Juvenile:** All morphs fledge wholly ash-brown and have blackish-brown bills, purplish facial skin and yellowish-grey legs. Maturity is reached over 2–3 years.
HABITS: Smallest booby; breeds colonially in trees on marine islands. Gregarious, undertakes long foraging trips, when it freely approaches ships, perching in rigging etc.
DISTRIBUTION: Pantropical; breeding dates vary according to location.
SIMILAR SPECIES: Compare with other boobies (p. 226, p. 227, p. 228).

Blue-footed Booby *Sula nebouxii* L80cm/31in W152cm/60in **P** p. 88

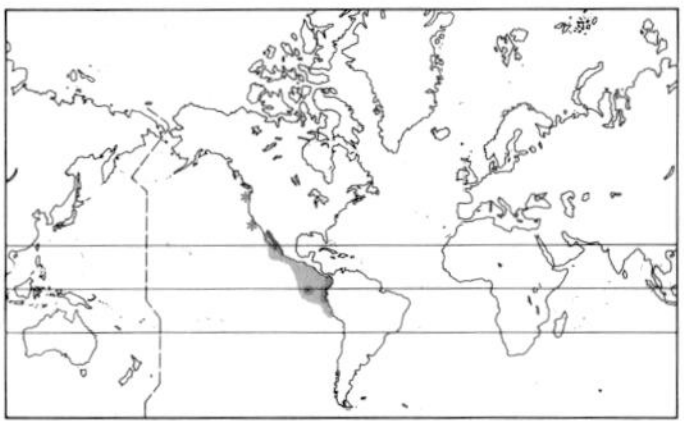

IDENTIFICATION: **Adult:** Large booby, mostly brown above, white below, with streaked head; blue feet diagnostic. Differs from adult Peruvian in streaked brownish head, white patch at junction of hindneck and mantle and white rectangular axillary patch. **Juvenile:** As adult, but legs grey, head dark brown extending to include chin, throat, foreneck and upper breast. Differs from Brown Booby in white patch at base of hindneck, white rump and white rectangular axillary patch. From juvenile Masked Booby in lack of white cervical collar, in white rump patch and white rectangular axillary patch. Maturity is reached over 2–3 years.
HABITS: Colonial breeder on marine islands; gregarious throughout year. Feeds mainly inshore.
DISTRIBUTION: Pacific coasts of central South America, dispersing north to California and south to northern Chile during oceanic fluctuations. Breeds islands off Mexico, Ecuador, northern Peru and at Galapagos Is; dates dependent upon location.
SIMILAR SPECIES: Compare adult with Peruvian Booby, juvenile with juvenile Masked and Brown Boobies (p. 228, p. 227).

Peruvian Booby *Sula variegata* L74cm/29in W? **P** p. 88

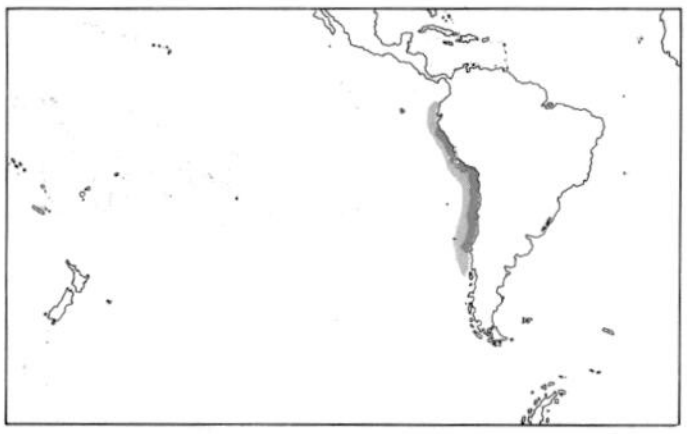

IDENTIFICATION: **Adult:** Medium-sized booby, mostly brown above with white head and underparts; feet blackish-blue. In flight underwing mostly dark, with whitish stripe through centre. Differs from Blue-footed in white head, black face mask, underwing pattern and dark feet. **Juvenile:** Much as adult, but head and underparts mottled with pale yellowish-brown.
HABITS: Colonial breeder on marine islands; gregarious throughout year. Often joins with cormorants and pelicans to form impressive feeding flocks of many thousands.
DISTRIBUTION: Coasts of Peru and Chile; normally sedentary, but during oceanic fluctuations disperses north to northern Ecuador and south to Chiloe Is, Chile. Breeds throughout year from Point Parinas, Peru, south to Concepcion, Chile.
SIMILAR SPECIES: Compare Blue-footed Booby (above).

New Zealand King Cormorant *Phalacrocorax carunculatus* L76cm/30in W? **P** p. 90

IDENTIFICATION: Large black and white cormorant. **Adult Summer:** Upperparts black, glossed blue, with white dorsal patch; upperwing shows two white bars, one on inner median wing-coverts and a second, shorter bar across scapulars. Underparts white, thigh blackish-blue. During courtship has a short crest on head and nape. **Adult Winter:** Similar, but white bar on wing-coverts and dorsal patch reduced or absent; lacks crest on forehead and nape. **Juvenile:** Pattern much as adult winter, but upperparts mouse-brown with indistinct bar on wing and dorsal patch; underparts dirty-white. All ages differ from Pied Cormorant, the only other large black and white cormorant of the area, in darker sides of face, pink (not black) legs and white on wings.
HABITS: Exclusively marine. Colonial breeder; gregarious throughout year.
DISTRIBUTION: Endemic to New Zealand, where a few hundred breed Jun–Sep Cook Strait area. Sedentary.
SIMILAR SPECIES: Compare Pied Cormorant (p. 232).

Stewart Island Cormorant *Phalacrocorax carunculatus chalconotus*
L68cm/27in W?

P p. 90

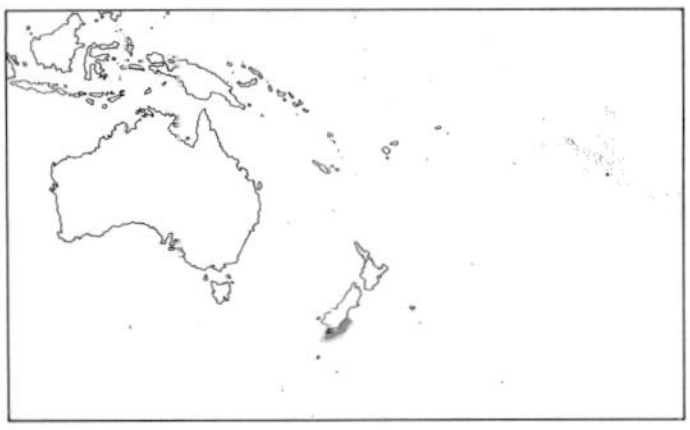

IDENTIFICATION: Usually considered a polymorphic southern representative of New Zealand King Cormorant; occurs in three morphs. **Adult Summer Pale Morph:** Differs from King Cormorant in greener lustre to upperparts, only one white bar on upperwing, and in much smaller, barely discernible white dorsal spot. **Adult Summer Dark Morph:** Wholly blackish, with rich oily-green lustre. **Adult Summer Intermediate Morph:** As for dark morph, but with irregular white spotting on underparts; palest examples have white belly and undertail-coverts. **Adult Winter:** Lacks crest on forehead and nape, white alar bar and dorsal patch reduced or absent. Pale morphs differ from Pied Cormorant in darker sides of face, pink (not black) legs and white on wing.
HABITS: Exclusively marine. Colonial breeder; gregarious throughout year.
DISTRIBUTION: Endemic to South Island, New Zealand. Breeds Jun–Sep from Otago Peninsula south to Foveaux Strait and Stewart Island.
SIMILAR SPECIES: Compare Pied Cormorant (p. 232).

Chatham Island Cormorant *Phalacrocorax carunculatus onslowi*
L63cm/25in W?

P p. 90

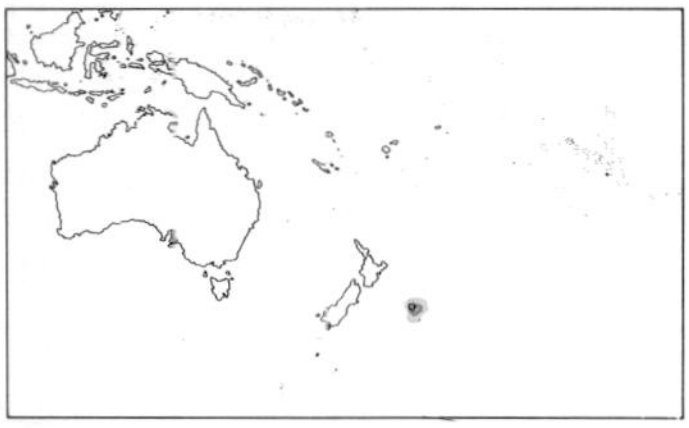

IDENTIFICATION: Usually considered an island form of the larger New Zealand King Cormorant. **Adult Summer:** Differs from King Cormorant in brighter red facial skin and gular, larger white dorsal patch, and deeper, more velvety-black upperparts with stronger iridescence. **Adult Winter:** Upperparts and bare parts duller; lacks crest. **Juvenile:** As adult winter, but upperparts brown with indistinct white alar bar. All ages differ from Great Cormorant and Spotted Shag, which also occur at Chatham Is, in white underparts and pink feet.
HABITS: Exclusively marine. Colonial; gregarious throughout year. It is smaller than the New Zealand King Cormorant, with a more compact, more delicate jizz.
DISTRIBUTION: Endemic to Chatham Is, New Zealand; sedentary.
SIMILAR SPECIES: None within area, but compare Great Cormorant and Spotted Shag (p. 235, p. 232).

Campbell Island Cormorant *Phalacrocorax campbelli*
L63cm/25in W105cm/41in

P p. 91

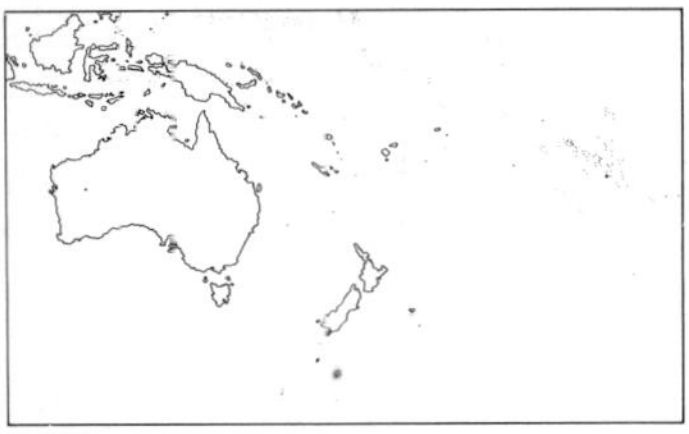

IDENTIFICATION: Medium-sized black and white cormorant. **Adult Summer:** Upperparts, including most of head and neck, blue-black, with recurved wispy crest on forehead; chin, foreneck and underparts white, with blackish thigh. Upperwing has white alar bar. **Adult Winter:** Upperparts and bare parts duller; crest and white alar bar reduced or absent. **Juvenile:** As adult winter, but brown above with brownish chin and throat. All ages can be separated from Little Pied Cormorant, which also breeds at Campbell Is, by plumage pattern and pink (not black) feet.
HABITS: Exclusively marine. Colonial breeder; highly gregarious throughout year, forming large rafts when feeding. Jizz recalls that of Imperial Shag, but with more laboured flight.
DISTRIBUTION: Sedentary, occurs only at Campbell Is, south of New Zealand. Breeds Sep–Mar.
SIMILAR SPECIES: None within range, but compare Little Pied Cormorant (p. 231).

Auckland Island Cormorant *Phalacrocorax campbelli colensoi*

L63cm/25in W105cm/41in **P** p. 91

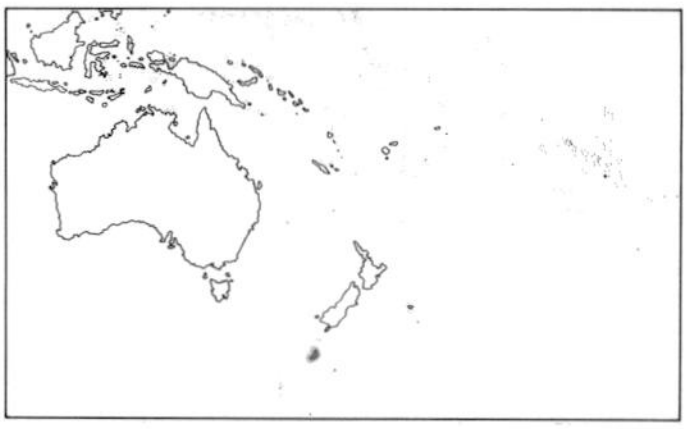

IDENTIFICATION: Medium-sized black and white cormorant, usually regarded as a race of Campbell Island Cormorant. **Adult Summer:** As for Campbell Island Cormorant, but less white on chin and throat; some may show narrow black necklace or complete band at base of foreneck and a small white dorsal spot. **Adult Winter:** Upperparts and bare parts duller; crest and white alar bar reduced or absent. **Juvenile:** As adult winter, but upperparts brown, with dark chin, throat and foreneck. The only resident cormorant at Auckland Is; differs from Little Pied and Great Cormorants, which occur as vagrants, in plumage pattern and pink (not black) feet.
HABITS: As for Campbell Island Cormorant.
DISTRIBUTION: Sedentary, occurs only at Auckland Is south of New Zealand; breeds Sep–Mar.
SIMILAR SPECIES: None within range, but compare Little Pied and Great Cormorants (p. 231, p. 235).

Bounty Island Cormorant *Phalacrocorax campbelli ranfurlyi* L71cm/28in W? **P** p. 91

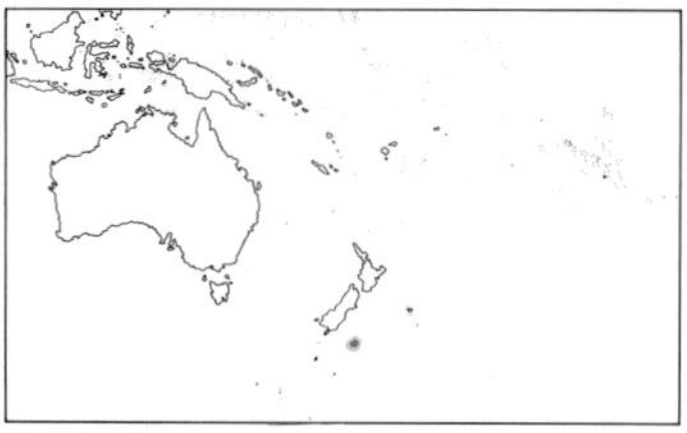

IDENTIFICATION: Usually regarded as a race of the smaller Campbell Island Cormorant. **Adult Summer:** As for Campbell Island Cormorant, but white on chin and throat extends broadly down centre of foreneck; white alar bar on upperwing more pronounced, with a variably sized white dorsal patch. **Adult Winter:** Upperparts and bare parts duller; crest reduced or absent, lacks white alar bar and dorsal patch. **Juvenile:** As adult winter, but brown above. No other cormorant occurs within range.
HABITS: As for Campbell Island Cormorant.
DISTRIBUTION: Usually sedentary, occurs only at Bounty Is southeast of New Zealand; breeds Sep–Mar. Stragglers have reached Antipodes Is, 190km to the south of Bounty Is.
SIMILAR SPECIES: None within range.

Imperial Shag *Phalacrocorax atriceps* L72cm/28in W124cm/49in **P** p. 94

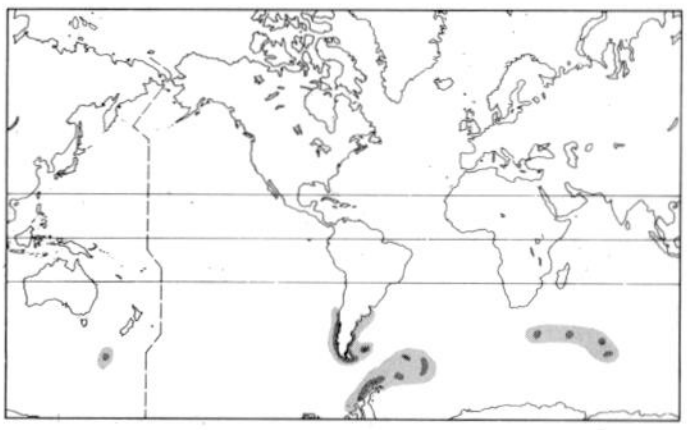

IDENTIFICATION: A widespread black and white sub-Antarctic cormorant formerly treated as several species (Blue-eyed, King, Kerguelen etc), but now generally regarded as a single species with dimorphic plumage. **Adult Summer:** During courtship has bright yellow or orange caruncles, wispy recurved crest and white filoplumes on sides of head. Upperparts black, glossed blue, underparts mostly white, thigh black. Birds with extensive black on face usually lack the white dorsal patch found on whiter-faced birds. Both types show white alar bar. **Adult Winter:** Upperparts and bare parts duller; wispy crest, alar bar and dorsal patch reduced or lacking. **Juvenile:** As adult winter, but duller and browner above. Identification usually straightforward as in most parts of range no other cormorants occur. Differs from Rock Shag in blue eye-ring and yellow caruncles, white foreneck and alar bar.
HABITS: Exclusively marine. Breeds colonially; gregarious throughout year, often forms dense rafts of many thousands.
DISTRIBUTION: Southern Oceans. Breeds Aug–Apr on islands adjacent to Antarctic Peninsula, South Sandwich, South Orkney, South Georgia and Falkland Is, mainland of South America, and at Crozet, Marion, Prince Edward, Kerguelen and Macquarie Is.
SIMILAR SPECIES: Compare Rock Shag (p. 232).

Black-faced Cormorant *Phalacrocorax fuscescens*
L65cm/26in W107cm/42in **P** p. 92

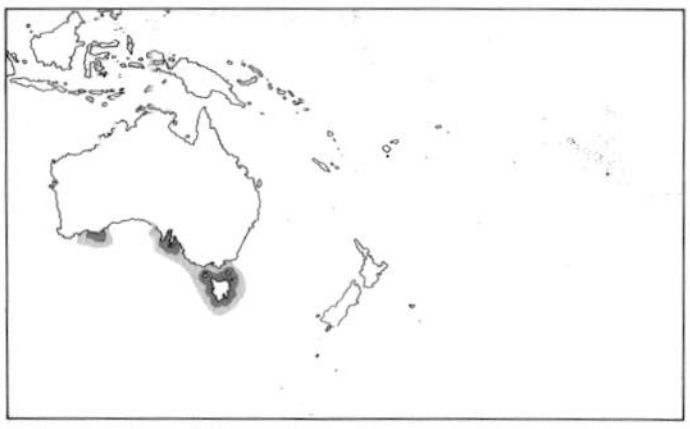

IDENTIFICATION: Medium-sized black and white cormorant. **Adult Summer:** Plumage pattern recalls more widespread Pied Cormorant, but differs in diagnostic black facial skin and gular with demarcation between black and white occurring below eye on sides of face. During courtship there are dense white filoplumes on the hindneck, rump and thigh. **Adult Winter:** Upperparts duller black; lacks white filoplumes. **Juvenile:** As adult winter, except for greyish cheeks and brownish wash across foreneck and upper breast; upperparts browner in tone. Differs from juvenile Pied Cormorant in grey (not yellow) skin before eye and darker face and foreneck.
HABITS: Exclusively marine. Breeds colonially; gregarious throughout year. In flight, the head and neck are held lower than in Pied Cormorant, creating a more humpbacked jizz.
DISTRIBUTION: Usually sedentary, endemic to coasts of southern Australia and Tasmania; breeding dates normally Sep–Jan.
SIMILAR SPECIES: Compare Pied Cormorant (p. 232).

Little Black Cormorant *Phalacrocorax sulcirostris*
L61cm/24in W81cm/32in **P** p. 92

IDENTIFICATION: Small, wholly dark cormorant. **Adult Summer:** Wholly black, with green or purple sheen; small white filoplumes on side of head and neck, behind eye, are lost after pair formation. Differs from Great, dark-morph Little Pied and Javanese Cormorants in diagnostic dark purple-grey facial skin and lead-grey bill. **Adult Winter/Immature:** As adult summer, but plumage duller, more brownish-black.
HABITS: Prefers freshwater locations, but also on tidal creeks; occasionally coasts. Breeds colonially; highly gregarious, indulges in co-operative fishing.
DISTRIBUTION: Malay Archipelago and Australasian region. Breeds from Borneo through Moluccas to New Guinea, Australia, Tasmania and North Island, New Zealand; dates dependent on food supply.
SIMILAR SPECIES: Compare Great, Javanese and dark-morph Little Pied (p. 235, p. 238, p. 231).

Little Pied Cormorant *Phalacrocorax melanoleucos* L60cm/24in W87cm/34in **P** p. 93

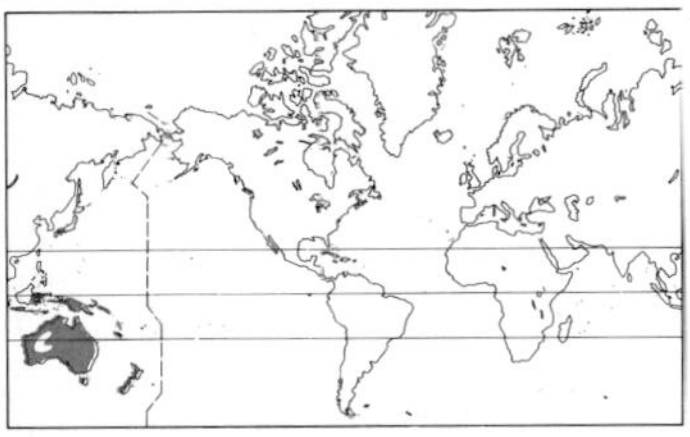

IDENTIFICATION: Small, polymorphic cormorant occurring in pale, intermediate and dark forms. Pale morph is the typical form occurring from Java to New Zealand. Dark and intermediate morphs are restricted to New Zealand. **Adult Pale Morph:** Black above, white below. Unlike the larger Pied Cormorant, the white extends narrowly over eye and the thigh (in most) is white; best distinction is its short, stubby yellow bill and brown eye. **Adult Dark Morph:** Mostly black, usually with white flecking on chin and throat. Differs from Little Black Cormorant in short yellowish bill and brown (not green) eye. **Adult Intermediate Morph:** As for dark morph, but with white sides to face, chin and throat, extending in some to include upper breast.
HABITS: Prefers freshwater locations. Colonial breeder; gregarious throughout year. Smaller than Pied Cormorant, more compact, with longer tail and more upright perching posture.
DISTRIBUTION: Mainly Australasian region. Breeds from Java, New Guinea and Solomon Is, south to New Zealand; dates dependent on food supply.
SIMILAR SPECIES: Compare pale morphs with Pied Cormorant, dark morphs with Little Black and Javanese Cormorants (p. 232, p. 231, p. 238).

Pied Cormorant *Phalacrocorax varius* L75cm/30in W121cm/48in P p. 92

IDENTIFICATION: Large black and white cormorant. **Adult Summer:** Facial skin yellow or bright orange, with pink gular and pale yellow bill. Upperparts glossy black, underparts white, the demarcation between black and white occurring above eye. **Adult Winter:** Duller black above, with duller bare-part colours. **Juvenile/Immature:** Upperparts brown, extending across foreneck to divide whitish throat from streaked brown and white underparts. In New Zealand some immatures are all-dark. Adults differ from those of Black-faced Cormorant in bright facial skin and gular pouch; juveniles have yellow (not grey) skin before eye, and have paler face and foreneck than Black-faced juveniles. Little Pied Cormorant is much smaller, with dark skin in front of eye and smaller, more compressed bill structure.
HABITS: Freshwater and marine locations; breeds colonially, gregarious throughout year.
DISTRIBUTION: Coasts and larger inland waters of Australia and New Zealand; not Tasmania.
SIMILAR SPECIES: Compare Black-faced and Little Pied Cormorants (p. 231).

Spotted Shag *Phalacrocorax punctatus* L69cm/27in W? P p. 93

IDENTIFICATION: Distinctive species with colourful breeding plumage. **Adult Summer:** Head and neck mostly greenish-black, with pronounced double crest and conspicuous white stripe curving from eye to sides of lower neck. Upperparts greenish-grey, each feather with blackish tip giving spotted appearance. Underparts pale grey, thigh black. The Pitt Is race, confined to the Chatham Is, lacks white stripe on sides of face and neck. **Adult Winter:** Lacks double crest and white stripe on sides of face and neck, head and neck appearing mostly dark. **Juvenile/Immature:** As adult winter, but upperparts mouse-brown with pale grey underparts; chin and throat whitish.
HABITS: Exclusively marine. Breeds colonially; gregarious throughout year.
DISTRIBUTION: Coasts and islands of North and South Islands, New Zealand, also at Chatham Is; egg-dates Jul–Oct.
SIMILAR SPECIES: None.

Rock Shag *Phalacrocorax magellanicus* L66cm/26in W92cm/36in P p. 93

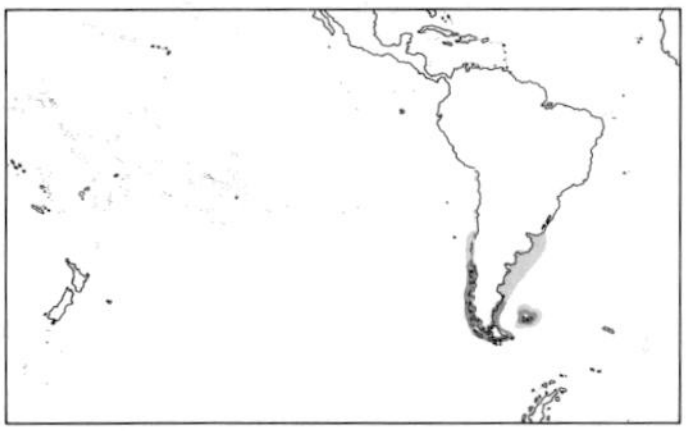

IDENTIFICATION: Medium-sized cormorant with bright red facial skin and black bill. **Adult Summer:** Upperparts, including foreneck, upper breast and most of head, black with green or violet gloss; chin and tuft on side of head white, with white filoplumes on sides of neck (latter lost during pair formation). Underparts silvery-white, thigh black. **Adult Winter:** Browner above, with variable amounts of white on chin, throat and foreneck. **Juvenile:** Mostly dull brown, with whitish belly and ventral area. **Immature:** Upperparts mostly brown with scattered greenish feathers, underparts brownish with scattered white tips on belly and ventral area. Adults with red facial skin, tufted head and white patches on sides of face distinctive. Juvenile/immatures differ from corresponding Olivaceous Cormorants in dark bill, facial skin, smaller size, more slender jizz, thinner neck and smaller head.
HABITS: Marine locations. Breeds colonially on exposed sea cliffs; gregarious throughout year. Flight usually low with rapid wingbeats, very little gliding or soaring.
DISTRIBUTION: Coasts of southern South America and the Falkland Is, with post-breeding dispersal north to 33°S in Chile and to 35°S in Uruguay. Breeds in southern Chile from about 37°S to Cape Horn and then north to about 50°S in Patagonia; egg-dates Oct–Dec.
SIMILAR SPECIES: Compare Olivaceous and Guanay Cormorants (p. 233).

Guanay Cormorant *Phalacrocorax bougainvillii* L76cm/30in W?

P p. 94

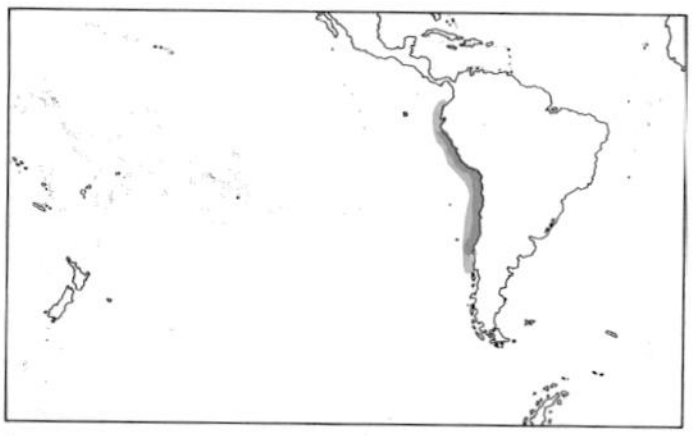

IDENTIFICATION: Large cormorant, dark above, white below. **Adult Summer:** Facial skin bright red, bill yellowish. Upperparts, including foreneck, black with blue or violet gloss; underparts and small area on chin white. During breeding has small erectile crest on forehead, with white tuft on sides of head and scattered white filoplumes. **Adult Winter:** Duller and browner, head lacks crest, white tuft and filoplumes. **Juvenile:** As adult winter, but white underparts sullied with brown. All ages differ from Olivaceous in colour of facial skin, pink (not black) legs and white underparts. From Rock Shag in larger size, yellowish bill, less extensive red on face, whiter upper breast and lower foreneck.

HABITS: Exclusively marine. Highly gregarious, often joining other cormorants, boobies and pelicans to form rafts of many thousands. When swimming sits very low in water, upperparts awash. Breeds colonially in vast colonies of up to 6 million on flat or gently sloping areas.

DISTRIBUTION: Western South America; breeds islands and headlands of Peru and Chile.

SIMILAR SPECIES: Compare Rock Shag and Olivaceous Cormorant (p. 232, p. 233).

Red-legged Shag *Phalacrocorax gaimardi* L76cm/30in W91cm/36in

P p. 94

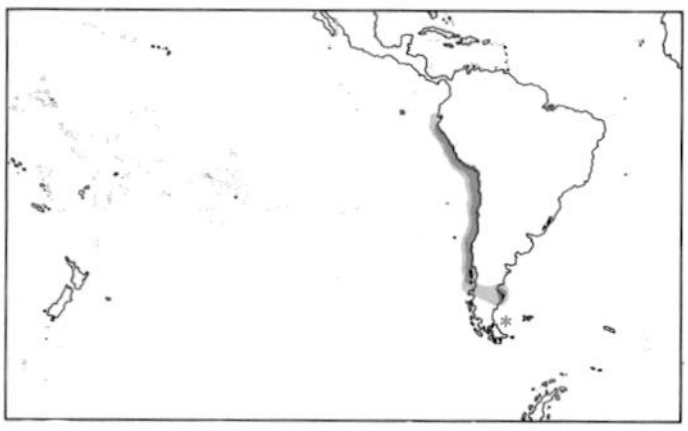

IDENTIFICATION: Large colourful cormorant with distinctive plumage. **Adult:** Base of bill, feet and legs red. Plumage mostly silvery-grey, with conspicuous white patch on side of neck; in flight, whitish blocking on upperwing-coverts forms obvious pale forewing patch. **Juvenile:** Much as adult, but brownish-grey above, with white chin, grey-brown breast and white belly. At all ages, easily separated from other Humboldt Current cormorants by greyish or brownish-grey plumage, white patch on side of neck and red feet.

HABITS: Exclusively marine; nests singly or in small groups, usually in caves.

DISTRIBUTION: South America. Breeds from about 6°S in Peru south to about 46°S in Chile, with a small colony on eastern littoral near Puerto Deseado; dates dependent upon food supply.

SIMILAR SPECIES: None, but compare Rock Shag and Guanay Cormorant (p. 232, p. 233).

Olivaceous Cormorant *Phalacrocorax olivaceus* L65cm/26in W101cm/40in

P p. 95

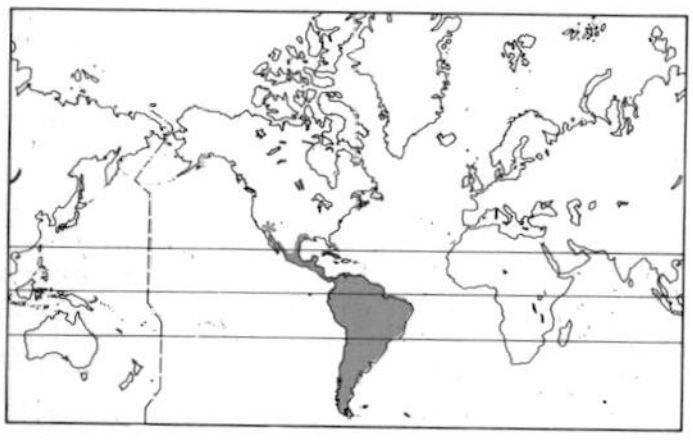

IDENTIFICATION: The only wholly dark adult cormorant in South America. **Adult Summer:** Plumage black with blue-green gloss; a conspicuous white tuft on side of head is lost during pair formation. Differs from larger, shorter-tailed, more robust Double-crested Cormorant in diagnostic, narrow, white triangular-shaped border to yellowish gular. **Adult Winter:** Similar, but plumage browner, more olive in tone. **Juvenile/Immature:** Wholly brown at first, lacking white border to gular; with advancing maturity, attains white border to gular and brownish-white underparts. Differs from corresponding Double-crested in whitish border to gular and dirty, brownish-white foreneck and underparts.

HABITS: Occurs at both marine and freshwater locations. Colonial breeder; gregarious throughout year. In flight the head is slightly hunched back.

DISTRIBUTION: Throughout much of Central and South America, including Cuba and Bahamas to northwest Mexico; smaller numbers in southern USA. Breeding dates vary.

SIMILAR SPECIES: Compare Double-crested Cormorant (p. 234).

Double-crested Cormorant *Phalacrocorax auritus*
L84cm/33in W134cm/53in **P** p. 95

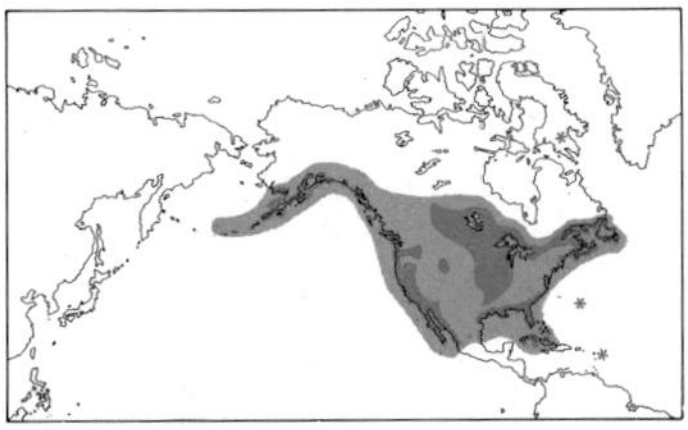

IDENTIFICATION: Most widespread North American cormorant. **Adult Summer:** Plumage wholly black with greenish gloss. During pair formation adult has short crest of curly tufts on sides of head, which are white in western birds, black in eastern birds. **Adult Winter:** Browner, without crest or filoplumes. Differs from Brandt's Cormorant in slightly larger size and bright orange facial skin and gular pouch; from Great Cormorant in smaller size, bare-part colours, and lack of extensive white on head and thigh. **Juvenile/Immature:** First-year birds are brown, with variable pale whitish-brown foreneck and upper breast.
HABITS: Colonial breeder at marine and freshwater locations; gregarious throughout year. Smaller than Great Cormorant, with more slender bill and smaller, less angular head. In flight, differs from Brandt's and Pelagic in its comparatively large bill and head carried on crooked neck.
DISTRIBUTION: From Aleutians and Gulf of St Lawrence south to Cuba. Breeds Apr–Sep.
SIMILAR SPECIES: Compare Great, Brandt's and Olivaceous (p. 235, p. 234, p. 233).

Brandt's Cormorant *Phalacrocorax penicillatus*
L85cm/33in W118cm/46in **P** p. 96

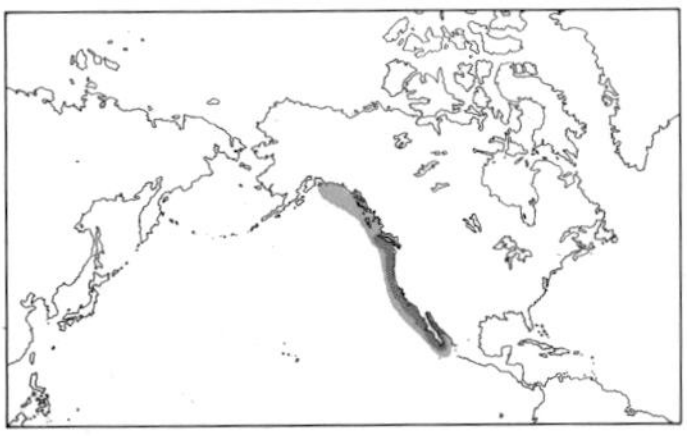

IDENTIFICATION: Wholly dark marine cormorant, distinguishable at any age by a band of pale yellowish or tan feathers bordering gular. **Adult Summer:** Plumage mostly blackish, with oily-purplish gloss on head and rump. Differs from Double-crested Cormorant in dark facial skin, diagnostic sky-blue gular with yellowish border, and white hair-like filoplumes on sides of head. **Adult Winter:** Similar, but plumage duller, lacks white filoplumes and sky-blue gular. **Juvenile/Immature:** Browner than adult winter, with paler underparts and indistinct paler 'V' across upper breast. Differs from juvenile Double-crested in pale border to gular and darker underparts.
HABITS: Exclusively marine. Breeds colonially on cliffs, islands etc; gregarious. Almost as large and bulky as Double-crested, but with more upright stance; in flight head and neck usually carried straight, not crooked.
DISTRIBUTION: Commonest cormorant of Pacific coast of North America. Egg-dates Mar–Jul.
SIMILAR SPECIES: Compare Double-crested Cormorant (above).

Pelagic Cormorant *Phalacrocorax pelagicus* L68cm/27in W96cm/38in **P** p. 96

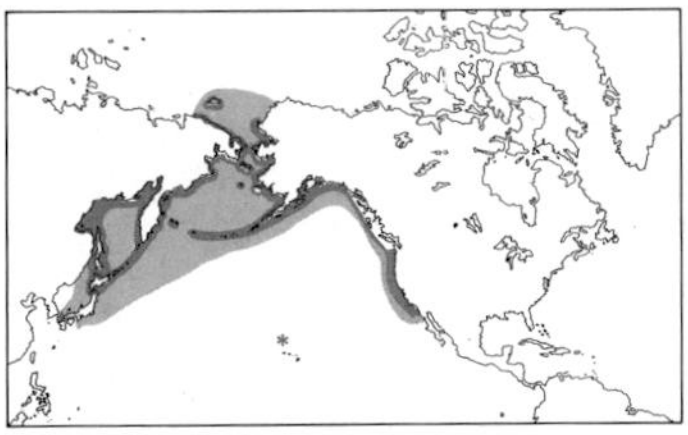

IDENTIFICATION: Small, mostly dark Pacific cormorant. **Adult Summer:** Wholly black, with violet gloss on head and neck and rich green iridescence on body. Differs from larger Brandt's and Double-crested Cormorants in red facial skin, double crest on head, and white flank patch. Differs from Red-faced Cormorant in absence of yellow on bill, red facial skin not meeting over bill, uniformly coloured upperwings and back. **Adult Winter:** Duller, less glossy, without double crest or thigh patch. **Juvenile/Immature:** Uniformly brown, never shows the contrast shown in corresponding Brandt's and Double-crested Cormorants. Difficult to separate from corresponding Red-faced; differs only in smaller size and less extensive facial skin.
HABITS: Exclusively marine. Less gregarious than Double-crested Cormorant, but breeds colonially. In flight, head appears small with slender neck held straight out.
DISTRIBUTION: Asiatic and American coasts of North Pacific; breeds May–Aug.
SIMILAR SPECIES: Compare Brandt's, Double-crested and Red-faced (p. 234, p. 235).

Red-faced Cormorant *Phalacrocorax urile* L84cm/33in W116cm/46in **P** p. 95

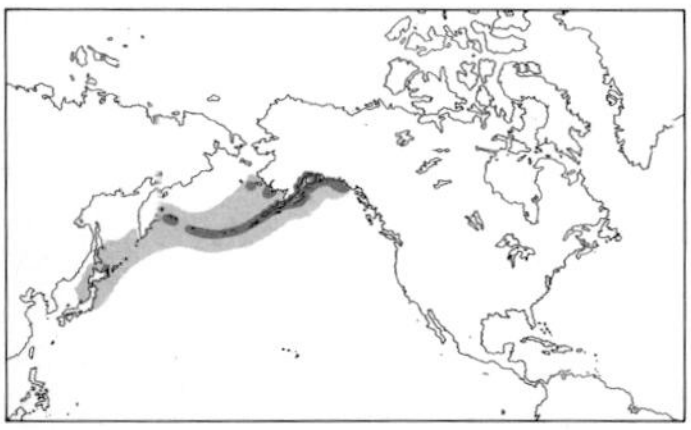

IDENTIFICATION: Medium-sized, wholly dark Pacific cormorant. **Adult Summer:** Plumage mostly black with greenish iridescence; thigh patch white. Differs from smaller Pelagic Cormorant in diagnostic red facial skin extending broadly across forehead to join over upper mandible. Base of bill yellow, with bright blue gape. In flight, the wings appear browner than in Pelagic Cormorant and contrast with iridescent body. **Adult Winter:** Duller, less glossy, without double crest or white thigh patch. **Juvenile/Immature:** Very similar to juvenile Pelagic, but larger, with continuous brownish-red or grey facial skin joining over bill.
HABITS: Exclusively marine; breeds colonially. Has same flight profile as Pelagic, but is slightly larger with thicker neck and proportionately longer bill.
DISTRIBUTION: North Pacific. Breeds from Moyururi Is, Japan, north and east to Commander Is, Aleutian Is and to Cordova, Alaska; egg-dates May–Jun.
SIMILAR SPECIES: Compare Pelagic, Brandt's and Double-crested Cormorants (p. 234).

Great Cormorant *Phalacrocorax carbo* L90cm/35in W140cm/55in **P** p. 97

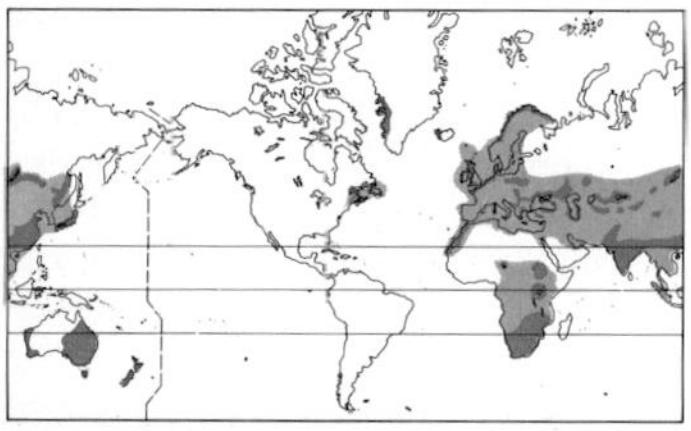

IDENTIFICATION: Largest and most widespread cormorant. **Adult Summer:** Mostly black with green or blue gloss; white border to yellow gular and white thigh patch. Some races have pronounced white filoplumes on head and neck during breeding. *P.c. maroccanus* in northwest Africa has white throat and upper neck, while African *P.c. lucidus* has white extending to include upper breast. **Adult Winter:** Duller and browner, without white filoplumes or thigh patch. **Juvenile/Immature:** Mostly dull brown above, with whitish chin and throat. First-years have white belly, which becomes progressively darker in the second year, wholly dark by third year. Best separated from congeners, at all ages, by larger size and obvious yellow facial skin which, in adults, is bordered with white.
HABITS: Colonial breeder at freshwater and marine locations; gregarious throughout year. Flight rather goose-like, with slower wingbeats than Shag; longer neck supports heavier, more apparent head.
DISTRIBUTION: Almost cosmopolitan in Old World; smaller numbers breed in North America along Canadian coast south to Nova Scotia.
SIMILAR SPECIES: Compare Shag, Double-crested and Japanese (p. 235, p. 234, p. 238).

Shag *Phalacrocorax aristotelis* L72cm/28in W97cm/38in **P** p. 96

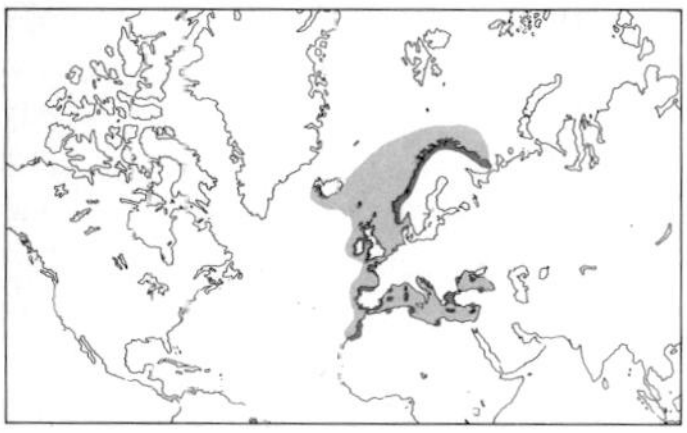

IDENTIFICATION: **Adult Summer:** Wholly black with rich green iridescence. Differs from sympatric Great Cormorant in much smaller size, lack of white on head, throat or thigh, with diagnostic wispy, recurved crest and thin yellow gape; the crest is absent after pair formation. **Adult Winter:** Duller, less glossy, with paler throat; yellowish gape reduced, crest absent. **Juvenile/Immature:** Mostly dull brown, with whitish chin, throat and foreneck.
HABITS: Almost exclusively marine; breeds colonially, loosely gregarious. Unlike Great Cormorant, rarely perches in trees. In flight wingbeats quicker than Great Cormorant, with smaller, more rounded head and thinner neck held lower.
DISTRIBUTION: Breeds coasts and shores of northwestern Europe from western Iceland south to Mediterranean and northwest Africa; egg-dates usually Apr–Jun.
SIMILAR SPECIES: Compare Great Cormorant and any winter diver sp. (p. 235, p. 182, p. 183).

Bank Cormorant *Phalacrocorax neglectus* L76cm/30in W132cm/52in

P p. 97

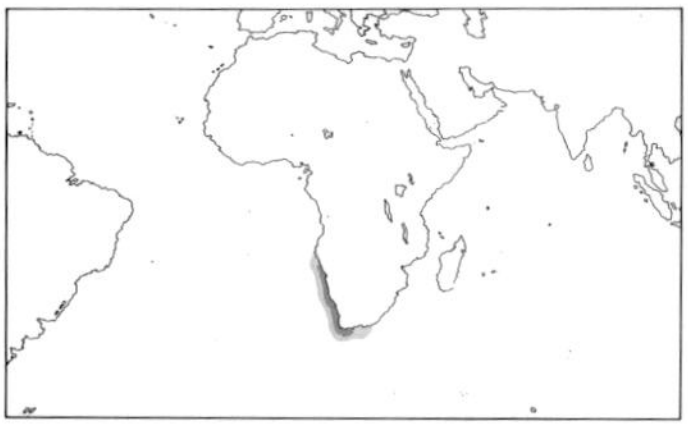

IDENTIFICATION: Large, mostly blackish marine cormorant. **Adult Summer:** Plumage dull black, except for diagnostic white patch on rump and small white filoplumes on head and neck, which are lost after pair formation; short erectile crest on forehead. **Adult Winter/Immature:** Wholly dull brownish-black. **Note:** Leucistic individuals with varying amounts of white on face and neck are frequently met with, but differ, at any age, from all other South African cormorants in blackish facial skin and gular pouch.

HABITS: Entirely marine; usually met with singly or in small parties hunting among inshore kelp beds. Colonial breeder on marine islands and cliffs. Size intermediate between sympatric white-breasted form of Great and smaller Cape Cormorants, with rotund pot-bellied jizz.

DISTRIBUTION: Endemic to cold-water zone off Namibia and South Africa; breeds throughout much of year. Rare east of Cape Agulhas.

SIMILAR SPECIES: Compare Cape and white-breasted form of Great Cormorants (p. 236, p. 235).

Cape Cormorant *Phalacrocorax capensis* L63cm/25in W109cm/43in

P p. 98

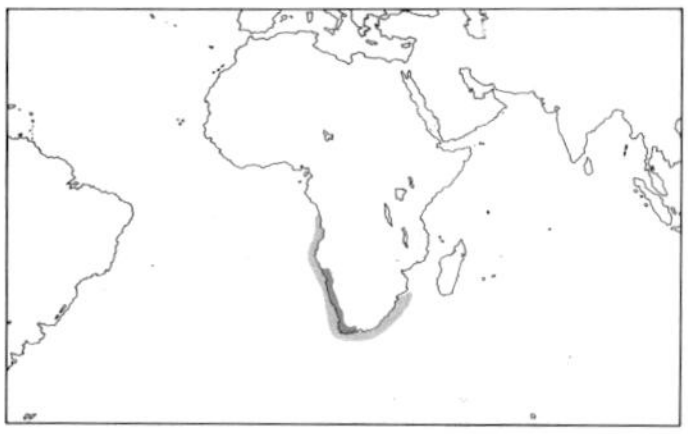

IDENTIFICATION: Small to medium-sized cormorant with rather short tail. **Adult Summer:** Combination of glossy blackish-blue plumage and bright yellow gular diagnostic within its limited range. **Adult Winter:** Mostly dull brown, with greyish-brown chin, foreneck and upper breast; gular dull yellowish-brown. **Juvenile/ Immature:** As adult winter, but whiter below.

HABITS: Almost exclusively marine. Breeds colonially on headlands, cliffs and islands. Highly gregarious, the most abundant cormorant species off coasts of Namibia and South Africa, where its long skeins are a characteristic sight.

DISTRIBUTION: Endemic to southern Africa. Breeds Sep–Feb coasts of Namibia and South Africa, dispersing north to Congo River mouth and Mozambique.

SIMILAR SPECIES: Compare Bank, Long-tailed and Crowned Cormorants (p. 236, p. 237).

Long-tailed Cormorant *Phalacrocorax africanus*
L53cm/21in W85cm/33in

P p. 98

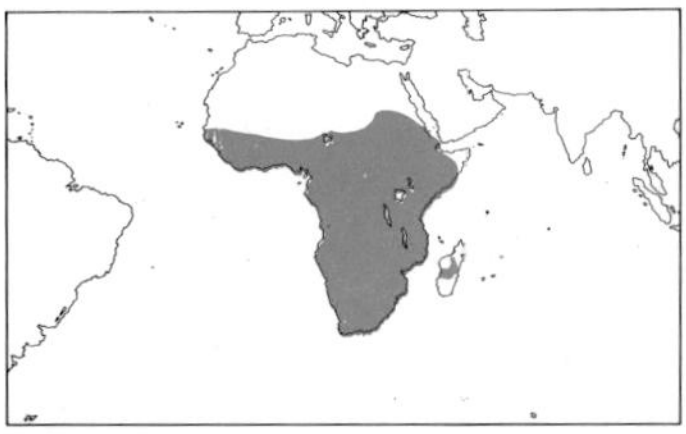

IDENTIFICATION: Small black cormorant, with long graduated tail, yellow bill and red eye. **Adult Summer:** Mostly black, with green iridescence; wing-coverts silvery-grey, each feather with large dark tip giving spotted appearance. During courtship has short erectile crest and white filoplumes on sides of head. **Adult Winter:** Bare parts duller, lacks white filoplumes and crest. Adults differ throughout year from Crowned Cormorant in spotted upperwing-coverts. **Juvenile/ Immature:** Dark brown above, with off-white underparts. Juvenile Crowned Cormorants are wholly brown, except for pale throat.

HABITS: Prefers freshwater locations, but also on coast in some localities. Breeds colonially; loosely gregarious.

DISTRIBUTION: Throughout Africa south of the Sahara, also at Madagascar. Breeding dates dependent on food supply.

SIMILAR SPECIES: Compare Crowned, Bank, Cape and white-breasted form of Great Cormorants (p. 237, p. 236, p. 235).

Crowned Cormorant *Phalacrocorax coronatus* L50cm/20in W85cm/33in P p. 98

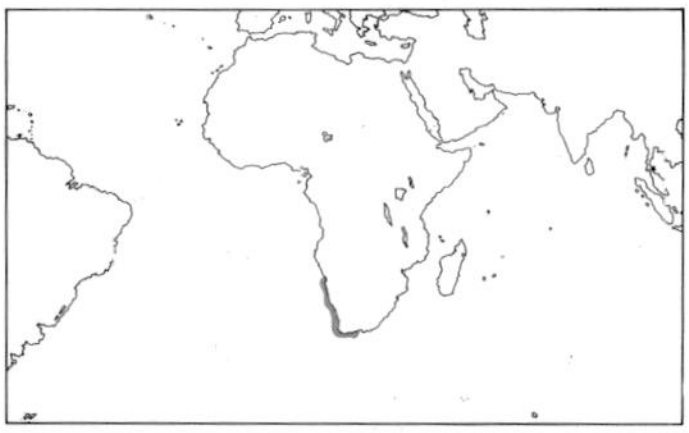

IDENTIFICATION: Small black cormorant, with long graduated tail, yellowish bill, red eye and facial skin. **Adult Summer:** Mostly black, with green iridescence. Differs from Long-tailed in brighter red facial skin, longer crest and shorter tail; best distinction is that the upperwing-coverts are uniform with upperparts without large black tips, and thus lack the distinctly patterned appearance of Long-tailed. **Adult Winter/Juvenile:** Mostly brown, with pale chin and throat.
HABITS: Almost exclusively marine. Breeds in small colonies on cliffs and islands; loosely gregarious.
DISTRIBUTION: Endemic to southern Africa, breeding Namibia and Cape Province, South Africa; egg-dates Jul–Apr.
SIMILAR SPECIES: Compare Long-tailed Cormorant (p. 236).

Socotra Cormorant *Phalacrocorax nigrogularis* L80cm/31in W106cm/42in P p. 99

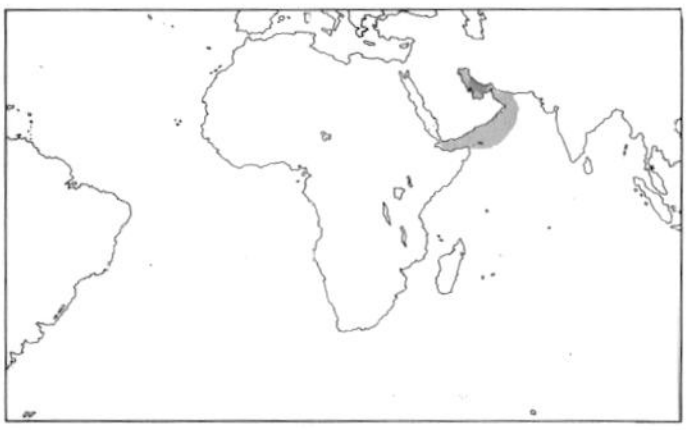

IDENTIFICATION: Large blackish marine cormorant. **Adult Summer:** Mostly glossy black, with purple sheen on head and neck. Wing-coverts glossed green, with darker centres giving spotted effect; white tuft on sides of head and white filoplumes on neck are lost after pair formation, and rarely seen at colonies. **Adult Winter:** Duller and browner, lacks white on head. Differs from Great Cormorant in smaller size, dark facial skin, and lack of pronounced white bordering gular, on head or thigh. **Juvenile/Immature:** Upperparts, head and neck brownish, underparts white; with advancing maturity, underparts become brown with blackish feather tips.
HABITS: Exclusively marine, where highly gregarious, often gathering in dense flocks of several thousands. Breeds colonially on marine islands. Resembles Eurasian Shag in flight and jizz, but flies in close 'V' shaped skeins.
DISTRIBUTION: Southern Red Sea and Persian Gulf, dispersing beyond Straits of Hormuz south to Gulf of Aden. Breeds islands in Persian Gulf, perhaps also islands off Dhufar, Aden, and Socotra; egg-dates Jan–Mar.
SIMILAR SPECIES: Compare Great Cormorant (p. 235).

Pygmy Cormorant *Phalacrocorax pygmeus* L50cm/20in W85cm/33in P p. 99

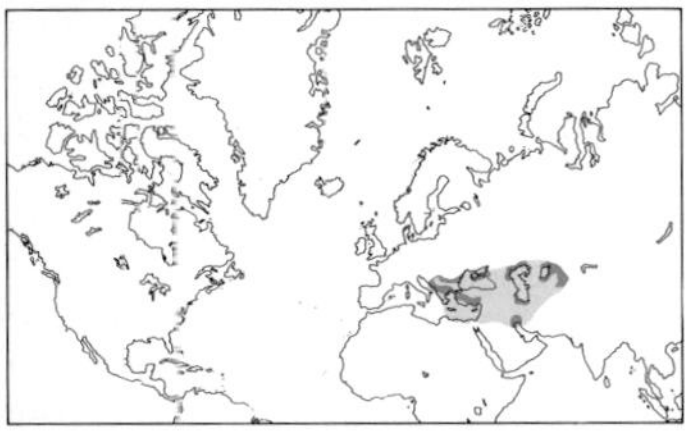

IDENTIFICATION: Small freshwater cormorant with long graduated tail. **Adult Summer:** Mostly black, with short, tufted crest on forehead and dense white filoplumes on sides of head and neck. As season progresses, head becomes rich velvety-brown with fewer filoplumes. **Adult Winter:** Upperparts dull brown with pale feather edges; whitish chin and foreneck, crest absent. **Juvenile/Immature:** As adult winter, but underparts mostly white. About half the size and bulk of Great Cormorant, the only other cormorant of the region; confusion should not therefore arise.
HABITS: Freshwater species. Breeds colonially; gregarious throughout year. Flight buoyant, with rapid shallow wingbeats alternating with short glides, during which small size, short neck and long tail at once apparent.
DISTRIBUTION: Eurasian. Usually breeds Mar–Aug from southeast Europe east through Black and Caspian Seas to Aral Sea. Most populations probably sedentary, but north Caspian population disperses southwards during northern winter.
SIMILAR SPECIES: None within limited range.

Japanese Cormorant *Phalacrocorax capillatus (=P. filamentosus)*
L92cm/36in W152cm/60in **P** p. 97

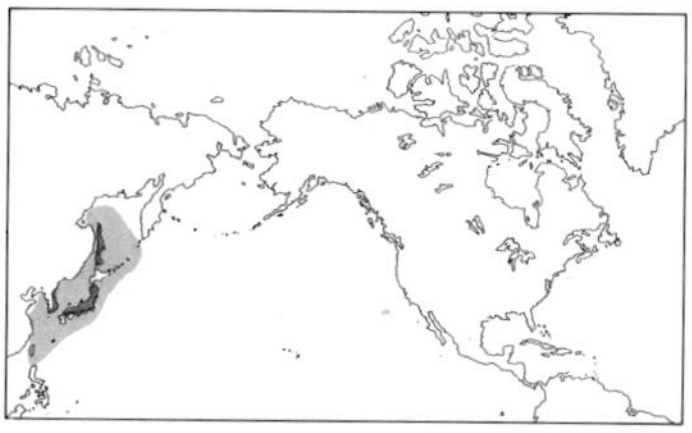

IDENTIFICATION: Large marine cormorant. **Adult Summer:** Mostly black with greenish gloss, white border to yellowish facial skin and gular, white filoplumes on neck and thigh patch, thus very like Great Cormorant. Differs in more marine habits, green (not bronze) wing-coverts, narrower, longer white filoplumes on sides of neck, and white of lower face extending forwards below lower mandible (in Great Cormorant the white on lower face is separated from base of lower mandible by yellowish gular). **Adult Winter:** Duller and browner, without white filoplumes or thigh patch. **Juvenile/Immature:** Mostly dull brown above, with whitish chin, throat and underparts. With advancing maturity underparts attain scattered dark tips, becoming wholly dark in about third year.
HABITS: Almost exclusively marine; flight and jizz as for Great Cormorant. Breeds colonially on rocky islands; gregarious.
DISTRIBUTION: Asiatic. Breeds rocky cliffs of Korea and in Japan, from Kyushu northwards to Sakhalin Is. Dispersal poorly known; winters from Honshu, Japan, southwards; Japanese birds have reached China.
SIMILAR SPECIES: Compare Great Cormorant (p. 235).

Javanese Cormorant *Phalacrocorax niger* L56cm/22in W90cm/35in **P** p. 99

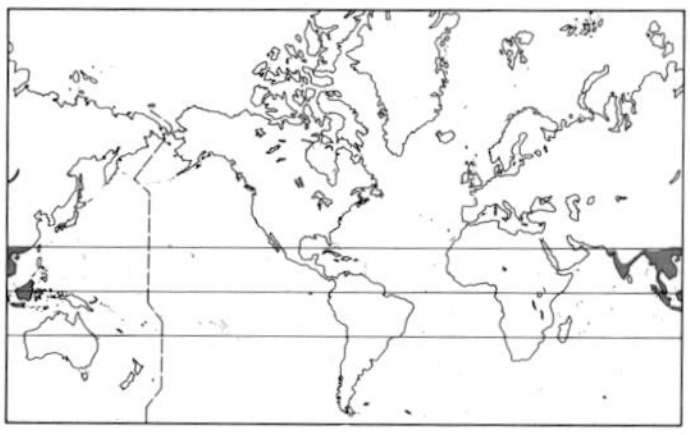

IDENTIFICATION: Small freshwater cormorant with long graduated tail. **Adult Summer:** Wholly black with strong greenish iridescence; during courtship, has short erectile crest and scattered white filoplumes on head. **Adult Winter:** Duller and browner, with pale chin and throat. **Juvenile/Immature:** As adult winter, but chin and throat greyish-brown, merging into upper breast. Differs from Indian Cormorant in smaller, more compact jizz with shorter bill, proportionately larger head, and less scaly upperparts.
HABITS: Prefers freshwater locations; breeds colonially, loosely gregarious throughout year.
DISTRIBUTION: Asiatic. Distributed through lower-altitude regions of India, Pakistan, Sri Lanka, Burma, Thailand, Malay Archipelago, Borneo and Java; breeding dates vary.
SIMILAR SPECIES: Compare Indian Cormorant (below).

Indian Cormorant *Phalacrocorax fuscicollis* L65cm/26in W? **P** p. 100

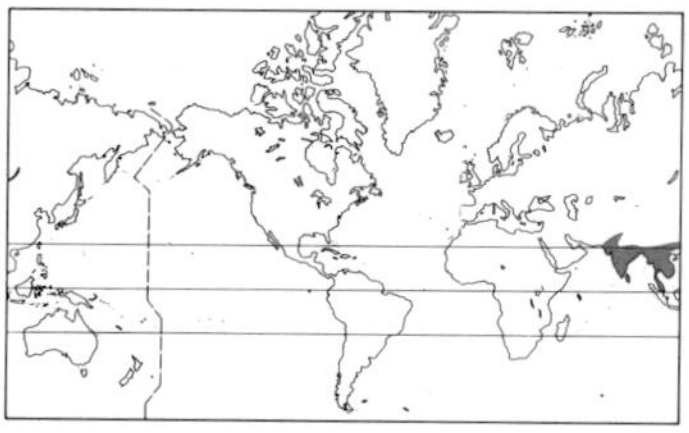

IDENTIFICATION: Medium-sized cormorant with long, graduated tail. **Adult Summer:** Mostly blackish-bronze, with darker feather edges producing scaly pattern on mantle, scapulars and wing-coverts; facial skin pale green, with yellowish gular. White tuft on side of head is lost after pair formation. **Adult Winter:** Browner and duller, with dull whitish chin and throat; lacks white filoplumes. **Juvenile/Immature:** As adult winter, but whole of underparts dingy-white. Differs from Javanese Cormorant in larger size, with proportionately longer, darker bill, more scaly upperparts and different jizz. Great Cormorant is much larger, with stouter bill and yellowish facial skin.
HABITS: Breeds colonially; gregarious. Frequents freshwater and marine locations. In flight appears larger and slimmer than Javanese Cormorant, with longer neck and tail.
DISTRIBUTION: Asiatic. Breeds India, Sri Lanka, Burma, Thailand, Kampuchea and Cochin-China; egg-dates Jul–Nov.
SIMILAR SPECIES: Compare Javanese and Great Cormorants (p. 238, p. 235).

Galapagos Cormorant *Nannopterum (=Phalacrocorax) harrisi*
L95cm/37in **P** p. 100

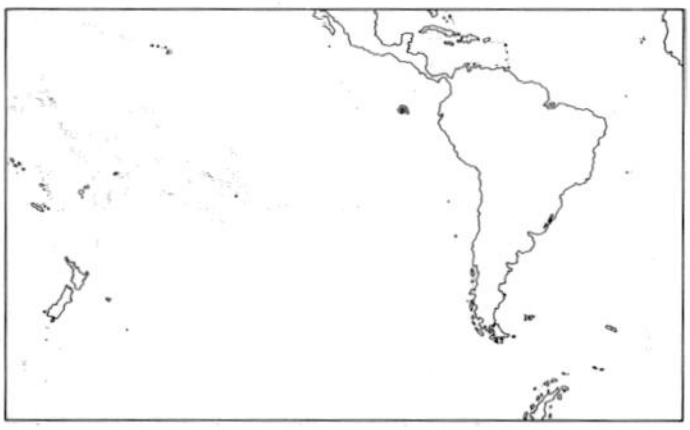

IDENTIFICATION: Unmistakable. The only species of cormorant at the Galapagos. **Adult:** Plumage dull blackish, with greyer wing-coverts and slight ochreous hue to underparts. **Juvenile/Immature:** Uniformly brownish-black.
HABITS: Exclusively marine, sedentary, rarely venturing even a kilometre from natal shoreline, returning each evening to roost on rocks. Swims low in water, back awash, with distinctive 'large-headed' jizz.
DISTRIBUTION: Endemic to Galapagos Is, where about 1,000 pairs breed on Fernandina and Isabela.
SIMILAR SPECIES: None.

Ascension Frigatebird *Fregata aquila* L91cm/36in W198cm/78in **P** pp. 100–1

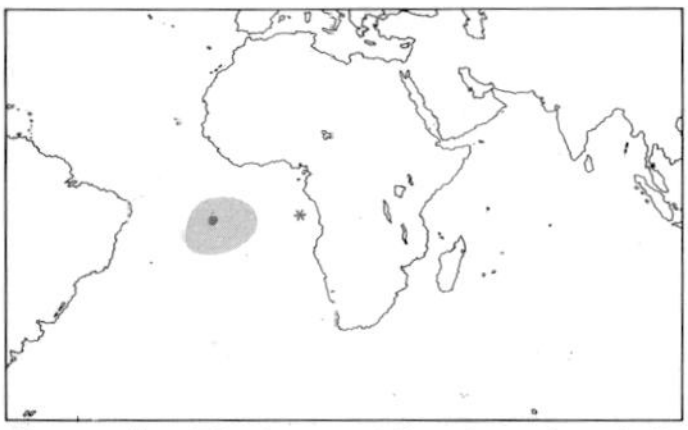

IDENTIFICATION: Sexually dimorphic. **Adult Male:** Wholly black, with green iridescence; legs black. Probably indistinguishable from adult male Magnificent Frigatebird, but ranges not known to overlap. **Adult Female:** Two forms. Typical form is as male, but with brownish nape and hindneck extending in continuous band across upper breast, legs reddish; the white-breasted form differs from typical dark females in white breast and belly, with square white 'spur' on axillaries. **Juvenile:** Fledges with white head, breast and upper belly; the underwing shows a noticeable and diagnostic square white 'spur' on the axillaries. This latter character is shown to some degree in all subsequent plumages, except that of adult male and dark-morph adult female. Consult Harrison (1983) for black and white plumage key showing 9 transitional immature plumages.
HABITS: Breeds colonially on ground. Gregarious; follows ships. See p. 18 for further notes.
DISTRIBUTION: Tropical Atlantic Ocean and adjacent seas. Breeds May–Mar, Bosun/Boswainbird Islet, Ascension Is.
SIMILAR SPECIES: Compare with other frigatebirds (p. 239, p. 240).

Lesser Frigatebird *Fregata ariel* L76cm/30in W184cm/72in **P** p. 102

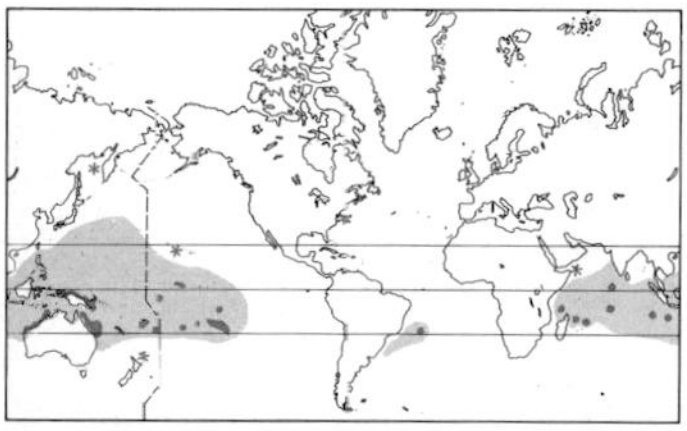

IDENTIFICATION: Sexually dimorphic. **Adult Male:** Mostly black, glossed green, with diagnostic white 'spur' across flank and axillaries. **Adult Female:** Very like female Magnificent, but smaller, with more noticeable white collar on hindneck, triangular, more apparent white 'spur' on underwing, and pointed (not square) division between white and black on lower belly. **Juvenile:** Fledges with rusty head and white breast and belly broken by partial or complete breastband; underwing with triangular white 'spur' as in adult female. All subsequent immature plumages of both sexes differ from corresponding Great Frigatebird in axillary colour and distribution of white on underparts. Consult Harrison (1983) for plumage key showing 9 transitional immature plumages.
HABITS: Breeds colonially, usually in trees/bushes. Gregarious; follows ships. Smaller size apparent only when viewed with other frigatebirds. See p. 18 for further notes.
DISTRIBUTION: Widespread in Indian Ocean and tropical western Pacific, with small numbers in Atlantic at Trinidade and Martin Vaz; breeding dates vary with location.
SIMILAR SPECIES: Compare with other frigatebirds (p. 239, p. 240).

Magnificent Frigatebird *Fregata magnificens* L101cm/40in W238cm/94in **P** p. 104

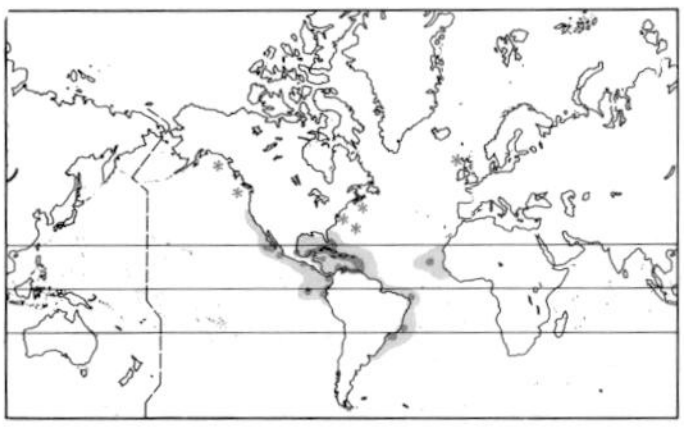

IDENTIFICATION: Sexually dimorphic. **Adult Male:** Wholly black, glossed green; legs black. Differs from male Great Frigatebird (usually) in blackish feet, lack of pale bar on upperwing, but some overlap in these characters reported. **Adult Female:** Mostly black above, with greyish cervical collar and pale brownish bar across upperwing-coverts. From below, chin and throat are black and end in sharp 'V' at white upper breast and belly. White tips to black axillaries form 3 or 4 wavy lines; this character is present in most immature stages. Female Great Frigatebirds have pale grey chin and throat and all-black axillaries. **Juvenile:** Fledges with white head and diagnostic dark wedge-shaped 'spurs' on sides of breast, enclosing triangular white belly patch. Consult Harrison (1983) for key showing 7 immature plumages.
HABITS: Breeds colonially, usually in trees/bushes. Gregarious; follows ships. See also p. 18.
DISTRIBUTION: Tropical Pacific and Atlantic Oceans; breeding dates vary.
SIMILAR SPECIES: Compare with other frigatebirds (p. 239, p. 240).

Great Frigatebird *Fregata minor* L93cm/37in W218cm/86in **P** p. 103

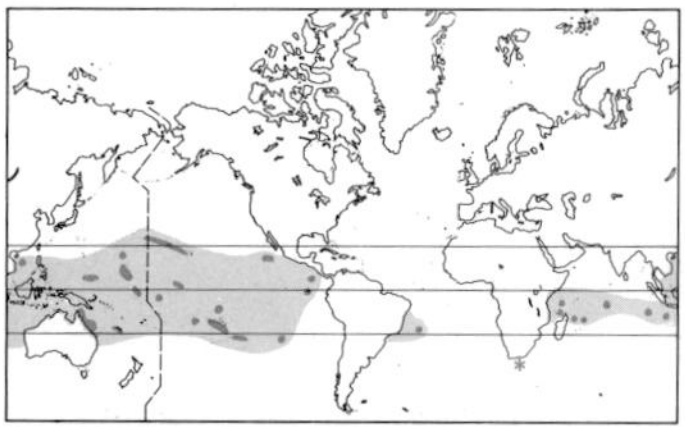

IDENTIFICATION: Sexually dimorphic. **Adult Male:** Mostly black, glossed green, with paler bar across upperwing-coverts; legs red. **Adult Female:** Mostly black above, with greyish cervical collar and pale, brownish bar across upperwing-coverts. From below the chin and throat are white; differs from female Magnificent, Christmas and Lesser in uniform black axillaries. **Juvenile:** Usually fledges with dark rusty head (some have white head) and partial or complete breastband enclosing white belly patch. The axillaries in this species are usually dark, but in some populations (e.g. Kure Atoll, northwest Hawaiian Is; Dry Tortugas, Florida) axillaries may show irregular white blocking or white tips as in Magnificent. Consult Harrison (1983) for key showing 10 immature plumages.
HABITS: Breeds colonially, usually in trees/bushes. Gregarious; follows ships. In flight, always more compact and with broader wings and distinctly shorter tail than Magnificent Frigatebird. See p. 18 for further notes.
DISTRIBUTION: Widespread throughout tropical Pacific and Indian Oceans; also at Trinidade and Martin Vaz in Atlantic. Breeding dates vary with location.
SIMILAR SPECIES: Compare with other frigatebirds (p. 239, p. 240).

Christmas Frigatebird *Fregata andrewsi* L94cm/37in W218cm/86in **P** p. 101

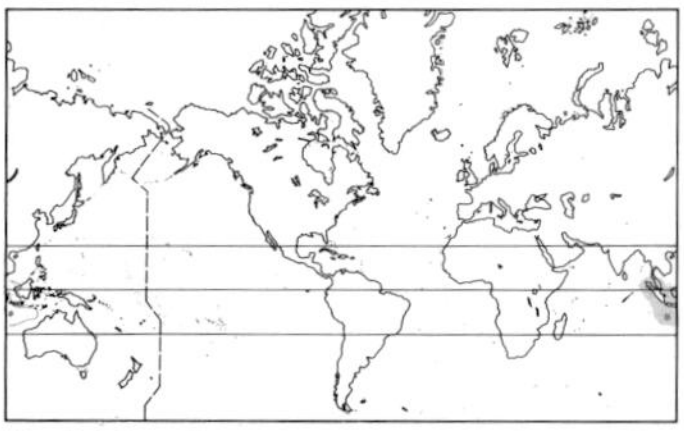

IDENTIFICATION: Sexually dimorphic. **Adult Male:** Mostly black, glossed green, with diagnostic white patch on lower belly. **Adult Female:** Mostly black above, with whitish cervical collar and pale brownish bar across upperwing-coverts. From below, breast and belly white with dark 'spurs' on sides of upper breast and a short white 'spur' extending from sides of breast to axillaries. **Juvenile:** Fledges with pale tawny-yellow head; otherwise resembles adult female, but with blackish sides of breast extending to form continuous breastband. Consult Harrison (1983) for key showing 7 immature plumages.
HABITS: Breeds colonially. Gregarious; follows ships. See p. 18 for further notes.
DISTRIBUTION: Breeds only at Christmas Is, Indian Ocean; egg-dates Apr–Jun. Disperses to coasts of Java and Borneo, some north to Thailand; vagrant Australia.
SIMILAR SPECIES: Compare with other frigatebirds (p. 239, p. 240).

Red Phalarope *Phalaropus fulicarius* L20cm/8in W37cm/15in P p. 105

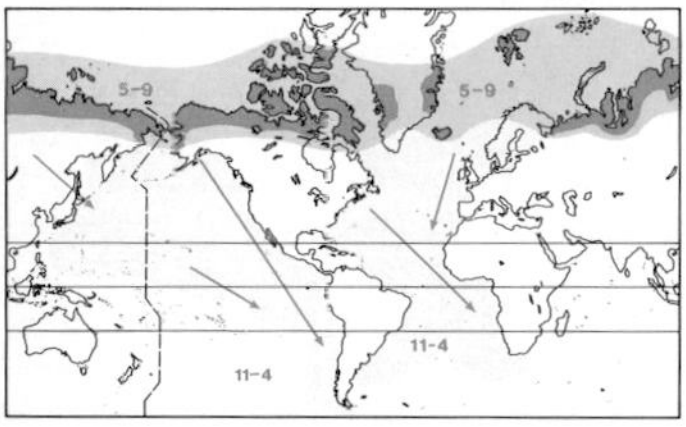

IDENTIFICATION: Sexually dimorphic during summer, females more brightly coloured. **Adult Summer:** Combination of blackish cap, white sides of face and brick-red underparts diagnostic; bill yellow, with black tip. **Adult Winter:** Mostly pale grey above, extending to sides of breast, with darker wings; underparts white; head mostly white, with blackish eye patch and darker nape. Differs from smaller, more slender, winter Red-necked Phalarope in thicker bill, usually with yellowish base, and more uniform grey upperparts. **Juvenile:** Briefly held plumage resembles summer male, but duller with white chin and throat.
HABITS: Breeds singly at freshwater pools, bogs etc; winters on open ocean. See also p. 18.
DISTRIBUTION: Breeds May–Aug in high Arctic, where circumpolar. Moves south after breeding to winter at sea: main concentrations occur Gulf of Guinea, south to Cape of Good Hope, and from Panama south to Chile.
SIMILAR SPECIES: Compare Red-necked and Wilson's Phalaropes (below).

Red-necked Phalarope *Phalaropus lobatus* L17cm/7in W34cm/13in P p. 105

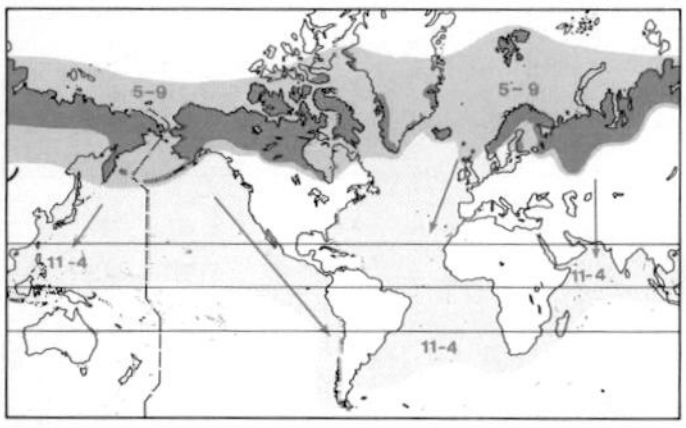

IDENTIFICATION: Smallest phalarope; sexually dimorphic during summer, females more brightly coloured. **Adult Summer:** Combination of slate-grey or brown head with white chin and red stripe on side of neck diagnostic; bill wholly black. **Adult Winter:** Mostly pale grey above, extending to sides of breast, with darker wings; underparts white; head white, with blackish eye patch and darker nape. Differs from winter Red Phalarope in smaller size, dainty jizz, needle-like black bill, and white 'braces' along outer edges of mantle and scapulars. **Juvenile:** Resembles summer male, but lacks red on neck; underparts white and buff. In first-winter plumage has diagnostic flame striping along edges of mantle and scapulars.
HABITS: Generally as for Red Phalarope but, in flight, appears smaller-winged with faster beats, more erratic twists and turns. See also p. 18.
DISTRIBUTION: Breeds May–Aug in low-Arctic regions, where circumpolar. Moves south to winter at sea: main concentrations occur off coasts of Peru, equatorial West Africa and in Arabian and South China Seas.
SIMILAR SPECIES: Compare Red and Wilson's Phalaropes (this page).

Wilson's Phalarope *Phalaropus tricolor* L22cm/9in W37cm/15in P p. 105

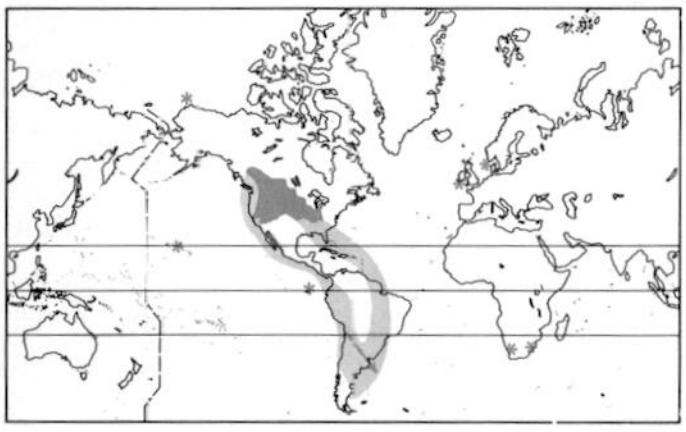

IDENTIFICATION: Largest phalarope; sexually dimorphic during summer, females more brightly coloured. **Adult Female Summer:** Mostly grey above, white below, with diagnostic black stripe beginning at eye and sweeping down neck to chestnut markings on side of lower neck, breast and back. **Adult Male Summer:** Mostly warm brown above, with short, pale supercilium; underparts whitish, with buff breastband. **Adult Winter:** Unmarked pale grey above, with whitish rump and underparts. **Juvenile:** As male summer, but upperparts browner with broad buff margins. Can be separated from winter-plumaged Red and Red-necked Phalaropes by larger size, longer bill, lack of distinct eye patch or wingbar, pale rump; long legs project past tail in flight.
HABITS: More terrestrial than other phalaropes; rare on ocean. See p. 18.
DISTRIBUTION: Breeds May–Aug inland North America. Migrates south to winter lakes and marshes of South America, mainly Patagonia, some south to Tierra del Fuego.
SIMILAR SPECIES: Compare Red-necked and Red Phalaropes (above).

Great Skua *Catharacta skua* L58cm/23in W150cm/59in **P** p. 106

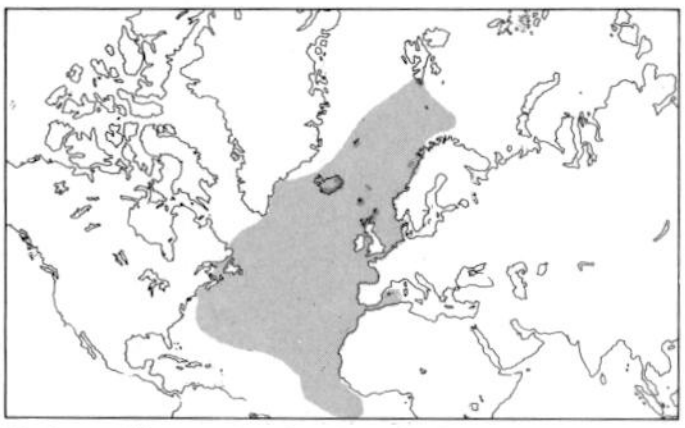

IDENTIFICATION: Largest, most powerful and predatory of the northern skuas. **Adult:** Appears uniformly brown at long range, with darker secondaries and primaries contrasting with large white flash at base of primaries. At closer range, plumage streaked/spotted rufous and buff; some have darker cap. Old/aberrant types are heavily marked with buff/cinnamon on body and upperwing-coverts, which contrast with darker primaries and secondaries. Differs from typical South Polar Skua in lack of distinct pale nuchal collar, and in reddish-brown tones in plumage, streaks/spots on upperparts and wing-coverts, little or no contrast between underwing and underbody. **Juvenile:** As adult, but upperparts much more uniform, colder brown, white in wing often reduced; underparts more rufous. **Immature:** As juvenile, but underbody sometimes paler through wear and bleaching inviting confusion with South Polar, but tone always distinctly warm (not cold, creamy-buff as in South Polar) and lacks pale nuchal collar.
HABITS: Loosely colonial; piratical feeding habits. Flight strong, purposeful, sometimes up to 50m above ocean, when broad wings, barrel-chested body and short rounded tail are easily seen.
DISTRIBUTION: North Atlantic. Breeds Apr–Sep mainly Iceland, Faeroes, Shetland and Orkney, with post-breeding dispersal to seas off northwest Africa.
SIMILAR SPECIES: Compare South Polar and Pomarine Skuas (p. 243).

Antarctic Skua *Catharacta (skua) antarctica* L63cm/25in W? **P** p. 108

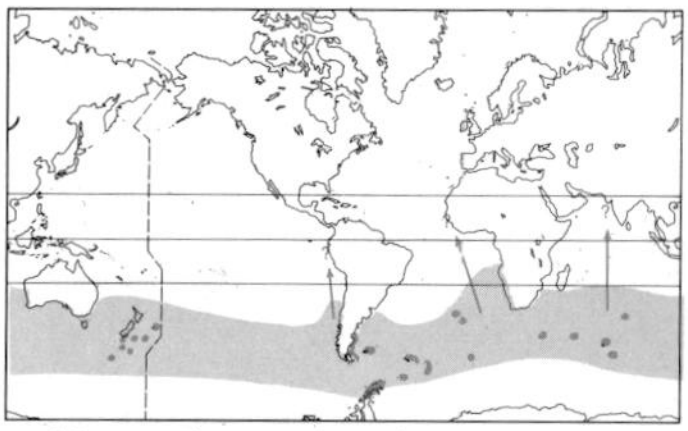

IDENTIFICATION: Resembles Great Skua in all respects and may be only a southern form of that species. Most differ in more uniform, browner upperparts, although *C. (s.)/a. hamiltoni* from Gough and Tristan da Cunha usually shows distinctly paler feather tips to upperparts (photograph p. 108). Differs from South Polar in larger size, lack of pale nuchal collar, pale feather edges on mantle, upperwing-coverts and underbody producing generally more variegated, less uniform plumage with warmer overall tone, little or no contrast between underwing and underbody. **Juvenile/Immature:** As corresponding Great Skua, but darker, more uniform.
HABITS: As for Great Skua. Compared with South Polar, larger with barrel-chested jizz; in flight tail usually lacks noticeable central projections (see South Polar and Chilean Skuas).
DISTRIBUTION: Breeds Sep–Feb coasts of Antarctic Peninsula and at many sub-Antarctic and Southern Ocean islands, dispersing north to about 30°S during austral winter. Hybridises to limited extent with Chilean Skua in southern Argentina (Devillers 1977).
SIMILAR SPECIES: Compare Chilean and South Polar Skuas (p. 242, p. 243).

Chilean Skua *Catharacta chilensis* L58cm/23in W? **P** p. 109

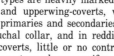

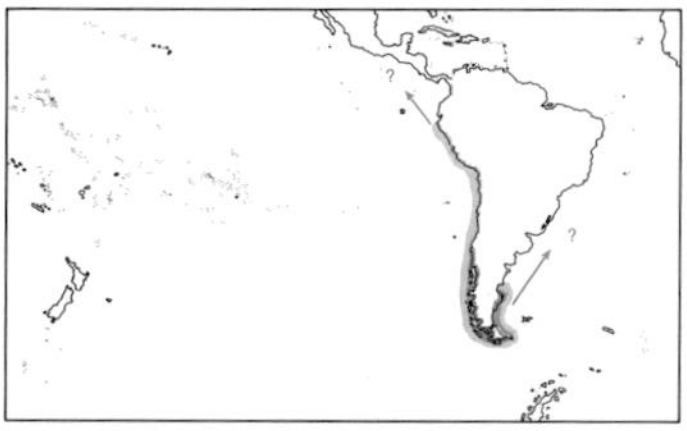

IDENTIFICATION: Bulk and jizz recall Antarctic Skua; differs in darker, more uniform upperparts, dark grey cap, and diagnostic cinnamon-coloured underbody and underwing-coverts (become paler, less noticeable in old birds). **Juvenile:** As adult, but cap greyer, with almost brick-red underbody and underwing-coverts.
HABITS: As Antarctic Skua but much less aggressive, does not attack intruders at nest. In flight, from below, tail usually shows short, blunt central projection.
DISTRIBUTION: Breeds Oct–Apr southern Chile and Argentina, where limited hybridisation occurs with Antarctic Skua (Devillers 1977); post-breeding dispersal north to at least Peru.
SIMILAR SPECIES: Compare Antarctic and South Polar Skuas (p. 242, p. 243).

South Polar Skua *Catharacta maccormicki* L53cm/21in W127cm/50in P p. 107

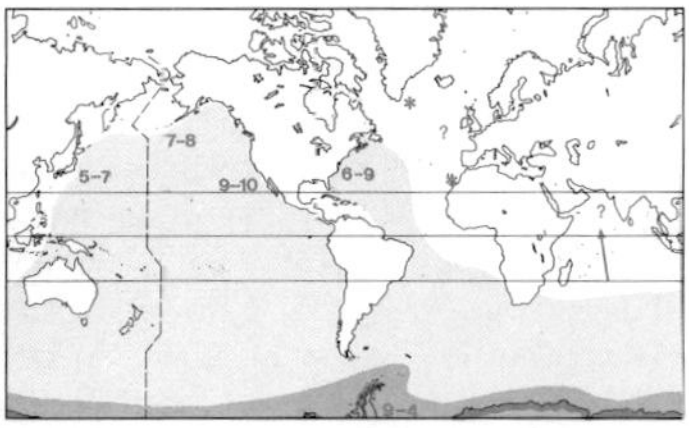

IDENTIFICATION: Smallest and only polymorphic member of *Catharacta* genus; occurs in pale, intermediate and dark morphs, with continuous intergradation between the three colour types. Most forms differ from those of Great and Antarctic Skuas in smaller size, pale nuchal collar contrasting with colder, more uniform upperparts, pale underbody contrasting with blackish-brown underwing; short, rounded tail projection. **Adult Pale Morph:** Creamy-buff head and underparts contrast with uniform brown upperparts. Some have darker cap and paler tips on upperparts (see photograph 413). **Adult Intermediate Morph:** Pale nuchal collar and underbody contrast less with dark upperparts. **Adult Dark Morph:** Almost wholly cold slate-brown; most show faint nuchal collar. At close range, look for diagnostic pale 'nose-band' around base of bill. **Juvenile:** Slate-brown; wing flashes often reduced.
HABITS: As Antarctic Skua, but shows smaller head and bill.
DISTRIBUTION: Breeds Sep–Apr Antarctic continent/Peninsula, with transequatorial migration in all three oceans but rare eastern North Atlantic, northern Indian Ocean.
SIMILAR SPECIES: Compare Great, Chilean, Antarctic and Pomarine Skuas (p. 242, p. 243).

Pomarine Skua *Stercorarius pomarinus* L56cm/22in W124cm/49in P p. 112

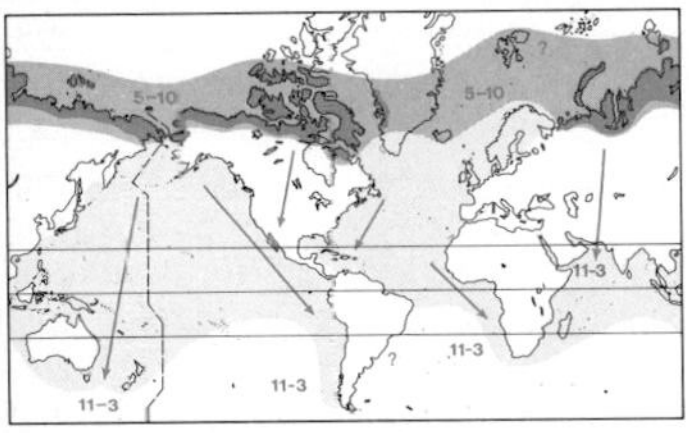

IDENTIFICATION: Polymorphic, with seasonal variation. **Adult Pale Morph:** Differs from pale Arctic in diagnostic, twisted spoon-shaped tail projections and, usually, larger size and jizz and darker cap, breastband, flanks and undertail-coverts. **Adult Summer Dark Morph:** Mostly dark brown, except for pale yellowish suffusion on cheeks and white wing flashes. **Adult Winter:** Lacks tail streamers; upper- and undertail-coverts widely barred; pale morphs have chin, throat and sides of neck darker, giving hooded effect. **Juvenile:** Mostly brown above heavily barred white and brown below. Differs from Arctic in broader, more distinct barring in more equal parallel divisions of dark and pale; unlike Arctic has pale crescent across underwing primary coverts, head usually paler or with darker cap, paler collar. Tail has small rounded projections.
HABITS: Piratical; usually larger than Arctic, with barrel-chest, broader bases to wings, larger head and heavier bill. Flight more measured, less flicking.
DISTRIBUTION: Circumpolar; breeds May–Aug, dispersing south to oceanic habitat.
SIMILAR SPECIES: Compare Arctic and Great Skuas (p. 243, p. 242).

Arctic Skua *Stercorarius parasiticus* L45cm/18in W117cm/46in P p. 110

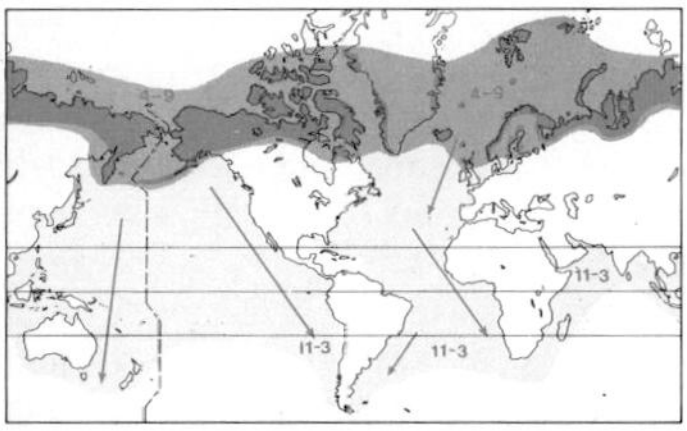

IDENTIFICATION: Polymorphic with seasonal variation. **Adult Summer Pale Morph:** Differs from pale Pomarine in shorter, pointed tail projections and, usually, smaller size and jizz, in less clear-cut cap, paler breastband, flanks and undertail-coverts. **Adult Summer Dark Morph:** Mostly dark brown, except for yellowish suffusion on cheeks and white wing patches. **Adult Winter:** Lacks tail streamers chin, throat, flanks and tail-coverts barred, but not so heavily as in Pomarine. **Juvenile:** Mostly brown, with underparts barred though not so heavily nor in such equal divisions as in Pomarine, with less distinct nuchal collar and barring on uppertail-coverts. Pointed central tail feathers project up to 2cm.
HABITS: Piratical; breeds singly or in loose colonies. Jizz and flight midway between larger, heavier, Pomarine and smaller, daintier Long-tailed, though some size overlap occurs with both.
DISTRIBUTION: Circumpolar in Arctic. Breeds Apr–Sep; disperses south to oceanic habitat.
SIMILAR SPECIES: Compare Pomarine and Long-tailed Skuas (p. 243, p. 244).

Long-tailed Skua *Stercorarius longicaudus* L54cm/21in W111cm/44in **P** p. 111

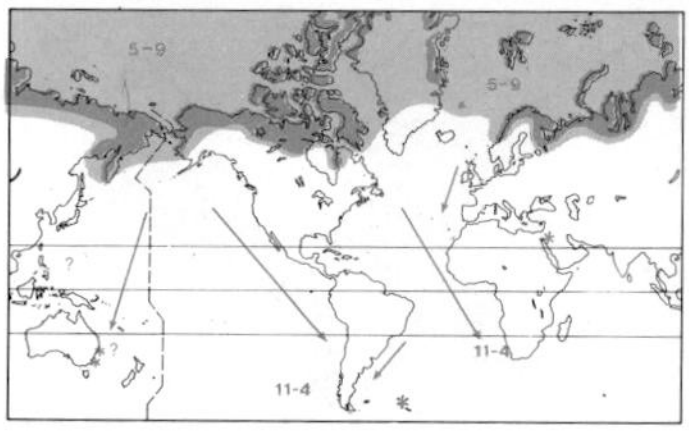

IDENTIFICATION: Polymorphic, with seasonal variation, but wholly dark morph extremely rare. **Adult Summer Pale Morph:** Differs from pale Arctic in much longer, floppy tail projections and, usually, smaller size, daintier jizz, more distinct cap, greyer upperparts contrasting with blackish trailing edge to upperwing, lack of breastband, less white on outer primaries. **Adult Winter:** Lacks tail streamers; sides of face, throat, breast and flanks darker, giving hooded effect; tail-coverts barred. **Juvenile:** Plumage colder, more grey than Arctic Skua, with wider, more apparent barring on tail-coverts, scapulars and underwing; head often whitish, with indistinct breastband. Upperwing shows only 2 white primary shafts; rounded central tail feathers project up to 4cm.
HABITS: Piratical; breeds singly or in loose colonies. Smallest, most lightly built skua, with small head, slim body, narrow-based wings and proportionately longer-based tail than Arctic; flight lighter, more buoyant.
DISTRIBUTION: Circumpolar in high Arctic. Breeds May–Sep; disperses south to oceanic habitat, mainly off Atlantic and Pacific coasts of South America and off South Africa.
SIMILAR SPECIES: Compare Arctic and Pomarine Skuas (p. 243).

Western Gull *Larus occidentalis* L64cm/25in W137cm/54in **P** p. 118

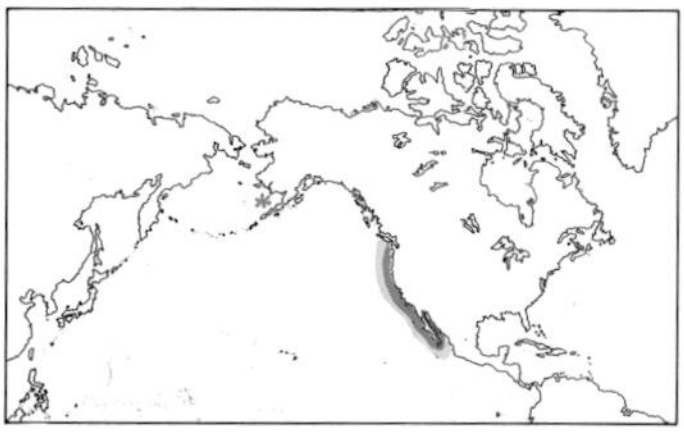

IDENTIFICATION: Large, dark-mantled gull; adult plumage acquired fourth year. **Adult:** Differs from both Herring and California Gulls in darker, slate-grey saddle and upperwings, different wingtip pattern and dusky trailing edge to white underwing. Northern birds have paler upperparts and darker eyes. Differs from Yellow-footed Gull in pink legs. **First Winter:** Difficult to separate from corresponding Herring Gull, but generally darker and greyer with denser markings on head and breast, saddle more spotted, less barred. In flight, inner primaries not so conspicuously pale as in Herring Gull. In all subsequent plumages, difference in colour of saddle enables ready separation from Herring Gull.
HABITS: Breeds colonially; almost exclusively marine; gregarious. Averages larger than Herring Gull, fiercer, more menacing jizz and heavier, more pot-bellied stance.
DISTRIBUTION: Pacific coast of North America. Breeds from British Columbia south to southern California; egg-dates May–Jul. Winters mainly within breeding range.
SIMILAR SPECIES: Compare Yellow-footed, Herring and Slaty-backed (p. 244, p. 245, p. 252).

Yellow-footed Gull *Larus livens* L69cm/27in W152cm/60in **P** pp. 118–9

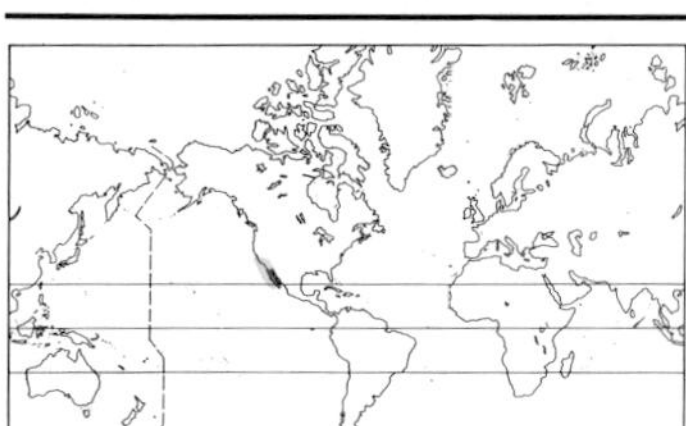

IDENTIFICATION: Large, dark-mantled gull formerly treated as a subspecies of Western Gull. Adult plumage acquired third year. **Adult:** Differs from Western Gull in larger bill and yellow (not pink) legs, yellow eye and darker grey mantle. **First Winter:** Differs from corresponding Western in whiter head, rump, lower belly and undertail-coverts, with grey feathers on mantle and back. Second-year birds differ from Herring and Western in yellow legs and black tail.
HABITS: As Western, but moult sequence 2–3 months earlier.
DISTRIBUTION: Resident Gulf of California, visiting Salton Sea and San Diego area.
SIMILAR SPECIES: Compare Western and Herring Gulls (p. 244, p. 245).

Herring Gull *Larus argentatus* L61cm/24in W147cm/58in **P** p. 114

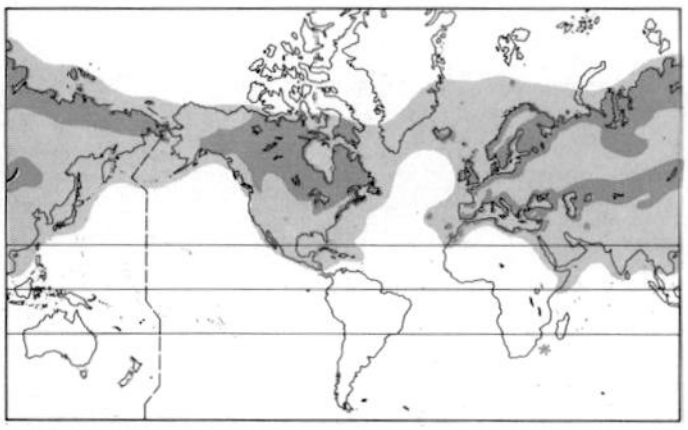

IDENTIFICATION: Most familiar large gull in North America/Europe; adult plumage acquired fourth year. Following notes refer to *L.a. argenteus* (see Grant 1982, Harrison 1983 for other subspecies). **Adult:** Head white (streaked brown in winter), mantle and upperwing pale grey with blackish primaries, the 2 outermost showing white mirrors. Differs from any race of Lesser Black-backed in paler grey upperparts; Common Gull is smaller, with larger white mirrors on outer wing, and has different bare-part colours. **First Winter:** Differs from corresponding Lesser Black-backed in pale window on inner primaries, single subterminal bar on trailing edge of upperwing, and little contrast between grey-brown rump, tail base and scapulars. In subsequent immature plumages, pale grey mantle and back enables ready separation from Lesser and Great Black-backed.
HABITS: Loosely colonial; gregarious. Opportunistic scavenger.
DISTRIBUTION: The various races have circumpolar distribution; egg-dates Apr–Jun.
SIMILAR SPECIES: Compare Lesser Black-backed, Thayer's, Western and California Gulls and immature Great Black-backed and Great Black-headed Gulls (p. 252, p. 245, p. 244, p. 245, p. 252, p. 254).

Thayer's Gull *Larus thayeri* L59cm/23in W140cm/55in **P** pp. 114–5

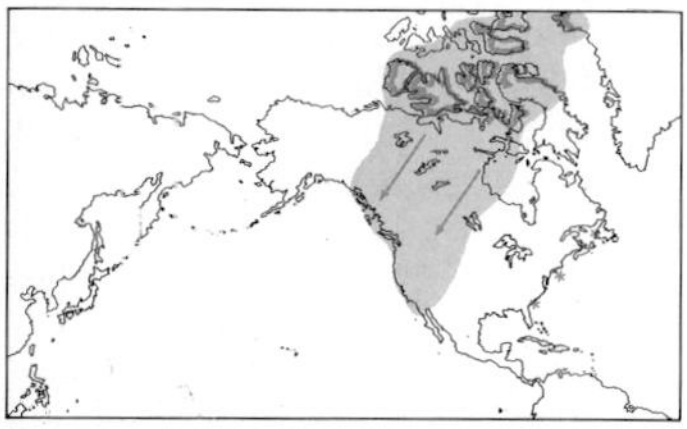

IDENTIFICATION: Formerly considered a subspecies of Herring, probably conspecific with Iceland; adult plumage acquired fourth year. **Adult:** Differs from Herring Gull in dark eye and less extensive blackish-grey wingtip with little or no black on underwing. In winter, head and sides of breast streaked grey-brown. Kumlien's Gull is smaller, with yellow eye, paler mantle and different wingtip pattern. **First Winter:** At rest Thayer's Gull is more uniformly tan-grey, with finer, more marbled plumage than Herring; the folded primaries range from tan-grey to chocolate-brown (never black) and have noticeable pale edges. In flight, from below, underside of primaries white; from above there is little contrast in plumage, inner primaries being paler with dark subterminal marks and a slightly darker trailing edge to secondaries, but never approaches contrast found in first-year Herring Gulls. In subsequent immature stages, always shows paler wingtip than Herring Gull, with white underside to primaries.
HABITS: Colonial; gregarious. Head shape rounder, bill smaller than Herring Gull.
DISTRIBUTION: Breeds northwest/Arctic Canada; egg-dates May–Jun. Winters south to Mexico.
SIMILAR SPECIES: Compare Kumlien's and Herring Gulls (p. 251, p. 245).

California Gull *Larus californicus* L54cm/21in W137cm/54in **P** p. 115

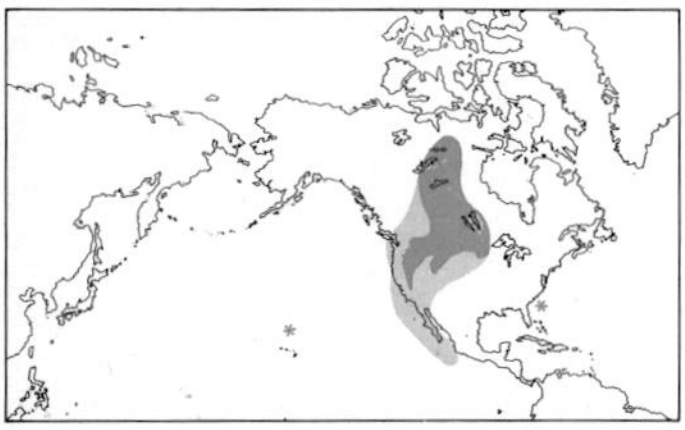

IDENTIFICATION: Abundant, grey-mantled American gull; adult plumage acquired fourth year. **Adult Summer:** Smaller than Herring Gull, differs in dark eye, greyish-yellow legs and darker grey saddle and upperwings; bill usually shows blackish mark next to red gonys. Ring-billed Gull is smaller, with shorter, banded bill, yellow eye, paler saddle and upperwings. In winter, head and nape spotted with greyish-brown. **First Winter:** Differs from most Herring and all Western Gulls of same age in clear-cut black tip to pink bill. In flight, upperparts more uniform than Herring Gull, lacking obvious contrast, tail mostly black. Second-calendar-year birds have mostly greyish-yellow bill and legs (pink in Herring Gull), with neater, greyer plumage.
HABITS: Colonial breeder; gregarious. Between Herring and Ring-billed in jizz.
DISTRIBUTION: Breeds Apr–Aug interior lakes, marshes etc of western North America, dispersing southwest to Pacific coast from British Columbia to Baja California.
SIMILAR SPECIES: Compare Herring, Ring-billed and Western Gulls (p. 245, p. 246, p. 244).

Common Gull *Larus canus* L43cm/17in W120cm/47in **P** pp. 126–7

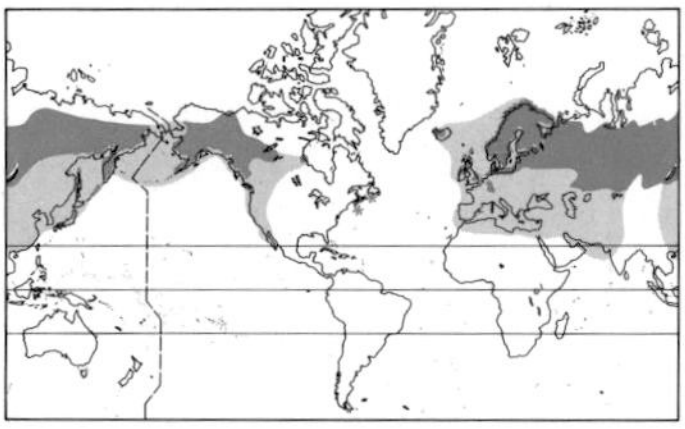

IDENTIFICATION: Medium-sized grey-mantled gull; adult plumage acquired third year. **Adult Summer:** Smaller than Ring-billed Gull; differs in shorter unmarked yellowish-green bill tapering to fine point, dark eye and darker grey upperparts. In flight, blackish outer primaries show larger white mirrors than either Ring-billed or Herring Gulls. **Adult Winter:** Bill sometimes banded. Differs from Ring-billed in more diffuse markings on head, breast and flanks, more prominent white tertial crescent when perched. **First Winter:** Differs from first-year Ring-billed in more diffuse markings on head, breast and flanks, paler carpal bar and secondaries, more prominent darker grey saddle, often mixed with brown, neater tail band. Second-year birds resemble adults, but head less white, with more black on outer wing and a smaller white mirror.
HABITS: Colonial breeder at freshwater locations.
DISTRIBUTION: Almost circumpolar in Northern Hemisphere; breeds Mar–Jul.
SIMILAR SPECIES: Compare Herring and Ring-billed Gulls (p. 245, p. 246).

Ring-billed Gull *Larus delawarensis* L45cm/18in W124cm/49in **P** p. 126

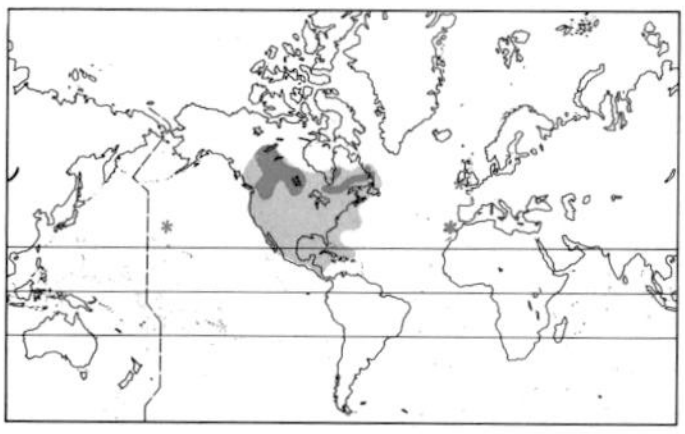

IDENTIFICATION: Medium-sized grey-mantled gull; adult plumage acquired third year. **Adult Summer:** Recalls smaller Common (Mew) Gull; differs in yellow eye, diagnostic banded bill, paler grey upperparts, smaller white mirrors on outer wing. Herring Gull is larger, with unbanded bill, pink legs, different wing pattern. **Adult Winter:** Differs from Common Gull in colour of bare parts, heavier spots (not streaks) on nape. **First Winter:** Differs from Common in longer, thicker pink bill with pronounced gonys and dark tip, spots on hindneck, crescentic markings on sides of breast and flanks, unmarked paler grey mantle and back; in flight, upperwing has paler midwing panel with darker carpal bar and secondaries, giving more contrast. From second-year Common Gull in only one small mirror, partial tail band, yellowish legs and distinctly banded bill.
HABITS: Breeds colonially at freshwater locations. All ages differ from smaller Common Gull in longer, thicker bill, heavier thickset body, fiercer facial expression and longer legs.
DISTRIBUTION: Breeds lakes, prairie marshes etc of North America; egg-dates May–Jun.
SIMILAR SPECIES: Compare Herring, Common and California Gulls (p. 245, p. 246, p. 245).

Black-headed Gull *Larus ridibundus* L38cm/15in W104cm/41in **P** p. 127

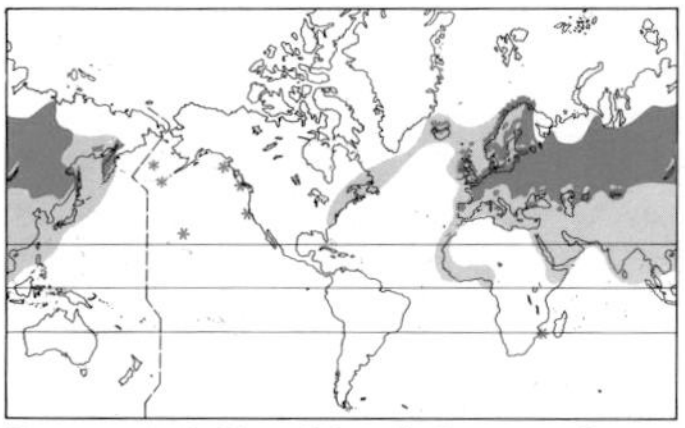

IDENTIFICATION: Small dark-hooded gull, with red bill and legs; adult plumage acquired second year. **Adult Summer:** The only European gull with brown (not black) hood and, unlike congeners, hood extends only to nape. **Adult Winter:** Head white, with dusky spot on ear-coverts. Differs from larger Mediterranean Gull in wing pattern and smaller ear-covert mark; from smaller Bonaparte's Gull in red bill and dusky inner primaries on underwing. Slender-billed Gull differs in diagnostic bill and head shape, pale eye, and lacks dark ear spot. Grey-headed and Indian Black-headed Gulls have different wing patterns. **First Winter:** As adult winter, but with black tip to bill, legs pinker, brown carpal bar on upperwing and dark band across tail. Differs from corresponding Bonaparte's in two-tone bill colour, dusky underside of primaries. **First Summer:** Has partial brown hood, tail band and carpal bar.
HABITS: The familiar small gull of Europe, found on both coasts and inland waterways. Colonial breeder, often at freshwater locations; gregarious.
DISTRIBUTION: Eurasian. Breeds Mar–Aug from Iceland and British Isles east through Europe and Asia to Kamchatka. Winters south to Florida, northwest Africa, India, China and Japan.
SIMILAR SPECIES: Little, Mediterranean, Slender-billed and Bonaparte's (p. 248, p. 249, p. 247).

Laughing Gull *Larus atricilla* L40cm/16in W103cm/41in **P** p. 124

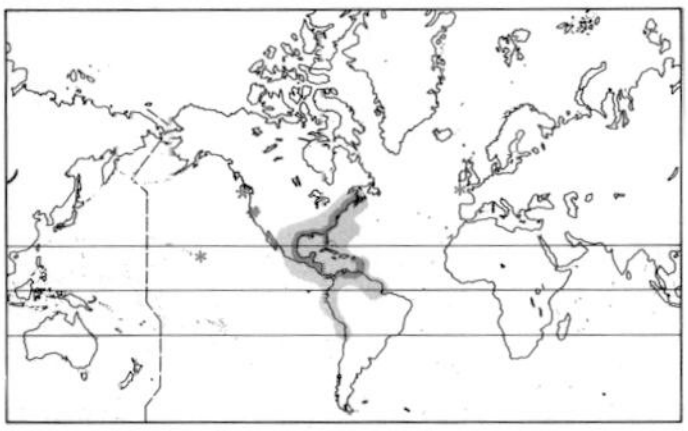

IDENTIFICATION: Small dark-hooded gull, with dull red bill and legs; adult plumage acquired third year. **Adult Summer:** The deep grey upperwing and black outer primaries lack the bold apical spots and white dividing band of Franklin's Gull; eye-crescents less prominent than in that species. **Adult Winter:** Differs from Franklin's Gull in darker wingtip pattern and less pronounced partial hood and eye-crescents. **Immature:** Less pronounced partial hood and eye-crescents than Franklin's; first-winter has more extensive tail band, darker, more dusky breast and flanks.
HABITS: Colonial breeder along coasts; gregarious. Has more rakish attenuated jizz than Franklin's, with longer, flatter crown and heavy (particularly at tip) drooping bill. In flight, wings longer and narrower, tapering to thin points, giving jaeger-like flight.
DISTRIBUTION: Eastern North America; breeds Apr–Aug from Nova Scotia south through Caribbean to Venezuela. Winters south to Brazil and northern Chile.
SIMILAR SPECIES: Compare Franklin's and Black-headed Gulls (p. 247, p. 246).

Franklin's Gull *Larus pipixcan* L35cm/14in W90cm/35in **P** pp. 124–5

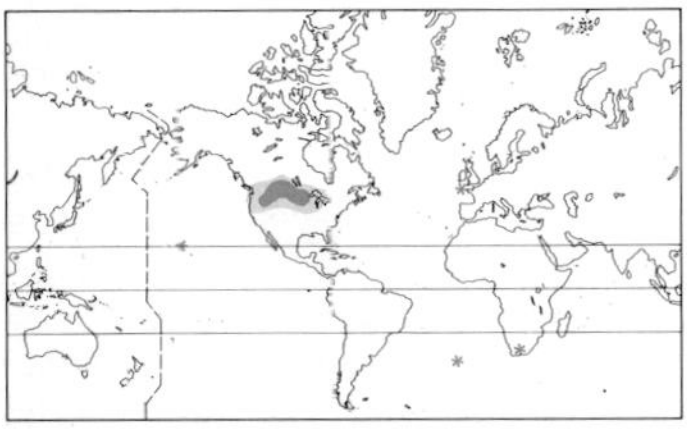

IDENTIFICATION: Small, thickset, dark-hooded gull with red legs and bill, latter with thin black subterminal band; adult plumage acquired second year. **Adult Summer:** Differs from larger, more rakish and attenuated Laughing Gull in prominent white tips to primaries and whitish band dividing blackish subterminal tip from deep grey upperwing; white eye-crescents larger, more goggle-like, an important character in all plumages. **Adult Winter:** Differs from Laughing in wingtip pattern and much more pronounced hood and white eye-crescents. **First Winter:** Head pattern as adult winter, banded tail with white outer feathers and grey centre; breast and flanks much whiter than in first-winter Laughing. **Second Year:** Differs from Laughing in darker partial hood, more pronounced eye-crescents and apical spots on wing.
HABITS: Colonial breeder; gregarious, migrates in large flocks. At all ages stockier than Laughing Gull, with more rounded wings, shorter neck, tail and legs giving chunky jizz; bill shorter, less drooping.
DISTRIBUTION: Breeds Apr–Aug inland marshes etc of North America from Canada south to Minnesota. Winters south to Peru and southern Chile.
SIMILAR SPECIES: Compare Laughing Gull (above).

Bonaparte's Gull *Larus philadelphia* L31cm/12in W82cm/32in **P** p. 125

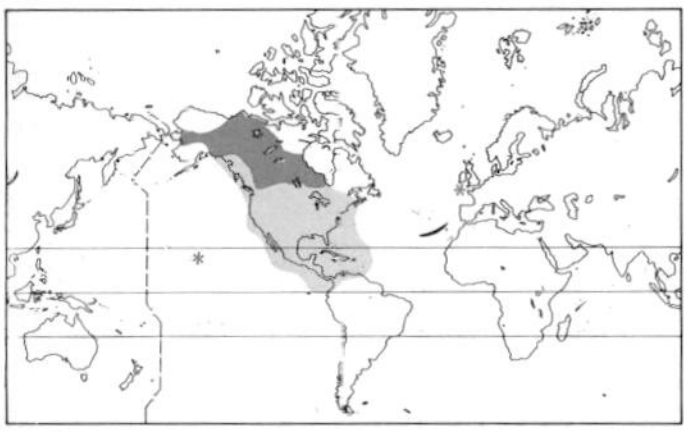

IDENTIFICATION: Tiny dark-hooded gull, with black bill and red legs; adult plumage acquired second year. **Adult Summer:** Much smaller than Laughing or Franklin's Gulls. Differs in thin white eye-crescents and distinctive white leading edge to outer wing. **Adult Winter:** Differs from larger Black-headed Gull in smaller, thinner black bill, grey wash to sides of breast, and neat black trailing edge to white (not dusky) primaries on underwing. **First Winter:** Head and sides of breast as adult winter. In flight, upperwing differs from Black-headed in darker carpal bar; underwing as adult.
HABITS: Colonial breeder, nesting in trees; gregarious, often migrates in flocks. Compared with Black-headed Gull, smaller, daintier, with dipping, buoyant flight recalling Little Gull.
DISTRIBUTION: Breeds May–Aug in North American forest belts; winters south to Mexico.
SIMILAR SPECIES: Compare Black-headed and Little Gulls (p. 246, p. 248).

Little Gull *Larus minutus* L27cm/11in W64cm/25in — **P** p. 128

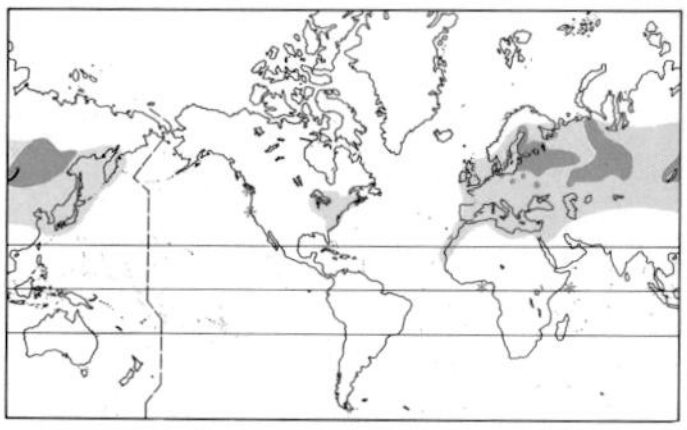

IDENTIFICATION: Smallest gull, bill blackish-red, legs red; adult plumage acquired second year. **Adult Summer:** Combination of blackish hood and dark underwing with conspicuous white trailing edge diagnostic. **Adult Winter:** Small size and diagnostic underwing separate it from all other gulls. Bonaparte's Gull is larger, has white underwing, and lacks dark cap of winter and immature Little Gulls. **First Winter:** Small size and distinct blackish 'M' mark across upperparts separate this from all gulls but larger Ross's. Differs from Ross's in dark cap to head, more black on outer primaries, and has dusky (not white) secondaries. Immature Black-legged Kittiwake is larger, with dark nape. Second-year birds resemble adults, but have less black on underwing, outer primaries marked with black above.

HABITS: Breeds colonially; gregarious. When perched, dainty compact stance, rounded crown and short legs give tern-like jizz. Flight tern-like and buoyant, dipping to surface, legs trailing.

DISTRIBUTION: Breeds Apr–Aug eastern and western Siberia, Baltic Basin, southeast Europe and North America; winters south to Florida (rare), Mediterranean, Black and Japanese Seas.

SIMILAR SPECIES: Compare Ross's and Bonaparte's Gulls, Black-legged Kittiwake and Black-headed Gull (p. 248, p. 247, p. 253, p. 246).

Ross's Gull *Rhodostethia rosea* L31cm/12in W84cm/33in — **P** p. 129

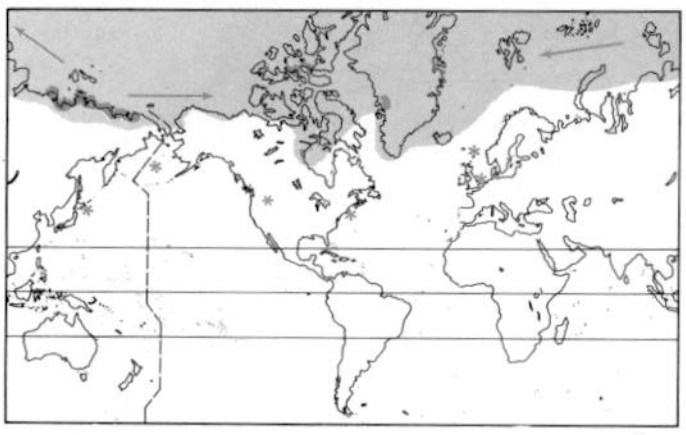

IDENTIFICATION: Small distinctive gull, bill black, legs red; adult plumage acquired second year. **Adult Summer:** Combination of black necklace, pale grey upperparts, rosy underparts and wedge-shaped tail diagnostic. **Adult Winter:** Lacks collar; pink underparts reduced or absent. Differs from Black-headed and Bonaparte's Gulls in lack of black on primaries, dusky eye-crescent and diagnostic wedge-shaped tail. **First Winter:** As adult winter, but has 'M' mark across upperparts and partial tail band. Differs from corresponding Little Gull in lack of distinctive cap, less distinct 'M' mark but which joins across back, wedge-shaped tail.

HABITS: Small high-Arctic gull; breeds on river deltas, frequents pack ice in winter. In all plumages note chunky compact body, long narrow wings and wedge-shaped tail.

DISTRIBUTION: Confined to high Arctic; breeds May–Aug. Usually winters within Arctic Circle, vagrants south to USA, British Isles and Japan.

SIMILAR SPECIES: Compare Little and Bonaparte's Gulls, Black- and Red-legged Kittiwakes (p. 248, p. 247, p. 253).

Sabine's Gull *Larus sabini* L34cm/13in W89cm/35in — **P** pp. 128–9

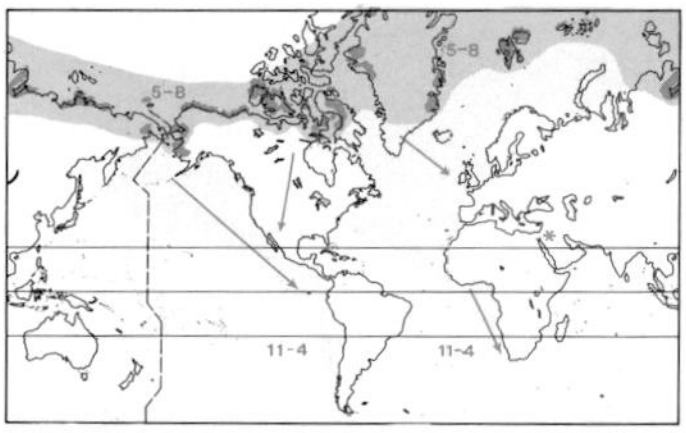

IDENTIFICATION: Small distinctive gull, bill black with yellow tip; adult plumage acquired second year. **Adult Summer:** Combination of small size, forked tail, dark hood and striking tricoloured upperwings diagnostic. **Adult Winter:** Black on head confined to patch or half collar over nape. **Juvenile:** Combination of tricoloured upperwings, brownish crown and nape with scaled brown and white upperparts diagnostic; underwing has dusky bar. At longer range can be confused with first-winter Black-legged Kittiwake, but is smaller, with lighter more tern-like flight, darker head, tricoloured upperparts.

HABITS: Breeds colonially; gregarious, migrates in small flocks; exclusively marine. Flight tern-like, with wings rising and falling well above and below body in steady rhythm.

DISTRIBUTION: Circumpolar in high Arctic; breeds May–Aug. Migrates south to winter off western South America and coasts of Namibia and South Africa.

SIMILAR SPECIES: Compare Black- and Red-legged Kittiwakes (p. 253).

Audouin's Gull *Larus audouinii* L50cm/20in W127cm/50in **P** p. 132

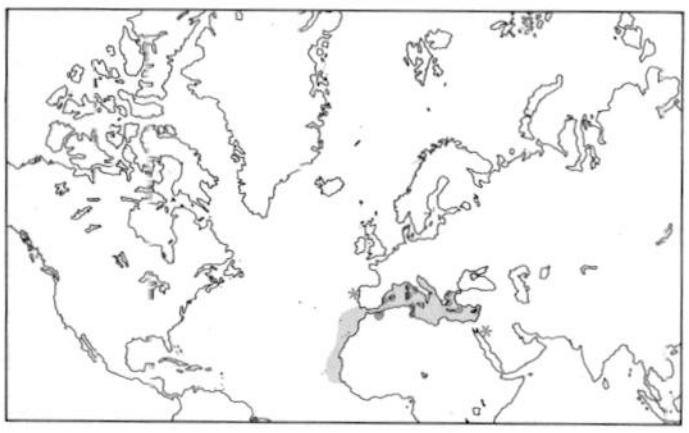

IDENTIFICATION: Large grey-mantled gull; bill dark red with black subterminal band and yellow tip, legs olive. Adult plumage acquired fourth year. **Adult:** Recalls larger Herring, but dark bill and eye impart distinctly different facial aspect. Blackish outer wing more prominent than Herring and lacks that species' prominent white mirrors. **Juvenile:** Diagnostic grey legs. Whiter-headed than corresponding local race of Herring; more uniformly black primaries, secondaries and tail contrast with whitish 'V' shape across tail-coverts. At close range, pale flanks show diagnostic, almost triangular-shaped dark marks (E. Mackrill pers. comm.). In all subsequent immature plumages, primaries, secondaries and their coverts remain darker than in Herring.
HABITS: Colonial breeder; gregarious; exclusively marine. Smaller than Herring Gull, more slender, with smaller head, more sloping crown and shorter, deeper bill
DISTRIBUTION: One of world's rarest gulls. Breeds Apr–Aug Mediterranean Sea, dispersing west to winter Atlantic shores of Morocco, south to Senegal.
SIMILAR SPECIES: Compare Herring and Lesser Black-backed Gulls (p. 245, p. 252).

Mediterranean Gull *Larus melanocephalus* L40cm/16in W106cm/42in **P** p. 131

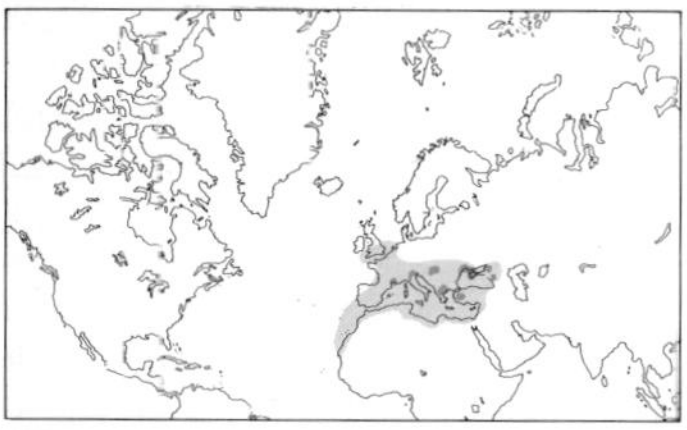

IDENTIFICATION: Medium-sized; the only hooded gull in Europe with unmarked, white wings; bill and legs scarlet. Adult plumage acquired third year. **Adult Summer:** Combination of jet-black hood, scarlet bare parts and wholly white wings diagnostic. **Adult Winter:** Hood replaced by dark eye-crescent and dusky ear-coverts (usually forming extensive patch and extending diffusely over crown). Differs from Black-headed in duller bare parts, different wing pattern and larger ear spot. **First Winter:** Recalls corresponding Common, but has different structure, blackish bill and legs, ill-defined partial hood, more contrasting upperwing pattern, narrower tail band. Subsequent plumage stages more likely to be confused with Black-headed but, at all ages, is larger, more robust and domineering, menacing facial expression, broader, more rounded wings and longer, thicker, slightly drooping bill; plumage differs in wing pattern, colour and extent of hood.
HABITS: Colonial breeder; loosely gregarious.
DISTRIBUTION: Breeding confined mainly to islands in Black and Aegean Seas north to Crimea; egg dates May–Jun. Winter range south to Mauritania and north to British Isles.
SIMILAR SPECIES: Compare Black-headed and Common Gulls (p. 246)

Slender-billed Gull *Larus genei* L43cm/17in W105cm/41in **P** pp. 132–3

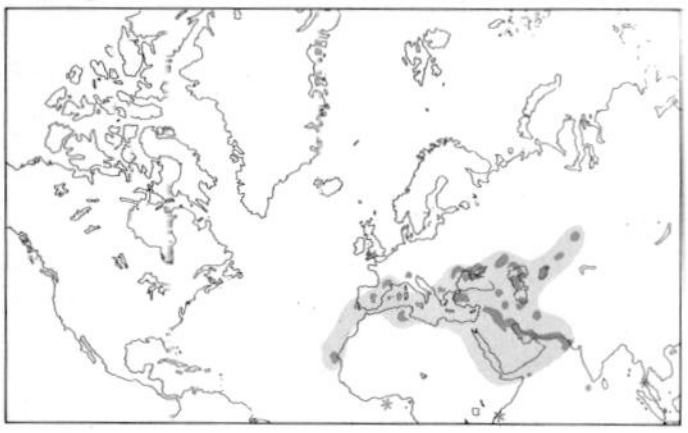

IDENTIFICATION: Medium-sized white-headed gull, scarlet bill and legs; adult plumage acquired second year. **Adult Summer:** Upperwing pattern recalls Black-headed, but head and iris white with noticeably longer bill, and pink flush to underparts. **Adult Winter:** Head shows barely perceptible ear spot, but never so pronounced as in Black-headed. **First Winter:** Resembles smaller Black-headed, but paler, more washed-out pattern on upperwing and virtually all-white head (ear spot shows only at close range); legs and bill pale orange. In winter and immature plumages, best separated from Black-headed by structural differences: Slender-billed is slightly larger, with distinctly longer, more sloping forehead running into a longer, more drooping bill. In flight, has distinctive long-necked, long-tailed jizz with humpbacked profile.
HABITS: Nests colonially in marshes and swamps; gregarious; winters along shorelines.
DISTRIBUTION: Eurasia. Breeds Apr–Aug western Mediterranean, Black and Caspian Seas to Karachi, also Mauritania; winters Mediterranean Basin, Red Sea and Persian Gulf.
SIMILAR SPECIES: Compare winter Black-headed Gull (p. 246).

Glaucous-winged Gull *Larus glaucescens* L65cm/26in W147cm/58in **P** p. 120

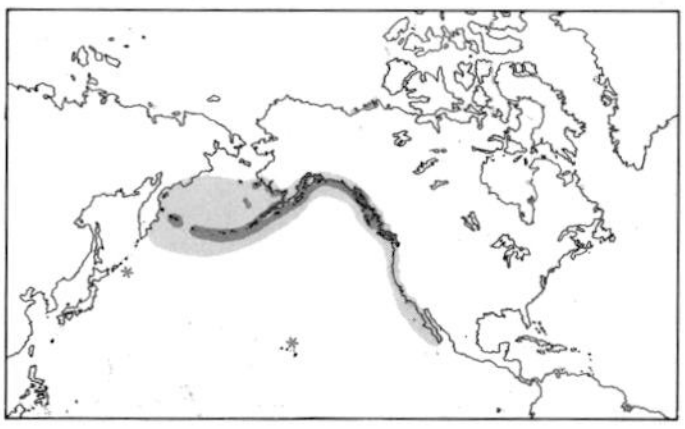

IDENTIFICATION: Large, grey-mantled gull; bill yellow, legs pink; adult plumage acquired fourth year. **Adult Summer:** Differs from Herring in slate-grey (not black) tips to outer primaries and white undersides to all primaries. Thayer's and Kumlien's are smaller, with different wingtip pattern; at rest their folded primaries project well past tail. Glaucous and Iceland have unmarked silvery-white primaries. **Adult Winter:** Head and hindneck streaked grey-brown. **First Winter:** Differs from Herring and Western in uniform, pinkish- or buffish-grey primaries; from Glaucous in mostly black bill and uniform brown tail. In all subsequent stages, combination of large size, outer primary colour and white underwing enables separation from all congeners.
HABITS: Most abundant gull of northeast Pacific; colonial; feeds along coasts, rubbish tips etc. Compared with Herring Gull, larger, more menacing.
DISTRIBUTION: North Pacific; breeds May–Sep, winters south to California.
SIMILAR SPECIES: Compare Glaucous, Herring and Thayer's Gulls (p. 250, p. 245).

Glaucous Gull *Larus hyperboreus* L71cm/28in W158cm/62in **P** pp. 120–1

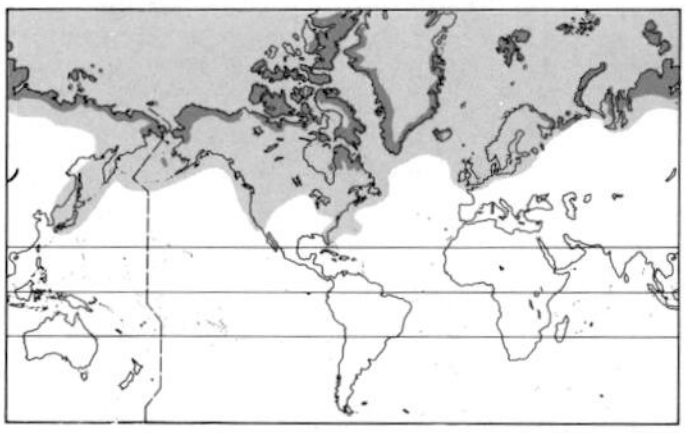

IDENTIFICATION: Large, white-winged gull, bill yellow, legs pink; adult plumage acquired fourth year. At any age, the white outer primaries distinguish it from all other gulls except Iceland. **Adult Summer:** Differs from smaller Iceland in heavier pot-bellied jizz, flatter crown giving fiercer facial expression, and proportionately longer, more massive bill. At rest wings project only a little past tail, giving rear end a decidedly blunt appearance, increasing disparity with more elegant and attenuated Iceland Gull. These structural differences are useful characters at all ages. **Adult Winter:** Head and sides of breast streaked grey-brown. **First Winter:** From Iceland Gull by structural differences and diagnostic black-tipped pink bill. In subsequent plumages, use structural differences to separate from Iceland. From adult Glaucous-winged Gull by unmarked primaries, from first-winter Glaucous-winged by two-toned (not black) bill.
HABITS: Solitary or colonial breeder; gregarious; feeds along coasts, rubbish tips etc.
DISTRIBUTION: Circumpolar; breeds May–Sep mainly north of Arctic Circle, wintering from southern parts of breeding range south to California, Florida, France, China and Japan.
SIMILAR SPECIES: Compare Glaucous-winged and Iceland Gulls (this page).

Iceland Gull *Larus glaucoides* L61cm/24in W140cm/55in **P** p. 121

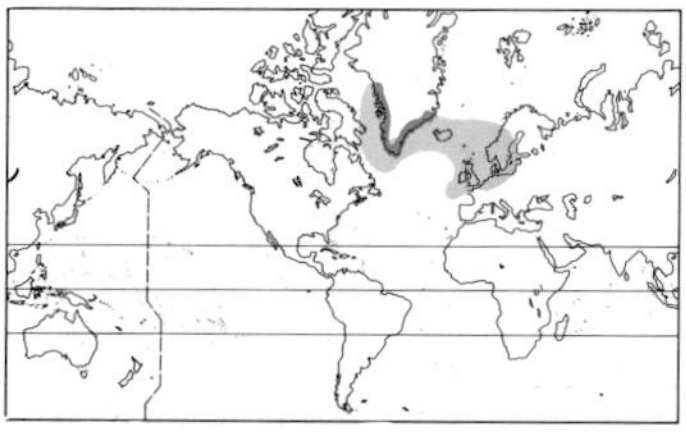

IDENTIFICATION: Large, white-winged gull, bill yellow, legs pink; adult plumage acquired fourth year. At any age, the white outer primaries distinguish it from all other gulls except larger Glaucous and dissimilar Ivory Gull. There is some overlap in plumage features of Glaucous and Iceland Gulls, and structural differences between the two are therefore important field characters. Compared with Glaucous, Iceland is usually distinctly smaller, more petite, with more rounded crown giving more gentle facial expression; proportionately shorter, less heavy bill; wings narrower, projecting well past tail when perched. Plumages develop as Glaucous, but first-winter more deeply barred, with mostly dark bill, pinkish at base, whiter terminal fringe to tail.
HABITS: Less predatory than Glaucous Gull, otherwise very similar.
DISTRIBUTION: North Atlantic. Breeds May–Sep from Ellesmere Is and Greenland south to Baffin Is, Canada; occasionally Iceland. Winters south to Virginia and northern France.
SIMILAR SPECIES: Glaucous, Thayer's and Kumlien's Gulls (p. 250, p. 245, p. 251).

Kumlien's Gull *Larus (glaucoides) kumlieni* L61cm/24in W140cm/55in **P** p. 122

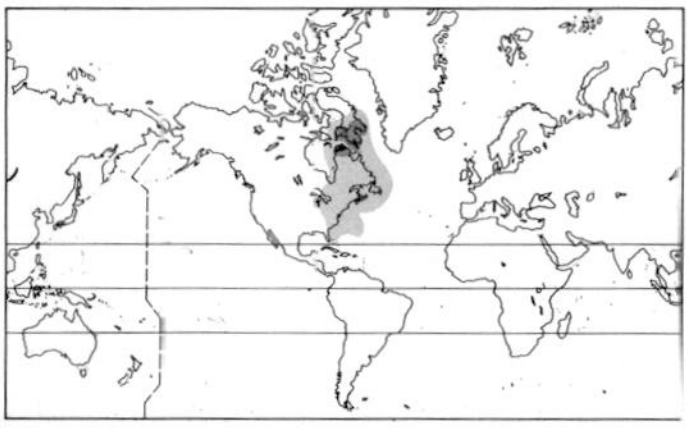

IDENTIFICATION: Large pale-winged gull, bill yellow, legs pink; adult plumage acquired fourth year. The taxonomic status of this gull is still vexed; it is variously considered a subspecies of Iceland, a hybrid population of Iceland x Thayer's or even a separate species. **Adult:** Differs from typical Iceland in variable slate or black outer web and subterminal bar on outer 5 primaries and deeper pink legs. Differs from Thayer's in paler iris, less black or slate on outer primaries, with paler grey mantle and upperparts. Separation of immatures from those of true Iceland remains questionable (the possibility of hybrids should always be considered), although typical Iceland have silvery-white outer primaries whereas Kumlien's have grey or buff-grey outer primaries with a more uniform pale grey tail. From first-winter Thayer's by lack of solid brown or dark grey subterminal tail band, and uniform whitish flight feathers, paler than upperwing-coverts.
HABITS: Little known; presumably as for pure Iceland.
DISTRIBUTION: Breeds May–Sep Baffin Is, Canada, wintering on Atlantic coasts south to Long Is, USA.
SIMILAR SPECIES: Iceland, Thayer's and Glaucous-winged Gulls (p. 250, p. 245, p. 250).

Ivory Gull *Pagophila eburnea* L43cm/17in W110cm/43in **P** pp. 122–3

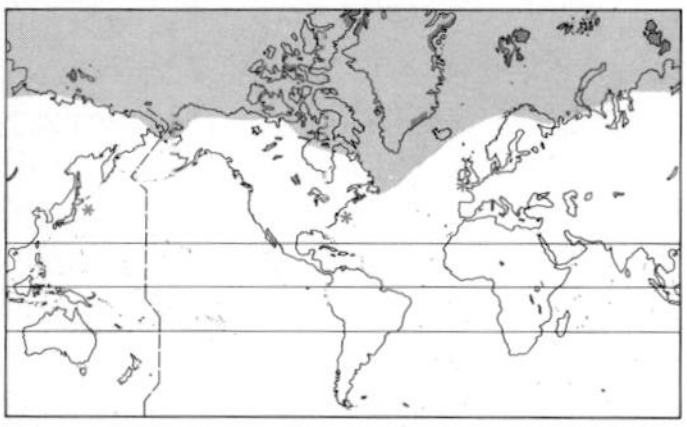

IDENTIFICATION: Medium-sized, pigeon-like gull; bill greyish-green with yellow tip, legs blackish. Adult plumage acquired second year. **Adult:** Distinctive, the only all-white gull. **First Winter:** Unlike any other gull, mostly white with blackish face mask and varying amounts of black spots on upperparts; at close range, shows black tips to primaries and tail.
HABITS: A characteristic bird of Arctic pack ice, strikingly white at all ages. When perched, high-domed crown, plump body and short thickset legs impart pigeon-like gait and jizz. Flight buoyant, rather light and graceful for such a long, broad-winged and heavy-bodied gull. Solitary or colonial breeder; loosely gregarious outside breeding season.
DISTRIBUTION: Confined to high Arctic; breeds Jun–Sep. Winters within drift ice south to Newfoundland.
SIMILAR SPECIES: None, but beware any albino gull.

Heermann's Gull *Larus heermanni* L49cm/19in W130cm/51in **P** p. 123

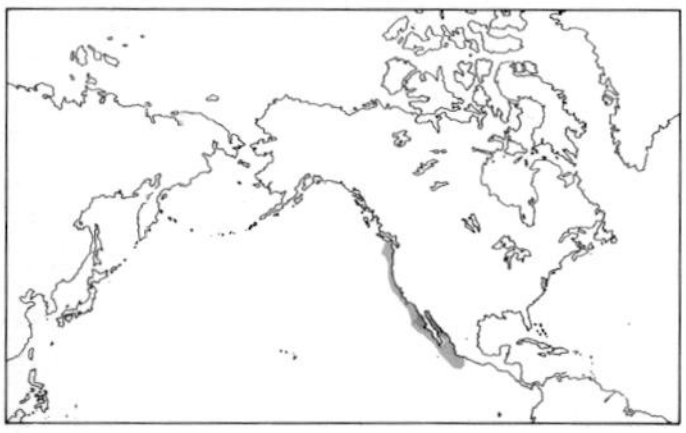

IDENTIFICATION: Distinctive gull, bill red with black tip, legs black; adult plumage acquired third year. **Adult Summer:** The only dusky gull of western North America. Combination of red bill, white hood and grey plumage diagnostic. **Adult Winter:** Similar, but with dusky hood. **Juvenile:** Wholly brown, but with paler feather edges giving scaled appearance; bill pink, with dark tip. **First Winter/Immature:** As juvenile but more uniform, lacks pale edges to feathers, becoming greyer with advancing maturity; bill first yellow, then red, as adult.
HABITS: Breeds colonially; almost exclusively marine. Flight buoyant, with long, angled wings and rhythmic flicking wingbeats; brown juveniles/first-winters at long range can thus suggest skua spp.
DISTRIBUTION: Pacific coast of North America; breeds Mar–Jun mainly on Raza Is, Gulf of California, dispersing north to British Columbia, south to southern Mexico.
SIMILAR SPECIES: None within range.

Great Black-backed Gull *Larus marinus* L75cm/30in W160cm/63in P p. 116

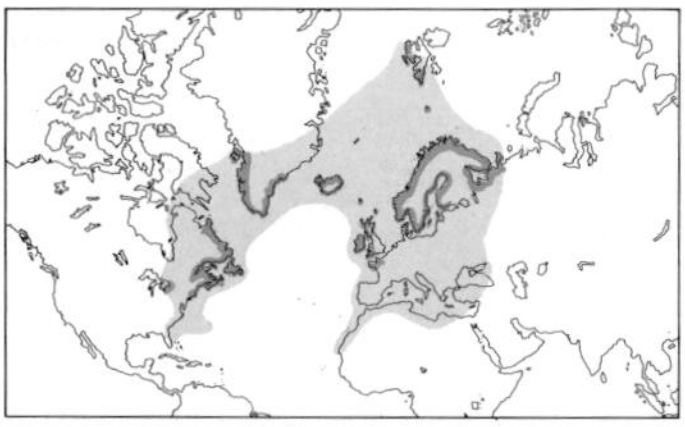

IDENTIFICATION: Largest black-backed gull in North Atlantic; bill yellow, legs pink. Adult plumage acquired fourth year. **Adult:** Differs from nominate Lesser Black-backed Gull in heavier bill, pink legs and diagnostic mirror pattern on upperwing. **First Winter:** Very like first-winter Herring and Lesser Black-backed Gulls, but head whiter with more distinct openly chequered upperparts and upperwing-coverts. From second year onwards, combination of whiter head and darker saddle enables separation from all subsequent ages of Herring Gull; from nominate Lesser Black-backed Gull by structure and upperwing pattern.
HABITS: Colonial or solitary breeder; loosely gregarious. Feeds along coasts and rubbish tips, and offshore over ocean. The sheer bulk and domineering jizz are distinct from both Herring and Lesser Black-backed, with heavier bill, fiercer facial expression and barrel-chest.
DISTRIBUTION: Breeds Apr–Sep coasts of North Atlantic from North Carolina north to Spitsbergen, coasts of Russia, south to France. Winters south to Florida and Mediterranean Sea.
SIMILAR SPECIES: Compare Herring and Lesser Black-backed Gulls (p. 245, p. 252).

Lesser Black-backed Gull *Larus fuscus* L56cm/22in W140cm/55in P pp. 116–7

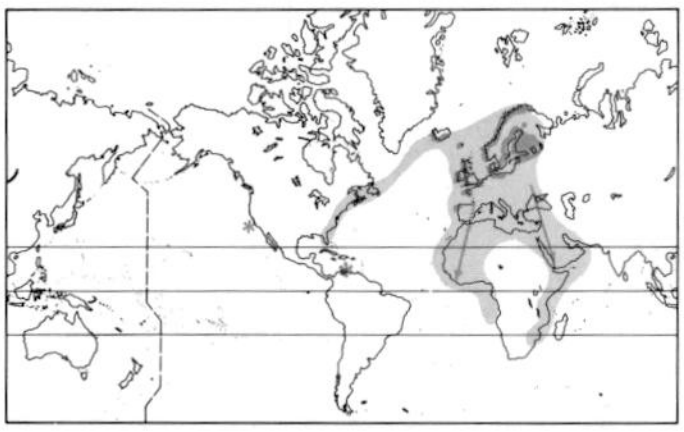

IDENTIFICATION: Large black-backed gull, bill and legs yellow; adult plumage acquired fourth year. **Adult Summer:** Colour of upperwings and saddle varies between blackish (*fuscus*) and slate-grey (*graellsii*). Both races differ from much larger Great Black-backed Gull in yellow, not pink, legs and in wingtip pattern. **Adult Winter:** Little difference in *fuscus*, but *graellsii* has heavy grey-brown streaking on head and sides of breast. **First Winter:** Legs pink, bill black. Differs from corresponding Herring Gull in uniformly dark outer wing and broader dark trailing edge, imparting more uniform darker appearance to upperparts which contrast with whiter rump and uppertail-coverts, tail band also more distinct. In subsequent plumages, differences in colour of saddle enable ready separation from Herring Gull.
HABITS: Colonial breeder; gregarious. Averages smaller than Herring Gull, with lighter jizz.
DISTRIBUTION: Northeast Atlantic; breeds Apr–Aug Scandinavia and British Isles, south to northwest Spain. Winters south to southwest Africa and Tanzania; casual eastern USA.
SIMILAR SPECIES: Compare Great Black-backed, Herring, Kelp and Audouin's (p. 252, p. 245, p. 253, p. 249).

Slaty-backed Gull *Larus schistisagus* L64cm/25in W147cm/58in P p. 117

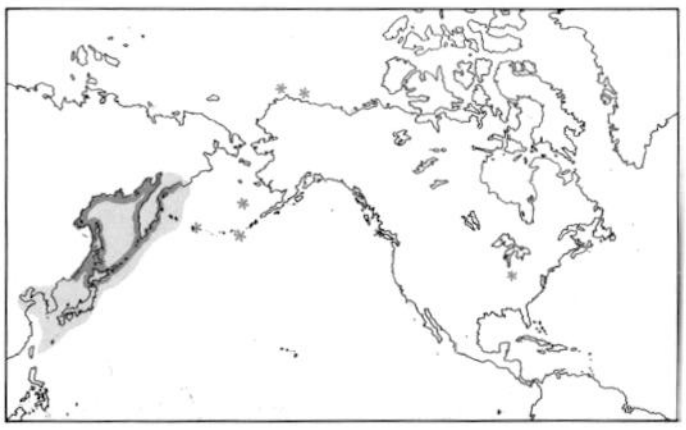

IDENTIFICATION: Large, dark-backed gull, bill yellow, legs pink; adult plumage acquired fourth year. **Adult Summer:** Differs from Western Gull in darker, almost black saddle and upperwings, with broader, more conspicuous white trailing edge to wing and tertials. From above, blackish tips to outer 4–5 primaries are usually separated from slate-grey upperwing by indistinct whitish band; from below, outer primaries are grey (not black). Black-tailed Gull is smaller, with banded bill and tail, yellow legs. **First Winter:** Differs from corresponding Western Gull in white head and paler underparts, with distinct pale window on inner primaries and broader dark band along trailing edge of upperwing. **First Summer:** Very much paler than any stage of Western Gull, more like a large, bleached-out Herring Gull. **Second Winter:** More marked on head and underparts than Western Gull, with darker saddle.
HABITS: Colonial breeder, gregarious. Slightly heavier, more powerful jizz than Western.
DISTRIBUTION: Breeds May–Aug Asiatic coasts of North Pacific. Winters south to Japan.
SIMILAR SPECIES: Compare Black-tailed, Western and Herring Gulls (p. 258, p. 244, p. 245).

Kelp Gull *Larus dominicanus* L58cm/23in W135cm/53in **P** p. 136

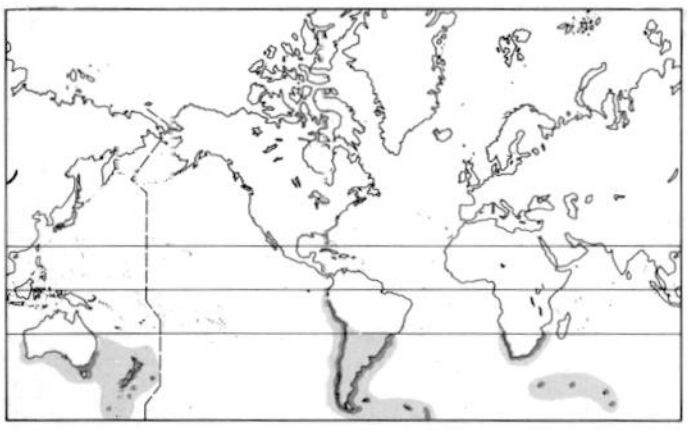

IDENTIFICATION: Large black-backed gull, bill yellow, legs olive; adult plumage acquired fourth year. **Adult:** Distinctive; the only large, black-backed and wholly white-tailed gull breeding in Southern Hemisphere. Differs from migrant Lesser Black-backed Gull in dark iris, olive legs, larger size, more thickset jizz, the wings projecting only a short way past tail when standing, blacker saddle and upperwings. **First Winter:** Differs from Pacific Gull in smaller size, smaller blackish bill; from first-winter Lesser Black-backed in structure and brown (not pink) legs. In all subsequent plumages, bill and tail colour enables separation from other Southern Hemisphere dark-backed gulls.

HABITS: The most widespread and frequently met with black-backed gull in the Southern Hemisphere. Colonial breeder; gregarious; feeds at sea and inland, follows ships.

DISTRIBUTION: Circumpolar in Southern Hemisphere; breeding dates dependent upon location.

SIMILAR SPECIES: Compare Pacific, Lesser Black-backed, Dolphin and Band-tailed Gulls (p. 257, p. 252, p. 259, p. 257).

Black-legged Kittiwake *Larus tridactyla* L41cm/16in W91cm/36in **P** p. 130

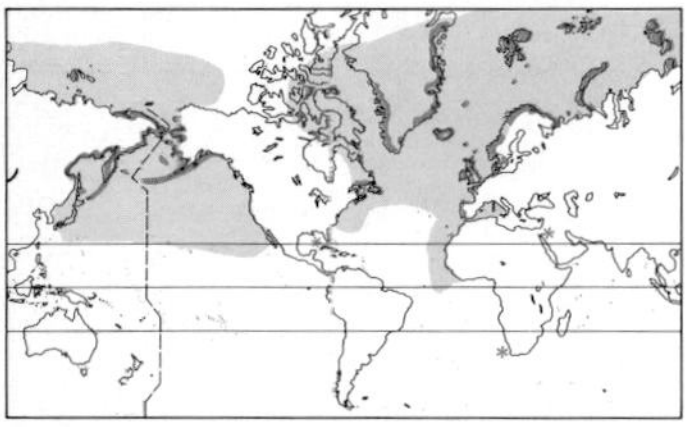

IDENTIFICATION: Medium-sized pelagic gull; adult plumage acquired second year. **Adult Summer:** Combination of unmarked yellow bill, black legs and wholly black wingtips diagnostic. Differs from Red-legged Kittiwake in paler grey upperparts, black legs. **Adult Winter:** Head and nape smudged with grey. **First Winter:** Bill black; head pattern as adult winter, but with black hindcollar; broad blackish 'M' mark across upperparts and black tip to slightly forked tail. Differs from juvenile Sabine's Gull in larger size, nape collar and 'M' mark; from Ross's Gull in hindcollar, more definite 'M' mark and tail shape. First-winter Red-legged Kittiwake lacks 'M' mark.

HABITS: More pelagic outside breeding season than most gulls; attends trawlers, follows ships, an accomplished marine scavenger. Colonial breeder; gregarious.

DISTRIBUTION: Almost circumpolar; breeds Apr–Aug Arctic coasts of America and Asia, and in North Pacific and Atlantic Oceans. Winters south to California, New Jersey and Mediterranean.

SIMILAR SPECIES: Compare Red-legged Kittiwake, Ross's and Sabine's Gulls (p. 253, p. 248).

Red-legged Kittiwake *Larus brevirostris* L38cm/15in W85cm/33in **P** pp. 130–1

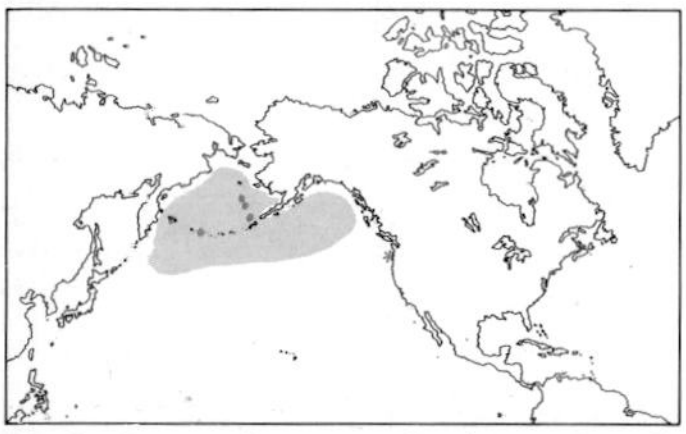

IDENTIFICATION: Medium-sized pelagic gull; adult plumage acquired second year. **Adult Summer:** Differs from slightly larger Black-legged Kittiwake in darker, more uniform grey upperwings with wider white trailing edge, less defined black wingtips, greyer underwings and bright red legs. **Adult Winter:** Head and nape smudged with grey. **First Winter/Immature:** Unlike Black-legged Kittiwake, lacks both the 'M' mark across upperwings and black tip to tail, has paler hindcollar and a ragged white triangle midway along trailing edge of upperwing.

HABITS: As Black-legged Kittiwake, but smaller, more compact, head rounder, bill shorter.

DISTRIBUTION: Breeds islands in or bordering Bering Sea; egg-dates Jul. Winters within breeding area.

SIMILAR SPECIES: Compare Black-legged Kittiwake and Sabine's Gull (p. 253, p. 248).

Great Black-headed Gull *Larus ichthyaetus* L69cm/27in W160cm/63in **P** p. 134

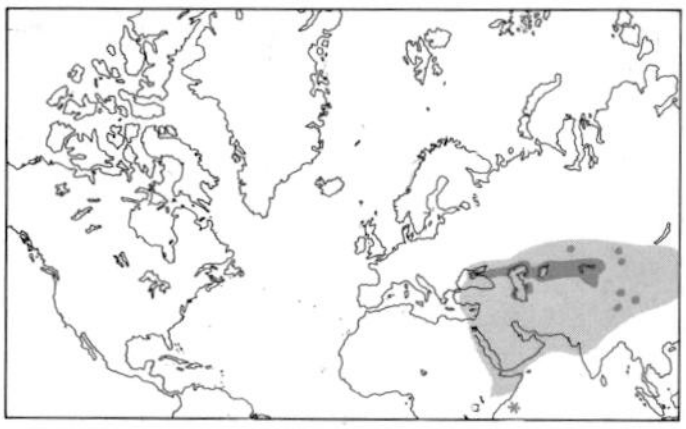

IDENTIFICATION: Large, distinctive gull, bill yellow with black band, red tip; adult plumage acquired fourth year. **Adult Summer:** The only large gull with full black hood and heavy banded bill. **Adult Winter:** Differs from Herring Gull in larger size, banded bill, darker ear-coverts and, in flight, different wingtip pattern. **First Winter:** Differs from second-winter Herring Gull in larger size, banded bill, darker ear-coverts and lower hindneck, greyish, more olive legs. In flight, look for distinct pale midwing panel, with white rump and tail contrasting with clear-cut black subterminal band. In subsequent plumages, banded bill, yellow legs, head and upperwing pattern allow separation from Herring Gull.

HABITS: Colonial breeder at freshwater locations; gregarious. Larger than Herring Gull, with proportionately longer wings which project well beyond tail at rest. Head has distinctive long, sloping forecrown which peaks well behind eye and accentuates length and heaviness of bill; yellow legs are noticeably long.

DISTRIBUTION: Asiatic. Breeds discontinuously from Black Sea east to Mongolia; winters from eastern Mediterranean south to Yemen, India and Burma.

SIMILAR SPECIES: Compare Herring Gull (p. 245).

Indian Black-headed Gull *Larus brunnicephalus* L42cm/17in W? **P** p. 135

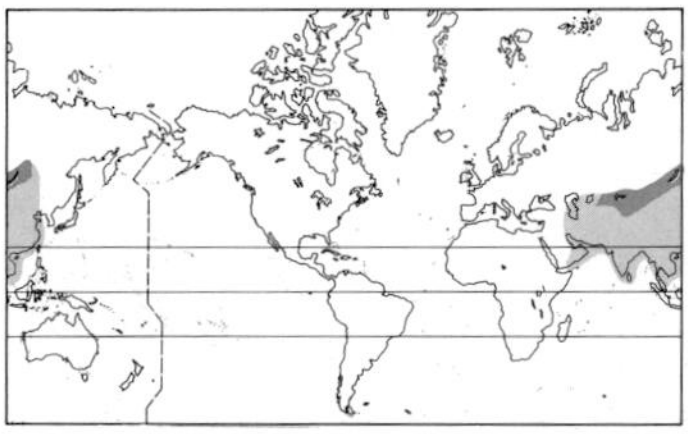

IDENTIFICATION: Medium-sized hooded gull, legs bright red, bill red, tip dusky; adult plumage acquired second year. **Adult Summer:** Wing pattern recalls more widespread Grey-headed Gull, but with chocolate-brown hood. Differs from smaller Eurasian Black-headed Gull in larger, brighter, black-tipped bill, pale iris and black wingtip with two large white mirrors on outermost primaries. **Adult Winter:** Head white, with dusky eye-crescent, mark on nape and ear-coverts. **First Winter:** Head as adult winter; differs from corresponding Black-headed Gull in broad dark trailing edge to upperwing formed by black primaries and secondaries.

HABITS: Colonial breeder on lakes, marshes of central Asia; gregarious.

DISTRIBUTION: Asiatic; breeds May–Sep central Asia, wintering along coasts and harbours of southern Asia from Persian Gulf east to Burma and Thailand.

SIMILAR SPECIES: Compare Eurasian Black-headed Gull (p. 246).

Chinese Black-headed Gull *Larus saundersi* L32cm/13in W? **P** p. 143

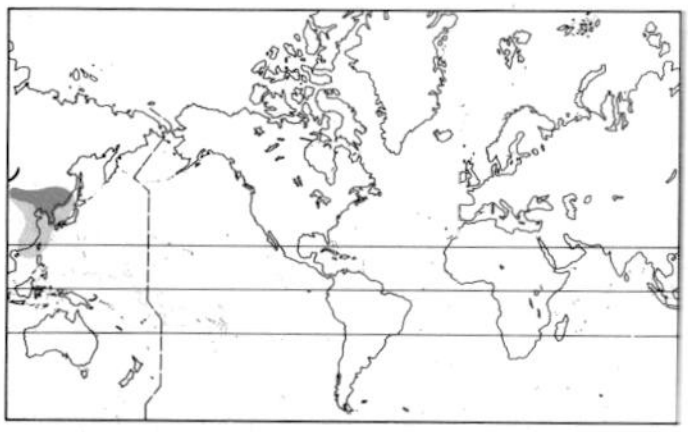

IDENTIFICATION: Small hooded gull, bill black, feet dark red; adult plumage acquired second year. **Adult Summer:** Blackish hood and white leading edge to upperwing recall smaller Bonaparte's Gull, but underwing has distinct blackish patch at base of outer primaries contrasting with translucent inner primaries. This character is found at all ages and coupled with upperwing pattern enables instant separation from all congeners. **Adult Winter:** Head white, with dusky eye-crescent, ear spot and band over crown. **First Winter:** Head and underwing as adult, with dark 'M' mark across upperwing and dark tip to tail.

HABITS: Virtually unknown; probably breeds inland lakes, marshes etc.

DISTRIBUTION: Thought to breed in eastern China. Winters south to Japan.

SIMILAR SPECIES: Compare Indian and Eurasian Black-headed Gulls (p. 254, p. 246).

Relict Gull *Larus relictus* L? W?

P p. 133

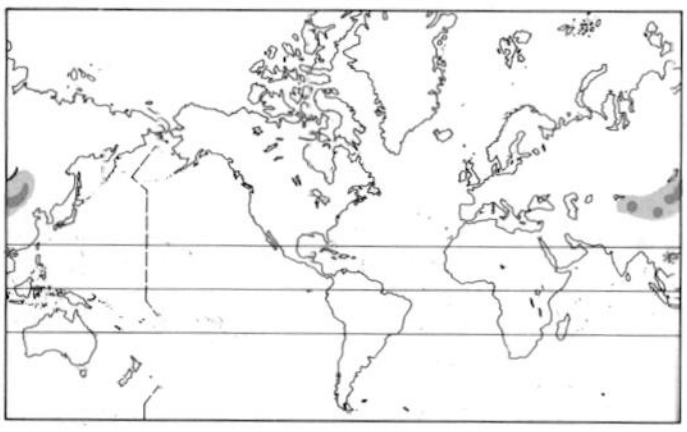

IDENTIFICATION: Medium-sized, recently rediscovered (1970) hooded gull; bill and legs dark red. Adult plumage probably acquired third year. **Adult Summer:** Combination of blackish hood and upperwing pattern recalling that of much larger Great Black-headed Gull diagnostic. **Adult Winter:** Unknown; presumably similar to that of winter Mediterranean Gull. **First Summer:** Head white, with traces of partial hood; pale grey mantle, brownish upperwing-coverts and dark tail band.

HABITS: Colonial breeder at freshwater locations. Superficially resembles miniature Great Black-headed Gull, but with red bill and legs. Differs from Mediterranean Gull in larger size, with longer wings, tail and legs; bill duller red, and black hood ends at hindcrown (not lower nape).

DISTRIBUTION: Asiatic; breeds Apr–Aug at several lakes in central, eastern and southeastern Asia (Kitson 1980). Wintering area unknown; perhaps in East and South China Seas.

SIMILAR SPECIES: None within range, but compare Great Black-headed and Indian Black-headed Gulls (p. 254).

Grey-headed Gull *Larus cirrocephalus* L42cm/17in W102cm/40in

P pp. 136–7

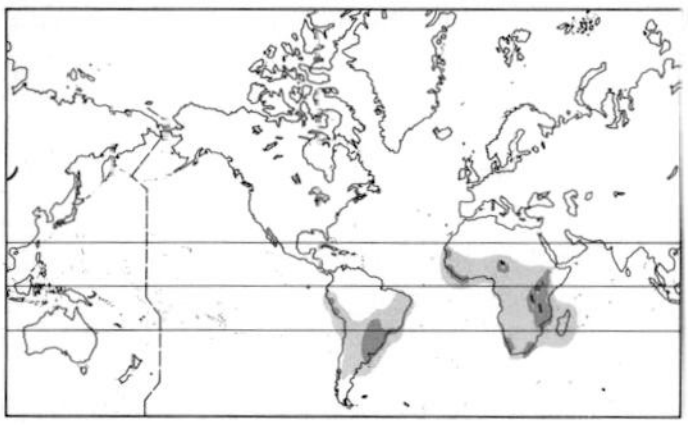

IDENTIFICATION: Medium-sized, grey-hooded gull; bill and legs crimson; adult plumage acquired third year. **Adult Summer:** Lavender-grey hood and distinctive wing pattern enable ready separation throughout most of range. In southern Africa differs from Hartlaub's Gull in much darker grey hood, brighter red legs and bill, pale eye (beware: some Hartlaub's have pale eyes). **Adult Winter:** Head mostly white; many show traces of grey hood, sometimes with faint ear spot. Differs from Hartlaub's in brighter legs and bill, pale eye; from Andean and Brown-hooded Gulls in different upperwing pattern. **First Winter:** Differs from Hartlaub's in bare-part colours, bold smudge on sides of head, more pronounced tail band and 'M' mark across upperwings.

HABITS: Colonial breeder at freshwater marshes/lakes; gregarious. Larger than Eurasian Black-headed Gull; in flight, wings noticeably broader.

DISTRIBUTION: South America and Africa; breeding dates vary with location. In South Africa hybridises to limited extent with Hartlaub's Gull.

SIMILAR SPECIES: Compare with Hartlaub's, Andean and Brown-hooded Gulls (p. 255, p. 256).

Hartlaub's Gull *Larus hartlaubii* L38cm/15in W91cm/36in

P p. 137

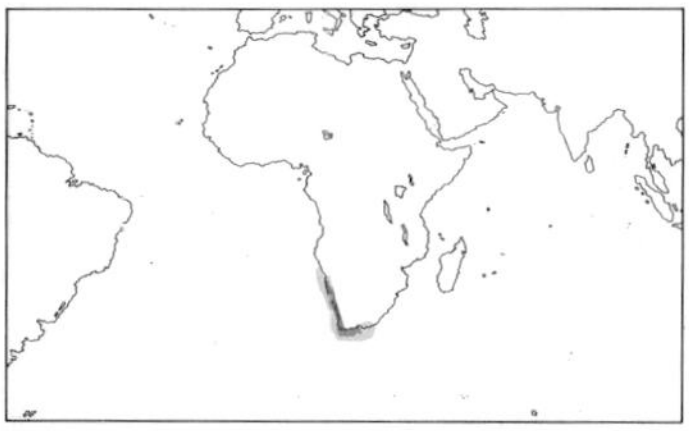

IDENTIFICATION: Medium-sized, pale-headed gull, bill and legs deep maroon; adult plumage acquired second year. **Adult Summer:** Differs from Grey-headed Gull in much paler head (most have wholly white head, others show faint suggestion of grey hood), darker bill and legs; most have dark (not pale) eyes. **First Winter:** Easily separated from those of Grey-headed by blackish bill, lack of bold smudge on ear-coverts, less black on tail. In all subsequent stages differs from Grey-headed in head and bare-part colours.

HABITS: Colonial breeder on marine islands and coasts; gregarious. Smaller than Grey-headed Gull, with proportionately thinner bill and shorter legs.

DISTRIBUTION: Sedentary; endemic to the western shores of South Africa and Namibia. Breeds Apr–Dec. Occasionally interbreeds with Grey-headed Gull.

SIMILAR SPECIES: Compare Grey-headed Gull (above).

Andean Gull *Larus serranus* L48cm/19in W?

P p. 140

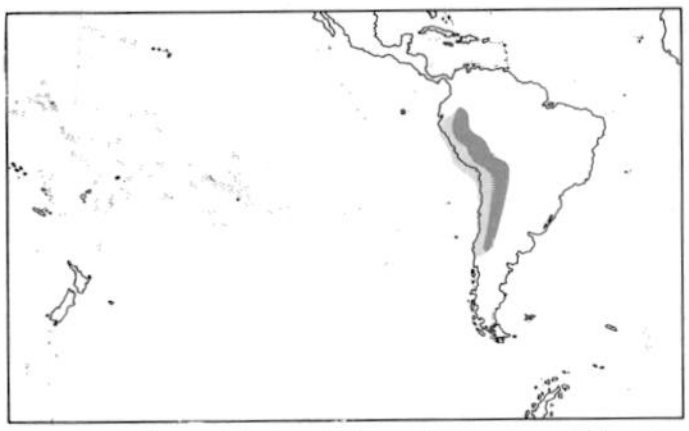

IDENTIFICATION: Medium-sized, black-hooded gull, legs and bill deep maroon; adult plumage acquired second year. **Adult Summer:** Combination of blackish hood and white wedge on leading edge of upperwing diagnostic. From below, dusky underwing shows distinctive white subterminal tip to outermost primaries, a useful character at all ages. **Adult Winter:** Head white, with dusky ear spot and eye-crescent; differs from Brown-hooded and Grey-headed Gulls in wing pattern, dark bill and legs. **First Winter:** Head as adult winter; dark 'M' mark across upperparts and tip to tail.

HABITS: Colonial breeder; gregarious. Larger and stockier in build than either Grey-headed or Brown-hooded Gulls, with broader, more rounded wings and heavier body.

DISTRIBUTION: South America; breeds mountain lakes and marshes in Andes, egg-dates Nov–Jan. Some disperse to coasts of Ecuador, Peru and Chile during winter.

SIMILAR SPECIES: Compare Grey-headed and Brown-hooded Gulls (p. 255, p. 256).

Brown-hooded Gull *Larus maculipennis* L37cm/15in W?

P p. 141

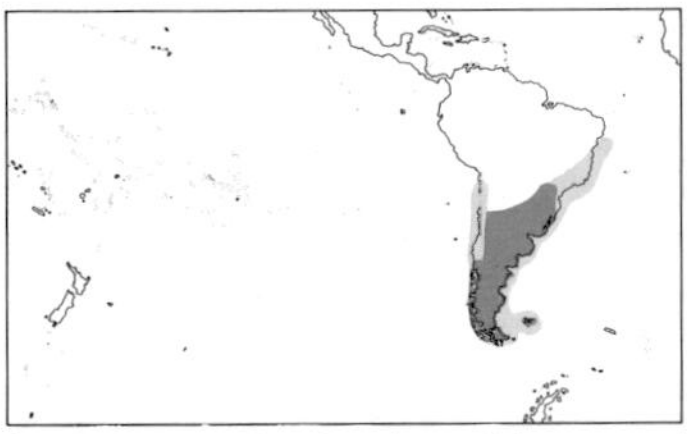

IDENTIFICATION: Medium-sized, dark-hooded gull, bill and legs crimson; adult plumage acquired second year. **Adult Summer:** Differs from both Andean and Grey-headed Gulls in chocolate-brown hood, and wing pattern recalling that of Eurasian Black-headed Gull. **Adult Winter:** Head white, with dusky marks on ear-coverts and crown; body occasionally with pinkish wash. **First Winter:** Differs from corresponding Andean Gull in black-tipped orange bill; from first-winter Grey-headed in darker head markings, much less black on primaries and secondaries.

HABITS: Colonial breeder; gregarious.

DISTRIBUTION: South America. Breeds from Tierra del Fuego north to about 33°S in Uruguay and to 40°S in Chile; egg-dates Dec–Jan. In winter disperses north to about 10°S in Brazil and to about 18°S in Chile.

SIMILAR SPECIES: Compare Andean and Grey-headed Gulls (p. 256, p. 255).

Silver Gull *Larus novaehollandiae* L41cm/16in W93cm/37in

P pp. 138–9

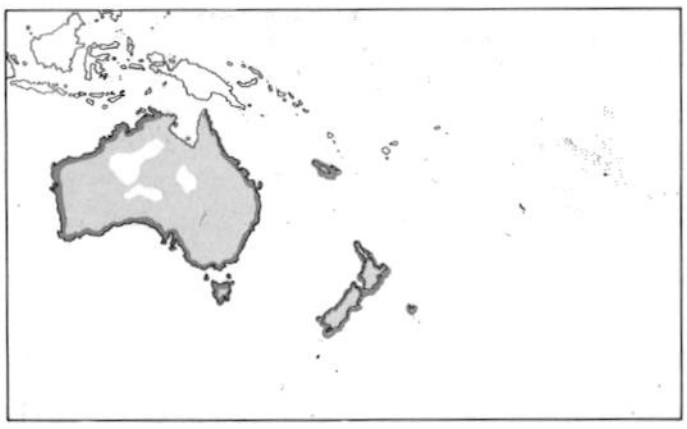

IDENTIFICATION: Medium-sized, white-headed gull, bill and legs crimson; adult plumage acquired second year. **Adult:** The bright red legs and bill coupled with distinctive black patch on upperwing separates this species from Black-billed Gull. **Juvenile/First Winter:** Differs from corresponding Black-billed Gull in white head with heavier, thicker bill, larger more rotund jizz, and upperwing pattern.

HABITS: Colonial breeder; gregarious. The only small gull in Australia, where common along coasts and on inland waterways. In New Zealand, range overlaps with smaller, daintier, Black-billed Gull; see notes under that species.

DISTRIBUTION: Australasian region; breeds Apr–Dec New Caledonia and all coasts of Australia and Tasmania south to New Zealand and its outlying islands.

SIMILAR SPECIES: Compare Black-billed Gull (p. 257).

Black-billed Gull *Larus bulleri* L36cm/14in W?

P p. 139

IDENTIFICATION: Medium-sized, pale-headed gull, bill black, legs dull red; adult plumage acquired second year. **Adult Summer:** Differs from Silver Gull in blackish bill and an upperwing pattern recalling that of Eurasian Black-headed Gull. **Adult Winter:** Many show faint grey wash over crown, giving slightly hooded effect. **First Winter:** Differs from those of Silver Gull in faint smudges over crown and on ear-coverts, different wing pattern. Immature plumages are often confused with those of Silver Gull because bill on present species is pinkish-orange with black tip, while immature Silver Gull has a blackish bill; separation is straightforward if differences in head and wing patterns are looked for.

HABITS: Colonial breeder; gregarious. Smaller than Silver Gull, daintier, with much thinner less robust bill.

DISTRIBUTION: Endemic to New Zealand; breeds chiefly South Island, nesting along inland lakes, rivers etc; egg-dates Dec–Jan.

SIMILAR SPECIES: Compare Silver Gull (p. 256).

Pacific Gull *Larus pacificus* L62cm/24in W147cm/58in

P p. 138

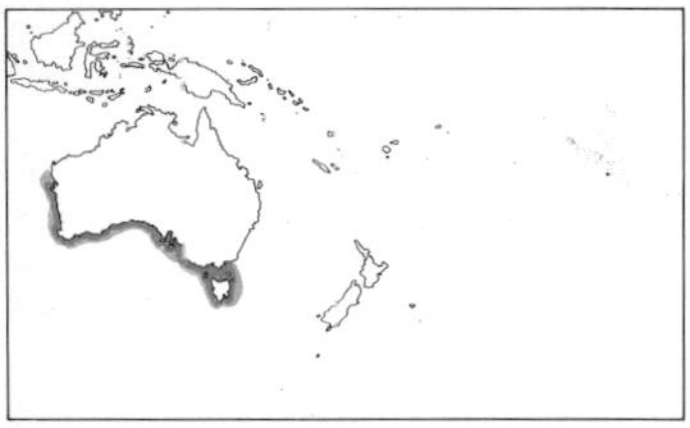

IDENTIFICATION: Australia's largest black-backed gull; bill yellow, tip red. Adult plumage acquired fourth year. **Adult:** The only adult black-backed gull in Australia with a black subterminal band to white tail; at close range, look for diagnostic massive bill. Differs from adult Kelp Gull in much larger size, more bulky jizz, upperwing lacking white mirrors, black tail band. **First Winter:** Averages darker than corresponding Kelp Gull, particularly underparts, with massive pinkish bill tipped darker. With advancing maturity, saddle, then wings become black, head and underparts whiter; at all ages, massive bill enables separation from Kelp Gull

HABITS: Breeds in loose colonies along coasts and islands; exclusively marine. Solitary outside breeding season.

DISTRIBUTION: Endemic to southern and southwestern Australia and Tasmania; egg-dates Sep–Jan.

SIMILAR SPECIES: Compare Kelp Gull (p. 253).

Band-tailed Gull *Larus belcheri* L51cm/20in W124cm/49in

P p. 142

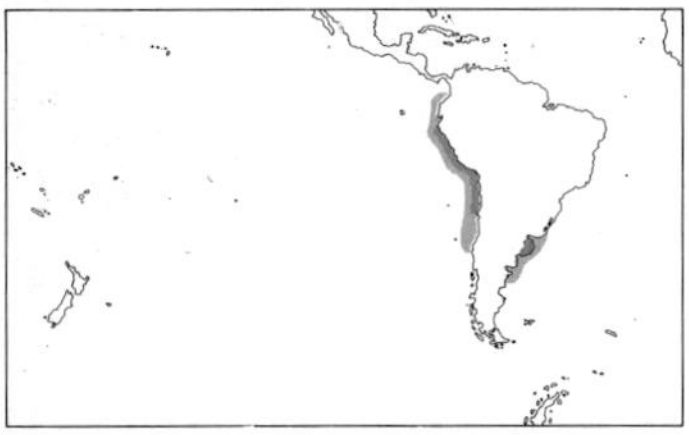

IDENTIFICATION: Large black-backed gull, bill yellow with black band and red tip; adult plumage acquired third year. **Adult Summer:** The only adult black-backed gull in South America with a black subterminal band to white tail; unlike Kelp Gull, upperwing lacks white mirrors. **Adult Winter:** Similar, but with full dark brown hood. **Juvenile:** Combination of pale yellowish bill with black tip, dark brown hood, and brownish upperparts scaled with buff diagnostic within range. With advancing maturity, scaly plumage fades rapidly, becoming more uniform above with pale collar. All ages have diagnostic banded yellow bill and are thus easily separable from Dolphin and Kelp Gulls.

HABITS: Exclusively marine; rarely follows ships; loosely colonial.

DISTRIBUTION: South America. Breeds from northern Peru south to Coquimbo, Chile; egg-dates Nov–Dec. Disperses north to Panama and south to central Chile. On Atlantic coast a small population breeds at San Blas Is, Argentina, dispersing south to Patagonia in winter (treated by some authors as a separate species: Orlog's Gull).

SIMILAR SPECIES: Compare Kelp and Dolphin Gulls (p. 253, p. 259).

Black-tailed Gull *Larus crassirostris* L47cm/19in W120cm/47in P p. 119

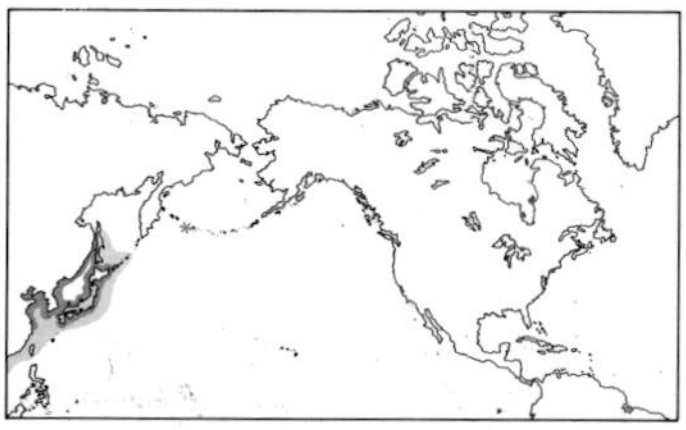

IDENTIFICATION: Medium-sized, dark-backed gull, bill yellow with black band and red tip; adult plumage acquired third year. **Adult Summer:** The only dark-backed gull in Japan with a black subterminal band to white tail; unlike the much larger and darker Slaty-backed Gull, blackish primaries lack white spots or mirrors. **Adult Winter:** Similar, except for grey streaks on crown. **First Winter:** Bill pink, tip black. Head white, with grey streaks over crown; upperparts mostly brown edged buff, with blackish primaries, secondaries and tail contrasting with whitish-grey rump. Second-calendar-year types generally resemble adults, but wing-coverts browner.
HABITS: Abundant resident along coasts; loosely colonial.
DISTRIBUTION: Asiatic. Breeds north coasts and islands of Sea of Japan bordering eastern Siberia, China and both islands of Japan; in winter disperses north to Sakhalin and south to Hong Kong.
SIMILAR SPECIES: None within range, but compare Slaty-backed Gull (p. 252).

Sooty Gull *Larus hemprichii* L45cm/18in W112cm/44in P p. 146

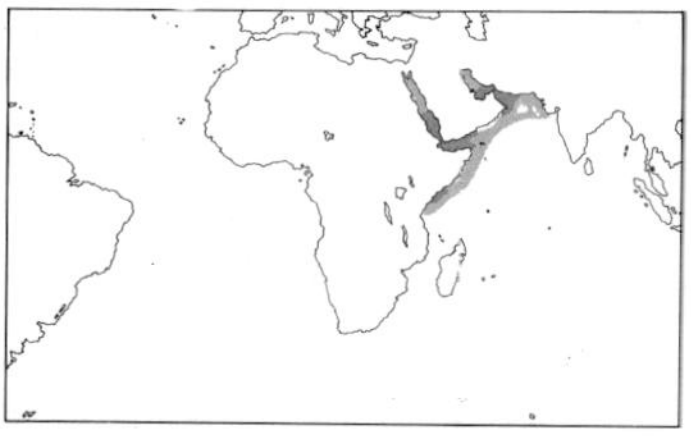

IDENTIFICATION: Medium-sized, hooded gull; adult plumage acquired third year. **Adult Summer:** Differs from smaller, less robust, White-eyed Gull in diagnostic yellow bill, tipped black and yellow, duller yellow legs, indistinct white eye-crescents, browner hood and upperparts. **Adult Winter:** Upperparts much browner in tone, white hindcollar less distinct. **First Winter:** Differs from corresponding White-eyed Gull in diagnostic grey bill with black tip, greyer legs, paler head lacking obvious eye-crescents, paler brown upperparts with conspicuous pale edges giving noticeable scaled effect. With advancing maturity, upperparts greyer; partial hood acquired second summer. At any age, Sooty Gull is larger, more robust in appearance than White-eyed Gull, with broader, more rounded wings. When seen together, the thicker bill and larger gonys of present species are easily seen and, coupled with differences in bill colour, at all ages, are perhaps the best means of separating the two.
HABITS: Solitary or colonial breeder; exclusively marine.
DISTRIBUTION: Northwest Indian Ocean. Breeds southern Red Sea off Mekran coast and then locally south to Kenya; egg-dates Jul–Aug. Disperses north to Elat, south to Tanzania and east to Pakistan.
SIMILAR SPECIES: Compare White-eyed Gull (below).

White-eyed Gull *Larus leucophthalmus* L39cm/15in W108cm/43in P pp. 146–7

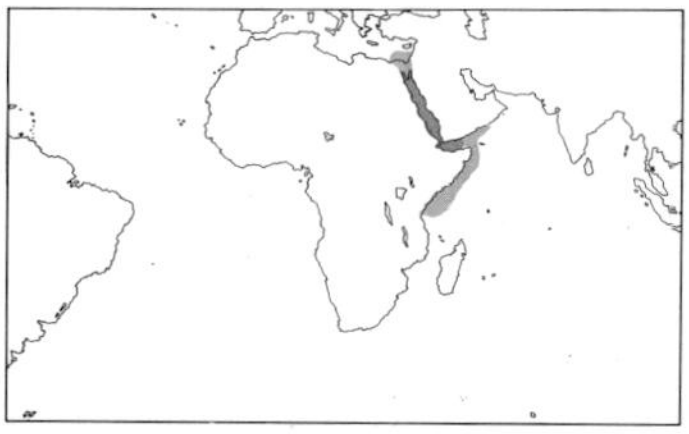

IDENTIFICATION: Medium-sized, black-hooded gull; adult plumage acquired third year. **Adult Summer:** Differs from larger, more robust Sooty Gull in diagnostic reddish bill with black tip, more prominent white eye-crescents, blacker hood, greyer upperparts. **Adult Winter:** Similar, but hood grizzled with white. **First Winter:** Differs from corresponding Sooty Gull in darker head with obvious white crescents and more uniform brown upperparts; it lacks white fringes of Sooty Gull, and the bill is wholly dark. With advancing maturity, black hood develops and upperparts become greyer. At any age, can be separated from Sooty Gull by smaller size and more slender, darker bill, slimmer jizz, thinner, more pointed wings.
HABITS: Not well known. Loosely colonial; exclusively marine.
DISTRIBUTION: Endemic to Red Sea; egg-dates not certainly known, perhaps Jun–Sep. Winters Gulf of Aden and adjacent Somalia coasts, occasionally north to southeastern Mediterranean.
SIMILAR SPECIES: Compare Sooty Gull (above).

Dolphin Gull *Larus scoresbii* L44cm/17in W104cm/41in **P** p. 144

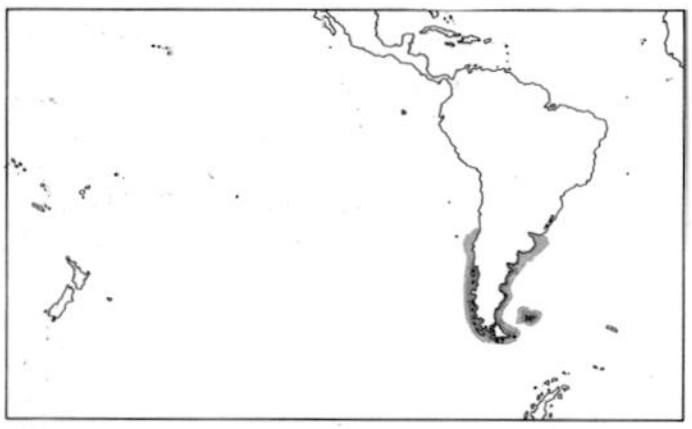

IDENTIFICATION: Medium-sized, dark-backed gull; adult plumage acquired third year. **Adult Summer:** Differs from much larger Kelp Gull in diagnostic blood-red bill and legs, whitish-grey head and body. **Adult Winter:** Head mostly dark grey, giving hooded appearance. **Juvenile:** Pattern as winter adult, but hood and upperparts browner; tail white with black subterminal band. With advancing maturity, upperwings blacker, tail wholly white

HABITS: Colonial breeder; opportunistic scavenger along tidelines, urban areas and seabird colonies.

DISTRIBUTION: Restricted to southern South America. Breeds Falklands, Tierra del Fuego and north to about 42°S in Chile and Argentina; egg-dates Dec–Jan. In winter disperses north to about 35°S.

SIMILAR SPECIES: None, but compare Kelp Gull (p. 253).

Lava Gull *Larus fuliginosus* L53cm/21in W? **P** p. 145

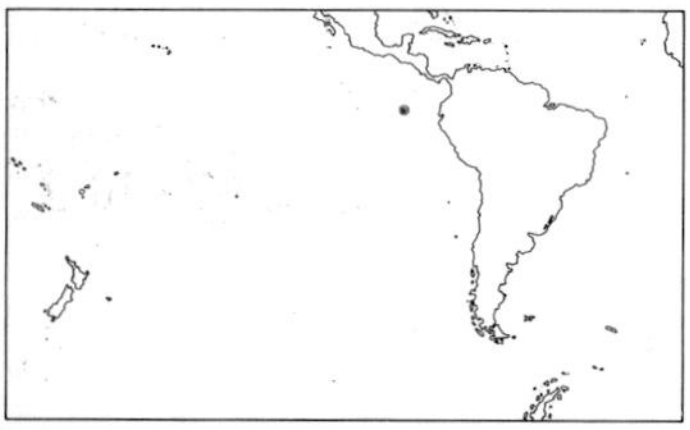

IDENTIFICATION: Large, dusky gull; bill blackish, tip red; adult plumage acquired third year. **Adult:** Appears mostly grey, with sooty-brown hood. The only dusky gull of the Galapagos. **First Winter:** Plumage mostly dull sooty-brown, slightly paler on rump, belly and undertail-coverts. With advancing maturity, becomes greyer in tone with darker head.

HABITS: Breeds singly; opportunistic scavenger along tidelines, urban areas and seabird colonies.

DISTRIBUTION: Endemic to Galapagos Is, where some 300–400 pairs breed (Snow & Snow 1969); sedentary.

SIMILAR SPECIES: None within area.

Grey Gull *Larus modestus* L46cm/18in W? **P** pp. 144–5

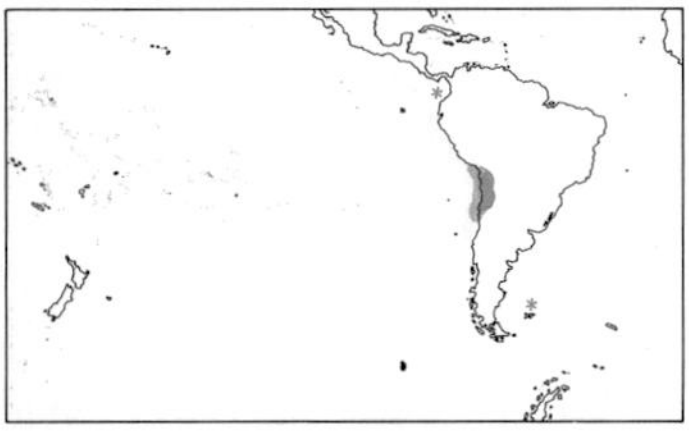

IDENTIFICATION: Medium-sized dusky gull, bill and legs black; adult plumage acquired third year. **Adult Summer:** Distinctive; combination of whitish hood and grey plumage diagnostic within limited range. **Adult Winter:** Similar, but hood brownish. **Juvenile:** Mostly greyish-brown, with blackish primaries, secondaries and tail. At close range, the paler feather edges on upperwing-coverts form paler area on closed wing. With advancing maturity, becomes more uniform dark brownish-grey and then gains grey of adult with pure white trailing edge to wings and tail.

HABITS: Colonial breeder in harsh coastal deserts. Forages along coasts and beaches of Chile and Peru, running over sand like a sandpiper, snatching at shrimps and sand fleas; large numbers congregate around trawlers.

DISTRIBUTION: West coast of South America; breeds Nov–May coastal deserts of northern Chile. Undertakes post-breeding dispersal north to Ecuador, occasionally Colombia, and south to at least Valparaiso, Chile.

SIMILAR SPECIES: None within range.

Swallow-tailed Gull *Larus furcatus* L57cm/22in W131cm/52in **P** p. 113

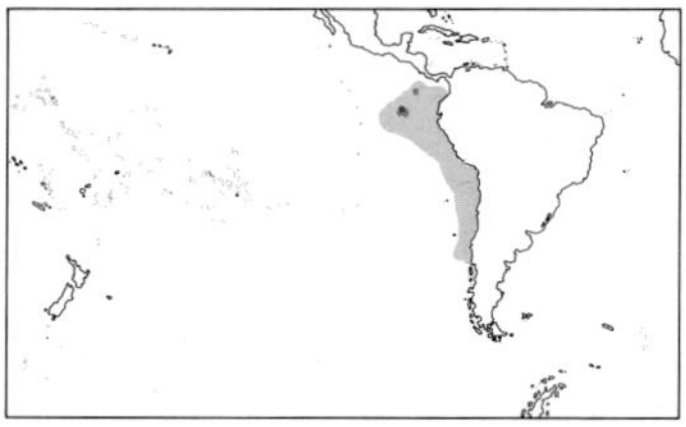

IDENTIFICATION: Large, hooded gull, bill black with grey tip, legs pink; adult plumage acquired second year. **Adult Summer:** Distinctive; combination of large size, dark hood and striking tricoloured upperwings diagnostic. **Adult Winter:** Head white, with black eye-crescent and dark eye creating large-eyed appearance. **Juvenile:** Head as adult winter. Upperparts scaled brown and white, with broad black tip to deeply forked tail.
HABITS: Recalls Sabine's Gull, but much larger with more rakish jizz and proportionately longer bill; often timid at sea, where it feeds mainly at night. Colonial breeder; gregarious.
DISTRIBUTION: Southeast Pacific. Breeds mainly at Galapagos Is, with a few pairs at Malpelo Is off Colombia. Disperses widely after breeding, reaching north to Panama and south to Chile.
SIMILAR SPECIES: None, but compare Sabine's Gull (p. 248).

Trudeau's Tern *Sterna trudeaui* L33cm/13in W77cm/30in **P** p. 155

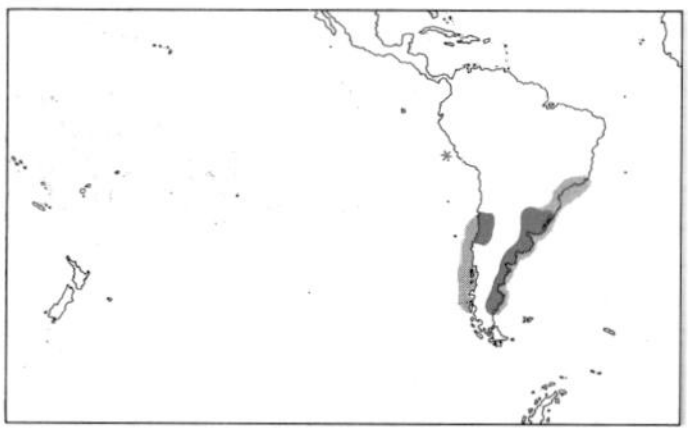

IDENTIFICATION: **Adult Summer:** Distinctive; combination of banded yellow bill, pale whitish-grey plumage and black eye patch diagnostic. **Adult Winter:** As adult summer, but bill mostly black with yellow tip, eye patch greyer, underparts whiter. **Juvenile:** Much as adult winter, but bill black with yellowish base, upperparts faintly tipped with brown, heaviest on tertials.
HABITS: Loosely colonial; feeds over both freshwater and marine locations. Flight and jizz recall Forster's Tern, but tail averages shorter.
DISTRIBUTION: South America. Breeds coasts and interior of Uruguay and Argentina; egg-dates Oct–Jan. Disperses south to Straits of Magellan; also reported from western littoral in Chile from Aconcagua south to Llanquihue.
SIMILAR SPECIES: None within range, but compare Forster's Tern (p. 263).

Gull-billed Tern *Sterna nilotica* L39cm/15in W94cm/37in **P** p. 149

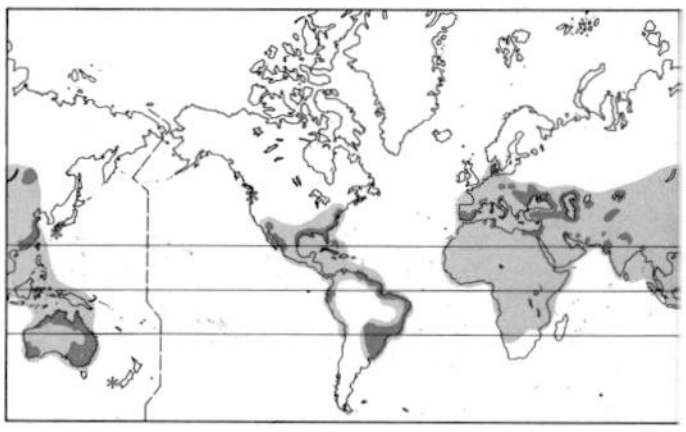

IDENTIFICATION: **Adult Summer:** Recalls Sandwich Tern, but with stout, wholly black bill, uncrested black cap, grey tail and longer, thickset black legs. **Adult Winter:** Similar, but head mostly white or with conspicuous black patches on ear-coverts. Appears white at distance, with rather broad, rounded wings, heavy body and shallow-forked tail giving stockier, more thickset jizz than Sandwich Tern; at rest, stout bill and longer legs obvious. **Juvenile:** As adult winter, but faint brownish wash over crown; saddle and upperwing-coverts tipped brown, primaries darker.
HABITS: Breeds colonially at freshwater locations, rare over ocean. Flight like that of marsh terns; feeds by hawking over marsh, mudflats or even fields, dipping down to pluck prey or seize insects in mid air; occasionally surface-plunges.
DISTRIBUTION: Widespread; egg-dates vary with location. Breeds North and South America, western and southern Europe east through Black and Caspian Seas to Indo-China and Australia. Northern populations more migratory, dispersing south to Peru and Botswana.
SIMILAR SPECIES: Compare Sandwich Tern (p. 264).

Whiskered Tern *Chlidonias hybridus* L25cm/10in W69cm/27in

P p. 152

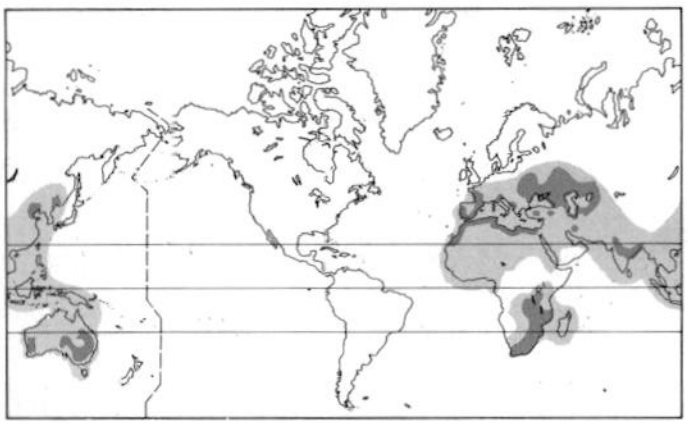

IDENTIFICATION: **Adult Summer:** Combination of black cap, distinct white stripe across cheeks, and dark grey underparts with white ventral area diagnostic. Bill and legs dark blood-red. **Adult Winter:** Head white with dark eye patch extending over crown, giving *Sterna*-like appearance, but lacks a white hindcollar; rump grey, different wing pattern from Common, Roseate or Arctic Terns. From winter and immature White-winged Black Terns by larger, deeper bill, darker rump, *Sterna*-like jizz, more forked tail. **Juvenile:** Upperparts recall White-winged Black, but greyer rump and leading edge of wing. Bill thicker, more dagger-like.
HABITS: Freshwater tern; breeds colonially. Compared with Black and White-winged Black Terns, jizz much closer to *Sterna*, but smaller, with shorter, more rounded wings.
DISTRIBUTION: Resident and migratory throughout much of Old World, from Europe and Africa east through India to Australia; egg-dates vary with location.
SIMILAR SPECIES: Black, White-winged Black, Common and Arctic (p. 261, p. 264, p. 265).

Black Tern *Chlidonias niger* L23cm/9in W66cm/26in

P p. 152

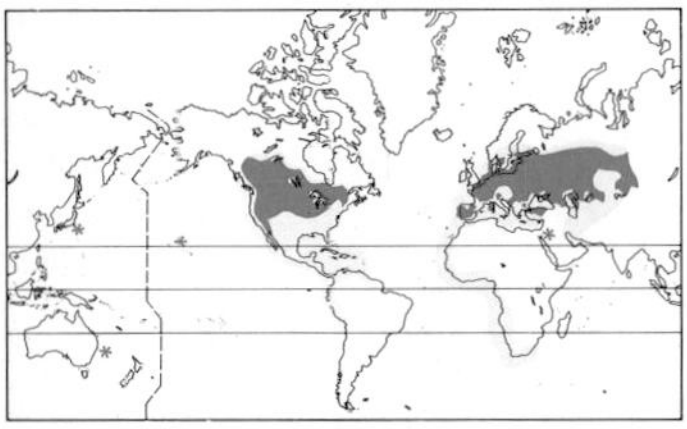

IDENTIFICATION: **Adult Summer:** Upperparts mostly dark uniform grey; blackish head and body contrasts with white undertail-coverts. Differs from White-winged Black Tern in uniform upperwing, grey rump, tail and underwing-coverts. **Adult Winter:** Head white with blackish cap extending down to ear-coverts, underparts mostly white; differs from White-winged Black Tern in much darker, more extensive cap, greyer rump, and diagnostic dark smudges on sides of breast. **Juvenile:** Head pattern and breast mark as in adult winter; lacks noticeable dark brown saddle and paler midwing panel of juvenile White-winged Black Tern.
HABITS: Breeds freshwater locations. In winter more marine than White-winged Black. Flight differs in deeper, faster wingbeats with longer, slimmer wings, more forked tail and longer, slightly drooping bill, giving more rakish jizz.
DISTRIBUTION: Breeds North America and Europe east to Caspian Sea and central Russia; egg-dates May–Jul. Winters south to Chile and Surinam; also South Africa.
SIMILAR SPECIES: Compare White-winged Black and Whiskered Terns (this page).

White-winged Black Tern *Chlidonias leucopterus* L23cm/9in W66cm/26in

P p. 152

IDENTIFICATION: **Adult Summer:** Distinctive; combination of blackish head, body and underwing-coverts contrasting with whitish wings, tail and ventral area diagnostic. **Adult Winter:** Always has whiter head than corresponding Black Tern, with paler grey upperparts, shorter bill, white sides to breast and paler, almost white rump. Many retain scattered dark feather tips on underwing-coverts. From winter Whiskered Tern by smaller, shorter bill, lack of *Sterna*-like jizz, white hindcollar and whiter rump. **Juvenile:** Resembles juvenile Black Tern; differs in paler, less extensive head markings, dark brown saddle contrasting with white rump, paler midwing panel on upperwing, and lacks dark mark on sides of breast. From juvenile Whiskered Tern by darker saddle, white rump, and darker leading edge to basal portion of upperwing.
HABITS: Breeds and winters at freshwater locations.
DISTRIBUTION: From central and eastern Europe east through central Asia to Russia and southern China; egg-dates May–Jul. Winters south to South Africa and Australia.
SIMILAR SPECIES: Compare Black and Whiskered Terns (above).

Caspian Tern *Sterna caspia* L53cm/21in W134cm/53in

P p. 147

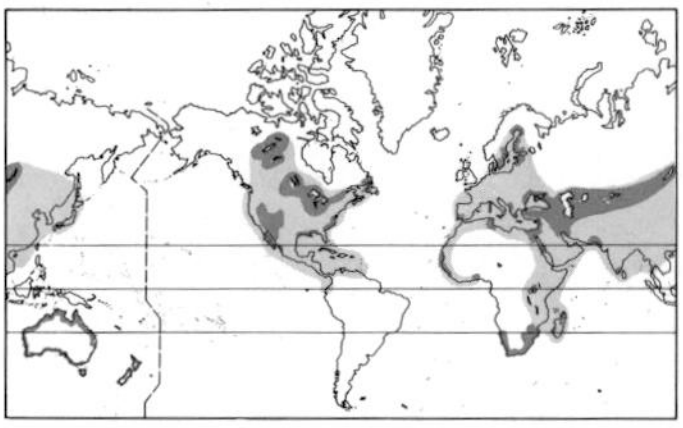

IDENTIFICATION: **Adult Summer:** Distinctive; combination of enormous size, large dusky-tipped, blood-red bill and wholly dark outer primaries on underwing diagnostic. Smaller Royal Tern has unmarked orange bill and different underwing pattern. **Adult Winter:** As summer adult, but cap streaked with white; some occasionally show mostly white heads with dusky eye patch. **First Winter:** As winter adult, but bill more orange, saddle and upperwing-coverts scaled with brown. Differs from first-winter Royal Tern in almost solid dark cap, lack of obvious dark carpal bar and of pale midwing panel, wholly dark outer primaries on underwing.
HABITS: Breeds singly or colonially at freshwater locations. Flight strong, swift and graceful, although size and bulk near that of Herring Gull.
DISTRIBUTION: Widespread. Breeds North America and northern and central Europe east to Siberia, also in Australia, New Zealand and southern Africa; egg-dates vary. Northern populations more migratory, wintering south to Caribbean, northwest Africa, South Africa and Japan.
SIMILAR SPECIES: Compare Royal Tern (below).

Royal Tern *Sterna maxima* L50cm/20in W109cm/43in

P p. 147

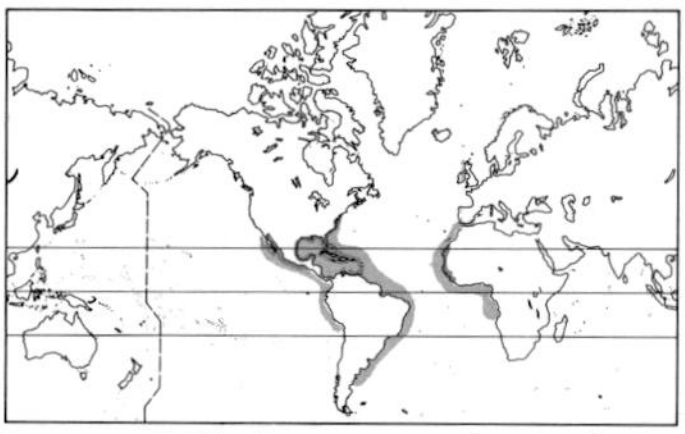

IDENTIFICATION: **Adult Summer:** Large, orange-billed tern with shaggy black crest; combination of large size, bill and crest separates it from all but Caspian, Elegant and Lesser Crested Terns. Differs from Caspian in unmarked orange bill, shaggy crest, black on underwing restricted to tips of primaries, deeply forked tail. From Elegant and Lesser Crested in larger size, deeper orange bill, which is stouter and thicker particularly at base. **Adult Winter:** Head mostly white; crest reduced to ragged black nape patch which does not usually extend to encompass eye (unlike Elegant Tern). Differs from Caspian in colour of bill, underwing, white forehead contrasting with black nape. **First Winter:** Head and underwing as adult; differs from both Caspian and Elegant Terns in dark carpal bar and distinctive pale midwing panel on upperwing-coverts.
HABITS: Strictly marine; colonial breeder. Second largest tern; unlike congeners, retains full black cap for only short period at beginning of breeding season.
DISTRIBUTION: Breeds Pacific and Atlantic coasts of southern USA, south to West Indies and Mexico, perhaps Venezuela; also equatorial West Africa. Egg-dates Apr–Jul.
SIMILAR SPECIES: Compare Caspian, Elegant and Lesser Crested Terns (p. 262, p. 263).

Crested Tern *Sterna bergii* L46cm/18in W104cm/41in

P p. 148

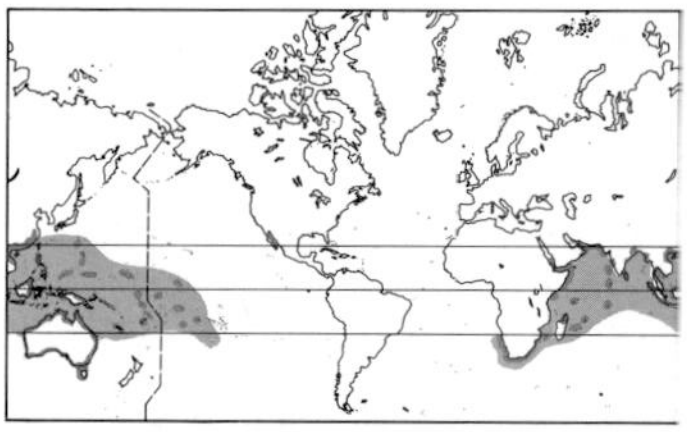

IDENTIFICATION: **Adult Summer:** Large, yellow-billed tern, with shaggy black cap separated from base of bill by narrow white forehead. Differs from Caspian and Lesser Crested Terns in yellow bill, narrow white forehead. **Adult Winter:** Forehead and crown mostly white, with ragged black nape patch extending through eye. Differs from winter Lesser Crested and Royal Terns in bill colour, more extensive black nape and dirty-white crown giving scruffy appearance, darker grey upperparts. **Juvenile/First Winter:** Head similar but browner than winter adult; upperparts dark brown, fringed white, becoming more grey on mantle and back with advancing maturity. Differs from Royal and Lesser Crested in yellow (not orange) bill.
HABITS: Exclusively marine; breeds colonially. Third largest tern, close to Royal in size, with longer, more drooping bill than smaller Lesser Crested Tern.
DISTRIBUTION: Throughout much of tropical and subtropical Indian and Pacific Oceans, coasts of South Africa and Namibia; egg-dates vary with location.
SIMILAR SPECIES: Compare Royal, Caspian and Lesser Crested Terns (p. 262, p. 263).

Lesser Crested Tern *Sterna bengalensis* L40cm/16in W92cm/35in

P p. 148

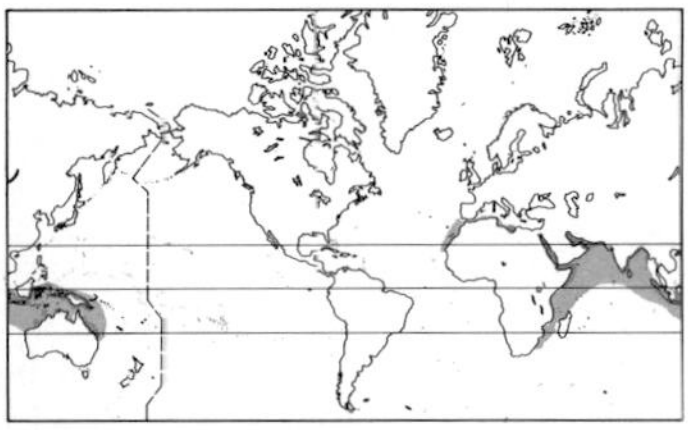

IDENTIFICATION: **Adult Summer:** Medium-sized, orange-billed tern with shaggy black crest. Smaller, more slender than Royal Tern, differing in smaller bill, silvery-white primaries on upperwing, grey rump, slightly darker grey upperparts. **Juvenile/Immature:** Very like immature Royal Tern, with dark carpal bar and pale midwing panel; differs only in smaller size, darker, more spotted rump, shorter, darker, less forked tail; with advancing age, rump and tail become paler.
HABITS: Exclusively marine; colonial breeder. Smaller than Crested, Caspian or Royal Terns, but slightly larger than Sandwich; bills of Mediterranean population average longer, more drooping, recalling bill proportions of Elegant Tern.
DISTRIBUTION: Mainly southwest Pacific and Indian Oceans, extending to Red and Mediterranean Seas; egg-dates usually Jun–Nov. Northern populations disperse in winter, reaching south to Mozambique, occasionally South Africa.
SIMILAR SPECIES: Compare Royal Tern (p. 262).

Elegant Tern *Sterna elegans* L41cm/16in W86cm/34in

P p. 148

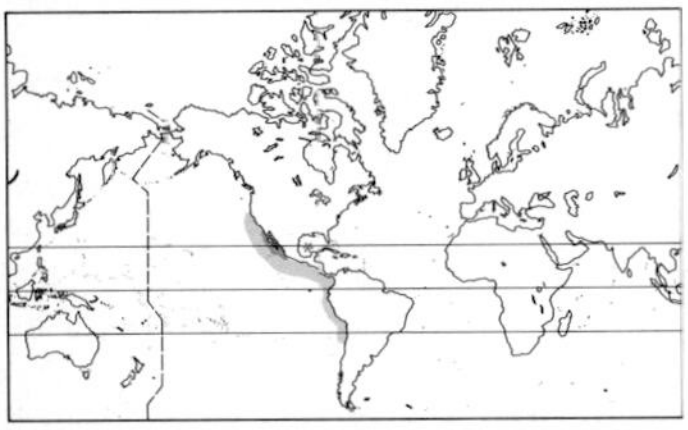

IDENTIFICATION: **Adult Summer:** Medium-sized, orange-billed tern with shaggy black crest. Differs from Royal Tern in smaller size, slimmer body, longer, thinner, more decurved orange bill which is usually slightly paler towards the tip, more ragged crest on nape, and variable pinkish flush on underparts. **Adult Winter:** Black crest reduced to ragged patch on nape which extends forward through eye; most western winter Royal Terns have eye surrounded by white. **Juvenile/Immature:** Bill more yellow; upperparts spotted with brown, primaries and secondaries mostly dark dusky-grey.
HABITS: Subtropical; frequents beaches and estuaries. Colonial breeder
DISTRIBUTION: Breeds Mar–Sep southern California, coasts of Baja California and northwest Mexico. In fall, some disperse north to San Francisco, most head south towards Peru and Chile.
SIMILAR SPECIES: Compare Royal Tern (p. 262).

Forster's Tern *Sterna forsteri* L37cm/15in W80cm/31in

P p. 151

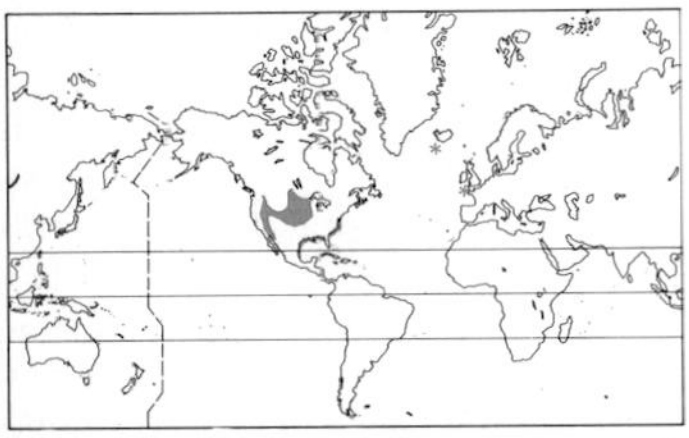

IDENTIFICATION: **Adult Summer:** Medium-sized, black-capped tern with black-tipped orange bill. Differs from similar Common in proportionately larger, heavier, more orange bill and longer orange (not crimson) legs. In flight, upperwing shows diagnostic silvery inner primaries which lack the distinctive dark wedge found in Common; webs of outermost tail feathers are white. From Roseate by orange bill and upperwing pattern. **Adult Winter:** Bill mostly black, base reddish; dark cap reduced to large oval-shaped eye patches, nape and crown faintly dusky. **First Winter:** Much as adult winter; the distinctive black eye patches and lack of obvious carpal bar prevent confusion with Common, Arctic or Roseate Terns. Differs from larger Sandwich Tern in reddish base to shorter bill and orange legs.
HABITS: Colonial breeder at both freshwater and marine locations; gregarious. Compared with Common Tern, larger, more robust with proportionately larger head, and longer tail streamers which, when perched, project past wingtip. During winter, at long range, its pale appearance and head pattern can suggest Sandwich Tern. In flight, has a distinctive metallic 'kick' note.
DISTRIBUTION: Breeds May–Aug temperate North America from prairie provinces of Canada south to Texas and Mexico. Winters south to California and Panama.
SIMILAR SPECIES: Compare Common, Gull-billed and Sandwich Terns (p. 264, p. 260, p. 264).

Sandwich Tern *Sterna sandvicensis* L43cm/17in W92cm/36in **P** p. 149

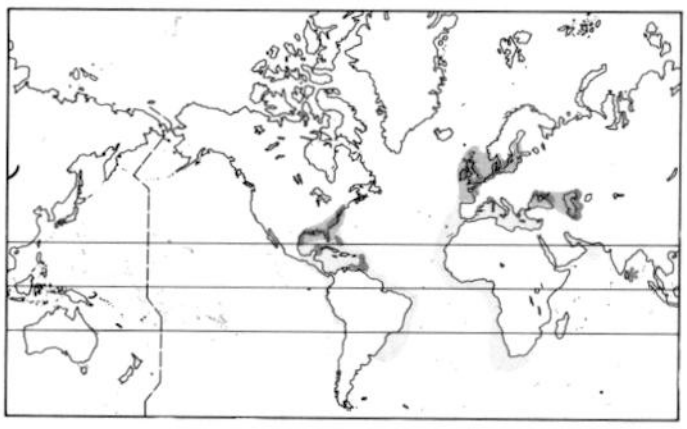

IDENTIFICATION: **Adult Summer:** Medium-sized tern with shaggy black crest and diagnostic yellow-tipped black bill. Upperparts appear very pale in flight, with dark outer 3–4 primaries forming small wedge; tail rather short, but deeply forked. Differs from Gull-billed in bill colour, shaggy crest, shorter legs, longer, more deeply forked tail, more slender jizz and different feeding habits. **Adult Winter:** Black crest reduced in many from July onwards to ragged black patch on nape, extending forward to eye. **Juvenile/First Winter:** Head as adult winter; black bill shorter, usually without yellow tip. Pale grey upperparts have brown 'V' shaped feather tips which soon abrade to give mostly clear upperparts; tail shorter, tipped brown.
HABITS: Colonial breeder; feeds over beaches and estuaries, flight strong and swift, plunge-diving to secure prey. Appears more elegant in flight than Gull-billed, with longer, more slender, more pointed wings, slimmer body and longer, more forked tail; longer, slimmer bill.
DISTRIBUTION: Breeds Mar–Aug in New World and in Eurasia from Ireland east to Caspian Sea. Disperses south to Uruguay and South Africa in winter.
SIMILAR SPECIES: Compare Gull-billed Tern and winter Forster's Tern (p. 260, p. 263).

Cayenne Tern *Sterna (sandvicensis) eurygnatha* L42cm/17in W96cm/38in **P** p. 149

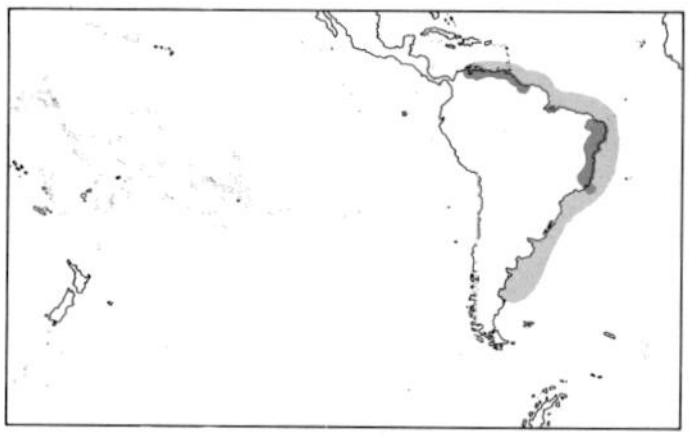

IDENTIFICATION: The only medium-sized tern in South America with a yellow bill. Regarded by many authors as a yellow-billed race of Sandwich Tern, with which it appears to be involved in a cline and/or hybridisation all along the Venezuelan coast (Alden pers. comm.). **Adult Summer:** As Sandwich Tern, but bill ranges from wholly yellow or orange to black with yellow tip; legs and feet vary from wholly yellow to black. Winter and immature plumages as for Sandwich Tern, but with variable bare-part colours.
HABITS: As for Sandwich Tern.
DISTRIBUTION: Poorly documented. Thought to breed from Venezuela south to Rio de Janeiro, Brazil; disperses north to Caribbean and south to Argentina.
SIMILAR SPECIES: None within range, but compare Amazon and Large-billed Terns (p. 271).

Common Tern *Sterna hirundo* L36cm/14in W80cm/31in **P** p. 150

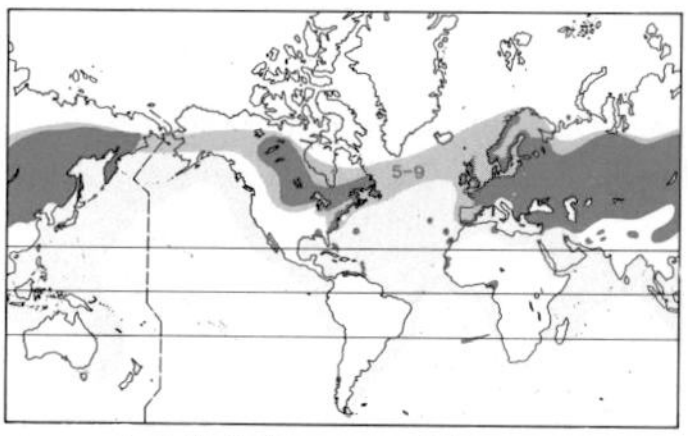

IDENTIFICATION: **Adult Summer:** Medium-sized, black-capped tern with black-tipped crimson bill (Siberian race has black bill). Upperparts mostly medium-grey, rump and tail white; underparts washed with pale grey, darker than either Roseate or Forster's Terns but paler than Arctic Tern. Differs from Arctic Tern in black tip to bill, variable but distinct dark wedge on outer primaries of upperwing, and a wider, rather smudgy black border along primaries on underwing. **Adult Winter:** Bill blackish, forehead and lores white. **First Winter:** Head and underwing pattern as adult winter. Differs from corresponding Arctic Tern in pronounced carpal bar and dusky-grey (not white) secondaries on upperwing, greyer rump and tail, giving overall dirtier, more unkempt appearance. Immature Roseate has darker cap and saddle, whiter underwing.
HABITS: Breeds colonially at freshwater and marine locations; gregarious. Compared with Arctic Tern, appears longer-billed with longer flatter crown; at rest, tips of wing and tail more or less equal. Flight silhouette of summer adult differs in proportionately broader, shorter wings, heavier body, more projecting head and noticeably shorter tail.
DISTRIBUTION: Widespread; breeds North America and Europe east through much of central Asia; egg-dates May–Aug. Winters south to Argentina, South Africa and Australia.
SIMILAR SPECIES: Compare Arctic, Forster's and Roseate Terns (p. 265, p. 263, p. 265).

Arctic Tern *Sterna paradisaea* L36cm/14in W80cm/31in **P** p. 150

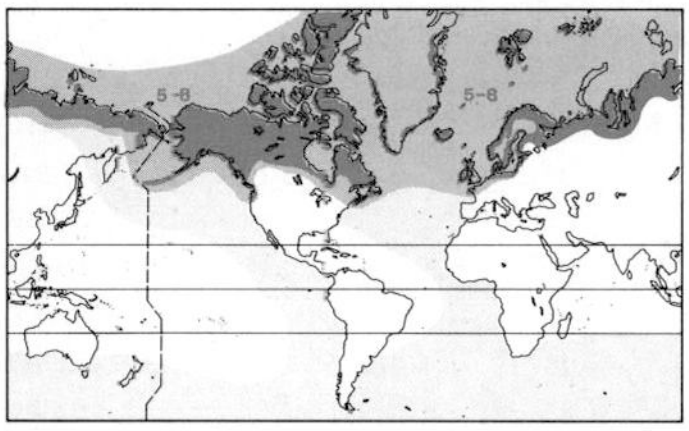

IDENTIFICATION: **Adult Summer:** Medium-sized, black-capped tern with unmarked crimson bill and legs. Upperparts mostly medium-grey, rump and tail whiter; underparts grey, darker than Common, Forster's or Roseate, with more noticeable white streak across cheeks. Differs from similar Common in unmarked bill, lack of dark upperwing wedge, and neater, narrower black margin to underside of primaries. **Adult Winter:** Bill blackish, forehead and lores white; differs from Common in whiter rump and tail, different wing pattern. **First Winter:** Head and underwing as adult winter. Differs from corresponding Common in lack of obvious carpal bar; the white secondaries, whiter rump and tail contrast more with slightly darker grey upperparts giving overall neater, more two-toned appearance. From Roseate in paler saddle, dark trailing edge to tip of underwing.
HABITS: Colonial breeder at marine locations; gregarious. Compared with Common, has shorter bill and legs; more rounded head; at rest, tail streamers usually project well past wingtip.
DISTRIBUTION: Circumpolar in Arctic and sub-Arctic regions; egg-dates May–Jul. Winters south through all oceans, reaching even to Antarctic pack ice.
SIMILAR SPECIES: Compare Common, Roseate and Antarctic Terns (p. 264, p. 265, p. 267).

Roseate Tern *Sterna dougallii* L39cm/15in W78cm/31in **P** p. 150

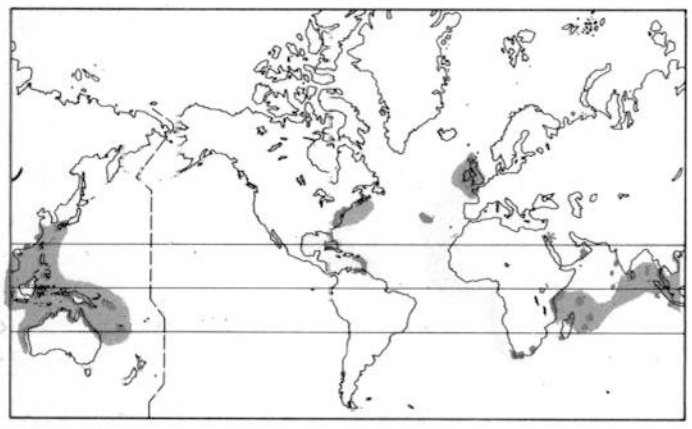

IDENTIFICATION: **Adult Summer:** Medium-sized, black-capped tern, bill black with reddish base, legs pale crimson. Upperparts very pale grey, appearing almost white at distance (some show small dark wedge on outer 3–4 primaries); underparts white, usually with strong pink suffusion at beginning of breeding season. Differs from Arctic, Common and Forster's Terns in blackish bill, paler overall plumage, wholly white primaries on underwing, and longer tail streamers. **Adult Winter:** As adult summer, but bill wholly black, forehead, crown and lores white extending forward to eye; head pattern thus whiter than in Common Tern. **Juvenile/First Winter:** Retains darker, more extensive cap than Common or Arctic Terns, with browner scaling on mantle and back forming darker 'saddle'; lacks dusky trailing edge to tip of underwing.
HABITS: Marine; breeds colonially. When perched, tail streamers project well past wingtip.
DISTRIBUTION: Widespread; egg-dates vary with location. Northern populations more migratory, wintering south to South Africa.
SIMILAR SPECIES: Compare Common, Arctic and White-fronted Terns (p. 264, p. 265, p. 266).

Little Tern *Sterna albifrons* L24cm/9in W52cm/20in **P** p. 151

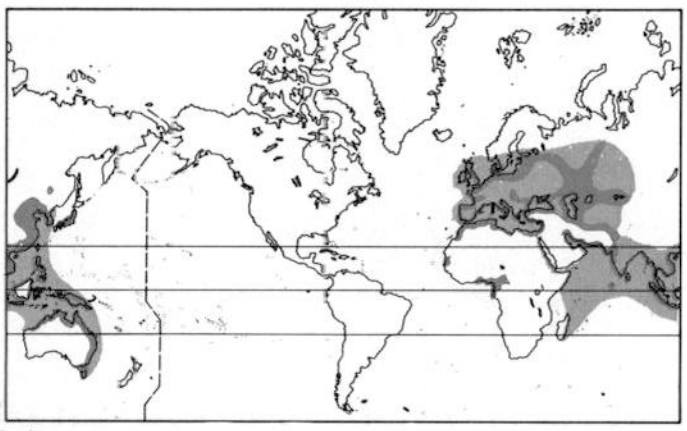

IDENTIFICATION: **Adult Summer:** Small, black-capped tern with white forehead, black-tipped yellow bill and yellow legs. Upperparts mostly grey, with blackish-grey outer 3–4 primaries forming small dark wedge; underparts mostly white. Differs from most of congeners in small size and yellow bill; from Saunders' Little Tern in paler outer primaries, slightly darker grey upperparts, white forehead extending over eye as narrow white supercilium, and yellow (not brown) legs. **Adult Winter:** As adult summer, but bill blackish with yellow base, legs brown; forehead, crown and lores white. Differs from Damara Tern in shorter, straighter bill, slightly darker upperparts. **Juvenile/First Winter:** Head pattern as adult winter, but crown browner, upperparts tipped with brown; upperwing has dark carpal bar.
HABITS: Colonial breeder at marine and freshwater locations.
DISTRIBUTION: Breeds coasts and rivers of Eurasia east discontinuously to Australia and Japan; egg-dates vary with location. Northern populations winter south to South Africa.
SIMILAR SPECIES: Compare Saunders' Little and Damara Terns (p. 268).

Least Tern *Sterna antillarum* L23cm/9in W51cm/20in

P p. 151

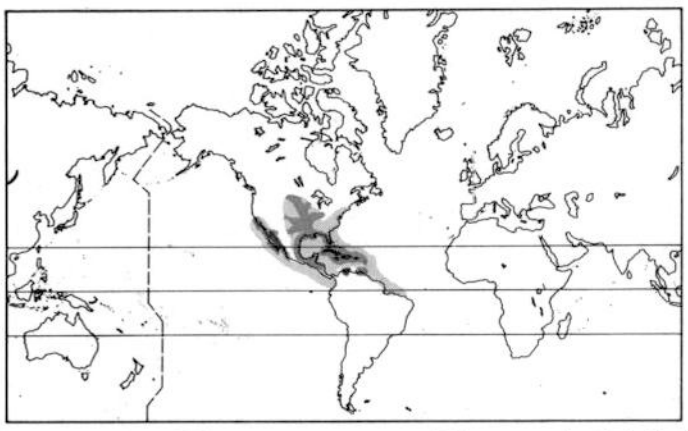

IDENTIFICATION: **Adult Summer:** Small, black-capped tern with white forehead, black-tipped, yellow bill and yellow legs. Upperparts mostly grey, with blackish outer 3–4 primaries forming dark wedge; underparts mostly white. Differs from all congeners in tiny size and black-tipped yellow bill. **Adult Winter:** As adult summer, but bill blackish-brown with yellow base, legs brown; forehead and lores white. **Juvenile/First Winter:** Head pattern as adult winter, but crown browner. Upperparts uniform pinkish-buff or brown with dark carpal bar, becoming paler and greyer with advancing maturity, but retains dark carpal bar.

HABITS: Colonial breeder at marine and freshwater locations. Smallest American tern. Flight hurried and dashing with wader-like wingbeats; hovers before plunge-diving.

DISTRIBUTION: Breeds in North America from California south to Mexico on Pacific coast, and from southern Maine south to Florida Keys; also along major inland waterways. Winters south to Venezuela and Brazil.

SIMILAR SPECIES: None within normal range, but see Amazon Tern (p. 271).

Fairy Tern *Sterna nereis* L25cm/10in W50cm/20in

P p. 157

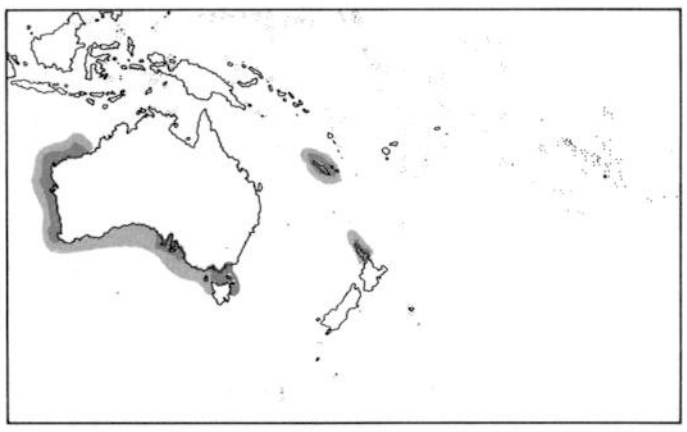

IDENTIFICATION: **Adult Summer:** Small, black-capped tern with white forehead and lores, unmarked yellow bill and bright orange legs. Upperparts mostly grey, outermost primaries only slightly darker than rest of upperwing; underparts wholly white. Differs from Little Tern in unmarked yellow bill, orange legs, white lores, lack of obvious dark wedge on upperwing (beware worn birds), pure white underwing. **Adult Winter:** As adult summer, but bill blackish, centre often yellow; crown white. **Juvenile/First Winter:** As adult winter, but crown and upperparts mottled with brown.

HABITS: Exclusively marine; breeds colonially, otherwise as for Little Tern but bill proportionately shorter, deeper at base.

DISTRIBUTION: New Caledonia, and in northwest Australia from Dampier Archipelago south and east to Victoria and Tasmania; a few pairs also breed in northern New Zealand. Egg-dates Aug–Mar.

SIMILAR SPECIES: Compare Little Tern (p. 265).

White-fronted Tern *Sterna striata* L41cm/16in W76cm/30in

P p. 156

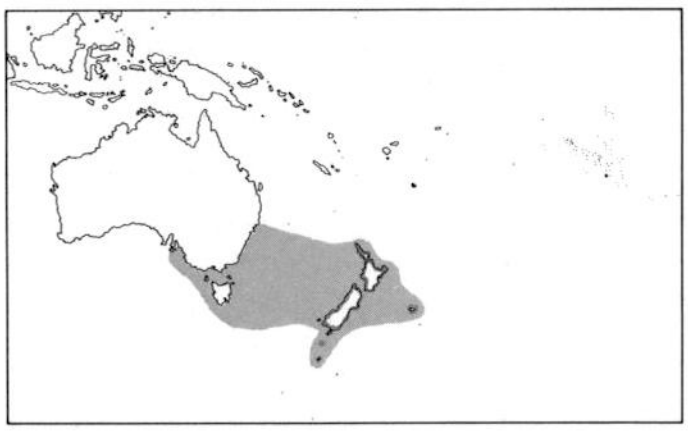

IDENTIFICATION: **Adult Summer:** Medium-sized, black-capped tern with white forehead, black bill and dark red legs. Upperparts very pale grey, appearing almost white at distance; underparts white. At rest, folded primaries show a broad continuous white edge along their upper sides. **Adult Winter:** As adult summer, but crown white. Adults differ from those of migrant Common and Arctic Terns in paler upperparts and lack of noticeable dusky trailing edge to underside of primaries; from Roseate Tern in white forehead, dark legs. **Juvenile/First Winter:** As adult winter, but crown and upperparts edged with brown; with advancing maturity, mantle and back become clear grey, with dark carpal bar, duskier outer primaries, brown tips to outer tail feathers.

HABITS: Colonial breeder; exclusively marine; gregarious.

DISTRIBUTION: Breeds Aug–Jan at New Zealand and its outlying islands, where commonest tern of coastal waters. Disperses after breeding to adjacent seas; some, perhaps mostly first-winter birds, move northwest to winter southern and southeastern Australia.

SIMILAR SPECIES: Compare Common, Arctic, Antarctic and Roseate Terns (p. 264, p. 265, p. 267, p.265).

Black-fronted Tern *Sterna albostriata* L32cm/13in W? **P** p. 157

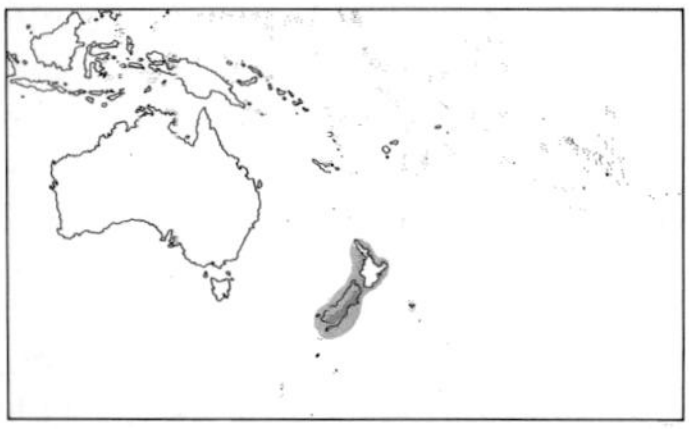

IDENTIFICATION: **Adult Summer:** Rather small, black-capped tern with bright orange legs and bill. Plumage mostly uniform mid-grey, with white stripe separating black cap from grey underparts; rump and tail white. **Adult Winter:** As adult summer, but bill yellow with tip black, forehead, lores and crown white, underparts whiter. **Juvenile/First Winter:** As adult winter, but with brown saddle and dark carpal bar. At any age, small size and yellow or orange bill enable separation from larger, black-billed White-fronted Tern.
HABITS: Appearance and habits recall Whiskered Tern, of which it may be only a race. Breeds singly along dry riverbeds; hawks for insects over rivers, lakes, agricultural crops etc.
DISTRIBUTION: Breeds South Island, New Zealand; egg-dates Sep–Jun. Disperses in winter to shores and estuaries from South Island north to Auckland.
SIMILAR SPECIES: None, but compare White-fronted Tern (p. 266).

Antarctic Tern *Sterna vittata* L41cm/16in W79cm/31in **P** p. 156

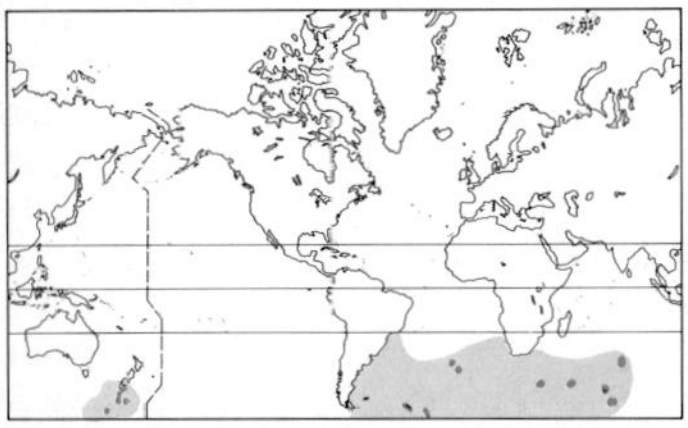

IDENTIFICATION: **Adult Summer:** Medium-sized, black-capped tern with bright red bill and legs. Upperparts mostly grey, the outer primaries edged and tipped slightly darker grey, rump and tail white; underparts variably grey, usually with whitish streak bordering black cap. **Adult Winter:** Bill and legs duller, forehead, crown and lores whiter than in Common Tern, more like winter-plumaged Arctic. Kerguelen Tern is smaller, with distinctive marsh-tern-like jizz, more obvious white streak across cheeks and much darker grey underparts, and smaller, more dusky bill. Differs from South American, Common and Arctic Terns in shorter, deeper bill, lack of distinct wedge on upperwing, and/or lack of pronounced dusky trailing edge on primaries of underwings. **Juvenile/First Winter:** As adult winter, but head and upperparts heavily marked with brown, becoming greyer with advancing maturity; bill blackish-red, legs pink
HABITS: Colonial breeder; exclusively marine; gregarious.
DISTRIBUTION: Breeds Sep–May at many islands in southern Atlantic and Indian Oceans and south of New Zealand, dispersing north after breeding to reach shores of South America and South Africa.
SIMILAR SPECIES: Compare Kerguelen, South American, Common and Arctic Terns (p. 267, p. 270, p. 264, p. 265).

Kerguelen Tern *Sterna virgata* L33cm/13in W75cm/30in **P** p. 156

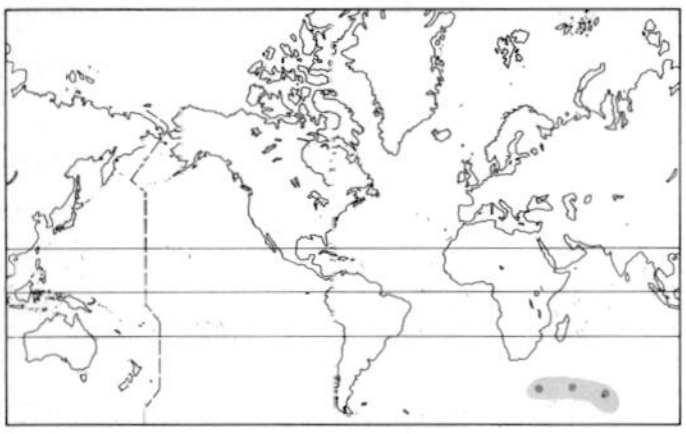

IDENTIFICATION: **Adult Summer:** Smaller, black-capped tern with dusky-red bill and legs. Plumage recalls larger Antarctic Tern; differs in smaller, duskier bill, more obvious white streak across cheeks, much darker grey body and upperwings. **Adult Winter:** As adult summer, but bill mostly black, forehead grizzled white. **Juvenile/First Winter:** Compared with Antarctic Tern, has darker, almost complete brown cap and is more heavily marked with brown on upperparts.
HABITS: Loosely colonial; gregarious; feeds over sea and crater lakes. In all plumages darker than corresponding Antarctic Terns, with smaller, weaker bill and shorter legs. Has distinct marsh-tern jizz; in flight, tail is distinctly shorter and less forked than in Antarctic Tern.
DISTRIBUTION: Southern Indian Ocean. Breeds Oct–Jan Prince Edward, Marion, Crozet and Kerguelen Is, perhaps Heard. Sedentary.
SIMILAR SPECIES: Compare Antarctic Tern (above).

Damara Tern *Sterna balaenarum* L23cm/9in W51cm/20in **P** p. 153

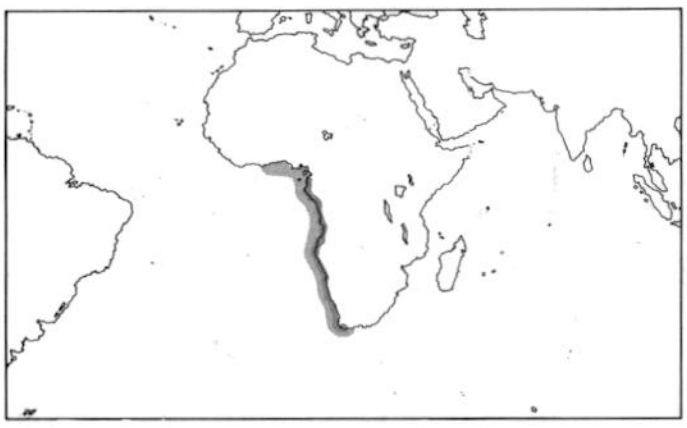

IDENTIFICATION: **Adult Summer:** Small, black-capped tern with blackish bill and brownish or black legs. Upperparts mostly grey; outermost 2–3 primaries black, forming dark leading edge to wing; underparts mostly white, sides of breast faintly grey. Differs from Little Tern in black forehead, black bill and slightly paler grey upperparts. **Adult Winter:** As adult summer, but forehead and crown white. **Juvenile/First Winter:** As adult winter, but crown and upperparts barred with brown, rump white, dark carpal bar on wing. With advancing maturity, mantle and back clear grey, carpal bar retained.
HABITS: Exclusively marine. Differs from Little Tern in longer, thinner, slightly decurved bill, with stockier body shape and stronger, less jerky flight.
DISTRIBUTION: Breeds coasts of South Africa and Namibia, perhaps also further north in Angola; egg-dates Nov–Feb. Disperses north after breeding to Gulf of Guinea.
SIMILAR SPECIES: Compare Little Tern (p. 265).

Saunders' Little Tern *Sterna saundersi* L23cm/9in W51cm/20in **P** p. 153

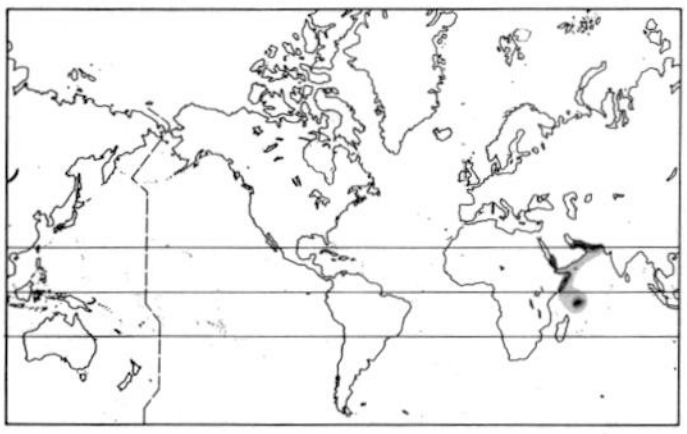

IDENTIFICATION: **Adult Summer:** Small, black-capped tern with white forehead, black-tipped yellow bill and brown legs. Formerly considered a subspecies of Little Tern; differs in blacker outer primaries giving more distinct wedge on upperwing, white forehead not extending over eye, slightly paler grey upperparts, brown (not yellow) legs. **Adult Winter:** As adult summer, but bill and legs blackish, with forehead, crown and lores whiter than in winter Little Tern, recalling pattern of Lesser Crested Tern. **Juvenile/First Winter:** Head pattern as adult winter, but crown browner; upperparts brownish-buff, becoming paler with age, dark carpal bar on upperwing.
HABITS: Much as for Little Tern.
DISTRIBUTION: Biology and dispersal little known; breeds southern half of Red Sea east to Iran, Seychelles, possibly Madagascar.
SIMILAR SPECIES: Compare Little Tern (p. 265).

White-cheeked Tern *Sterna repressa* L33cm/13in W79cm/31in **P** p. 153

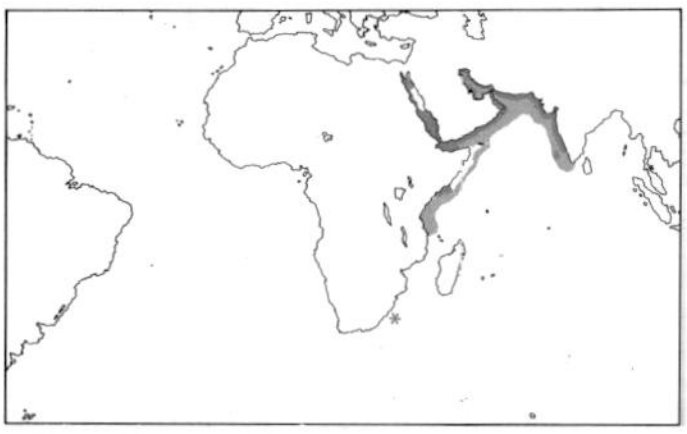

IDENTIFICATION: **Adult Summer:** Medium-sized, black-capped tern with red legs and black-tipped red bill. Differs from Common and Arctic Terns in much darker, mostly uniform dark grey plumage, with obvious white facial streak dividing black cap from grey underparts; rump and tail dark grey. **Adult Winter:** Forehead mottled white; underparts wholly white. Differs from Arctic, Common and Roseate Terns in grey rump and tail, and darker upperwings contrasting with silvery bases. **First Winter:** Bill black, legs yellowish-brown. Plumage similar to Common Tern; differs in obvious grey rump and tail, blacker, more extensive carpal bar on upperwing.
HABITS: Mainly coastal and inshore; colonial breeder; gregarious.
DISTRIBUTION: Breeds Apr–Aug coasts and islands of Red and Arabian Seas west to India, smaller numbers also off Kenya; most appear to disperse east towards the shores of Pakistan and India.
SIMILAR SPECIES: None, but compare Arctic and Common Terns (p. 265, p. 264).

Black-naped Tern *Sterna sumatrana* L31cm/12in W61cm/24in P p. 157

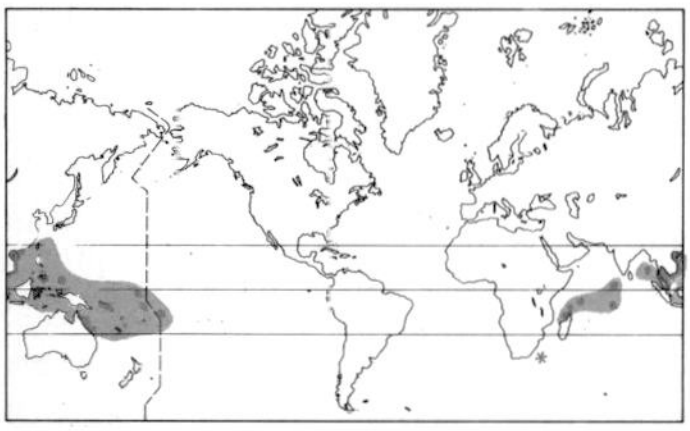

IDENTIFICATION: **Adult:** Distinctive, rather small tern with black bill and legs. White head has characteristic narrow black band running from eye to eye, broadest across nape but not extending forwards to reach bill. Upperparts pale grey, looking almost white at distance; underparts white. Differs from winter Roseate Tern in smaller size, black (not orange) legs and whiter upperparts. **Juvenile/First Winter:** Bill dusky-yellow at first, but soon darkens to black; head as adult, but black band less distinct, upperparts broadly tipped black with dusky carpal bar on upperwing.
HABITS: Exclusively marine; breeds colonially; gregarious. Feeds like a noddy, skimming low over open sea or shallow lagoons, snatching at surface prey.
DISTRIBUTION: Breeds on islands and coasts of tropical Indian and Pacific Oceans, normally between Sep–Jan. Thought to be sedentary.
SIMILAR SPECIES: Compare winter Little, Fairy and Roseate Terns (p. 265, p. 266, p. 265).

Indian River Tern *Sterna aurantia* L40cm/16in W? P p. 161

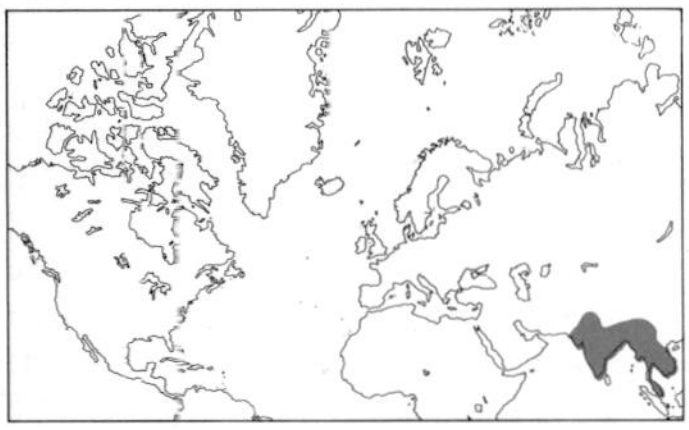

IDENTIFICATION: **Adult Summer:** Medium-sized, black-capped tern with large yellow bill and red or orange legs. Upperparts, including rump and tail, dark grey, with white outer tail feathers; worn/abraded outermost 6 primaries and their coverts often blackish, forming dark wingtip. Underparts mostly white. **Adult Winter:** Bill tipped black; forehead and crown whitish. **Juvenile/Immature:** As adult winter, but crown and upperparts tipped with brown, sides of breast grey-brown. All ages differ from Black-bellied Tern in much larger size, white underparts.
HABITS: Freshwater tern, occasionally straying to tidal creeks. Flight purposeful and strong, with long wings and long-streamered tail imparting distinctive jizz.
DISTRIBUTION: Breeds along inland rivers of Asia from Iran east through India, Burma, Malay Peninsula, where an uncommon resident in Thailand; egg-dates Mar–May.
SIMILAR SPECIES: Compare Black-bellied Tern (below).

Black-bellied Tern *Sterna melanogastra* L31cm/12in W? P p. 161

IDENTIFICATION: **Adult Summer:** Small, black-capped tern with bright yellow bill and orange-red legs. Upperparts, including rump and tail, pale uniform dove-grey; underparts white, with diagnostic black belly patch. Differs from Indian River Tern in smaller size, paler, more uniform upperparts and black belly. **Adult Winter:** Bill tipped black, forehead mottled with white; black belly patch reduced to scattered dark feather tips or, more rarely, wholly white.
HABITS: Freshwater species, often loafing with skimmers or associating with larger Indian River Tern, from which it further differs in less robust bill and lighter jizz. In flight forked tail appears disproportionately long.
DISTRIBUTION: Restricted to Asia; breeds from Indus Valley east and south through India, Burma, Sri Lanka and Thailand. Egg-dates Mar–Apr.
SIMILAR SPECIES: Compare Indian River and Whiskered Terns (p. 269, p. 261).

South American Tern *Sterna hirundinacea* L42cm/17in W85cm/33in **P** p. 155

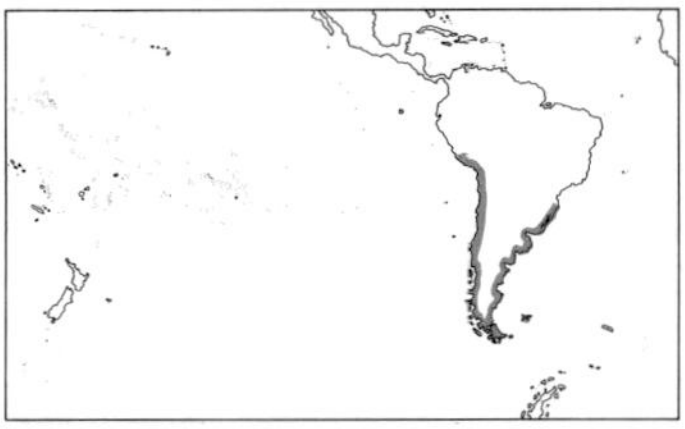

IDENTIFICATION: **Adult Summer:** Medium-sized, black-capped tern with bright red legs and bill. Upperparts mostly pale grey, with whiter rump and tail; underparts white. Differs from similar Antarctic Tern in longer, more dagger-like bill, paler grey upperparts, and white (not grey) underparts. In flight, outer 6 primaries on upperwing show darker outer webs and tips, forming dark outer wedge; from below, primaries have darker tips forming distinct trailing edge to wing. **Adult Winter:** Forehead and crown white; differs from Antarctic Tern in bill proportions and darker outer primaries. **First Winter:** As adult winter, but saddle, upperwing-coverts and scapulars scaled with brown; bill black. Compared with corresponding Antarctic Tern, upperparts, particularly scapulars, are more heavily and clearly marked, the cap more grizzled, giving paler-headed appearance.

HABITS: Breeds colonially at marine locations; gregarious. Slightly larger than Common and Antarctic Terns, with heavier, longer, more drooping bill.

DISTRIBUTION: South America. Breeds Sep–Apr on Falkland Is and from Tierra del Fuego north to about 25°S in Brazil and to about 15°S in Peru; disperses after breeding, reaching to about 15°S in Brazil and to about 5°S in Peru.

SIMILAR SPECIES: Compare Antarctic Tern (p. 267).

Peruvian Tern *Sterna lorata* L23cm/9in W50cm/20in **P** p. 155

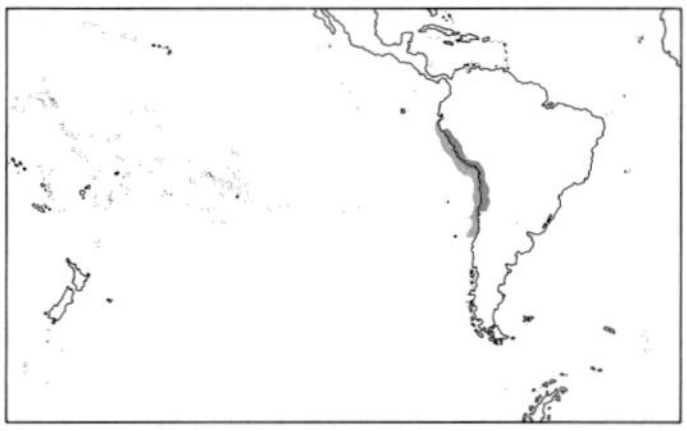

IDENTIFICATION: **Adult Summer:** Small, black-capped tern with white forehead, brownish-yellow legs and black-tipped yellow bill. Upperparts, including rump and tail, mostly pale grey, with outermost 2–3 primaries edged darker; underparts pale dusky-grey. **Adult Winter:** Bill blackish, base yellow; crown tipped with white; underparts whiter, with grey wash across breast. Differs from all congeners in small size, yellow and black bill.

HABITS: Smallest Humboldt Current tern; size and plumage recalls Least Tern, but rump and tail grey. Feeds over shoreline and brackish lagoons, flight hurried and fast, hovers before surface-plunging. Colonial breeder; gregarious.

DISTRIBUTION: Western South America; breeds coasts of Peru and Chile, dispersing north to Gulf of Guayaquil and south to at least 23°S. Egg-dates Dec–Jan.

SIMILAR SPECIES: None within range.

Inca Tern *Larosterna inca* L41cm/16in W? **P** p. 154

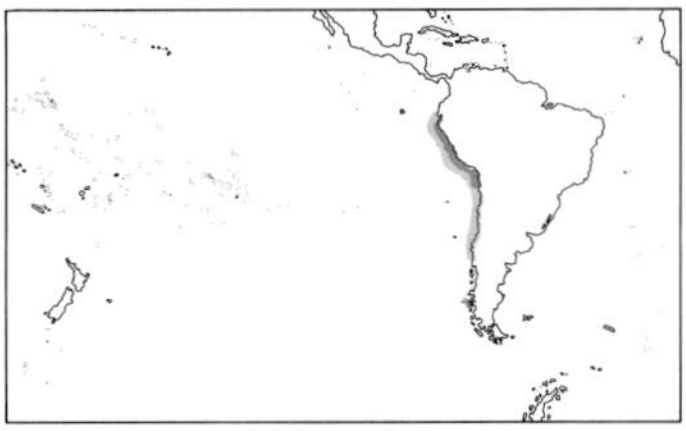

IDENTIFICATION: **Adult:** Virtually unmistakable; a large dusky tern with bright red legs and bill, with yellow wattle at gape. Plumage mostly dark bluish-grey, with conspicuous white moustachial streak, white edge to wing and blackish cap. **Juvenile/Immature:** Mostly uniform dark greyish or purplish-brown, with blackish bill and white trailing edge to wings; with advancing maturity, acquires paler moustachial streak and dusky-horn bill with reddish tip.

HABITS: Strictly marine; gregarious. Roosts with gulls and terns. Flight shows surprising agility and grace for so large a tern, hovering before dipping to surface to make quick darting manoeuvres.

DISTRIBUTION: Endemic to Humboldt Current, from Gulf of Guayaquil, Ecuador, south to Iquique, Chile. Ranges south to Chiloe Is, Chile, during periods of oceanic fluctuations.

SIMILAR SPECIES: None.

Large-billed Tern *Phaetusa simplex* L37cm/15in W92cm/36in **P** p. 154

IDENTIFICATION: **Adult Summer**: Large, black-capped tern with yellow bill and legs. Virtually unmistakable. Upperparts mostly dark grey, with striking black, grey and white upperwings, white hindcollar, grey rump and tail; underparts mostly white. **Adult Winter:** Crown mottled with white. **Juvenile:** As adult winter, but head paler, with blackish band from eye to nape; upperparts browner in tone, tail tipped brown.
HABITS: Distinctive, the only large, yellow-billed freshwater tern in South America; at all ages shows striking tricoloured upperwings. Gregarious; breeds colonially. Follows ships along Amazonian waterways surface-plunging into wake to secure prey.
DISTRIBUTION: South America. Breeds from Colombia, Trinidad and Venezuela south through Amazonas to Brazil, Uruguay and northern Argentina; vagrants occasionally reported from Ecuador and Peru.
SIMILAR SPECIES: None.

Amazon Tern *Sterna superciliaris* L23cm/9in W50cm/20in **P** p. 154

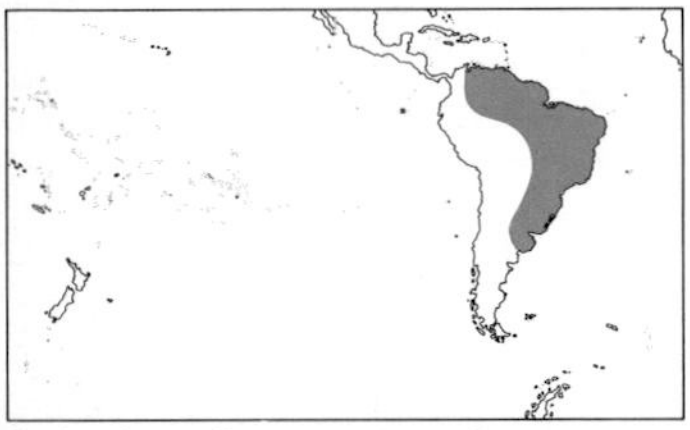

IDENTIFICATION: **Adult Summer:** Small, black-capped tern with white forehead, yellow legs and bill. Upperparts, including rump and tail, pale grey, with outermost 2–3 primaries edged darker forming dark leading edge; underparts white. **Adult Winter:** Crown and lores white. **Juvenile/Immature:** Bill dull yellow, brown at base and tip. Plumage as adult winter, but crown and upperparts scaled with brown. At all ages, differs from Large-billed Tern in much smaller size, lack of tricoloured upperwings.
HABITS: Tiny freshwater tern, recalling Least Tern of North America, but with greyer rump and tail, unmarked yellow bill. Gregarious; colonial breeder. Flight hurried and swift; hovers before plunge-diving.
DISTRIBUTION: Inland waterways of eastern South America from Colombia south through Venezuela to Uruguay and Argentina; egg-dates Jul–Sep.
SIMILAR SPECIES: None within normal range.

Chinese Crested Tern *Sterna bernsteini* L38cm/15in W? **P** p. 161

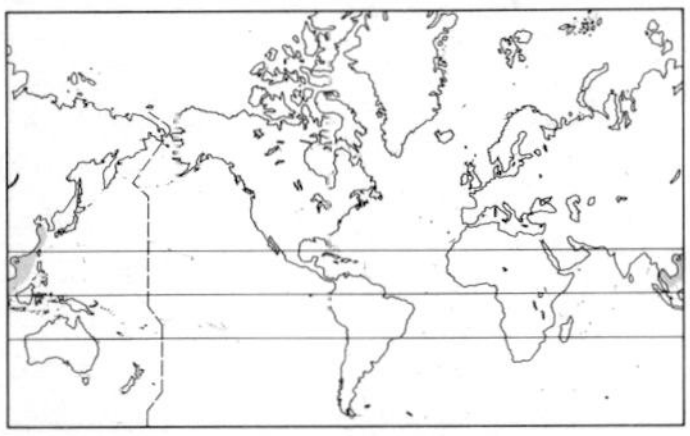

IDENTIFICATION: **Adult Summer:** Medium-sized, black-crested tern recalling more widespread Crested Tern, but with black tip to yellow bill. Upperparts pale pearl-grey, rump and tail white; underparts white. **Adult Winter:** Extreme tip of bill yellowish; forehead and crown white. **Juvenile/Immature:** Undescribed.
HABITS: Virtually unknown; compared with Crested Tern, smaller, with proportionately longer, more deeply forked tail.
DISTRIBUTION: Breeding area apparently unknown. Frequents coasts of China north to Shantung in summer and south to Thailand and Philippines in winter.
SIMILAR SPECIES: Compare Crested and Lesser Crested Terns (p. 262, p. 263).

Aleutian Tern *Sterna aleutica* L36cm/14in W78cm/31in P p. 158

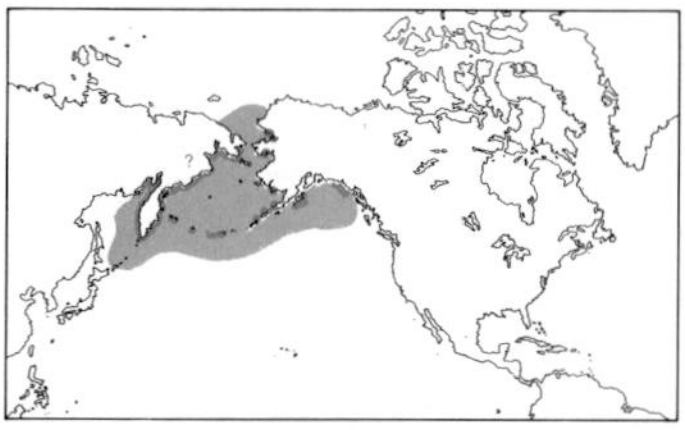

IDENTIFICATION: **Adult Summer:** Medium-sized, black-capped tern with white forehead, black bill and legs. Plumage mostly dark grey, with white facial streak separating black cap from grey underparts; rump, tail and ventral area white. In flight, from below, look for diagnostic dark subterminal bar and white trailing edge along secondaries. **Adult Winter:** Crown and underparts white. Adults differ from Common and Arctic in blacker bill and legs, greyer plumage and diagnostic underwing pattern. **Juvenile/Immature:** Legs and base of lower mandible dusky-red; buff-brown cap and upperparts, becoming greyer with age; underwing as adult.
HABITS: Gregarious; breeds in small colonies, occasionally with Arctic Terns. Flight strong, direct, with slower, deeper wingbeats than Arctic; diagnostic wader-like 'twee-ee-ee' flight call.
DISTRIBUTION: Breeds May–Sep along coasts of Siberia and Alaska. Absent from breeding areas Oct onwards, but movements/winter area unknown; probably south into oceanic habitat.
SIMILAR SPECIES: None within range, but compare Arctic and Common Terns (p. 265, p. 264).

Grey-backed Tern *Sterna lunata* L36cm/14in W74cm/29in P p. 158

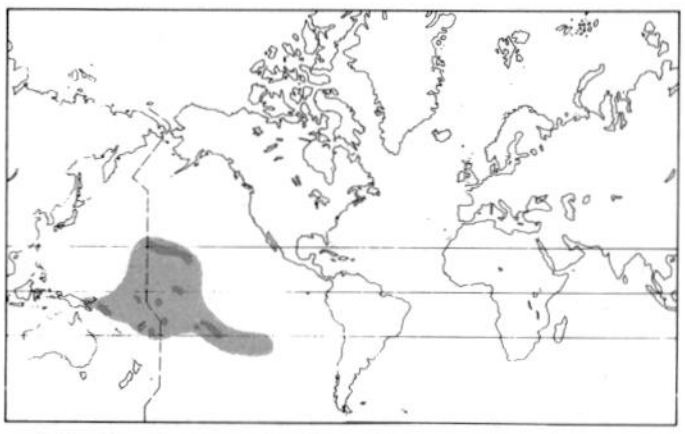

IDENTIFICATION: **Adult Summer:** Medium-sized, black-capped tern with large white forehead extending broadly over eye, black legs and bill. Upperparts mostly deep blue-grey, rump and tail paler grey, becoming slightly brown in worn plumage, with darker primaries; underparts white. **Adult Winter:** Crown mottled with white. Adult differs from Bridled and Sooty Terns in grey (not brown) upperparts, more extensive white forehead. **Juvenile/Immature:** Head mostly white, with dark cervical collar extending narrowly forwards through eye; upperparts mostly pale grey, with blackish primaries and arrow-like marks across mantle, back, scapulars and upperwing-coverts; with advancing maturity, upperparts less marked. Differs from juvenile Sooty Tern in grey upperparts and white underparts; from juvenile Bridled in paler head with more contrasting hindcollar, grey upperparts and dark arrow-like markings.
HABITS: Exclusively marine; breeds singly or in loose colonies, perhaps preferring cliff situations. In flight, easily separated from both Sooty and Bridled Terns by grey upperparts recalling Aleutian Tern, but with white underparts.
DISTRIBUTION: Central tropical Pacific, but range/movements poorly documented. Probably sedentary. Egg-dates Dec–Jan.
SIMILAR SPECIES: Compare Sooty and Bridled Terns (p. 273, p. 272).

Bridled Tern *Sterna anaethetus* L36cm/14in W76cm/30in P p. 158

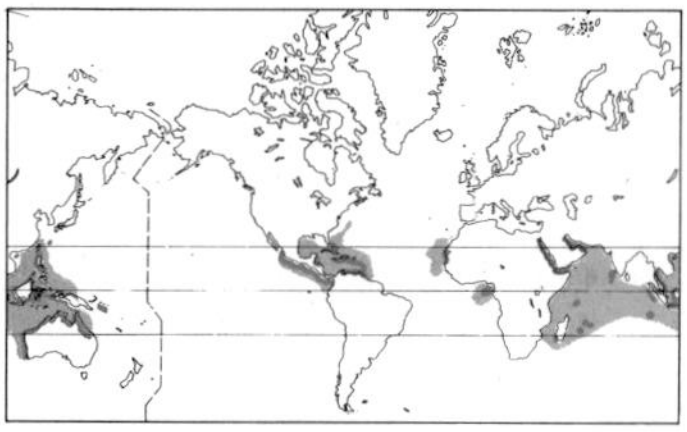

IDENTIFICATION: **Adult:** Medium-sized, black-capped tropical tern with white forehead, black legs and bill. Upperparts brown or brownish-grey; underparts white. Differs from Sooty Tern in paler upperparts, white forehead extending narrowly over eye, diffuse hindcollar between cap and mantle (often hard to see), whiter underwings and outer tail feathers. Grey-backed Tern is grey above, with more extensive white forehead. **Juvenile/Immature:** Pattern much as adult, but paler, more buff-brown above, with darker forehead, and pale tips to upperparts. Differs from corresponding Sooty Tern in paler upperparts and wholly white underparts; from Grey-backed Tern in darker head, browner upperparts with pale tips (not pale grey with blackish tips).
HABITS: Exclusively marine; breeds colonially, occasionally with Sooty Terns.
DISTRIBUTION: Breeds at many tropical and subtropical islands in all the major oceans, although absent from central and eastern Pacific; egg-dates vary with location.
SIMILAR SPECIES: Compare Sooty and Grey-backed Terns (p. 273, p. 272).

Sooty Tern *Sterna fuscata* L43cm/17in W90cm/35in **P** p. 159

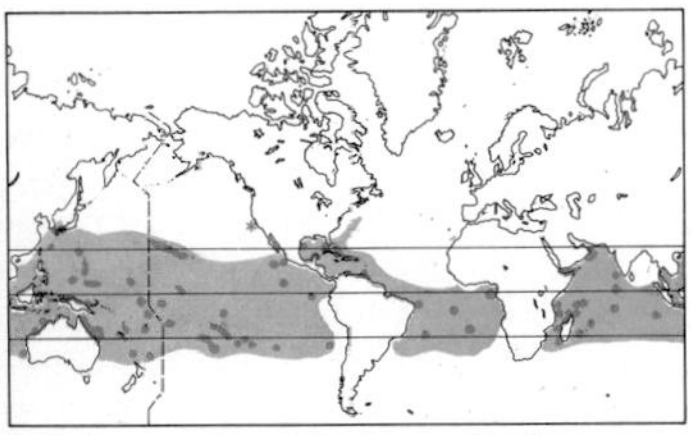

IDENTIFICATION: **Adult:** Medium-sized, black-capped tropical tern with white forehead black legs and bill. Upperparts blackish-brown; underparts white. Differs from Bridled Tern in larger size, blacker upperparts, white forehead does not extend past eye, lacks pale hindcollar, has broader, dark trailing edge to underwing. **Juvenile/Immature:** Mostly dark brown, with white lower belly, ventral area and underwing-coverts; upperparts broadly tipped white or buff at first, but less noticeable later. Differs from corresponding Bridled Tern in wholly brown head and upper breast.
HABITS: Highly pelagic, usually returns to land only to breed (unlike Bridled Tern). Colonial breeder; gregarious throughout year. Flight graceful and buoyant, dipping down to water to snatch surface prey; does not plunge-dive.
DISTRIBUTION: Pantropical; breeds at many islands, egg-dates dependent upon location; disperses to oceanic habitat after breeding.
SIMILAR SPECIES: Compare Bridled Tern (p. 272).

White Tern *Gygis alba* L30cm/12in W78cm/31in **P** p. 159

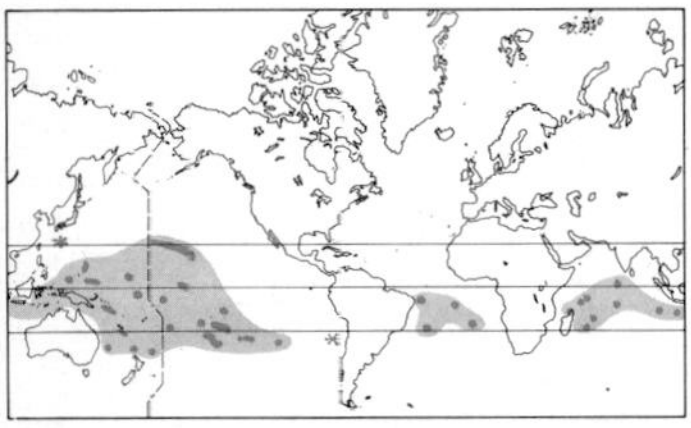

IDENTIFICATION: **Adult:** Also known as Fairy Tern; unmistakable, the world's only all-white tern; bill black, base blue. **Juvenile/Immature:** As adult, but with variable pale brown mottling on mantle, back and wing-coverts.
HABITS: Small, delicate, exclusively marine tern, with large black eye and slightly upturned bill. In flight, wings appear broad and rather rounded, which, with large head and eye, imparts distinctive 'chunky' jizz while remaining buoyant and graceful. This ethereal quality further enhanced by translucent quality of wings when directly overhead. Inquisitive and tame, hovering before human intruders at nest site. Breeds singly, laying single egg on branch of tree without any nest (unique).
DISTRIBUTION: Pantropical, breeding at many islands throughout tropical and subtropical oceans; egg-dates dependent upon location.
SIMILAR SPECIES: None.

Grey Noddy *Procelsterna cerulea* L27cm/11in W60cm/24in **P** p. 159

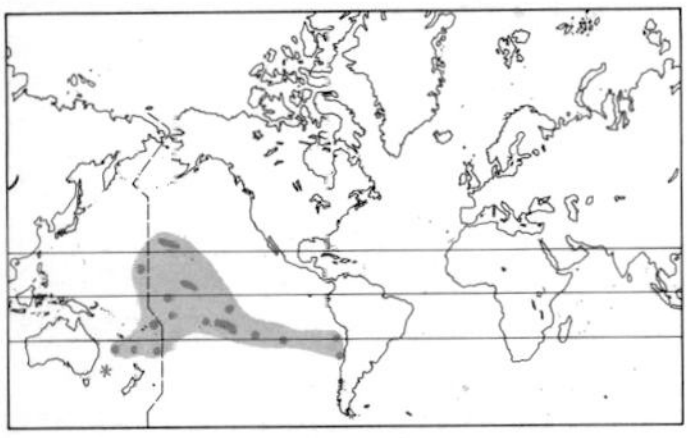

IDENTIFICATION: **Adult:** Small, dimorphic, blue-grey tern with black bill and legs, yellow or pinkish webs. Pale morphs have whitish-grey head, underwing-coverts and underparts; dark morphs have darker grey head, underwing-coverts and underparts. Small size and grey plumage should prevent confusion with any other species, although at long range pale morphs could perhaps be mistaken for White Tern by the unwary. **Juvenile/Immature:** As adult, but with brownish cast to plumage and darker primaries.
HABITS: Small size and soft grey plumage imparts distinctive appearance; flight graceful and buoyant; occasionally paddles on water. Breeds singly or in small loose colonies; sedentary.
DISTRIBUTION: Tropical and subtropical Pacific, breeds from Hawaiian Is south to Easter and Kermadec Is; egg-dates vary with location.
SIMILAR SPECIES: None.

Brown Noddy *Anous stolidus* L42cm/17in W82cm/32in

P p. 160

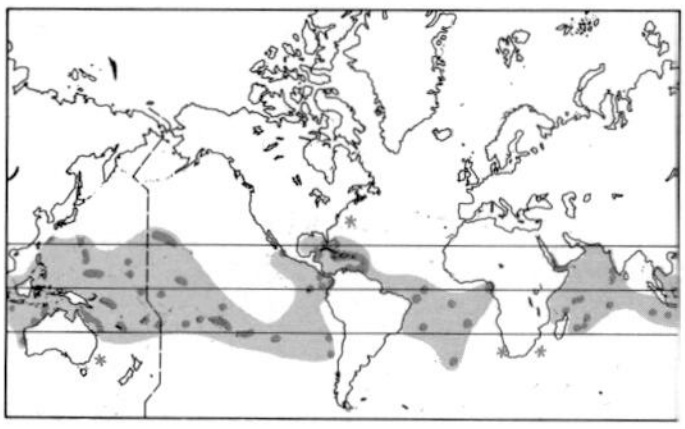

IDENTIFICATION: **Adult:** Medium-sized dark brown tern with greyish-white forehead, black bill and legs. Differs from Black Noddy in larger size, heavier, deeper, more robust bill, greyer cap which has curved demarcation with black lores, browner upperparts, and distinctive two-toned underwing. Lesser Noddy smaller, greyer, and usually lacks demarcated lores. **Juvenile:** Very like adult, but with dimorphic head pattern; some have pale smoky-brown caps with narrow white line over black lores, others have prominent white forehead ending abruptly at crown.

HABITS: Highly pelagic, usually feeding far out at sea, where gregarious, often feeding in large flocks over shoals of predatory fish. Unlike other terns, noddies have long, rather wedge-shaped tails with small central notch. They rarely land on water or plunge-dive, dipping down to snatch at surface prey. Colonial breeder.

DISTRIBUTION: Pantropical; breeding dates vary with location. Some populations migratory and dispersive, others remain at breeding islands throughout year.

SIMILAR SPECIES: Compare Black and Lesser Noddies (below).

Black Noddy *Anous minutus* L34cm/13in W76cm/30in

P p. 160

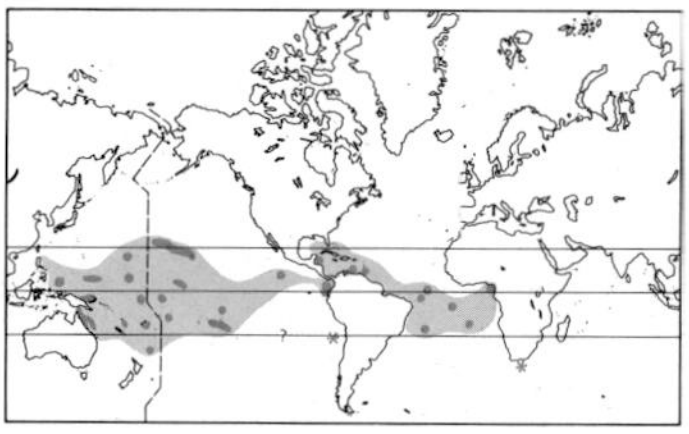

IDENTIFICATION: Some authors consider Black Noddy to be a race of Lesser Noddy. **Adult Summer:** Small to medium-sized blackish tern with white cap, black bill and legs. Differs from both Brown and Lesser Noddies in blacker overall plumage, longer, thinner bill, and whiter cap with straighter demarcation at lores than in Brown Noddy. **Juvenile:** As adult, but with only the forehead white, ending abruptly at crown. Differs from pale-headed form of juvenile Brown Noddy in smaller size, bill proportions, and blacker plumage contrasting more with brilliant white forehead; uniform underwing.

HABITS: As for Brown Noddy, but bill proportionately longer, finer; more lightly built jizz, with faster, more fluttering flight.

DISTRIBUTION: Breeds at many islands in tropical and subtropical Atlantic and Pacific Oceans; egg-dates depend on location.

SIMILAR SPECIES: Compare Brown and Lesser Noddies (this page).

Lesser Noddy *Anous tenuirostris* L32cm/13in W60cm/24in

P p. 160

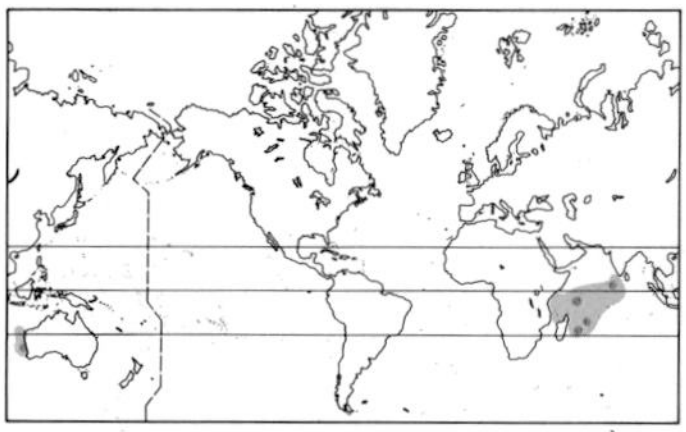

IDENTIFICATION: **Adult:** Small brownish-grey tern with diffuse pale greyish-white cap, black legs and bill. Plumage mostly brown, except for pale greyish-white cap which merges without obvious demarcation with nape and lores; atypical forms show sharp demarcation between pale greyish-white forehead and blackish lores. **Juvenile:** As adult; some, apparently, with whiter caps (Serventy *et al.* 1971). All ages differ from Brown and Black Noddies in smaller size and generally greyer head, which usually lacks obvious loral demarcation.

HABITS: As for Brown Noddy, but smaller, with narrower wings, lighter jizz and faster wingbeats.

DISTRIBUTION: Tropical and subtropical Indian Ocean; breeds Seychelles, Reunion, Maldives and off Australia at Abrolhos Is. Egg-dates Sep–Jan.

SIMILAR SPECIES: Compare Brown and Black Noddies (above).

Black Skimmer *Rynchops niger* L46cm/18in W112cm/44in **P** p. 162

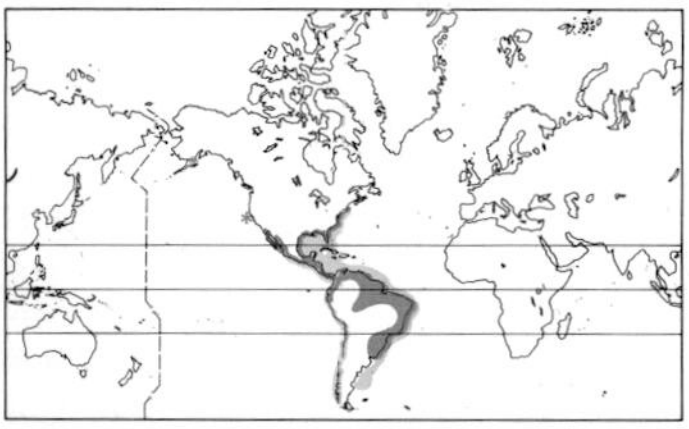

IDENTIFICATION: **Adult:** Unmistakable; black above, white below, with black-tipped red bill and white forehead, cheeks and outer tail feathers. In winter, upperparts browner, with whitish hindcollar. **Juvenile/Immature:** Pattern much as adult, but bill shorter, duskier; head white, mottled with brown, upperparts with obvious white feather edges.
HABITS: No other group of birds has a lower mandible longer than the upper. Flight graceful and buoyant, skimming low over surface while ploughing steady furrow through water with bill. Breeds colonially, often with other terns.
DISTRIBUTION: Coasts, rivers and larger waterways of North and South America. Breeds from Massachusetts and California south to Argentina; egg-dates May–Sep.
SIMILAR SPECIES: None within range.

African Skimmer *Rynchops flavirostris* L38cm/15in W106cm/42in **P** p. 162

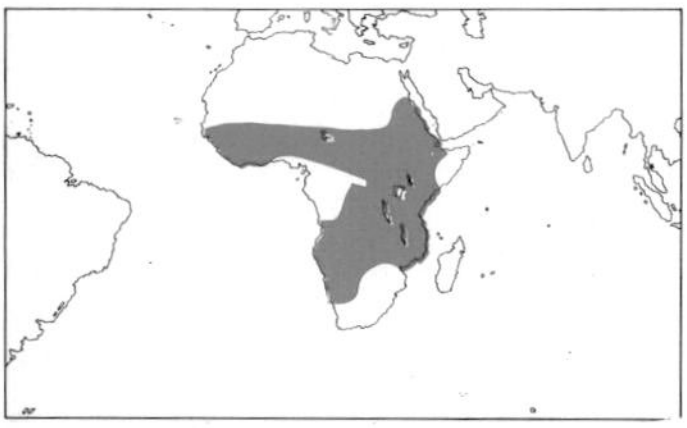

IDENTIFICATION: **Adult:** Unmistakable; black above, white below, with vermilion or deep orange bill, white forehead, cheeks and outer tail feathers. In winter, upperparts browner, with broad whitish collar over nape. **Juvenile/Immature:** Patterned as adult, but head paler, upperparts with obvious white edges.
HABITS: As for Black Skimmer (above), but smaller, with unmarked bill.
DISTRIBUTION: Coasts and rivers of Africa from Sudan south to Natal and the Zambezi and west across central Africa to Senegal. Partial migrant within range, movements dependent upon local rains. Egg-dates Apr–Sep.
SIMILAR SPECIES: None within range.

Indian Skimmer *Rynchops albicollis* L43cm/17in W108cm/43in **P** p. 162

IDENTIFICATION: **Adult:** Unmistakable; black above, white below, with yellow-tipped orange bill, white forehead, cheeks and outer tail feathers. In winter, upperparts browner. **Juvenile/Immature:** As adult, but head whiter, with whitish feather edges to upperparts.
HABITS: As for Black Skimmer, but found mainly at freshwater locations.
DISTRIBUTION: Restricted to larger rivers and lakes of Asia from Iran east through India, Burma and Indo-China. Partial migrant throughout range, movements linked with local rains. Egg-dates Mar–May.
SIMILAR SPECIES: None within range.

Guillemot *Uria aalge* L42cm/17in W71cm/28in **P** p. 164

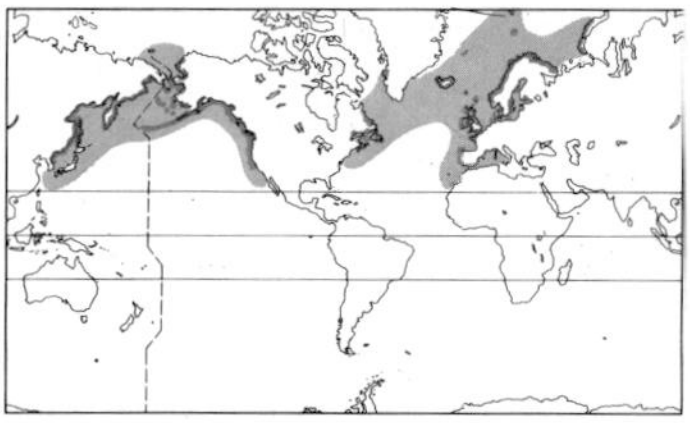

IDENTIFICATION: **Adult Summer:** Large, long-necked auk with dark head and upperparts, white underparts; legs and bill black. Upperparts, including head and foreneck, dark brown, ending at white upper breast in shallow, inverted 'U'; underparts white, except for diagnostic brown striations on flanks. The bridled form, found only in Atlantic, has a narrow white eye-ring and post-ocular line. Differs from Brünnich's Guillemot in browner upperparts, particularly head and back, flatter demarcation line between brown and white on lower foreneck, striated flanks, and longer, thinner, wholly black bill which gives head more attenuated appearance. **Adult Winter:** Throat, chin and sides of face white, with diagnostic black post-ocular line. **First Winter:** As adult winter, but bill shorter, cheeks darker, lacks post-ocular stripe.
HABITS: Breeds colonially on cliff ledges; gregarious throughout year. Flight fast, usually low over water, turning from side to side, neck extended, wings beating rapidly.
DISTRIBUTION: North Atlantic and Pacific Oceans; egg-dates May–Aug. Winters south to Japan, California and Mediterranean.
SIMILAR SPECIES: Compare Brünnich's Guillemot and Razorbill (below).

Brünnich's Guillemot *Uria lomvia* L45cm/18in W76cm/30in **P** p. 164

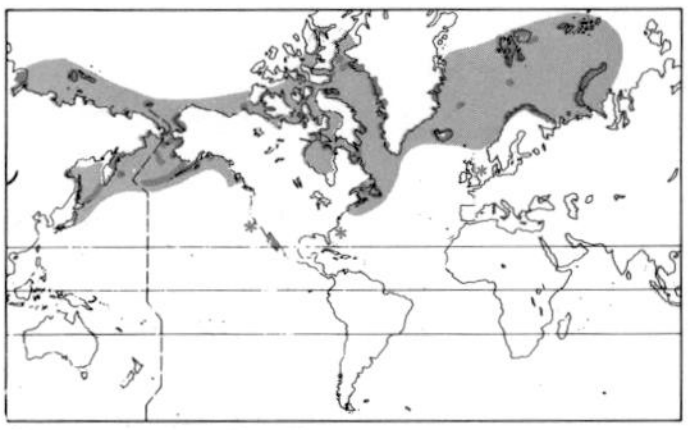

IDENTIFICATION: **Adult Summer:** Large, stocky auk with dark head and upperparts, white underparts; bill black, with thin white line on cutting edge of upper mandible. Differs from Guillemot in slightly larger size, diagnostic white stripe along thicker, heavier bill, which has an evenly decurving culmen from base to tip, and unmarked white flanks; upperparts average blacker, and end at white upper breast in inverted 'V'. **Adult Winter:** Chin, throat and foreneck white; differs from winter Guillemot in bill, dark cheeks, lack of post-ocular stripe, white flanks. **First Winter:** As adult winter, but bill smaller, chin and throat slightly more mottled.
HABITS: Breeds colonially on cliff ledges; gregarious throughout year. In flight, breeding adults usually blacker than Guillemot, with larger bill and head, shorter neck and stockier jizz.
DISTRIBUTION: North Atlantic and Pacific Oceans, where generally more northerly than Guillemot; egg-dates Jun–Aug. Winters south to northern Japan, southeastern Alaska and Iceland; casual further south.
SIMILAR SPECIES: Compare Guillemot and Razorbill (this page).

Razorbill *Alca torda* L43cm/17in W64cm/25in **P** p. 165

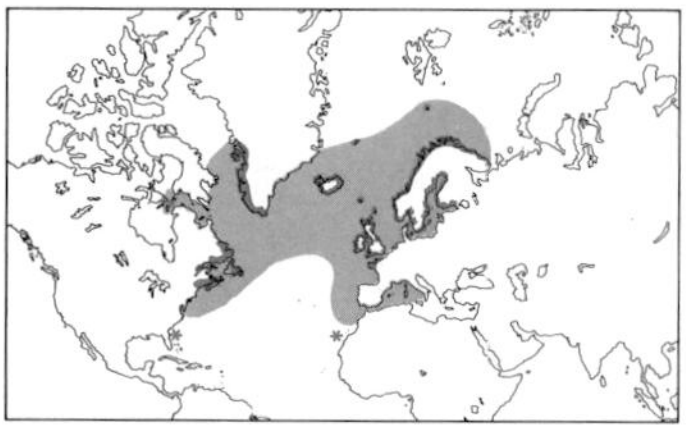

IDENTIFICATION: **Adult Summer:** Large, big-headed, thick-necked auk with dark head and upperparts, white underparts; bill black, with diagnostic vertical white band and a horizontal white stripe from base of upper mandible to eye. **Adult Winter:** Chin, throat and ear-coverts white. Differs from both guillemots in large head, short thick neck, longer pointed tail which is often cocked when swimming, and massive, blunt-tipped bill. **First Winter:** As adult winter, but bill smaller without white bands.
HABITS: Breeds colonially on cliff ledges; gregarious throughout year. In flight, appears blacker above than most alcids, with large head, torpedo-shaped body and long tail imparting distinctive jizz; sides of rump white.
DISTRIBUTION: North Atlantic. Breeds from Bear Is south to Maine in the USA, and to northern France in Europe; egg-dates May–Jul. Winters south to New York and Mediterranean.
SIMILAR SPECIES: Compare Guillemot and Brünnich's Guillemot (above).

Little Auk *Alle alle* L22cm/9in W32cm/13in P p. 163

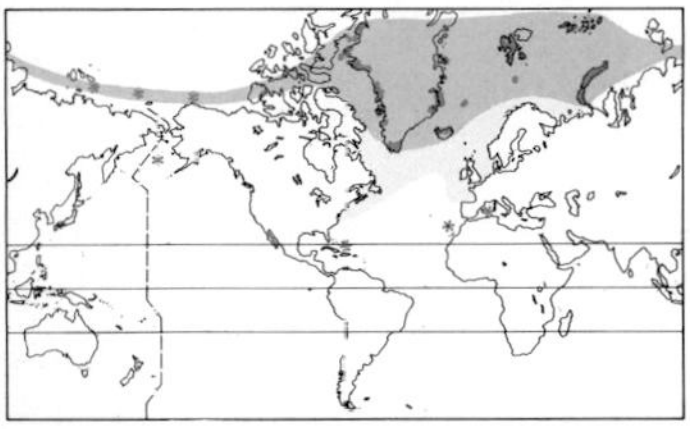

IDENTIFICATION: **Adult Summer:** Tiny, plump, short-necked auk, black above, white below, with small, stubby, black bill. Small size and whirring flight should prevent confusion with all other Atlantic auks. Upperparts, including head and upper breast, black, with white streaks on scapulars and tips to secondaries; underparts white. **Adult Winter:** Chin and throat white, curving upwards behind eye across ear-coverts. **Juvenile/Immature:** As breeding adult, but upperparts slightly browner, paler on chin, with smaller bill. In Alaska, no other small auk is so starkly black and white with all-black head and foreneck.
HABITS: Breeds colonially among boulders and rubble; gregarious throughout year. Flight low and fast; its small size, short neck and rotund body imparts distinctive chubby jizz.
DISTRIBUTION: Primarily North Atlantic, where abundant, but recently found in small numbers in Beaufort, Bering and Chukchi Seas, where it may also breed; egg-dates Jun–Jul. Winters south to Long Is, USA, and France.
SIMILAR SPECIES: Swimming juvenile Razorbills or Guillemots fresh from ledges (p. 276).

Black Guillemot *Cepphus grylle* L33cm/13in W58cm/23in P p. 165

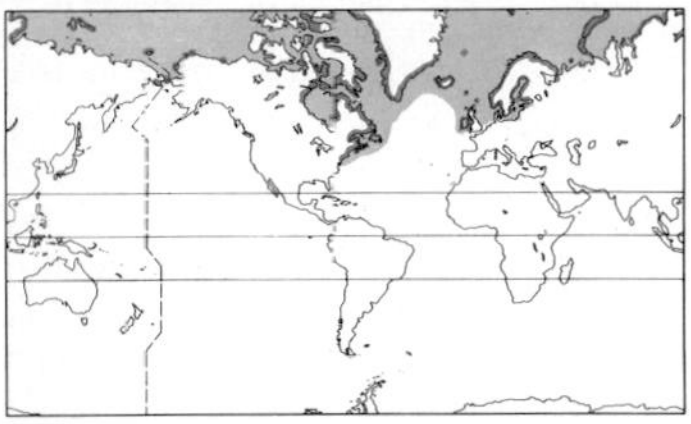

IDENTIFICATION: **Adult Summer:** Medium-sized, mostly black auk with conspicuous white wing patch; slender black bill, coral-red legs and mouth. At any age, unlikely to be confused with other auks except in Bering and Chukchi Seas, where range overlaps with Pigeon Guillemot. Differs in unmarked white secondary coverts, white (not dusky) axillaries and underwing-coverts. **Adult Winter:** Head mostly white, crown and lores mottled with black; upperparts mottled grey and white. **Juvenile/Immature:** As adult winter, but duskier on head, with mottled upperwing-coverts which, by first summer, can resemble those of adult Pigeon Guillemot (see photo p. 165).
HABITS: Prefers shallow coastal waters throughout year. Breeds in loose colonies among boulders/cliff rubble. In flight has pot-bellied jizz, skimming over waves with rapid wingbeats.
DISTRIBUTION: Circumpolar, although uncommon in Bering Sea; egg-dates May–Jul. Winters mostly within breeding range; casual south to Long Is, USA, and north France.
SIMILAR SPECIES: Compare Pigeon Guillemot (below).

Pigeon Guillemot *Cepphus columba* L32cm/13in W58cm/23in P p. 166

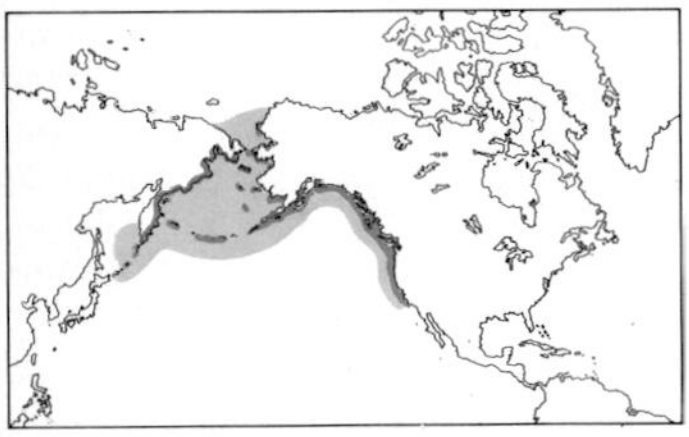

IDENTIFICATION: **Adult Summer:** Medium-sized, mostly black auk with conspicuous white wing patch broken by dark triangle; slender black bill, coral-red legs and mouth. Unlikely to be confused with any alcid except for Black Guillemot; differs in dark triangle across white upperwing-coverts and dusky axillaries and wing linings. **Adult Winter:** Head and neck mostly white, with variable dusky markings on crown and nape; upperparts mottled grey and white. Differs from Black Guillemot in marked wing-coverts, dusky underwing linings; winter murrelets are much smaller, with shorter bills and darker heads and upperparts. **Juvenile/Immature:** As adult winter, but head and upperwing-coverts duskier.
HABITS: A familiar bird of the intertidal zone; breeds singly or in loose colonies among boulders, piles of driftwood etc. Like the Black Guillemot, it sits high in water, the combination of slender bill, rounded head, thin neck and pointed tail imparting distinctive grebe-like jizz.
DISTRIBUTION: North Pacific; breeds from northeast Siberia south to northern Japan and southern California; egg-dates May–Jul. Many vacate inshore breeding areas after breeding, but winter range largely unknown.
SIMILAR SPECIES: Compare Black Guillemot (above).

Atlantic Puffin *Fratercula arctica* L32cm/13in W55cm/22in **P** p. 163

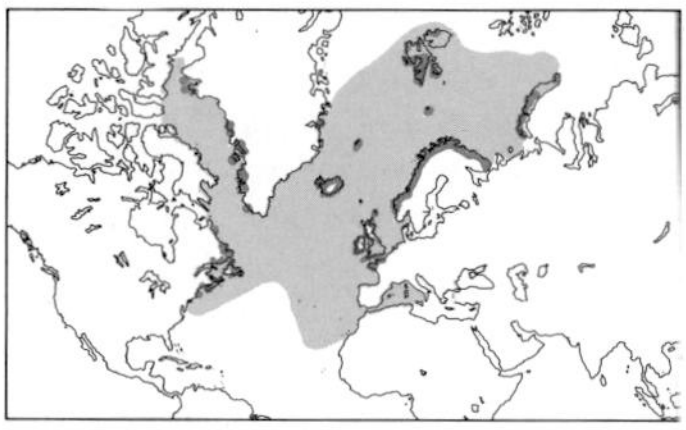

IDENTIFICATION: **Adult Summer:** Unmistakable; a medium-sized plumpish auk, black above, white below, with large head and brightly coloured red, yellow and blue bill. Head has greyish-white sides to face, with black crown, nape and collar; underparts mostly white, flanks and underwing dusky. **Adult Winter:** Sides of face and bill dark dusky-grey; colourful bill sheath shed. **Juvenile/Immature:** As adult winter, but bill smaller, more pointed, sides of face duskier, looking almost black at distance.

HABITS: Colonial, breeds in burrows; gregarious throughout year. In flight, appears distinctly smaller than either Guillemot or Razorbill, with more rounded wings and tail giving distinctly chunky, rotund appearance. More pelagic outside breeding season than either Guillemot or Razorbill.

DISTRIBUTION: North Atlantic. Breeds from Spitsbergen south to Maine, USA, Britain and northern France; egg-dates May–Jul. Most winter at sea, from southern breeding range south to Morocco.

SIMILAR SPECIES: None within range, but compare Little Auk (p. 277).

Spectacled Guillemot *Cepphus carbo* L38cm/15in W? **P** p. 166

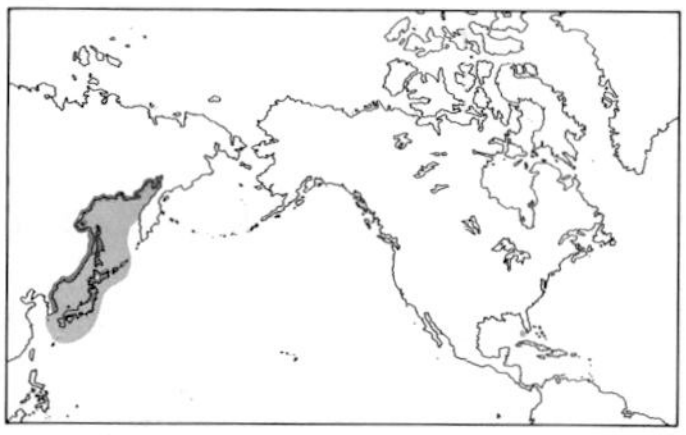

IDENTIFICATION: **Adult Summer:** Distinctive, largish, mostly sooty-black auk with conspicuous white spectacles and post-ocular stripe on head. Bill black, with coral-red legs and mouth. **Adult Winter:** Retains spectacles, but chin, throat, sides of neck and underparts white. Differs from Pigeon Guillemot in darker head, nape and hindneck, uniformly dark upperparts.

HABITS: Larger and stockier than Pigeon Guillemot; prefers rocky coastlines; breeds among loose boulders, rocks, crevices etc.

DISTRIBUTION: Northwest Pacific. Breeds from Kamchatka Peninsula south to Sea of Japan; locally common along Japanese rocky shores; egg-dates unrecorded, probably May–Jun. Disperses to adjacent coasts in winter, with limited southwards dispersal.

SIMILAR SPECIES: None.

Crested Murrelet *Synthliboramphus wumizusume* L26cm/10in W? **P** p. 167

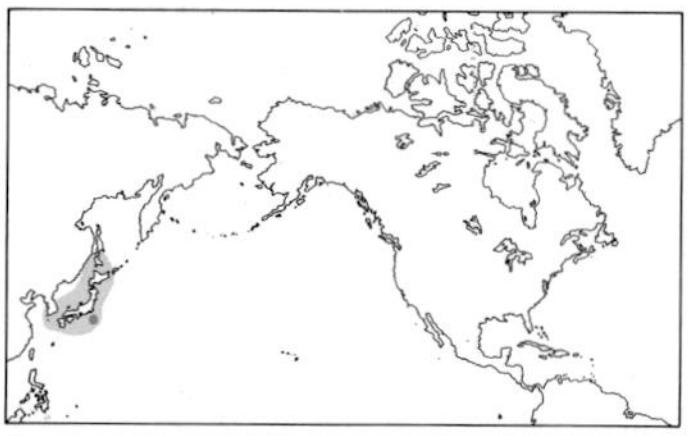

IDENTIFICATION: **Adult Summer:** Small grey-backed auk with crested head, patterned face and stubby white or horn-coloured bill. Head, including crest, black, with broad white stripes running down from sides of head and nape to join on lower hindneck; underparts white. Differs from Ancient Murrelet in black hindcrest and white neck stripes. **Adult Winter:** Lacks crest, white neck stripe less defined.

HABITS: Little known, presumably much as for Ancient Murrelet; breeds in boulder rubble.

DISTRIBUTION: Endemic to Japan, where an uncommon local breeder on isolated islands from central Honshu (Izu Is) south. In winter, disperses to mainland coasts from Sakhalin south to Korea.

SIMILAR SPECIES: Compare Ancient Murrelet (p. 281).

Crested Auklet *Aethia cristatella* L27cm/11in W? P p. 170

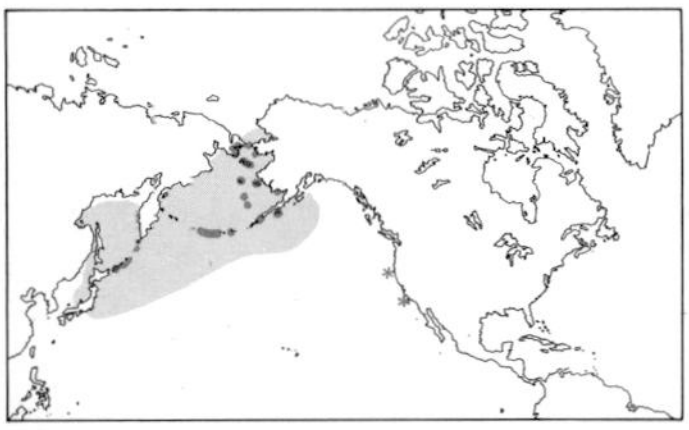

IDENTIFICATION: **Adult Summer:** Medium-sized, mostly sooty-grey auklet with conspicuous recurved crest springing forward over stubby, swollen red bill; a small white plume also extends backwards over ear-coverts from whitish eye. Differs from Whiskered Auklet in larger size, larger bill and lack of white loral plumes. **Adult Winter:** Bill browner, smaller; facial plume absent, crest reduced. **Juvenile/Immature:** Resembles adult Cassin's Auklet; differs in lack of white eye-crescent, paler bill, darker belly and ventral area.

HABITS: Breeds colonially in crevices and under beach boulders etc. Flight usually low and direct on fast-whirring wings, characteristically in small compact flocks, occasionally in large swarms.

DISTRIBUTION: North Pacific. Breeds from Bering Strait south through Aleutians to central Kurile Is; egg-dates Jun–Aug. Winters in ice-free waters of breeding range south to northern Japan and Kodiak, Alaska.

SIMILAR SPECIES: Compare Whiskered and Cassin's Auklets (p. 280).

Parakeet Auklet *Cyclorrhynchus psittacula* L25cm/10in W? P p. 170

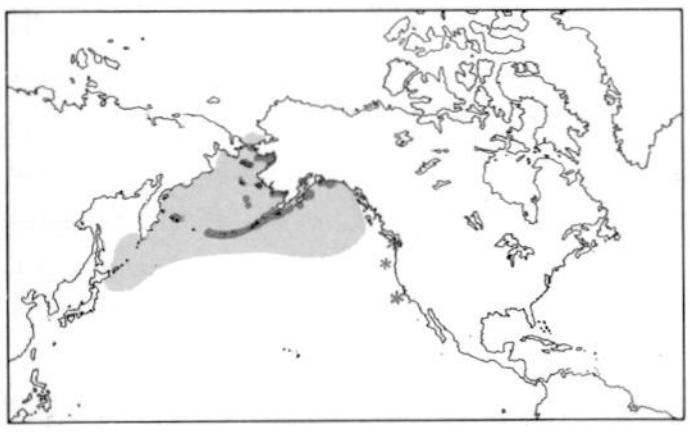

IDENTIFICATION: **Adult Summer:** Medium-sized auklet with dark, sooty-grey upperparts, mottled breast, conspicuous white underparts and a short stubby red bill, the lower mandible of which curves strongly upwards. The head shows a single thin white auricular plume stretching backwards and downwards from white eye. **Adult Winter:** Bill dull brownish-red; chin, throat and foreneck whitish. Differs from Cassin's in larger size, reddish bill and white underparts; from breeding Rhinoceros in smaller size, reddish bill, only one white facial plume, whiter underparts.

HABITS: Less gregarious than most auklets; nests singly or in small colonies deep within rubble and crevices of sea cliffs and boulder slopes. Flight strong and direct, normally higher than congeners, rolling from side to side.

DISTRIBUTION: North Pacific. Breeds from Diomedes south through Bering Sea to Commander and Aleutian Is and east to Prince William Sound; egg-dates Jun–Aug. Thought to winter in ice-free waters of breeding range.

SIMILAR SPECIES: Compare Cassin's and Rhinoceros Auklets (p. 280).

Least Auklet *Aethia pusilla* L15cm/6in W? P p. 171

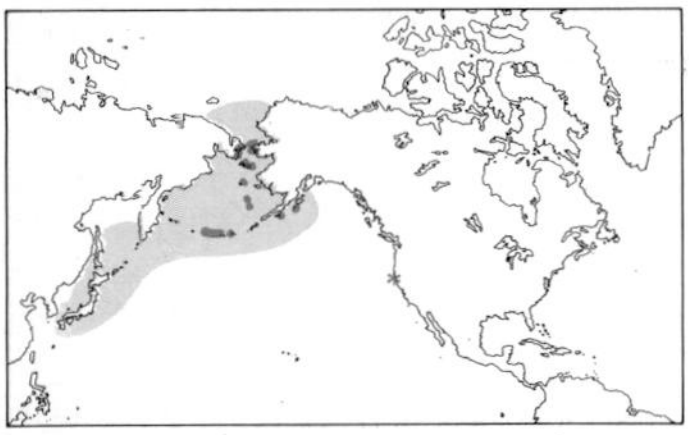

IDENTIFICATION: **Adult Summer:** Tiny, chubby, short-necked auklet, dark above with white-tipped scapulars, underparts whitish, variably mottled with grey; stubby red bill has small knob at base of upper mandible. At close range, head shows fine hair-like white streaks on lores and behind eye. **Adult Winter:** Similar, but white scapular stripe more apparent. Underparts wholly white. Differs from winter Marbled and Kittlitz's Murrelets in smaller size, darker head, whitish auricular streak.

HABITS: Smallest alcid. Reputedly one of North Pacific's most abundant birds, wheeling like swarms of twittering bees over colonies, some of which exceed one million birds. Nests in crevices.

DISTRIBUTION: North Pacific. Breeds from Bering Strait south to Aleutian Is and east to Semidi Is, Gulf of Alaska; egg-dates Jun–Jul. Winters within ice-free seas of breeding range.

SIMILAR SPECIES: None, but compare Cassin's and Whiskered Auklets and winter Marbled and Kittlitz's Murrelets (p. 280, p. 282).

Rhinoceros Auklet *Cerorhinca monocerata* L37cm/15in W? **P** p. 172

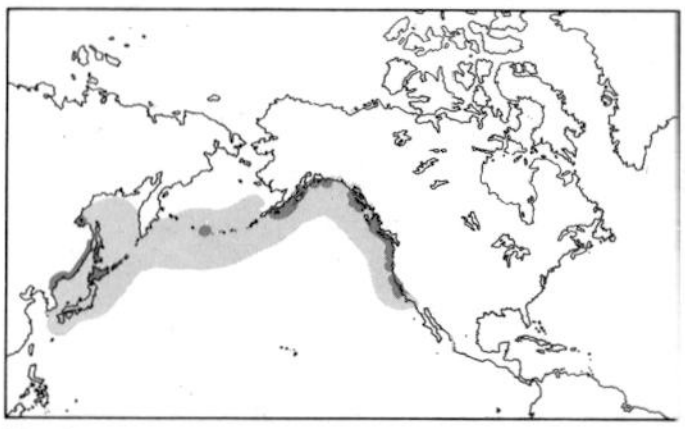

IDENTIFICATION: **Adult Summer:** Large sooty-brown auk with two thin white plumes across sides of face and pale yellow 'horn' at base of orange bill; belly and ventral area whitish. **Adult Winter:** White facial plumes reduced or absent; bill duller, lacks 'horn'. **Juvenile/Immature:** As adult winter, but darker, lacks head plumes, has a smaller, more pointed bill. Winter adults and immatures differ from winter/immature Tufted Puffin in whiter underparts (visible only in flight) and proportionately smaller, less deep bill. Parakeet Auklet is smaller, with small red bill and much whiter underparts.

HABITS: A mis-named puffin. Nocturnal at colonies; breeds in burrows. Resembles Tufted Puffin in flight, but wings more pointed, head smaller, with contrasting white belly. In winter, at night, often forms large roosting rafts in sheltered bays.

DISTRIBUTION: North Pacific. Breeds discontinuously from Alaskan Peninsula south to Korea and California; egg-dates Apr–Jun. Winters within breeding range; general movement south.

SIMILAR SPECIES: Parakeet Auklet, juvenile/immature Tufted Puffin (p. 279, p. 281).

Cassin's Auklet *Ptychoramphus aleuticus* L23cm/9in W? **P** p. 172

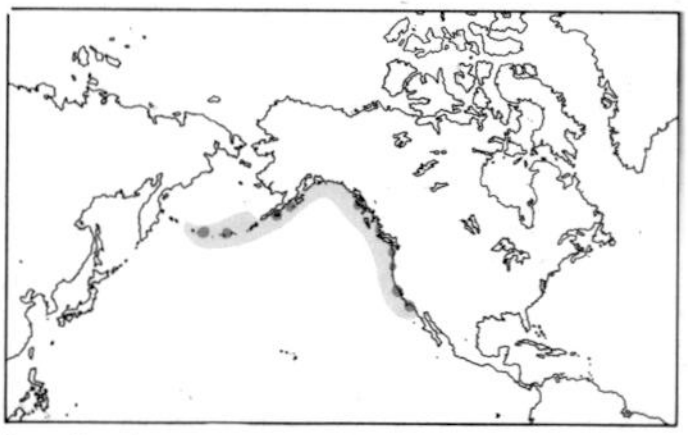

IDENTIFICATION: **Adult:** Small, plump, rather drab, dark grey auklet which lacks obvious plumage features. At close range, has pale eyes with prominent pale eye-crescents above and below eye and pale yellow or whitish base to lower mandible; underparts paler grey than upperparts, shading to whitish on belly and ventral area. Differs from very similar juvenile Whiskered Auklet in longer, thinner bill with pale base, paler belly and ventral area, proportionately larger head, shorter neck and more rounded wingtip. **Juvenile/Immature:** As adult, but paler, with whitish chin and throat.

HABITS: Nocturnal at breeding colonies, which vary from burrows under bare, flat ground to marine terraces and sea slopes with heavy covering vegetation.

DISTRIBUTION: North Pacific. Breeds from Buldir Is, Aleutians, eastwards through Gulf of Alaska and then south to Baja California; egg-dates Mar–Jul. Winters within breeding range, with general southwards dispersal.

SIMILAR SPECIES: Compare with juvenile Whiskered Auklet (below).

Whiskered Auklet *Aethia pygmaea* L20cm/8in W? **P** p. 171

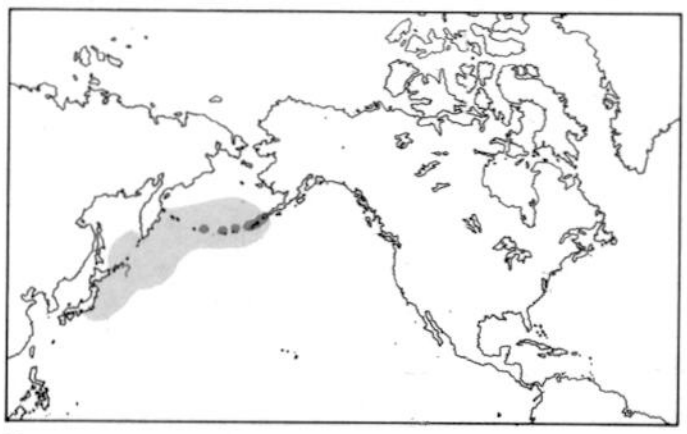

IDENTIFICATION: **Adult Summer:** Tiny, mostly sooty-grey auklet with short red bill and diagnostic ornate head plumes. Of the 3 white facial plumes, one runs from the eye backwards and 2 are joined at the lores, one of which springs upwards to project at crown, the other backwards below eye. A further recurving plume of dark feathers springs forwards from forehead to hang over the bill. **Adult Winter:** Bill brownish-red; facial plumes shorter, much reduced. **Juvenile/Immature:** Wholly sooty-grey, slightly paler below, with weak facial stripes and pale eye. Differs from adult Cassin's Auklet in shorter, more conical bill, more uniform underparts, smaller head, longer neck and more pointed wings.

HABITS: Rarest Alaskan Auklet. Nocturnal at colonies, which are situated under boulders and in rock crevices. In summer forages close to shore, and flies low and fast on whirring wings.

DISTRIBUTION: North Pacific. Breeds at about 10 Aleutian islands, perhaps also at Commander and Kurile Is; egg-dates Apr–May. Disperses to adjacent seas in winter.

SIMILAR SPECIES: Compare Cassin's and Crested Auklets (p. 280, p. 279).

Ancient Murrelet *Synthliboramphus antiquum* L26cm/10in W? **P** p. 167

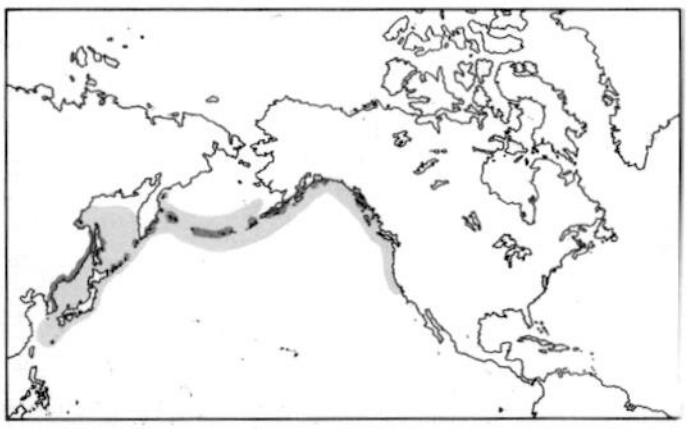

IDENTIFICATION: **Adult Summer:** Small, grey-backed auk with patterned black and white face and yellowish or pale grey bill. Black of head extends down as short bib to upper breast, with white patch extending upwards on sides of neck and lower face; a narrow white plume extends from above eye to nape; underparts mostly white. Differs from Crested Murrelet in lack of crest and lack of white stripes down hindneck. **Adult Winter:** Similar, but white plume reduced or absent, black bib speckled with white. **Juvenile/Immature:** As adult winter, but chin white; differs from juvenile Marbled Murrelet in heavier, paler bill, blackish head contrasting with uniform grey back.

HABITS: Adults are nocturnal at colonies; chicks leave burrows or natural cavities when only 2 days old, and are then reared at sea. In flight, head normally held higher than in other murrelets.

DISTRIBUTION: North Pacific, from Aleutians south to Japan and Korea and east to Queen Charlotte Is; egg-dates May–Jun. Winters within breeding area and south to Baja California.

SIMILAR SPECIES: Compare Crested Murrelet (p. 278).

Horned Puffin *Fratercula corniculata* L38cm/15in W57cm/22in **P** p. 173

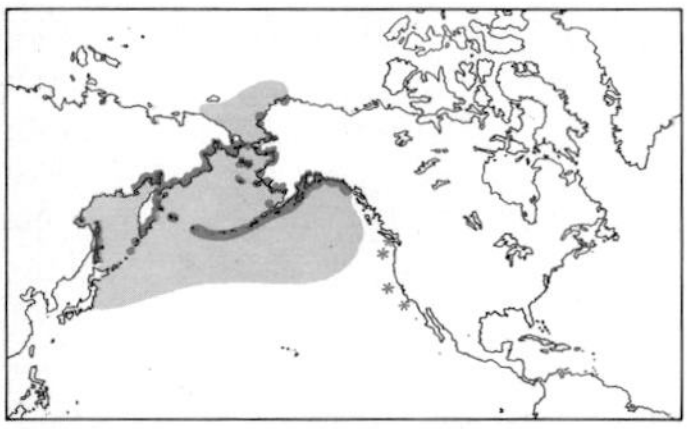

IDENTIFICATION: Unmistakable; a medium-sized plumpish auk, black above, white below, with large head and brightly coloured red and yellow bill. Head has greyish-white sides to face, with black crown, nape and collar; underparts mostly white, flanks and underwing dusky. **Adult Winter:** Sides of face and base of bill dark, dusky-grey. **Juvenile/Immature:** As adult winter, but bill smaller, more pointed, sides of face duskier.

HABITS: Colonial, breeds in burrows, under boulders, natural cavities, crevices etc; gregarious throughout year. In flight, its large-headed, big-fronted jizz is further emphasised by short rounded wings and tail.

DISTRIBUTION: North Pacific. Breeds from Chukchi Sea south to Kurile Is and east to Queen Charlotte Is, British Columbia; egg-dates Jun–Jul. Disperses to pelagic habitat in winter south to California.

SIMILAR SPECIES: None within range.

Tufted Puffin *Fratercula cirrhata* L38cm/15in W? **P** p. 173

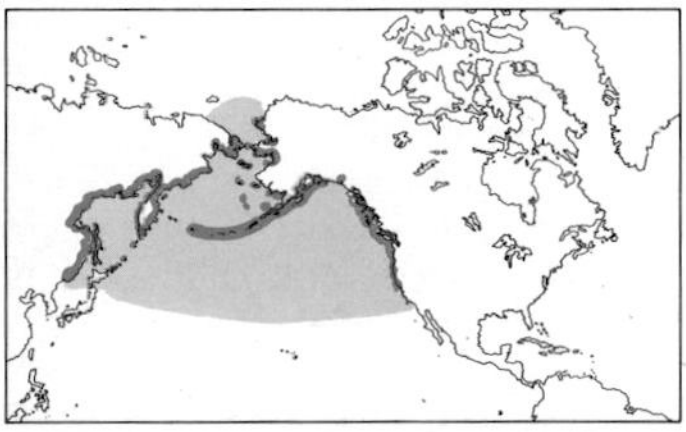

IDENTIFICATION: **Adult Summer:** Unmistakable; a largish mostly black auk with white face mask, flowing yellow head plumes and massive reddish-orange bill the base of which is greenish; legs orange. **Adult Winter:** Head mostly dark; yellow tufts much reduced or absent, bill smaller and duller with dusky base. **Juvenile/Immature:** As adult winter, but with smaller, more pointed dusky bill and grey or buffish-white underparts. Differs from immature Rhinoceros Auklet in larger, less pointed bill and larger, more rounded head; first-summer Tufted Puffins show obvious greyish stripe behind eye.

HABITS: Colonial, breeds in burrows along clifftops or in steep talus slopes; usually solitary at sea. Appears stockier than Horned Puffin, with heavy, rotund body and short rounded wings.

DISTRIBUTION: North Pacific. Breeds from Chukchi Sea south to Sea of Japan and California; egg-dates Jun–Jul. Disperses to pelagic habitat in winter, south to about 35°N.

SIMILAR SPECIES: Compare immatures with those of Rhinoceros Auklet (p. 280).

Marbled Murrelet *Brachyramphus marmoratus* L25cm/10in W? P p. 168

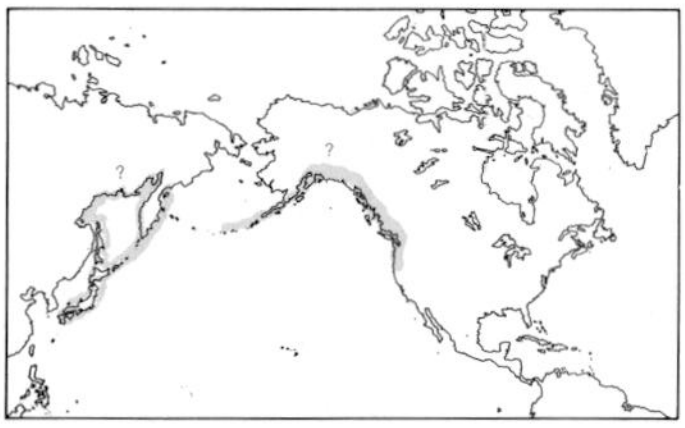

IDENTIFICATION: **Adult Summer:** Rather small, dark alcid, mostly brown, mottled with grey or reddish, the scapulars edged paler; chin, throat and belly whitish, mottled with brown. Differs from summer Kittlitz's Murrelet in longer, thicker bill, browner, less cryptic upperparts, more capped appearance, and darker belly and ventral area. **Adult Winter:** Mostly sooty-grey above with black cap extending well below eye; white underparts and scapular stripe. Differs from Kittlitz's in bill size, cap extending below eye, dark hindneck, less obvious dark necklace across white lower neck.

HABITS: Little known; few nests have ever been found, but it is nocturnal and apparently non-colonial, breeding up to 20 miles (32km) inland, nesting on limbs of evergreen trees or on ground. Flight swift and direct, skimming low over water.

DISTRIBUTION: North Pacific, but limits unknown; probably from Aleutians and Kamchatka south to Japan and California; egg-dates unknown. Winters south to Japan and California.

SIMILAR SPECIES: Compare Kittlitz's Murrelet (below).

Kittlitz's Murrelet *Brachyramphus brevirostris* L23cm/9in W? P p. 168

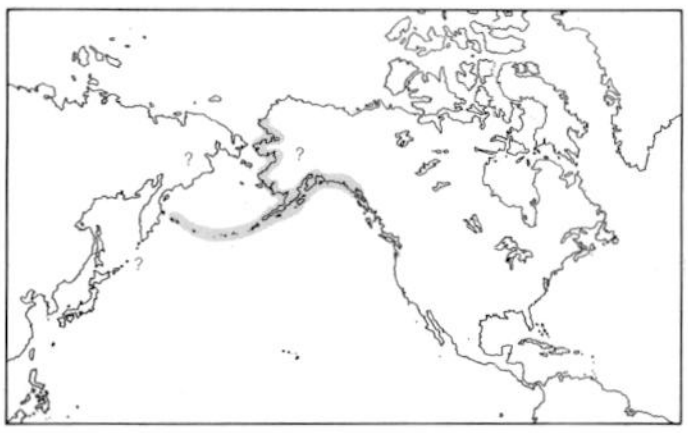

IDENTIFICATION: **Adult Summer:** Very like Marbled Murrelet; differs in shorter bill, more cryptically marbled, sandy-brown upperparts, whiter belly and ventral area, and white outer tail feathers (easily seen when landing). **Adult Winter:** Mostly sooty-grey above, white below, with conspicuous white scapular stripe and a small black cap on crown. Differs from winter Marbled Murrelet in smaller bill, cap not reaching eye, white hindcollar, darker necklace across whiter foreneck, and white outer tail feathers.

HABITS: Breeding biology little known but parallels that of Marbled Murrelet.

DISTRIBUTION: North Pacific, but limits of breeding range unknown; probably extends from Bering Strait south to Aleutians and Commander Is and east to southeast Alaska; egg-dates unknown. Winters within presumed breeding range.

SIMILAR SPECIES: Compare Marbled Murrelet (above).

Xantus' Murrelet *Synthliboramphus hypoleucus* L25cm/10in W? P p. 169

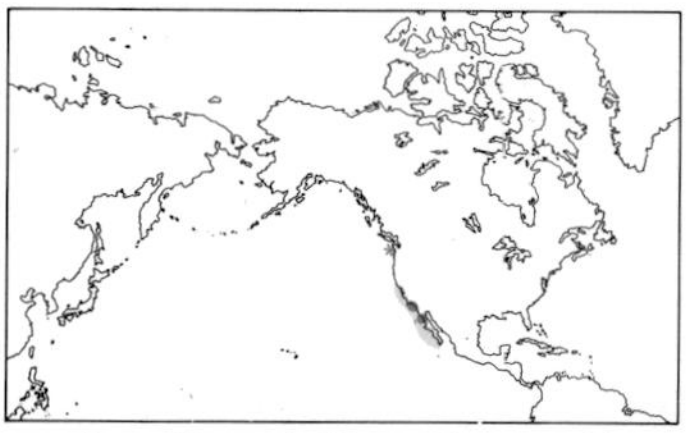

IDENTIFICATION: **Adult:** Medium-sized alcid, black above, white below, with black bill and bluish legs. The southern Californian form *S.h. scrippsi* has a partial white eye-ring. Both forms differ from Craveri's Murrelet in slightly shorter, stouter bill, demarcation of black and white on sides of face occurring just below eye, level with gape, lack of partial dark collar, and, in flight, whitish axillaries and underwing-coverts.

HABITS: Nests in crevices among rocks, under driftwood etc. Precocial juveniles, unable to fly, join adults at sea 2–4 days after hatching. Gregarious, normally encountered in small groups or in pairs on open ocean, swimming with neck stretched upwards giving grebe-like jizz. Flight is swift and low, groups moving in straight lines.

DISTRIBUTION: Breeds on islands off Baja California and western Mexico; egg-dates Mar–Jul. Winters offshore seas adjacent to breeding islands, wandering north to Oregon in fall.

SIMILAR SPECIES: Compare Craveri's Murrelet (p. 283).

Craveri's Murrelet *Synthliboramphus craveri* L25cm/10in W? **P** p. 169

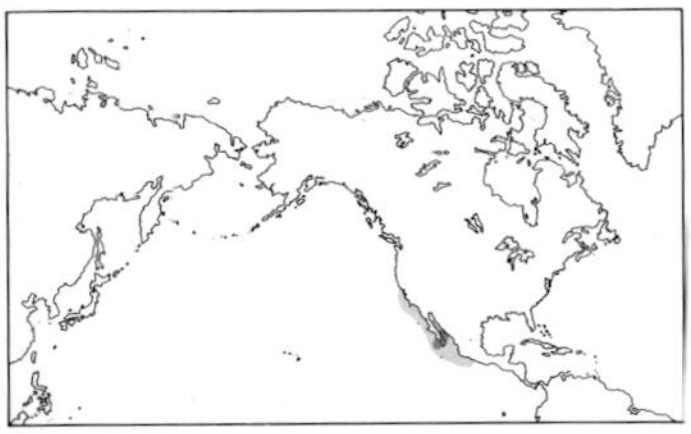

IDENTIFICATION: **Adult:** Medium-sized alcid, black above, white below, with black bill, bluish legs. Differs from similar Xantus' Murrelet in slightly longer, finer bill, demarcation between black and white on the side of face occurring level with bottom of lower mandible, partial black collar on sides of breast which, in flight, extends into white underparts as dark triangle forward of leading edge of wing; dusky underwing linings.

HABITS: Much as for Xantus' Murrelet, but ranges further south in winter.

DISTRIBUTION: Breeds on islands in Gulf of California and off Baja California; egg-dates Feb–Jul. Winters offshore in waters adjacent to breeding areas, south to Mexico and north to Monterey Bay, California.

SIMILAR SPECIES: Compare Xantus' Murrelet (p. 282).

TUBENOSE IDENTIFICATION KEYS

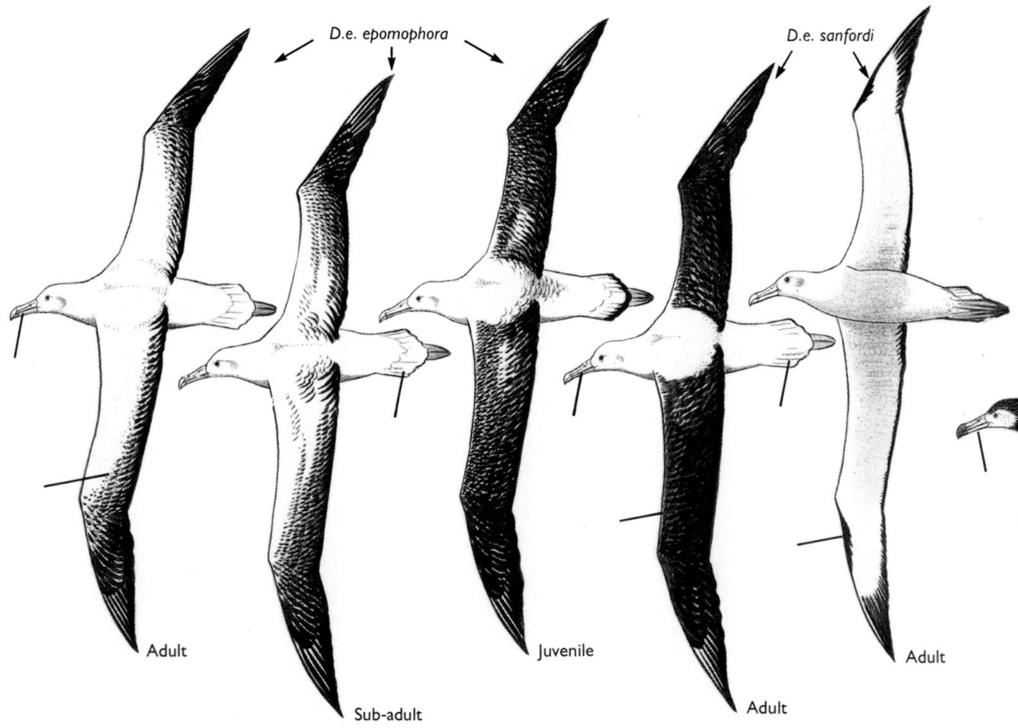

Royal Albatross p. 186. L115cm/45in W330cm/130in

D.e. epomophora: Unlike Wanderer, body and tail mostly white at all ages and upperwings whiten from leading edge backwards. At close range, both subspecies show dark line along cutting edge of bill.

D.e. sanfordi: At all ages, upperwing mostly black. Underwing shows diagnostic mark near carpal.

Amsterdam Albatross p. 186. L ? W ?
Resembles juvenile Wanderer, but with dark tip and cutting edges to both mandibles; more extensive dark line along leading edge of underwing.

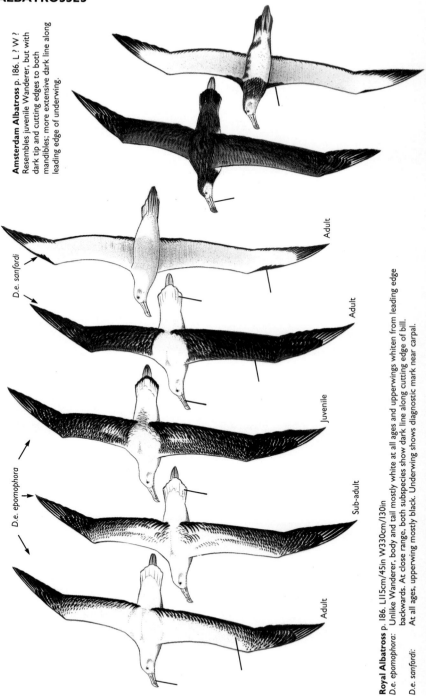

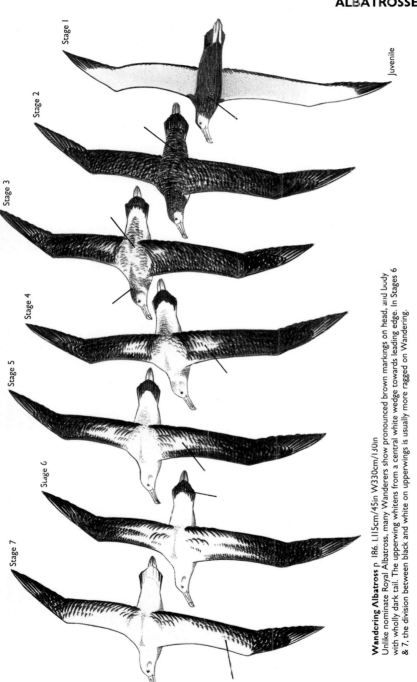

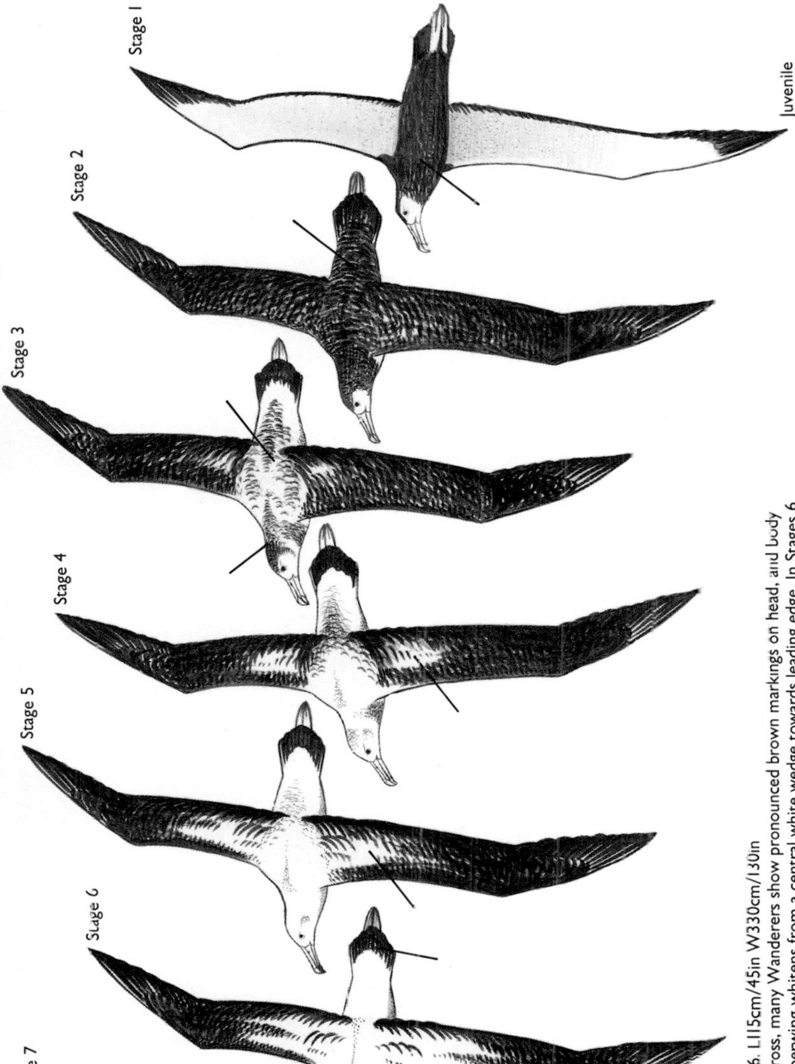

Wandering Albatross p. 186. L115cm/45in W330cm/130in
Unlike nominate Royal Albatross, many Wanderers show pronounced brown markings on head, and body with wholly dark tail. The upperwing whitens from a central white wedge towards leading edge. In Stages 6 & 7, the division between black and white on upperwings is usually more ragged on Wandering.

ALBATROSSES

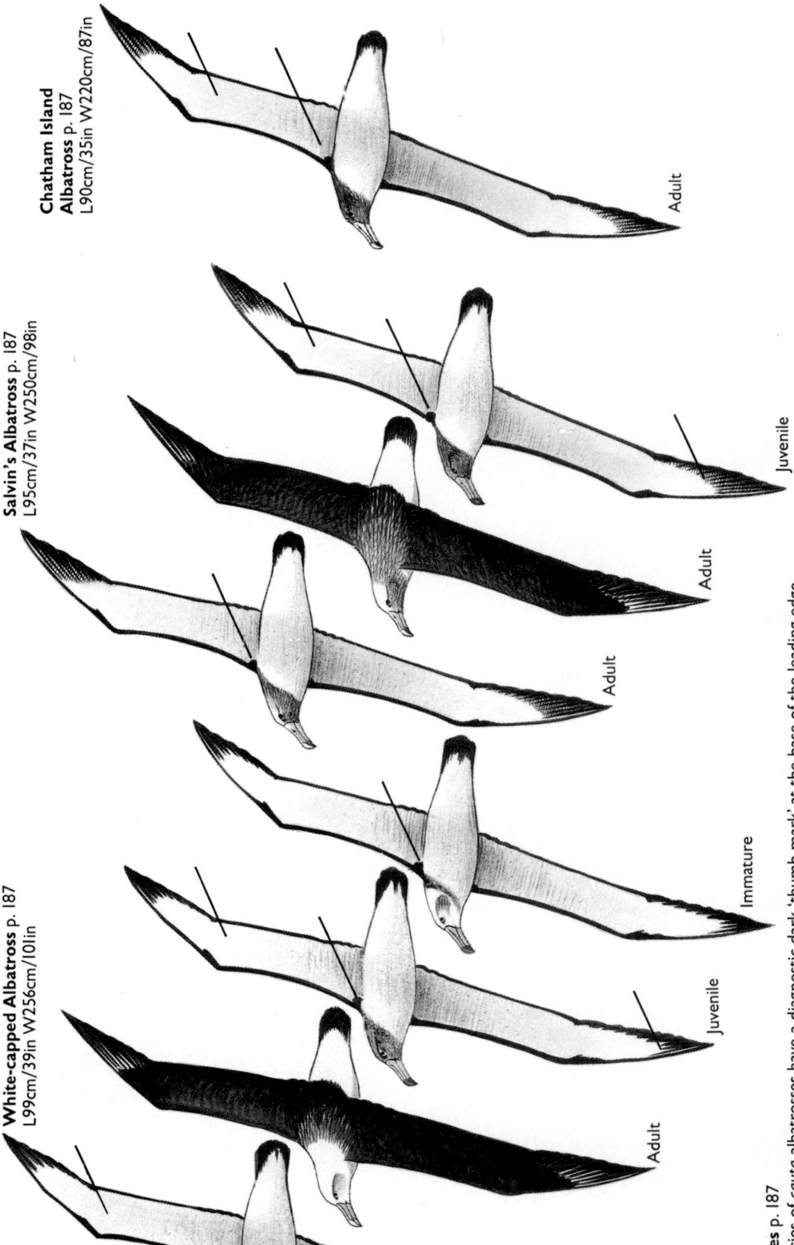

cauta **Albatrosses** p. 187
All three subspecies of *cauta* albatrosses have a diagnostic dark 'thumb mark' at the base of the leading edge on underwing, and narrower black margins on underwing than any other dark-backed Southern Oceans albatross. Immature *cauta/salvini* can be separated by difference in amount of black on tip of underwing.

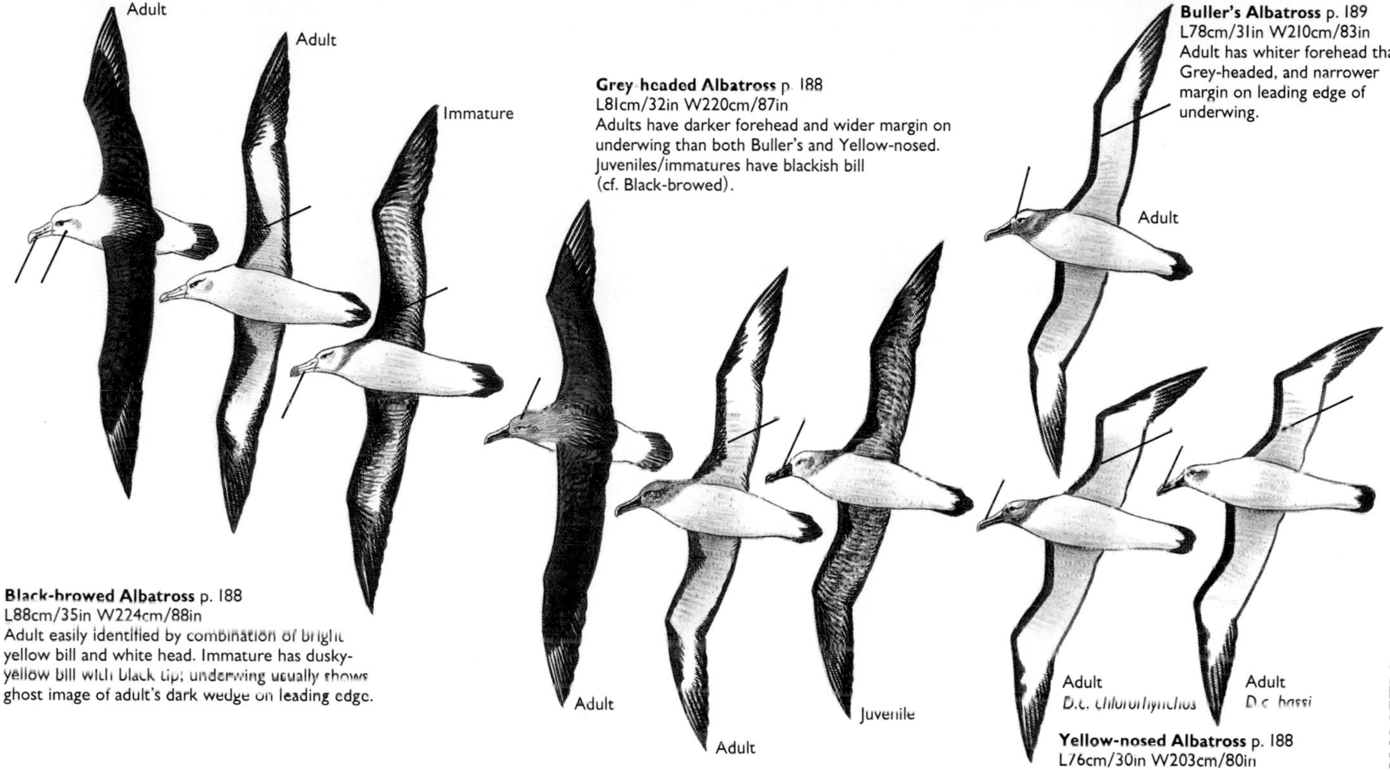

Black-browed Albatross p. 188
L88cm/35in W224cm/88in
Adult easily identified by combination of bright yellow bill and white head. Immature has dusky-yellow bill with black tip; underwing usually shows ghost image of adult's dark wedge on leading edge.

Grey-headed Albatross p. 188
L81cm/32in W220cm/87in
Adults have darker forehead and wider margin on underwing than both Buller's and Yellow-nosed. Juveniles/immatures have blackish bill (cf. Black-browed).

Buller's Albatross p. 189
L78cm/31in W210cm/83in
Adult has whiter forehead than Grey-headed, and narrower margin on leading edge of underwing.

Yellow-nosed Albatross p. 188
L76cm/30in W203cm/80in
Two races, one with white head, one with grey. Look for narrow underwing margins and yellow confined to top ridge of bill.

ALBATROSSES and GIANT PETRELS

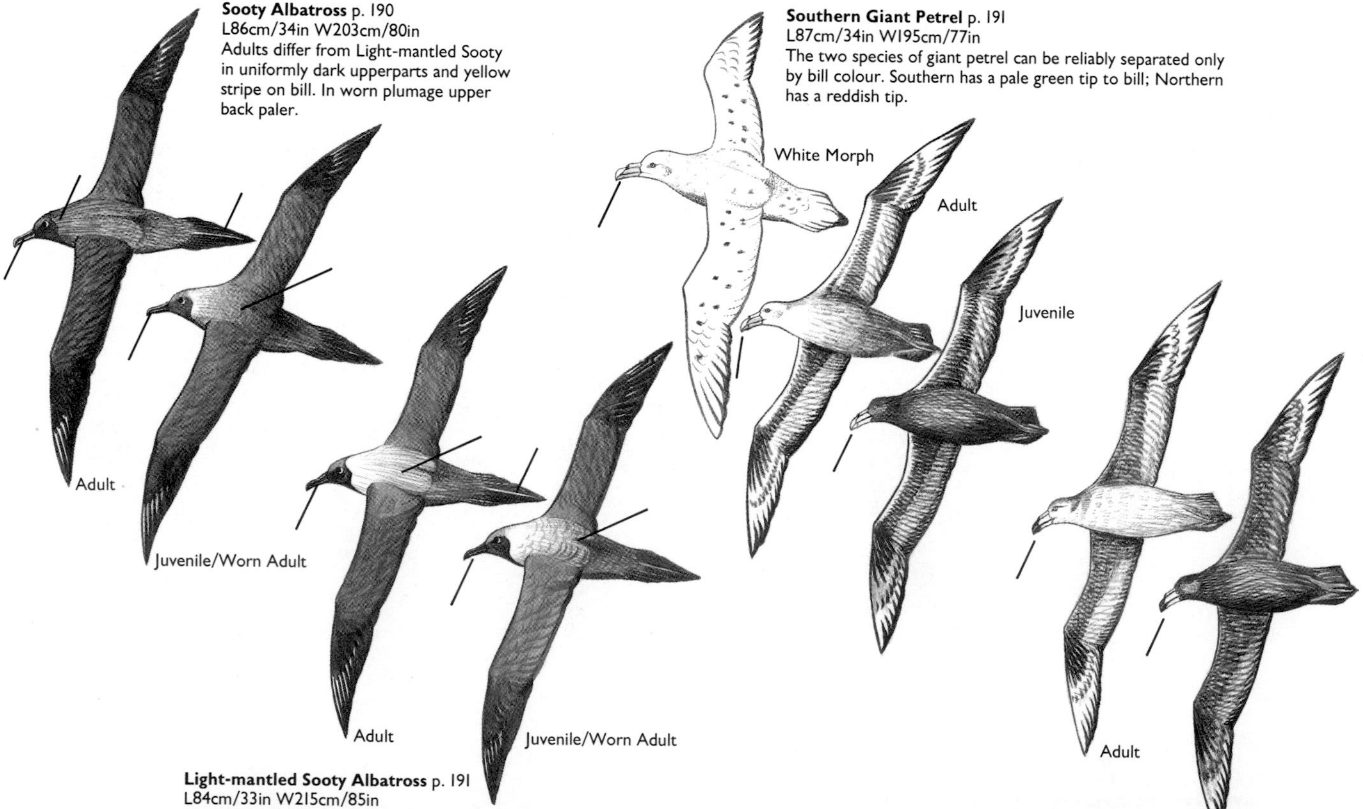

Sooty Albatross p. 190
L86cm/34in W203cm/80in
Adults differ from Light-mantled Sooty in uniformly dark upperparts and yellow stripe on bill. In worn plumage upper back paler.

Light-mantled Sooty Albatross p. 191
L84cm/33in W215cm/85in
From Sooty Albatross by blue stripe on bill and frosty-grey mantle and lower back.

Southern Giant Petrel p. 191
L87cm/34in W195cm/77in
The two species of giant petrel can be reliably separated only by bill colour. Southern has a pale green tip to bill; Northern has a reddish tip.

Northern Giant Petrel p. 191
L87cm/34in W190cm/75in

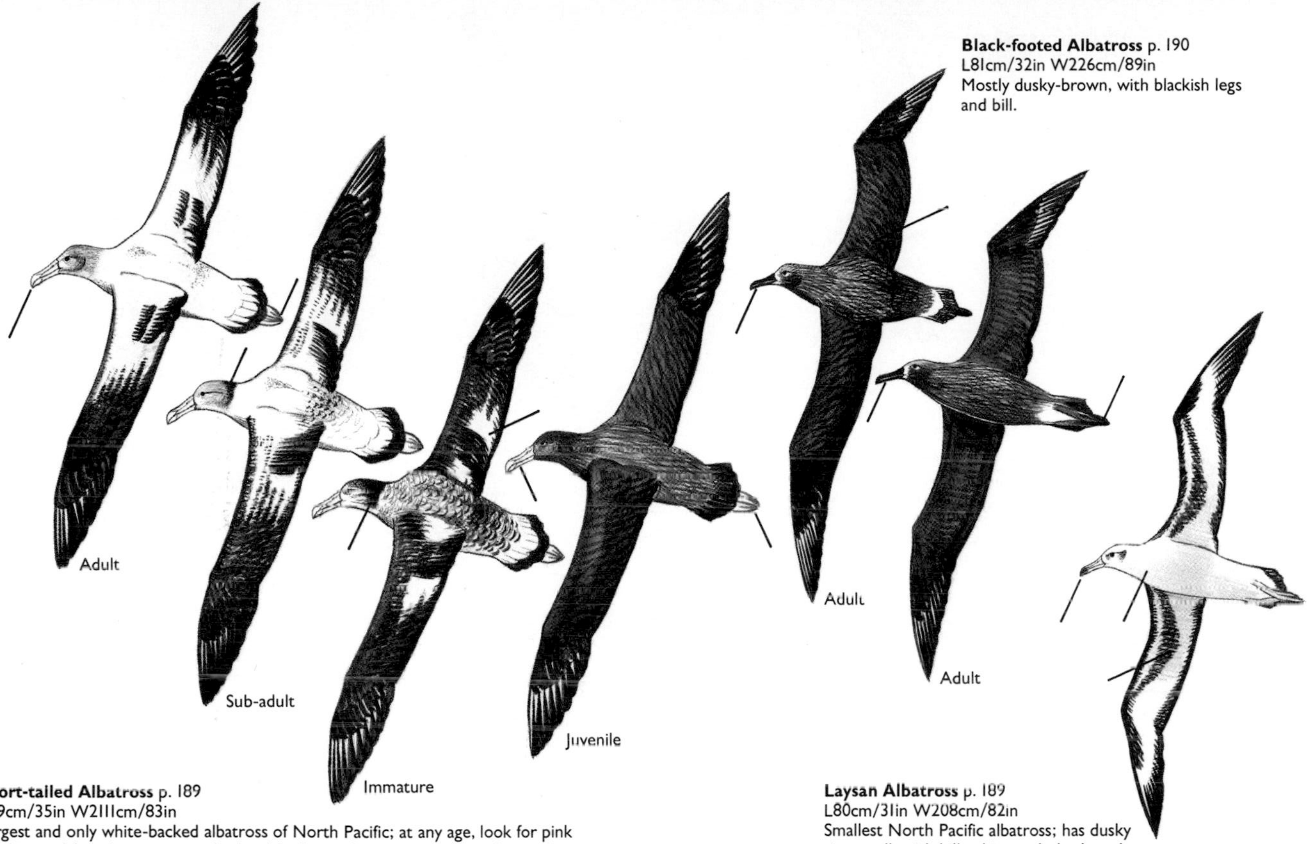

Black-footed Albatross p. 190
L81cm/32in W226cm/89in
Mostly dusky-brown, with blackish legs and bill.

Short-tailed Albatross p. 189
L89cm/35in W211cm/83in
Largest and only white-backed albatross of North Pacific; at any age, look for pink bill, legs and feet. Immatures and sub-adults have white upperwing patches and dark cervical collars.

Laysan Albatross p. 189
L80cm/31in W208cm/82in
Smallest North Pacific albatross; has dusky tip to yellowish bill, white underbody and diagnostic underwing pattern.

Waved Albatross p. 190
L89cm/35in W235cm/93in
The only albatross of Galapagos seas.

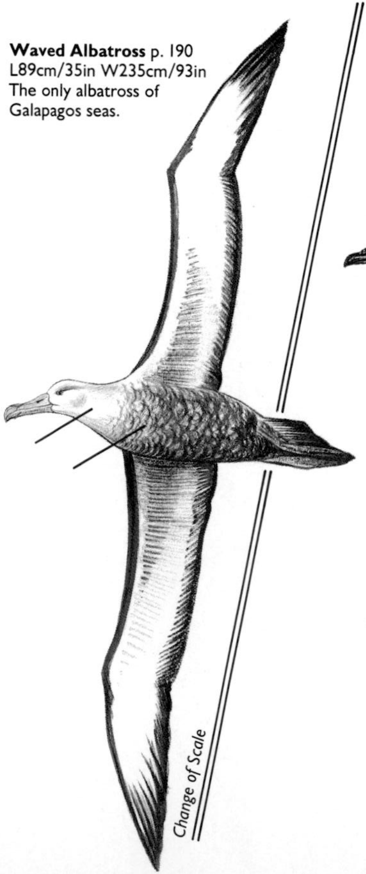

Diving-petrel spp. pp.220–1
Identification of most diving-petrels at sea is impossible owing to small size and whirring flight.

Magellan Diving-petrel p. 221
Differs from other diving-petrels in conspicuous, crescent-shaped half collar on side of neck.

Identification of diving-petrels in the hand (Based on Murphy & Harper 1921; Payne & Prince 1978)

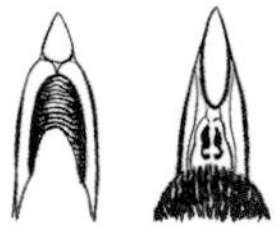

Common Diving-petrel p. 221
L23cm/9in W35cm/14in
When viewed from underside, sides of bill nearly parallel, converging only at tip. Tarsus lacks posterior black line.
Bill depth: 6.0–7.3mm
Wing length: 106–130mm

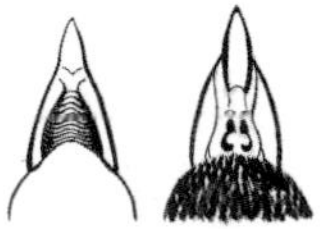

South Georgian Diving-petrel p. 221
L20cm/8in W32cm/13in
When viewed from underside, bill broad at base, converging gradually into 'Gothic' arch. Tarsus has posterior black line.
Bill depth: 5.0–5.7mm
Wing length: 104–122mm

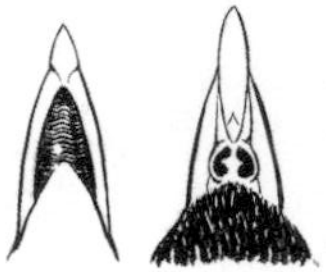

Peruvian Diving-petrel p. 220
L22cm/9in W ?
When viewed from underside, bill tapers evenly from wide base to pointed tip.
Bill depth: 7–9mm
Wing length: 130–144mm

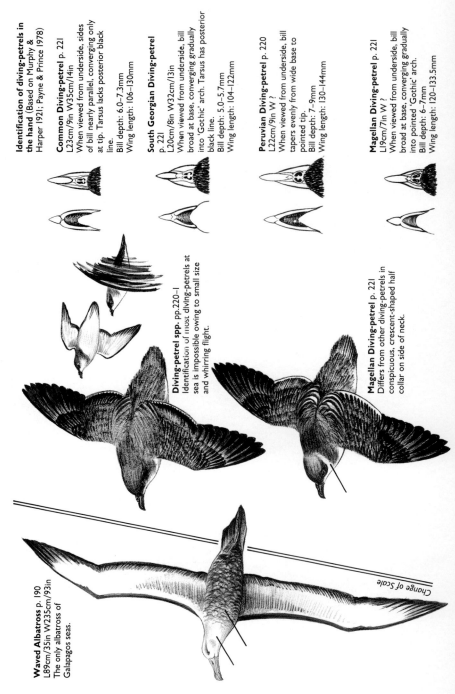

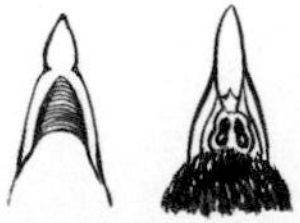

Magellan Diving-petrel p. 221
L19cm/7in W ?
When viewed from underside, bill broad at base, converging gradually into pointed 'Gothic' arch.
Bill depth: 6–7mm
Wing length: 120–133.5mm

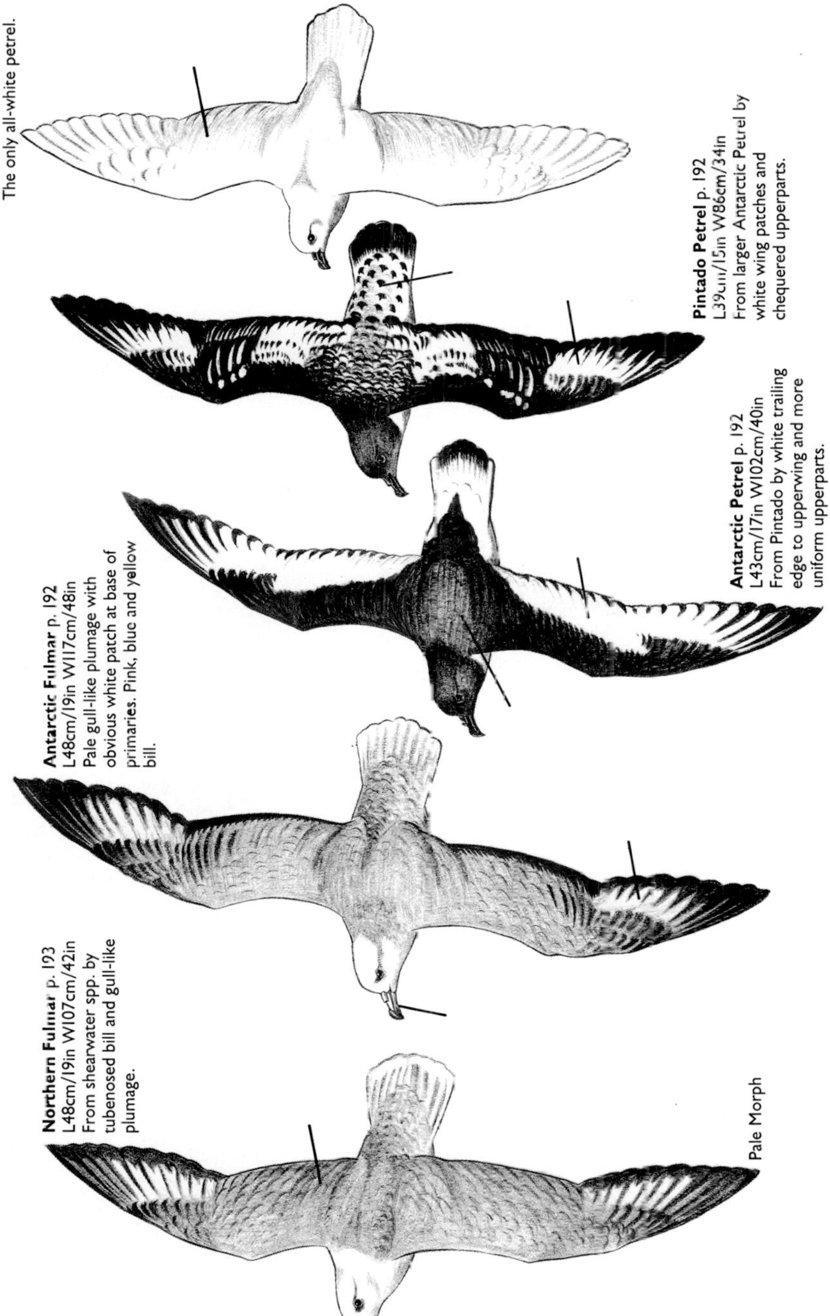

Snow Petrel p. 193
L32cm/13in W78cm/31in
The only all-white petrel.

Pintado Petrel p. 192
L39cm/15in W86cm/34in
From larger Antarctic Petrel by white wing patches and chequered upperparts.

Antarctic Petrel p. 192
L43cm/17in W102cm/40in
From Pintado by white trailing edge to upperwing and more uniform upperparts.

Antarctic Fulmar p. 192
L48cm/19in W117cm/48in
Pale gull-like plumage with obvious white patch at base of primaries. Pink, blue and yellow bill.

Northern Fulmar p. 193
L48cm/19in W107cm/42in
From shearwater spp. by tubenosed bill and gull-like plumage.

Pale Morph

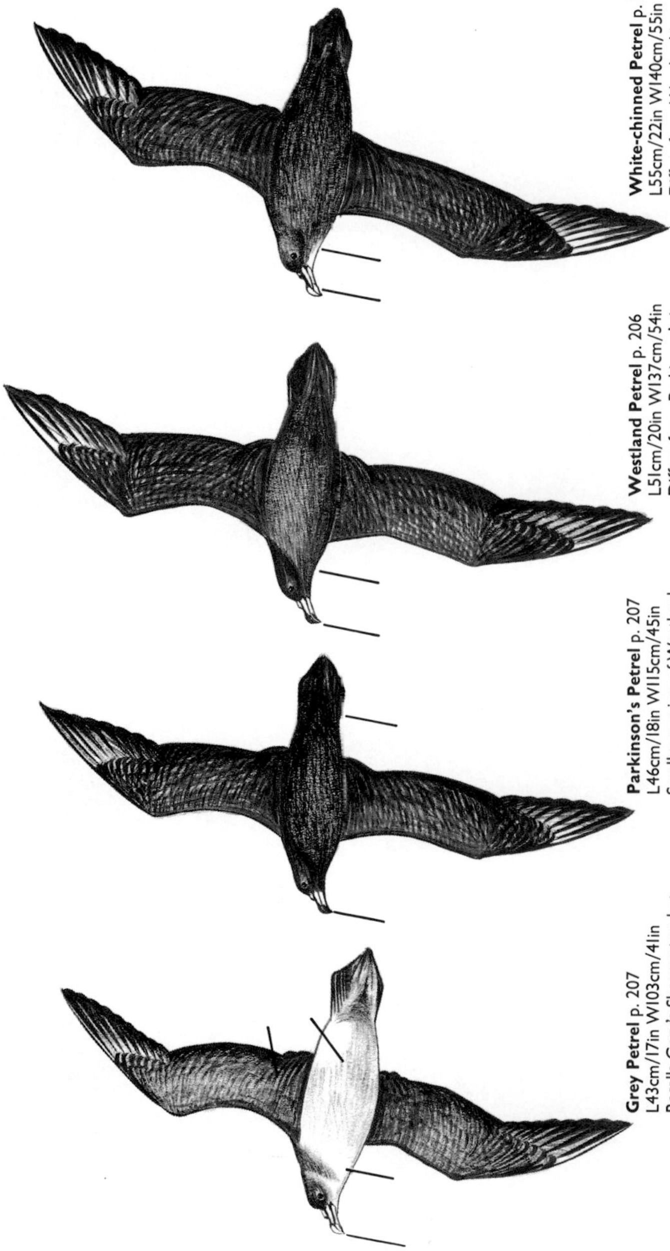

Grey Petrel p. 207
L43cm/17in W103cm/41in
Recalls Cory's Shearwater, but has dark underwing and tail. From Atlantic Petrel by lack of breastband, pale bill.

Parkinson's Petrel p. 207
L46cm/18in W115cm/45in
Smaller version of Westland Petrel. Differs from Flesh-footed Shearwater in more thickset jizz and dark feet.

Westland Petrel p. 206
L51cm/20in W137cm/54in
Differs from Parkinson's in larger size. From White-chinned in dark tip to bill and dark chin.

White-chinned Petrel p. 206
L55cm/22in W140cm/55in
Differs from Westland in unmarked ivory bill and (usually) white on chin.

Cory's Shearwater p. 208
L46cm/18in W113cm/44in
From Great Shearwater by lack of pronounced cap or white hindcollar. At close range, look for diagnostic yellow bill.

Manx Shearwater p. 209
L34cm/13in W82cm/32in
Longer-billed than Little Shearwater, with darker underwing margins and sides of face; different jizz.

Great Shearwater p. 208
L47cm/19in W109cm/43in
From Cory's by darker cap and white hindcollar. At close range, look for black bill and belly patch.

Balearic/Levantine Shearwaters p. 209
L37cm/15in W87cm/34in
From Manx by diffuse division between upper- and underparts; darker axillaries and underparts. See also Sooty (p. 208).

LARGER SHEARWATERS

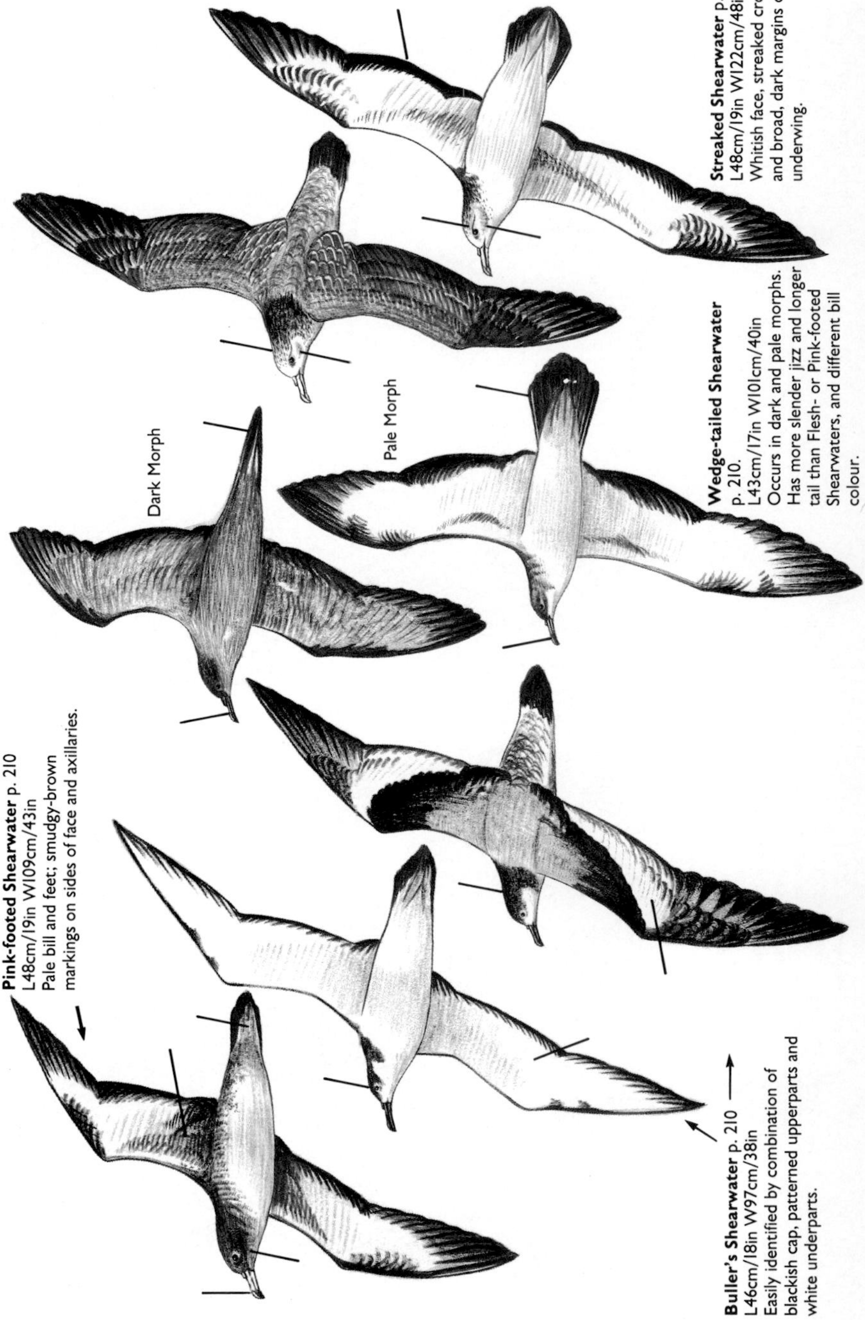

Pink-footed Shearwater p. 210
L48cm/19in W109cm/43in
Pale bill and feet; smudgy-brown markings on sides of face and axillaries.

Buller's Shearwater p. 210
L46cm/18in W97cm/38in
Easily identified by combination of blackish cap, patterned upperparts and white underparts.

Wedge-tailed Shearwater p. 210.
L43cm/17in W101cm/40in
Occurs in dark and pale morphs. Has more slender jizz and longer tail than Flesh- or Pink-footed Shearwaters, and different bill colour.

Streaked Shearwater p. 211
L48cm/19in W122cm/48in
Whitish face, streaked crown and broad, dark margins on underwing.

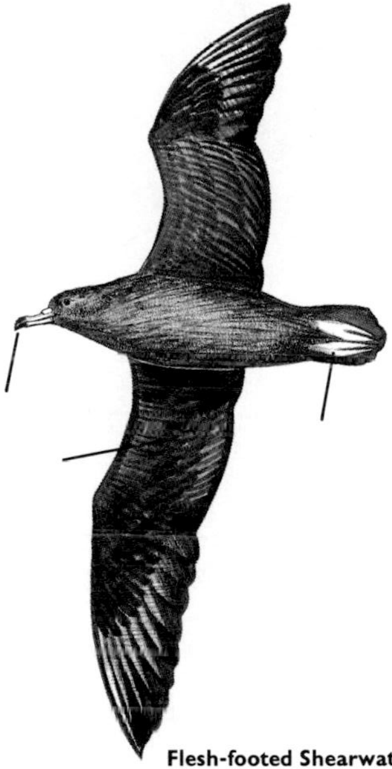

Flesh-footed Shearwater p. 207
L43cm/17in W103cm/41in
Darker underwing than Sooty or Short-tailed Shearwaters, with dark tip to pale bill. Shorter tail and more thickset jizz than dark morph Wedge-tailed Shearwater.

Christmas Shearwater p. 211
L36cm/14in W76cm/30in
Smaller than Sooty or Short-tailed, with darker underwing.

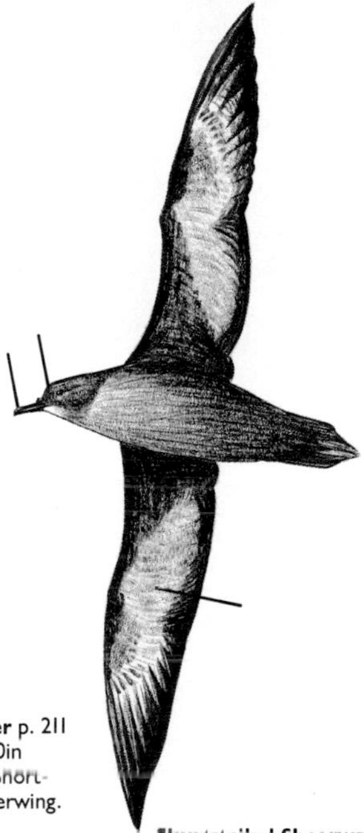

Short-tailed Shearwater p. 211
L42cm/17in W98cm/39in
Shorter-billed than Sooty, with steeper forecrown and greyer, less silvery underwing-coverts.

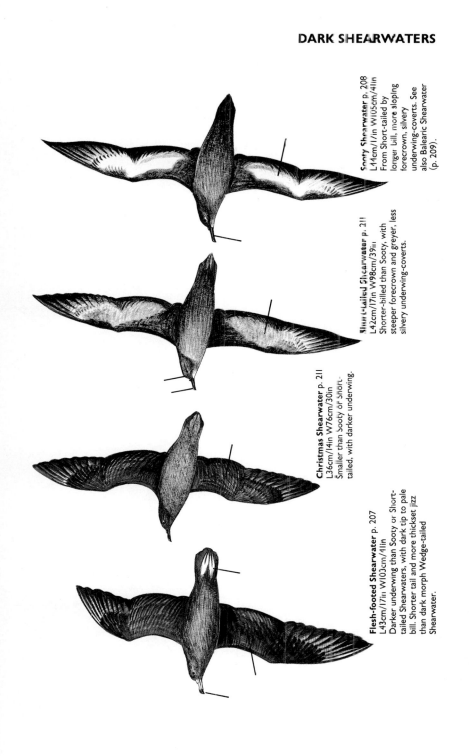

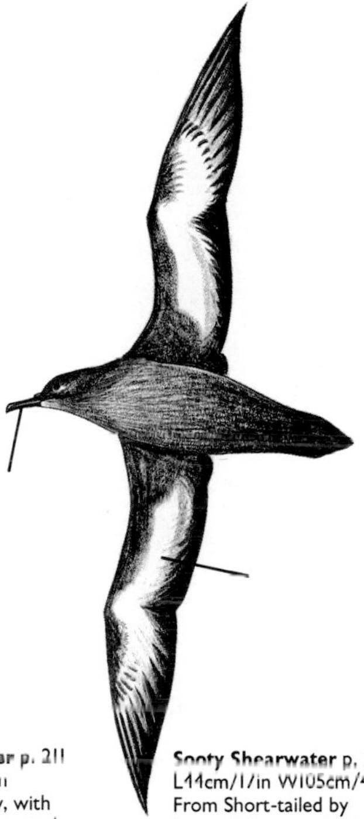

Sooty Shearwater p. 208
L44cm/17in W105cm/41in
From Short-tailed by longer bill, more sloping forecrown, silvery underwing-coverts. See also Balearic Shearwater (p. 209).

SMALLER SHEARWATERS

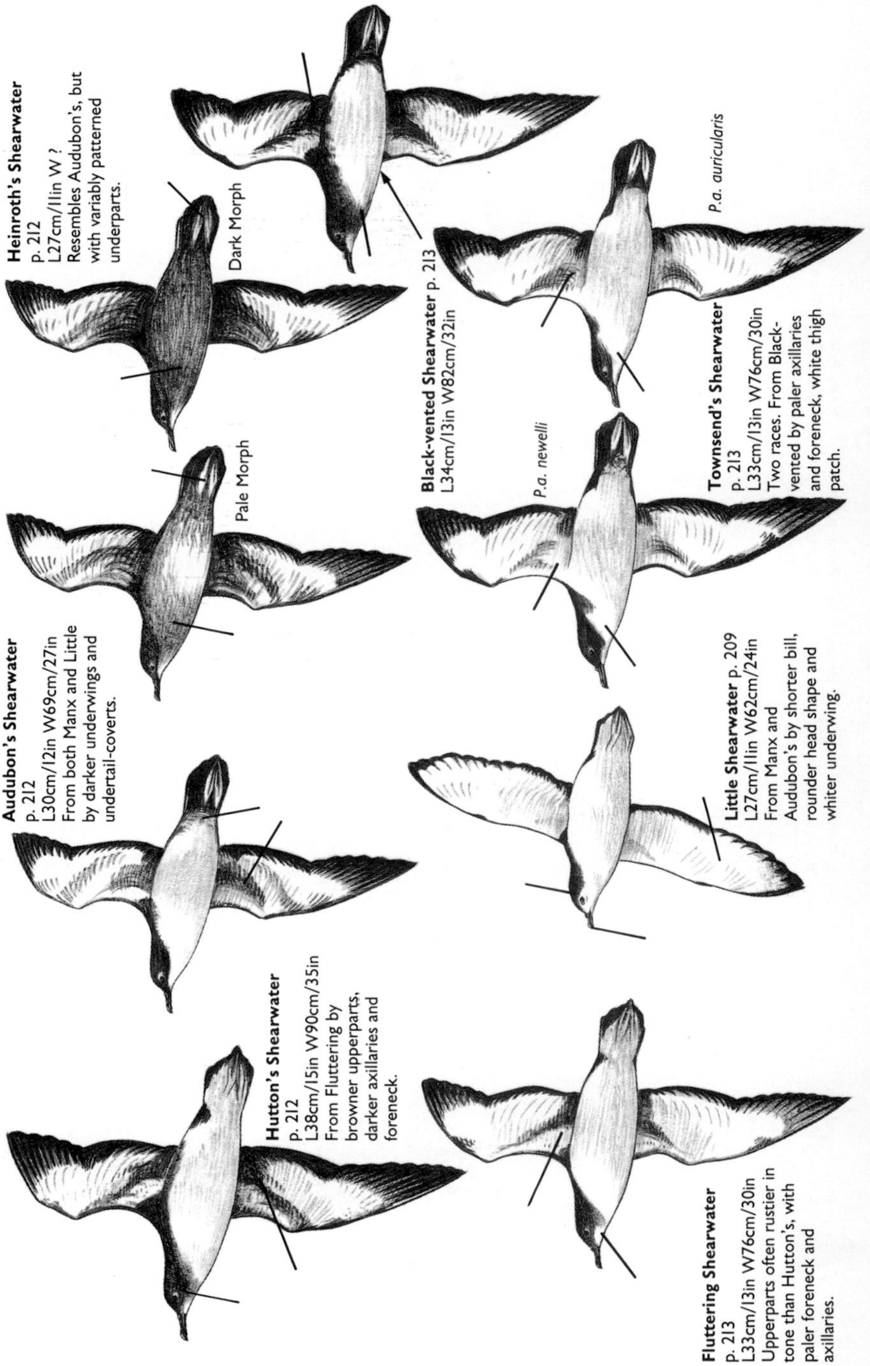

Heinroth's Shearwater
p. 212
L27cm/11in W ?
Resembles Audubon's, but with variably patterned underparts.

Audubon's Shearwater
p. 212
L30cm/12in W69cm/27in
From both Manx and Little by darker underwings and undertail-coverts.

Hutton's Shearwater
p. 212
L38cm/15in W90cm/35in
From Fluttering by browner upperparts, darker axillaries and foreneck.

Black-vented Shearwater p. 213
L34cm/13in W82cm/32in

Townsend's Shearwater
p. 213
L33cm/13in W76cm/30in
Two races. From Black-vented by paler axillaries and foreneck, white thigh patch.

Little Shearwater p. 209
L27cm/11in W62cm/24in
From Manx and Audubon's by shorter bill, rounder head shape and whiter underwing.

Fluttering Shearwater
p. 213
L33cm/13in W76cm/30in
Upperparts often rustier in tone than Hutton's, with paler foreneck and axillaries.

Blue Petrel p. 193
L29cm/11in W62cm/24in
Easily separated from all prions by combination of black cap and white tip to tail.

Antarctic Prion p. 194
L27cm/11in W61cm/24in
Like Broad-billed, but smaller bill and more extensive collar.

Broad-billed Prion p. 194
L28cm/11in W61cm/24in
Largest prion, with massive black bill and broad black tip to tail. Paler head and collar than Antarctic.

Fairy Prion p. 195
L25cm/10in W58cm/23in
From Broad-billed and Antarctic by paler head, broader black tip to tail. From Thin-billed by head and tail pattern.

Thin-billed Prion p. 195
L26cm/10in W56cm/22in
Differs from Fairy Prion in distinctive head pattern and smaller black tip to tail.

PRION BILLS

Fulmar Prion (Not illustrated, see p. 195)

Salvin's Prion (Not illustrated, see p. 194)

Antarctic Prion

Broad-billed Prion

Fairy Prion

Thin-billed Prion

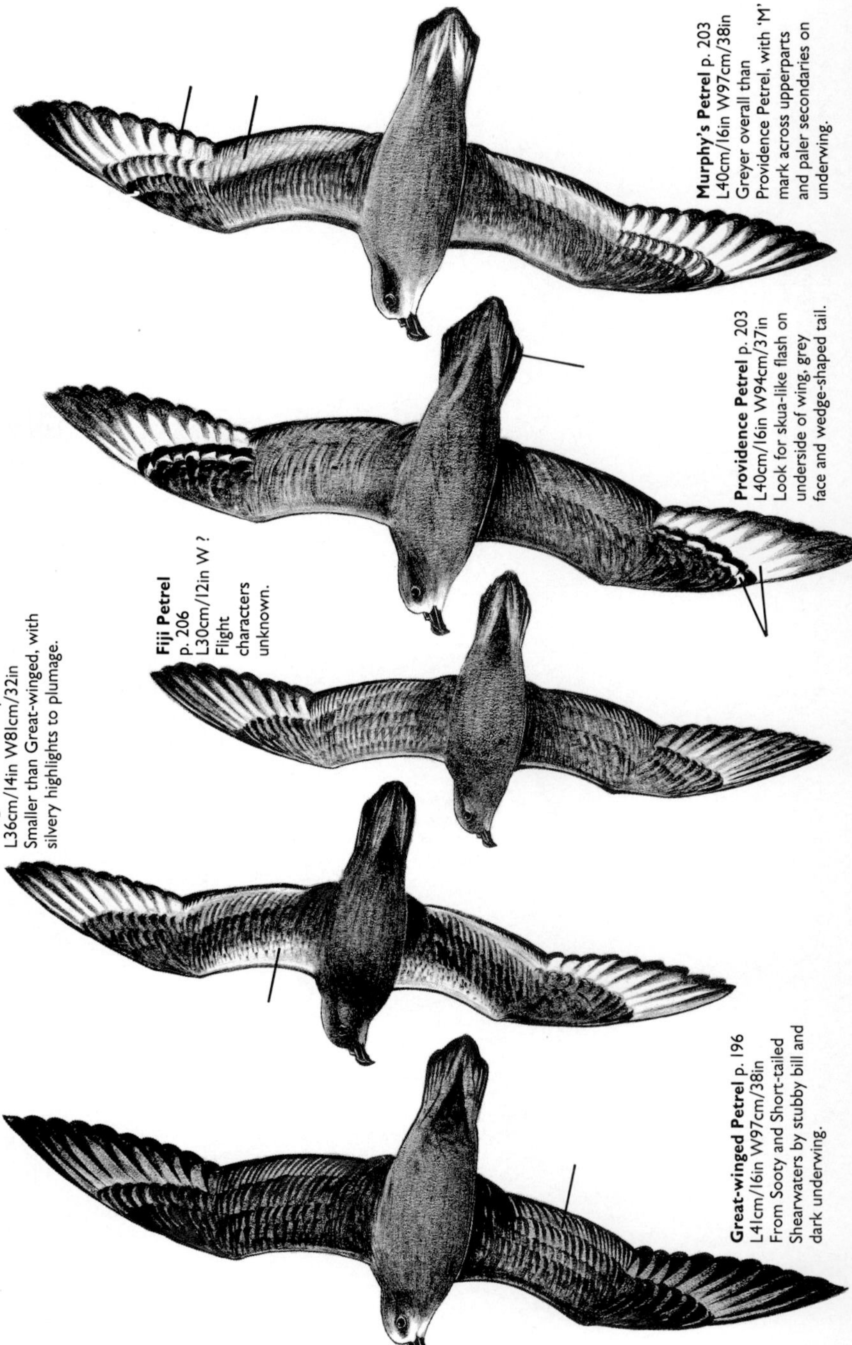

Murphy's Petrel p. 203
L40cm/16in W97cm/38in
Greyer overall than Providence Petrel, with 'M' mark across upperparts and paler secondaries on underwing.

Providence Petrel p. 203
L40cm/16in W94cm/37in
Look for skua-like flash on underside of wing, grey face and wedge-shaped tail.

Fiji Petrel
p. 206
L30cm/12in W ?
Flight characters unknown.

Kerguelen Petrel p. 196
L36cm/14in W81cm/32in
Smaller than Great-winged, with silvery highlights to plumage.

Great-winged Petrel p. 196
L41cm/16in W97cm/38in
From Sooty and Short-tailed Shearwaters by stubby bill and dark underwing.

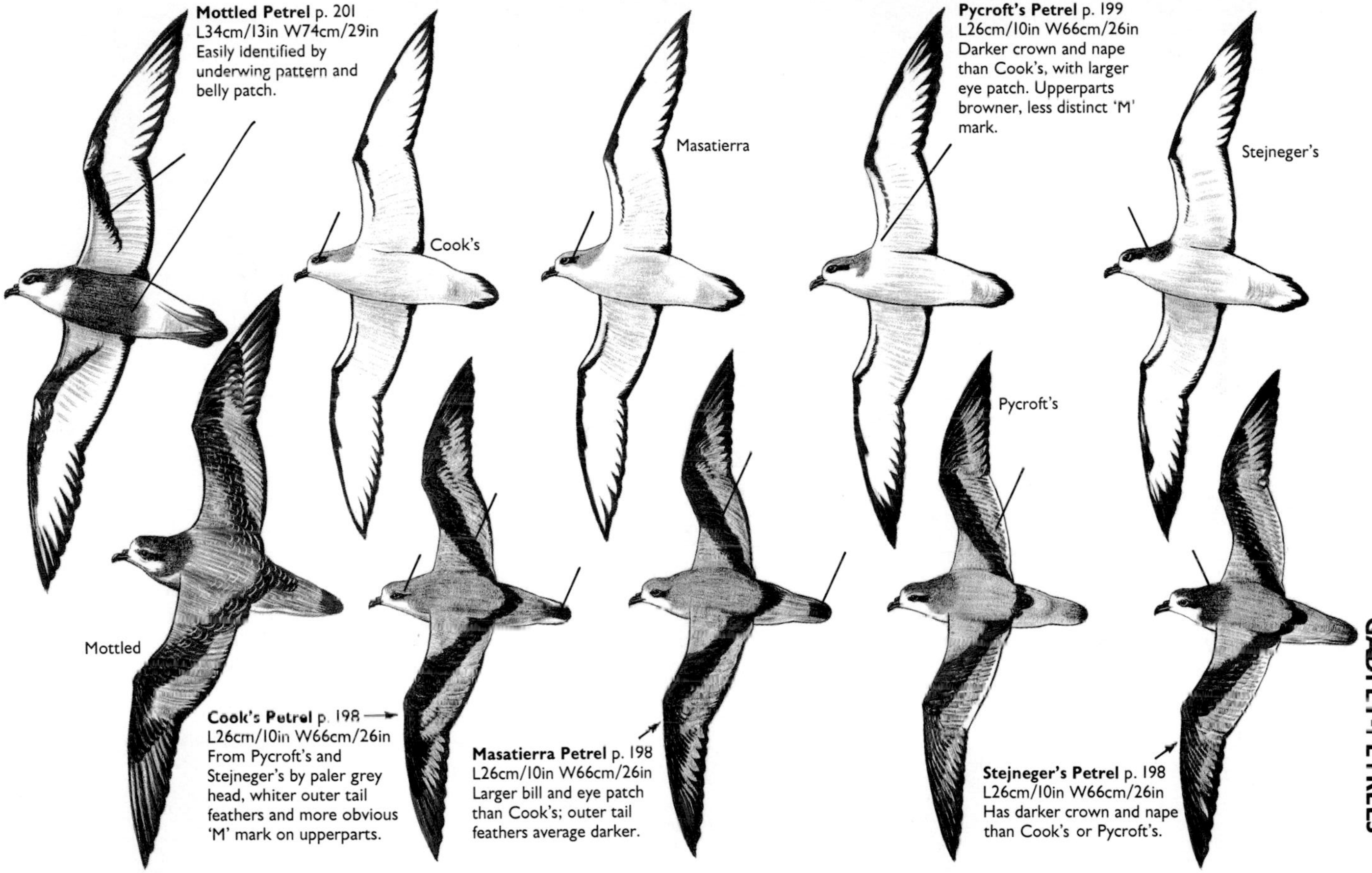

Mottled Petrel p. 201
L34cm/13in W74cm/29in
Easily identified by underwing pattern and belly patch.

Cook's Petrel p. 198
L26cm/10in W66cm/26in
From Pycroft's and Stejneger's by paler grey head, whiter outer tail feathers and more obvious 'M' mark on upperparts.

Masatierra Petrel p. 198
L26cm/10in W66cm/26in
Larger bill and eye patch than Cook's; outer tail feathers average darker.

Pycroft's Petrel p. 199
L26cm/10in W66cm/26in
Darker crown and nape than Cook's, with larger eye patch. Upperparts browner, less distinct 'M' mark.

Stejneger's Petrel p. 198
L26cm/10in W66cm/26in
Has darker crown and nape than Cook's or Pycroft's.

GADFLY-PETRELS

Bonin Petrel
p. 200
L30cm/12in
W67cm/26in
Has dark cap and diagnostic underwing pattern.
Chatham Island Petrel
p. 200
L30cm/12in W67cm/26in
Differs from Black-winged Petrel in black axillaries.
Black-winged Petrel
p. 200
L30cm/12in W67cm/26in
Has diagnostic underwing pattern and pale grey crown and collar.
Dark Morph
Intermediate Morph
Collared Petrel p. 199
L30cm/12in W71cm/28in
Occurs in pale, intermediate and dark morphs.
Pale Morph
Gould's Petrel p. 199
L30cm/12in W71cm/28in
Differs from Cook's, Pycroft's and Stejneger's in obvious underwing margins and darker head. Black-winged Petrel has pale grey head.

GADFLY-PETRELS

White-headed Petrel p. 197
L43cm/17in W109cm/43in
From Grey and Atlantic Petrels by whitish head and tail.

Magenta Petrel p. 210
L ? W ?
Very like Phoenix Petrel, of which it may be only a southerly form.

Barau's Petrel p. 197
L38cm/15in W?
No other Indian Ocean gadfly-petrel has combination of white forehead, dark cap and white underwings with diagonal black bar.

Mascarene Petrel p. 205
L36cm/14in W ?
Flight characters unknown.

GADFLY-PETRELS

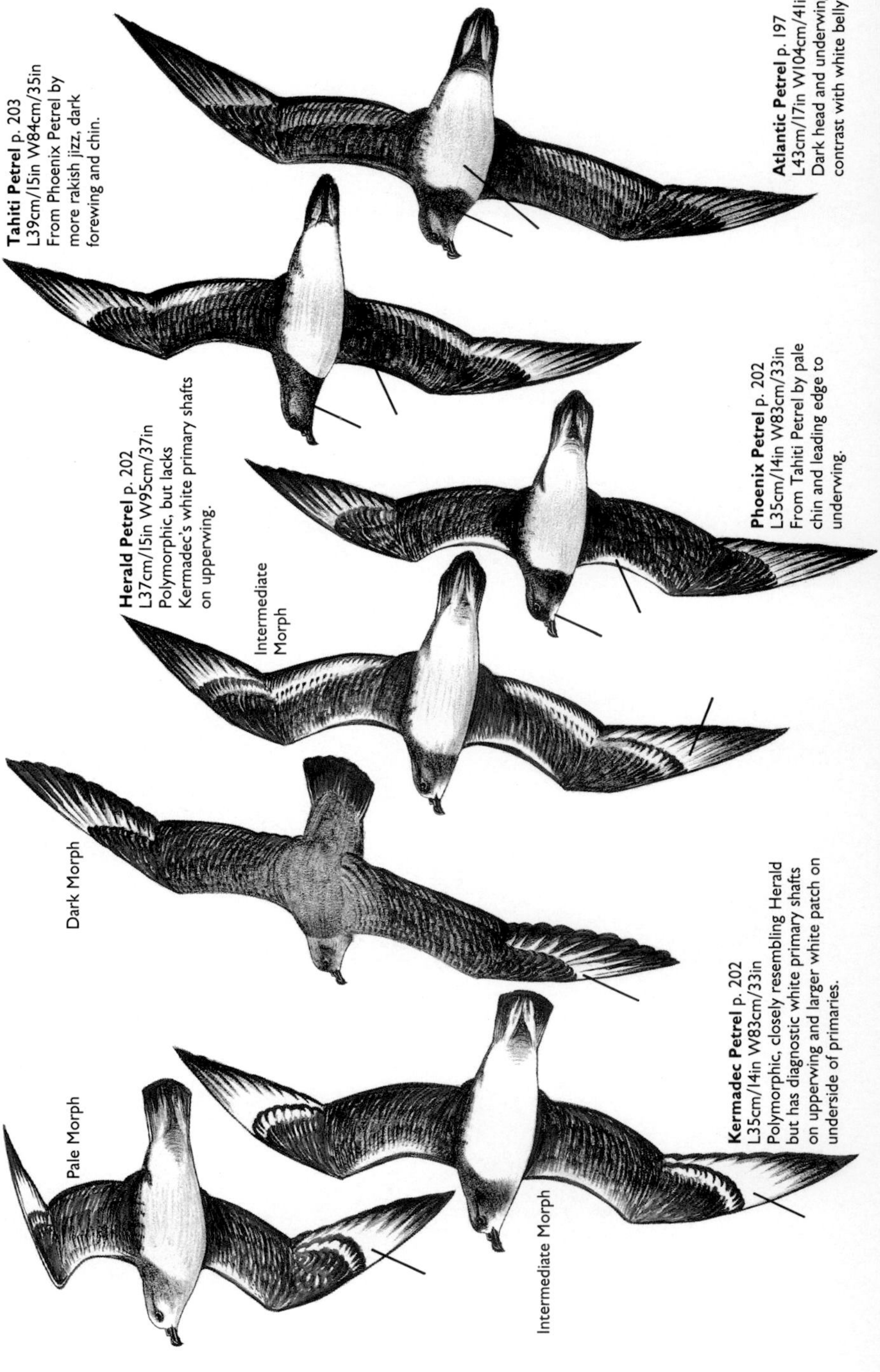

Tahiti Petrel p. 203
L39cm/15in W84cm/35in
From Phoenix Petrel by more rakish jizz, dark forewing and chin.
Atlantic Petrel p. 197
L43cm/17in W104cm/41in
Dark head and underwings contrast with white belly.
Herald Petrel p. 202
L37cm/15in W95cm/37in
Polymorphic, but lacks Kermadec's white primary shafts on upperwing.
Phoenix Petrel p. 202
L35cm/14in W83cm/33in
From Tahiti Petrel by pale chin and leading edge to underwing.
Intermediate Morph
Dark Morph
Kermadec Petrel p. 202
L35cm/14in W83cm/33in
Polymorphic, closely resembling Herald but has diagnostic white primary shafts on upperwing and larger white patch on underside of primaries.
Pale Morph
Intermediate Morph

Hawaiian Petrel p. 204
L43cm/17in
W91cm/36in
Browner above than Juan Fernandez, with darker head and underwing.

Juan Fernandez Petrel p. 201
L43cm/17in W97cm/38in
Greyer above than Hawaiian, with paler head and underwing margins.

Black-capped Petrel p. 204
L40cm/16in W95cm/37in
Differs from Bermuda Petrel in obvious white collar and rump patch.

Soft-plumaged Petrel p. 196
L34cm/13in W89cm/35in
Smaller than Atlantic Petrel, with white throat and forehead.

Bermuda Petrel p. 204
L38cm/15in W89cm/35in
Darker hindneck and rump than typical Black-capped Petrels.

PETRELS and STORM-PETRELS

(Note: figures not drawn to same scale on this key.)

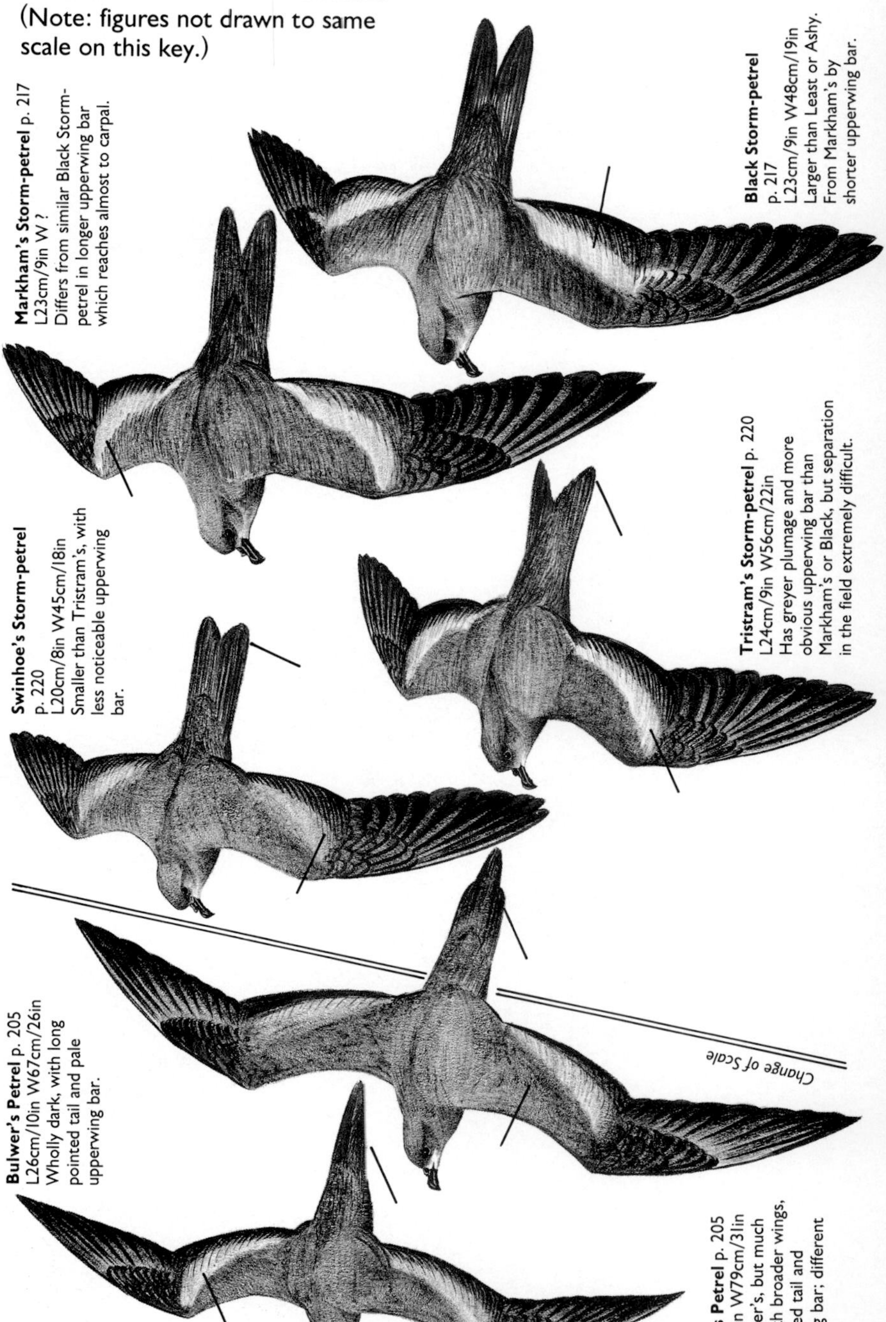
Markham's Storm-petrel p. 217
L23cm/9in W ?
Differs from similar Black Storm-petrel in longer upperwing bar which reaches almost to carpal.
Black Storm-petrel p. 217
L23cm/9in W48cm/19in
Larger than Least or Ashy. From Markham's by shorter upperwing bar.
Swinhoe's Storm-petrel p. 220
L20cm/8in W45cm/18in
Smaller than Tristram's, with less noticeable upperwing bar.
Tristram's Storm-petrel p. 220
L24cm/9in W56cm/22in
Has greyer plumage and more obvious upperwing bar than Markham's or Black, but separation in the field extremely difficult.
Change of Scale
Bulwer's Petrel p. 205
L26cm/10in W67cm/26in
Wholly dark, with long pointed tail and pale upperwing bar.
Jouanin's Petrel p. 205
L31cm/12in W79cm/31in
Like Bulwer's, but much larger, with broader wings, less pointed tail and upperwing bar; different flight.

STORM-PETRELS

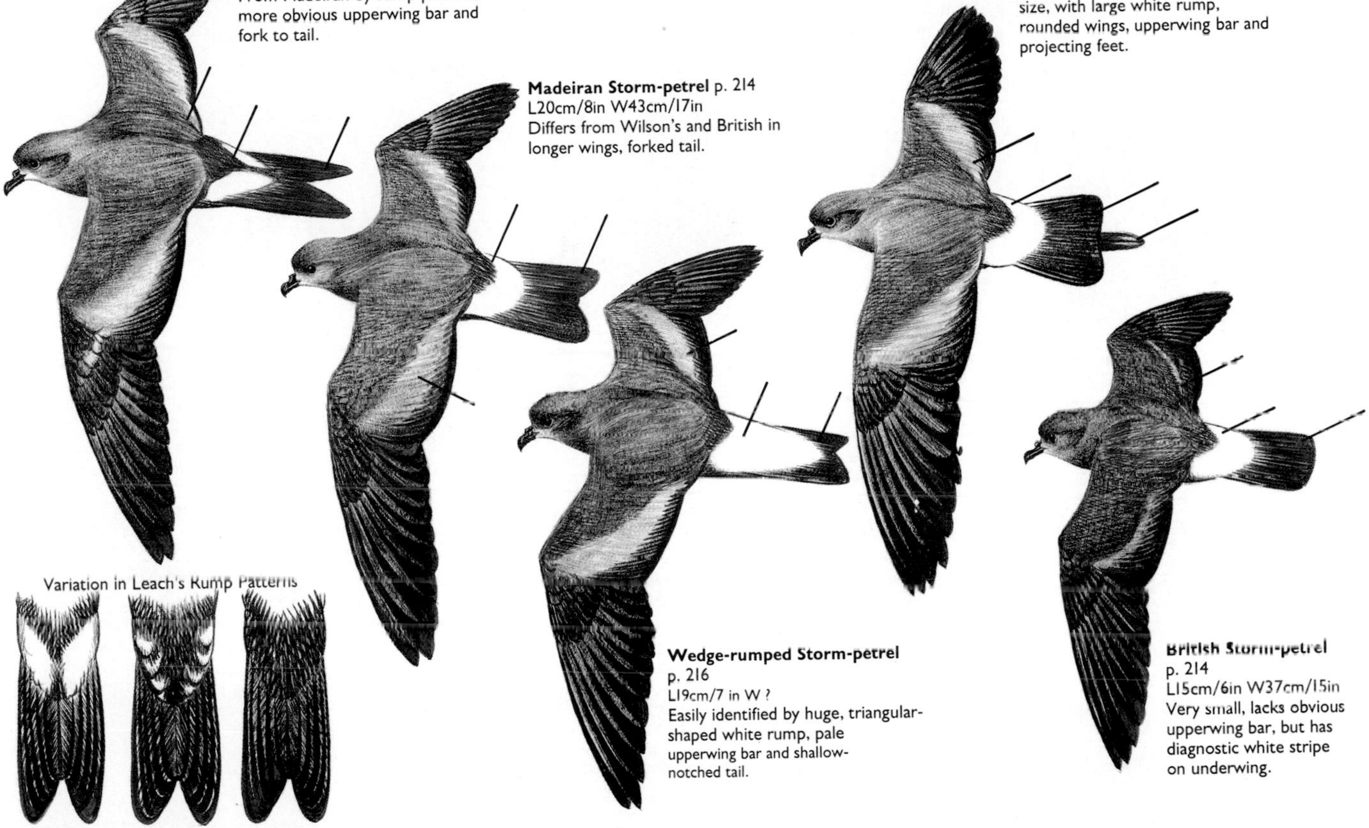

Leach's Storm-petrel p. 214
L20cm/8in W46cm/18in
From Madeiran by rump pattern, more obvious upperwing bar and fork to tail.

Madeiran Storm-petrel p. 214
L20cm/8in W43cm/17in
Differs from Wilson's and British in longer wings, forked tail.

Wilson's Storm-petrel p. 215
L17cm/7in W40cm/16in
Between Leach's and British in size, with large white rump, rounded wings, upperwing bar and projecting feet.

Wedge-rumped Storm-petrel p. 216
L19cm/7 in W ?
Easily identified by huge, triangular-shaped white rump, pale upperwing bar and shallow-notched tail.

British Storm-petrel p. 214
L15cm/6in W37cm/15in
Very small, lacks obvious upperwing bar, but has diagnostic white stripe on underwing.

Variation in Leach's Rump Patterns

Typical
Intermediate
Dark

White-faced Storm-petrel p. 215
L20cm/8in W42cm/17in
Easily identified by patterned face, upperwing bar, grey rump and projecting feet.
Ashy Storm-petrel p. 217
L20cm/8in W ?
From Black Storm-petrel by smaller size, pale suffusion on underwing
White-bellied Storm-petrel p. 218
L20cm/8in
W46cm/18in
From Black-bellied by unmarked white belly.
Intermediate Morph
Pale Morph
Fork-tailed Storm-petrel p. 216
L22cm/9in W46cm/18in
The only North Pacific storm-petrel with grey plumage and black face mask.
White-throated Storm-petrel p. 219
L25cm/10in W ?
Pale morph most typical, with white throat and breastband. Feet project past forked tail.
Black-bellied Storm-petrel p. 218
L20cm/8in W46cm/18in
From White-bellied by black stripe down centre of belly.

Hornby's Storm-petrel p. 219
L22cm/9in W ?
Easily identified by dark cap, breastband; grey upperparts and forked tail.

Least Storm-petrel p. 216
L14cm/6in W32cm/13in
Smaller than Black or Ashy, with wedge-shaped tail.

Grey-backed Storm-petrel p. 218
L17cm/7in W39cm/15in
Readily identified by blackish head, grey rump and white underparts.

Matsudaira's Storm-petrel p. 219
L24cm/9in W56cm/22in
White primary shafts form obvious pale patch on primaries.

Elliot's Storm-petrel p. 215
L15cm/6in W ?
Like Wilson's, but smaller, with white on lower belly and vent.

SELECTED BIBLIOGRAPHY

Alexander, W.B. (1955) *Birds of the Ocean.* New York.

Bourne, W.R.P., & Dixon, T.J. (1972) *Sea Swallow* 22:29–60; (1975) *Sea Swallow* 24:65–88.

Cox, J.B. (1980) *Rec. S. Austr. Mus.* 18:91–121.

Cramp, S., & Simmons, K.E.L. (eds.) (1977–1985) *The Birds of the Western Palearctic*, Vols. 1–4. Oxford.

Dementiev, G.P., & Gladkov, N.A. (1951) *Birds of the Soviet Union*, Vol. 3. Moscow.

De Schauensee, R.M. (1966) *The Species of Birds of South America and Their Distribution.* Acad. of Nat. Sci; (1971) *A Guide to the Birds of South America.* London & Edinburgh.

Devillers, P. (1977) *Auk* 94:417–429.

Dwight, J. (1925) The Gulls (Laridae) of the World: their plumages, moults, variations, relationships and distribution. *Bull Amer. Mus. Nat. Hist* 52:63–408.

Grant, P.J. (1982) *Gulls: A Guide to Identification.* Berkhamsted.

Harper, P.C. (1980) *Notornis* 27(3):235–286.

Harper, P.C., & Kinsky, F.C. (1978) *Southern Albatrosses and Petrels: An Identification Guide.* Victoria.

Harris, M.P. (1974) *A Field Guide to the Birds of the Galapagos.* London.

Harrison, P. (1983) *Seabirds: An Identification Guide.* Beckenham.

Howard, R., & Moore, A. (1980) *A Complete Checklist of the Birds of the World.* Oxford.

Jehl, J. (1982) *Le Gerfaut* 72:121–135. (The biology and taxonomy of Townsend's Shearwater.)

Jouanin, C. (1963) *Oiseau* 37:1–19; (1969) *Oiseau* 40:48–60.

King, W.B. (1967) *Preliminary Smithsonian Identification Manual: Seabirds of the Tropical Pacific Ocean.* Washington.

Kitson, A.R. (1980) *Bull. BOC* 100 (3):178–185.

Kurata, in Hasegawa, H. (1978) *Pacific Seabird Group Bull.* 5 (1):16–17.

Mayr, E. (1945) *Birds of the South West Pacific.* New York.

Mayr, E., & Cottrell, C.W. (eds.) (1979) *Checklist of the Birds of the World.* Vol. 1, 2nd ed. Mus. of Comp. Zool., Cambridge, Mass.

Meeth, P., & Meeth, K. (1977) *Ardea* 65:90–91.

Murphy, R.C. (1936) *Oceanic Birds of South America,* Vols. 1 & 2. New York.

Naveen, R. (1981) *Birding* 13(6):14(1–3).

Nelson, J.B. (1978) *The Gannet.* Berkhamsted; (1980) *Seabirds: Their Biology and Ecology.* Feltham, England.

Palmer, R.S. (1962) *Handbook of North American Birds,* Vol. 1. Yale.

Payne & Prince (1978) *New Zealand Journal of Zoology* 6:299–318. (Identification and breeding biology of the diving petrels *Pelecanoides georgicus* and *P. urinatrix exsul* at South Georgia.)

Peterson, R.T. (1980) *A Field Guide to the Birds.* Boston.

Roberson, D. (1980) *Rare Birds of the West Coast of North America.* Woodcock Publications, California.

Roux, J.P., Jouventin, P., Mougin, J.L., Stahl, J.C., & Weimerskirch, H. (1983) *Oiseau* 53, 1:1–11.

Rumboll, M.A.E., & Jehl, J.R., Jnr (1977) *Trans. San Diego Soc. Nat. Hist.* 19(1).

Serventy, D.L., Serventy, V., & Warham, J. (1971) *The Handbook of Australian Seabirds.* London.

Sinclair, J.C. (1984) *Field Guide to the Birds of Southern Africa.* London.

Snow, B.K., & Snow, D.W. (1969) *Ibis* 111:30–35.

Stallcup, R. (1976) *Western Birds* 7:113–136.

Terres, J.K. (1980) *The Audubon Society Encyclopedia of North American Birds.* New York.

Tuck, G.S., & Heinzel, H. (1978) *A Field Guide to the Seabirds of Britain and the World.* London.

Tunnicliffe, G.A. (1982) *Notornis* 29:85–91.

Watson, G.E. (1975) *Birds of the Antarctic and Sub Antarctic.* Washington DC.

Watling, R. (1986) *Bull. BOC* 106(2):63–70. (Notes on the Collared Petrel *Pterodroma (leucoptera) brevipes.*)

Woods, R.W. (1975) *The Birds of the Falkland Islands.* Salisbury, Wilts, England.

INDEX OF ENGLISH NAMES

The main entry for each species is listed in boldface type and refers to the text page; the entry in italics refers to the photograph page number and the entry in roman type to the identification key page number.
A check-off box is provided next to each common name entry so that you can use this index as a checklist of the species you have identified.

INDEX OF SCIENTIFIC NAMES